TOUCH
OF
DANGER

Vol. 1 of the Three Worlds Saga

Carol A. Strickland

Other books by Carol A. Strickland
Lost in the Stars– vol. 2 of the Three Worlds Saga
Stalemate– vol. 3 of the Three Worlds Saga
Worlds Apart– vol. 4 of the Three Worlds Saga
Applesauce and Moonbeams– wacky soft sci fi
Nothing Personal– ditto but wackier
Burgundy and Lies– sweet historical romance

NOTE: A version of the first half of this novel was first published and copyrighted under the name *Touch of Danger* in 2009, then re-edited and re-copyrighted in 2011. The second half of this book was first published and copyrighted in 2011 under the title *Star-Crossed*. In 2013 the two books were combined into one volume and re-edited.

Published by Carol A. Strickland
www.CarolAStrickland.com

Publisher's Note: This is a work of fiction. Names, characters, places, and incidents are a product of the author's imagination. Locales and public names are sometimes used for atmospheric purposes. Any resemblance to actual people, living or dead, or to businesses, companies, events, institutions, or locales is completely coincidental.

Book Layout © 2017 BookDesignTemplates.com

Exterior cover by Strick. Interior cover illustration by Colleen Doran.

Touch of Danger / Carol A. Strickland. – 2nd ed.
ISBN Print edition 978-1-941318-20-1
ISBN Digital edition 978-1-941318-21-8
IISBN IngramSpark Print edition 978-1-941318-30-0
ISBN IngramSpark Digital edition 978-1-941318-28-7

WITH THANKS…

...to Romance Writers of America, especially the members of our local chapter, the Heart of Carolina Romance Writers. They are steadfast, encouraging and always willing to offer their opinions and expertise.

...to my own guides, who sent me an amazing Dream ten years before this was first published– the same week they cracked my noggin with a metaphorical frying pan and yelled, "Hel-LO! It's mid-life! Start doing what you're supposed to be doing!" What a fun bunch of guys!

...to Raelene Gorlinsky of Ellora's Cave, who gave me the thrill of being a real, published author by believing in me and my work. Indie is a very good place to be, but it wasn't so much in those days.

…Thanks to Samantha Gordon at Invisible Ink Editing for editing the 2013 composite book. I didn't have to take her direction, so if you have probs with this novel, bring them to me. For the 2017 version, all blame to be assigned belongs to me.

...*Mille fois merci* to Timothée Hayes and (so long ago!) Geneviève/Glortie, for helping with my Québécois and French. Yes, it's really *"marde"* and not *"merde"* if you're in Montréal. Timothée also explained why it's so important for French Canadian cursing to include obscure Catholic rituals. (YouTube helped with their many "How to Swear in French-Canadian" videos.) And to Christophe Raoux for enlightening me about a line of French love-speak. Oh, those French speakers! (And to the internet community, who informed me that some of what these people told me was incorrect. Do you see bad French/Québeçois? Too bad! *Dommage!* Live with it.)

…to Tony Lavely, who bravely critiqued the original second half of this manuscript. He not only had problems with *"marde"*, but also with "god" only being capitalized when someone actually addresses the Source. Hope none of that bothers the readers. He also made great observations and generally helped me a lot.

…to Tish Shaffer and Marcia Colette, for checking out an early version with patience and lots of Café Carolina pastries.

Part One

1

White fear washed through her like ice. Once again Carolina O'Kelly asked herself if now wasn't a good time to take another step back from life. She couldn't think straight. This was all getting too real. If she got flustered she'd die.

The hotel was burning down around her.

Wishing wouldn't stanch the smoke. She shivered despite the warmth of the tropical morning.

Come on, do *something!* she ordered herself through the numbing daze. *Focus on goal A. Okay, this is me now, doing something.* She sat frozen on the bed. *Move! Move!*

The hotel posted no fire instructions on the door that allowed tendrils of smoke to curl into the room, despite the wet towels stuffed under it. No fire trucks had yet shown up here in the middle of nowhere.

Hard reality was that no matter how much she wished, the ParaNet was probably on the other side of the world stopping some war or another. The harder reality was that Lina O'Kelly was too damned unimportant for even the most minor of ParaNetters to care about.

It was up to her to save herself. As usual.

"This is not funny, God," she muttered, and the flames of righteous indignation blazed through her inner freeze.

She jerked the knot on the sheets in her lap tighter, letting out an "umph!" for her efforts. It didn't feel secure to her. She stepped on one sheet and pulled up, testing–and the knot slipped.

Damn.

So she reknotted it and pushed the thought of failure away as if it were a physical thing. It was five long stories to the ground from this rapidly-crumbling firetrap someone had advertised as a hotel. A bitter, dark fume oozed out of the electrical outlet next to her.

She set to work on the next sheet, tying it to the thin blanket with renewed determination. All she had to do was plan and take action: one, two, three, like all the Zig Ziglar motivational speeches she listened to.

Goal A? Get out of hotel. Alive.

Dying was not on her list of life goals. She might break a leg on the way down, but if she did, she'd still be able to crawl to safety.

She tugged on the new knot. This one held– good. Hope bloomed within her. Gathering up her prize, she ran to the balcony and threw it over the railing. It unwound down the side of the ugly cement structure– less than halfway. The bloom soured into a tight ball in her gut.

You'll need more sheets, *they* told her.

"I noticed," she replied. She closed her eyes, took a deep, cleansing breath and tried to filter out the burning taint that came with it. Squaring her shoulders, she hauled the life rope back up. Long locks of dark hair still wet from her shower slapped against her face as she looked desperately around her room. The room's curtains were already ripped; they'd never begin to hold her. Where could she get more sheets? How much time did she have?

Damned cheap hotel! She should have paid more and stayed down the road in St. Catherine, at one of the nice, nonflammable hotels there. Trying to save a few bucks– *stupid! Stupid!* Lina cursed herself as she dragged her chain of sheets back inside.

She grabbed some clothes, her wallet and her iPad, and stuffed them into her beach bag before she paused to stare at it. What was she doing? Having something to wear besides this nightgown was a B goal at most. This was not survival.

She was getting rattled again. Remember Goal A. Everything was expendable except herself. Still, the bag was packed. She tossed it onto the balcony to grab on the way out.

She fumbled at sneakers, but her hands shook too badly to pull the laces into any kind of bow or knot. *Get hold of yourself, Muttbutt!* She hurled the shoes out over the balcony, venting her rage and frustration. Put the shoes on once she was down and safe.

Lina wanted to kick the walls and scream. This damned cardboard hotel didn't offer much for survival. Hell, the fire alarm hadn't even peeped yet. She'd used up all her room's resources. What was left? Oh– other rooms. Behind a chair stood a connecting door to the room next door.

Of course it was locked. Nothing in this life came easy. *Damn you, door!* She hurled herself at the door– *yowch!*– did it again– and it shifted. One more heave crashed it open.

The cloud of dark gray smoke hanging in this room whirlpooled from the disturbance. After she pulled her nightgown's bodice up to cover her nose and mouth, Lina yanked one corner of sheets and blankets off the bed there as quickly as she could. Still she had to pause to cough out the bitter smoke.

Suddenly the hallway door boomed with pounding. The sound stopped. She heard male coughing in the corridor, then the slams resumed. *Please, God, let it be a fireman!*

"Hold on!" she cried as she unlocked the door. It stuck. Whoever it was behind it threw himself against it, sending Lina tumbling back as the door gave. A new, darker cloud of smoke and heat poured in like a wave from the hallway. Lina doubled over in a paroxysm of coughing. The blind sound of man-coughing echoed her. He wheezed as he shoved the door closed behind himself and then pulled Lina closer to the balcony and fresh air.

She gasped it in and rubbed her tearing eyes.

"You okay?" the man asked.

She blinked against the blur. Tall. Brawny. Dark hair, medium-brown skin. A familiar, chiseled jaw line and even more familiar black clothing. Valiant? Awright, Valiant! Yes!

Valiant of the ParaNet!

Valiant equaled safety. Lina's shoulders sagged with relief.

But... But he wasn't *doing* anything. He wasn't putting out the fire with his parapowers, wasn't sweeping her up in his arms to fly her from this horrible mess. This had to be someone dressed like the famous parahero.

But no. The right sleeve of the costume might be in shreds, but the face was definitely his.

"I'm, I'm fine. Thanks," she managed to say. One step farther back; this wasn't reality, was it?

"*Oui*, I'm the real thing," he assured her, and his voice held Valiant's French-Canadian accent, the rich timbre. "But *non, maintenant* I have no powers. Sorry. Don't worry. We'll get out."

He scanned the area outside the balcony to assess the situation much as she'd done. Then he turned back into the room to circle the place as he kept low out of the smoke, checking what was in drawers, searching... Valiant tried the phone but put it back when someone told him no one was answering downstairs. Oh– she had. Her body was talking while she numbly stood somewhere behind herself.

Too far from reality, Lina. Come back. Don't forget the fire.

Valiant without powers! How had that happened? And a helluva time for it to happen. God was certainly having a good belly laugh at her expense today, but He had no business laughing at Valiant. Valiant was one of the good guys. He was Important.

Valiant went out to the balcony again.

"There's no way down out there," she told him. "I think we have to make our own rope. Help me with these sheets. Please?"

He grunted his acceptance of her plan and together they wrestled the final sheets off the bed. While he dragged the bundle to her room she retrieved towels out of the bathroom.

Once back, she wet the towels and stuffed them around the connecting door as... Valiant... snapped off the TV. CNNi had been airing *PanRand*, with that spectacular footage of Valiant towing a transatlantic jet on his back to a safe landing. The powerless version here sat on her bed and knotted cheap sheets together.

He nodded with his chin at the sheets she'd already worked. "They'll never hold," he declared. "Watch."

He made some kind of sailor's knot with his sheets: over, over and through. He gave it an ineffectual tug and frowned.

"I'll get used to this," he muttered, and then jerked the knot tight with more force than was necessary. He displayed the result to her before starting on a new sheet.

Lina quickly undid her knots and retied them the way he did. When she pulled on the two ends, the connection was definitely stronger.

Her guides' warning cut through Lina's concentration. **Get out now.**

"You could have given me a little more warning," she griped.

"Warning?" Valiant asked.

"Sorry, not you," she said quickly. "Um, we've got to get out now."

He fished inside his black vest. "I have some twine we could add to these knots. You have a scissors or knife?" he asked.

"Sorry," she told him, trying not to panic at the stream of **hurry, hurry, hurry,** in her mind, "but we've got to get out now, ready or not." She knotted her first sheet to the balcony railing. Throwing the line of sheets over the edge, she caught the last corner. "Come on, give me yours," she demanded.

"Not yet. We're in enough trouble as it is. We have time to make this safer."

"No, we don't," she told him. "*They* say we have to get out now. Hurry!"

"*Qui?* Who says?"

"My guides. Please don't argue with my guides; they're usually right. Usually."

He sat there on the bed, frowning at her and not moving.

"I know it sounds weird, but please. Please! *Now,* they say."

Tell him to roll when he hits.

"And they say to roll when you hit," she added as she grabbed the sheets from him. He opened his mouth to say something when she held up a warning finger. "Tell me I'm crazy once we're down. We've got to get out now!"

He shook his head in surrender and worked the final knot himself. "It should be more secure," he warned, then shrugged. "The cards we're dealt," he said as if that decided things.

Lina watched the line of sheets and blankets fall. The final length was close enough to the ground; good. "Okay, you go first. I have to get my—"

But he was already lifting her up, swinging her over the railing as if he'd done this a million times before. "You're first. Make it quick."

She jerked away from his invading touch and overbalanced. Grabbing the balcony rail, she took an instant to steady herself, then started down.

"Toss me my bag!" she called to him and hoped he could hear her over the bass roaring of the fire. By now it howled like a high wind. Currents of scorched, super-heated air clung to the sides of the building. Tiny square pieces of smoky soot swirled upward around her.

Lina shimmied down the fragile lifeline as fast as she could in the thickening haze, but it took forever. The flimsy fabric started to rip already. As soon as she thought it was safe, she jumped off the sheets to save them for Valiant's trip. No broken leg!

"Go!" she shouted up at him but he was already scrambling over the railing. The sky hung black with smoke above him. Was that a lick of flame on the balcony curtain?

It really was him, she decided in wonder. The most amazing man in the world. The hero constantly in the news, battling all kinds of para-criminals, clearing out natural disasters. Flying through the sky, a leader among Earth's paraheroes. The pride of Canada and New York City.

But he was having trouble handling the shifting make-do rope shredding from above him. The rip began with him still up high.

"Roll when you hit!" she shouted. Pressing her hands against her mouth, she begged his angels to protect him as the sheets disintegrated under his weight. She watched him fall in slow motion. Too high! He twisted stiffly and landed hard on his left shoulder.

"Jesus!" Lina cried.

Between yelps of pain, Valiant let out a string of curses in English, French and some other language she'd never heard before— but at least that meant he was alive.

She ran to help him sit up. "Are you all right? I mean other than the shoulder?"

He shouted some more curses at the world. "*Que je suis bête!* I forgot to roll. It feels–" Valiant groaned as he tried to move his shoulder. "Dislocated? Hurts like hell and a half!"

A faraway look hazed her eyes. "Dislocated, yes," she agreed. "Nothing's broken. But there's something terribly wrong. Show me, please."

"Who–"

She held up her hand and listened to something he couldn't hear. "I'm sorry. What is that? A microscope? Oh, okay." Her eyebrows knit in concentration. She shook her head, disturbed at something. "What's the cure?" she asked.

On top of it all, I'm stuck with a lunatic, Londo decided. Talking to herself. The girl was bi-polar or something.

A beautiful lunatic.

"Your cells are in deep shock," she told him. "*They* say you need to rest and keep warm, treat yourself as if you were in shock and not just your cells. The longer you put off resting, the longer it'll take to heal."

Lon hissed at the pain and glanced up to see flames founting from the fifth floor windows, the same room they'd just so hurriedly left. The girl looked back, too.

"Aw, shoo!" she cried. "My bag's up there!"

Black smoke settled and coalesced to form a cloud around the building. Good thing they'd gotten out when they did. "I don't think there's much left of your bag now." Lon scowled as he wobbily shifted to get up, with a sharp intake of breath for his pain.

The girl eased him back down onto the lawn using just a fingertip. "Sit," she suggested. "Enjoy the show, I guess. Rest while we wait for the fire department."

"I'm in shock and I need to rest," he condescended to repeat as he sized up their situation. Push the pain back and down. Keep Crazy Girl thinking that he thought she was normal so she wouldn't freak out.

He needed to get her to safety– no, get both of them to safety. Time to start thinking like a norm and not a megapara. His sharp mind cut through the momentary uncertainty of his situation to formulate strategy.

He rolled to put his weight on his good right hand, and then gingerly stood up. He told himself he could ignore the shafts of pain ripping up his arm to the top of his head. He ordered his body to shut up. He had to hold his left arm with his right so it wouldn't drag at his shoulder, but at least then he could think. Priorities and strategy: those were their only hope, his sudden humanity be damned.

"No," the girl declared. "*You're* not in shock, not on a level of your body being in shock in a holistic way. On a smaller scale– a cellular level– that's where you're in shock. Your cells can't operate like they normally do. They're sort of shut down or something."

She gestured with her hands: big, then small, and he didn't get any of it. In this situation it wasn't important to understand a crazy person.

"So you don't feel like you're in shock even though you are," she finished as if that explained it all.

He gave her a clear look of disbelief. "And just where are you getting all of this?" he asked her. "Are you some kind of psychic friend? Shirley MacLaine in disguise?"

"Who are *you* in disguise?" she asked archly. "The Valiant I've seen flies and doesn't fall. Doesn't get dislocated shoulders because he's invulnerable. And he could put this fire out in a couple of minutes."

Few people had *l'audace* to stand up to him. He could tell when she realized who she was talking to because she bit her lip and dropped her gaze.

"I'm, I'm sorry. I know what I say sounds funny, sounds loony tunes, but I really think it's true."

He gave her a half-frown. Even if she were crazy, it was difficult to be too frustrated with her. She had big, innocent green eyes and dark wet hair with reddish tints in it. If her skin had been brown, she could have passed for part Polynesian by the ovalness of her face, the wide cheekbones, the hint of a slant to her eyes. But the lips were full only by Caucasian standards, the skin a peach-tinged ivory.

She was tall and awesomely buxom, wearing only a little white nightie that came down almost to her knees, thin material trimmed in eyelet lace. "Don't let a pretty face fool you," Hal had taught him, but he'd always been a sucker for them.

He couldn't let himself be distracted from the mission at hand. Londo turned and squinted at the fire, already down to the third floor. It moved like arson, feeding on something deliberate. "It would take me more like ten, fifteen minutes to put this out, especially since there's no one to rescue."

He turned back to her and took her measure from a more professional standpoint. Was there anything in her open and rather inept body language that disguised deceit? "Except you."

"What? Where are all the others?" She snapped to attention, her gaze raking the windows and grounds of the hotel. "But just thirty or forty minutes ago, there were maybe six people in the pool, another fifteen or so just walking around. I was surprised because it was so early. There was a big group of Australians or New Zealanders here, some sort of convention. They were all men. Creepy men. They've been running around drunk all night. I bet you anything one of them started this."

"*Eh bien,* they're not here now."

"That's impossible," the girl said flatly. "They must be on the other side of the hotel."

There was no one trapped in any windows. Lon's paravision still operated to an extent. Through the fog of smoke the beach showed deserted as well. The girl ran across the lawn to the other side of the building and the gravel parking lot there– empty.

Lon followed her, holding his mangled arm and grunting. "We need to get out of here," he told her. "The reason I'm powerless–"

As she turned to face him her eyes went wide. She sucked in a breath and leapt for him.

"Get down!" she yelled, taking him down with her onto the sharp gravel with no regard for his shoulder.

Ba-whu-whoom! A curtain of fire and glass, cement and wood splinters blasted through the smoke.

Valiant looked up through the pain to see a sheet of glass flying through the space he'd just been taking up. If he had been standing there–

The girl put her palm on his forehead and pushed down. "There's something else," she said, and then another explosion went off, this one even closer than the last.

Shock wave! A wall of air lifted them up and threw them across the hotel lawn. He heard her cry out as she landed, but then he did, too. It felt like someone sledge hammered his shoulder. All his senses except touch blanked as agony jolted through him down to his feet.

He shouted his torment. Tears of pain ran down his face. *Stop it, stop it! Get control!* He was still alive. He needed to protect the girl!

Cracking his burning eyes open, he squinted back at the hotel. Everything was gone– leveled. Only piles of cement blocks and debris remained. A pea-soup haze of yellow dust left from disintegrating masonry swirled in a sour, choking cloud he could feel as distinct particles when he breathed. Where was the girl? Londo coughed through the filter of his hand as he peered around.

A hundred feet from him the ocean breeze lifted the dust-covered hem of her nightie, but she lay very still.

In his life he'd seen far too many other still bodies.

Cringing at the pain, he pulled himself up and tried to run to her. The best he could manage was a lopsided lope through the sea of crumbled brick and cement blocks. The girl lay face-down, surrounded by brick fragments and glass– and one desk phone, incongruously intact. Yellow dust coated all except for a tiny, liquid trickle of crimson running from under that thick mass of dust-caked hair.

Was she alive? He'd never before administered manual CPR. What if she had spinal injuries? Warily he reached for a pulse at her neck. There it was. How odd to feel such delicate movement. He watched. Her shoulders rose and fell. Deep breath; she moaned and started to raise up, coughed.

"Steady." He put his hand on her shoulder. She seemed to twitch fully awake at his touch and jerked away from him. "Take it slow." He realized he didn't even know her name. He should ask–

"L-Lina. Carolina O'Kelly." She wiggled her fingers, testing, then pulled herself up, twisting to a sitting position. She batted at the air, trying to make a window through the gritty fog, and then gingerly patted the back of her head. "Ooo."

Valiant one-handedly parted her hair to examine the wound. "Something caught you good," he said. It was a nasty rip of a cut, already swelling blue-black and crusting blood. It needed antibiotics at the very least. *Don't alarm her.* "It doesn't look too bad, but we'll keep an eye on it. Blurred vision? Double vision?" The girl slowly shook her head. "Anything else major?"

"Um... no. How about you?"

"I don't think I have anything new to report." Except that now the pain was maybe twice as much as it had been. Still he could smile to himself about one thing. Well, two. As she reached around to set herself straight and smooth her nightie back into place, Lina didn't notice how that thin cotton, wet from where she'd fallen on dewed grass, let him see the shadows of her nipples underneath. He forced himself not to stare.

"Shoo," she muttered as she slapped at the dust on herself. It left a pale yellow stain on her chemise. "I didn't achieve Goal B-for-Bag. Maybe it's time for Goal C-for-Cry? At least we managed to meet Goal A."

"Goal A?"

"Getting out."

"Ah. *Très bien.* Sorry about B."

"I had some real clothes packed in it. This is not the way one wants to meet a parahero."

He grinned and eased down next to her, carefully, carefully. "But it's the way every parahero wants to meet a lady. Don't sweat it. On some worlds, you'd be considered prudish to wear anything besides shoes and a hat. I don't mind."

"I bet. You're really Va–? Are you sure you're okay? You don't look so well."

Lon tried to feel how he felt. He was a norm now. His body seemed like he'd stepped into that of a stranger– of another species. He wasn't supposed to feel pain. He wasn't supposed to feel– anything. Suddenly there was an entire world pressing down on him with its presence, even invading his lungs, as well as a body that was screaming its wounding.

It wouldn't do to let another know how much he hurt. If someone thought about it too long they'd realize the falseness of his ordinary life. And worst of all– he'd seen ordinary norms in far worse situations, braving their way toward survival despite impossible conditions. If he slacked now, Lina would think he was a coward. Hell, he'd think he was one, too.

He was no coward. No mere norm. He was a man, Valiant, and even as a norm he had duties he could never dream of ignoring.

"It's hard to tell," he hedged. "The shoulder is taking up all pain frequencies." Valiant picked up the desk phone with his right hand and set it back down. Its cord was still intact and he swung it thoughtfully. "If I can find a jack for this, we can get a rescue squad out here, *peut-être*." Asking for help was embarrassing, but sometimes it was all one could do. The important thing was Lina's safety and health. Then his own.

He took a breath, then painfully rose and offered his good hand. Instead she shook her head and got up on her own, brushing off the chemise and her hair in great clouds of dust amidst the general yellow haze.

As he ran a hand through his own grimy hair, he swiped what he'd hoped was an unnoticed tear off his cheek. Push the pain back harder. This was no time to give in to human frailty. Maybe he could work his vest into a sling later.

The distant but distinctive sound of helicopter echoed in the yellow fog.

Local emergency systems wouldn't have helicopters at their disposal.

Valiant twisted, trying to pinpoint the direction with his diminished hearing. "They're coming." He reached out to grasp Lina's upper arm to lead her, but closed on only air as she stepped away.

"Who?"

"I ran into terrorists about three or four miles from here. They had very specialized munitions."

Lina squeaked as her hand flew to her throat. "When I was in the shower I heard thunder–"

"That was them. And up close, the guns sound more like an atomic blast. They did a job on me." He indicated his torn sleeve and reached again for her. Again she pulled away from his touch.

"It's just–"

"It's supposed to be indestructible," he explained briskly. "Of course, so am I." The melted metal remains of a computerized ring still held to the middle finger of his right hand, yet the skin wasn't blistered. "I was getting ready to call for backup when they hit. C'mon, we've got to get out of here."

She began to trail him just out of arm's reach. Lina squinted at him before her face smoothed into understanding. "So the guns threw your cells into shock. No powers."

"I barely managed to fly here before that gave out, too. I was hoping to find a phone and call the Network that way. But I spotted the fire, and then I saw you–"

"You *saw* me?"

"Vision powers are still on so far. Mostly. Can you run? We've got to make some time."

Lina blinked to come back to the Real World and take in all this. He really was Valiant, and he was hurt. So many new things to think about; her head was spinning around that awful ache. But there was no excuse for hiding from reality when someone was in pain.

"Here I thought the management were just Nazis about guests stealing sheets." She nodded at his arm as she sorted through new goals. "Let me fix that shoulder first."

But again came the sound of the 'copter, closer this time. She peered up into the dissipating fog. "Terrorists," she whispered to herself.

"They'll be coming to finish their job. I don't think they get paid unless they can present a body."

"Good god."

"Are you coming?"

The extent of their situation hit Lina with the abruptness of an electric shock. Valiant had turned toward the beach and the easy, hard-packed sand route there, and she'd automatically begun to follow him. "I can work on your shoulder later."

"I agree." He asked hopefully, "Are you a medic?"

"Beggars can't be–"

He began to trot.

"Valiant! Not that way."

He turned toward her. She shook her arms to rid herself of the worst of the fear and exhaled in an *oo*, looking beyond Valiant and shaking her head.

"I see it," she muttered to her guides, then directed her words at him and the beach. "The worst danger is that way." She pointed in the opposite direction, into the forest, toward new Goal A: escape the whoevers who were after him. "There are nature trails that go way back into the island. We could keep to those or go into...

the... woods..." She looked down to her feet and then up at Valiant in utter surprise. "I'm wearing my shoes. Did you–?"

"You'll need 'em," Valiant replied. "*D'accord*, you've been right so far. We'll take the trails and see how it goes."

"But, Valiant–"

"The name's Londo Rand. You can call me Londo. Or just Lon, since we're going to be traveling together. C'mon, Lina. Move it."

Reluctantly, she did. "But your arm–"

He grimaced despite his determination. "My arm can wait. Right now we run."

"But–" They reached the first of the paths into the forest. Lina slowed down to look back uncertainly at Valiant. Obviously he was in great pain, but he pushed her with one hand to urge her forward.

More important than running was getting away from that touch! Lina sucked in her breath. Maybe he hadn't noticed her jump from it. She didn't want to look stupid in front of Valiant. She didn't want to die in front of him, either.

"No arguments. Shut up and *run*," he ordered. So together they fled down the pebbled pathway into the deepening forest.

2

ina was in good shape and kept up with the now-powerless Valiant as they logged a quick half-mile, then a mile. His shoulder didn't seem to slow him. He cursed as an occasional hard step joggled it. Sometimes he cursed in French. He was from Montreal, after all.

Lina hurt just from the glass still embedded in her and that throbbing lump on the back of her head. *Please-please-please–* With every stride she wished that they could take a rest so she could do what she could for the both of them. Valiant ordered them to a walk every few minutes, but he kept them at a quick pace. Lina was out of breath and so was he.

This was all wrong! Valiant should be flying heroically across the sky, or leading a troupe of paraheroes, or maybe the entire United States Army, into action. This was *Valiant*, the number-one hero ever. Ever! (Well, maybe tied with his father, Maximus.)

He should be uprooting trees barehanded and flinging them like javelins toward their pursuers. He should be ripping great canals into the soil of the island and letting the sea fill them, cutting those goons off with a giant moat. And she should be watching it all safely at home in front of a TV.

But this wasn't TV, and this Valiant had to be a little stronger than a norm still, or how could he run so hard with his injury? This Valiant was certainly taller than he looked on the tube. He stood inches higher than she, and she wasn't used to having to look up to that many people. Solidly– no, heroically built, his skin was a honey brown, with medium-length hair that was dark underneath all that dust.

The explosion had laid a sheet of dirty yellow over the familiar Valiant costume of gray shirt, black leather pants, boots and black hunter's vest. Now with movement it was flaking off. And of course the small circular silver pin closed the shirt's neck.

It flashed color and pattern as he moved. She wondered what it was. It always seemed just a little white dot in pictures.

The unreality of celebrity sighting tried to disguise real exhaustion and that horrible pain in her head. Lina clung to her goals for clarity. Don't think; just run. Except–

"Rest break," she dared. They must have come over five miles already. She wasn't prepared for a marathon and Valiant couldn't be used to this, even without the band of agony he was broadcasting. Mustn't let him overextend himself in these circumstances. "Please."

"*D'accord*. Five minutes."

A short log bench marked a curve in the path just ahead. Lina sank onto its far end. Valiant reached out with his right hand to lean on a tree branch, but it broke as he touched it. As his injured arm slammed into the tree trunk, he cried out horribly. He squatted on the path, grinding his teeth, and hugged his limp arm against himself. "Goddam *marde*-sucking *skurn*!" His body shook from his head to his boots.

"That's it!" Lina growled. She sat down cross-legged beside him. "We're doing something about that shoulder right now."

Valiant started to protest.

"Be quiet," she said and shoved his good shoulder down before he could stand up. "Let me help. We won't be going much farther unless we get this fixed."

He finally relaxed under her hand, so she kept it there through sheer determination. Maybe that way he would sit there for a while at least.

"It's dislocated," he said. "Hurts like hell. And running isn't doing it any good."

"I know, and you know what I'll have to do. Give me a few minutes to catch my breath and I'll take care of it." She snatched her hand back from him. Apparently her determination wasn't that strong.

Valiant grunted. "Do you have any experience at all?"

"Do you see anyone else around here who has more? No, I've never done this but I've seen it done. On TV."

He groaned.

She gave him a steely stare in return. "Or we could ask one of those nice terrorists to do this."

Oh god, terrorists. How were they traveling, what did they look like? They wanted Valiant dead! If she could just help him, they'd be all right. Valiant always came through. People were always safe around Valiant.

He leaned back against the tree, rolling his eyes to Heaven. "It has to be set exactly right," he finally said. "When my powers come back, there won't be a second chance."

She nodded solemnly. "I'll ask your shoulder to guide me."

"*Comment?*"

"Your shoulder knows how it's supposed to connect."

She couldn't tell if the sound he made was a groan or a curse. "Listen," he said, "do you want me to catch you a snake so you can hold it over me and dance, eh?" The next sound he made was definitely a snort. "Eye of newt and lizard lips."

"If I were in your position, I wouldn't be so smart with someone who had just offered to help." Now that she was breathing normally, Lina knew he'd be ordering her to run again unless she worked on him right now. She'd gotten mad at his stubbornness so of course he was mad back. This wouldn't accomplish anything.

"I'm sorry," she lied as she focused herself to calm. "It's just that we don't–"

He held up his hand in a "stop" gesture as he twisted, every feature alert.

Gas motor. Coming closer.

"*Kicking frickurnen,*" he muttered, or that's what it sounded like.

"We've got to get–" Lina began, but Valiant had already grabbed her. He pulled her into the forest with his good hand, so swiftly she couldn't even think of getting away.

The motor became much louder all too fast. Valiant pushed her to the forest floor, scooped up foul-smelling, leafy humus, and dumped it all over her. Then he dropped and, with groans he couldn't withhold, did his one-handed best to cover himself in the same way.

He glanced at her. In one quick movement he spat into his hand, rubbed it in the dirt, and scoured Lina's face with what she supposed was a dulling coat of ick.

They lay mere inches from each other, facing the path through the undergrowth. "Now quiet," he growled at her.

Irritation kicked through her fear. What was she, an idiot? There was no time to argue as a dark green ATV *vroom*ed up the path toward them. Two men in camo, dark face paint, and big guns manned it. Equipment bristled from under straps on a mini-trailer.

With a squeal of brakes, the ATV came to a halt. Right in front of them. Had they given themselves away? Lina couldn't breathe. Her heart pounded as if it would burst. Her body vibrated with the force of it.

The two terrorists held a terse English conversation filled with abbreviations and slang of the trade: "coord another LP," "flag the DR-m and give it a double lick." Apparently they were setting up a post of some kind. Silently Lina cursed them.

Kicking *bastard mercenaries. More organized than I expected,* Valiant thought next to her, focused enough to broadcast.

Lina watched the mercs unload the equipment. They didn't act like they'd seen them. Instead they set up a vertical dish on a tripod, fumbling with some of the connections. Now their language consisted of four-letter words and variants thereof, delivered in Aussie accents.

****I don't see any sleeping rolls or cooking equipment,**** she telepathed to Valiant.

He jumped. A clump of leaves avalanched off him. Luckily, the scrape of equipment and mutters ahead of them covered the sound, and the men were looking in the other direction.

****Christ!**** Valiant stared at her. ****A telepath.****

****They don't seem like they're setting up camp. Does that mean this is temporary? They'll leave eventually?****

Valiant's mouth opened and closed. ****I've teamed with telepaths enough to know how it works: I talk to myself as loudly as I can, and you pick it up if you're listening, right?**** His attention returned to the men. ****Oui, that's a listening post. Doesn't look permanent. I estimate fifteen minutes to a half hour. They'll hear what they can hear and then head on. We'll move off then.****

So they lay and waited. And waited. The two mercs put on headphones. Then they silently aimed the dish into the forest and checked their instruments. Every minute or so they'd turn the dish slightly.

Out of the corner of her straight-ahead view Lina watched a beetle make a tour of Valiant's face, just to disappear into his hair. The hero never moved anything other than his eyes, trying to track it as it crossed his nose.

Then it was her turn. Something crawled very slowly across her back. She scrunched her muscles so she wouldn't shudder. Think about something else. Anything. Nice little bug. He wouldn't bite her, would he?

She took a step back from the real world, then another one just for more distance. No bugs there. No mercenaries, either. No guns. No fear. She began to drift...

****Stop!**** Valiant commanded her.

Lina's awareness popped back to reality. ****What was I doing?****

****Moving your head. Up and down.****

She gave herself a grimace. Stupid Muttbutt. ****Sorry. I had "Into the Woods" going through my mind. You know, "Into the woods you have to go, you must begin the journey." I think that was my guides telling me that we have to get off the– ****

****Obviously,**** he retorted and let a beat pass. ****Tell me why you're here.****

****Why–? Because you pushed me down.****

****How did you get here? What brought you here now? I need to know that you're not tied up in any of this.****

He must have shifted and done something to his shoulder because he sucked in a great, silent breath as all the muscles in his face and neck contracted.

The mercs repositioned their dish so it pointed directly past their heads.

Lina thought her hands were well-hidden. Within her mind she reached for white light, centered her chakras in it, and pictured Valiant's etheric body– his shoulder– under her fingers. She could do a rough remote healing at least. She willed warm energy into him.

How's that feel? she asked.

He didn't move. **Is that you? Are you doing that?** Though his position didn't change, Lina thought he was relaxing, sinking deeper into his pile of humus. **How–? Crisse, I can feel that.**

One of the mercs looked around, obviously bored with his job. His gaze dropped to the forest floor just off to Lina's left. If he looked closer... Lina felt dizzy as the fear rushed back full force.

Let me worry about them. You tell me now. Everything.

She kept her eyes riveted on the two men facing her as again they shifted the dish's position by a few degrees, this time to Lina's right. Though she never said a word out loud, she explained haltingly to Valiant how she'd gotten a phone call saying that a travel agent had underbooked and she could win a vacation to exotic Tiawa if she could leave immediately and make her own way to LA.

A blind call?

She told him that she'd checked with various agencies to make sure that this one was on the up-and-up, and how she'd recently had a few clients– **Come to think of it, they've all been new clients,** she mused– give her rave reviews about this particular agency. **I just assumed that they'd gotten my name from one of my regulars.**

Clients.

Psychic readings.

Ah. Here we go.

The mercs had said something Lina hadn't caught, and now they began to disassemble their equipment. They packed it securely in the trailer, radioed someone who answered back with a static-y male voice, and then took off farther in the direction they'd been traveling.

The two of them waited a few minutes before they shook themselves out of their hiding place. Lina opened her mouth to tell Valiant that it was time to see to his shoulder, but he just steadied his sore arm with his good hand and waved her across the path with his chin.

"Into the woods," he ordered her.

"But—"

"Four more ATVs heading this way. I want us deep in the woods by the time they get here. If we want out of this mess, we've got to stop hiding and put some miles between us and them." The stare he gave her was steely. "We must begin the journey."

She had to help him as they trampled through the rough terrain of the jungle. Farther and farther from the path, they pushed through wads of ferns, through sticky spider webs anchored by hanging vines. Some of the vines had needle-like thorns and somewhere out there an animal scurried through the undergrowth. Though he grimaced in disgust at himself each time he did so, Valiant whimpered when he had to slap at mosquitoes.

"Guess we should have gone by beach instead," Lina muttered. She felt stupid for bringing Valiant this horrible, dangerous way. In addition to it all, she was responsible for his shoulder. If she'd let him go first down the rope, he wouldn't be hurt.

"No, you were right about that. That's the first route they took, the easiest. Next they take the easy inland routes— the paths and roads— until they establish a search perimeter."

"And then?"

He frowned as if he considered more possibilities than he was telling. "And then they start moving into the woods. Working backward."

"Valiant, how long—"

"Londo." He stopped, slightly out of breath more from the pain then the exertion, and gave her a don't-argue-with-me look. "My name is Londo."

"How long before they start coming our way?"

He began to shrug and must have thought the better of it. "*Sais pas.* I don't know. I don't know how big this operation is. Is Terry just after me, or something more? Maybe it's all terrorist war games, and I'm just a bonus."

"Who's he?"

"Who?"

"Terry."

"She. Teresa Rhodes. Major mover and shaker on the terrorist supply circuit."

"Oh." Lina had never heard the name.

But Valiant wasn't going to explain. Instead he turned and took a step in the direction they'd been moving, but stepped on a rock and stumbled. He winced with a withheld gasp. From his twitches she could almost trace the shot of pain as it jolted through him.

"What we're doing now," Lina commanded, "is taking care of that shoulder."

"Not now."

"We can't do it if we're hiding, Valiant."

He shook his head violently, as if shaking the pain off. "I said, call me Londo."

Lina stuck her chin out in defiance. "I will if you let me work on it. Besides," she cajoled as he didn't look convinced, "I've got some glass in me that I'd like to attend to."

Sure enough, that decided it. She'd always imagined that he was chivalrous. He turned back to her with a reluctant nod. "You're going to do that whatever you did back there?" he asked. "I could feel that. It was warm."

"No, this calls for a different technique at first," she told him. "I'll need a snake and lots of lizard lips."

That got a chuckle out of him. He seemed to relax. His glance slid over her body, then up to her face, meeting her eyes. How sharp and bright his eyes were, as if he could see right through her. This wasn't some man on TV; Valiant was real. She looked away and pretended to take in their surroundings.

"*D'accord*," he said, "I may have deserved that. Now say it."

"L– Londo."

"There. Not so hard."

Getting the vest off him proved difficult and unnecessarily painful, so they left his shirt on. From the way the shoulder didn't fit right she could tell that it must be awfully swollen under there. Londo leaned against a tree to provide support and even out their height difference.

"This may be a little rough," Lina warned him.

Lon sucked in his breath as Lina eased his arm to a level position, then braced it under her own arm. She held it lightly just below the shoulder.

"Do it!" He hissed at her hesitation.

"I need to match your etheric field perfectly," she replied with all the authority she could muster. Sue had taught her always to keep the client calm and informed. Lina tightened her grip, pulled out– twisted– and eased the shoulder back in.

Londo yelled and tried to jump away despite the tree at his back, but she kept him firmly in her grasp.

"Agh, f– , aw christ," he groaned. She released him. "Next time, try to make it hurt a little more." He heaved a sigh and slid down the tree. "Sorry. I mean, it feels much better." But he was panting.

"The worst part's over. I know what I'm doing now," Lina said. She sat on her knees next to him and placed both hands lightly on his swollen shoulder in proper position. "Hot for pain again, then cold for swelling."

"Make it quick. We need to be moving."

She should tell him out loud he was being tyrannical– many non-Southern men didn't understand the significance of the baleful Gaze of Doom she gave him– but didn't. "The healing will be incomplete. I'll have to finish it later. All you have to do now is relax and talk while I work, okay?"

"Yes, mother. *Skurny marde*, I can feel that. This must be what a hot compress feels like." His chin dropped as the tension lessened. "Is it always like this? Do norms go through this *pain* every day?"

"Dislocated shoulders aren't that common," Lina said.

He grunted affirmation but it also seemed to be a cover for a groan. She told his cells to relax and let her work.

"Is this doing anything for my... other condition?" he asked hopefully.

Goodness, she'd actually forgotten that for a moment. "I think I'd need a lot more time to fix that," she told him. "Maybe a few hours or more someplace where I could concentrate and figure things out. And well, it's not like I'm a doctor. These methods aren't guaranteed. Oh right, I was supposed to tell you that before we started. Psychic ethics, you know."

"Hmf." He shifted but at least this time he didn't look like it caused him agony. "We're making toward safety as it is. Once we reach it, you'll get that time you need."

He looked at her strangely, like he had other ideas for how he'd spend safe time. But he couldn't be thinking anything like that. Lina reminded herself of her Muttbutt loser status.

"Please," she said as she worked, "tell me what's going on. I don't think you're here on vacation?"

He shook his head with a grim set to his mouth. "*Mais non*, I was tracking Terry. She's been too quiet lately. I think she gets more insane every time I see her– and I run into her every few months. She's into aiding large-scale terrorism, and I just happened to catch wind back in New York that she was planning something big and soon, somewhere." He gave little laugh. "Not much to go on. An informant of mine got me a lead that pointed here."

Lina struggled to keep her mind on both the conversation and the healing. "Terrorism in the tropics? I didn't think there was any religious war here. This is a pretty out-of-the-way place."

"*Oui*. French Polynesia; this is about as out of the way as it gets. Which island is this? Bora-Bora? No, this isn't–"

"Tiawa," Lina said.

He nodded. "Ah *oui*, Tiawa. Let's just say that my informant is my informant no more. This was obviously a set-up." Londo's eyes darkened as his eyebrows drew together. His nose wrinkled in distaste. "Obviously. I should have realized... I could have taken some precautions."

"But you didn't, so there's no need to worry about woulda-coulda now," Lina told him. She shifted to brace his shoulder so she could reach the muscles in back better. Under the subtle gray-on-gray stripes, warm flesh filled the satiny shirt. Her hands touched firm muscle and not just an image on a TV screen. This was a being as real as she was. Here was Valiant, really and truly in person!

She forced her mind back to what she was doing as well as what he was saying. This was no time for star-struck mooning, as if she were some kind of stupid para-groupie. Her membership in the Valiant Fan Club had expired years ago. Snap out of it! It was just that he looked exactly like his pictures only more so, and here he was in person– so incredibly handsome and heroic. Hell, he'd come to her rescue! A pleasure of warmth washed through her at the thought. Maybe reality wasn't that bad.

"You said this Terry was a terrorist..." she prompted.

"Usually she targets scientific or arms materiel for resale. Every now and then she comes after me. Who can understand Terry? Sometimes she acts like... like... And sometimes she's determined to kill me." His voice lowered to a confidential level. "We used to be an item– before I realized how crazy she was. *En fait*, I was crazy in my own way back then."

"Crazy? You?" The warmth in Lina's hands had slacked off with her inattention. She summoned the healing energy again and Londo shifted to get more comfortable.

"*Eh bien*, I was a little– no, a lot desperate. And frustrated as hell. I was–" His mouth worked and he turned his face entirely from her.

Lina returned to her position in front. She was ready to start the cooling phase of the healing, but she hesitated. She needed to reassure him somehow. Ordinarily the healer could give a neutral touch on the arm. The healer/client relationship could be misunderstood, she'd been taught, so always be extra careful to be neutral. But though she could touch if she had to in order to heal, she couldn't touch to reassure someone. She had to keep her distance. Instead she put the reassurance into her voice.

"It's okay if you don't want to tell me, Londo. But you should know that I'm an ordained priest. Anything you say to me in confidence will stay that way."

"Good lord!" Lon exclaimed with a laugh. "I mean, good grief. A psychic healer and a priest. They let you become a priest? I mean, the church and psychics..." Again he eyed her up and down. "Not to mention the female thing–"

She blushed at the perusal and hoped he didn't notice. "There's no church involved; it's not that kind of order. Most of the members are psychics of some kind. Psychic work is illegal in a lot of places, you know. But if you can say that you're practicing your religion–"

"Ordination to escape prosecution–"

"I can understand that there're a lot of so-called psychics out there fleecing people, but there are more who are trying to help, and they're getting harassed by the legal system."

"So you all set up a phony order." Sensing illegal activity, Londo was beginning to sound more like Valiant with each passing moment.

Lina's defenses sprang into full operation. "It's not phony! It's legitimate. I've never met a member who wasn't an honest person– well, pretty much as people go. And quite a few Near Death survivors swear that the Order's got an excellent reputation on the Other Side."

"Oh, the *Other Side*. Now I know I'm talking to a gen-u-ine psychic," Londo drawled.

Lina forced herself to calm down. Healing a client while upset was unprofessional and counterproductive. Primly she placed her hands on his shoulder in proper position and summoned a cooling energy. "*Surely* in your business you know lots of psychics. You must deal with all kinds of people."

"I told you, call me Londo," he said, and they both chorused, "Don't call me Shirley."

"Old joke." Lina wrinkled her nose for his efforts.

"Not that old. Psychics. Well, I know one telepath very well, but she's not from Earzh. I've never heard her say anything about guides or the Other Side or psychic healing."

"Golly day, what kind of telepath is she?"

"Highly trained."

Lina made a rude noise. "It doesn't sound like it. I'm a Sagittarian; I talk first and think later, and so I usually tell my clients about guides and such. Maybe what she's highly trained in is not saying weird things in front of people who don't want to understand."

Was he looking to the heavens, or was that a half-roll of his eyes? "She's always seemed very skilled to me. *D'accord*, what's this order about?"

She changed her hand positions and gave a tentative smile. "About fifteen years old." The smile he returned was relaxed and generous. "Really, the only requirement for joining is that if someone asks you for help, that's what you give them."

"*C'est tout?* That's it?"

"Isn't that enough? I mean, it's pretty close to what you do for a living, isn't it?"

"I suppose so. Close enough." Londo rotated his shoulder under her hands. She clucked a warning. "And I guess that I shouldn't question the motives of anyone who can do what you've done with this shoulder."

"How's it feeling? I'm doing a feedback loop on it and it seems to me like it's getting there."

"What does that mean, that you're feeling what I feel?"

"Something like that. To make sure that I'm doing it right." She shook her hands out away from the two of them, wishing she had some salt water to rinse her arms. "Tell you what, I'll stop it there and we'll finish up later. I've got some pieces of glass in me that are driving me crazy. How about you?"

Londo said, "Most just bounced off my clothes." He flexed his spine and shoulders, testing. "Oh. Ah *oui*, I think I may have some still, too. Ouch, in my neck." He reached around with his good hand and picked something out, glancing at it before he threw it to the ground.

"I can work on the cuts later," Lina said, twisting to get at that annoying piece of glass in the center of her back. She cursed under her breath as she couldn't reach it.

"Something stuck?" Londo asked, and she nodded. "Here, let me try." He touched her back.

Lina flinched as if he'd shocked her with a live wire. "Ow! Yes, that's it. I think you just drove it in deeper."

"*Pardon!* I'm not used to this level of strength yet. You're going to have to... give me access." He paused. "Oh hell, I won't look." *Damn it anyway.*

She waited a second and then turned her back to him. She slipped the tiny straps off her shoulders and eased the chemise down in front so that it cleared her back.

Lon brushed her long auburn hair out of the way. It was thick and ropy and just a little frizzed, as if the curl were natural. She hadn't had a chance to brush it since it dried. "*Voici*, here it is," he said. "Hang on." He picked at the sliver of glass, about four inches above her waist. She held herself stiff and trembling. "I'm trying to be as gentle as I can. Did I tell you yet that you're very pretty?"

"Very f-funny," she said through gritted teeth. "I believe you had just gotten off-subject so you w-wouldn't have to tell me how you came to be here in your particular condition."

"Got it. Whups, it's bleeding. Let me apply pressure for a minute and then you can cover up." He passed the sliver to her for her inspection and tried to peer over her clenched shoulders before he remembered that he'd promised not to. "Where was I?"

"T-Terry Whatsherface."

"Ah *oui*. Like I said, I ran into Terry Rhodes. But she was waiting for me with a trap and about a hundred armed mercenaries. I'm usually very careful, especially when it comes to Terry– she's damned crafty– but I didn't even notice most of the bastards until it was too late. They sucker-blasted me with some über-bazooka, and suddenly I'm losing power and on the run, fast as I can. I even had my ParaNet cell out to signal for help, but the gun disintegrated it– and made a mess of my Legion com-ring as well. It was sheer luck that I managed to get away. I don't know what she thinks she can get out of me this time. I mean, my powers will return. It's just a lucky coincidence that I happened to see you before they gave out completely."

"So everything's out except your v-vision?"

"Mm," he growled a positive response. "In an emergency you use what you've got. I looked everywhere for someplace to get myself together, call for help. I wandered around the empty hotel pretty damn dazed until it felt like something was going to happen. Then I saw the fire and then I saw *you*–"

"And you came running to my rescue. Thanks." As soon as he released his fingers from her back, Lina scooted away to secure her chemise. "I wouldn't put much into that coincidence theory of yours, though," she said. "Well, from your point of view finding some bystander is a fluke, but from mine it was the difference between life and death. Besides, there's no such thing as coincidence. Maybe you should reexamine the situation."

"What do you mean?"

She fluffed out her hair, getting rid of more dust and grit as she turned back to him. Londo reminded himself to keep his eyes on her face, not on what were shifting around, pressing against the bodice of her nightgown.

"Oh, I don't know."

Almost offhandedly she began to pick out little pieces of glass from her arms. How could someone be so insensitive to pain? Londo had relearned today all about hurting. He didn't think he would need another lesson for the rest of his life.

And yet Lina continued to peel off the slivers with nary a wince. "All the tourists and workers disappearing from the hotel but me. Ouch."

That "ouch" made him feel better. Perhaps he hadn't acted like a baby in front of a beautiful woman after all. Would she mind if he ran his hands up her legs to help her look for glass shards? Images began to fill his mind about just how helpful he could be. *Just lendin' a neighborly hand, ma'am.* He wore a cowboy hat, boots with spurs, and nothing else. She wore her tiny white nightie that– oops!– somehow fell down around her ankles....

Lina continued, "I'm here because I just happened to win a vacation. From people recommended to me by clients that I've only started seeing within the last six weeks. And then when the hotel's about to blow to smithereens, poof! There you are." She shrugged. "Like I said, I don't know what it all means, but it certainly sounds like something's up. Oww." She gingerly touched the back of her head at that swelling.

Immediately Londo returned to the real world. "Let me see," he said and examined the site. The swelling was more extensive than before. He didn't like the way it looked, but then he never liked injuries of any kind. Norms shouldn't get injured. They died all too easily. He thrust two fingers in front of her face. "How many?"

"Two."

"Are they blurred? Do you feel dizzy?"

"What, you think I've got a concussion?"

"Just being cautious," he told her. Concussions were tricky things. He'd have to keep an eye on her.

"I don't think it's a concussion," Lina said. "My guides are giving me the thumbs up."

"Guides. Where'd they get their medical degrees?" Londo leaned back and picked at his own skin, examining blue bruised patches there. Bruises– him! He lifted the shoulder of his shirt to scowl at the swollen, discolored mass that used to be a good shoulder. He didn't like this. He didn't like being a norm.

Lina tilted her head as if listening to someone not there. "*They* say they attended Wattsamotta U."

That made Lon laugh despite himself. "Them and Bullwinkle, I get it. They really say that?"

"No, I just made that up." She sat back on her heels, plucking a final splinter of glass off her legs. "I'm done," she announced, watching him as he flexed his arm and rotated it experimentally. "How are you feeling?"

"Ahem. *Ben*, it seems I owe you an apology– a big apology. I guess snakes and lizard lips work after all. It feels almost as good as new." The tiny lie made him feel better. Valiant didn't do pain.

"I take it we need to be moving along. At the next rest stop I'll see if I can't do more. I'll heal up some of those cuts." She gestured at his face.

Londo ran a tentative touch over his face and came away with dirt, bits of leaves and spider webs... and grainy bits of dried blood. "I'm bleeding." He opened and closed his mouth a few times before determinedly clamping it shut. Valiant didn't bleed either.

"You were," Lina reassured him. "Nothing's bleeding any more as far as I can tell. It'll wash off, if we can find some water."

"*D'accord.* I'm just not used to being a norm, if you'll excuse the expression. Which way?"

"How should I know?"

"You're the one with the guides."

"And you're the one with the para-vision. All my guides tell me is to move north, north, north, and I have no idea which direction that is."

"North is that way," Londo pointed. He stood up uncertainly before he found his balance. When he reached down to pull her up, she ignored his hand and stood on her own. "And I meant it when I said you were pretty– very pretty. That's a nice dress, too. A little thin, even for this climate, *non*?"

Lina knew that she'd started to blush and tried to hold her arms nonchalantly to cover her chest. "Perhaps I should have stopped and changed into something more formal back at the hotel."

"*T'inquiète pas*; don't worry about it," he said. He took a sighting through the forest for direction. Mercs there, there, spreading out there. He turned back to her and reached behind himself for her to take his hand.

Lina said, "I think we'll need both our hands to get through this."

With a nod, he led the way.

3

They kept to the deep forest. Sometimes they had to force their way through brush that slapped at them as they squeezed by. Now and then a wide canopy of densely-rooted banyan trees let so little growing light through that the forest floor cleared enough for them to run.

Skitterings through the humus hinted at the large rat population, and Lina wished even one of her cats were along to scare off the critters. Terrorists and her cats? She took it back. At least the cats were back home and safe. Unlike her.

"There's steady traffic on all the footpaths I can see," Londo reported. "Someone should charge a toll."

They had no choice but to keep to the woods. At last the two of them came upon a stream. Londo pronounced it reasonably safe, and Lina checked its vibes to see what "reasonably" was; she'd never had to check anything like that before. She saw "reasonably" rather graphically illustrated in her focused imagination: don't drink too much or you'll regret it a few hours later. Best not to drink any, but they needed to rehydrate. So they drank a little and cleaned up as much as they could, but it was quick and Londo insisted that they be off to put as much space between themselves and danger as possible.

From then on they stopped briefly whenever they came to water, but almost not long enough to catch their breath. Lon kept track of the increasing patrols to either side of them on the paths. Finally around midmorning they came to a little hollow in the hills. Lina, who'd set her inner antenna toward looking for water, peered around determinedly.

"I know it's here somewhere," she said. She'd psychically opened herself so much for so long that the world seemed faintly immaterial, although she could still count Lon's fingers whenever he held them up for her. She pointed. "There. Fresh water, and it's clean. Drink your fill."

Londo peered at the small spring. "You're right," he said after a few moments. "Pure water. You'd probably pay six dollars for a bottle of this back home. Let's take a break."

"Good." Lina collapsed onto the moss next to the stream and scooped her hands in for a drink. She waited until Londo had drunk, too, and then immersed her arms up past the elbows. Refreshing coolness washed through her. She directed the waste energies from the healing down into the willing earth, leaving herself unburdened and free. With a sigh of relief she splashed water on her sweaty face, then glanced around.

Londo was looking at something in the trees: brown, over-ripe bananas that might have been good a week ago, but definitely weren't now. He scouted the area and then made a satisfied sound as he disappeared behind some undergrowth.

A spindly coconut palm suddenly swayed dangerously– then swayed again. And again. At last a coconut fell and the sound of impact included a sharp crack. Holding three pieces of mostly shell, Londo returned in triumph.

"Your brunch, *mademoiselle*." He offered one of the larger pieces to her across his forearm like a fancy waiter displaying a wine bottle.

"Thanks." She eyed it. The central portion was nestled in a thick and unappetizing nest of shaggy fibers. "How do you eat it?"

He made a noncommittal sound and examined his prize critically as she looked around for suitable rocks. Lina put the coconut piece on top of a flat one and hit it with a smaller stone until she could pry the meat from the rest. "You may want to wash it first," she suggested as she handed it to Londo.

"Thanks," he said and passed her the other pieces. "What about the brown stuff?" It had a hard membrane around it.

"I have no idea. I'm used to this coming shredded in little plastic bags."

He dipped his in the spring before trying it. "Not too great," he pronounced. "Tastes like... like a macadamia nut on a bad day."

"Wonderful."

"It doesn't taste at all like coconut. Hm, coco-nut. Pretend it's just another kind of nut, and it'll taste all right. It's calories."

He watched her as she hit the other pieces, and Lina got the uncomfortable impression that he was not appreciating her culinary technique. In fact, it seemed to her... The phrase "undressing her with his eyes" suddenly took on a new meaning. She whirled on him.

"Are you using your para-vision on me?" she demanded.

He reared back. "*Non*," he said, and it seemed an honest answer. "No, sorry. I didn't realize I was staring. You just happen to be a very beautiful girl."

But his cheeks flushed. He must have been using his imagination– almost as bad.

"And of course you're catching me on a good day," Lina said. She flipped a sweaty strand of hair out of her face. "Don't tell me that it's tr–" She caught herself. Just because he upset her didn't mean that she had to be petty and upset him in return. "How does the coast look? How many are out there?"

Her next strike freed a good piece of coconut. She sat back to try it. It tasted... not at all like coconut. Was it even ripe? How did you tell?

It did taste like a nut, but it held the slightest of hints that maybe with some processing it could taste like coconut. It needed to be shredded with lots of sugar. And maybe some chocolate and real nuts and a big dollop of whipped cream with some frozen vanilla yogurt, followed by a nice chilled vegetable of some kind to cut it all. With some iced tea. Or a big glass of anything wet and cold.

Londo looked for terrorists through the dense woods. "There are enough around." He shrugged his head as if so what, he couldn't do anything to change things. He'd sat down next to her. She eased away as casually as she could.

Londo didn't notice. "They seem to be covering this section of the island with all due speed, but they aren't leaving the paths. They should do that soon."

At that Lina put down her coconut and moved back to him to use the time to finish up on his shoulder. He watched her without comment. It only took a few minutes; there was only mild swelling. He'd been healing naturally for all the time they'd been traveling. Even as a norm his healing rate was astounding.

"Any reason why you think so?" she asked as she worked.

"It's what I'd do. They won't be able to travel in large groups. I should be able to handle it if we run into any of them."

"Without powers?"

He reared back and looked insulted. "I do have some skills besides my powers," he said.

"Sorry," she muttered. "That's nice to know. Is there anything you can teach quickly? I'd hate to wind up being the red shirt in this episode."

"Red shirt? What are you talking about?"

"*Star Trek*. Classic *Trek*– original series." She shook her arms out after she finished the shoulder. "Hold on a sec while I get your face." She positioned her hands just an inch above the skin there.

He made a wry mouth. "Okay, thanks. *Star Trek*. Sorry, I've heard of it, but never seen it. Any of them. I mean, I've seen real starships."

She tried to imagine such a thing, but… really? "Well, anyway. There was usually an extra security person– security people wore red shirts– and by the end of the episode they were almost always dead, leaving the stars alive to go on to the next episode. The legend of the red shirt, the expendable character. I'm not keen on being one here."

"I'll keep you alive."

"Thanks." She moved to the spring to dip her forearms again and shook them out afterward. When she came back she sat an arm's length away from Londo. "Do we have any kind of real goal? Or are we just staying one step ahead of the bad guys?"

He put down his coconut. "We're going to outdistance them. Maybe they'll think that I managed to get off the island, and they'll give up looking. Maybe they'll narrow the search and we can slip by." He cocked his head the other way. "And maybe my powers will come back soon and we can leave 'em behind in the dust."

"I like that one best. Let me check something."

Her green eyes unfocused and her mouth screwed into a puzzled frown. "Aw, come on," she urged someone. "It's not that hard a question. When?" She blinked out of it and slapped at a mosquito. "Sorry. I was hoping to get a little information from my guides, but they're being obtuse. All I asked was when were your powers coming back, and they hand me a bunch of symbology: circles and triangles and starbursts, and nothing looked like a clock to me."

"Are they usually like this?"

She talked around a new bite of coconut. "Not really. They have their moods, although they say it's their reasons. I suppose that when I look back, if… *when* we get out of this, I'll say, oh yes, that triangle means that it was… oh, three o'clock for the three sides of the triangle, when your powers returned. But it sure would help if they'd just show me a clock. They'll usually do something like that."

"It still seems quite handy."

"Oh it is, it is. I like channeling. My guides are fun. It's nice to know that the Infinite has a sense of humor, you know? That it's all not as serious as they'd have us believe back in Sunday School."

"Guides." Londo rubbed the bridge of his nose. "I'll have to ask Chimrin if we ever get back."

"*When*," Lina said firmly. "Be positive; set your future."

"*When* we get back." Londo nodded to her. "Chim's the telepath I know. I'll have to ask her if she's got guides, too."

"Everyone's got guides," Lina said. "You just have to learn how to listen to them."

"How did you?"

"My dad says I was always talking to someone he couldn't see," Lina said. She didn't mention that he always accompanied that comment with a hard slap to her face. "Of course he says that I was just doing it to draw attention to myself. He made me stop. But when I got involved with the New Age people, they actually had classes in it. You can learn how to channel real quick. Practice makes you good at it."

"You seem very good."

"I practice. I do this kind of stuff on the side."

"The side of what?"

"My regular paycheck comes from commercial art. But every now and then people ask for a reading."

"And because you're a priest, you can't say no."

She smiled at him. She had a bright smile, a smile that warmed. "That's right. I enjoy helping people. Of course, there are those who just hang on and expect you to make their decisions for them. It's very irritating; you sit there and say, '*You* see your choices; *you* make the decision,' and they beg you to run their lives." Lina shook her head with a snort. "Some people."

Londo was trying to contrive how to bring up the subject. "So did you ask your guides about coming here to Tiawa?"

Lina laughed. "There goes my reputation. They said, 'Go ahead, have a swell time,' and didn't mention anything about explosions or terrorists. I must not have communicated with the highest level I should have. Although it has been interesting so far. As long as nothing really bad happens, it'll be an adventure I can look back on someday and tell everyone about. I mean at the very least, I got to meet Valiant himself."

Londo smiled. "And I got to meet Lina O'Kelly herself. Psychic healer extraordinaire."

That made her laugh again as she regarded the remaining slice of coconut and his empty hand. "Want some more? I'm in a bludgeoning mood right now."

"*Bien sûr, merci.*" Londo took the opportunity to slide closer. "So you haven't left anyone missing back at the hotel? Traveling alone?"

"It was a vacation for one," she said as she positioned the coconut on the large rock. "Odd, isn't it? I mean, they're usually for two."

"So who'd you have gone with if it had been for two?"

Lina considered. "I guess I'd have tried one of my friends at work." She paused again, as if listening to the air. "Oh. No, no boyfriend or anything like that."

"Your guides seem to be blunt."

"Better blunt than obtuse." She cracked the hard outer coating off and handed the result to Londo. He'd noticed that she tended not to look at him when she spoke, so he raised the coconut as he accepted it, forcing her gaze to follow the movement so it met his eyes.

"Thanks," he said, and held her gaze for a split second before she looked away.

"You're welcome."

"You're between boyfriends..."

"No."

"Divorced?"

"Never married," she said. She glanced around the clearing, not at him. "Never involved with anyone. Never been out on a date."

He stared. He couldn't help it. Here was one of the most beautiful women he'd ever seen– not glamorous, to be sure, but an earthy, natural kind of beauty– young, buxom, thick auburn hair and bright green eyes filled with life. "How does that happen?" he had to know.

"It happens," she said vaguely. "For instance, there's a certain parahero I know of who's never been associated with anyone. Not seriously. I mean, I've heard about him escorting this woman and that woman and the date contest winners and all, but his love life's never made the cover of *People* two issues in a row."

Londo drew back from her. "Euh... What do people think?" he asked in a tight voice.

Lina knew what he was talking about. "Maybe you were... too busy," she hedged. "Saving the world all the time. You give up a personal life to be a parahero. A megaparahero. Unless... Unless you have some kind of secret identity thing going–"

"Secret identities are a royal pain." He gave a snort at the idea. "You should talk to some of the people who have them. *Non*," he shook his head, "megaparas don't have time for secret identity crap."

"No time for a personal life?"

"Everyone's got to take time for a personal life or they go crazy."

"And no one would want Valiant to go crazy."

He smiled sadly. Now he was the one who looked anywhere but at her. "*Non.* Crazy Valiant would cause too many problems. Been there."

"Um." Lina sat and considered the rumors she had heard over the past few years as if one of them might be true. The leading contender, of course, was...

"I have too many problems as it is." Londo frowned down at his coconut. There was only a sliver left. He crushed it between his fingers and flung it away.

"So it's what they say? Don't answer if you don't want to. But remember, I'm a priest. It won't spread from me."

Londo saw only concern on her face. "Yeah," he finally confessed. "Too powerful for my own good."

"I'm sorry," she said softly, and looked away to give him his privacy. Maybe even famous people had miserable lives. It didn't seem fair for a hero like Valiant. When did karma kick in? Or was karma just a hoax, something that someone had dreamed up to give people like her hope?

"Of course, there is this one thing."

"Hm?" Lina found a forgotten piece of coconut and tried to figure out how to break the shell away from it without destroying it completely. She lifted her rock in preparation for a precision strike.

"It seems that I don't have any powers now."

Her hand stopped in midair.

"And there's this beautiful woman who happens to be here, and who doesn't have attachments anywhere else..."

Lina gaped at him but he smiled encouragingly back. "So do you think you might be available tonight... for a date?"

Now the world seemed to take its own step back from her. This was unreal. He couldn't mean... She closed her mouth and put the rock down. "I don't think it's just a date that you want," she said slowly. He must be utterly desperate, that was it. Poor man.

Londo edged closer. "No, it's not," he admitted. He reached out to touch her hair and twisted a curlicue lock around his finger. "Lina, if we're in safer territory tonight, and if my powers haven't come back, would you...?" He let the question hang in the air between them.

"Londo..." She didn't know how to say it. She moved away from him, but he came with her, still holding her hair.

"You have the most beautiful eyes," he said and leaned in closer. Suddenly he straightened and gave her a *hush!* signal. In an instant he was up and running close to the ground, keeping the forest undergrowth between him and... whatever.

Seconds passed before Lina realized that he was responding to some kind of danger. She sat paralyzed until he disappeared into the forest. Only then did she pick up a fallen branch of fronds and run it through the clearing as quietly as she could, obliterating the evidence that they had been there while trying not to think about anything except gun-toting terrorists with hard faces. She scattered the coconut shell under some leaves and then bent down for a final drink from the spring.

Good, she heard Londo say silently as he came up behind her. **Let me get one, too. They've started to come into the forest. Let's move out.**

They marched north in general, with Londo maintaining a constant eye and Lina an inner one for danger. Twice they skirted squads whom Lina couldn't see against the forest foliage, but Lon could. Often they'd crouch rock-still to hear a walkie-talkie go by some distance away.

Londo regarded her, aware that the situation was escalating. He could see the tightness in her face, how she trembled when they had to wait. **You okay?** he asked. He slipped his arm around her shoulders to comfort her, but her trembling increased. She pried his fingers off and twisted away.

I'm fine, she replied. **I'll just conveniently forget that yellow is the color that the newer Treks used for Security forces. Or that it makes me stand out like a sore thumb.**

He frowned at her nightgown. The staining dust from the explosion had made it a light yellow and white flag against the dark forest. Lon shrugged off his vest, dropped it on the ground, and started to take off his gray-striped shirt. His left shoulder held blotchy bruised patches. Most were turning yellow and green as his injuries healed. The swelling had gone.

Lina gaped as his upper body stood revealed. Michelangelo would have killed to get a model like him. She hurriedly looked away from his nakedness and licked her suddenly dry lips.

Take it off, he ordered her. **The dress. Wear my shirt instead. It's darker than what you've got on, and patterned. You'll blend into the shadows better.**

He secured the vest back over his broad chest and shoulders and politely turned away while Lina slipped her gown off to don the shirt with its shredded sleeve. It closed with what looked like Velcro, but this stuff didn't make any ripping noise when pulled apart.

The small metallic circle lay next to the collarless neck of the shirt. It contained a hologram with Valiant's symbol, the V surrounded by the starburst. But more than just a hologram, the starburst was a bursting, colorful sphere, rotating and changing direction, collapsing in and then exploding again. Lina had never seen such a complete and spectacular hologram before. It was a regular mini-movie.

Leaving the shirt open a couple inches at the top made it less confining, even though the neck opening was comfortably large. Thank goodness the shirt covered her well. She was a very tall woman, just shy of six feet, but Londo was maybe four or five inches taller than she was, and the difference between the broadly-defined muscles of his shoulders and her feminine ones let the shirt hang a reasonable length on her. If only she were tanned darker, that would help, too. She hadn't yet had time on her vacation to get a tan.

How long does it take? Londo demanded.

Sorry! I'm done. She folded up the gown and wondered what to do with it. She might be able to use it as a skirt when they stopped next time, if they got to some territory where the color wouldn't make her a walking target.

Londo looked her up and down. His mouth quirked into a smile. **My shirt looks good on you,** he told her.

He stuffed her dress into a pocket on his vest. Now she noticed that the vest had a number of deep pockets, and wondered what was in them. Not emergency supplies or rations, that was for sure.

Londo looked around to assess their situation. **Five minute break,** he announced, and Lina took the opportunity to sit on a fallen log. Carefully; this now took a little finesse. Londo sat beside her. His hip and arm touched hers, and she eased away.

There's a small patrol next hill over, not moving in this direction. He pointed. **Another patrol over there, going away from us.**

Lina squinted her eyes and tried to match Lon's para ones without success.

So if you've never been on a date, he asked, **does that mean you're a virgin?**

She looked at him as if he were a dolt, but he just smiled, wide-eyed and innocent.

Yeah. As if it were any of your business, she admitted. **Two hundred percent.**

How two hundred percent? Are you counting past lives now?

She ignored him.

C'mon. Two hundred percent. Are you celibate because you're a priest?

No. I've just never been kissed. Never been touched. By anyone.

Londo considered that. **How did that happen?**

I have a little phobia about being touched. Actually, a pretty big phobia.

He opened his mouth to accuse her of lying. Then his eyes moved as if he remembered how she'd pulled away every time he'd offered his hand or sat down beside her. Closing his eyes, he shook his head at himself. **Oh great. God is laughing at me.**

She grinned. At least she was safe from him, now that he knew. **Yes, He is. So you're a virgin too, and against your will.**

But only about, oh, twenty percent.

It was her turn to pause. **Hold on. I'm trying to figure it.**

Let's just say that I've experimented a number of times. I can get a couple bases into the process. Foreplay– I'm good at that, I've been told. Or maybe they were just trying to be nice when I couldn't...

When you couldn't or wouldn't?

Wouldn't. Can't risk injury, especially anyone who'd get into that position with you.

A considerate lover.

Why wouldn't she at least look at him? He had to gain her attention somehow, make her realize that this was far from trivial. **Very considerate, Lina. You'd like it. Don't you ever get lonely?**

Lina was silent for a while. **I've been alone all my life,** she finally told him. **What is loneliness? I get by. I'm fine with just myself.**

Denial.

Is it? I call it adaptation. Whatever it is, I'm locked in to it. I don't get close to people, and they don't get close to me. You seem to have adapted well, too. I mean, I've never heard of you going on any wild rampages in frustration.

I'm lonely all the time. I'd give anything to be truly intimate with someone.

What to say to him? Did he need a counselor or someone to point out hard reality? **You... You could be intimate without having sex. There are thousands, maybe millions of disabled people having satisfactory relationships.**

Let's just say that I'm very, very close to a couple of people. But close and sex close– those are two different things.

Especially for a man, I suppose. Is there any chance to contact those people now? To take advantage of the situation?

Less than zero, Lon told her. **Why especially for a man?**

Women get intimacy first, then go to sex. Men get sex first, then go to intimacy. Different genders, different ways of thinking.

Mon dieu, not the old Venus and Mars thing. You don't believe any of that tripe?

A lot of times it's true tripe.

Londo sighed. He rubbed his nose. Ground the heels of his hands into his eyes. He stared openly at her, this sleek woman dressed only in gray-striped silk. Her long, curving legs. The way she filled out his shirt. She was straight out of one of those early Sixties bachelor movies, where the exotic virgin stewardess winds up– quite innocently– in the hero's shirt and nothing else.

Lon wanted to make it a more modern movie, R at the very least, triple-X and banned in Canada if he could. There had to be a way, a starting point. **You seemed to be able to touch me well enough back there.**

I can touch for healing. That's business, not personal.

Why the phobia? Or don't you know?

Oh, that's easy. Emotional deprivation as a child compounded with lack of self-esteem. In other words, I can blame it all on my parents. Handy.

So see a shrink.

Shrinks are expensive. I've got a slew of self-help books at home and I've taken bunches of psychic courses, but I've never been able to make real progress in this area. I guess I'm too embarrassed about the problem to help myself.

Londo brushed mosquitoes away from himself, wanting to curse out loud. This was one hell of a situation! Easy, easy. **You can heal emotional problems?**

There are lots of non-mainstream techniques, but when you're too close to the problem, they don't work well. She paused and met his gaze. **I'm sorry.**

Don't be. He snorted softly and his eyes crinkled as he looked at her. **I'm going to work on you all day.**

One eyebrow arched. **And how are you going to do that?**

You mentioned three things. Never been on a date. Well, consider this a date. Voilà, we're at Adventureland. He gestured to take in the forest.

Lina shook her head and gave a soundless laugh.

Lon slipped his arm around her waist, caught her by her cheek and turned her. He gave her a quick kiss before she could protest. **A touch and a kiss. Now you're at 100 percent; I've cured half your problem. I can cure the rest, too.**

With a gasp, she pushed away but didn't get anywhere. He still held her by the waist and now his other hand slid from her cheek to stroke her neck and chin. He moved in so his mouth, his nose, his eyes were only inches from hers. **Get used to my touch, Lina.**

Londo!

It's not so much to ask. Just let me touch you.

She trembled until she shook. He could see her grit her teeth and try to fight it even as she pushed away.

It's a for real phobia, Londo. Please stop. Stop it! Stop it!! She made an inarticulate sound and was about to make another when Londo clapped his hand over her mouth. The quick, short breaths she sucked in and out pulsed against his palm. Her pupils shrank to pinpoints.

QUIET! he ordered. **Do you want them to hear?!**

Ohgodohgod, let go. Please let go, letgoletgoletgo LET ME GO!!

4

She scrabbled against him, and when that didn't work she shoved her own hand under his against her mouth. He let her loose then. She fell to the ground: shaking, teeth chattering. She pressed both fists against her mouth and curled into fetal position. Faint, inarticulate squeaks emerged despite her efforts.

To Londo it looked like a seizure.

Lina! Are you all right? Lina!!

She spasmed. Great shudders rocked her, as if she'd been stranded in the Antarctic, shivering for her very life.

Lon fell to his knees beside her. He reached to touch and then hastily drew back. **Lina. Talk to me.**

The shudders subsided little by little.

Lina? Lina?

Eventually her hands de-clamped from her mouth. She covered her eyes. **Give me a few minutes. Please. I'm sorry. I'm sorry.**

Dizzy with relief, Lon sat back on his heels. He studied the way she shook out her arms as if she were releasing something clinging to her. She tried to breathe rhythmically, couldn't quite do it. Then she shook her arms out again.

How long have you been like this? Londo demanded. Great waves of quaking overtook her with every third breath. He wanted to help her, but how? How without touching her again? How without the patrols hearing them?

It was a long, long while before she could reply. **I don't know. A little ever since I can remember. Really bad since fifth grade or so. I'm better than I used to be.**

Better? This is better?

Used to be I couldn't touch anyone. Now I can heal. I'm sorry. She just lay there, a wrung-out rag. She panted shallowly behind the hands that hid her face.

And no one notices this? Again he reached out to help, but caught himself and backed away in a crouch.

She shook her head. **We're not a very touchy society, Londo. How often do you go around touching people?**

I like to touch people. I just have a problem with controlling my strength when I'm doing it. Why didn't your parents do anything?

Lina gave a soundless laugh. Her eyes peeked out above her hands. **They would have had to care first.**

Londo digested that. **D'accord. So what are you going to do about it now? You, yourself?**

I hadn't planned on doing anything.

So you'll live the rest of your life not being able to touch or be touched? You're planning on dying a virgin? Is that Goal A?

Lina's eyes narrowed as she raised up, her shoulders squaring. **I hadn't put it in writing.**

So when are you going to get over this? When are you going to want someone to touch you, to have sex with you? Will you wait until you're eighty or ninety, and then suddenly decide you don't want to be lonely anymore?

She sat silent, hands clasped, and stared into the woods.

You've got to get past this sometime. Today's as good a day as any, and maybe better than most. Have your phobia for everyone else, not for me. Please. He leaned in to her line of sight, so close she couldn't turn away.

"Help me, priest," he whispered. His brown eyes held a sharp sheen of desperation as he took her hands firmly in his own. He held them up so she could see that was all he was doing.

Lina gasped at his temerity. **That's a dirty trick,** she said. She began to squirm in his solid grasp. He gave a nod as if she'd done well and released. Lina gulped her relief.

You have to help anyone who asks. Please, Lina, you've got to do this for me. Get over this touching thing. Let me have sex with you tonight— if I can find us a safe place. If my powers haven't returned.

Her green eyes flashed outrage. **You'd force me to do it?**

I'm not going to rape you.

She scrambled out of his reach. **By asking me as a priest, you're taking my free will away. This is a legitimate request, I can't refuse. I took a vow.**

Maudit! he exclaimed and threw up his hands in surrender. **D'accord, *I'm not asking you as a priest. I'm just asking you to tell me what might put off this phobia so that maybe you'd consider having sex with me tonight.***

She rubbed her hands as if she were washing his presence off herself. Somehow he had to get through to her!

It would just be a... *an hour, a night, maybe an entire day. Just a few hours out of your lifetime,* he pleaded with her. **But for me it would be something I could look back on for the rest of my life.***

She didn't look at him as she sat on the ground. **It, *it's probably impossible.***

We don't know until we try. *Consider this: there are times when you can touch and you're fine. All you have to do is to enlarge that idea to include me in it.*

I'll think about it, Lina told him.

About what we can do about the phobia, or about– *the proposition?*

Let. Me. Think about it, she said.

Londo huffed in frustration. **Okay, *you do that while we get out of here. Don't forget to come up for air every now and then to check in with your guides.***

She nodded, afraid to respond? Not looking at him at all. He stood up and took her hand firmly in his, crooking an eyebrow at her. She met his eyes dangerously: watch what you're doing. He smirked back. He knew exactly what he was doing.

For the most part.

C'mon, he said as she snatched back her hand, and led her back into the forest.

The next hour they spent scrambling through rough terrain that quickly rose to long, lumbering ridges. Once Londo got stuck in a briar and fought against it, entangling himself so thoroughly that he was forced to a standstill. He fluently cursed the entire time it took Lina to pry him loose and then gave what he could of the sprawling briar a good kick of *adieu*.

They pushed through thick stands of forest only to come unexpectedly upon sun-lit clearings where massed orchid blooms made delicate mosaics upon tree trunks. The sudden beauty made even Londo pause– for a few moments. They continued on.

Lina knew Londo was tired, but then so was she– exhausted– and terrified as again and again they stopped when they spotted a patrol of big men with guns. Yet she found herself dozing for the fifteen minutes they took to make sure that a patrol was far enough away from them before they resumed their journey north, always north.

Once she woke wondering what the weight on her back was. It turned out to be Londo asleep. He wouldn't trigger any of her fears that way. They had both fallen asleep sitting up, their backs to one another. She let him rest for a few more minutes while she sank into a deep session with her guides, a thorough clairvoyant scan of the area.

You wanted adventure, her guides reminded her. Other than that, they said very little. Still no word of when Lon would get his powers back (but yes, she knew in her gut that he would, if they could survive long enough). Still the information was that north was the safest way. Nothing else.

So she let her thoughts slide through the forest, picturing the island as a map in her mind to pinpoint where they were on it. Ah, there: crosshairs on the map, practically in the middle of the lower half of the bloated C-shaped island. She zoomed in, asking: closest phone, closest *working* phone. Little arrows flickered across the landscape, very possibly indicating phones, but judging from the map, the size she knew the island was, and the fact that the majority of Tiawa was a private eco-preserve, they were too far to do any good– except for that one there. That arrow held steady and didn't blink. It wasn't too far away, considering how far they'd already come. Northwest. North-northwest. Try to get it exact so they wouldn't overshoot it.

Londo. She was afraid to speak out loud, for fear that someone would be listening.

Judging from the jerk he gave, he woke instantly. A second to get his bearing. **How long–?**

Just a few minutes. I was asleep for a while, too. Which way is north?

He pointed.

She considered and pointed just off to the left of that. **About two or three miles. A phone, I think.**

He squeezed her shoulder and she tensed. **Good girl.**

Arf.

Oh be quiet, he said with a smile as he stood up. He held out his hand to her.

This touching thing was ridiculous. Lina set her jaw and took his hand– a small victory.

That way's north. Which way is it again?

You know. She pointed definitely. **North-northwest.**

Just making sure that you're sure. He squinted in that direction, then nodded. **Voilà, I see an estate. There's a stone wall on this side, but I think it's climbable. Come on, hup hup.**

The rough wall was indeed climbable if they made sure their handholds and toe-holds were secure. A novice to rock climbing, Lina took her time on the fifteen-foot wall. Lon went first and checked at the top that she was climbing well. By the time she reached the top to pause and rest, he was scouting on the ground beyond.

There didn't appear to be anyone around, but this was a forested corner of the estate. Well-kept gardens and a swimming pool lay next to a villa about a half mile away. The house was two stories, an uncomfortable pink mix of modern and pseudo-Italian renaissance, lavish in a nouveau-riche way.

"Come on down," Lon called softly from the ground. "I'll help you."

"Don't! I can make it on my own."

Lina searched for good handholds on the hot, pocked stone. Then she slipped. She scrabbled to get a secure toehold.

"Just drop," Londo commanded.

"No!" Lina closed her eyes and double-checked by feel what holds she did have. Left, left... there. Yet her toe still wanted to slip.

Londo's arm wrapped around her waist. He'd climbed up to her. "I've got you," he said in her ear as she flinched. His legs pressed against hers; his stomach squeezed up against her butt.

"Lon–" A suffocating white curtain of fear wrapped itself around her. Her left hand lost its grip as the world faded away.

"Don't panic because I'm touching you. Now *I'm* helping *you*; I'm allowed to do that. Concentrate on your handholds, on your toeholds. I'm just here to steady you, got that?"

With a ragged breath, she tried her damnedest to focus. Lina crept down the wall with him beside her, his hand on the small of her back. Almost down, and he dropped to the ground below her. Now that she was within reach he caught her, sliding his hands up her hips to her waist. The shirt slid as well. Londo took firm hold of her to lower her gently to the ground, and then loosened his grasp to allow the shirt to slide back down.

"You've got nice legs, too," he said softly as she looked up at him.

She just wasn't used to having to look up at that many men, but Londo stood over her, all broad shoulders and thick, bare arms. He made her feel small and vulnerable in comparison. He backed her up against the wall so that their bodies brushed together. There was no place for her to go.

"Londo, please..."

"Feel me touch you, Lina," he whispered. His eyes said *you're mine tonight.*

"I don't belong to you," she said. She knew she was blushing. No one had ever looked at her with this intensity. He radiated a tightly-controlled lust. She clenched her jaw to keep it from touching her.

He played with her hair with one hand, regarding her chin and mouth before he gazed into her green eyes. "I can't imagine fate being any clearer than this," he told her. "Me, powerless, and along comes you. On a tropical island, yet. Is the moon full? That would make it complete."

"It isn't," she said. She didn't tell him that it was gibbous, close enough to full.

"Close enough to full." He laughed softly. Damn, had he read her? They had been using telepathy a lot.

He stood there with one hand still on her waist. "It's working, isn't it?" He trailed the other down a curlicue of hair and suddenly that hand was on her arm. He pressed her closer to him and leaned in for a kiss. His clothed legs brushed the naked skin of hers.

In order to escape the hand he had in back now she'd have to move forward, but there he was. She couldn't escape backward, because of the wall. Sideways? He had her trapped. The entire expanse of her skin tried to shrink away from him. The only parts of her that could roll up upon themselves were her hands, and they balled into fists.

Heart pounding, Lina fiercely ordered herself not to faint, dammit! The world narrowed into far-off tunnel vision. She shuddered against the cold numbness of panic. The only action she could take was turn her face away from his.

"Car," she gasped, and his lips brushed her cheek when she said it.

"Hm?"

"Jeep," she said, nodding to the distant driveway through the trees. A camouflage-colored Jeep sat outside the ornate entrance to the pink villa, incongruous at best. There were no people around, though a cloud of dust hung behind the Jeep as if it had just arrived. They must have missed hearing it while she was having her panic attack. Lon leaned away from Lina to look in the car's direction.

Then he sighed. "Woman, why can't you keep your mind on the important things?"

"Silly me," she replied, easing him farther away using just the tips of her fingers on his shoulder blades. "I thought you might be interested."

He closed his eyes in defeat and shook his head. "You arranged this, didn't you?" He lowered his hands. "*D'accord*, don't move too quickly. They might see the movement."

They kept to the purple shadows of the trees as Lina took deep breaths, trying to counteract her shudders.

"There are three of them," Lon reported as they crouched behind a thick stand of bushes near the house. "They're inside, checking it out."

With the slightest of leftover trembles, Lina asked, "Do you know how to hot-wire a car?"

The question must have surprised him because he blinked twice at her. "No," he finally said. "That's a skill they missed in self-defense class. Seems stupid now that they did that." He gave a slight snort as he eyed the car again. "Quick escape, transportation, maybe a cell phone...."

"How difficult can it be? Kids do it all the time. Let me try."

"I don't see keys in the ignition," Lon said. "If I give you an all-clear signal from the side second-story window, or maybe the first floor, then you try hot-wiring. But stay hidden here until I signal you, you got that?"

She considered. "You don't have any powers," she said. "We should try the car. Leave the bad guys in the house; get away while we can."

He shook his head, his eyes on the house. "No arguments. I'm in charge of battle teams." He glanced back at her. "I'm not used to explaining myself," he said and nodded to the house. "There are three highly-professional, heavily-armed mercenaries in there, and they're moving around at a good clip. By the time we figured out how to get the car going, they'd probably draw a bead on us. And if we can start the car, we've made a little noise, maybe attracted attention. *Non*, I take care of them first, and you try the car when I signal you. Those are your orders."

Lina thought about it for a moment. He certainly had more experience at this kind of situation. Follow Valiant and be safe. "You don't have to signal; just give me a call." She tapped her forehead.

"Even better."

"And remember that you aren't up to your usual standards. Don't overestimate your abilities."

That provoked a scowl. "You don't question team leader in the midst of battle," he said.

"We aren't in the middle of battle," she retorted.

"That shows how much you know," he told her with a grim smile. "We've been in a battle all morning. Now stay out of sight." He patted her on the butt as he left, chuckling quietly.

Lina watched him as he slipped through the noon-day shadows, stealthy and powerful as a hunting lion, grace and taut energy dressed in tight black leather. He was Valiant; he could take out three goons, couldn't he?

Valiant or not, he was certainly sex personified. She wanted to respond to him. She wanted to enjoy his touch, maybe even try to touch him herself, but her brain just wouldn't let her. Every time he got close, a switch inside her mind labeled "FEAR" clicked on and obliterated any rational thought with panic.

But maybe he was right.

Maybe just being around him so closely with his desires so easily read, was doing something. Now that he was gone she could still feel his hands on her, warm and firm. The softness of his lips. Hear his sweet whispers. Here and now it wasn't frightening at all. It was, well, rather arousing.

Thrilling, really. The memory of him made her feel tingly all over. Warm. Excited.

What the hell was wrong with her that she couldn't feel that way when he was doing it? Stupid, stupid Muttbutt!

Only one day in his whole life that this opportunity would present itself to him. Who was she to refuse Valiant, the champion of Earth? But what he wanted was more than she could give.

Maybe they would find another woman somewhere on this island. At the very least, there was that Terry person. She had the hots for Lon, and he could probably call up some reciprocal feelings if the situation presented itself. Lon was very resourceful that way.

Lina wondered: Terry's plot had condemned Lon to this condition. Was this the plan, so Terry and he could have sex? It made sense. But if it was, where was she? And why send all these mercenaries or terrorists after them? It seemed to Lina that a bouquet of flowers or an invitation to a candle-lit dinner would get Terry what she wanted a lot more efficiently.

It also occurred to Lina that if Terry were romantically pursuing Lon then her own female presence so near to him might not be in Lina's own safest interests. Still she felt much, much safer with Lon around than she would ever have out on her own, trying to survive the jungle. Even powerless he seemed to be a lot savvier in stealth matters than anyone else she could think of.

She watched Londo disappear behind a corner to enter the front door of the villa–without bothering to check in any windows. Of course. He could see the men's locations right through the walls. With a shock Lina realized again that this was Valiant, not just Londo. What a shame. Valiant remained too far beyond her reach, but Londo might not.

What was she thinking?! With her phobia, any man fell beyond her reach, and no one but a very desperate man would ever want the likes of Lina Muttbutt. She groaned at her miserable reality and waited for Lon's signal.

Londo crept silently into the house. Thank god he still had his vision powers. If he hadn't he would have dreaded doing this. He would have felt human and helpless.

But he was Valiant, ParaNetter and Mega-Legionnaire. These were merely Terry's hired men. Enough already! She dogged him, always testing him with something worse than the time before. She needed to be taught a lesson and he'd teach her so she would never forget.

But just for now he must lay low, protect himself until all his powers came back. Protect Lina, the civilian caught in all this. Protect Lina, who held his dreams in her hands. And other places.

God, she was a luscious woman. Between the thin material of her dress and his shirt pulling up on her, Londo had gotten a very good look at what lay underneath those clothes, and he was going to enjoy it just as soon as they got to safety, wherever that might lie. He'd work around her phobia somehow.

He smiled to himself before he remembered his new vulnerability and the three well-armed men in the house. Concentrate on the here; concentrate on the now. Kuttr and Jae's voices echoed in his head as years of combat lessons rewound themselves for him. How would Jae handle this?

As Lon advanced his smile returned, a grim promise to those who would stand in his way.

Upstairs first. That would put him above the other two on the way back. He kept his steps on the supporting framework of the stairs, lessening the possibility of squeaks. The house was quiet but not silent; that helped. Birdsong and a breeze's rustle came through open windows.

Londo watched his target in the master bedroom checking into closets, into the ensuite, anything that had a door. Assured that there was no one here, the man slung his rifle up and back on his shoulder and then shuffled his hands through dresser drawers. There he found some jewelry: rings, a watch. He stuck them in his pocket and moved to more drawers.

The door from the hall to the bedroom had hinges that would swing in, so Londo couldn't hide behind it for an ambush. A shallow linen cabinet stood in the hallway adjacent to the next door, one to a bathroom. Londo took his position inside that door, hidden by the cabinet. He waited patiently. Professionally.

The man finished his search of the room. Peering all around, he emerged into the hall. He held his rifle stiffly in front of himself, ready to fire.

Now Londo took the pill he'd found in the bathroom and threw it hard against the top of the wall, above the man's line of sight. *Tok.* The man and gun whirled to the slight sound.

Lon shot out of his hiding place. He rammed three fingers unmercifully into the nerve cluster in the man's neck, right off the jugular. Lon's thumb dug at the top of the spinal column. The rifleman crumpled. Lon caught him, grabbing his rifle lest it go off. He eased the man to the floor. No noise.

With the first one tied, gagged, and left lying in the bedroom, Lon peered through the floor to see where the other two men had gone. One was entering the back door. He must have gone outside to search.

Lina! Was she all right? Londo's breath caught as he sought her. There. She still sat behind those bushes, well-hidden from the house. Still, it seemed to him that she looked up directly at him as he looked at her. Such a strange girl.

The remaining mercenary slunk through one of the wide, elegant rooms downstairs. The first floor sprawled about four times as large as the second, numerous salons crowded with modern western furnishings, wet bars and electronics. This must be quite the party house when people were here.

The merc found a painting on hinges that swung out to reveal the door of a wall safe. He glanced around before rummaging through a small pack on his belt.

From his position, Londo smiled. This one would be last.

Padding to the back stairs, Lon positioned himself almost on the opposite side of the house from man number three, but around the corner from the one who'd just come inside. He stood above where the wall opened over a pantry or butler's supply room with neat cabinetry hiding dishes, cleaning supplies, and canned goods.

Below him, the second man emerged. Londo vaulted the stair rail and landed squarely on him. The merc rolled as they fell. Though the impact knocked his breath out, he still grabbed Londo. That powerful hand sinking into his flesh shocked Lon to the core. He was human now. What wouldn't have affected him in the least now *hurt*. He could feel himself bruising from the fall, from the attack. He had bones that could be broken. A body that could be killed.

Save it for later– this man had a bear grip! The mercenary hooked his arm around Lon's neck and clutched with his great paw of a hand, aiming for Lon's eyes. Lon buried his elbow in the man's stomach. It worked so well he repeated it hard as he could, then hauled the gasping man's hand away from his eyes, pinning it to the wall.

But the bear-man surprised him. Even without breath he rose up reaching for his gun as Londo loomed above him. The parahero kicked him down again, slammed the man's head against the floor and grabbed the pressure points under both ears. He pressed and held until the man slumped. Lon punched him with dagger-like fingers on the pressure point to the heart, then on the back of the neck. The man lay limp on the floor.

"Ow," Londo allowed himself the luxury of saying as he rubbed his sore hand. He stretched and massaged the back of his neck, then tested the ankle he'd fallen on, before he tied this one up. One more to go.

Man number three and last was up to his elbows reaching into the back of the safe. He dredged out small notebooks and boxes of jewelry that fell to the floor in front of him. Londo took advantage of the noise to creep across the rug behind him.

The thief pivoted, swinging his rifle down level and ready. A second of surprise bloomed on his face, then fear as he beheld Valiant before him– but Londo froze and the man's features slowly hardened into a sneering grin.

"Valiant himself, eh? One more step and you're hist'ry." He had a broad Australian accent. "Ralpho!" he shouted. "Barnes!" He waited for some acknowledgement. Londo smiled dangerously at him.

"I don't think they'll be coming to help. Drop the gun and I won't hurt you. Tell me what this operation is."

The thief eyed him warily before his hard face eased. "What's going on is that you don't have any pow'rs, Valiant, do you? If I let loose with a couple here, you'd be on the floor dead in your own blood, right? Your hands won't stand you much good against my gun."

Damn himself anyway! Lon never operated with guns. It had never occurred to him to take one of his captives' weapons. Stupid! Now what were his options? "I take it that means that you're not going to cooperate," Londo growled.

The man laughed at him. "You've still got your balls, at least," he said. "Now hands on your head. Get over there." He motioned with his gun to a velvet chair. "Looks cushy, don't it? Sit down."

Lina! Lina!

Londo? Time to–?

Shut up and listen. He held a terse conversation with her as he slowly, so slowly retreated in front of the man's gun.

"What," the man said, "are you slower than a wet week when you don't have your powers? Now, Valiant!"

Lon grudgingly turned and sat in the chair, watching the man's every move. The thief already held a length of rope. Lon could see tapes and cords in his backpack, ready for use. **Now, Lina, now!**

"Yoo hoo! Sue, are you in there?!"

The man startled at the sudden female halloo from outside. Londo sprang up, sending him sprawling on the carpet. The rifle went off– just one round. Londo slammed his fist hard into the back of the man's neck and he went limp.

Lina's face appeared at the window. Her eyes opened wide as she took in the scene and then focused on Londo. "Are you–"

"And what would have happened if he'd won and there you are with your head in the window?" Londo chastised her. "Just a little more caution, Lina. Just a bit."

She frowned uncertainly at him. "Yes, Commander. Are you all right?"

He let himself relax as he sat on top of his prisoner. "I'm fine. Consider this a signal to figure out the car while I truss up this one."

She nodded and disappeared. Londo got to work.

5

She'd been gone a long time. Londo took extra care to bind these mercenaries thoroughly. They'd have been trained to free themselves.

How's it coming? he asked her at one point.

Damn. I guess I'm too dumb to be a criminal. Let me try something else.

Lon couldn't find keys on the thief anywhere. He dragged the first man downstairs, letting the body bump-bump, bump-bump with every step, and brought him in to join his comrade on the living room floor. Then he went to retrieve the last one. He got a good grip on the bear man's bindings and began to drag him.

Abruptly the front windows blew in. Glass cascaded in daggers as something outside exploded with a roar. The Jeep! Jesus christ, Lina! He heard timbers breaking, followed by a smaller secondary explosion. Metal on metal. A momentary overwhelming stench of gasoline.

Lon used his para-vision to find the Jeep beyond the front wall of the house, only to see pieces of twisted metal, shards of glass and tire and cloth lying on the ground. Hardly any smoke. Spatters of crimson dotted everything. He clamped his eyes shut; he didn't want to see body parts. Not Lina's. Oh lord. A human caught in that would have been blown to pieces instantly.

He turned from the scene as the bear stirred. Lon kicked him hard and he lay still. The bastard must have had some kind of remote incendiary device wired to the Jeep in case it fell into enemy hands.

Christ, Lina. Lina! As he dragged the bear behind him, Lon wanted to cry. She'd been so beautiful, so brave. So perfect for him for tonight. He felt guilty to dismiss her entire life just thinking about the night he had lost, but here it was. She was gone.

But in addition to the promise of the night, he realized that part of the magic of the world had drained away with her loss. Spirit guides and psychic healing and mind talking that seemed so much more intimate than ordinary talk. That smile of hers. Those guileless eyes. His insides twisted in anger, in frustration, in loss.

Another one gone.

He wouldn't think about it. He refused to think about it! Instead he roughly checked his three prisoners, their own handcuffs now contributing to their detention. He added a loop of twine from the cuffs to their necks– a little trick he'd learned so they wouldn't squirm too much. Londo took pleasure in imagining their dread when they woke up, the defeat and fear they'd experience. Just a start of the payback they owed him, owed Lina.

He used his newly-won knife deftly in cutting twine and knotted it too tight. A part of him wanted to lay their throats open for what they'd done to his Lina. Instead he let them fall hard to the floor when he was through with them. *Bâtards!*

She deserved a burial. He'd have to go out and–

"Jeez, do you have to be so rough?"

Lon spun at the voice, dropping the dagger. Lina stood in the dining room doorway. She held a cloth sack stuffed with bottles of water and newspaper to keep them from clinking.

"Lina!" He crossed to her in a second and took her in his arms to clutch her to him. She went stiff as she tried to pull away.

"I thought you were caught in the explosion." Relief flooded him. God, he wanted to kiss her all over, hold her forever. That damned phobia! "You're alive."

He put down the bag for her, trying to slow himself. Then he used just two fingers to place her arms gingerly around his neck. She immediately started to draw away. "You kiss back," he told her in a no-nonsense voice, and went in for a kiss. After a moment's hesitation, she eased forward and their lips touched. The taste was sweet if reserved.

She broke from it almost immediately. Her face blossomed rosy pink as she didn't meet his eyes. He lay one finger on each of her arms to keep her in position. She pinched her lips together and her brows contracted at the constraint.

"See?" he said softly. "It's not fatal. It can even be kind of nice."

He ran the very tip of his finger so lightly along her jaw line. Her eyes widened; her lips parted slightly with a tiny gasp.

"Now relax along here," he said. "I'm so glad you're alive."

He took her mouth for a long kiss. She kept withdrawing her arms but brought them back again, as if she were forcing herself to touch him.

"Very good." He kissed her again, daring to gently touch her waist and draw her close. She stiffened even more at that.

You're alive, you're alive...

Through the thin material of her shirt he could feel her heart speeding up, but this was a panic speed. Her breathing became erratic. She pushed him away and he backed off without protest, still smiling to see her. He could only repeat, "You're alive."

"I do appear to be," she said, trying to look anywhere but at him. If anything, she turned redder. She clutched at the neckline of her shirt and gulped in air.

"Darned if I could get the car started or find a hidden key, so I figured we might need some supplies. I looked around as long as you were busy. The phone's still working, but I had no idea who to call. The woman who lives here must be a midget, I mean little person, because her clothes are all so small. Windows are open, so whoever was here must have left in a hurry. The fridge is still pretty cold even though the electricity's off. These people haven't been gone that long."

Londo had to laugh at the thoroughness of her practical search. Her face was clean now, no longer covered with the dirt of their march, and her hair had been brushed and tied back. "Very good reconnaissance, Lieutenant," he said, and that made her smile and look quickly at his eyes.

She turned curiously to the prisoners. "Ah," she said.

"Ah what?"

"Now we know what happened to some of the people at the hotel," she said. She bent down to inspect the bear in particular. "This guy gave me the creeps all afternoon yesterday. I was afraid to go exploring with him around. The hotel never told me that their convention was for mercenaries."

A knot somewhere between Lon's shoulders melted away now that one big mystery was solved. "What, the seminar about the proper application of camo makeup didn't give them away?"

"Couldn't get in without a membership badge."

"Can you find out from them what's going on?" Lon asked. "Read their minds?"

Her mouth twisted in consideration. "It'll work better when they're conscious. I think that'll take a while." She cocked her head at him. "Care for some lunch in the meantime? Do we have time?"

"I'm famished. For whatever reason, these men are far from the others, not following the search patterns. I bet they wanted to loot this place in peace, or at least before anyone else could. We have a while. I'll make sure we're out in time."

"Then I'll see what I can whip up." She took her sack and walked into the kitchen. Londo followed, savoring the sweet sway to her as she moved.

"I saw some bedrooms in the back of the house and upstairs," he mentioned. "There are king-size beds on the second floor– just in case those fellows are out for a long time." She didn't reply and he smiled to himself.

They explored the extensive pantry and kitchen and found enough to make soup and some very acceptable sandwiches. Even with a good sniff, Lon was unsure what the meat was, but they were in no position to be choosy. They found some fruit, a few vegetables, and what they didn't eat that was portable went into Lina's bag for later. There was cold fruit juice for now. Lon grabbed a couple cans of Coke to add to the bag. Simultaneously they spotted the wine.

"It's a good relaxer," Londo said. "All you need to do is to relax, and I bet that'll be the end of that phobia. Or our virginity at least."

"I'm sorry, Londo," she said miserably. "I'm screwing up everything. Alcohol doesn't make me drunk; it puts me to sleep. That's a little too relaxed, isn't it?"

"Shit," he said before he could stop himself. "*Eh bien*, it was a good idea."

"Maybe they have some tranquilizers around here somewhere."

He regarded her wryly. "It's a good thing I have no ego, or it would be shattered by now. Apparently we need to get you drunk or doped in order for us to have sex. You don't find anything you like about me? Nothing to start us off?"

Lina looked away from him. "I never said that."

"You've been acting like that all day. You and that damned phobia of yours."

"I'm sor–"

"So tell me, is there anything at all about me that you like? Anything that attracts you, so I can use that as a starting point?"

Her blush reappeared rosy and deep. She turned her back to him. He ran his fingers through her ponytail. "Hal always told me," he murmured, "he said, 'Londo, if a woman grows her hair so long that you can't stop yourself from touching it, well, maybe that's why she grew it that long to begin with.' Is that right, Lina? Who did you want touching your hair?"

She said nothing and he placed his hands lightly on her shoulders. "Let me touch you. I won't hurt you." Only the tiniest of trembles reached him. She turned her face slightly and he leaned to kiss her on the cheek.

"They say a woman's skin is ten times more sensitive than a man's," he whispered in her ear, "and today my skin is a million times more sensitive than it usually is. My hand– it's only my hand. And it's only your arm." He ran his palm as slowly as he could down her left arm, and she followed it with her eyes. Then he did the same with her quivering right arm. He caressed her fingers, stroking them, and slid his hands back up to her shoulders. She shuddered under his touch but did not pull away.

"You're living in fear, not enjoyment," he told her. "Switch gears. Time for pleasure, beautiful Lina. Carolina in my mind. Give it five minutes to see if it isn't pleasurable. Just five minutes."

Her breathing ran ragged and sharp despite her attempts to quiet it. She couldn't speak, only shake her head. "Let me... Let me try to find some tranquilizers," she managed to say at last.

"And there go the last shreds of my self-image." He let go of her with a heavy sigh.

"Londo, it's not you at all. I'm sorry."

"Just let me gather myself together and do what I can before I collapse in utter shame. Tell you what, I'll mosey around and see what else we can find here. If you hear anything, anything at all from either those guys or outside, give me a call and I'll come running."

"Okay." The smile she gave him was watery. "Can you give me five minutes first before I have to keep an ear out? Do we have time?"

"Five minutes?"

"I was thinking about a shower."

He sidled close to her again. "That might be a very good idea. But the water's probably gone cold by now. You'll need someone to warm you up in there."

"You've been watching too much *Playboy* Channel."

"Uh huh."

"Give me my dress while you're at it." She reached to the pocket he'd put it in and pulled it out before he could protest.

"What do you need that for?"

"I'm going to try something." She glanced sharply at his questioning face. "You have first watch," she told him.

"*D'accord*; all right. But don't use up all the water. I wouldn't mind getting clean again, too."

"And don't you dare watch me through the wall!"

"What kind of gentleman do you take me for?" He tried to sound hurt but laughed to himself as she left. Lon turned with a sigh and looked around to figure a quick way out of this mess. The wine rack stood in a corner like a beacon. Crap vintage. Screw top. He stashed a bottle in their bag.

Lina came back into the kitchen almost exactly five minutes later, her hair up in a towel and carrying her nightgown and a comb. She was still dressed in his shirt, he was disappointed to see. He'd hoped she'd only have a tiny towel wrapped around herself, like in a 007 movie. One wrong move and the camera would cut to a scene of the two of them lying in bed so satisfied while the soundtrack played cool jazz.

He snapped back to reality. "My turn," he told her. "I might be a little longer."

"I'll yell," she promised.

Lon caught sight of himself in a mirror before he got in the shower and inhaled sharply. Not James Bond at all. No wonder he wasn't making any headway with her! Streaked with sweat and dirt, scratches on his face, his hair half building powder, eyebrows still dusted with white– Still... She could tell that he was pretty good underneath the damage. He ducked into the shower and gasped at the shock of the water. Cold– the memories of cold crashed back to him. It had been a long time...

When he finished he found his comb in his vest and worked diligently to get everything just right. One of his vest pockets held his stash of hair gel– never go anywhere without the gel– and he used it now.

These scratches weren't all that major. Norms healed from scratches all the time, didn't they? He'd heal from these. Lon grabbed some toothpaste and did what he could using his finger, then gave himself a brilliant smile. Um hum. Lina tonight, maybe sooner. He patted his muscled belly as he preened before the mirror. At last he reached down to pick up his clothes and shake them. Just to be thorough, he beat them against the wall.

What the heck are you doing back there?!

Movement outside the window attracted his attention. She was hanging that nightie up wet over a trellis. It was now a dark color, a bluish charcoal gray.

Nothing much. I see you found some dye.

She glanced up at that and spotted him at the window. He settled on the wide ledge and propped his foot against the sill. Then he slapped his pants hard against the outside wall. That raised a nice cloud of yellow dust that hadn't gotten out before.

Lon! She turned her back hastily.

Tell you what, chérie, he laughed. **Why don't you wash that shirt of mine, too, while you're at it? We can both sit out in the sun where it's nice and warm while everything dries. You'll like that. We won't have to touch; we can just look.**

She kept her back to him as she took the towel off her hair and began to comb it out so the breeze and sun would dry it. **I don't remember hearing about this side of you when they showed you on Biography.**

So you keep up with me on TV?

...Doesn't the entire world?

Some do. Some don't. I'm honored that such a beautiful girl does. Did you see anything– on Biography– that you liked? Is there anything about me that you like, Lina?

Of course there is.

Like what?

Well... You're the greatest hero in the world. Everyone knows that.

Most people would say Maximus, if they're naming paras.

Well, some people would say his son.

Do you like heroes, Lina? Londo emptied the pockets of his vest as he prepared to slap it against the outside wall.

Everyone needs an inspiration, be it human or para. Or angel, for that matter.

Before he hit his vest on the wall he paused to savor Lina and her hair. The comb picked up a mass of auburn and feathered it until it fell, golds and reds and browns in the midday sun. It curled in long, loose ringlets far down her back.

Londo tried to swallow but his mouth had gone dry. **What else? Flatter me.**

You don't get enough flattery? I thought you said that you were tired of women throwing themselves at you. That you were tired of going to places where women would make a point of parading themselves in front of you. Or they'd conveniently lose parts of their clothing in your presence.

You don't look like the kind of girl who reads Playboy.**

It was on the lunch table at work.

At work? Businesses are a lot more liberal than I thought. That woman who did the interview, she was the one whose blouse conveniently untied as she leaned over. Trying to make it like other women did that, too. The editors wrote me an apology.

So she was sorta like all those women who said you fathered their kids? Lina sounded amused now.

Do you have any idea how much time it takes to go to court?

Why don't you just tell them you're a virgin? Hm?

Because maybe I don't want them to know. Dearest Lina, being a male virgin is not at all the same image as being a female one.

So you'd go to court rather than confess in an interview and then dare any woman to claim you lied.

Are you listening to the prisoners?

I'm listening. I've got guides standing by, too. They agree with you about time.

All right. I remember one woman reporter. She printed that I was brave, loyal, thrifty, and devoted to God and King and country, and then turned around and said that I spent money like there was no tomorrow, was hopelessly atheist, hated politics in any form, and looked at least twice at every female who crossed my path. I liked that article. I kept it.

It had a nice picture of you on the cover.

Oh? You're a* Cosmo *girl?

Only when I like the cover. As I recall, it had the year's astrological calendar in that issue. I might still have it at home.

And you framed the issue to cover a crack in your wall?

Don't be silly. Did you date the reporter afterward?

She was a very nice lady, a grandmother of three. Does that make you feel better? Tell me you like me, Lina.

Of course I like you, Lon. You've rescued me a few dozen times today. Other than being a little bossy and a lot horny, what's not to like about you?

That's my girl. Now get back inside where you can actually hear those prisoners. It's not that I don't trust those guides of yours, but—

But you don't trust my guides.

Exactement.

Yes, Commander.

He flashed her his best smile as she glanced at him before she went inside. So she read articles and watched shows about him, did she? Thought he was better than Hal, did she? Humming to himself, he got dressed and checked his hair again.

He took a few minutes to explore the place with wider attention. Only the servants' quarters had any kind of lived-in look. The owners must use this as a vacation home. Out of curiosity, Lon opened a closet in what looked like feminine living quarters and laughed. "Little person" wasn't quite right, but it was close. The maid must be a tiny but robust woman, and his Lina was very tall and where she had any extra fat, it was located in just the right places. He wandered on to a male bedroom looking for a shirt for himself, maybe a larger shirt or dark robe that Lina could wear, but again the occupant seemed to be very small.

Lina had stuffed a can of insect repellent into their bag and now Lon thought that might have been a wise move. His first experiences so far with the mosquitoes of the tropical forest had been unpleasant. This had not been the right day not to have thrown on an undershirt before he left home. He scratched his bare chest and looked down. Maybe he should leave the vest open. Women liked bare chests, and he knew his was impressive. In fact, maybe he should ditch the vest altogether... and maybe not. He'd see how it went.

He ventured out to investigate the Jeep for salvage. He might use a short-wave radio or satellite transmitter to contact the Network. Instead he found two axles, half an engine block, and not much else. Terry did like her high explosives. This had been particularly compact and efficient. It was a wonder that more of the house hadn't been damaged. And it was true enough that reddish liquid was sloshed about: transmission fluid.

Lon ground his teeth at the thought of what might have happened. He'd been able to spend most of his life feeling a little– no a lot– cocky. He couldn't afford to make that mistake or any other now. He didn't have any intentions of dying, and he was damned if anyone was going to harm Lina!

Absolutely, especially before they had some very special time together.

He returned to her in the kitchen where she sat beside a battery radio, fiercely listening to one station that he realized was broadcasting in French. "No tranquilizers," he reported.

She nodded at him absently. "They're not mentioning anything amiss. Business as usual. They're not local, but I think they're from this island chain. I don't think anything from here is actually broadcasting, not that I've found."

"You understand French?"

"Not enough to carry on a real conversation," she told him. "I can understand it better than I can speak it. With me it's one phrase at a time."

He nodded sympathetically. "I remember how it was learning English," he said.

Lon didn't try the landline yet. With this kind of operation, someone certainly had a finger in communications. They'd use the phone the last thing, on the way out. Still, the phone sat there like the ultimate temptation. He desperately wanted to try it now to see if they could get through. If that happened they could be rescued within minutes. The Network could have this island secured in no time.

Then he would go home to recuperate and take Lina with him. Even she'd appreciate his bed after a day like this. She wouldn't refuse him. He pictured her there, naked under the sheets, holding out her arms and welcoming him as he slid in beside her. Inside her.

Londo jumped as the walkie-talkie of one of the men in the next room crackled with a garbled voice. He shook himself into sharp awareness. It was time to get back to work. How long had it been since the explosion? He'd thought that they could be remote enough from the nearest of the other troops for it to have passed unheard, or at least vague in direction.

"Get in your dress if you're going to," he told Lina as he repacked their bag more efficiently before he returned to the main salon.

Two of the men were stirring. He shook the third awake. They lay there sullenly, glaring at him though the fear crawled up their faces to live in their eyes. Valiant.

Alert as a hawk, he leaned on the edge of a table, taut and dangerous. "Anyone want to start?" Lon asked them in a voice that made Lina shiver where she was, hidden from the men.

Valiant was known to be the warrior Rand, as opposed to his father. Now she could see it. She'd hate to be on the receiving end of Londo's hard eyes.

The walkie-talkie interrupted again, a male voice asking for check-in. Someone missed these men.

"We've got you surrounded, Valiant," the bear-man sneered. He had an Australian accent also. "Everyone knows you're operating widout yor pow'rs."

As he stood, Lon considered the man. He propped his foot on the seat of the chair next to his captive's head. "Oh, there are powers enough at my disposal," he said. The man started to say something and then cried out as Londo twisted the twine that wrapped around his throat. His cry turned into a gargle. "The power of breath, for one. I know lots of little tricks. And of course, there's my partner here." He released the twine.

The man's squint shifted as Lina stepped into the room. It started at her sneakers and ran up her legs to the dark skirt of her chemise, until it got to what was obviously Valiant's shirt. Up to her face. His gaze widened to a stare. Obviously, she wasn't supposed to be there.

"They know I'm a telepath," Lina said wonderingly. "How'd you know that?" She turned to Londo. "There's something about the two of us. Something… If they found the two of us together, they were supposed to… leave us alone? Or herd us... I'm not sure." She turned back to the mercenary. "What does that mean? Why?"

The man's face screwed up in concentration.

"Very good," Lina said. "Someone's been teaching them how to close their minds. That works great for telepaths, you know that?" she told Lon. "For psychics, though, there are ways around it. Why don't you ask some questions, see what we get?" She tried to mimic Lon's swagger and threat in her own manner. This was no time to play the fainting female.

Londo gave an evil smile to the men, and Lina could almost see them quake in their boots. "*D'accord*, it's *Jeopardy* time, but the answers don't have to be phrased in the form of a question." He turned to the lead man, the bear. "Where's Terry?"

The man didn't say anything, but stared stonily ahead at nothing.

"That looks like St. Catherine, some kind of mansion there," Lina said. "It feels like it's their headquarters. People talking… I guess that's a communications center. Vehicles. Oh, helicopters." **Do you know how to fly one?**

I can get by. "How many of you are there?"

Lina considered. "Hard to get an exact count. Over your hundred, that's for sure." She looked at the leader, the one whose face was so contorted. "Two hundred infantry," she said. "Thank you."

"So the expression doesn't really do that much for the effect?" Lon asked.

"Oh no It just makes him look silly."

"Stay out of my mind," the bear-man said, but the demand was cast in fear.

Too calmly, Londo replied, "But we have questions we want answered. You want her out of your mind, you're going to have to speak out loud to me."

"We'll keep her out of our heads."

Lina gave him a kindly smile as she sat in a red-upholstered chair and made herself comfortable for effect. If they saw she was at ease, they would automatically relax. "I'm so sorry," she said in a sincere voice, just a tone or two lower than her usual speaking pitch. "I know it's impolite. But down inside, you want to tell us; I can feel it. You know that it's the right thing to do, and deep in your hearts you want to do what's right.

"Each of you is not the horrible person you'd like the others to think you are, not really. Inside you is your true self. You know your true self; you want to do what's right. You want to live in the truth. It's so much easier to tell the truth, to help people, isn't it?"

She went on like that for a few minutes more. Londo admired the way she used her voice. She sighed a lot, and he noticed the men relaxing more each time she did it. He recognized the technique. He'd been put under hypnosis and through guided meditations before. It was the voice of quiet, unthreatening authority that bent the strongest will.

The first man's face evened out. He gave an earnest little smile as he gazed at Lina. **You've got one,** Lon told her. **Maybe that other one there. I don't think the big guy's going for it too much, though.**

Well, it only takes one. Keep your voice soft, Lina told him. **Ask.**

You do it. You're the one they're listening to.

Lina's voice didn't pause, didn't vary in timber. "What we're offering you is a chance to live that inner truth, to let the good in you shine through. Remember, you are the light of the world, I can see that; I can see that. Now, tell us what—"

"Death before dishonor!" the bear-man barked. He'd been the least glazed over. His abrupt words awakened his teammates. They glanced at him, at each other.

"No. No! You can't! Londo!" Lina jerked alert in her chair. "Stop them!"

"What?"

She could communicate quicker telepathically. **Pills. Suicide pills. Oh lord—**

Londo pulled open the jaws of the man who'd almost been entranced just in time to see the pill go down the man's gullet. He flipped him over and performed the Heimlich maneuver, but the man was dead before it could do any good. He jerked as he died. The other two lay still around him.

"Oh my god!"

Lina gaped at the bodies on the floor, both hands splayed over the lower half of her face. Her wide eyes stared, unfocused. "I've never seen anyone die before," she finally said slowly as she rose from her chair. "Yes, you're dead," she said to the air. "Why do you think you're standing there when you're lying there, too? That's what being dead means."

Londo stood slack-armed. Lina was in earnest conversation with someone, something.

"Suicide," she said. "You took life and threw it away. All right, so you've done that with others, too. Now you've done it to yourselves. You know how wrong that was, don't you?" She paused. "Good. So why don't you tell us what we want to know? They can't hurt you now for telling us. It would help us and make you feel better. Answer Valiant's question. What's the safe way off the island?"

Pause again. "*North half unguarded; it's too far for them to penetrate on foot. They couldn't be there.* Thanks. Now, what was this... about us? That you weren't supposed to bother us if we were together?" She nodded. "*We didn't know you were together; we just saw Valiant. Orders were to bring him in if he was alone. To kill you if you were alone. To follow and observe absolutely undetected only if you two were together.* Why? Wait a minute. Please. Just a minute."

She held one hand up in halting motion, her face drawn and anxious. "Wait. Don't take them just yet. Let them stay just a few minutes. What is time to you? We have questions." Pause. Then, much chastised: "Of course I do. Yes, this is more important. I understand. Wait– do you think you might help us?"

She listened for a moment and took a deep breath. She closed her eyes and then looked up at Lon. "I'm sorry. That guy–" she pointed at the bear. "He saw the tunnel and went in immediately. The other two– an angel came to show them the way. It was time for them to go." She looked so contritely at Londo. "You don't argue with the angels when they're on a mission. But he said... He said..." She seemed confused.

Londo still reeled in shock. Had she really talked to the dead?! Was she so insane, or was this real? "What?"

She shook her head. "He said that the way off this island lay within us. '*Within you,*' he said, and I don't think he was talking about you." She pressed her lips together. "I don't know; maybe I got it wrong. Maybe he means that your powers will come back soon. I'm sorry that I can't be more exact."

Londo blinked and nodded. He hadn't expected to be able to get anything out of dead men anyway. Hearing her grill ghosts– and somehow he knew that that's what she'd been doing– had chilled his bones.

"All right," he finally said. "They haven't answered their check-in call, there's been an explosion and a mangled vehicle is sitting out front, visible from the air.

Someone will be out here soon. They're still a couple miles away, on the road. Let me try the phone and then we're out of here."

Surprised to find a dial tone, he punched the international ParaNet emergency number. When it picked up on the first ring, the tightness in his back relaxed.

"ParaNet emergency." Tara's voice.

"*They* say we need to leave, Lon," Lina said urgently.

He nodded, not pausing. "Code Armageddon, Londo here. I'm on–"

The phone went dead.

"*Maudit*!" he exclaimed. "Okay, we're really on our own now. Let's move." He reached over to the table where he'd put the men's rifles and slung one over his shoulder, shoving two extra clips of ammo in a pocket. He held out his hand to her. "Lina?"

With a shaky nod Lina gathered up the supply bag and ran after him, out the back. They had known she was a telepath. Somehow she wasn't just a civilian caught up accidentally in all this. They were after her, too. She looked at Londo and knew that he'd either caught the thought or had realized the same thing.

Why? They both asked themselves as they ran.

6

Within a half-hour the forest tops clattered with the sound of helicopters: ten in a perfect row, flying in a search pattern. The two of them huddled under the thickest leaf cover they could find.

"Will they see us?" Lina whispered to Lon. In her fear of being discovered she didn't notice his protective arm around her.

"No, not in this place," Londo lied. "Even if they use scanners, there's a lot of heavy growth and we've been keeping under it."

"But still, a human registers differently than plant life."

He nodded grimly. "We can only do what we can do."

Lina ducked her head as the helicopters thrummed overhead. She pulled the lines of nature like a blanket to cover the both of them. Hide away. *We aren't here!*

Londo studied the skies. Of course they could track them. Surely they had sophisticated enough equipment to do this much. But the helicopters stayed on track, never wavering. No, wait– one of the helicopters slowed, breaking formation. It hung over where they'd been about twenty minutes ago. Londo's hard eyes sized up the situation as Lina's fingers dug into his shoulder. He could feel her heart pound against his chest.

"Sh-should we make a break for it?"

"*Non.* We stay here. The copters that went past us didn't seem to see us, but they could very well have motion detectors."

"Oh god."

The helicopters circled, regaining their formation as they backtracked. Lina tucked her head under Londo's chin and hid them under a thick blanket of earth energy.

Puzzled, Lon watched as the copters cut by them and did not pause. Did they not carry IR scan units? Those sure looked like Heinzig-Barre models, but his view was from below– not a good angle. He couldn't imagine anyone not equipping a search squadron with them.

Damn not having powers! He wanted to fly up and take some of those copters out of action with his bare hands before they could even react. Throw them into the Pacific, put the fear of god into them!

Lina whimpered only once as the helicopters returned. Lon held her close, watching for any hesitation in the copters' courses. Preoccupied, he rubbed her back to calm her. "It's okay, it's okay," he murmured in a sing-song.

Finally he began to believe it, too. The helicopters continued westward above the forest. "They're gone," he could finally announce.

He let out a breath he didn't know he'd been holding and there was Lina's head under his chin. She was plastered against his body, clinging for life. Slowly she raised her eyes to the sky, and then looked down to see her hand on Lon's shoulder, her arm wrapped around his back. How she'd almost crawled onto his lap.

"Oh," she said.

He kissed her. They were already in a tight embrace, and now he kissed her hard. His fingers sank into flesh that resisted his touch instead of disintegrating at it, and he pulled her even closer. Her arms locked around him. Her hands pressed against the muscles of his shoulder and back. Her mouth answered his. She gasped a little when they broke apart, but so did he. He didn't let her think as he kissed her again and again.

He didn't care if the little sounds she made were of protest or passion. She was kissing him back. He let his hands explore her. He was eager for her, unleashing the ardor chained for so very many years. He could have her now. Here.

She smelled of sweat and dirt, her hair tangled with the odor of crushed leaves. He moved down her neck and she clutched helplessly at him. Her breasts were so soft. Her heart fluttered under his hand. This was what he wanted; human-to-human contact, no fear of hurting her, no terror that the slightest misstep could kill. For once in his life he could let go completely!

"Londo..." she whispered. Was it a warning or a plea for more?

He wanted her. No time for preliminaries. Now, now, now! He pushed up her skirt and kneaded her butt.

She squirmed. "Londo. Mmph. No. Londo..."

He began to pull her panties down.

"Oh! Stop. Stop it, Londo!"

Kissing her on the mouth muffled her protests. She tried to push him away, but he held her head steady with one hand and stroked her inner thigh with the other. He rubbed her soft, fuzzy warmth.

"Londo!" With a sudden burst of strength, she pushed his shoulders away.

With a start, Londo flashed from a warrior's frenzy back to sobriety. What was he doing?

She slapped his face. Hard. "Stop it, dammit!" she hissed.

"Augh!" The sharp sting woke him further from his primal fantasy. He touched his chin as the wave of unfamiliar pain pulsed in his cheek. Lina rolled away from him.

"Aw, jesus," he groaned. "Ah god, I'm sorry. I'm so sorry. I don't know what came over me."

Lina lay there on the ground, staring at him in shock. "Ohmigod," she whispered to herself. Remorse bubbled like a cauldron in him, the animal in him pushed back down to wherever it had come from, leaving bitter shame. She saw the mark of her hand against his cheek. Valiant's cheek, and she had slapped him!

His face turned stark red. Lon couldn't look at her. "I'm sorry," he repeated. "I didn't mean it. Not that way. I'm not like that. I'm not!" And yet a small, dark corner of his mind whispered, *So close...* He shunted that down, pushed it as far away from himself as he could.

He didn't watch her as she straightened herself. "Are you all right?" she finally managed to say.

He glanced at her and then away. "How can you ask me that? I practically mauled you." That tiny voice in his mind whispered *rape*, and he cringed from the thought as if it were a knife pointed at his very soul. "Forgive me. I'm so sorry. I am so sorry." He finally managed to look at her and knew that she was back to being her untouchable self, so separate from him. "It won't happen again. Not that way. Please believe me!"

She licked her lips as she considered. After a very long moment she said, "I do."

Londo dragged his hand down his face. "I don't know what came over me. All of a sudden, I... I..."

"I understand," she said shakily. She reached for their bag. "Let's get going, shall we?"

He stood up alongside her, but when he went to take her hand she pulled away from him. With a nod, he led the way through the forest. North.

The next time the copters came from that direction, a double line. The two shrank back into the forest, and this time the fact that Lina didn't hug to Londo for protection seared his conscience. They hid under the exposed roots of a cluster of banyan trees and watched what they could of what was happening in the sky. Londo reached for Lina's hand, pausing just inches from her. She took it. As the copters got closer and closer she squeezed it and inched to Londo's side. He pressed his other hand around hers, rubbing her knuckles as she shut her eyes.

"Angels and devas protect us."

Even Londo offered up a prayer to protect this innocent girl who was under his care. She trembled against him, and he put his arm around her waist gently, as a comfort and nothing else.

"It'll be all right," he murmured to her. "It'll be all–" Suddenly he tensed. "What–?"

Be quiet, he told her. **Mercs coming.**

She pressed a fist to her mouth.

When I leave, stay put. Stay still. Wait at least twenty minutes before you move, and then go north. Take your time, keep your antenna up, and don't take chances.

**Londo– **

He checked his rifle and replaced it on his back. **Do as I say, cherie.**

Lon didn't wait for the nearest soldier to come into sight. If they were going to spot him, they were going to do so before they could get in range of Lina. He crept through the undergrowth. He still held the advantage of being able to see his enemy while they couldn't see him.

Gunfire would draw too much attention. Londo hefted some rocks and kept two, one in each hand. Now was not the time to play the dainty megapara who had to hold his punches. Now was not the time to stun them for a few moments. These men had orders to kill Lina, and there was no way in hell he was going to let them do that.

He melted into the shadow of one tree, blending into the landscape like Jae or Kuttr would have done. The mercenary didn't even notice him until Lon slammed the rock into his skull from behind. The man dropped with a grunt, but that was all. Blood streamed from the back of his head and Londo forced himself to remember what the man had planned for Lina.

Past a stand of slender trees stalked a second soldier in the squad of four, spread out in their search. Londo tossed up the second rock in his hand, experimenting with its weight. Motion was a hazard, but he'd only get one chance. He wasn't para in strength now. He tossed it again, trying to figure how much power he still had, and then crouched motionless, watching and waiting.

The merc scanned the forest using a portable sensor, moving it in an arc. The sensor swung closer and closer until Londo finally fired the rock from his hand like a cannonball. It hit its target square on and the soldier fell, his body letting out a soft *clump* as it hit the earth.

Where was the other one?

A heavy-booted foot slammed into his back. Londo fell forward, rolling, his mind racing. *Don't stand up where they think you will.* He pivoted to the side and kicked out, targeting the ribs. A double-fisted smash into the mercenary's jaw sent him reeling backward. The merc regained his feet. He ducked unsteadily to butt Lon in the belly with his head and got in a hard punch as a follow-up. Lon staggered.

A small "Oh!" distracted the mercenary even as he reared back to connect with Lon's jaw.

Blood shot in a spit from the merc's nose as Lon's fist cracked against it. Lon followed through with a battering of blows to the man's head and stomach, using his knee to deliver the telling stroke. He secured the merc with a hard press to the familiar nerve center in the neck. If nothing else, that much guaranteed unconsciousness for at least an hour.

Lon crouched on the ground trying to catch his breath. ***I told you to stay put,*** he accused.

I did.

Sure enough, Londo had unknowingly circled back. The fight had been within sight of the banyan stand. Stupid.

One more, he told her.

Londo! Behind–

The sharp butt of a gun barrel poked into Londo's spine. "Hold it right there, Valiant," a gruff American-accented voice told him. "Not a move, or I'll kill you where you stand. Or at least injure you so you wished you was dead."

Get ready! Lina's clear voice rang out from the foliage: "Your orders are that no harm is to come to Valiant!"

Londo seized the moment of hesitation. He rotated his body against the gun so it swung away from Lina's position. The barrel seared his back as it fired past him. Lon continued the smooth motion, using the momentum to add force to a smashing blow.

Before his eyes the fight concentrated into slo-mo: the Australian hat falling away from the man's face, a stream of spittle spraying out of his surprised mouth as it opened, the hands releasing their hold on the rifle.

Londo punched him hard in the side, kicked him in the balls when he was down and then kicked him under the chin. Blood spewed out of the man's mouth as Lon gave the final blow to the nerve cluster.

Gasping for breath, Lon wiped the sweat off his brow. He surveyed the area, searching for more soldiers– there were none– and estimating the extent of injuries he'd inflicted in the enemy. Good enough. He yanked the rifle from the mercenary beside him and then removed its ammunition. A knife and more ammo clips he stowed in his belt and vest. Finally he straightened and held out his hand toward the banyans. Lina's relieved face appeared in the foliage. She darted out to him, taking his hand.

"You're hurt," she said. "Let me–"

"Later," he told her between gasps as he caught his breath. His ribs throbbed. Lon bent down to the soldier who'd come after him hand to hand and took his gun, too. All extra clips he could find went into his vest or their supply bag. The extra knife he threw into the deep woods.

Lina followed him as he examined the remaining two. "These men. I don't think–"

"This is war, Lina. Sometimes men die."

He could see worry and fear and uncertainty mixing in her face. By now she must think him a monster. He couldn't help what he was. Lon turned back to strip the other soldiers of their weaponry. The one's walkie-talkie didn't take much to de-commission: throw its battery pack down a ravine. He handed extra clips of ammo to Lina and she stashed them in their overstuffed bag.

"We don't set up a Red Cross station for them," he told her.

She nodded reluctantly and then reached into their pack to hand him a water bottle. He hadn't realized how thirsty he was. Now he drank half the bottle before he recapped it and passed it back.

She looked everywhere but at the downed mercs. Dark blood streamed from a knot on the second one's forehead.

Lon placed a reassuring hand on Lina's arm. "These men aren't the type to obey orders they don't agree with," he told her. "I don't think they're just going to leave us alone because we're together. It's too easy to separate the bodies after the deed is done."

She nodded again, but she didn't look at him, either.

He squeezed her arm and she met his eyes. She didn't pull away when he leaned forward; his lips brushed hers and then kissed very softly. His hand stayed precisely where it was, and he didn't touch her with the other.

"Forgiven, *cherie*?" he whispered when they were done. "Please."

She said nothing. Then she reached up to touch both palms so lightly to the sides of his face. She kissed him now, and it was all he could do to restrain himself. He rubbed her arm only the tiniest bit.

It was a gentle kiss, but a long one. The tension in his shoulders began to drain away. The sting of the bruises on his face started to–

"Hey!" He broke them apart. "You were healing me!"

"Maybe."

"I said to save that for later."

"And I thought you wouldn't object if we got two things done at once."

"There's a time and a place for efficiency," he growled– but softly and with a smile, hope in his eyes. "Not just after a gun discharges. We need to clear this area." He glanced around and pointed with his weapon. "North," he said.

They disappeared into the deep forest.

Lina clutched at the outcropping hiding her from the next patrol. She hated guns. She hated the anger and fear associated with them. Londo crouched next to her, peering through his rifle sight at these living, breathing men below them. They all had guns.

Men and their awful games! They took them much too seriously. People could get hurt. People had already gotten worse than hurt this afternoon. She knew that two of those last men Londo had taken care of wouldn't last much longer. One had already died maybe twenty minutes ago. She could sense angels waiting patiently and lovingly to take the others away. No one ever died unloved.

Angels, make it so Londo doesn't have to hurt anyone else! She knew deep in her heart that he didn't like this. He hurt himself whenever he hurt others, and she couldn't bear to see that.

There was something about him that wailed in the etheric wind, howling of lone-liness and a soul so injured it bled. *Angels, don't let Londo hurt any more!*

Lon eased back on his heels, lowering the rifle. **They're moving on,** he re-ported. **We rest here for fifteen minutes, make sure they're away.**

Lina waited three before she reached to hand him the water bottle. He was a soldier now and she carried his battle supplies. Tonight she was supposed to be the camp follower to service his other needs.

This Londo scared her. He was all war and fighting efficiency, his nerves taut, his senses alert. He didn't need these skills normally. Brute, undiluted mega-force should accomplish everything he needed to do. He must have had extensive training somewhere. Who would train Valiant for this?

But she had to admit that he was good– good enough to take out a four-man squad with only the most minor of injuries. She put her hands on his vest in the center of his back. Time to heal that nasty burn from the gun. He sat still, scanning the forest, almost oblivious to her.

Where was the laughing, joking man of earlier? The man who didn't have twenty layers of steel over his heart? Where was that beautiful smile of his? Now his eyes burned almost black, his brows dark as he considered their situation. This was no man; this was someone who had turned himself into a fighting machine. Survival was his only goal. And she was only holding him back.

"Lon, maybe I should stay here," she said. He turned to regard her with a neutral gaze. "This seems safe enough. There's already been a patrol past, so they know this area's clean."

"No."

"But you can move a lot quicker without me. You can find some way to signal the Network, and then when they arrive you can come back to pick me up."

"I said no. That's final. Don't argue." He kept looking around, pausing as he must have spotted soldiers how far away? Lina rummaged through their bag, now a lot lighter than it had been, and drew out the can of insect repellent. "Thanks," he said as she handed it to him.

"Have you been inoculated for malaria?" it occurred to her to ask.

He stopped at that. "Malaria?"

"Mosquitoes, the tropics..." she said.

"*Non.*" He spritzed the stuff on himself, wrinkling his nose and waving the spray off as he forgot to protect his eyes. "My powers will come back and all my immunities with them. No problem."

She nodded and he returned the can to her. As their hands met, the ground trembled. They both reached out for a tree to steady themselves.

"Oh!"

"Did the earth move for you just then?" Lon asked. Branches swayed as if a stiff, circular breeze blew. A few coconuts fell to the ground.

"They said at the hotel that earthquake activity was increasing. There's a volcano on the island, you know."

"Jeee-zus. *Non*, I didn't know. I saw a couple of mountains..."

"Volcano. My guidebook said that this island gets hundreds of micro-quakes every day."

"That wasn't micro. Just what we need added to all this. Anything else your guidebook warned you about?"

"Um. This is still the rainy season, the end of it..."

"I wish. Does this seem overly hot to you, or is it just me?" Lon wiped the sweat from his forehead. Damn it, being a norm reeked.

"It ain't the heat, it's the humidity," she told him and he smiled a little for her sake. "Yes, it's very uncomfortable. The book said the farther inland you went, the worse it got. The ocean breezes..."

"Mm." There wasn't a hint of a breeze now, just a ton and a half of hot, wet atmosphere trying to drown him.

"And there was something about a purple-veined leaf that's like poison ivy, but I've been looking and I still haven't seen it."

"Those snakes that we saw..."

"There's only one kind of poisonous snake, and the book said that you practically had to stick your finger in its mouth to get it to bite you. Wild pigs, lots of rats, poisonous fish like lionfish, sharks... That's all I remember as warnings. Plus you have to ask before you go into villages, and dress up not down outside of St. Catherine. People will think you're being suggestive."

"These people? I've seen how they dress."

"And they know how Westerners dress. Wear jeans and tee shirts, the book said. No swimsuits unless you're in tourist territory."

Lon nodded. "We'll just keep you away from any natives, then."

"If we can find any. Are you sure–?"

"There's no one. No one except all these mercenaries, Lie."

Lina frowned. "You don't think that there was a warning about the volcano, do you? That they might have evacuated the island?"

"Don't even think that." Still, he clenched his jaw at the thought. "We've got enough trouble as it is."

Nodding, she adjusted the packing on their sack. "Earth says that it's waking up, but still at a half-doze. It shouldn't blow for a while yet– maybe a couple years."

"Earzh says."

"Yes."

Lon tried not to roll his eyes and didn't succeed. He grunted and slung the rifle onto his back. "We'll have to circle around a half-dozen squads," he reported, pointing at what Lina could only see as more forest. "It's going to take some rough climbing. Do you think you can do it?"

Silence. Londo looked back at her and saw how subdued she was. "I can't make it if I have to carry you over my shoulder," he told her.

"It would be so much better for us both if I weren't such a burden. I'll be fine here."

"Come on, Lina. Get that round butt of yours in gear and let's move." He stood up and then grasped her arm to pull her up with him. She let him. "I know you're tired. I'm tired. And this next part isn't going to be easy. I need your cooperation."

"I can handle it," she said with a sigh.

"Good girl."

"Arf."

They set off through dense forest before starting up a butte of basalt, rough volcanic rock that looked like it had been torn in creation. Ancient roots the width of Lon's arm clung to the rock, occasionally producing thin bushes that they used to hide behind.

Lon glanced back at Lina. She was obviously exhausted, her hair tied back in a long braid with tendrils sticking to her sweaty face. In the heat she'd taken off his shirt, and used it as a sling for their pack.

He tried not to notice how much her sweat-soaked dress clung to her as she moved up the rock, how her breasts swung when she moved. Now and then she cursed softly and sucked her palm as the rock cut her, the same as it had been cutting him.

Blood and dirt covered his arms and chest. He had to wipe the sweat out of his eyes every few minutes. How could normal humans take this pain all the time? Londo had never realized that his isolation was also a gift of sorts. He'd never had to go through any of the agony he'd experienced so far today– well, not for some years. He tried to forget that time as best he could.

He gave her a wan version of an encouraging smile. The afternoon's humidity sucked at his energy. If only it would rain and clear things out! **Penny for your thoughts.**

They're unprintable, she responded, and continued her slow ascent.

So think of something better. Like what you're going to do when this is all over.

What am I going to do? Her mind paused although she kept climbing. **I'm going home and buying a dozen really big bottles of hand cream, and I'm going to dump it all on me and wrap myself in a sheet. And then I'm just going to soak in it until all these nasty cuts and bruises and chapped places go away. And then I'll–**

He imagined Lina in that sheet. Lina in bed, wrapped in a sheet, those leaf-green eyes of hers gazing into his as he entered the room. He'd strip slowly and she'd watch every move. And then he'd sit on the side of the bed and lift one corner of the sheet and unwrap her.

In his mind the sheet became a long strip of silk sliding across her skin, baring parts of her and leaving others still tantalizingly covered, like a sexy mummy. Her hair would be splayed out around her on his pillows and curling over her bare shoulders. The strips of silk immobilized her as he uncovered her breasts, then revealed her thighs as he paused to caress her. He could hear her sighs of pleasure at that, her soft croon as he entered her, as she wrapped her now-naked arms and legs around him...

His indestructible pants were much too tight.

And a glass of iced tea with some kind of robot or something that would keep 'em coming, she was telling him. **Oh yeah– one of those automatic massage recliner chairs. I'd get one of those and damn the cost. Instant shiatsu.**

Not a masseur.

I have a little phobia...

Londo pulled her up to the ledge where he had stopped. She sat down with a groan. After a moment she wrestled with the sling and produced the last water bottle. She handed it to Londo. He took a few swigs and passed it back.

"I'll go over there and take a look around." He pointed vaguely into the distance.

"What's the matter with right here?" she asked before taking a drink herself.

He looked at her, her thin gown plastered against her, her bare legs moist with sweat. Her breasts rose and fell as she caught her breath after the hard climb.

"I'll be over there," Londo said again.

"Oh hell, Lon, even I can see that you'll be out in the open. There's no cover. People will be able to see you for miles." She took in the view, seeing not the green bounty of the land below but only hiding places for terrorists who might look up at this next level of the island.

"There are times, Lina, when a man can't be trusted with a lady."

She regarded him without sympathy. "So you're an animal and not a person? You can't control yourself?"

"This is an unusual day for me. Pardon me if I can't take some things in stride. Being side by side with a beautiful girl whom I tried to rape a couple hours ago... *Non,* Lina, I'll just–"

"Try to commit suicide as some kind of penance," she bit out. "No, Londo Rand, you are going to remain here, under cover. And you're going to be just fine. I apologize for being female, okay? Sor-ree. The story of my life, the sin of double-X chromosomes. I'm just one of the boys here. You want me to burp... or maybe fart? Hey, how about them Packers in the big game last Sunday?"

"Football season's over. Besides, I don't follow football. Much." He hesitated, then settled back down beside her.

"Well, that's ten points in your favor. It's a violent sport."

"My game's hockey."

"Shoo, talk about violent."

"I like it. The Canadiens; I've got season tickets. They're winning again, you know."

She considered that. "I suppose you don't have to worry about being hit by a runaway whassis."

"Puck. *Non,* I don't. Just overenthusiastic fans trying to get in my box."

She nodded. "Autograph hounds? Paparazzi."

"And more. The one thing I can say about this place is that it's quiet," he said as he stretched in the heat. He picked up the bag and peered inside. "What are you hungry for?"

"Mm. Corn on the cob, dripping in butter. Potato salad. Cole slaw and fresh, perfect tomatoes, maybe with a few cold cukes on the side..."

"Steak just off the grill." Lon settled into a lazy smile. "Home fries with cheese and gravy. Beer in frosted mugs."

"Tea," Lina countered. "Heavy on the ice."

"*D'accord,* I'll have the beer and you can have the tea. I'll even refill your glass for you."

"Very nice." She shared his fantasy as he handed her the last apple, taking a couple of carrots for himself. Neither of the selections was very crisp, but they sat in silence feasting on their dream meal as they ate.

Lon reached for the water bottle again. "We'll refill this when we get back down," he told her. "Shall we?" He began to get up.

Lina reached out and almost touched his arm. "Please," she said. "Just a few more minutes. My muscles are like jelly."

He nodded and sat back down.

"I can tell you're still Valiant, despite everything," she told him. "I'm jealous of your stamina. It's not quite at norm levels."

He shrugged. "Then why is the heat getting to me so much?"

"Maybe it's those leather pants. I don't see how you can stand them. Aren't you steam-cooked yet?"

"Faux leather. I'm told it breathes." He smiled crookedly. "I never appreciated the difference until now. If it were real, I suppose I would be running around like you to keep cool. Then we both would have to stay out of the locals' way."

She chuckled and they both gazed at the vista before them for some time. "What's the scenario down there?" she finally asked.

"What you'd expect. They're thick over there–" he pointed.

"Direction?"

"South."

"Ah. Good. Send 'em all thataway, angels! Go south, young mercenaries, go south!"

"Fine with me."

"There was no way the Network could have traced the call?" she quietly asked.

Londo shook his head. "Not in that amount of time." He examined his rifle, made sure it was functioning smoothly, and double-checked that he had extra ammunition easily available in the pockets of his vest.

"Those men back there are dead now," Lina said. He didn't respond. "I've never thought of you that way."

"As a murderer?"

"As someone whose job sometimes requires them to kill. You've killed before this."

"Entire populations have been at stake. When there's been no other way out– Yes, I've killed people. Down there it was either them or us. You saw."

She nodded. "I saw. Intellectually I understand. I'd much rather be the one still alive now than them. But how do you deal with it?"

"It's part of my training."

"Just training? No follow-up?"

"And my therapist handles a lot of it. I have a very good therapist."

Lina nodded at that. "Good. Are we going to get out of here?"

He turned to look her straight in the face. "Of course we are," he said, and she knew that he truly believed it. The confidence of the man was unbelievable! "Don't let me catch you thinking differently. We're going to get you home and safe!"

She caught a thought behind that: a picture of a strange bed, and her in it.

He knew she'd seen it. "Well," he admitted, "maybe a little detour first." He gave her a small smile. "Now you know I'll get us rescued. There's no way I'm going to miss *that.*"

He leaned toward her desperately, his mood change swift and terrible. "God, Lina, say you forgive me. I don't know what came over me. I vow to you, it won't happen again. I'd never hurt you, never in a million years!"

She didn't look at him. "I know. This has been as strange a day for you as it has for me. People do things sometimes... Sometimes events trigger buttons that people never even knew they had."

"It'll never happen again. Never ever."

"I know, I know. It's all right. You just scared me, that's all."

"I'm so sorry." He reached for her hand and she drew it back automatically. "And damn, we're back at square one."

"No we aren't." She set her jaw, her lips forming a hard line of determination. "A phobia is merely a conditioned response to a situation. I've learned a way to react to other people that suits me. And today, for a little while, I saw another way to react. I've just got to remember how I was thinking when that happened."

"You were more scared of the helicopters than you were of me," Londo said. "All we have to do is find something to scare the crap out of you, and we've got it made."

Lina nodded glumly. "Doesn't this island have anybody else on it?" She rubbed her tired eyes. "I know about all the nature preserves, and the Sherridan estate takes up a lot of space, but supposedly there are still a few villages left and one fair-sized town. Where the hell is everyone?"

"How should I know? Maybe Terry gave them all twenty dollars and sent them off to see a movie. Maybe she killed them all. Maybe she's got them all rounded up somewhere behind barbed wire. So now you're thinking about fixing me up with a nice girl?"

"The thought had entered my mind."

"I like the girl I'm with."

"How about Terry?" Lina asked. "Is that why you're not to be harmed? Maybe she's had an intimate luau she's been trying to keep warm for you all day. A poor little roast pig with an apple in his mouth. Maybe some of that beer you mentioned. And a candlelit table for two with a big ol' bed in the next room."

Londo gave a grunt. "I don't think she'd send out two hundred men with invitations for that. Maybe a few years ago, she'd have pulled something like this for that, *peut-être*."

"Nuts about you?"

"Just plain nuts. And I was crazy enough not to notice. Or maybe I just pretended not to notice. We came so close once..."

"You did? How?"

Londo opened his mouth to reply and then stopped, looking at Lina. "Are you jealous?" he asked.

She blinked at that. "Of course not. I'm just curious. I suppose it's your business."

"I suppose."

Lina stared into space. "She's older than you."

"Eh. *Oui.* I was practically still a kid when we first met, and she was the glamorous older woman. Maybe fifteen years difference. She told me she could teach me a few things." He gave a pained laugh. "Well, she did at that. But not really what she wanted."

"So she resorted to a bazooka thing today. How Freudian. I hope she realizes that."

"It was about twenty times bigger than a bazooka and plugged into the world's biggest portable electric generator, but yes, it was a bazooka thing." He let out the merest *humph* of a chuckle. "I'll remind her of the symbolism next time I see her."

"And she's gotten rid of everyone besides the mercenary conventioneers..."

"And you."

"And me." Lina tried to figure it out. "It makes my head hurt," she finally decided. "This whole thing makes my head hurt. I've never had to keep my antenna up for so long before. I feel like my mind's been blown open."

"How many fingers?" He held four up and saw her blink, try to focus.

"Four," she said after a beat.

"And how much of that was cheating with those guides of yours?"

"I've got a headache, all right? Sometimes headaches make your eyesight fuzzy. I am not concussing on you."

Lon checked the back of her head again, as if that could help, and finally reached into his vest to draw out a plastic pouch. "First aid supplies from our friends out there. I see some aspirin inside."

"Thanks." She found two tablets, double-checking to make sure they really were aspirin and not just marked that way. For some reason she didn't trust those mercenary soldiers with their poison pills. Her guides assured her they were okay.

They sat there for a few more minutes. Nothing moved in the jungle below. "C'mon, get a drink and we'll start down again," Lon said as he reached for the bag on top of his shirt. Instead, he knocked it over and before he could grab, the bag tumbled down the side of the rock. The water bottle, insect spray, and other luxuries of home spilled out of it as it went, raising tiny rackets of clinks and clunks against the rustling forestland. Lina reacted quick enough that her foot stepped on Lon's shirt, holding it in place.

They stared at the path of their survival kit. "I'm not going back down to get it," Lina finally declared.

Londo heaved a sigh of surrender, shaking his head at his own clumsiness. "Neither am I. *D'accord*, our target will be to find clean sources of water on our way to the north side of the island. Maybe we can pick up a canteen along the way." He slung the rifle back over his shoulder

Lina picked up his shirt. Hoping that it would keep some of the mosquitoes off her bare back, she tied it around her neck. It was certainly too warm to wear it.

They edged around the butte, kept to what vegetation had managed to anchor itself to the rock, and were finally rewarded with a view that included a narrow ocean bay cutting into the island from the east. Above it lay a strip of green stretching to the horizon.

"The north side of the island," Londo announced.

7

The journey to the bay took three hours, ending at bluffs that overlooked a wide, rock-strewn shore. Tall blowing grasses and the edge of the palm forest surrounded them. Almost a mile down the beach were at least twenty soldiers and their equipment spread out on the sand above the high-tide level.

Lina said, "Twenty here, a lot in the forest and in helicopter crews. What would you say that leaves us? About twenty-five or so unaccounted for? Less?"

She set their canteen on top of the pile of other things Lon had taken off that last soldier: compass, another knife, more packs of ammo, a walkie-talkie, first-aid kit, blanket, some plastic. It was a good thing they'd gotten the backpack, too. Her left nightgown strap had given out, and although Londo didn't mind that a bit, she was wearing his shirt over the gown now instead of using it as an equipment sling.

"More. The two hundred was only infantry, remember?" Lon gestured to the land beyond the water west of the garrison here at the end of the bay. The stiff salt breeze barely rifled his sweat-matted hair. "I don't see any of 'em beyond about there. North seems to be clear."

"Just one little problem..."

"How do we get over there? They've got the forest blanketed at this point." Lon scowled as he considered the problem. He kept eying the bay, sparkling in the late afternoon.

Lina regarded that, too, the cool expanse of blue. The air was fresh with ocean spray. A bath– that's the one thing she wanted in this world, after a long, cold drink of water that she didn't have to worry about saving some for Lon or for later. She felt as if she'd been rolling in dirt all day.

She pulled out a new mat of spider webs from her hair. At least there weren't spiders in it this time! She used her other hand to roll the sticky webbing off her fingers, back and forth, until it separated from her skin and she could toss it to the ground.

She was literally covered in dirt, her very cells outlined in black. The same black traced her wrists and knuckles in deep lines. Her fingerprints stood out as if she had inked the finger pads herself. Absolutely filthy! The shower from earlier was long forgotten. She didn't know how Lon could stand to look at her. Of course he was the same way.

It didn't happen like this in the movies. Action Hero X would stomp into the jungle and when he stomped out he was clean and fresh-looking, maybe with a few spots of someone else's blood spattering his pressed camo outfit. Lina guessed people didn't want to see other people dirty, much less stinking like she and Lon were.

Reality wasn't pretty sometimes. Every breath of sweat, every sting from where some thorn had scraped her, reminded Lina that this was as real as it got. She scratched at yet another mosquito bite. Did she have any blood left?

Lon squinted into the sun's reflected glare. "How good a swimmer are you?" he asked.

"In the ocean, not much. A past life of mine, a World War II guy– he committed suicide by drowning himself. His sub was about to boarded by the Japanese. He was terrified." She winced at the past-life workshop memory that had taken so long to retrieve, and then had arrived in a spine-chilling flash of knowing.

"How interesting. And that's relevant because–?"

"I'm not too cool about waves breaking over my head. I have a lot of fears, I guess."

"Can you rise above this one?"

"Oh, I've been in the ocean lots of times. I just don't like doing anything besides jumping waves. Short waves. Now, swimming pools– I do pools very well. How good are you, without your powers? I keep seeing you looking far out to sea. You've never claimed to be related to the merpeople."

Londo paused. "I can do it."

"Are you sure?" Lina gestured at the horizon, where the moon would soon be showing its face. "We're at low tide now. The last I heard, last night, Typhoon Whatsherface–"

"Xandra. Ah *oui*. Shit."

"Typhoon Xandra was a few hundred miles off the coast. Not close enough to endanger the island, but near enough to stir up rip currents. They're sometimes fatal for even experienced swimmers. They were warning the tourists."

"Lina," he tried to be reasonable with her, "the only way I can see for us is to go by sea, and so far out they don't spot us. Do those guides of yours have any suggestions?"

Her green eyes unfocused. "Wait a while, *they* say. *Let the waters return.* I think they're showing me rip currents that will go away when the tide comes back. *Keep closer to the shore; Londo can't do as much as he thinks he can.*" She looked over to him apologetically. "Sorry, that's what they said."

"So how are we supposed to remain unnoticed if we cross right under their noses?"

"Let's wait a while and see what happens, an hour or so. Any fruit trees around here? I'm a little hungry." The last soldier they had pilfered from had had only a candy bar left of his rations. They'd split it. Half a candy bar didn't go far.

"Just all these coconut palms. I don't see us creating a scene just to get some coconut."

Londo stifled a groan of frustration as Lina nodded agreement. All the downed coconuts they'd found along the way had been previously investigated by the rat population of the island, or were moldy. If they were going to eat coconut, they were going to have one fresh from the tree.

"*D'accord*, we wait one hour. What can we do in the meantime? I know. We have some retraining to do." As they lay together in the grass Lon touched the middle of her back and rubbed a soft circle there.

"Londo–"

"Don't complain until you actually don't like it. You opened your mouth as soon as I touched you. If you can hold my hand, you can take this much."

"All right." She looked at him out the corners of her eyes as he began to massage her back. He used two hands now, and bent low over her to escape notice.

"How's that?" he asked, but it was obvious. Her hands clenched in the beach grass and her shoulders moved away whenever his hands came near them. The muscles resisted his touch. "Relax. It's a massage."

"I'm trying," she said. "It's just not working. It's not going to work." A sudden thought came to her and she laughed once in spite of herself.

"What was that?"

"I was just thinking, 'Oh god, I'm stuck with Pepé Le Pew.'"

Londo harumphed at that. "I'm not that bad, am I?"

"*Mais oui.* You seem to have a one-track mind on certain things, Pepé."

The humor seemed to relax her; at least she wasn't fighting him now. "So ah'm a skonk..." he used his French accent to its fullest, "an' yu are ze leetle poosy cat. Don' be afraid, *chérie.*"

"The... intensity is a little daunting, Londo," Lina said. His hands had started to slide down her back to her buttocks. "Don't."

"Pepé never had the deadline I have."

"And those cats never had a phobia. I don't think this is going to work at all." She pulled his hands from her, shivered and then rolled away from him onto her side.

"I thought you said we were supposed to talk positively about the future." Lon settled himself right behind her, almost touching her with his body. He swept her hair out of his way. "Let me talk positively about tonight. Tonight, under the light of the almost-full moon in some perfectly safe clearing with a lovely spring and fruit trees all around us..."

Lina shook her head at the wishful thinking. He used that as a signal to massage her shoulder lightly, but she clenched and pulled away.

"This is just your shoulder. I want you to visualize. I'm not doing anything. Let your imagination take over." He used the soft, deep voice of persuasion and she nodded, though she was still tight with fear.

Lon pitched his voice as compelling as possible. "Tonight I am going to make love to you, Lina O'Kelly. It's going to be like nothing you or I have ever imagined. It's going to be gentle and wild. It's going to be magic."

"Please..."

"Oh yes, I'm going to please you, don't worry about that." He nudged her hair back from her ear, though she jumped even at that.

He whispered right next to that ear, "Visualize; don't feel me here. Tonight, Lina, I am going to kiss your warm mouth until you're dizzy. Until you're hot." He nuzzled the outside edge of her ear, moving down its short length and then along the back, tickling her with the very tip of his tongue where her ear met her head.

"Don't, Lon." Her hand reached back to brush him off, but he caught it and kissed it, then placed it on her hip.

"What was that? 'Don't stop'?"

She was trembling.

"This is all in your imagination, *chérie*. Just imagine. I'm going to move down to those beautiful breasts of yours– you thought I'd forgotten about them, hadn't you? Just because you've got 'em covered up now. I haven't. I've been thinking about them all day. I'm going to lick my way down to them and then I will worship them with my mouth and my hands. And you're going to beg me for more."

She squirmed, but he held her shoulder steady and bent to suck lightly on her ear lobe. What an intriguing texture. Londo took a moment to savor his new senses– and to shift slightly, to get more comfortable without distracting her. He needed to adjust his pants.

He hoped she was beginning to feel similar sensations.

"That's your nipple. Feel it." He sucked again. "I'm sucking them, licking all around. Can you feel me tonight? Feel the pleasure. Only the pleasure." He gave her ear a long lick and whispered, "Can you feel my mouth on you?"

Her voice was almost inaudible as she hunched her neck to keep him farther away. "Yes..."

"That's good, baby," he purred at her. He muttered words of encouragement, sighing to relax her as he moved his hand down her arm. Then he dared to stroke the top of her hair with one hand as he let the other outline her down to her hips. He painted a word picture of the night to come, of flowers blooming in the moonlight all around them. He felt her trembling ease. Time to move on.

Now Londo gathered the hem of her shirt. He inched it up. His fingertips brushed so close to her thighs. Feeling through the thin material of her nightgown and running up just under the edge of the panty there, he could sense her skin turning cooler as she tensed. She eased away from his hand only to be restricted by him behind her.

"Picture it in your mind. I'm not doing anything here. You can let yourself imagine anything. You'll enjoy this. Feel it. I'm going to taste you between your legs."

He licked the folds of her ear, then came back and did it again slower. He traced the hem of her panty, just enough to draw her attention down there. Did she shiver? Did she ease closer?

"I'm going to run my tongue up and down you until you come like you've never come before. You masturbate, don't you?" He got no answer. "C'mon, you've masturbated, right?"

"Yes," she said so quietly the surf almost drowned the word.

"This is going to be ten times better. You're going to shake under my mouth, under my fingers. And you'll ask me, you'll plead with me, 'Oh, Londo, take me now.' You'll be all wet and ready for me, won't you? Won't you? You can allow yourself to feel it. The hunger, the passion– it'll take you over. You want me inside you. Spreading you out and entering you. Gently. Slowly. It feels so good. Oh god, Lina, you want it."

Damn, *he* wanted it bad. Now. Lon ground his teeth against the primal urge that he'd held in for so many years. His body was making his priorities known as it pressed against her backside. How much of a trance was she in?

Not enough. She was trying to curl into a little ball. He kept his mouth at her ear, just touching her there, just brushing her leg and her hair when he wanted to grind himself against her. He whispered, "'Take me, Londo.' 'Oh, Lon, you feel so good.' 'Lon, I'm coming. Make me come...'"

Easing forward, he lay spooned against the length of her. Let her feel his arousal. His breath took in the forest fragrance of her hair. She shifted to roll away, and he caught her gently on the stomach, holding her in position. She didn't resist.

"We'll ride for the rest of the night, just you and me." Between his hand and his hips, he rocked her gently. "You're going to moan with pleasure and I'm going to enjoy hearing you do it. And I'm going to come a hundred times inside you. We're going to make up for years tonight. The world's never seen the likes of what we're going to do. Me in you." He nuzzled her neck. "I'll fill you up. I'll give you sensations you've never dreamed of. Tell me, Lina. Tell me."

He rolled her over to crouch above her, gazing into her wondering eyes. Were they dark with anticipation? It was difficult to tell in the bright sunlight. Heaving breasts might merely be a sign of panic.

No. She had to be aroused. "Tell me you want me," he ordered her, an expectant smile playing on his face.

Her mouth opened and nothing came out. Her hands made fists and then opened; fists and open. She tried to edge away from him, pushing against his thighs before she realized where her hands were.

"Say it," he whispered. "They're just words."

She shook her head. Her long fingers swept across her mouth, covering it and then uncovering. Covering.

"Repeat after me: 'I want you, Lon.'"

"I... I..."

"Good enough." He pulled her up and guided her lips to his. Wonder of wonders, she kissed back. He slid one arm down her spine, rolling her over as he rolled, bringing both of them down to the ground and out of sight of anyone. One hand secured her butt, the other kept her head in position. Her lips were hot and moist over his.

She started to tense up.

"Don't even think about doing that," he told her between kisses. "You like this, and it's too late for your body to tell you you don't." He explored the taste and feel of her lips, but she held back. No arms wrapped around his neck, yet her kisses were real enough.

Londo eased her onto her back and began to explore down her neck with his lips.

"Oh no. No no no no." This time the pushes away were real, but she pushed like a girl– ineffectually. Still, he retreated.

"Off," she ordered in a tight voice. "Get off me. Please. Off. Get offgetoff!"

Immediately he rolled onto his side. He watched her come up to panic speed, then try to calm down as she panted and pulled the beach grass with her fists. She shook her head angrily at herself. "I'm sorry," she said. "Look, I–"

"You did great. We can do this. We need to keep this new reaction going until it's a learned reflex. Concentrate on the pleasure. Our plan of action is to neck here for twenty-five more minutes."

Lina gaped at his audacity. "Just, just kiss?" There was a sharp note of doubt in her voice, and more than that of distress in her eyes.

Londo looked a little sheepish. "Well... maybe a little feeling up, too. You're a very tempting morsel, *chérie*." He paused. "If I go too far or too fast, just say no. I'll stop."

"You'll stop."

"I promise; I swear. Twenty-five minutes. Maybe a half-hour."

"Are you wearing a watch?"

"Has anyone ever told you you talk too much? I'll know." He pulled off his vest. With satisfaction he noted the way Lina gave his chest the once-over and came back for more. "Why don't you take the shirt off? I think you'll be more comfortable. It's awfully hot today."

"This sounds a lot like lines a good girl is supposed to be on the lookout for."

Still, she slowly unfastened the non-Velcro Velcro and eased the shirt off, trying to ignore the way he gazed at her left breast with the gown riding so low on it. She pulled the bodice up even as he put his arm around her, drawing her to him. Automatically she defended herself with the palms of her hands on his chest.

"Maybe this isn't going to work after all," she said. "I really don't think–"

"So don't think. Just kiss, sweetheart, twenty-five minutes."

"Your arm. Do you have to touch me?"

"Yes, I have to. Otherwise we'd look like kissing fish." He stuck his lips out to cartoonish proportions and made kissy noises. As he'd hoped, she laughed, but still looked beyond doubtful. She squirmed in his embrace.

"What do you suggest?" he asked with all the patience he could muster.

"I don't know. It's just not going to work this way."

"Of course it'll work." He huffed in frustration. "Look; this is a meditation. I know you've meditated."

Her eyebrows lifted at that.

He gave a sharp nod, affirming his own new direction. "Kissing as meditation. Let your mind go blank. Any time a thought comes around, you bat it out of the way and ignore it. We'll get spiritual enlightenment together."

The corner of her lips twitched into a snicker and he caught it quickly with his own mouth before she could protest again. He began with soft kisses, pilgrim's kisses, and she relaxed... slightly.

Lina was amazed. Swatting away thoughts actually seemed to help. Then he slid both hands around her waist, and the center of her back started to crawl away from his touch. She pushed him away and breathed out the tension there as it rose to the surface. Maybe that was how she could get through this.

"Rebirthing," she told him as hope dawned. "We need to stop now and then and let me do that."

He cocked his head at her. "Re-*birthing*?" The slightest of snorts escaped him. "Do I need to call a midwife? Boil hot water?"

"It's called that because... Oh, you don't need to know that. It's just a breathing technique. As things bubble up to the surface, you can breathe them out."

"Are things bubbling?"

"Yes." She pushed him farther away. "Just every so often we need to let me get rid of it. Please."

He watched as she did it, taking about thirty seconds before she relaxed again. This phobia of hers was a royal pain.

"A royal pain," she agreed out loud. "You don't know any Tony Robbins techniques, do you?"

"I only go to certified shrinks."

"Too bad. I've seen him get rid of major phobias in minutes. I've almost done the same thing with some of my clients." But it hadn't worked to do it on herself. Maybe she just hadn't been properly motivated before.

"Maybe you haven't had the motivation." Londo smiled knowingly and moved in for more kisses. After a few minutes they had to stop for her to rebirth, and then began again. He held her head so she couldn't squirm away. She made a sound, an *oh*, and he introduced her to the fine art of fully French kissing. They had to rebirth almost immediately, and Lon tried hard not to chuckle at his innocent partner. He ran his fingertips up and down her arms as she breathed.

"That's not helping," she warned him.

"So rebirth it." He pulled her to him for another session, and now he allowed a little feeling up, non-major erogenous zones only. He could feel her go rigid whenever he encountered new territory.

"It's just a little too much," she whispered. "Please."

"Live in the present," he murmured into her ear as he backed off. "Don't dredge up bad memories. Concentrate on how it feels now."

"Just on the moment," she breathed, her eyes half-closed.

"Good," he said. She relaxed again. Time to move onto new territory. He rested his palm on her shoulder and then eased it down. Bingo.

"Lon." She squirmed. "Too far."

"You're doing great. If it feels good, enjoy it, *chérie*." He stroked the covered breast lightly, amazed at the give of it. Her breathing was deep and hard. He could feel her heart under his hand as well as through the pulse point under his mouth at her neck. It sped up– too fast.

"Biofeedback," he whispered. "You must know that. Match my pulse. Match my breathing."

"Back– back off, Lon."

"Biofeedback. You can do it." He moved back up to her mouth, still holding her breast.

"You promised!"

"*Chérie*, just give me a chance–"

"Getoffgetoffgetoffgetoff–!"

Londo pushed himself away hurriedly. "Sorry! I'm off, I'm off!" He watched her attempt at rebirth. "What can I do to help?"

She lay there panting, glaring at him. "You can keep your promises," she finally gasped.

"I didn't think..." he realized the stupidity of it as he said it, "...that you were serious."

"I was serious!"

"I'm sorry. I apologize, I really do. It's just that... Women say things they don't mean. You know. Society forces them."

The glare darkened. Perhaps it was accompanied by tiny lightnings. Her fists tightened around the grass she'd pulled. "Like society forces men to have no respect for women."

"I have respect. Great respect for women. Some of my best friends are women." He frowned at himself. "And I know one woman who'd clobber me if she could for what I just said. She's been threatening me with bodily injury for years. I'm sorry, Lina. I said I'd stop when you asked, and I didn't. My fault completely. You can hit me if you want."

He looked like a puppy dog caught with a shoe in his mouth. "I don't hit people," Lina finally decided to say. "I've only hit one person in my life. This afternoon. I don't want to do that again."

"I have no excuse."

"Well. You're forgiven, I guess."

"You're an angel, love." His face brightened. Was he a man or a little boy to rebound this quickly? Hope blossomed in his eyes as she watched him. "So tell me, can you do biofeedback?"

"I can do it in my sleep," she retorted.

"I don't want you to be asleep when you do it."

He really thought they were still going to go through with this! The utter confidence of the man! "Londo, in case you haven't noticed," she said in exasperation, "this is not going well. And we're not that far into it."

"I wouldn't say that, *pantoute*." He lay on his side and looked at her with that sly, crooked smile of his as she adjusted her clothes. "Not at all. This morning, as I recall, you were a 200% virgin. Now we've gotten to second base, and you've enjoyed it– to a point. I know I certainly have." He fastened his eyes on hers. "Did you think you could get that far? In less than one day, with a perfect stranger?"

"So you think you're perfect now?"

"Lina..."

"All right, no I didn't," she told him. "But I don't see how I can go much further."

"Come over here, *chérie*, and I'll show you."

She had to chuckle behind splayed fingers at that. "You are a big ol' horndog, you know that? One thing on your mind. Must I remind you that there are a couple dozen big, burly men down there a piece on the beach, and they've got guns? We're both filthier than dirt right now. If we must be frank, Lon, you don't smell so good, and I'm surprised that those guys down there can't smell me from where they are."

"Details," Lon tossed it away. "We can forget it all in the passion of the moment. Come here and give me a kiss, my fragrant little cabbage."

"Do you act this way when you're out gallivanting with the ParaNet?"

"They're not here now," he murmured as he touched the remaining strap of her gown. "Let's just loosen this up, shall we? As long as we're on Tiawa, we can go native."

She put her hand on his to stop him. "Let's not." She craned her neck to make out the mercenaries down the beach. "You're crazy, you know that? Doing this with them there– on a time schedule yet. You've been listening to 'Sixty Minute Man' too much: fifteen minutes of this and fifteen minutes of that.

"Look," her voice took on a desperate edge, "this island has a few villages. Everyone can't be gone. If we can make it to one, I know that every woman in it would throw herself at you and demand that you take her right then and there."

His eyes narrowed into triumphant slits as he found it. There, behind the embarrassment: her attraction to him, pulsing to the beat of her heart, after he'd thought that maybe she didn't feel anything for him other than a priestly duty. "And why is that?"

She gave him an exasperated look. "Because you're who you are. Because you're the handsomest, most heroic man on the planet. And that French accent would drive any sane woman crazy with desire."

He wrinkled his nose at the compliments, unable to hide his smirk. "Mmm. Except you."

"I said sane." She shook her head at him. "Look at me. I'm a walking basketcase of fears and phobias. I'm terrified of everything."

"I wouldn't say that."

She snorted. "That's because you don't know me."

"But I do," he said in all seriousness. "When you thought you were in danger this morning, you came up with a plan of action and executed it with those god-awful sheets. You protected me against that blast. You were afraid of working on my shoulder, but you pulled it off– well, not exactly the shoulder, though you sure as hell tried, but the procedure. We've been wandering around all day with terrorists on our heels, and you've kept your head and helped out. Lina, six men died at your feet and you stayed fairly calm. I know full-blown paraheroes who would be gibbering idiots by now if they had to go through this. But not you."

"That's because I *had* to do all that."

"That's how everyone gets through life. Doing things because they have to get done."

"You mean, *Do It Despite Your Fears*." She made two-finger air quotes.

"What is that, a book?"

"Uh huh. It's in my room... I mean, it was blown up this morning. I've been studying it."

"So do it despite everything. And have fun while you're doing it. This is Adventureland, after all."

"Now I know you're crazy."

"My shrinks have been telling me that for years." Londo checked the position of the sun and then returned his gaze to Lina. "I can afford the best."

"I can tell you've learned some visualization techniques from them." Lina blushed.

He grinned at her. "*Tsé*, I can do it, too. You were an inspiration. It's an adaptation of some things I've had to do." He raised her chin so she looked into his eyes "Maybe we'll just repeat it tonight, eh? The pattern I'm seeing is that you need to get revved up before you relax and let go."

"Tell me something. Are you ever unsure of anything?"

"Never." He leaned in for a kiss. She drew back automatically. "C'mon," he urged, and she met his lips, but quickly.

"We're going to have to have another session. You seem to have forgotten how to do it." His eyes crinkled. It was fun to tease her. "We'll do that after we get across the bay. It's been almost an hour; is anything different? Tide's back in, pretty much. It'll be dark in a couple hours."

Lina checked in her own way as Lon scanned their environs with his para-vision. "The currents seem to have eased, but there's something else. Something in the air..." Her eyes focused again and she looked around. "Do you smell fresh air... like ozone?"

Lon sniffed. "*Ouais*, there's a storm over there." He nodded his head at a cloud wrapped around a mountain down the coast.

Lina smiled slowly. "Maybe that's it. Come here, little cloud deva," she said to the air.

8

"Cloud deva? What's that?"
Can you link with me? Like a conference call.
I don't know. What's a deva?
A spirit or sentient force in charge of something that's not human, like an animal or a thing or a concept. In this case, a storm. You'll like storm devas. They're almost always happy and half-crazy, like a kid on a roller coaster. The worse the storm, the happier they are– except for the really bad storms. Use your imagination. Picture a being sitting on top of the cloud there.

Just visualize?

And listen. It's like, like a whisper in your mind. You'll think it's you thinking to yourself at first, but let it whisper.

Londo tried it to humor her as a tradeoff for the night ahead. He pictured a genie riding the cloud like a magic carpet, and the image morphed into that of a rather calm but happy bodiless face, blessing the earth by raining on it.

Hello, Lina said to it. It smiled pleasantly at her, recognizing a human who could speak to devas, although it was not incredibly interested in doing so. It wanted to bless the earth instead. ***Could you work up a bit of a storm for us here? We really need one.***

The deva lowered its eyelids benevolently, and there was a feeling, a whisper, that full-blown storms were not what it wanted to do, but that there was a system just upwind that might be interested.

Thank you, Lina said and dissolved the connection. "Be polite to entities," she told Londo. "It's always appreciated and it gives you good habits."

That was a deva? No, that was just Londo's imagination... wasn't it? Of course it was. Was he so desperate that he'd see nature spirits? "I'll keep that in mind. What's this storm you want?"

Lina gestured at the beach. "If we had a nice downpour, we could go across close in, maybe even at a deep wading depth. You wouldn't have to swim all the way across. The creeps down there would be taking cover from it. They wouldn't be looking."

"That's an awful lot of if's," Londo mused. "So you're saying you can control the weather now? How about lightning?"

"No, I can't control the weather. But the devas who make it can sometimes– *sometimes*– be talked into doing things, as long as it won't cause any harm that would counter the Universal Will. Humans are pretty powerful beings. We have free will, and no one else in the cosmos does. At least that's what Sue says. Devas are confined by the Universal Will, but sometimes the two go hand-in-hand. Then you can control the weather."

"Now we're getting to the fine print." Londo rubbed his nose. Pretty weird stuff. Maybe... maybe he'd give her the benefit of the doubt. Options were running low. "Where's this other deva?"

"Let's see..." Lina's eyes got dreamy, and Londo almost bent down to kiss her. She refocused. "You're interfering," she accused.

"Sorry," he said. "Just let me get comfortable here." He settled onto his back, same as her, but he lay his head on her shoulder and placed his hand on her stomach.

"Londo."

"What?" he asked innocently. He rolled onto his side, keeping his head and hand in place.

"I can't concentrate."

"Good." He snuggled, getting comfortable on her shoulder, and kept his hand quietly where it was. The more points of contact, the better. "How's that?"

"Move over."

"Baby, this is as good as I'm going to give you," he said. "Work with the cards you're dealt. Now, where's this other storm? Concentrate on it, not me."

She huffed at him in frustration, giving him a nice sensation as he watched breasts rise and fall. When her eyes unfocused he tried to tune into her, tried to figure out what she was thinking. He seemed to be resonating to her thoughts now. Surely he could do this.

Lying above the ocean to the west of the island was a mass of clouds like a tightly-packed herd of animals, heavy with rain and off-balance with electrical potential. Londo pictured another genie riding the herd, but the image changed into that of a wild stallion, a frenzied dancer. He tried to force the image back.

Let your mind picture what it wants to; don't control it, Lina instructed him. **Imagine what the images are saying. Play with it.**

The images went through all kinds of wild and crazy permutations including a berserk clown, a daredevil motorcycle rider. The clouds bubbled and the bubbles were laughter and the image steadied even as the bubbles bounced along.

A man... Lon thought it was male. Yes. Chubby, dressed in a loose jogging outfit, an iPod clipped to his belt. Balding and happy– joyful with life. Delighted with his situation.

Lon had to smile just to imagine him. The deva that danced on these clouds chortled, letting the clouds roll under him as he somersaulted over them as if they were trampolines strung together for his personal recreation.

Hello, Lina said. **Could we ask a big favor, please?**

Lon couldn't hear until the reply echoed, amplified, through Lina's mind: **Of course, of course. I've seen your request coming for days now, and I've been gathering myself.**

Really? Lina beamed to Londo: **That's new.**

Oh yes, rain is needed, rain is needed. Recycle that atmosphere, stir things up! In the human realm, too, a great stirring begins. I am pleased to be part of it. A nice storm you'll get. Dancers of lightning! Dancers of rain! A chorus of wind!

Then dance and sing! Lina laughed at the deva's enthusiasm. **How long from now will you be where we are?**

Not long, not long.

Londo got the feeling of a half-hour to the beginning, until they had to take their places for their run.

Can you spare striking the ocean with the lightning? We don't want to get hit.

Ah, this bay is a lazy bay. It doesn't want to be awakened. I'll strike out to sea. And there are some trees who want to go home. I'll take them.

Thank you. Thank you very much!

Have fun, Speaker. Don't forget to dance to life. And you too, other human– the Protector. He learns about us today, no?

He learns, Lina said.

Good. Teach them all.

Lina opened her eyes to see Londo rising up on one elbow and blinking. He shook his head incredulously. "I feel I was just talking to Yoda on happy pills," he said with a wondering half-smile. "I feel... I think..." He looked at her, wanting to say something and not at all sure what. "It was real. It was real?"

She nodded. "It's a different vibration from what we normally perceive."

"Do you do this kind of thing all the time?"

"This is after-hours stuff, if I still have any energy left after my regular job."

"But you could make a living at doing this, couldn't you?"

Lina eased herself into a sitting position and brushed sand from her hair. "I know people who do. But to me it's like donating blood. Some people give blood to get paid, and I don't like doing that. You give blood, you do psychic work, because it's your duty as a human being."

She blushed, realizing that she probably sounded sanctimonious. "It's too bad that mortgage companies and grocery stores don't barter for psychic readings. If clients pay, that's great, but if they can't you do the work anyway."

"It still seems to me like you could be wasting your time at your day job," Londo told her. "If– *When* we get out of this, I'm telling the ParaNet about you. They'll want you to perform a demonstration or two. All this could be very useful. Maybe they'd put you on the payroll."

She sniffed. "Of course they will. Y'know, Londo, for being Valiant, you seem easily impressed."

"Y'know, Lina," Londo retorted, "you'd better check in a mirror before you start telling other people what's wrong with them."

"Okay, okay," she said to keep the peace. She turned to settle onto her stomach, protected by the tall, blowing grasses from view of the mercenaries as she pointed at the beach with her chin. "Now where do you think we need to be when all hell breaks loose? If indeed it does? Storm devas can change their minds pretty quickly."

"How reassuring. *D'accord,* we want to come out up there..." Lon leaned over her and pointed so she saw the same target he did. She nodded. He traced the route, following just behind the line of breakers, to a point below them. If the storm suddenly slackened or didn't arrive as planned, he made a contingency plan for them to head far out into the bay and try to make it across.

"We're going to hold hands the whole way," he told her firmly. "We're not going to lose each other in crazy storm currents. I don't want to hear any arguments about touching."

She agreed.

A sudden blast of wind bore down on the island from the west, sweeping the trees in front of it in mighty bows.

"Storm outflow," Lina said. "It'll be here in minutes." She pulled on Lon's shirt.

"I'll carry the pack," Londo said as he stuffed their booty into it. Wrapping the rifle in the plastic, he then threaded it through the top of the rucksack.

"It'll still get wet," Lina said.

"Probably. Guns can withstand a little water."

Lina helped him put the loaded pack on his back.

"Keep low," Londo said.

They scrambled down the bluff to the beach. An outcropping of black rock lay between them and the mercenaries.

Lina considered the route. It still seemed awfully long. During a storm those waves would get worse. Already whitecaps frothed in the bay. Seagulls shrieked as they hurried to shelter. She glanced at Londo. Damned if she was going to let him get hurt again. He didn't have any idea how much stamina he had as a normal human now, and the day had been a hard one already. She'd have to keep an eye out for him to make sure he didn't do anything stupid out there.

"I'm not going to do anything stupid," he said, looking at her out of the corner of his eye as he faced the bay. "I've been through a helluva lot worse than this."

"But not as a norm," Lina reminded him. "Just remember your limits now. Don't try to push yourself, because you won't make it if you do."

"Lina."

She glanced up at him expectantly.

"Shut up." He kissed her hard. "For luck."

With a sudden crash of thunder the sky turned black, just like that. Lina had never in her life seen such a thing! It was like tales of dark magick, a malevolent, blanketing spell–

"This is the tropics," Lon said. "Storms work like this here."

Rain fell in hard sheets to the ground and the mercenaries ran to their tents. The force of the rain kept them from seeing beyond where they were.

It did the same for Lon and Lina. "That's our signal," Londo said. "*Allons-y!* Go!" He pulled her after him into the wilding surf and they dragged themselves out beyond the breakers. They swam when they could, but often had to stop and bob their way across. Lightning split the skies everywhere but directly over the bay.

The struggle proceeded slowly. The sea would yank at their feet, and they'd hold onto one another as if two people could really fight the Pacific Ocean. Sometimes a rogue wash of freezing water swept in from nowhere only to vanish again. An eon passed as the storm roiled overhead and they hadn't reached shore yet.

"Just a... Just a little more to go," Londo shouted in her ear so she could hear him over the din. The ocean dragged at them, so low down. Lina lost her footing for a moment and then found it again before she could be pulled under. She pointed behind them: a huge wave rolling up, foaming already this far out from shore.

"Ride it as much as you can," she shouted back, "but we're going under that." She grabbed Lon's hand tightly and then pushed off in the trough right before the wave, sucking in as much oxygen as she could. Of everything having to do with the ocean, she hated going under waves the most. She felt so mortal in the grasp of primal forces.

Lina rose with the wave, but it was breaking above her with a roar. There was only time for one final gasp of air before it hit and knocked her sideways. Londo hadn't risen as far in the wave as she had. He was below her, and their grip on each other faltered.

Londo, hang on. I'm just below the surface.

No, I am.

No, you're below me. As the wave surged past her, she tried to grab his arm and pull him up. His fingers slipped. **Londo!**

He was gone.

Pounding panic amped his thoughts. **Jesus! I'm caught in some kind of current!**

Just hold your breath. If you touch bottom, kick off. Swim sideways to the shore. I'll find you.

Ow! I think I'm sideways to the bottom.

There'll be another good-sized wave to counteract the current, she assured him as she tried to remember every iota of rip current safety she'd ever heard. **Stay calm. Remember that the bubbles from your breath will show you which way is up.**

She could feel claustrophobia pressing in on him. His panic was infectious. Lina couldn't think through it as the world began to dissolve into an unbeatable, all-crushing, end hand of Destiny.

Goals.

Goal A: rescue Londo. Keep him breathing at least. From there she'd figure out B and C. There was no room for panic.

Kick off the bottom, she repeated. **Get your head above the water. I'll see you when you hit the surface.**

I'm trying, dammit. His thoughts drained her with their exhaustion. **There.**

She felt him emerge, take a breath and cough, breathe and cough. Where? Good lord, he was clear out there.

I'm coming! she told him. **I see you now. Just tread water if you can't swim.**

Lina swam her hardest. All the waves rose up tall and angry, breaking farther from shore now that the storm was lasting so long. They broke over her head, driving her back even as she tried to move forward. Fury boiled in her for them being in her path, and she battled her way through. They were between her and Londo, so she kept going.

She lost sight of him. **Where are you?**

Coughing. "Here!" His head bobbed to the surface, peering around. He looked so wretchedly weary!

Finally Lina reached him. She supported him in the waves as he couldn't stop coughing. "If you're going to be a norm for a while, you should know: we don't breathe water well," she chided.

"I'll remember that," he said between spells. "Where are we?"

Lina pointed through the black torrent toward what she thought was the shore. A flash of lightning illuminated it for them. **Thanks,** she told the storm deva, just in case he'd done it on purpose.

"Good. Not far," Londo choked. They made their way now slowly and carefully, not attempting any speed records, as the storm churned on. Londo had to stop a couple times to lean on Lina to catch his breath. His progress took on a doggedness based on determination instead of strength.

Lina began to fall behind, but he pulled her along. "You can do it," he assured her. They fought outflow currents right up to the beach. Lon had to talk Lina into not collapsing right there, but to make it to the rocks instead. When they'd reached the side away from the sheltered mercenaries, she fell to her knees. He sat heavily beside her.

Just as suddenly as it had started, the rain slackened and then almost disappeared, sprinkling for a few final minutes. The clouds streamed out over the eastern edge of the island.

"Jesus, that was rough," Londo muttered. He looked at the sky. "Thank you, deva. We appreciated it a lot," he said with a weak wave and added for Lina, "Just being polite."

She helped him shrug off the rucksack and soggy rifle. He lay back on the sand and held out his hand for Lina to take. "I'm going to take a little nap right now," he announced through his exhaustion. "Seems I don't have as much energy as I usually do."

He pulled her down next to him and wrapped his arms around her. "We can keep up the training while we sleep, though. Feel me touch you, *chérie*," he murmured, snuggling to her. He fell asleep almost instantly, and she gazed at his head next to her neck, the tousled, almost black hair already starting to dry as the lowering sun broke through the retreating storm.

C'mon, Lina, she told herself firmly. *We've got to get it together for him. I'm not afraid of him.* No, affirmations should be positive. *I feel safe around Londo.* That's it. *I trust Londo.* She paused in her thoughts and added another affirmation. *It's okay to feel passion toward Londo.* She repeated the affirmations until she, too, fell asleep in his arms.

She woke when he stirred. Purple twilight swathed the sky and gentled the surf. Lina's shirt and gown were still damp from contact with the sand and Londo.

For a few minutes she lay studying him, so warmly handsome. Strong lines of his face and body added to his aura of masculine confidence. Relaxed like this, the slight signature scowl disappeared to reveal a youthful, innocent smoothness of brow.

His open vest displayed that powerful chest. Deeply tanned and glistening with ocean salt, it rose and fell as he slept. Washboard muscles on his stomach echoed the powerful knots that defined his arms. Those faux-leather pants showed off long, strong legs as well as an area Lina was embarrassed to catch herself studying.

This man wasn't Valiant now, not the ParaNetter she'd seen on television lifting trucks with ease, flying through the air, bracing himself against spectacular attacks. Powerless, but for how long? Unfathomably frustrated all his life.

After his powers returned, he'd be frustrated again– and gone. She'd never see him again. It was just a fluke that she was the available woman while he was like this.

They wouldn't fool themselves if they went through with this intimacy. Of course Lon would be sensible enough not to get emotionally involved. Lina could keep a firm picture of Afterward in her mind and protect her heart.

Always hide her heart. Always keep it untouched– that was the key to surviving life. She wouldn't allow it anywhere near Londo. She could do this and come out unscathed... if she could reach down inside herself and find some guts.

C'mon, she reprimanded herself. *You're a healthy female. Women have been doing this for millennia and liking it. This touching thing– Grow up! Get over it! You've got how long until he wakes up? And then you've got to be able to touch him, you've got to be able to receive his touch. At the very least, grit your teeth and think of England.*

Think of Valiant.

When he'd been in college, the press had called him the All-Canadian boy, the guy every girl wished lived next door. He'd had that wholesome look back then that had sharpened with maturity. Nowadays he was Valiant, the warrior Rand. Protector of Earth. Fierce and commanding and sexy as hell.

For so many years on television and so many magazine covers, he'd smiled seductively out at her: the slight, teasing twist to his mouth promising that he'd never be serious about any romantic entanglement. So many women used him for their fantasies and now here he was, needing her.

How long will he be like this? One day in his entire life that he has this chance. You are not going to blow this for him. You are going to come through. This isn't just a goal, it's goal A, goal A-plus. You can do anything if you absolutely–

She jerked away from him as she realized that she was shaking in fear, already gasping from fright. *And he isn't even touching you,* she berated herself. *It really is all in your head.*

Instead she hugged an outcropping of rock. She hid within the sheer inhumanity of it. Nothing of it could judge her. She shared the rock's calm immortality and imperviousness here in the deepening darkness. It anchored her as she tried rebirthing, breathing out the fear, trying to cast it off as it crawled so close to the surface.

His words still whispered in her ear, his promises of what he was going to do to her. He'd awakened something...

She'd been alone for as long as she could remember, and this afternoon she'd been touched by another. God, she wanted that again. But how could she convince all those fears she had that they had to let up, just for the next few hours? They could come back later, but she needed them gone now. *Please, God, just give us these few hours. For him, if not for me.*

She buried her face against the rock and tried to release the panic that clambered up through her from places she didn't know she had. It was worse now than before. It seemed every fear she had clawed right below the surface of her skin, screaming at the danger of the world and of other people. She couldn't release it. Long ago she'd sworn she'd never be vulnerable again. She hit the rock with her fist.

"It's only me," Londo's deep masculine voice said behind her. His hand touched her back and she twitched away from him.

"I can't do this," Lina said. "I just can't. Oh god, I am so sorry."

Silence. He began to rub her between her shoulder blades. Gently, comfortingly. She trembled under his touch.

"I'll never hurt you," he finally said. "I'm not going to force you to do anything you don't want to do. Don't be afraid."

She gritted her teeth. She needed to explain herself to him. "It's not any of it you, Lon. It's just–"

"Just what?"

"Just... just..." She struggled to admit it: "You don't want me. I'm not worthy of anyone caring for me, especially you."

"Just because I'm Valiant?"

"No, because you're Londo. If you really knew me, you..." her voice almost disappeared, "you'd get as far away from me as you could. I'm a terrible person."

He kept the massage going as she clung to the rock. "So terrible," he said softly. "How?"

"In every way."

"Who's told you this?"

"I just know it. I'm not stupid. I realize what I am." Muttbutt. Stupidhead. Clumsy bitch. "There has got to be someone else on this island. You'll want them."

"I want you, Lina."

In desperation and shame she wrapped herself over the rock outcropping. "No you don't."

"Are you telling me who I can or can't care for?" Lon teased. "And next you'll be telling me what to think. Where does it end? Maybe a little mind control?"

Lina straightened like a gunshot, whirling around to face him. "Mind control! How could you say such a thing?"

Shock shot across his features, quickly replaced by a calming, slow smile. "But you just said that you were going to decide what I should think." His hands had dropped when she moved, but now he replaced them on her waist.

"You know that's not what I meant. No one should force their will on another. Lon, this may be a joke to you, but to a psychic, controlling someone is a very real possibility. People who fire mental hooks into– I even–"

"You even what?" he asked curiously.

"I almost did it once," she whispered, still horrified at herself for ever considering it. But he had to know what kind of person she was.

"Mind control, you?" Suddenly all business, he studied her. "Tell me."

She took a breath. "I was in sixth grade, and one day this big guy from the seventh grade– heck, he was probably held back, probably should have been in high school– comes looking to beat me up."

"Why?"

"How should I know? Maybe he just liked to beat up ugly tall girls. He backed me into a corner on my way home. Suddenly I knew I could take over his mind if I wanted. I knew I could stop him that way."

"So what'd you do?"

Her shoulders sagged. "I let him beat me up. He did a very good job of it, too. X-rays and shots and lots of stitches."

"Jesus, Lie. So what happened to him?"

She shook her head. "Nothing. Well, except that I got in a couple of good bites. He got his kicks and moved on to other victims. I think eventually they sent him off to military school."

His eyes narrowed into slits. "Your parents didn't call the cops? Or his parents? What'd they do?"

Shrug. "My dad yelled that I was trying to put him in the poor house with the doctor bill."

"He was joking."

"He locked me in the basement for three weeks without electricity and told me that I could make up for the extra money he had to spend on me by not having breakfast or dinner for two months."

"And your mother let him get away with that?"

She gave him a faint smile. "She was the one who talked him down to only two months."

"*Sacré*– What'd you do?"

"I snuck out, of course. I discovered the fine art of dumpster-diving. I scrounged candles and matches, too. Mom sneaked me down some food a few times."

His face had contorted, so she tried to reassure him. "It was good, Lon. I can look back at it and see that it showed me not to rely on anyone else. It taught me not to be caught vulnerable."

"So the next time that happened, did you have the good sense to–"

"No!" She wanted to shake him, but of course she couldn't touch. "Mind control is wrong, even in a good cause. Even back then I knew that it was a can of worms I don't ever, ever want to open. You set yourself down the wrong path that way. Humanity's gift from the universe was free will, and no one has the right to tamper with that. Everyone should have the freedom to decide for themselves–" She stopped, realizing the situation they were now in. "No matter how foolish their decisions."

"So I'm allowed to make foolish decisions?" Londo gathered her in his arms. At first she held back and he didn't force her. He tried again, and she hid her face in his shoulder.

And he began to sing softly:

Some people stay far away from the door
If there's a chance of it opening up.
They hear a voice in the hall outside
And hope that it just passes by.
Some people live with the fear of a touch
And the anger of having been a fool....

I'm only willing to hear you cry
Because I am an innocent man.

He sang to her in his deep voice there in the waxing moonlight, her so tense and trembling and trying not to be.

Some people sleep all alone every night
Instead of taking a lover to bed..."

He cradled her in a light, unconfining hold.

But I've been there and if I can survive,
I can keep you alive;
I'm not above going through it again...

She was silent as the song ended. Considering? Her breath lightly fanned Londo's neck.

"A safe place," she finally whispered. "Find us a very, very safe place."

9

"**M**aybe what we need is to find a nest of mercenaries and do it right next to them."

She stared at Londo.

"That way you could differentiate your fears. See which one was bigger and which was the preferable one. Rev you up."

Lina gave a helpless laugh at that. "You *have* been through therapy."

"I speak fluent Freudian– with a Jungian accent."

"A safe place, Londo. Please."

He gave her an encouraging smile and bent to place a gentle kiss on her lips. They trembled ever so slightly as she returned the light pressure.

"I know you might not have much time–" she began.

She lowered her head but Lon lifted her chin with a finger so she would look directly at him. "We're going to make this as long and as slow as you need. There's no hurry. All you have to do is relax and enjoy it."

Before she could ask again, he confirmed, "A very safe place," and got up, holding out his hand. She hesitated before taking it. "You are so beautiful," he told her.

She frowned.

Londo cocked his head at her doubts. "Someone has been doing some hardcore PSYOPS on you, Lina. Psychological warfare."

"Don't be–"

"He's been telling you that you're not good, not beautiful, and that the world isn't safe for you. I can't believe you bought into it. You seem... *Eh bien*, don't take this the wrong way, *chérie*."

He tried to gauge her expression. "Strong-willed. Too strong a person to believe others when they try to deceive you." She didn't seem insulted, so he started up the slope. He helped her as she couldn't see well in the rapidly-falling darkness.

"Some lies are truths to people," she eventually said.

"Let me tell you a few truths. You're a beautiful, caring woman, and every now and then you can trust the world and the people around you. Choose good people to join your team, and then trust them with your life."

"Most people just want me to help them somehow." *Like now*, but Lina didn't say that.

Londo stopped. "You can trust me," he said. He squeezed her hand and turned to continue the climb. "Watch out here. You say your parents did this to you? Your father?"

"I did it to myself," Lina said. "People can tell you things and you don't have to take it to heart. I am responsible for my own state."

"And I don't believe that for a minute. Take it from me, sometimes things can happen to you when you're too young or defenseless to control them. You're at the mercy of the world."

Of course Lina knew his origin story, just as everyone did. "Something like that happened to you when you were– kidnapped."

"*Oui*. Something happened," he said too sharply.

"You're a Cancer."

"What?"

"Sun in... No, moon in Cancer, Cancer the Crab. Fierce emotions. Loyal. Family first. I think it's easier for you to maintain trust in a person than it is for other people."

"Cancer?" Londo tasted the concept as signifying birth instead of disease.

"You feel like some people I know, Cancers. It's just an energy you have."

"When's that?"

"Moon signs change every two hours of the day. Sun sign... I think... You're a Leo. Yes, a Leo definitely."

"Leo the Lion." Some shaft of moonlight caught the brilliance of Lon's sudden grin. "He's the guy with the corn flakes, right?"

"That's Tony, and he's a tiger, not a lion."

Lon shrugged. "Both good Italian names. When's Leo?"

"Ah. I think August, last bit of July. You didn't–?"

"I don't know my birthdate. I was adopted; no birth record."

"Oh, right." He'd been kidnapped from his parents and then adopted years later by Maximus; everyone knew that. "Well, if you're not a Leo, then your rising sign is. But I'd be willing to bet real money that you're sun in Leo, moon in Cancer.

"Leo is the guy who likes the limelight; lots of actors are Leos, usually as a rising sign though. The ego dominates, not necessarily in a bad way. I think it's a fire sign. Your moon in Cancer means that if you make a friend, they stay friends no matter what they do. If you make an enemy–"

"I've got too many enemies as it is." His voice sounded bitter as he helped Lina over another run of rock.

"They experimented on you." She tried to remember everything she'd ever heard from Lon's early life. They almost always glossed over that part, leaving it as one of Valiant's mysteries. "They wanted to make another Maximus."

"Yeah. Change subjects. What's your sign, babe? You come here often?"

All right. "Sagittarian," she replied as she tried not to trip in the dark. The cliff here rose a long way. Maybe that's why the soldiers hadn't come this far. It still loomed over them.

"Ah *oui*. And when is that?"

"December."

"A nice Christmas gift for your family."

"Not for Dad." Lina kicked a good-sized stone that was in her way. It clattered behind her into the dark. "There were four miscarriages and one stillborn between my sister Barb and me, all boys. Dad really wanted that son and all he got was Muttbutt. He always said it was a crime that you couldn't exchange kids."

After that Londo climbed in silence for a while. Finally he asked, "Did he abuse you?"

"Did he beat me? Not much. Some families, the kids get beaten all the time."

"And some families, the authorities haul the parents to jail."

"Not mine. Can we skip subjects again?"

"Okay. Big step here; let me help– *D'accord*, tell me more. If Leos are stuck on ourselves, what do Sagittarians do?"

He put his hands on her waist and lifted her over an obstruction she could barely make out. While Lina grimaced at the touch, she didn't draw away. The shadows along this way were inky black, edged on the west with a disconcerting highlight from dusk's afterglow that made depth perception difficult. The only way to safety lay literally in Londo's hands.

"Ah." She tried to concentrate on her astrology lessons. "It's a fire sign, same as Leo. A tendency to jump first and ask questions later. I do that all the time."

"I've already noticed that. But it has nothing to do with phobias?"

"Nope. Thought that one up all on my own. Sags are very creative, you know. Love to learn and teach."

"So do you want to learn anything new tonight?" They'd reached the top of the slope. Holding both her hands, Londo eased her over the last rise.

"I said I would," she said quietly. "I keep my word."

They stood on the precipice, the almost-full moon rising over the bay. Londo pointed at vague movement along the beach. "They're packing up for night maneuvers. Away from us." He regarded her. "I was almost serious, *chérie*. Get closer to them so you can see the difference between fears– of being in a life-threatening situation versus an unreal fear. Your father's creation."

"I accepted and created the fear for myself." In her frustration Lina slammed a tree with her fist. "I just can't release it. God! I am so stupid!"

Gingerly Lon wrapped her in his arms. "It'll be okay, I promise you." He rocked her as he would a child, and eventually she put her arms around him, her palms to either side of his backpack. "I'll share your fear, Lina. I'll make it easier for you."

"Oh god, Billy Joel," she murmured from his neck. How could she tremble this much and still be able to stand?

He laughed lightly. "I even remembered all the words, miracle of miracles. Safe place. Let's try over there." Disengaging except for her hand, Londo led her deeper into the forest. Shortly he found a clearing with a small stream trickling nearby from the evening's storm.

"No fruit trees, but it's safe," Londo said. His fingers squeezed hers tightly, hopefully.

The moon shone through the gap in the forest canopy, providing light. But it also created dark, moving shadows in the warm ocean breeze. The animals of the forest made themselves known by their night sounds.

"Are you sure?" Lina started at the unfamiliar noises and peered suspiciously into the shadows. She checked with the deva of the place.

Safe, it said as it settled for the night.

Londo watched her every move even as he eased the pack off his back and pulled out the blanket. "Safe," he unknowingly echoed the deva. "Lina..." Would she? Had she changed her mind? They stood so close; he could feel his breath as it hit her cheek and rebounded.

Looking at his shoulder and not in his eyes, Lina reached up to the collar of her shirt and slowly began to unfasten it.

Lon let out a breath he hadn't realized he'd been holding. He touched her fingers with his to stop her and she looked up at him in question. Lovely green eyes in the moonlight.

"Carolina O'Kelly... is that the whole name?"

She blinked. "Angelina," she said after a hesitation. "Carolina Angelina."

He repeated the name in his mind, nodded, and then took a breath. "Carolina Angelina O'Kelly..." His eyes fastened upon hers and held them. "I need to make things clear. I want to have sex with you. That means going all the way. If we start, there's no pulling back."

Lon paused to let her absorb that. "I don't think I'll be able to stop if you ask me." He remembered the afternoon and forced himself not to wince with shame. "I'll go slow and I'll be as gentle as I can. But I'm going to do it."

They stood inches apart. Through her fingertips he could feel her quiver just at their closeness.

She looked away. "You're supposed to ask... before you do."

"Ask what?"

"I don't have any diseases."

The edge of his mouth quirked at that. "Neither do I. That would be difficult to do."

"Um... Condoms?"

"I've been accused of carrying a little of everything in my vest," he said, a glow of delight in his belly at finally having this conversation with someone, "but not condoms. And I'm afraid there isn't a drug store nearby. We've been living dangerously all day. We'll just have to find our way safely through unsafe sex."

She pursed her lips and then nodded. "This isn't going to be easy," she told him. "I can't guarantee you anything. Londo Rand—"

"Falcon. Londo Falcon."

A ghost of a smile came to her face. The name fit him with his tendency to scowl and his sharp, far-off eyes. "Londo Falcon Rand," she said, "I will try. This Sagittarian has jumped. I will do my absolute best to go as far with you as you want. But take it slowly." She swallowed. "And if... and if I can't do it... You have my permission to, to do whatever you have to."

"I'm not going to rape you, *chérie*."

She gave him a stern stare to reinforce her declaration. "No. It's not rape if I give you permission. I understand a little of what you've been through. I can feel the terrible need in you for this. Now you do whatever it takes. I mean it."

"Don't worry about it." Londo reassured her and took her by the shoulders as she flinched and then tried not to flinch. "Relax," he told her. "We've done this much before."

He gave her a light kiss before starting a slower, deeper kiss. He kept his hands on her shoulders. He had to be sure about how and where he touched her, never letting himself advance too far too fast.

"You can do this. Just relax and enjoy it. Learn to concentrate on the pleasure in life and not the pain. Tonight we're going to solve both my problem and yours, and we're going to have a wonderful time doing it."

Londo had formed a quick plan: treat this like a war campaign. Take it one sure section at a time, make sure that area was subdued, and then move on. Celebrate the victory only after the entire area had been secured.

"I am not a b-battlefield," Lina whispered to him.

"Allow me my own fantasies, *cherie*." He turned to study the clearing. It held several rock intrusions and a few downed trees, normal conditions for the forested basalt island. "Here." He led her to one outcropping. This was pillowy and smooth, unlike the butte this afternoon. After he spread the blanket on it, he seated her on it and settled next to her. "How's that?" he asked.

"A little h-hard, but an o-okay bench."

"Consider it a couch. We've just gotten in from our date and your parents are upstairs asleep."

"Parents?"

As she tensed at the word Londo cursed himself for mentioning them. Time to twist the imagination harder to take her away from the reality. "It's high school, when we both should have done this the first time."

"Th-that would make us... what age? Maybe sixteen for me..."

"Let's live dangerously. Fifteen for you."

"Uh oh. Here comes the shotgun and the sheriff."

He shook his head. "No one's going to catch us. *Voyons.* I figure fifteen for you lets me be in town visiting from college. There was a high school prom and I crashed– no, I was in the band, yeah, the band– and then I saw you and fell madly in love."

"The band. Instrument?"

"Lead guitar. And vocals."

"You do have a very n-nice voice. Formal or informal?"

He wiggled his eyebrows at her. "I look great in a tux."

"Yes, you do." She smiled at him despite herself. The cover of *Cosmo* had been in a tux, headlined "The World's Sexiest Bachelors." It now hung on the bulletin board over her home office desk.

"I drove you home in my Shelby GT-500." At her blank look, Lon added, "My black convertible. In the moonlight. You invited me in to talk."

"Oh. What do we talk about?"

"We both know we're not here to talk. You're in a strapless number that's driving me crazy. With a coat. Let's get rid of the coat." He helped her out of his shirt and flung it on the ground.

"That's very expensive," Lina protested. She decided to help him weave his story. Maybe that would help. "Fake... silver fox."

"I'll pay for the dry cleaning. Let's make this strapless, shall we?" He reached for her gown.

"I thought it already was."

"Ah. So it is. It makes you look like a goddess."

She gave him an indulgent smile. "Watch it. The dog's going to bark at you."

"I gave him my leftover steak from dinner." Lon sidled closer. "He'll be quiet." He put his hand on her knee and leaned in for a kiss and then another as he slid his hand up her leg to settle on her hip.

"Arm around my neck," he whispered, and she awkwardly obeyed. He pulled her closer and though she tried not to, she still pushed off him with her elbows. "Relax. You can do it."

Lina scrunched her hip away from his hand and strove to concentrate on the kisses instead. Kissing closed-mouth wasn't bad. There was a method involved. His hands were the big problem, and where his body brushed up against hers. She might be able to get away with this if he'd just keep his touch to one area from which she could concentrate on keeping the fear. Two or more places, and the white fear swept in behind her barriers.

This was not going to go well, despite his encouraging murmurs.

Londo didn't notice anything amiss as his tongue delicately began to explore her mouth until he realized her pulse was pounding. Then it began to slow until it matched his own. She must be doing biofeedback.

"You okay?" he whispered.

She nodded, but when he regained his place and caught her tongue, sucking lightly on it, her shoulders contracted. Her fingers dug into his own shoulders and she pushed away hard. Her eyes seemed glazed over. Lon got the impression of a blinding whiteness inside her, a wall of panic and fear.

"Take it easy," he told her.

Through her gasps she nodded as she visibly fought against it. When she put her hand on his left chest he knew that she was trying to feel his heart through his vest. Her eyes closed in concentration. Her breathing slowed with effort.

"Shit," she said when she could talk. "I'm sorry."

"It's okay. Just keep matching me," Lon coaxed. "Keep your hand there if it makes it easier."

"It does."

He said, "We'll go at your pace. Don't worry about it."

"Um, maybe skip the French kissing," she offered.

"You don't like it?"

"It's so... Maybe if I knew you better."

"Baby, you're going to know me better than anyone in a little while. You can take it."

He brought her to him for another kiss, and another and another, his tongue probing her, stroking her until he realized how very cool she felt. She wasn't responding very well.

She wasn't responding at all.

"Lina," he whispered. No reaction. A little louder: "Lina. Come back."

She blinked. Blinked again. "It didn't work?"

He sighed and shook his head. "If the other person isn't there, it's just masturbation," he told her firmly. "This isn't going to do you any good if you retreat inside yourself."

He said it as if he knew what she'd been doing. "You've been there."

"Lots. Now we're here and I want both of us here, okay?"

"I thought it would make things easier."

"'Lovemaking is an art which requires at least two creators,'" he quoted to her. The echo of Jae's voice whispered in his mind: Jae, the expert on sex. Go away, Jae; this was Lon's turn tonight. Lon's turn at last.

"Yes, Londo. Sorry."

He forgave her with a kiss and felt her breasts press against his vest. Mustn't think of breasts yet. Just her mouth, just her face. One sector at a time.

Her right hand she kept firmly against the vest over his heart; her left she kept balled in a fist. How much concentration did it take to maintain her calm? She was so tense, it was almost like holding a statue. Um, a soft statue of Aphrodite. Without thinking he cupped a breast– She gasped as if she'd been struck by a spark and squirmed away from him.

"Match my breathing," he suggested. Her hand reached blindly, seeking his heart, and he guided it to him. Slowly she started to come out of it, her eyes focusing again as her breathing slowed.

"Okay now?" he asked, and she nodded as she caught her breath. "I should have warned you. I'm going to touch you here." His hand hovered in front of her breast, and she nodded tightly. "Let me massage you so you'll relax." He drew her to himself and squeezed her gently. "How's that feel?"

Trembling, biting her lip, she nodded her head. He could almost feel the cold panic through her now, feel her controlling her own body processes as she fought to calm herself by exerting sheer willpower.

"Don't manage yourself so much that you don't feel anything," he chided her. "You're supposed to enjoy this."

She squeaked out a sound and trembled, pushing him away but letting him come back. She still quivered. "Sorry, sorry," she repeated and he rubbed her, murmuring little encouragements, little sweet nothings into her ear until the trembling subsided to petite tremors. He worked his vest off and tossed it on the ground in front of them. "Your turn," he told her softly.

"P-please, not yet."

"*D'accord.* Anything for you." He licked her shoulders, nibbled at the base of her neck, and she arched it under him. It was a tiny movement. She wasn't relaxed in the least, but she was permitting this as if she'd seen someone do it in a movie.

He whispered, "Think of the pleasure and *relax.*" His fingers moved deeper on her breasts, soaking in the firm softness of them and she shuddered, shaking her head. "I'm sorry, I'm sorry." "Relax, baby." "I'm trying; sorry."

They had to stop for a few minutes while she rebirthed. She looked like she wanted to cry.

"*Chérie,*" he pleaded, "what can I do?"

Miserably she shook her head and blinked rapidly. "It's not you, Londo. I'm messing this up for you."

"You'll be fine. Don't try to rebirth; just relax."

So now she became a ragdoll, limp but there, trembling but pliant, trying to control her constant panic by shallow panting.

"No," he finally told her. "We'll go back to rebirthing. Don't do this. You're not some blow-up love doll."

"I'm sorry."

"Touch me. You haven't ever really touched me just for the sake of touching."

Timidly she reached, then snatched her fingers back as if he'd burned her.

"You can do it. Try again."

Her hand almost palsied. She scrunched her eyes shut and the hand shot out.

"Ow."

"Oh! I'm sor–"

Londo caught her hand before she could take it back and settled it back on his chest. Cautiously he let go and her hand remained. "That didn't kill you. You feel any pain from that?"

Lina shook her head quickly, absorbed in the sight of her hand on his skin. He wasn't objecting to it. Timidly she touched his neck and ran her fingers down the line of his shoulder, watching for any sign of displeasure.

"There are hundreds of kinds of touches," he breathed. "Try different ones."

So she began to experiment with light touches, heavier touches, massages and thumb-rubs, even found herself doing a T-touch like she gave her cats.

"That's nice," Lon told her.

This was wonderful. She didn't tremble a bit. She could outsmart her subconscious, have it believing that she was doing massage therapy. "I can do this," she told Londo triumphantly.

"You certainly can," he sighed. "Oh yeah, do that some more, *chérie*. Kiss me there."

So kisses were part of the therapy now. She worked on him, varying the touches, and tried to feel what he wanted her to do. She was reaching around to massage his right back shoulder when she felt him pull on the back of her dress. He tugged and tugged again, then followed the line of the bodice and pulled it down off her breasts. Diving from her shoulder blade, he wetly kissed down.

"Oh, stop. Stop!" Lina began to hyperventilate. No paper bag around– She needed to feel his breath pattern, but he was down *there* and she was up *here*...

"I'm stopping!"

He quickly guided her hand to his heart, but now it was his naked nipple under her little finger. They were sweaty skin against sweaty skin.

"C'mon, love, match me. You can do it." He exaggerated his breathing for her. That did the trick.

"I'm sorry."

"You're not sorry; you're goddam gorgeous. You ought to bronze these beauties. Mount them on a mantelpiece instead of running around with them."

Through the trembling, she shook her head at him. "You– You're ridiculous."

"Breasts are wasted on women," he declared as he nuzzled his nose against hers. "Here you walk around like they were nothing. Give a man a set like these and I guarantee he'd sit at home all day long just playing with them. A man knows what to do with boobs."

"Stop." She pushed against him, a nervous chuckle escaping like a hiccup. "Next thing I know you'll be telling me jokes."

"*Voyons.* A priest, a rabbi, and Dolly Parton walk into in a bar..." That made her giggle and he held her in his arms until she quieted. "All right, here's what we're going to do..."

Londo instructed her to pay attention to different touches and report on a scale of 1 to 10 of how pleasurable they felt. That would keep her mind just on the present, he knew; it would keep her concentrating on pleasure. "How's this? Uh huh, and this? Oh, you like that? Let me try it again..."

He could feel when she began to relax. Was that a sigh? She'd been so silent up to now. "Oooh, Londo," she whispered, and it was the most wonderful thing that he'd ever heard.

Her breasts rose and fell under his mouth with her deep breaths. She was definitely relaxing– and Lon was definitely getting harder. *Virgin!* his loins screamed at him as he spread the blanket wider on the rock. He eased her back down as his mouth settled on those full pink peaks.

After a while he told her, "Stretch," and she did, stretching out her long, slender limbs as he watched her. That relaxed her even more. Lightly he brushed her up and down. He slid her gown off completely, bending down to lick the sides of her knees and caress her calves. Her skin was sandy, salty, sweaty after the events of the day, and the sensation was his favorite in the entire world. Londo paused.

"Damn," he said to himself. Her eyebrows contracted as if she thought she might have done something wrong. "Boots," he said with an abashed look. "Let me get them." He reached down to pull them off with a grunt apiece. Socks and belt followed, and with a quick glance at her, he unzipped his pants and pulled them off, too. He dropped them on the ground next to the rock.

Londo looked down at her panties and then up to her face. Showtime. He worked his briefs off, maybe a little too quickly, and stood over her.

"Point of no return?" Her voice trembled as she looked away.

"*Chérie,*" he reached for her panties, "we passed that a long time ago." She eased her hips up as he pulled them down over her long legs, past her feet, to drop them next to his briefs.

Wonderingly he stood over her as she lay there breathing quick and shallow. This beautiful woman was his, his alone. "You are so lovely." He joined her again on the rock. He took her in his arms and explored the nakedness of her. The give of her body against his own bare skin filled him with new sensations.

Lina focused on his response to repel the pressing whiteness of her own fear. The pleasure he got out of her touch was palpable. Of course– he'd been invulnerable up to now. How sensitive could his sense of touch have been? Now it must be so different. This had nothing to do with her. This had everything to do with him. She truly was healing him. Nevermind what was pressing up against her thigh. *Concentrate, Mutthutt*

Suddenly everything went wrong. White panic swooped down. It wiped out all her logical thoughts. She couldn't breathe. She heard his compelling voice: "Match me. Match me." And she concentrated on her breathing, on his, and bringing them into synch.

"I'm here, Lina," she could hear through her ragged gasps, through the whiteness. "Focus." How he invaded her private world!

Fighting desperately for control, she shook her head to clear it as she came out of it. Jesus. She felt so weak after these things. Lost and alone.

"Are you okay now?" Londo asked.

"I think so."

He took her in a hug. "I'm here," he told her. "It's all right now. You're safe. Trust me." He smoothed her hair as if she were a child as her heart beat right next to his, slowing down from panic speed.

"Sorry." She summoned her courage to touch him again, to run her hands over the hard muscles of his back and arms. He was like that everywhere, well-defined muscles but not overly-defined, hard but not unyielding. Confident in his very structure, even his legs strong and determined as they slid over hers. His mouth was so soft and yet sometimes so hard, too, commanding her own to open to his. His hands pressed into her back and she felt the tensions melting away, warming now instead of cooling at his touch.

The barriers she'd set up to keep the panic away began to dissolve in that warmth. Instead of concentrating on the physical method of making love, Lina discovered that kissing Londo was rather... thrilling. His lips held a kind of promise as well as an invitation. Kissing was a way of communicating, just like telepathy and speech.

What his lips were telling her was scary in an exciting way. They invited her to come with him, sneak away and do what she'd never done before. Don't hide from the world now. This time would be different. This time things wouldn't go horribly wrong.

Just this time if she dared to reveal her awful Muttbutt self and touch life, the universe wouldn't punish her.

Londo guarded for another panic attack. Nothing came. Letting his hands slide so she would know where he was going, Lon lifted her hair so he could nuzzle the back of her neck, and she leaned to him. He caressed her shoulders and moved down to fondle her lovely breasts, knowing that the sound of his breathing filled her ears. It seemed to him that they had the same heartbeat now, the same breath. She was still stiff, but she was getting there.

He let his hands travel slowly down, outlining her navel. He rubbed himself against her and she moved with him, her breath soft and deep. His fingers inched down to her thighs, poised to stroke.

She screamed.

10

No sound accompanied it but it raked through Londo's mind like knife blades. Clapping his hands over his ears couldn't stop it. The scream paralyzed him as the forest erupted with animal and insect cries.

With one hard shove Lina knocked Lon's head into the rock. Rainbow lights cascaded across his retinas. She ran into the night forest shadows.

Lon had this advantage, that he could see and target her while she couldn't spot the obstacles in the darkness. Before she could get to the deep woods he caught her and pinned her within his arms. She beat at him. She growled like an animal, and pummeled him with her fists until he grabbed each of her hands in his.

"Lina. Lina!" He tried to sound authoritative, but the change in her terrified him. She needed tranquilizers. Professional aid. "You're safe! It's just me," was all he could say. He didn't think she could hear him this time. She struggled against him with eyes squeezed shut, audibly screaming in short pants.

He caught her when she collapsed.

Now the woods held absolute silence except for her whimpers as he carried her back to the rock. There she curled into a ball on her side. She gasped fast and shallow, her arms wrapped tight around her head. Londo was afraid to touch her. It would only make things worse.

Lina couldn't breathe. There wasn't enough air! She was going to explode from all the fear! The numbing whiteness of pure terror burned all around her. Go down into herself. Hide deep within.

"Lina. Lina!"

Was someone talking to her? Maybe... Lon? She could barely hear his voice, somewhere out there in the terrible, ringing whiteness. Was he there at all? Was he real?

Lina!

Lon?

I'm here, chérie. Calm down, calm, you're all right now.

Nothing existed in this world but white fear. Sky, earth and ocean: anchorless white storm. **Where are you?**

Right here. Breathe with me, baby. Breathe with me.

Lina hung on to his presence like a lifeline flung onto a tossing sea. She could sense him exaggerate his breathing, so she took a mimicked breath and another. There was his heartbeat. She struggled to bring hers into rhythm with his.

Finally she realized that her eyes were closed. When she opened them to the silver moonlight, Londo really was there. She reached out to embrace the reality of him, the safety of his shelter against the absolute panic.

"Oh god," she gasped. "I'm sorry, Lon. I'm so, so sorry." She was so frightened; she was so embarrassed. She was so disgusted at herself for doing this to him. Stupid, heartless little bitch! She wept into his neck.

Londo wondered at the way she clung to him. "It's all right," he reassured her as he stroked her hair. Wearily he sighed and closed his eyes. So much for his great plans. It was clear that they wouldn't be going any further after this. Instead he rocked her, cooing reassurance. How he hated the universe!

It was a long time before she eased up on him. Her breathing was ragged with her tears, but she forced deep, shuddering breaths. She sat back in his arms.

"Could I... could I have my dress, please?" She didn't look at his face.

"Sure, chérie."

Gently he let her go. When she stood up she swayed, and he retrieved the thin material from the ground where it had fallen. For a moment Lina clutched it to herself like a blanket. Then she scrabbled through the material, searching for a tiny pocket. There was a tissue in it, soggy from the ocean, and she pulled it out to blow her nose. After a chattering sigh and a hiccup she repocketed the shreds, wiped her eyes with the back of her hand, and took a clear breath.

With a sudden movement she snapped the blanket from the rock. It settled softly to the ground next to her chemise. Londo stood there, unable quite to comprehend it. She wasn't getting dressed again. There was a blanket on the moist earth. Lina reached for his hand as she knelt down on the blanket. He joined her in a daze.

"You can't be serious," he finally said. "Not after that."

"I promised." Her smile was tremulous but genuine. "I try never to break my promises." Another hiccup betrayed her determination.

"But... biofeedback..." He didn't know what to say. "Sweetheart, your biofeedback didn't work that time."

"It worked a little."

"It's not enough." He ached for her as the moonlight played upon her body like he wanted to. The triangle of auburn hair at the top of her long legs called out to him, the ultimate goal of human touch.

"No, not enough." She could admit defeat.

Desperation made him try to search for another avenue. "You can match me in breathing and heartbeat," he began. "Can you match me in... being relaxed?"

She gave him an ironic smile, still not quite looking at him. "You aren't relaxed, Londo."

He had to smile at that, too. "*D'accord,* granted. But it's a different kind of tension than what you have," he told her. "It's excitement. Passion." He took her hand and twined his fingers through hers, brought them to his mouth and kissed them. She watched with heavy-lidded eyes. God, she was a temptress! Her mouth beckoned him and he moved in to meet it with his own. "Match me," he urged. "Match what I feel."

"That would take more than biofeedback," she whispered, her eyelashes brushing his cheek. "That would take–"

He waited for her to complete the sentence. "What? Whatever it is–"

She moved a few inches back from him. "It would take a sharing of minds."

He considered the plan. "How do we do that?"

"I don't know," she told him. "I've never done it before."

"But others have?"

"I have no idea," she said. "I just read a lot of science fiction."

"But it can be done?" Ah god, he had to have her at any cost. Any cost.

Her forehead creased. "I'm not sure. I think–"

He took her by the shoulders to draw her to him as he gazed into her eyes. "Share minds with me, Lina," he said. "Feel my passion for you."

Tell me if you don't want to do this, or if I go too deep.

He was about to ask when she was going to start when he felt it. Her mind touched his tentatively, lightly as a rose petal. It wasn't silent speech; a tangible presence of *her*, of her true self grew within him. He lay his cheek on her shoulder, running his hands gently up and down her arm to quiet the tremors as he felt her come more and more deeply inside him, blooming, the petals of her mind unfolding hesitantly. How soft they were. How sweet. How afraid as she tasted what he was.

****I just want to go deep enough to tune into you,**** she said within him. ****I need to know what you're feeling. I won't go any deeper than that.****

****It would help if I knew what you were feeling,**** he suggested.

****Can you do the same thing, then?**** It seemed she held out some etheric hand to him. In his imagination he grasped it, and she pulled him inside her mind. ****Easy,**** she said as he breathed himself fuller, sharpening himself to look around.

This emotion almost felt as if it were his own, her overwhelming fear of him in addition to her fear of being touched. She was terrified. It was a wonder that she'd gotten this far. Fear of the actual act, fear of him, a stranger, fear of losing her very self in this too-personal act, fear of feelings that she'd never allowed herself before, fear of the power of his passion– and a smothering, overwhelming fear of his rejection.

Voices faintly echoed all around: "Good girls don't..." "You'll wind up in a gutter..." "Never trust anyone..." "Just a Muttbutt." Somewhere under everything was a great wall of determination, but it was all overridden with fear upon fear. Was there any passion? Anything at all like what he was feeling for her? If there were, it was only a pale, echoed whisper.

****I won't hurt you,**** Londo promised. ****Trust me.**** He tried to broadcast gentleness and relaxation in waves matching the rhythm of his hands on her legs. He knew she could feel his desperation, his lust, but hoped she could also feel his patience, the fondness he had for her.

It was a sleepy, totally relaxed kind of sensuousness that he tried to communicate as he felt the very edges of the tension in her begin to melt. He wrapped his arms around her and rocked her against himself, running his hand down to cup her buttocks, stroke her legs. He shared with her the primordial humanity of it. This was a part of her as well as him.

She relaxed with a slight sigh, and he ran his hand up her leg. As they kissed, Lon stroked her upper leg softly and then rubbed the bit between her legs he could reach.

"Lon–"

"Take it easy, *chérie*," he told her and kissed her cheek. He sent her a sense of excitement. Of daring. Of listening to what the body wanted. "Stay in the now. How does it feel *now*? Give me a reading, 1 through 10."

Her fingers gripped his upper arm hard. "Tell me," he urged.

"Four," she whispered.

"Good girl. This?"

"Ooo," she breathed.

****You're doing great. Just relax,**** he told her.

This is all so damned personal.

I won't ever tell your secrets. Ever. Now relax. Before she knew what he was up to, he'd pushed her down flat, kneeling between her legs. "Give me readings," he ordered. "Constant readings."

"Lon!" She tried to push his head away from her, clenching as his mouth descended, but he grabbed her wrists and held them tightly to the ground on either side. "One to ten!" he commanded as he came up for air.

But she couldn't; this was too new for her. Instead she flailed her legs until she realized that he wasn't going to stop. His tongue was warm and wet; it tickled– no, it *tingled*– where it should never be– and then he sucked on her. She couldn't help making noises when he did that!

When he finally released her wrists, she tried to slide away. "Don't," she gasped. "They'll hear. Oh god, Lon, they'll hear!"

"No they won't, baby, not a chance. Go on, scream if you want; I like it loud. I'm a little loud myself when I get going."

Londo went back to work, pinning her again.

"Stop, stop! They'll find us." But that and the guilt were the only reasons she wanted him to stop. He kept going.

She lay helpless under his assault and cried out in spite of herself. The sounds inflamed him; his passion started to crest and he knew she could feel it pulsing like a neutron star within him. He could sense a faint echo within her. Maybe she wanted him now, not just feeling pity for him. Her breath came in sharp, voiced gasps; her fingers dug into the dirt as she twisted under his mouth, breathless and swooning.

Ready? He waited for her to tense up again, hoping that she wouldn't but knowing she would.

Oh lord, I don't know. Please, please take it slowly.

He kissed her smooth stomach. He rubbed his hard, anxious penis up and down her wetness, then tried to ease himself in. She was too tight. Too tense. Reaching out with his mind, he took hers firmly and let her feel the full power of his passion. **Match me. Feel what I'm feeling. I've got to have you. Open up for me.**

She shook her head in a storm of hair. "No," she said. "Here." She drew herself up beside him.

"Baby, not a good idea–" Lon started, but the movement of her sliding up his body, of her lips– oh god, her tongue– slithering up his chest, up his neck, meeting his own lips, was electrifying. She hadn't kissed like this before. She hadn't touched him like this.

Lina gave herself permission to be wanton. *You're a dirty whore*, the voices said. She agreed and then stuffed them to the dark recesses in the back of her mind.

This is part of being human, Lon told her. **I'll never tell, trust me. Oh, do that again.** With a groan, he was lost in an apocalypse of sensations he'd never felt before.

Lina told herself that he didn't have to respect her in the morning. He'd probably never see her again. She was safe in her anonymity. She could let all her barriers down if she wanted– what would it matter, except that he'd finally get the experience that he needed?

And maybe just this once, she'd do what she wanted. Indulge in her own selfishness.

She let herself explore him, feeling the hot flesh and the immediacy of being that pulsed within him. He was Creation itself, quivering to create Life. She was yin to that primeval yang.

Her skin awoke. Her taut nipples raked him. Bunching his soft hair between her fingers, she pressed her mouth hard against his. Her breath ran fast and she relished it; she wanted to laugh. Just this once, let it loose! She kissed him everywhere she could find a spot to kiss. His nipples came erect under her mouth, too. His skin was salty, sweaty, sticky, and as she nipped at it he moaned.

Where else did he want to be touched, to be kissed? Her hands traveled down his belly, and then she eased herself back to stroke his thighs. He guided her hand in a tour of his penis as he let the tip of it run over her, back and forth.

Lina's mind moved deeper within his as she felt his passion consume him, drowning his thoughts in the thick liquor of lust. He fastened his mouth on hers as he rubbed himself between her legs.

Now, Lina. Now! Please!

Londo didn't know if he could hold himself back from her anymore. He was white-hot. He dug his fingers into her butt trying to spread her out more.

The curtain of fear threatened to descend again and Lina fiercely willed it back. She didn't know how long she could stave it off. **Do it!**

She was sitting straddled on him so he raised her up and guided himself in. As she clutched to him and made a soundless cry, he held his breath. He could feel her pain as something too large tried to get into something too tense to open to it.

Ohmigod, you're so big, you're so hard...

Londo's pride in himself swelled. He was big, he was a man, he was about to burst. She was so tight, but wet and so very warm. He fought against images of himself as a mighty Viking captain, a lusty Arab sheik, leaning over his virgin captive, spreading her legs wide open to him. She, terrified of her conqueror as he laughingly made her his. Not these images! Not now! He had to be gentle, go slow no matter what his private fantasies screamed at him.

Lina's fingernails dug holes in his back. He rocked with her, releasing his pent-up breath. Her hard nipples pierced him as she panted. She cried out and changed her death hold on him. Now it was she who held her breath.

"I want to go all the way in," he whispered desperately to her. "Open up some more, *cherie*. Breathe." She nodded silently and gasped out her held breath. "Match me, sweetheart." He let her pause for a second. Two.

"Better?"

She nodded again, lying. She clutched him as if she were drowning, gulping in air and holding, gulp and holding. "Please," she managed to say. "Please. I can't–" How much longer could she hold the white curtain back? Hurry, get it over with before she died of fright!

"Relax. Relax!"

God! He couldn't hold back! She was woman, open to him. She was his. Groaning in triumph, he plunged into her as far as he dared, held tight there.

She shrieked. She arched against the fear. Her fingernails scraped his back– Such sweet pain, Lon thought dizzily as her tightness encased him.

He wanted more. He'd always dreamed of having a beautiful, naked woman under him. "Here we go." He gathered Lina close and shifted position so that she was lying on the ground. When he raised up to support himself on his hands the tableau was complete: here was the beautiful woman, naked and sweaty. Brave Lina.

Hesitantly he began to move, then a little surer, a little deeper as she cried out with each stroke. It sounded like sobbing. He knew that he was hurting her even as he tried to be gentle.

"Look at me, Lina. Feel what I feel."

She opened glassy eyes to meet his, gasping as if she couldn't catch her breath as he shook her in his soft rhythm. He grunted with the effort not to go harder, not to go faster, and the sobs eased into mewling whimpers, the song of sex that he'd always wanted to hear sung just for him.

"Deeper now. Feel it with me." He drew her deeper into his mind as the universe churned around him. He groaned as he tensed. All of his energy gathered and screamed to be released. He couldn't contain it– he shouted and shivered as he came.

Londo reeled from the sheer physical experience. He murmured to her, "Sweet baby, sweet baby," and then pulled out of her with a wet sound. It was over. Too soon!

"Uff, so that's what it's all about." Lina blew out a deep breath now that it was over. Finally.

He smoothed her sweaty hair away from her face. "Oh yeah." As she raised herself up on her elbows he hovered over her. "It was wonderful, *incroyable*. Are you okay?"

He knew she was trying to find something nice to say. "I'll live," is what she came up with, an apologetic look on her face.

He grinned at her pronouncement and her predicament. "I have to say it..."

"What?"

"It was exactly as I'd always dreamed it would be. Heaven, and then some." He kissed her. "How can I ever thank you?" He fell into kissing her until she had to laugh weakly at his fervor.

"I want to do it again," he whispered. "And again and again. Longer this time. Much, much longer."

"I know." She stroked his cheek and shoulders as he embraced her. It was so odd to touch. Somehow her sense of touch had come alive. Feel the texture, feel the warmth, feel the structure underneath. Feel– Londo. Another wanderer in the darkness that was the Universe. He was real.

Lon twined his fingers through hers even as realization shocked through him. "I know you," he said. He'd seen through her pretenses. He'd glimpsed her essence. "I don't know anything about you," he told her, "but I feel like I've known you for years."

"For years... and yet not at all," Lina realized. He was as familiar to her as if they'd grown up together.

She trusted him. He amazed her: so confident, so brave. If anyone deserved the title hero, it was certainly him. She could serve his needs for this one night or day or however long it took. He deserved it.

Londo tipped her chin up. "My god, you're a mountain of courage. You have to be, to handle life with all that fear and not end up gibbering in some corner."

Lina sought the right words. "You're such a caring person wrapped around... a core of steel. One who stands in righteousness," How many people built their lives around human decency? His mouth twitched in a self-depreciating smile. "And you've been so lonely all these years." Pangs of isolation permeated the man.

Lon asked, "Anything else?"

"There's a bit of a devil in you, too," she shyly added. "Someone who likes to take chances. No, someone who's not afraid to take chances. There's a difference. Not afraid– How do you do it?"

Instead of answering, Londo laughed triumphantly to himself. He shouted inwardly with victory as he felt her naked body pressed against his. The drops of blood here were virgin blood that he'd spilled!

"And you weren't a virgin?" she asked.

He shook his head like a lion. Leo the Lion! "Not any more! And always enough non-virgin to truly appreciate the moment." He grinned at her. He was the Viking captain. He was the Arab sheik. She belonged to him now; his woman. Was she laughing at him behind her hand? "What?"

"Who'd have thought that I'd ever... do the deed?"

"And who'd have believed that I'd ever do it?" He gripped her in an enormous hug and they rolled through the damp forest ferns, laughing exultantly, until he became serious again. "So, are you up to a second try?" he asked her. He was going to be ready whenever she said yes.

Londo knew that she could sense the desperation still within him. He knew they had to have a few hours sleep, and soon. Who could tell what condition he'd be in when he woke up? This might be his last chance– for a lifetime.

But Lina wished they could wait until morning, until the soreness and the raw memory faded some more. However, that might be a luxury that they couldn't afford. "The first time was a little... awkward," she admitted. "I'm sorry I screwed up so bad."

"Awkward but very, very nice– for me, at least. Maybe for you this time. No panic attacks now, *peut-être*. Practice makes perfect." How the moonlight glowed on her! How the fragrance of crushed leaves, of rich forest humus and human sweat could be a sweet perfume on this night of nights!

Londo asked, "How do you feel now? Still afraid? You don't seem to be." He ran his hands over her slowly. "Any tender spots? Any panic triggers?"

"You're not testing for a panic attack," she told him as he squeezed her buttocks. She could feel the pounding beat of his heart, almost hear it within his chest. She heard the gushing of his blood through his veins, felt the give and take of his muscle groups as he moved, sensed the life that flowed through him as well as her.

Touching was a miracle. *Thank you, Lord, for this gift.* It made it easier to reciprocate for poor Londo in need.

Such a mischievous glint in those warm brown eyes! He said, "Let's make love, Carolina Angelina. Let's touch each other all over and really feel things for the first time in our lives." But he paused. "I'm sorry I... took the plunge so abruptly. I just couldn't hold back any more. Was it really that bad for you?"

"I understand, I really do." How could she assuage his guilt? "I liked what led up to it," she whispered. "It made the other part worth it, I guess. I think I might be able to stand it again."

"I hear that some women actually get to like the other part," he said and kissed her neck right below her ear. She would. She'd beg him for more before he was through with her. His woman.

His breath tickled and made Lina's head swim. Oh dear, she'd made so much noise before! "Are we still safe?"

"I'll check, *chérie*." He sat up and examined who knew where or how far, peering all around. While he did that, Lina quietly ran her hands down her etheric aura, smoothing the irritation, cooling the swelling. Damned if she was going to impede him any more than she absolutely had to. Maybe it wouldn't be so painful this time, now that she knew what it entailed. She was sure she could relax better if she could heal herself a bit.

Lon finally nodded to the south. "How about that; they've retreated. Moving back toward the hotel, tightening their net. We're miles from there now, and it's got to be what, nine, ten o'clock? We're safe enough. We should see how much ground we can cover before the sun comes up, though."

"Lon, I can't run through the forest in the dark."

"So we'll hit the beach instead. Run by moonlight." Even he winced at the idea of more running. Now that Lon could think about other parts of his body besides the one, he realized the burning soreness in his feet and lower legs from the day's ordeal.

"It's been a long day for both of us. Shouldn't we–"

Londo rolled onto his side so that she lay beside him. Trust was written all over her face. He took her hand in his. "I think we should make love again, long and slow, and then try to catch a few hours of sleep. Then before the sky gets light, we get out of here. Can you manage that?"

As his gaze traveled down the length of her, it struck Lina suddenly that she was absolutely naked, lying next to an absolutely naked man.

Londo slowly smiled at her. "Yes. Yes, you are," he said softly. "And you are the most beautiful naked woman I've ever seen."

His sweet lie made her blush. She picked some foliage from off his shoulder. "This is going to sound very strange," she said to him. "But I've never felt like a woman before this. Just a person who happened to be female."

He stroked her hair tenderly. "Never?"

She smiled and ran her fingertips down his cheek. "*You make me feel like a natural woman*," she sang so softly. "Do you want the entire song?"

"We're safe here now," he murmured into her hair. "I'll keep you safe."

"Is there anything up on the north end of the island that looks better than here? Or maybe a way out?"

Lon swam back to full consciousness and peered past her into the darkness. "I see a few estates, but they're surrounded by tall fencing. I doubt we could make it. Over there's a little cove that looks nice, but it's miles and miles from here."

"Oh, how pretty," she said, and he glanced at her in surprise. "Sorry. You were broadcasting the image. I don't look into people's minds unless– I guess it's because we were... so close."

"That's okay. *D'accord*, we'll try for the cove in the morning, but we'll have to keep under cover. Maybe we'll make it sometime late tomorrow. Maybe my powers will return by then and we can really get out of here."

"In that case, we don't have much time." Their efforts had rolled them a good distance from the blanket they'd started from. She sat up to return to the damp thing in the moon-dappled shadows.

Londo rose up behind her. "Come here." His voice purred husky and low as he caught her around the waist. "Sweet Lina."

This time, too, he took it slowly, pausing whenever it seemed as if a new panic attack hovered near, but Lina always managed to keep the white curtain at bay.

Thus things progressed faster than they had before. She still trembled at his touch but that excited Londo. These trembles were the dregs of her virginity which it was his pleasure to burn away. Now this captive girl was his; now she bent to his will, that of the pirate captain taking his prize. They were in his candlelit cabin, she in his feather bed at the bow with no hope, no wish for escape...

Her cry as he entered her brought him back to reality. "Relax, *chérie*," he crooned. "Tell me if I hit a six." Smiling at his cleverness in overcoming that damned phobia, he held her bent against the rock. This time had to last much longer, and he tried to remember conversations he'd overheard, videos he'd watched, articles... Jae's voice now came back to him, laughingly criticizing someone's technique, telling him what they were doing wrong.

Lina tried to catch her breath. She clawed to regain her handhold on the outcropping. This was taking too long– when was it going to be over? It wasn't that it hurt as much as the first time. It didn't hurt so much as make her feel like waves of trembling jelly.

Sometimes he'd pull out and she'd think he was done, but he didn't seem done– there was no climax– and he'd *do* things to her, things she knew about but never imagined would be done to her. He used words that polite men didn't say, but he didn't say them roughly or insultingly. The world spun around even as he was in her again, whispering that he wanted to go faster, harder. She tried to speak, but could only nod and try to relax for Londo's sake.

She called his name and his fierce lust coiled like a spring tightening. Lina's sensations began to focus deep in her belly. She gritted her teeth against it. This wasn't for her. Don't mess it up for him.

But she had to raise up against the pressure, standing erect with him reaching around to wrap one arm down her stomach, his other hand above it, trapping her breasts. She arched back against him. His jaw pressed into her cheek. His hips never paused their squeezing rhythm. She rolled her head helplessly on his shoulder as he leaned to kiss her. Damn, she couldn't stop it! She gasped and let out a moan.

"Come for me," he urged her.

She writhed against him, struggling for release, crying out as she couldn't. The pressure kept building. He pressed so far into her. She stretched herself upward and strained against him, almost growling, but his hands between her legs and on her breast kept her caged. The only hope for release was within.

With a shout that was half-shriek, all the tension climaxed and broke. She cried out again as a second wave hit, a third wave and a fourth, dozens of tiny wavelets rocking as it receded. Freefall buoyed her in some space beyond time.

Lon supported her as she sagged against him. He was still going, cooing to her. "That's a good girl. God, you're so hot."

She caught her breath as she remembered her duty. Dizzily she leaned forward again against the rock and he followed. His breath came ragged now, his grunting lengthening to groans.

"Hang on." He changed his position so he could take firm command of her hips. The groaning became cries and he trembled hard against her, then jerked suddenly as he came. Another jerk, and another. A noisy sigh.

"Ah god. Oh god." Londo pulled out but drew Lina with him, and together they slid down the side of the rock to the ground. "Ah *chérie*," he breathed, "that's exactly the way it's supposed to be." He held her on his lap as he sat against the rock. "How was it for you? I think I scored an eleven that time, *non*?"

She pressed herself against his warm chest as he wrapped her in his arms. Did she kiss him, or he kiss her? Did it matter? This was afterglow and it was so very nice. She felt a part of his reality, surrounded by trust and safety. Contentment.

He chuckled, a small sound of triumph, and they sat there in the shadows and the silence, the sea singing in the distance. "Oh God, don't let this end," he said, and it sounded like a real prayer. "It was even better this time. I felt like... I felt like... I didn't... realize... it would be... so..." His eyelids drooped.

"Here, let me get the blanket," Lina whispered, and shifted to get up. He reached out.

"Don't leave me!"

His hand clamped hard on her arm, and a sheen of desperation glinted in his eyes. Quickly she regained her position. His arms locked around her.

"I'm here, Londo. I won't leave."

"I'm sorry," he whispered. "It's... just... that..."

He was softly and contentedly asleep. The night and Londo were warm enough, so she snuggled against him with his arms around her. She tried to set her inner alarm clock for a few hours before dawn and asked her guides to act as backup. Without waiting for the response, she too, fell asleep in his arms.

11

She jerked awake well before dawn.

Lina lay on the ground, surrounded by the naked arms and body of a well-muscled man, musky with dried sweat and sex.

Londo, she recalled with amazement. Londo whom she had touched and who'd touched her back. The handsomest man she'd ever seen. Here in his warm arms she felt a safety she could never remember feeling before.

And here she was something new: a woman to his man. The entrancing wonder of it all kept her from realizing for some minutes that anything was wrong. Lon still slept beside her in almost the same position that they'd fallen asleep. His breathing was very deep but not to the point of snoring.

But the setting had changed completely.

The deep forest glade was now a sandy clearing. Palm forest surrounded them on three sides with a narrow wooded buffer from the night-darkened beach on the fourth. A softly-gurgling brook emerged from the trees and emptied by low waterfall into a manmade swimming pool. It was a miniature paradise, Lina thought, like something out of a travel brochure, but to wake up here out of the blue–?

She surprised herself by not panicking. Lina felt eerily calm and not quite real. Compared to yesterday's events, this was almost mundane.

How strange that Vallant had never let it be known that teleportation was among his powers. But if he was a teleporter, why did they do all that running yesterday? Maybe that bazooka thing had done it to him as a side effect and he didn't realize it?

Maybe she was dreaming it all. She dismissed that thought. Even though the change was fantastical, the circumstances themselves were very real, the sand a little too cool under her naked backside as she shifted around. Her legs ached; her feet were beyond sore.

Wait– This was the cove she had seen in Lon's mind!

Carefully Lina sat up and slid away from him. For a moment his arm draped like Adam's on the Sistine Chapel ceiling: relaxed, graceful and powerful at the same time.

He was that masterpiece in the sky and she was some nobody tourist craning their neck to gawk. Before she knew it they'd have to go back home, never to return again.

Guard her heart. Guard his as well. He didn't seem to be as sensible when it came to that as she was. Cancer energy was illogical stuff.

Hers was the practical world, so she searched for their clothes and supplies and found nothing. Why should she? Lina could clearly picture where everything was back in last night's glade. She'd left her nightgown fallen beside that big rock–

The dress dropped onto the sand in front of her.

Now, that wasn't mundane.

Lina gaped before crawling to it. Yes, same rips and everything, except that now it was its original pristine white, or at least much lighter than it had been. It was hard to tell color in the darkness. As if it could be a copy. All she had done was–

Where had Lon left his clothes? Careful, had to get these exactly right...

And they appeared on the sand, too. Her shoes– they materialized next to the chemise. And where was– ah. Her underwear. The knapsack. The blanket.

She sat back hard. First the explosion at the hotel. Now this: telekinesis or teleportation or something. *Beam me up, Scotty.* And over there– Valiant himself. Her lover.

Had she gone insane or had the world? Crazy, mixed-up things were happening. Wonderful things.

She needed a swim. How crazy wonderful that there just happened to be a pool around! Its cool water snapped her fully awake. It also washed away most of the sweat and salt and shock.

Yes, she was awake but unreal: Eve in Paradise, totally sated and contented, woman personified. A movie star on a romance set. She was the glamorous and sexy... who? Someone who had sultry dark eyes, cherry red lips, siliconed T and lipoed A. Anyone but Lina Muttbutt.

Or maybe someone really exotic. For a while she imagined herself a wanton mermaid with long seaweed hair, daring to swim naked with a human man nearby. She laughed at the stars and they twinkled back at her.

This mermaid hung weightless in her tranquil water womb for as long as she had breath to do it. There was time now to heal the ache in her lower legs as well as the embarrassing soreness between them. She stroked her own etheric field to smooth and cool the abrasion. And then she heard **Lina,** and knew that Lon was awake. The mermaid disappeared, leaving just her to face him.

He lay in the last of the moonlight next to the pool: one arm in the water, one hand propping up his chin as he lazily watched her. Such beautiful, mischievous dark eyes! His lips curled into a slow, tantalizing smile. "Lina," he said, and her name brought warm and tender images broadcast to her mind. He made it a love song. "For a moment I thought that you were trying to drown on me."

She swam to him, but kept just out of his reach. She felt very shy and couldn't stop her blush. They had made love. Now how was she supposed to act? It wasn't as if they had forever. Just a day. Smoothing her hair back gave her an excuse to non-chalantly cup her hands at the base of her neck so that her arms covered her breasts from his eyes.

"Londo," Lina murmured. She could tell he was hurt that she didn't come up to him, but he understood and let her be unsure. His eyes could see right through her, see that she didn't want to say anything about what they'd been doing.

What to say instead? "I, I told you I was pretty good in pools. And I never heard that you were a telepath," she added.

He cocked his head, puzzled at her pronouncement. "I'm not. Valiant, remember?"

"But you're sending out telepathic signals today. And you certainly were last night."

"Hmm. *Eh bien,* you never told me you were a teleporter."

"I still may not be. There are two possibilities here that I can see."

He put his head on his crossed arms and considered. "Two. I only see one." Still, his eyes moved as if he were gazing clearly at her body.

"There was an episode of *Star Trek* where an alien civilization had set up a park so that anything anyone wished for would suddenly appear."

"*Star Trek.*"

"Original series. First season."

He thought about it. "So you're saying there's some kind of technology or mag-ick going on that lets people teleport."

"Maybe. I left one thing back there: the rifle. Can you bring it here?"

"How do I–?"

"Just picture it in your mind, and then picture it being here."

Lon was quiet for a few minutes. "*Non,*" he said. "Unless you see it somewhere."

"It's still back there," Lina told him.

"So bring it in. Here." He patted the ground next to himself.

"Maybe over there," Lina said, pointing. "It *is* an explosive."

"Good point. *D'accord*, do it."

The gun appeared at that spot precisely.

"It's melted," Londo reported. Lina couldn't see that well in the dark to confirm it. He turned back to her. "Congratulations, love. You're a teleporter. Just don't think about teleporting me anywhere soon."

"The chemise is different, too," Lina said wonderingly. "Maybe... Maybe I need to take a little more time, focus more."

"Now why would all this happen tonight?" Lon murmured to himself.

"Not tonight," she said and Lon turned to her curiously. "Yesterday. I must have teleported on my shoes at the hotel, remember? And you were reading my mind all day, saying things before I could say them and repeating what I was thinking. It has to be an offshoot of the bazooka thing. You're radiating evolvo-rays or something."

"Evolvo-rays." He snorted.

"Well, hell, I don't know. You tell me." She shook her head, taking in the marvelous waterfall at the other end of the pool. "What is going on?"

He lifted himself up in one motion and dropped into the water with hardly a splash. He was a vision of perfect grace and power. She treaded water, unsure if she was afraid to move or afraid that he might not come to her. Her heart threatened to beat out of her chest.

Londo ducked under the water, rinsed off the same as she had, and surfaced. Running his fingers through his black hair, he ducked again; she could see dark movement rippling closer through the moonlight-silver pool. He broke surface. His eyes met hers as he took her into his arms.

"Right now I don't give a damn about teleportation or telepathy. The only thing that's important is you," he said. His kiss held a command of possession.

Lina didn't care either. He'd shifted her into selfish mode, and all she wanted was him. Here in the cool water heat flooded through her. Desire swept logic away.

Londo bore down on her lips as he clasped her to him firmly so she couldn't pull away even if she had tried. Pulling her to the side of the pool, he trapped her between him and it.

With a satisfied grunt, he set her on the lip of the pool so her legs draped over his shoulders. She had to pant, had to whimper to keep herself from exploding, and she knew each sound she made caused his passion to rise ever higher. She tried to twist away from his tongue, but he held her hips firm against him until all she wanted was more of him inside her.

Wordlessly she cried out for him. Londo lifted himself out of the water along the edge, rising up over her as she slid back to make room. Stalking toward her, dripping, his eyes never left hers. She was an animal in some delicious trap as he bore down on her. His body covered hers completely. He pinned her with his weight, and his teeth on the flesh of her neck claimed his prey as she cried her surrender. She gave herself up to him. She bent herself to his will completely and he knew it.

They lay locked together at the very edge of the pool, aware of the sky lightening in the east. "Sweet Lina," he murmured into her ear. "Beautiful Lina. Lina who likes it now, *n'est-ce pas?*"

She knew he could feel the beating of her heart just as she could feel his. "Oh yes, Lon."

"And I'm the best man you've ever had."

"Mm hm. Ever. Ever-ever."

That made him smile and lay his head back in the sand. "So we'll stay right here and I'll build a treehouse for us. We'll find everything we need washed up in the sand."

"Mm. And we can invite tourists to stay the night in the guest room for outrageous rates. What shall we name the coconut pie concession?"

"*Non non non.* Just the two of us forever, just you and me, *chérie.* Have everything stay like this." His stomach rumbled.

"Maybe you'd want some breakfast flown in every now and then?"

"Maybe. Lina—"

"Hm?"

He raised up to gaze earnestly at her. "I want to make love just as often as I can, while I can. We don't need to run today now that we're here."

"We're here and we also need to eat and find clean water. Goal A: survival."

He shook his head. "Goal B. The pool's clean enough. And as for food— I'll take you somewhere when the powers return. A five-star restaurant. Room service, anything you want— when it's over. For now— Say you will. Say yes, love."

How long did he have? She had no will of her own when he held her. "Yes. Anything."

"I love you," Lon whispered in her ear.

"Don't say that!" she blurted before she realized how he might take it. "Don't... Londo, you don't have to say that. Please."

"Yes I do. Because it's true." He pulled her back with a smile. "I. Love. You." He stopped when he saw her expression. "I didn't think I was jumping the gun here," he said slowly. "I may be new at this telepathy thing, but I have the distinct impression that—"

"Lon, I..." He'd entwined their fingers, and now she tried to unwind them. Too deep. Too much. Moon-in-Cancers fell all too easily. "I know it's not the right time to take a dose of the real world. Don't worry; I won't hold you to what you said."

He said it so it would sink in. "I love you. You love me."

"Look, Lon, it's a whole new experience today. Sex and emotions– they get mixed up so easily. We've got to keep a handle on what the future holds."

His face tightened. Lina urged, "Just say that you're enjoying it, that you're caught up in it. Everything will change– I don't know, tonight, tomorrow."

"You love me. Love me, Lina."

Those brown eyes of his blazed into her own, anxious, unsure and hurt. He was out of balance, too, and didn't realize it. This was impossible! "Lon, I don't know what I feel." She tried to sort it out, to give him something in return. "I like you very much. I respect you."

"Cold," he muttered.

"No, no." She ran her hand over his wonderful chest and shoulders. "Very warm thoughts. But it can't go farther than that. You know that. Skin-deep is all we have."

"And soon we won't have that much." He rubbed her hip. "So I can touch the outer you, but I can't touch your heart in any way?"

Her cheeks turned pink under his sweet offer. "I don't want you to say anything in the heat of the moment that you'll regret tomorrow."

"That's too sensible, Lina. Live for the moment, because it's all we have." He pulled her head to his shoulder so she'd relax again. "Say you like me at least."

"So very much."

"Tell me why," he teased.

"You're nice," she said.

"More."

"You're handsome and nice. Handsome and nice and fearless. And funny."

"And...?"

"And you have that romantic accent, Pepé."

"And...?"

"And you have no need for ego-stroking." She laughed. "You're a silly-billy."

He tickled her and she giggled, and tickled her some more until she was forced to tickle back. They rolled there in the sand laughing and wrestling until he was on top of her, his hands holding her arms out from herself. His gaze locked onto hers, suddenly serious. Eyes wide, Lina caught her breath.

"You're still afraid of me. Trust me. That thing we did the first time, when we shared minds. I want to do it again."

She looked away. "That's so private."

"What we've been doing is so private. I want to know you better."

"So let's talk."

"It's quicker this way. It's deeper." Lon realized what her main objection was. "Your mind is lovely, *chérie*. Don't be afraid that I don't like what I see there." A glint flashed in his eyes and the edge of his mouth crooked. "Or is what you're objecting to how ugly my mind–?"

In astonishment she blurted, "How can you say that?! Your mind– It's beautiful and focused. I could lose myself in that."

"I want to lose myself in you." His breath feathered her neck. He smiled when she closed her eyes with pleasure, and did it some more. "I've never known anyone like you. I want to know all about you. I want to have you in every way I can, while I can."

The hand on Lon's arm clenched. "No. Bad idea."

"It was fantastic. I want to do it again."

He reached for her mind and after a moment she opened to him as he opened to her. They blended into each other, melting with golden lights and pastel colors dancing softly around them. Music played somewhere in an etheric realm. He felt her gentleness, her givingness, and she his overwhelming need. As he moved deeper within her, she made a tiny frightened sound.

I won't hurt you,* chérie. *Let's go a little deeper.

Just a little, Lon. Remember tomorrow.

He tried something, merging his essence with hers as if he'd stepped into the same space she took up. All at once a whirlpool of emotions and attitudes engulfed them– Someone cried out; maybe both did.

What they shared matched up and grew stronger: integrity, courage, focus, caring. They could taste the other's abilities: Lon felt Lina's connectedness to the ordinary world; Lina, Lon's incredible self-confidence. Their attraction to each other grew as much as their wonder. And the lo–

Too much! Londo! Lina managed. She broke the connection abruptly, like ripping strong adhesive. It hurt. Some parts came with her; some didn't quite disengage from him. She felt dizzy and incomplete. "Too deep," she groaned.

Lon rubbed his forehead as if he were coming out of a headache. "You can take it," he growled. "That was... You–"

"Look," Lina told him, "you've got just a little time left and we haven't done experimenting with touch." She sat up and took a breath. "I know what all guys like. I've seen it done lots of times, but you're going to have to coach me. How in the world do you begin?"

"What are you talking about?"

"Um, ah. Oh hell. Fellatio. A blow job."

He blushed. It was a relief to see that he could blush at something. The irritation in his features turned to sharp interest as he sat up as well. "What do you mean, you've seen it done?"

"Well, ah, it's part of my job."

"I just got the impression that you were– some kind of graphic designer?"

"Yeah, you could put it that way," Lina replied weakly. "Very graphic."

"What's that mean?" He searched the outer layer of her mind– "You can't be serious."

"Londo, I'm a pornographer." She said it very quickly, as if he might not notice it that way. "There's nothing wrong with that. It's all very healthy and completely covered by the First Amendment."

Londo gave what sounded like a hiccup.

Lina bulled it through. "I'm in charge of putting out an adult products catalog. Midnight Delivery, have you heard of them? We're on-line, in the mail and on satellite, everything legal," she repeated, "and fairly respectable. Plus I review X-rated movies on the side, to help pay for the extras in life– like groceries."

He slapped his knees as he laughed uproariously. "You! I don't believe it." A thought hit him. "Lina... last night you were still–"

"A virgin. They didn't have a warning on the job application: 'No virgins accepted.' I got in. And I've helped sales hit record levels time and time again, so there," she added in defiance. "I guess it takes a subconsciously frustrated virgin to turn out really good smut. That was part of the reason why I took the job in the first place, to learn more about sex. I knew I'd never learn any other way."

Lon began to chuckle again and despite his best efforts, it turned into giggles. "I love it, I love it. It's so efficient."

"Obvious question..."

"Can you get me a catalog?"

"Everyone asks. Yes, I can. You can even use my employee discount."

He nuzzled her hair. "Great. I think we can put it to good use," he said with an occasional giggle.

Lina realized that they were talking as if they would still be together tomorrow or the day after that. But those powers would come back soon. "I need instructions," she whispered into his ear.

"Instructions?"

"For the– you know."

"Ah. *D'accord*, no need to rush." But they did, trying to fit everything they could into what time they had.

They spent time just touching each other, trying out the feels. Lon would rub her earlobe between his thumb and forefinger and then he'd press so gently on her lips. Her chin and cheek fascinated him with the firmness and then softness so close together. He explored all of her thoroughly.

But he was such a wonder to touch as well, the hard muscles under the tight covering of skin, rougher than her own. Such broad shoulders, the landscape of his chest, the surprising roundness of his butt.

Even more different was just being held, secure and safe. She could wind herself so deeply in that that she never wanted to find her way back.

Lina curled a lock of his hair around her fingers as she continued her exploration. "Do you mind me touching you like this?" she asked.

"Isn't that the pot calling the kettle black?"

"Sometimes you seem to draw back."

"I'm fine. I love you touching me, I love the way you touch. It's just that I've never been touched like this. If I can feel something at this level, it's usually trying to kill me."

"I'm not," she murmured, "believe me." He chuckled at that and she continued to investigate him.

Londo closed his eyes so he could better feel her exploration. Such a curious but tentative touch, like her mind. He hummed softly in time with the tide and realized that she hummed along in occasional harmony. *Don't let this end yet, God. Not yet.*

But– But– The world began to spin faster again as those sweet, tiny kisses and licks brushed his belly. Her fingers trailed slow lines up above his knees now.

No. He pulled her up to lie beside him.

"Let's take a break," he said, trying not to make it sound abrupt. "Figure this out. How the hell did you get us here? Instant teleportation for you. Instant telepathy for me."

Lon gazed anywhere but her, at the early-morning clouds rolling across the sky. "And here I am without my powers. Do you think that that may be why I have telepathy? That I suddenly developed it for survival..." He considered. "Or maybe to be better equipped to deal with you? To convince you to..." The sentence hung in midair.

"If that's true, then I became a teleporter because of the danger. I wanted to run. But why should it happen to both of us at the same time?" She shook her head.

"Evolvo-rays," Lon murmured.

"Don't quote me on that."

"Stranger things have happened, Lie."

"Stranger than this? Powers appearing, an entire population disappearing– oh, god, Londo..." She raised up, her eyes wide on his.

With a reassuring smile Londo chuckled her under the chin. "I definitely do not believe that you're responsible for the disappearance of an entire island of people. I bet that turns out to be very logical– even ordinary." But it was a possibility. He filed it in the back of his brain for later.

She settled on his shoulder. "If you say so. I don't believe in coincidence anyway, but right now the amount of coincidence is piling up too high to be... coincidental."

"Maybe the telepathy for me was a side-effect of the bazooka Terry hit me with."

"But I wasn't hit by it, Londo. That doesn't explain me." She paused. "Could we be, I don't know, in the Timeless Realms and not know it?"

"The Timeless Realms?" He rubbed his nose and frowned.

"Impossible things happen there, right?"

"Yes, but not like this." He cocked his head at her. "I've been there. You haven't."

Lina sucked in her breath in wonder. She kept forgetting that he was Valiant, with a lightyear's experience away from her own mundane world. "What are they like? Did you see magick? What kind of people live there?"

Lon shifted to tell the tale in comfort. "I've been there twice. Once because they were having a huge forest fire, and the other time to help them rebuild from an earthquake. It's not someplace you can visit any day, Lina. Those Scythians guard that Gateway very fiercely. People along the Borderlands inside don't trust us at all. Even the Green Mage can be hostile. He claims that Outerworlders are imperialists just waiting to conquer the Realms."

"Aren't there supposed to be places where you can just find yourself in the Realms without going through the Gateway?"

"Like a faerie tale, you mean?" Lon considered. The Green Mage could pop up in the most unexpected places...

Lina asked, "Isn't that where faerie tales and myths come from? The Timeless Realms?"

Lon scratched his head and then he scratched hers with a quick grin. "I'll tell you what all this reminds me of," he said. "There was this girl. This beautiful princess." He glanced quickly at Lina and then back into the distance. "With beautiful green eyes to match the beautiful girl. And she lived in the Timeless Realms."

"Why do I think you're making this up?"

"Hush. Anyway, this princess wakes up one day and everything's all crystal clear, not misty like it usually is in the Realms. And she hears horns, car horns outside her palace window, and people yelling and cursing at each other, and a whooshing sound, and she looks and there are metal tubes with wings flying through the sky. And she says, 'Oh goodie, I've fallen through a doorway into the Outer World!'"

"Can they do that, too?" Lina asked.

Lon waved her off. "Don't interrupt; I'm telling the story. Of course they can, or they should be able to. It only makes sense that a hidden doorway would go both ways. Where was I?"

"The princess is in the Outer World."

"Not just the Outer World, but in Montreal," Lon continued. He told Lina of how the princess went out exploring and met a policeman in the building next door who showed her the magic of the Outer World and saved her from dangers she didn't expect. How she realized that she didn't belong there and longed for her home. The tale was exciting, colorful, funny… and poignant. The policeman helped her find her doorway back, and they bade each other a tearful adieu before she left forever.

Lina drew a design on his chest with air. "I wish that he had kept her with him," she said. "Why couldn't the story have a happy ending?"

"Who said it didn't?" Lon asked. "Who says that the princess didn't go home and find happiness?"

"I suppose. It's just that things usually don't turn out well in the real world."

"Tell you what. The next time I tell it I'll have the policeman go into the Realms. Maybe he'll have an adventure."

"You should write it down," Lina told him. "You tell a very good story, Lon."

"I've got a million of 'em," he said with a faraway smile.

"Then you should write a book. If they're all that good, people would want to read them."

"Uh huh. Valiant writes children's books."

"So use a nom de plume if you think that people won't be able to read past your name. Oh– and hire some sleazy-looking guy for the author's picture, with a big ol' bushy beard, and craggy eyebrows. Don't forget the eyepatch."

Lon laughed at that. "Eyepatch."

"You never know what that eye's doing under there. He could go on talk shows and pretend he's the author. Give him an interesting background, you know, son of gypsies who worked on an oil rig in the North Sea, traveled to Atlantis on weekends…"

"Where he swilled ancient aged octopus ink with willing mermaids," Londo grinned. "I like it. Captain Miller, we'll call him. Scourge of the North Coast. Arr. Lock up yer kiddies, mate, Cap'n Miller's been spotted out in th' bay." Londo lay there smiling at the sky. "Maybe so. Maybe I'll try it."

"It'll work. I do know a little about marketing."

"Apparently. Tell you what, when we get back I'll hire you as Cap'n Miller's publicist."

That made her laugh. "I'll get someone to ban the book. That way everyone will run out to buy it."

"Such a devious brain! I like you, Lina. I like the way you think."

He put his arm around her and told her one of Cap'n Miller's adventures then, how he sailed the world round on his flying ship that could dive to the bottom of the ocean when it needed to because it wasn't just covered with barnacles, it was one big barnacle, able to trap a huge bubble of air with it when it dove.

Now Lon rubbed his face with his hand. "Ah, why'd you do that?" he asked her. "You got me started on those crazy stories."

"Magical," Lina said.

"Whatever. I shouldn't have talked about water so much," Lon said, getting up. "I'll be back in a few minutes." He trotted off to the forest and Lina turned her back.

She tried not to cry though her heart turned inside-out. She had lost him.

12

It was bound to happen, she reminded herself. She had thought that they might have this day together. Well, she was wrong. Even the world's most desperate man couldn't keep an interest in Lina Muttbutt for more than– how many hours had it been?

At least she wouldn't have to worry about protecting his heart. The old Muttbutt curse had done that for her.

She made a quick, bitter swipe at her eyes and then looked around for something– anything– to divert her. Her nightgown lay sprawled on the sand, white as the day she'd bought it. It showed not a trace of black dye, yellow dust or green vegetation stains. Too bad the shoulder strap wasn't fixed as well.

Lina pulled a long vine off a tree and morosely twisted it back on itself, plaiting it with the strap. After she tested it for strength, she put the gown on, drawing her hair out of it. She could make another tie for her hair with a vine, maybe. It had gone all frizzy and needed braiding.

"Qu'est-ce qu'il y a?!"

Lina twisted at the sound of his voice. Naked at the edge of the forest, he stood staring at her, his brows drawn into a frown.

She tried to sound peppy. "It's time to be up and about, isn't it? I suppose you'll be wanting to go find Terry Whatsherface today," she said and turned away from him. She took his silence as affirmation.

"We're staying here," he finally said. "I'm in no condition to find Terry."

"I'd say you were in fine condition to find her."

"What?"

"Look, Lon, you don't have to be nice to me. You don't owe me anything," she said. She sank to her knees on the sand, staring into nothingness. She didn't feel brave anymore, just lost. "I've known all my life I'm not what men look for when they want a woman. And I know you're Valiant and I'm nobody. So just go out there without me and I'll bet someone finds you and takes you to her. You can still have that day you can remember, but with her and not me."

He knelt behind her. "What makes you think that I want Terry more than I want you?" He twined her hair through his fingers.

"You don't have to do this," Lina choked. "I understand."

"But you do not understand, *pas pantoute*," Londo told her. "You don't understand that you're the most beautiful woman I have ever laid eyes on. The most exciting woman I've ever been with. There's absolutely no comparison between the two of you."

She shook her head. "Then I'm sorry I'm so stupid," she said. "I don't understand what you expect me to–"

Londo rubbed her soft shoulders. Touch seemed to make the telepathic contact come into focus.

"Ah," he said. She blamed herself. She could feel he was ready– past ready– to continue and yet they had lain in the sand and he had told her stories. Obviously, it was because he was tired of her.

She was inferior and ugly– how could she believe that?– and he was uninterested in her now that he'd had her virginity and a little more. He was just letting her down nicely.

Lon said, "What I expect from you is nothing. I only ask, and if you say yes then I am ecstatically happy."

"Then... why don't you ask?" The question was almost too soft to be heard.

"Look, I have these powers." He didn't mean for it to come out harshly, but it did. "I could split you wide open by accident if they were to come back."

"You don't have the powers now."

"And I have no idea when they're going to return." He put his arms around her and tasted her body with his fingertips. "You're the only woman I want," he murmured into her ear. "In all the universe, there's only you."

Her breath was warm and moist against his cheek.

He said, "If I could, I'd make love to you non-stop all day and all night, however long I have. If I never got my powers back I'd stay right here with you, and I'd never let you up from under me. Never."

"Your powers won't be back for hours," she told him. "Talk to your cells; they'll tell you."

"Talk to my– I don't know how to do that, *chérie*. You talk to them. Find out exactly how much time we have."

"Hours."

"Not days?"

"No."

He ran his finger over her lips. So wondrous, to feel softness like this. "So now you like it," he murmured to her. "You want it too."

"Please."

He combed his fingers through her hair. Take a chance? With Lina at stake? "Do you guarantee a few hours?" he asked. "Absolutely? One hundred percent sure?"

"I see a wave of time," she said in a distant voice. "It flows, adapting to things as they happen. It could happen sooner, it could happen later, depending on how things go. That bazooka thing didn't have a clock on it that they could set. There wasn't a scale for ten hours, twenty hours, thirty hours. And your cells need you to rest to get your powers back. The more you rest, the sooner they return."

"I don't want them back, not yet." Lon clenched his fist. Then his tone softened. "But we do have hours? At least?"

"At least a few, Londo. Until this afternoon or evening; it feels like it."

He turned to view the distance, miles and miles away. Maybe forty; hard to tell from this angle. Terry's men still scoured the forest on the south end of the island. No one was remotely near to the two of them.

Lina asked, "How do you think you feel?"

"Like maybe my regular powers will come back any minute. Damn, I wish I knew exactly," he said as he stroked her drying hair. He tangled his fingers in it and pulled her head to his to kiss her to show her it wasn't her fault. "It's not safe for you. What if we're right in the middle, and suddenly the powers come back? You've seen– Sometimes I can't control myself. We can't take the chance."

"They'd come back all at once?"

"No idea. This has never happened to me before."

Lina did not even want to think about it, but she considered the problem. "What if you had an early warning system?"

"Like what?"

"Like maybe that feedback loop that I did on your shoulder. I think you could tune in to me at a very easy level, so that when your powers turn back on you'd know immediately from the echo. That way we'd have right up to the last minute."

Lon sat up and wrapped his arms around his knees. He gazed out to the ocean horizon. Chances and possibilities... All his life he'd had to live with the terror hanging over him of accidentally hurting someone. Sometimes he had. Every incident replayed for him now.

He turned back and studied her. She hadn't moved, but her green eyes were wide on his. Her lips were a little swollen and parted, and beneath that white chemise her full bosom rose and fell exactly like those of the women he'd always dreamed about.

His throat went dry. "Do you... Would you want to try now?" he rasped.

"Oh yes," Lina whispered. How had this happened, that she could long for his touch so? She pressed his right hand against her breast and tried not to tremble. Londo breathed very carefully, as if he were about to take a step off the edge of some chasm.

"Now, feel from the skin's point of view."

"It would be easier if I did this first." He pulled her straps off her shoulders, her gown off her breasts, and took his previous position. "From the skin's point of view, you say?"

"Um hm." As his fingers moved over her skin, she tried to amplify the sensations and relay them to him. Touch— his fingertips left a trail of arousal wherever they went, and he picked up that emotion immediately. Now he began to realize the tactile sensations, too.

"Oh." His breath warmed her skin, and he looked up at her. "I get it." He cupped her breast and massaged it. It made her gasp, and then he realized that he had made a sharp intake of breath at the same moment.

"Oh yeah," he said in comprehension. He lowered his head to kiss the nipple, and then came down deeper, sucking.

Lina cried out. She couldn't breathe! His mind dove into hers. Unbidden memories began to bob up to the surface, forgotten emotions, a cold basement floor and blood–

"Stop! Lon– too deep!"

He startled as if she'd caught on fire, their minds tearing apart. "What?! Did I hurt you? Are you all right?"

Lina dropped her hands from where she'd covered her face and reached out to touch him with reassurance. "I'm fine."

His terrified expression disappeared, to be replaced with a question. "Then what...?"

"Mentally. You went much too deep. For a brand-new telepath, you're strong. We're looking for physical here, not mental. I don't know what we can– You need resistance."

"Resistance?"

"As in another person doing it, too. A double feedback loop with me on the other end. That way you'll have a kind of calibration going."

He grinned at her. He looked like a boy out for serious mischief. His uncombed hair stuck up in places. His eyes were laughing. "Sounds fun. Game to try?" He leaned in toward her.

He was a wild animal about to pounce, and instead of fright, Lina felt only a sudden flush of heat as her heart came alive again.

"Places?" he asked, moving his hand toward her breast.

"Just a second..." She felt inside that hand, felt the lust poised like summer lightning. She didn't have to tell him when to start– he knew.

They began awkwardly at first, overstepping boundaries and then withdrawing too far. They settled down to a balance that, if tipped, just added more excitement to the act. It made each touch memorable and alert.

Hold on here, Lon said as he began to thrust in a hard rhythm. With each movement he drove his mind farther into her, pressing through her emotions.

Not so deep, Lina insisted.

You can take it, he told her, but eased until she consented.

Deeper and deeper. Lina panted with every push of body and mind. The gasps became cries and Lon groaned with her. For a moment or two, he slowed down but then she took over the rhythm, urging him on until he took control again. Salty sweat dripped from his brow down onto her. Crying out, she arched and he came within her with a roar.

Firecracker cascades rippled through her, through *them*. It was a minute or more before Lina opened her eyes, drowning in the multi-layered revelations, gasping as if her life depended on it.

Lon watched her like a lion his prey, hair down in his eyes. He gulped air as if he'd just run a marathon. "On a scale of one to ten," he managed to say, "we just hit a thousand. Whoa."

She rubbed the edge of her mouth with her knuckles. "Anyone ever tell you you're one dangerous guy?" she asked him.

"Uh huh. But never in this position." He laughed suddenly and rolled next to her to take her in his arms. "Never ever in this position."

The vibration traveled through his chest into her own. She could feel his heartbeat thundering, feel the hot flashes of his breath against her neck, the length of his sweaty body stretched on her own. Laughing, he collapsed onto his back on the sand next to her. And she laughed with him in delight.

The downpour was almost as heavy as it had been yesterday but there was no lightning, so they huddled together under the hastily-hung blanket and plastic.

"Maybe you should talk to the local deva about getting rid of this," Lon suggested. He held her tightly in his arms, trying to keep her warm. His cheek rested against her soft one, but something was out of kilter. Disengaging them carefully, he rubbed his chin. A raspy stubble had appeared that registered sharply on Lina's double-loop.

"It looks very movie-star," Lina said, amused at the wonder he displayed when he scratched his jaw.

"Even so, I wish I had a razor," he replied. "Getting rid of this when my powers return will be a real pain. It always is." He gave it a good scratch. "Good thing it doesn't grow nearly as fast as a norm's."

"Ah." Lina cocked her head and wondered what her range was. If time and space truly existed only as human constructs, as she'd read, then distance wouldn't matter, would it?

She crossed her arms over her chest. After a long moment of concentration she gave a mighty blink and a curvy razor appeared in front of Londo, followed by a pink bottle of shaving cream. "Thy wish is my command, master," she said with more than a bit of surprise.

"My own genie." Lon grinned as he examined the equipment. It definitely wasn't mercenary issue. "Where'd this come from?"

"My house," she replied. "Hope you don't mind using female shaving cream. It's probably the same thing men use, but priced twice as much and stuck in that sickly pink bottle– with a lot of perfume thrown in."

"I don't mind if I don't have a choice. Thanks. Do you have a small mirror you can teleport in, too? Don't break it; seven years bad luck."

Lina searched with her mind but couldn't find one, so she examined his barely-bristly jaw. "How hard can it be? Shaving is shaving. I'll do it for you."

"How about some soap and maybe some toothpaste, too? Might as well take advantage of this big bathtub here. It's even got a shower." He nodded to the swimming pool, choppy with the downpour. "Big enough for two." He caught her hand and pulled. "C'mon, *chérie*. I'll scrub your back and you'll scrub mine. You'll like it."

It took her more than a moment to set aside the rush of excitement his invitation caused. She needed to concentrate completely on this teleportation stuff. Soon enough there appeared a wrapped bar of soap in her hand, along with a toothbrush. "Just a minute," she said. "I think I put it in the pantry." Another toothbrush appeared, this one in unopened packaging. Next came toothpaste and a couple of washcloths.

She beamed under his approval. "All the comforts of home. Towels?" Lon asked.

"Let's wait and see if the rain stops," Lina told him.

"Ah, efficient. How about a little champagne? Maybe some music?"

"How about me just teleporting us both out of here?"

He looked sharply at her. "Can you do that? If you took your time?"

Her smile disappeared. "I don't know. I'd hate to make a mistake. Wrong-colored dresses are one thing, but–"

"But melted guns and flesh are another." He nodded and looked around. "Then I guess we're just stranded in Paradise. We'll have to make do."

Surprisingly shy once they were in the pool, they soaped each other up, adding their lips to the process to make sure that every spot was attended to. Lina cornered Londo and very, very carefully shaved him as he gave her strict instructions as to sideburns. He thought at one point that she'd nicked him, and his outcry jogged her hand so she really did. She kissed the injured spot, healing it as her lips touched it, and he settled down.

As the rain lessened she scrubbed shampoo into his hair, letting the suds drip down into his eyes so they burned and he had to duck himself. He needed to learn all about what it meant to be a normal human. Then it was his turn to pour a stream of scented shampoo on her long hair and sensuously massage it clean.

Such a simple act, but she hummed her pleasure at it. She ducked under for a rinse and they played tag underwater. Splashing to the surface, they caught each other in a hug.

"One more little task," Londo chuckled as he held her so close. He steered the both of them to the edge of the pool. "Where's that razor?" he asked and spotted it. "Lina, can you get it?"

It was on the other side of the pool from them. She concentrated for a second, and it landed next to Lon's hand. Where had she missed? His chin looked good and clean to her. And then she realized–

"Oh no, you don't," she said, but he gave an evil laugh.

"Yes, I do." He boosted her onto the edge of the pool, brandishing the razor and cream. "Spread 'em, baby," he demanded.

"Lon, really!" She blushed furiously.

"Really, Lina." He rested his crossed arms on her clamped knees and stood there staring into her eyes, that crazy lopsided grin on his face.

Aroused in spite of herself, Lina growled, "You owe me big time for this," and Lon eased back so she could spread her legs.

"I'll make it up to you," he promised.

Afterward they both splashed in the pool again to get the sand out of their hair and then went for a quiet walk hand-in-hand along the damp beach, clad in Lina's towels.

Londo's hand in hers: it felt so different from the way he'd led her around yesterday. But something was bothering him now. She could guess what it was.

"Sweetheart." Lon finally had the courage to speak. "This isn't going to last."

She squinted at the sun peeking out from the clouds. "I knew that before and I know it now."

He squeezed her hand. "The mind-sharing we did. It's taken this a little– no, a lot farther than I thought."

"I'm sorry. It was the only way I–"

"I know. We had to do it that first time. But I goaded you into doing it again." He licked his lips and looked sideways at her, but her eyes focused straight ahead on the horizon at the black storm clouds streaming away, then down to their path ahead.

"I didn't have to agree," she told him as she kicked some shells out of their way.

"Yes you did. You've got this mixed up with your priestly vows. You think you have to do everything I ask you."

"Do not."

He stopped and turned her to face him. "Look, we're getting into deep water here. I'm just telling you that whatever happens, I won't be able to follow through on anything... afterward." Her face was calmly, maddeningly accepting. "But I want to do the sharing again. I want to do everything again."

Lina knew the truth: he was Valiant and she was no one. He'd be gone soon. Forever.

Goal A was to protect his heart. Her heart, too. She'd forgotten that for a while, but it wasn't too late. "I understand," she said in controlled tones. "But no more mind-sharing. We don't need to do it. It's just going to make things worse."

"I don't want to hurt–"

"Don't worry about me; I'll get by." He didn't reply. "Always make sure you're two steps back from the world, and that way it can't reach you to slap you down," she instructed him. "When this is all over, I'll just take two steps back. You, too."

He shook his head. "I can't do that. I don't want to do that, and I don't want you to do that either." He lifted both her hands to his lips and kissed the knuckles. "Lina," he began.

"No." Delicately she retrieved her hands as her mouth set in a firm line. "We switch subjects. Now."

So they strolled the beach without speaking. A long-ago lava flow on the beach set a boundary for them with a spill of high, undulating walls. They turned around to retrace their steps. Lon started to say something several times but stopped, and they continued in silence.

"Love," he finally said, "is something you don't cut yourself off from. Every little bit keeps you going through the bad times. Sometimes just the memory of love is enough."

"Love," she countered, "is wonderful for most folks. It's a gift past all understanding. But for those who aren't in step with everything else, it's the universe's way of tapping you on the shoulder so you look around at something that isn't there while it sucker punches you in the gut. It's God's practical joke, a two-edged blade that cuts you coming and going."

"That's a helluva way to look at it."

She wrapped her arms tightly around herself. "Sometimes reality isn't pretty. Let's face it, Lon, love hurts. Personally, I have enough wrong with my life that I don't ask for more trouble. Let's drop this subject, please."

Now it was his turn to look away from her. "Look. I truly think I'm... I think I–"

"No. No, you're not and no I am not, okay? I refuse to be pushed farther than–"

"Pushed?" He spun on her. "Pushed? Are you saying that I–"

"This situation!" she cried. "You just said it, but you don't *get* it. Tomorrow everything will be different. Everything. Forever and ever, amen. So just–"

She tried to summon up her indignation when she felt so helpless and he looked so hurt. "Just don't let all this get to you. You have to be strong in this world, and I don't mean Valiant-strong. I mean you've got to protect yourself when God throws these things at you. You have to take those two steps back or you don't survive."

He was silent for a long while before he finally said, "You want to talk survival? I've had to survive in this world– and in other worlds. My life was in shambles, dust at my feet, and I survived. And I have loved."

"And a lot of good it's done you, right?"

He grabbed her by the shoulders. "You don't have the right to–"

She had to be strong for him! "No, I don't. But you've loved and you haven't been able to do anything about it and you've been miserable, haven't you?" How his jaw tightened at that! "Haven't you?" She shook his hands off her. "Well, that's not going to happen this time. You're not going to go back miserable and lonely because of this. We can control things here. We don't have to let our guard down, do we?"

"Damn, you can't–"

"So I don't and you don't and we are going to drop this subject right now."

He fell silent. His face turned to blank stone as he gazed at her.

"You're a very practical girl."

"You have to be to survive."

"No, you don't. I know perfectly impractical people who have survived very well. Loving, warm, impractical people. It seems to me that you were pretty warm and impractical yourself just a little while ago. Maybe a couple times today already."

"No."

"Yes." His crooked smile returned to mock her. "I think you don't know yourself nearly as well as you think you do."

"Well, I can't love and I can't be loved. I know that much. That's my reality."

He ran his thumb along her cheek next to her mouth. "I'll work on you today," he told her, his eyes squints of mischief. "I got you to let me touch you yesterday, and today I'll get you to let me touch your heart."

"You're just asking for trouble if you try."

"Trouble is my middle name," he drawled.

"This is not a game to me, Lon."

"Games." What flashed across his face? Something of his lightning mind reflected in his features before he gave a sudden grin and announced, "Race you!" He whipped Lina's towel off her and ran away with it flying above his head like a flag.

She shrieked and tried to snatch it back, but his long arms kept it above her reach. Lon stopped to enjoy the show of her jumping, her eyes lit first with annoyance and then frustration, her breasts bouncing, that tiny triangle he'd left on her pointing the way between her legs. He'd notched out the top of it so it made a "V," for Valiant's woman. She was his; he just had to figure a strategy to keep her.

Huffing in mock anger, Lina tucked the towel back into place. "Touch it again and you're dead," she growled.

"Such a modest girl." Londo grinned at her. He lounged in the shade of the forest at the edge of their beach, in the crook of two fallen trees. "So where do we build the treehouse? Pick a spot."

Her gaze swept the forest for a moment and then took in the sea, at the seagulls screaming with laughter on the high breezes above them, at the glare from the bright sunlight that made her squint at the Pacific. There was nothing in the world as green as the trees, as white as the beach, nor as blue as the high tropical sky!

Lina straightened to take a deep breath. "What a great day!" The storm had left the sky washed clean. They could see for miles and miles, out to the edge of forever. "Wish I had my camera. Or a frisbee."

"What, play and not build houses?" He was about to make a joke when the ground trembled, just enough to feel it well. "Whoa. Easy, girl. The volcano's not going to blow today, is it?"

She frowned at that, her eyes going distant, and then shook her head. "Years yet. Two at the soonest, but no more than five before it wakes up, she says."

He nodded, not surprised at her any more. After all, yesterday he'd talked to a storm god. A deva. Whatever.

"And Earzh tells you this?"

Lina flicked a bug off the top of her towel and adjusted the fit again. "Earth's a very nice person. I'll introduce you sometime."

"You do that. Hey, I know where there's one, a frisbee," Lon said. "I'm not–"

"Clairvoyant," Lina supplied the word.

"Clairvoyant," Lon said. "But if I can picture where it is, can you pick it up from me?"

She blinked. "Never know until we try," she said. "Okay, picture it in your mind."

Fiercely he concentrated on his apartment and the particular souvenir cabinet. Lina's eyes unfocused, she chewed her lip, and suddenly he held a frisbee in his hand. "MONTREAL 1976" was emblazoned on its face, along with the five Olympic rings, gold writing on a black background.

"Very cool." He flashed a smile to distract her and then threw the disk hard down the beach. "Catch!"

She ran after it, laughing as she gauged the landing spot for the frisbee. The towel was lost within a few steps. Lon enjoyed watching all of her moving as she ran. She missed, but gave it a valiant try as it arced to a landing just out of her reach. Picking it up, she sailed it low back up to him. It streaked by before he realized how fast it was going. He didn't even bother to grab for his towel as he ran after the toy.

They played fast and hard. Lina saw just how much Londo was not himself. He'd leap for the frisbee as if he could fly but it'd be far out of his reach. He reacted as if his reflexes were twice as fast as they were now.

She didn't take it easy on him. She did try to cut him a break every now and then, but it was her responsibility to teach him how to be a norm for a day, and part of being a norm was being physically fallible.

Still, he amazed her at how fast he seemed to adjust, to assess his level of skill and play to it. He was sharp. And he looked so hot in action: sweaty and gleaming, his skin such a dark warm tan as if it were congealed sunlight. As if he were Hercules come to life in front of her eyes, a tropical god in earthly form.

She threw the frisbee into the wind over the ocean.

"Lina!" Londo shouted in disappointment. "That was a gift!"

Then he saw that the breeze was bringing it right back to shore, practically along the same course it had taken out. He ran to catch it, his eyes only on the frisbee. Leaping, trying to judge how far he could jump now, his fingers just closed on the edge. He sprawled onto soft sand with it and then reached up to gather Lina down to him. They rolled on the sand, laughing.

She was completely at ease. Off-guard. Londo reached with his mind to surround her with easy-going pleasure.

She stopped laughing, but kept her smile. "Not a good idea," she said. "Let's–"

Comfort. Safety. Despite herself, she relaxed next to him. He tipped her chin so she'd look directly into his eyes. Intimacy. As he opened his mind he reached out to hers. They meshed on a soul-deep level. He could sense mirrors of himself in her, places that held resonance to him. All he had to do was search. Fan them.

It all came down to Woman and Man. She was his woman, and he was all man.

She wrapped her arms around him to snuggle into how he made her feel.

And Londo gloried in his tactics.

Lon lay in a reverie at the edges of her mind, rubbing her butt under her shirt, as she lazily traced the lines of his pectorals.

He'd told her stories again, but this time they were of the groupie and the rock star, or the snooty socialite and her pool boy; Red Riding Hood and the wolf, or the detention hall teacher and her naughty student. Together they played all the parts.

Now Lon pushed her up so she was on all fours over him, looking down at him with a smile quirked in expectancy.

He had his hands on the shirt placket when he stopped. "What?" he asked, curious at her expression.

"I was thinking that it was about time on your schedule for you to be getting back to work."

He almost blushed. He'd been found out at least in part. "What, you tired out?"

Lina loosened the shirt and Lon pulled it off her with that dazzling grin of his. "It's just that I didn't think you were really serious when you said you were going to come a hundred times," Lina told him. "You know, the Guinness people require an official witness for world records."

He pulled her down to lie beside him where he could reach her well. "Too bad it's just the two of us then. *Eh bien*, let's see. From a purely theoretical view, with no scientific or psychic basis to it, I figure I have about 24 hours here in this condition. Maybe 25. One hundred divided by 25 means–"

"You'll have to develop bad habits. We're falling way behind schedule," Lina chided.

"I'm not finished yet," Londo said into her neck as he rolled her nipples between his fingers. "I'm a strong finisher. The best."

Amazing how his touch up there could stir fires down *there*. "Mm. I've noticed you're a leg man," she laughed softly.

"Lina O'Kelly," Lon said, "You have the all-time best boobs around, and I just gotta get me some." He rolled her over as she let out a shriek, until she lay on her back on the sand. Now he took his position over her.

"Mine," he said, kissing one breast, and "mine," kissing the other. He placed his index finger on her chin. "Mine," he pronounced solemnly, gazing into her eyes. Then he lowered his mouth to his favorite parts of her and went to work, leaving her to play with his soft hair, to run her hands over the contours of his strong shoulders and back.

"So is this what this segment is, or do we breast-ball?" she asked as she could.

He raised up at that. "We haven't done that yet," he considered and then added, "And there's something else that we haven't done." His eyes took on a sly squint. "Anal," he announced.

"Oh, no. No, no, no," Lina said. Lon kissed her breasts.

"Anal," he repeated.

"Nope," she said, and he moved up on her to kiss her mouth.

"Uh huh," he whispered with a smile. He put his arms around her and kissed her a little harder, pulling her hips insistently toward his.

She pushed him away. "Nuh uh. Most people go their whole lives without that."

"C'mon, Lie honey. Anal. Backdoor. Hershey highway."

"No," she declared. "I draw the official line at that."

Lon studied her eyes, sensing the strength of her refusal versus the importance of the request. "*D'accord*," he finally sighed and made a rude noise with his mouth against her skin. She giggled and kicked at his silliness. "So we'll just move along to Plan B."

"You know, Valiant, I get the feeling that this is just a little more than the average human male can accomplish. If you ever wanted to switch jobs, you could make a fortune in porn."

He grinned at her as he slid to her side. "I'll keep that in mind. Maybe I've just been saving up all my energy for today. All I know is that I'm not going to be able to walk tomorrow."

"So you'll fly instead."

"With a big stupid grin on my face," his smile faded. "Tomorrow–"

"There is no tomorrow; only today," Lina said quickly.

"Today could be a problem, too." He frowned. "Just one day, and damn it..."

Lina waited.

"What do you do to yourself?" he asked suddenly. "I've seen you. Healing your-self?"

She eased away, not knowing if she should feel embarrassed or not. "It's been a bit more than this average human female can take, Lon. I'm just trying to keep up with you."

"Do you think you could do that... with me?"

One day for Londo, just one day. How many times had they done it so far?

"Y'know, on those commercials they say that if it lasts for more than four hours–"

"Not the same thing." Lon shook his head at her. "There's plenty of blood getting to where it needs to go, believe me.

"I want to do it until we have to stop," he insisted. "I don't care if my balls turn green and fall off tomorrow, as long as they work today. Please."

"This is not what they taught us at psychic school." Lina pressed two fingers against her mouth, figuring what the best approach would be.

She showed him then: how to touch the etheric field, soothe it and breathe out toxins. Now when they made love, Lina made sure that every touch of hers stroked not only his skin and muscles but *him* as well. She breathed the white light love energy of the universe into him to cleanse and revitalize him. She felt like she was glowing with the energies she channeled into him; they swept her clean as well.

"Jesus, Lina," Lon whispered into her ear. "I can feel that. I can feel that!"

He came twice without resting, but they both collapsed to nap after that. Sun through the palm trees woke Londo to wonder at the world.

So this was what touch really was, he thought as he lay beside her. He stroked her lightly so as not to wake her, as she lay with her lovely head on his shoulder.

Skin had always been something to pretend to touch, or to allow the slightest of contact with. It was eggshells, it was thin glass, so easily bruised or broken. He'd learned that the hard way so long ago, but he'd learned it quickly and fortunately with people who loved him enough to forgive him.

But this. Skin was warm, it was cool. It was dry and it was moist. Firm, soft and hard. This was woman's skin, tasting of salt and sweat and sex and sand, smelling of the same, with shampoo and soap and... woman... mixed all together.

He ran his hand over her breast; she shifted in her sleep and the breast shifted, too. He loved breasts and nipples and women's bellies and hips and asses and legs and dark reddish hair and green eyes and soft pink lips wherever they might be.

She almost awakened as she turned over and slid her free arm over his shoulder. Londo loved this, too: the closeness, the intimacy, the trust that he'd earned from her despite everything. For all the years he'd railed at the universe bemoaning his fate and declaring sex overrated claptrap, there was this to counter it all, this day with this woman. He let his hands explore this new universe that she brought with her precious self.

This day. He could live with it now, maybe. The wonder of it would shine throughout the rest of his life. It would have to.

But he was damned if he was going to live that life without having *her* beside him. She still refused to say the obvious. She would. He'd make her.

His woman.

13

"Hungry?"

Lina hadn't realized it, but she was ravenous. It was well after noon. When was the last time she'd eaten? They'd been *exercising* since before dawn. They had caught rainfall for water, with a couple rows of coconut shells worth of clean pool water in reserve, but still... She raised her head from his sandy chest. "Did you pick that up from me?"

"*Non*," Lon said. "I'm hungry, too." He scratched his chest thoughtfully. "Maybe it's time for the big game hunter to do his job. All I can think of is a Big Mac. A dozen Big Macs." He eased her off himself so he could reach over to the pack and draw out the dagger there. Its cold steel flashed as a sparkle of sun caught it.

"*Voyons*... Setting traps..." Lon muttered, then, "Is rat good eating?" He made a sour face. "Feel like a fish dinner, *chérie*?"

"Can we make a fire? I'm really not into sushi." Lina peered inside the sack, trying to figure what could be used as a pan. What kind of leaves did people pack the pig in when they made a luau? The fire was underground, right? No smoke for anyone to see?

"Maybe I could go up there," Londo gestured at the high ridge to their west, "and try to spot a McDonalds."

"McDonalds again! I wouldn't think you'd go in for that kind of thing."

"Why not?"

"Paraheroes just don't go to McDonalds, right?"

"And how many paraheroes do you know?"

She smiled at him. "Just one now. He definitely goes to McDonalds; I stand corrected." One eyebrow went up and she squinted her eyes, looking far away. "You want fries with that?"

"What? What are you up to?" He flashed her a devilishly conspiratorial grin as he sidled close.

"I'm going to try something. I feel a little guilty because I'm not paying for this– all my cash got blown up in this terrible hotel fire, you know..."

"*Mais oui*, I'd heard."

"So, where is there a Micky D's that has a lot of Big Macs made up, some that they won't ever miss?"

Lon watched those dark-fringed eyes go out of focus. She slowly rubbed his stomach as she concentrated.

"Hm. Not there. It's the middle of the night back home... But all McDonalds are basically the same, right? Search for the *feel* and– There's one. Now let's see..."

A wrapped Big Mac appeared in the air next to Lon. It arrived on its side and dropped to the sand, but it seemed intact. Another one plopped down on top of the first.

Lina's mouth drew up in distaste as she drew away from Londo. "Oh bother!" she exclaimed.

"*C'est quoi, le problème?*"

"I think on top of everything else I just became a vegetarian. Dead cow vibes, ick."

"I hope you don't mind if I eat them."

She waved him ahead, and then a large carton of fries settled unsteadily next to the hamburgers. A stack of ketchup packs arrived one by one like a swarm of red fireflies suddenly come to light. Garden salad was next for her, with a fork; napkins emblazoned with the McDonalds logo.

"Coke? Sprite? What? There are some sitting ready to go."

"Coke, if I get a choice," Londo said. Her new power amused and delighted him. It was so very handy, even in this uncertain stage. The cup sat steadily next to him when it arrived, no lid but a paper-covered straw next to it. He took a sip. "It's flat," he said automatically, then realized she'd take it as a complaint.

She frowned at the drink. "Well, I definitely won't be porting people around anytime soon if I mess up a simple Coke. Lord only knows how I got the two of us here."

"Maybe it's been sitting out for a while. Don't worry about it, kitten," he said as he took a big bite. "The ol' powers will be back soon enough. I'll get us out of here on my own."

"Did I mention my fear of flying?" Lina asked, and he snorted through the hamburger. "Let's try it again."

Her eyebrows knit in concentration and a second drink appeared after a moment. He took a sip. "It's good."

She looked relieved and popped in a second drink, artificial lemonade for her. "Coke's not good for psychic work. The caffeine can knock you off-kilter."

Londo nodded as if he understood. Strange girl. Strange, wonderful girl. "How do you–?" He made a circling motion with his finger next to his forehead. Lina shrugged.

"I just see whatever it is and picture it here– and apparently now it comes in, poof."

"Poof." He considered as he munched on his burger. "Just see it?"

"Well... I have to have some idea of what it is I'm looking for. I need a picture, a memory, to start me out. I build up a mental image from that."

"Ah." He considered that. "Have you always been able to *see* things?"

She peeled the lid off her salad. "You mean, have I always been clairvoyant?" A small bag of croutons appeared in her hand and she ripped it open to sprinkle on her salad. "Let's just say it's a skill I learned out of boredom."

Lon maneuvered an errant pickle back onto his bun. "Boredom, eh? I remember being bored to tears in the back of my class at university."

"So what'd you do?"

He sucked sandwich sauce from the tip of his thumb and resumed eating between words. "Usually I'd pretend that some world-shaking emergency had come up and duck out, until the professors started to complain and Papa Mike heard about it."

"Papa Mike?"

"My grandfather. Mike Rand. You may have heard of him?"

"Oh. Of course I've heard of the Rands."

"Papa Mike called up the ParaNet and within twenty-four hours each of my classes was equipped with a special PA system that only went off when they needed me."

"Poor thing!" She chuckled.

He rolled his eyes. "Yeah. I had to buckle down and study then. So that's what happened to you? Bored, so you let your mind wander? You can really become clairvoyant that way?"

"I did. I have friends who've really improved by practicing, too."

"You know other psychics?"

She made an affirmative sound.

"Are they as good as you?"

"Oh, you should meet Sue, Sue Taylor. She can talk to disincarnates like they were regular people. She's amazing. Not too great in precognition though she says she is, and she's getting too preoccupied with other things these days to pay the kind of attention she should to her healing, but she's real good. And Dave and Dinah..." Lina sorted through her acquaintances. "And Rendi and Clarise and Tom. They're all very good, and they all live in my area."

"What, you have Psychic Bowling Tuesdays and get together?"

"We all went to Sue's psychic healing school. She started out with three different classes, jam-packed with people standing so close in her basement that you couldn't breathe– and each and every one of them were huggers! I thought I was going to die."

Londo chuckled around his second sandwich.

"By the end of two years she combined us all because there were just ten of us left. Sue teaches solid stuff. You just have to wait for her to finish her tangents, but eventually she says what she needs to say."

"And she taught you how to be a clairvoyant?"

Lina squirted out some more dressing for the dry salad. "No; I was already one. She had me teach the others how to really focus and get it down. They didn't have to– How're your Macs?"

There was a flash of something in Lon's mind then, a feeling more than an image: darkness and cold and an endless, mind-numbing emptiness in a night that went on forever. He knew that feeling, almost, but his emptiness had been filled with a light that was never extinguished except behind his closed eyes. He'd told stories to himself to fight the boredom, but she'd sent her mind out searching for the real-life stories...

"Best Big Macs I ever had. You're an excellent cook. Tell me, when were you locked up?" he asked her nonchalantly.

She froze. Interesting; he'd expected her to drop the fork or send some of the salad flying by reflex action. This was a frightened rabbit reaction, subtly done.

"What makes you think I was locked up?"

"I saw you somewhere dark. You were imprisoned."

"I was arrested once when I was in college..."

"C'mon. You can't lie to me."

She picked at her salad, moving it around but not eating it.

Lon kept his tone light. "Why is it that I get the distinct impression that your father had something to do with it?"

"Can we change subjects?"

"You were locked up for some reason and it was dark," Londo began to put it together, "and your father was the one with the key. This wasn't just the one time with the bully and the stitches. It was– How often did this happen, Lie?"

She kept poking at her salad until the silence demanded that she say something. "Often enough for me to become quite good at clairvoyance, okay? Is that enough information for you?"

"Why didn't you ever bring him up on charges?"

"Charges? He's my father. You don't have your father arrested. It would embarrass everyone."

"People's fathers are arrested every day."

"I'm sure it doesn't shock you. You're used to arrests and police and publicity. Next to Montreal or New York, the city Mom and Dad live in is small. Very... unsophisticated."

"You were going to say 'redneck.'" Lon smiled at his growing ability to read her, and she made a face at him.

"Okay, redneck, although they aren't, so you stop thinking of my family that way. My sister's family– they're redneck through and through. She's converted to redneckism, a born-again redneck."

"Oh, is that where you get it." He brushed his fingertips across her shoulders, flagging the shirt open so she could look down and see the patches of red, too. "Any sunscreen in that magic head of yours?" he asked. "I'd be happy to rub it on."

Lina adjusted the shirt back. "I see you don't have that problem." He was a bronze tan all over and had gotten a little darker as the day was progressing. "Is all that natural, or do you augment it at the ParaNet tanning emporium?"

A small bottle of tanning lotion with a deteriorated drug store price tag appeared on the sand, half-used. It had dust on it as if it had been stored over the winter. It was probably from her home, Lon thought. A new tube of Chapstik appeared, too, and Londo laughed outright as he saw it even though he thought it was a good idea. Now he knew what chapped lips felt like.

He crumpled his Mac wrappers. "It's all natural. Like it?"

"It fits you very well. It makes you look mysterious. Exotic." She gave a little laugh. "And yet it's ambiguous enough that certain people– if you know who I mean– don't know exactly what they can insult you for."

He rolled his eyes at that. "Oh I've heard more than a few comments along those lines. I've been called everything from a wetback to a nigger to dago to raghead to... well, no one's ever called me 'that damned mick.' I believe Senator Stern made a cloaked remark about my ancestry just last week."

"Senator Stern!" Lina sniffed.

"He's from your state, isn't he?"

She waved her fork for emphasis. "I have always gone out of my way to vote against him and anyone he's sided with," she declared hotly. "This world has no room in it for bigots, especially bigots with as much influence as Senator Mush-mouth Stern has. Why is it that so many politicians are in it for power and not to help people? How does Stern get away with what he does?"

"You don't like him, huh?"

"How observant you are."

He grinned sideways at her as he swigged his Coke, satisfied that he'd pegged her correctly. She really lit up when she got angry. The redhead in her came out. "Another, please?"

"Another?"

"The polite hostess doesn't count. I'm a growing boy." A new pack of fries appeared in the sand... alongside a salad.

"Euh…"

"Norms need roughage," Lina told him.

Making a play of pouting, Londo started on his fries first. He sucked in a breath. The heat was a nasty surprise. Did norms really eat their food this hot? Once he got used to it, it was an interesting effect if a little painful. Pain was thrilling, as long as it came in short bursts and then went away.

"And then this other guy discovers that someone's sent the papers false documents..." Lina was griping at length about election abnormalities centered around Stern.

Londo tried to comment around the thirteen fries he'd stuffed in his mouth. "Hm?"

"I said, struck a real chord, eh?"

She set her jaw. "I don't like that people look at North Carolina and say, 'Oh that's the place Senator Stern's from. It must be real Dark Ages down there.' Stern's a blot on the entire state. A blot on American democracy. A blot on racial equal–"

"Save it for your election speeches." Londo smiled. "So when you run against Senator Stern–"

She wrinkled her nose at him. "Oh yeah, like anyone would ever vote for Muttbutt."

"Who calls you that? Your father."

She shrugged. "It's all these weird genes I have. My ancestors were from all over. And despite it all I can't even get a good tan." Lina frowned at her skin. "Total whitebread; I was hoping for more whole wheat."

"Toasted whitebread today," Londo told her. "What kind of ancestors?"

He did seem interested, so she told him of the family's genetic brew, which seemed to come from every inhabited continent. "Dad calls Mom the Original Muttbutt. I'm just Phase II," Lina finished.

She was still famished. Fast food places didn't really cater well to vegetarians. Instead she stole a fruit salad and bagel from her favorite grocery store and crossed herself for her sins even though she wasn't Catholic.

"So what do you consider yourself?" Lina asked him. "Are you drawn to one culture or another?"

He shook his head noncommittally. "I was raised by Hal, and he was raised by Papa Mike and Mama Ruth."

Hal– Lina realized again that he was talking so casually about people she'd heard about for years only on the news, and then only in reverent tones. Hal Rand, Londo's adoptive father, was Maximus, the biggest megapara there ever was– next to Lon. And the Rands were the people who had raised Maximus from infancy. Of course they'd be Lon's adoptive grandparents– but she knew of them as "the Rands," not "Papa Mike" and "Mama Ruth." These were real people of whom Londo spoke, not just pictures on the news.

Londo continued, "They're from a middle-class black or African-American background– Mama Ruth says she wishes people would forget the 'n' word so everyone could go back to being 'negroes.' She thinks that that word is more romantic than all the other terms, that is, if you have to group every person of a certain color together for some reason. Of course Papa Mike started his stores–" Mike Rand had been CEO of the now-international Rand Drugs chain before he retired– "but they still have those middle-class roots that they're never going to give up."

Pictures of the Rands showed kind-looking people who avoided the spotlight.

Londo upended the fry carton to get the salty crumbs. "Hal– he's a product of his parents and his legend. He's always surprised when people call him the spearheading influence of racial equality these days, just because of his skin color. People think he's part or pure African, but he's not Terran at all. Well, maybe a few genes in the mix that made him, who knows? He does what he can for the Cause, but I think he feels a little guilty about it, as if he's doing it under false pretenses. Lord knows what he'd do if he ever got over that."

"Probably change the world more than he has," Lina said.

Londo shrugged. "Eh. Probably."

"What about you?" she asked him. "If Maximus raised you, but he didn't have a strong cultural background, what do you consider yourself?"

"I put down 'other' on forms when they ask for race," Londo told her. "Most of the media call me a 'man of color.' I've considered having a DNA check to see what ancestors I might have, but I've never gotten around to it. It's not that big a deal to me. I'm a citizen of Earzh."

"That's a nice phrase."

"That's why I use it." He waved at the sky. "Out There, that's the only way they think of me. They don't know from countries. I do a lot of work off-planet, so I just tell people that I'm Terran, not half-African, half-Canadian, half-god-knows-what."

"Certainly not half-mathematician."

He gave a little snort and then told her of the more interesting cultures of Earth that he'd wondered if he'd come from. "You're a psychic," he said. "You tell me where my people came from, eh?"

"Hm. Well." Lina tried to get the vibe. She'd always pegged Valiant as Caribbean or Mediterranean, but thought that someone had told her that when she was a child. It was difficult to figure out things psychically when you had a preconceived notion. "Let me think about it. You really want to know, don't you?"

"Eh, who cares about all that? When it all boils down, what good is any of it?" He threw his empty carton hard on the ground, but it merely bounced an inch and came to a rest. "I don't have anyone of my own," he muttered.

"It's a part of your background," Lina insisted. "You don't feel anchored in the world without knowing. It's living without roots, Malcolm X and all that."

He fooled with the straw in his drink. "Yeah. I guess."

"So make up your own roots. Go with what you've got and work from there. Don't turn your back on it."

"Easy for you to say. How far back do you know your family tree?" He knew that would hurt before he said it, but still he wished he hadn't. "Sorry."

"My family tree could use a trimming," Lina said. "Maybe a little gasoline and a match on a few limbs would do it good."

"You really hate your father, don't you?"

"Of course I don't," she said so quickly she almost dropped her fork. "I don't know why I said that. I love my father."

"Sure, baby. Well, whatever you are with all that crazy family of yours, I'm glad you got what you got. Toasted whitebread looks good on you, even with those patches of strawberry jam." He pointed to sunburned spots.

She made a face at him. "My fondest wish is to tan evenly, not in splotches. Perhaps it's time to get some real clothes and cover up some more."

Her eyes started to unfocus. They'd put on clothing for some reason, she in his shirt open almost to the waist, allowing him a teasing view; him in those tight faux-leather pants with nothing on underneath. They seemed to keep taking everything off all morning; maybe that's why they kept putting it back on.

"Must you?" Lon asked, almost shyly.

"What?" Her eyes focused again.

He ran his fingers up her leg, under the shirt. "I like what you're wearing now."

She paused and their eyes met. "I guess we're not going anywhere formal for a while," she admitted.

He shook his head. "No. Not for a while." That slow, crooked smile came back. He reached to take a grape from her fruit salad and pop it into his mouth.

Lina slapped him lightly. "Who taught you table manners?"

He stuck his tongue out at her, the grape balanced on its tip, and she returned the salute, sans grape. When she turned her attention to her salad, something flashed on her shirt: the silver holograph medallion.

"I've been meaning to ask wherever you got this," she said as she unpinned it to see it better. "It's a beautiful job. How–" she stopped, staring at it.

"What?" Something in her voice made Londo think something was wrong.

She handed it to him. "It's changed."

He looked at it. Now instead of the 3-D burst with the V in it, there was the burst, but inside it was no V, but rather a transparent sphere with a pyramid in its interior. They were all rotating and fluctuating as if part of one unit. It was perfect and striking.

"I can see my dress reverting in color; I must have missed the dye job," Lina said. "But changing a hologram? Maybe if something were missing from it, but this?"

Londo frowned hard at the symbol. "This is my Mega-Legion ID," he said. "Nothing could have–" Lon shook his head. "Nothing to do about it. You're a designer, right?" She nodded. "Well, this is a nice logo. Maybe your subconscious came up with it."

"And did a snazzy little hologram movie with it. That's one helluva subconscious. Somehow I don't picture myself unconsciously designing this and then arranging to split a beam of light and bend half of it around and do whatever it is that they do to come up with holograms. Much less a moving one like that." She paused. "Starburst, circle, triangle," she realized.

"That's what you saw when you asked when my powers would return."

"So it means something. Your symbol is a starburst. Somebody's trying to tell us something. But what? Is there someone with an insignia that has a circle or triangle who's supposed to... do something?"

Lon considered. "Forte. Impala. Galactic Guards. All the Dragons. Black Magnum– lots of people with circles in their symbols. Triangles, let's see..."

"But does it mean that they're going to come here before your powers return?" Lina weighed conflicting mountains of happenstance. "Lon, I'm beginning to think that we really are in a pocket of the Timeless Realms– gods and faeries manipulating mortals, that kind of thing."

Lon took her theory seriously. "There's weird and there's weird. I don't think any of the people or creatures there would dabble in pseudo-techno-magick like holograms. But don't quote me on that." He looked again at the medallion pin, wondering. "The Timeless Realms..."

He sighed. "Well, we'll just put this in the same column with all the other little things that we can't figure out," Lon picked up his vest from the sand and tucked the medallion inside. He took his time sealing it inside a pocket, and then gestured at her. "Let me see your head."

"Two fingers," Lina said before he could even put up any to test her. He harumphed as he parted her hair.

"It looks better today," Londo pronounced. There was just a little bump now, pinker than the surrounding area. But Lina had been healing herself all day; had it been that bad to take so long to heal? "What do you think the possibilities are of a brain injury giving a temporary para-power?"

"Brain injury?" Lina asked and then, "Temporary?"

"You think it's permanent?"

"I'd hate to lose it." All around them were items that had been ported into the clearing, making the place almost home away from home: blankets, pillows, toilet paper... "I don't think it's temporary. Porting's like– Well it's like something so obvious I wonder why I hadn't done it before. It's easy."

Londo chewed lightly on his thumb. "So," he said, "it's a knowledge and not a power? Anyone could do it?"

Lina blinked. "I don't know. They'd have to be clairvoyant."

"Call it a skill, then. Is it getting weaker? Do you find it's harder to remember how to do it?"

"As my head heals? Do you mean that maybe if the bump goes away, I'll lose it?" Intense disappointment gripped Lina. It was her power! It was her mind! She didn't want to go backward, not now, not when it was somehow connected to all this and to Londo!

"I'm just asking," Lon replied. "It's just some possibilities. Personally, I hope it stays around; it's so useful." He stared to the south. "And it's brought us so far away from Terry's goons that they'll never dream of looking for us here. Look at that– they're still wandering through the south island. Next thing you know, they'll be looking under rocks." He let out a low, evil chuckle. "Fooled ya, Terry!"

When he turned back to her the furrow in his forehead evened out. The slight snarl turned into a gentle smile. "I'll have to thank her someday for allowing me to meet you."

Lina didn't know what to say.

"You know," he said softly, "that self-esteem problem rears its head too much with you. You can't take compliments."

"No," she agreed. "I don't believe them."

Lon lay on his stomach in the clean white sand, propping his head up on his fist. "So you get to decide. Is the person giving you the compliments lying, or are you just lying to yourself?"

"Or is that person just desperate enough that he actually believes them for a little while?"

He nodded as he considered. "I can see where that might be an option, but it's not now. Believe me. I'm glad you were the one. I'm very glad you're here. You're like everything I ever hoped for."

Lina gave him a tolerant smile and shook her head.

Londo sat up and took her right hand between his. "Listen to me. I think you are one of the most beautiful women I've ever seen. Clothes or no clothes." He gave a sly smile that wrinkled his nose. "Especially no clothes. I love your body. It feels so good and it tastes so good. I love being able to feel what you feel; it's absolutely amazing. Just like you, like all that magical stuff you do, the porting, the healing, talking to your guides. Meeting a storm deva." He shook his head at her. "You're amazing. I'm so glad it's been you."

He gave her the courage to speak, but it came out in a whisper. "If it was anyone, I'm glad it was you, Londo."

He grasped her one hand and then took the other and swung her around so she straddled him, sitting on his thighs.

Lina said, "You're so confident, so unafraid. That's magic to me. And..." she touched his shoulders, his chest, "you're so strong; you exude an incredible feeling of masculinity. Mystery and power rolled into one."

Their eyes met in a riveting gaze. "You are a magnet, Londo Rand," she declared softly. "I can't seem to pull myself away from you."

He knew there was more. "And?"

She slid her arms around his neck and leaned in to whisper in his ear. "And I love the way you touch me. I love the way you feel." She kissed his neck under his ear, and he turned so their next kiss was mouth-to-mouth. They held on to it as they finished, quiet for a few moments.

Somewhere in the back of Londo's mind, a list ticked off. *She didn't say she loved me, but she came close.* He pushed the thought away before she could sense it.

Lina opened her eyes and leaned back to get a better view. "I said it before; you're the handsomest man on the planet."

He gave her a cocky grin, holding her hips against him. "I am? Still?"

"Um hum. Clothed or unclothed." Now she gave him a wily smile. "But if you have to be clothed, keep the black outfit."

"Hm?"

"I've always loved men in black. It reeks of romance. Of sex," she said. "The great mystery of manhood."

"You mean the great mystery of womanhood."

"No mystery to that. Men: that's life's big mystery." Her eyes moved distantly as she came up with a list. "Sexy men in black. Will Smith and those shades. Buffy's Angel in that big ol' black trench coat. James Bond in his tux. Luke Skywalker in *Star Wars* 5 and 6. I must have seen those movies forty times apiece, just to watch him. Mmm."

"Dragonlord?" Lon asked curiously.

"Too scary. Besides... those little antennas?"

Lon laughed at that. "Who else?"

"Valiant," Lina said. "Always Valiant."

He hugged her to him to kiss her, then kiss her again with all the passion he could muster. She sank against him and her soft lips pressed so tightly against his. Suddenly he pushed her away.

"Wait. Listen," he said tersely.

Lina strained her ears. Ocean surf. Birds. Wind.

Helicopter.

He gathered her up as he scrambled up himself, then pulled her into the cover of the forest. As he went he collected what he could of what they'd accumulated. Lina surveyed the clearing and teleported the leftovers into the forest with them, out of sight. They crept to the ocean edge of the woods, crawling under ferns and spider webs.

Three helicopters in formation swept up the beach toward them in quick but careful order. They were spaced so that they covered a large swath of forest as well.

"We're hidden enough," Londo assured her. She nodded, then spotted the frisbee on the beach, black against the sand. With a few seconds' concentration it disappeared, back to wherever that picture in Lon's mind had been.

Lon saw it just as it vanished. "Good," he said, trying to ignore the perfect little circle imprint left there in the sand or the tracks of bare feet running. If he had his powers, he could use his breath to blow it all askew. If he had his powers, he could do a lot of things. Maybe the brisk breeze today had blown the evidence enough. Maybe they'd think that this was left over from whoever had lived here yesterday or the day before. Maybe.

Within three minutes the helicopters were upon them. One came so close that they could see the people inside well enough to give an exact description.

We're hidden, Londo repeated.

They shouldn't notice us, Lina told him. She'd gathered the lines of force around them like a blanket. The soldiers in the helicopter were diligent, but not so much that she couldn't create an area where they wouldn't think of looking.

Neat trick, Lon said. **Teach me.**

She tried to show him what she'd done. It was an old childhood technique, one she'd used when she'd wanted to hide. She thought that maybe it had been what had shielded them yesterday.

Londo nodded. He thought he'd be able to do it, too, if he ever needed to. "Does it work on film? If they're filming as they search and then they look at the video later, will we show up?"

"I don't know. People don't usually shoot your picture when you do this. They have to be specifically looking for you and knowing where you are, I think, in order to see you."

The helicopters kept to their search pattern up the beach away from them. Again it occurred to Lina and she could feel it occurring to Londo, too, that he was not the only target of the search. What could anyone want with her?

"Let's put it this way, *cherie*," he whispered to her as if someone from the copters might hear. "When we get out of here, the first place I'm taking you is to ParaNet headquarters. You're going to put on some demonstrations."

She looked doubtfully at him and he gave her a no-nonsense stare. She sighed. "Yes, Londo," she said.

They watched the copters disappear over the horizon. Finally Londo rolled over to sit up.

"Urk," he said and stopped, a strange look on his face. He clutched his stomach and caught his breath.

"Bad food?" Lina asked.

He shook his head with a brusque intensity that frightened her.

Immediately Lina sent her mind into his body. "Time's running out," she said tightly. Something was leveling out in his cells, as if they were preparing to stabilize.

Through their loop, he could sense them, too. "We still have time. Maybe a few times more, if you're game. I can't believe I'm doing this at all. I'll take whatever you want to give me, *cherie*."

In a little while it would all be gone. Lina reached for Lon's hand.

14

The copters had been gone almost an hour. Lon couldn't detect any sign of increased activity on the south side of the island.

"Ah god, Lina, do that again," Londo moaned as he arched his back. "Oh. Just like that. Ah."

Lina rubbed the ball of his left foot hard, dragging her thumb down the center of his sole, then going back up to dig in.

"*Skurny marde*, not that hard!"

"Oh, be quiet. You have some stuck energy here. This is the way to release it. Might as well get it now while I can."

"I walked ten million miles yesterday; give me a break. Ah *oui*." He leaned back again on the fallen tree and pillows as Lina softened her touch. Suddenly he pointed up into the sky. "Look at that!"

With a gasp of apprehension, Lina dropped his foot, following his finger's direction– No helicopter, just sky and clouds.

"Richard Nixon!" Londo declared, shaking imaginary jowls. "'I am not a crook!'" The imitation was scathingly accurate.

"What?!" Darn him anyway. He was looking at the clouds, not mercenaries. "Lonnn!"

He grinned at her exasperation. "Look, you see him too."

"You're crazy. Crazy! Oh, I don't see Nixon."

"Then who?"

She studied the cloud formation, which might have two appendages giving a peace sign, but only if you had a very good imagination. "Rudolph," she finally decided. They could be antlers.

He made a face at the sky and shook his head. "No visits from Santa for you this year," he told her, "insulting his reindeer like that. What's that cloud over there?"

They compared pictures with Londo always coming up with the more fantastical story and a matching mimicked line from this famous person or that. Lina began to wonder if he were really seeing these people in the clouds or just inventing excuses to do impressions. He did them very well, usually with a pun or two to set off a famous line.

"George Washington as a vampire," he finally decided for one cloud. "I really hate vampires. D'you think one could do anything with wooden teeth?"

"Paul Revere could make him silver fangs," Lina theorized, "but would that kill him, like a silver bullet?"

"Could be, especially if he bit himself in the lip." Londo stretched lazily, wiggling his toes. "No wonder Gary married Gina," he said. "He says she gives great foot."

Lina laughed and moved up to settle next to him. "Who's Gary?"

He took her hand in his to explore its firm softness. "You know– the Bolt. Gina's his third wife. You should see the two of them. Sometimes I wonder they didn't get divorced the first month after they got married, arguing all the time. Guess they like to fight."

"The Bolt." The famous parahero. How strange to just drop his name like that, as if he were part of the normal world. "He's from Chicago," Lina said. Lon made an affirming noise as he moved along to her forearm.

They talked of other heroes and how the ParaNet had divided the world into territories convenient to his members. Londo got eastern North America, the Bolt got the central portion, and Maximus patrolled the western.

Lon continued, "I kid Hal about that, I mean he's living in the middle of mudslides and forest fires, earthquakes and volcanoes, and he says it's all a lot better than blizzards and split-pea soup in Quebec."

Then he told her trivia about the major players in the organization: Bolt, the legendary Olympia, Impala, Forte, Sovereign, and the Dragons, especially their leader, Dragonlord. Lon's face soured when he came to the Galactic Guardian.

"Paul Granger. What a loser."

"A Galactic Guard?" The respected ranks of the Galactic Brigade were handpicked by the mysterious Galactic Sentinels. They chose only the best of the best to award conduits that funneled unlimited energy from the black hole in the center of the galaxy. Theirs was the mission to uphold basic justice and control chaos on planetary levels.

Londo looked as if he'd sucked on a lemon. "Let's just say– and this is absolutely off the record– that Granger's probably home right now lying around in his underwear drinking a beer and watching a basketball game on the tube– while logging in that he's stopping a riot somewhere." He glanced at her face. "Good," he said. "I was shocked, too. If it makes it any better, he's the only one I've ever met who was like that. It's too damn bad that Rico Carapella retired. Now, *he* was a Galactic Guard."

They covered a few more members before Lina asked, "Why isn't it '*Vaill...*'?"

"'*Vaillant,*'" Londo supplied the French version of his name. "I started out in the States, in English. That's what stuck, though some of the smart-ass newspapers in Quebec use the French every once in a while.

"Look at Forte," he continued. "She had a time when she first started out. Russian, but her first big public appearance was in France, so one of the brilliant reporters there named her 'Strong,' Fort, with the final 'e' because she's a girl. Then some music major who was reporting the news on CNNi that night pronounced it as if it were Italian music, so it's *for-tay*. That's what stuck.

"She actually likes how it turned out better than the Strong version. Says it gives her more subtlety or finesse or something. She likes to think that she's subtle. Don't get me wrong; she's very nice. You'd like her. But subtle she's not.

"So who else do you want to know about? I've got all the dirt. Ask me about the Dragons, go on..."

"You don't have any dirt on Maximus. There can't be any."

Lon gave an evil laugh. "The upstanding Boy Scout of all the paraheroes, of the galactic megaparaheroes. When the final biography's written about him, there'll be a few real surprises there. But for the most part, he's exactly what he portrays himself to be. There's no pretense. Just a few little hiccups in unlikely places."

"I'm afraid to ask." This was the world Lon would return to tonight or tomorrow when he left Lina behind.

"C'mon, more questions or else I'll ask for another Big Mac. Is it time for supper yet?"

"It hasn't been that long since lunch. Do you want one, seriously?"

"I've worked off a few million calories today." He theatrically drew the back of his hand across his forehead. "If ah don't eat ah shall faint dead away."

Then he belched.

It didn't shake the foundations of the earth, but it was loud enough. It left Londo speechless, sitting there wide-eyed and slack-jawed at himself. Then he rolled onto his back, dissolving into gales of laughter.

Tears streamed down his face and Lina couldn't help but laugh with him. "So that's how it works," he gasped, holding his belly. "I mean, *je m'excuse*." Then he lay back down and laughed some more. "It came out of nowhere," he claimed. "I didn't swallow any air and I still did it."

After a few left-over chuckles he sat up. "Jae will be so proud of me," he said. "And you know, Papa Mike was right. It does make more room. Think you could rustle up a shake, *chérie*? It must be tea time at least. Chocolate? If you can afford it."

Lina looked sideways at him. "Are you sure?" she asked. "Do you really know what feeling full is?"

He patted his stomach. "Much more room now." His face took on a crafty look. "I could make some more room, maybe. I think I can outdo that one." And he started to gulp air.

"Wait, wait!" Lina cried, holding up her hands in surrender. "No need to wake up the volcano. Ah, shakes. They don't make those up in advance, do they? It's not like I can operate the machinery from here..."

"That's okay." Still, he gave a start when a small, round carton of chocolate ice cream and a plastic spoon appeared on the blanket next to him. "Good enough," he said, and dug in. "Things taste so different," he declared.

"Okay. A question. If Maximus is on the West Coast, how'd you get to Montreal?"

"I'm allowed to travel. I'm not attached to his spleen or anything."

"Sorry. Didn't know it was a sore point."

Londo frowned to himself. "It shouldn't be, but it is. Everyone always brings up Hal whenever there's an interview. 'What does Maximus think of you doing...' well, whatever. Over and over again. Every now and then– not very often– I wish I could get out of his shadow. The man casts one hell of a shadow."

"Montreal..."

"It was the nicest city with any size to it I could find on the opposite coast from Hal. It was a definite plus that they speak French there."

As he continued to chat about his life, it gave Lina inexpressible satisfaction just to listen to him. Not only was he warm in body, he was the same in spirit.

And he was safe. This day had been a rare haven. Instead of jumping at every surprise, she knew she'd be safe so long as she was near him. Was it because he was a man? Yang energy was high in protective impulses. Maybe it was because he was Valiant. It was his job to keep people safe. Maybe it was because he was just Lon. Wonderful Londo. She snuggled closer. How lucky she was to know him for this day!

As she listened and fiddled with a sliver of driftwood, she happened to mention the watercolors she had brought with her on vacation.

"You paint?"

"No," she said, "that's the problem. No time for it, no time to get good at it so I can go pro, as if anyone actually buys original art any more. I thought this trip would inspire me to get up off my ass."

"So why is it you've never done anything with your other talent?" Lon asked gently. "Why haven't I heard before about Lina O'Kelly, the Healing Wonder?"

The sliver she'd been trying to bend finally turned upon itself into a small ring and Lina flipped it into the woods. "Anyone can do the healing work."

"Bullshit. No one can do it at this level or everyone would have heard of them."

"I've just been on an adrenaline high. You've seen my technique much more impressive than it usually is. But really, Lon. I could teach you if you wanted. It takes a little discipline, but not that much. It's basically focused good intentions. All it takes is a good heart– and that you have."

He touched her cheek. "And you."

His eyes could glow so warmly. Lina wanted to drown in them.

"Let's share minds again," he whispered in her ear.

Yes, yes, yes. "No," Lina said. Goal A was to protect her heart during all this.

No, that was wrong. Goal A was to protect *his* heart.

"I think we've shared minds enough, Lon. We can't do it any more," she said. "It's going to make it that much harder when we have to stop."

"*Pantoute,*" Lon said. "I'm fine and I'm going to be fine. I know your body so well now."

His breath was hot behind her ear. Lina closed her eyes as her body woke again to that sensation. It wasn't just his breath; it was his low, compelling voice. Music. Magic.

"I want to know it better." His music thrummed through her. She wanted so badly to listen, but she couldn't. Did he have any idea of what he did to her?

"I want to see *you,* to see your mind naked and open to my touch so I can know you like no one else has ever known you before. I want to feel the real you. I want to make love to you in your mind. I want to have you, body and soul."

"It would be different if we had more than today. No." She wanted to push away, but she loved being in his arms.

"Just today– a day to do everything we've ever imagined– and more. This is the more. Let's take it so we'll always have it to look back on." He kissed her forehead. "Let's jump again and see where we land."

"Tomorrow we'll hate ourselves for doing it. Three months from now we'll hate ourselves for doing it."

"But today, love, *today*..." His mind reached out to hers.

Only one day. How could she survive when he was gone? This was all she'd have to last her until eternity passed away. This would be the memory she could live on. "Has anyone ever said no to you?" she whispered.

"Come in my mind and see," he told her. "Oh, Lina, come in my mind and see!"

So deep now, his mind drowned in aching loneliness. **Touch me, touch me,** it called to Lina. **Talk to me, read to me, sing to me, let me know someone is there.**

I'm here, Lina replied.

But after a day you'll be gone.

There was no answer to that. **If you ever want to talk, I can be there.** She spread her essence through his mind, trying to reassure his entire being by her presence. **I'm here. I won't go unless you want me to.**

A little dark-haired boy stood lost and crying in front of her. He was all alone in the universe. She knelt to put her arms around him, and he hugged her fiercely around the neck.

Don't leave me, don't leave me! he snuffled and then raised his head. Someone was hugging him from the other side and he turned to her. "Maman!" he cried, but the shadowy woman let him go. She walked away and never looked back. "Don't leave me!" he screamed at her.

In a voice that echoed here in the dark, the woman said, "I don't love you any more." Then she was gone. Without her the universe stretched empty, devoid of life and feeling.

The child dissolved into a wild whirlpool of pain and rejection. If only he'd been better, she would have loved him enough to stay. If only he'd eaten his vegetables, or played nicer, or been quiet when she told him to... He didn't know what exactly it was, but if only he knew, then she wouldn't have left. It was all his fault that she was gone.

That's not true, Lina said. The boy turned to her and grew into the man. **Lon, you're a good person. A hero, renowned for your integrity. I don't know what happened here, but it couldn't have been because of you yourself. Whatever it was, you were a child, and children so often misread a world they don't understand.**

Don't leave me, Lina. He grabbed her shoulders and hugged her fiercely. **Don't ever leave me!**

This is just for a day. We can be friends for as long as you want. I'm not re-jecting you.

You are.

I'm not. It's a physical thing. The universe–

I hate the universe. I hate God. He did this to me!

And you helped plan it. On this plane she could feel the emotions that battered his features. Fear, helplessness, hatred, confusion.

Before you were born, Lon, you helped plan your life. Think about what being Valiant has given you that you couldn't have gotten any other way. There's at least one very important thing that you've gotten that you couldn't have otherwise. There are all the things that you've seen that I could never hope to imagine. Think about what you can do that no one else can.

The storm around him began to calm. Colors evened out from raging firebursts to short, choppy waves of cool greens and blues. **I like flying. I like leading people. I like knowing Hal, and all my other friends. There were some kids in an African refugee camp last year; I stopped a mob of assassins there. You should have seen their faces. They'd be dead if I hadn't been there to help.**

Lina could sense some of the images coming to him, more experiences that he was thankful for. She edged away to let him re-experience them as much as he had to.

But he looked around for her. **I'd never have met you if I were normal,** he said, and he drew her into an embrace. On this level the hug merged them and ran their essences together.

His innate confidence plowed through the heart of her. He fulfilled the world's faith in himself, while Lina– she knew exactly how much she was worth. She squirmed to get out of Lon's arms and away from him. Mustn't soil him with her presence!

"Who do you think you are, anyway? He's a famous hero. You're just a dirty little girl," Dad told her.

"Go wash up," Mom whispered.

"Always thinking you're better than other people," her father jeered. "Spoiled, ugly brat, putting on airs. Think you're so smart. Why can't you be like your sister?"

Mom nodded. "Barb's so pretty. She's just smart enough, so the boys will like her."

"Be quiet down there! We're trying to watch TV! I said, be quiet! I'll give you something to cry about, you stupid, ugly mutt-faced Muttbutt!" Dad drew his belt out of his pants and snapped it against the palm of his hand.

"Don't upset him," her mother told her. "You have to love him; he's your father."

"I love you, Dad," Lina said.

"Lina!" her father yelled. "Stop trying to attract attention! Don't lie to me! You go to your room right now, little miss bitch! You go down there and stay there until I tell you you can come out! No food, no drinks, no electricity for you!"

"But I wasn't doing anything," Lina wailed. "I was just talking to the angels, to the earth. They like me."

"You've embarrassed me for the last time. Why weren't you born a boy? You liar. You little whore!"

Lina! Lina! Don't listen to them!

As tears obliterated her sight, she pushed away from Londo even as he tried to take her in his arms. **Don't touch me, Lon! It might be catching. I'm no good!**

Lina chérie, don't listen to them. What do they know? They don't understand. They're coming from their own problems. They inflict their own fears on you. Come here: I'll touch you. I'll hold you.

Just to get some sex! You don't care about me at all. No one cares about me. I'm all alone– and I like it that way. Just me and the angels. The angels say there's no sin, so they don't mind being around me.

Londo crept closer. **So what do your parents know that the angels don't? They're the ones who are telling you how wrong you are. What do the angels say?**

In her misery Lina spiraled down through the darkness. Get away from Londo. Spare him from having to endure her presence.

But he followed her.

Lina tried to think through her confusion and shame. **They always say that everything's right, that the universe is doing what it's supposed to be.**

And does that include you? Are you doing what you're supposed to? Are you doing anything the angels say is wrong?

Her downward movement slowed to a halt and he caught up with her. **I...** She looked up to see him beside her, his presence wrapping her protectively. **I don't know.**

Touch me, Lina. Show me that you're here for me.

Touch me, Londo. Show me that I'm good enough.

They held each other in that timeless place for forever and a moment.

Back on a physical plane, their gazes opened into each other's for that heartbeat of eternity. Yet they were still totally together someplace where there was not-so-distant singing, where a breeze blew away the darkness and starlight fell like laughter upon and through them. A soft, cleansing wave of peace washed over each. It left them able to accept the sunlight, accept the breeze– accept each other.

Londo rolled away from her as she lay dozing beneath the twilight palm trees, her hair splayed around her in a dark halo, thick lashes closed against her cheek, sweet pink nipples on those beautiful white mounds rising and falling to the gentle rhythm of her breath.

Oh god, what had he done? He caught his head in his hands, afraid that he was going to be sick.

He was Valiant, for pity's sake. Honorable Valiant. He'd used this girl terribly, played with her heart as if she were his toy.

All for his own needs, his own raging passions. It was true; he was no better than Pepé le Pew, thinking with his cock. Just after a piece of ass at his first opportunity. His only opportunity– for life.

But what about her? Here at the end of this day, think about her for once! She had been innocent. She still was, except that he'd taken her virginity from her and painfully at that. All she'd wanted was to help him.

He'd constructed the perfect fantasy. Now the real world crouched nearby, ready to rip it to shreds.

Lon clenched his fist around the corner of their blanket in self-disgust. She'd helped him, she'd healed him and he hadn't been able to wait to spread those legs of hers apart. She was so vulnerable to him. But all this was coming too quickly to an end. He'd be damned if he was going to take advantage of her that way, too. Save her something.

But oh god, he wanted more! His gut clenched in longing. He wanted everything she could give. How he wanted her to love him– finish the fantasy, complete the tale. Fill the hole where his heart had once beaten. But she was right. What future was there in that besides misery?

"Second thoughts, Lon?" her soft voice asked from his shoulder.

He didn't turn. "Lina, after this is over..." He didn't know how to phrase it so it wouldn't sound so rough and unfeeling.

"I know that tomorrow you'll be gone," she finished for him. "I don't expect anything more from this."

Jesus. How could she say that? He'd wrecked her life. He pulled his hands over his head. "I'm sorry. My only job was to get you to safety. I should have paid attention to that."

"And ignored your soul," she replied. "You had a duty to yourself, too. Lon, there's no way we coulda or shoulda or woulda. No way to take back the past. Or is that one of your powers now? Can you give me back my virginity? Can you retrieve yours?"

He sat silent, consumed with guilt. The edge of the moon began to peek over the eastern horizon.

Lina rubbed the back of his shoulder. Her hand glided around to the front to stroke his chest. Now it was her warm breath on his neck, her soft cheek against him, her breast pressing against his spine. "Do you really want your virginity back?" she whispered.

"I never wanted to hurt you," he said between clenched teeth. "I don't want to give you any false expectations."

"I don't have any. This is just for now. No more than that."

He could hear her say that, but it seemed that her heart was saying something else. Lon turned his head to look at her. "No more?"

She sighed. "Well," she admitted, "if we should ever see each other again it would be nice if you could stop and say hello, or wave, or something. If you can't do that, a Christmas card would be okay. But if you can't do that..." She paused, and he could actually feel in her mind an image of her closing a door to the world, cutting herself off from it, stepping her two steps back. "I'll understand. It's an awkward situation."

"Awkward." He gave a choked laugh, his back still to her. How did she do it? How could she be here with him and yet be able to keep her emotional distance?

"We aren't kids," Lina told him. "We know how the world goes. Things happen. People sometimes have to handle awkward situations awkwardly. I don't want you twenty years from now to say oh, we still had seven hours left. That's..." she figured it up. "Twenty-eight times we missed because we were feeling sorry for ourselves. Or are you still thinking in fifteen-minute segments? We are sooo behind schedule if you are."

He tried to laugh at that but no sound emerged. "Twenty-eight times." With Lina. With her warm and soft in his arms, her sweaty and moaning under him, hot and wet and tight, her mind gently wrapped within his. He turned to her, his hand resting on her familiar thigh. "So what'll we do?"

"Debauch," she said very clearly, and this time he laughed. She could always make him laugh. "Whatever you want to do, we'll do it."

Lon's mouth opened to say something, and she beat him to it. "Except anal." He gave a snort and rubbed her in acquiescence. "And when your powers return, we'll say adios and keep our fond memories. Anything we say or do during this time will be rendered null and void."

"What about sharing minds?" Lon's eyes burned into hers. **Can we do that and just walk away?**

"We're going to have to, aren't we? We've already jumped," she reminded him. "It's a little late to go back."

Easy for her to say it. She'd have lovers after him. A sudden bitter taste struck Lon as he thought of those others. He hated them already. She'd forget him.

Lina shook her head. "No, I don't see that happening." She touched his cheek. "We've shared minds. I trust you, Lon. I don't trust anyone else. I don't think I can touch anyone else."

"So this is it for you, too." He ran his hands over her shoulders, feeling the human reality of her. "We just walk away and forget it afterward?"

"I'll never forget it," she said so softly he almost didn't hear her. "Never." She tried to summon a smile. "When I tell Katie about this, she'll–"

Lon's grip on her turned tight and sharp.

"Katie's a cat," Lina said quickly. "She doesn't speak English. She won't repeat anything."

"Lina." Lon took her firmly by the shoulders and stared at her with focused intensity as if he could hypnotize her to his will.

"I won't tell. No one. Ever." She opened up her mind to him so he could see the truth of it. "I will never betray you. Never embarrass you."

He cradled her face in his hands, feeling the sincerity, amazed at himself for being able to do so.

We'll need to talk– afterward, Lina's mind whispered to him. **To give things closure. Tie up loose ends.**

I don't want this to end! His lips came down on her mouth roughly. Then he pressed her onto the sand. He crouched over her like a cage, possessing her. She was his forever, no matter what the universe had to say about it!

Mine, mine, mine! "Tell me you love me," he ordered.

He needed this final step; he couldn't deny it any more. Instead she took hold of his head and raised up to meet his lips. He pushed her back.

"Tell me," he insisted. "Tell me." Gently he shook her. "Say it just once. It won't kill you. Just say, 'I love you, Londo.'"

"It wouldn't be right," she insisted. "This is just for a day."

"I want more."

"You always want more. Love is forever. Please don't make me."

He shook her again, this time a little rougher. "Tell me. Lie if you have to. Please!"

"Stop it, Lon! We agreed–"

"You agreed. Not me. Tell me now! They're just words!"

Her face hardened as she pushed him away. "You don't want just the words. Look, we're taking time away from your precious schedule. How much more do you have, anyway? An hour? Less?"

"Damn you anyway!" He jumped up and ran into the forest.

It was too dark to follow him, so Lina huddled in the moonlight shadows, starting at every strange noise. Terrorists or Londo?

God, Londo! He was going through hell, and she'd yelled at him! Of course he'd be having mood swings. Of course she shouldn't expect him to be reasonable. How stupid could she be? How insensitive? And how much time did he have? She'd promised: do it as long as he was still a norm. She always kept her promises.

It was probably not as long as it seemed before he trudged back into the clearing. "I'm sorry," he mumbled. "I was wrong." He came over to her to sink in the sand, his mind a jumble of dejection and misery as he collapsed upon himself. "You hate me."

"And here I thought you were trying an excuse to get out of proving your boast," Lina said as lightly as she could. She knelt next to him. "Whazza matter, can't get it up?" she whispered into his ear.

He blinked blankly at her.

"Finally ran out of steam, didn't you? I guess some guys have it and some guys just don't."

After the moment of astonishment, his eyes crinkled. "I was giving you a rest," he claimed.

"Like hell," she said. "You were flakking off. Lying down on the job. We aren't even going to come close to 100– I am *so* disappointed! What kind of parahero are you, Mr. Londo Rand? Can't keep to your own schedule. You should be disciplined." Lina slapped an imaginary whip against the palm of her hand.

"The kind who doesn't know who his partner is any more. So you've decided to go again?" He sat up but she pushed him back down and held him there.

"You're just not as tough as they say you are," she taunted him.

"So give me some of that special touch you have, baby."

"What you don't need right now is healing." Any more revitalizing energy would send his cells back to normalcy. They were only minimally still in shock right now. He was so close... "You don't have that strong finish you promised me. You're just a big... a big... honeybear." She had to grin at him. She couldn't think of anything nasty. Not for Londo.

Lon decided he'd liked how the situation had been going. "That's the last straw," he told her. "Nobody calls Valiant a honeybear."

"Poohbear then."

"Worse!"

"Sweedy teddy bear. With a little pink bow around his neck."

"Wrong answer!" He wrestled her so she was the one on the ground now, pinned by his hands on her arms. "Take it back. Say uncle."

"James Bond," Lina sighed with a faraway smile. "Now there was a strong finisher. James always comes through." She gave a sudden lurch and almost turned the both of them over until Londo bore down on her arms again.

"In your dreams, baby."

"Yeah, in my dreams."

"Uh uh. You want me. You can say that much. Say it." He shook her.

"Ooo, Luke Skywalker, use that Force again," Lina cooed. "What a lightsaber."

"Mine's not made out of light, baby. Say you want it. Just that much, say you want me."

Lina looked into his eyes and her smile faded into deadly seriousness. "I want you," she whispered.

"I didn't hear anything..." He glanced around innocently before he allowed his gaze to bore into hers. He wanted to hear the veneer of civilization fall away from her as she surrendered herself to lust. Lust just for him; the only man she'd ever know, and by default, the best man she'd ever know. He'd never be compared to others in her eyes, never fall under the shadow of anyone else.

"I want you." She said it louder this time. "Londo Falcon Valiant Honeybear Rand, I want you."

"Who do you want?" he hissed at her.

Desire and lust washed her face; her breath surged sharp and hot against him.

"I want you!"

"Tell me you love me. Now." He had her trapped physically and emotionally. She couldn't get out of this. "Tell me. Tell me!"

When she turned her face away he realized what he'd been doing. He loosened his grasp but something inside him wouldn't let go completely. "Please," he begged. "I–"

With a lunge, she rose up, shaking him off. She twisted him so he fell flat on his back, and she held his arms down. In the sudden shock of it, Lon laughed and Lina shook him. "You bullying teddy of a bear," she accused. "Can't keep to a schedule, can't follow the rules."

He couldn't get mad at her. She was so funny, always a surprise. And she was right. "That's no way to talk to an important parahero," he began as he started to rise up.

She pushed him back down with a sudden movement. "And now apparently I have to do everything for you. Let's see how you like it."

Now she was the one who got him ready, she the one who used her own mind to go too deep as she rode him until he gasped under her. She laughed.

"You can take it," she parroted to him as he'd done to her all day. She leaned over to stroke her mind into him like a piston to reflect her physical actions.

"Oh, *crisse*, Lina! God... jeeeeSUS!!"

"You can take it. You can take it," she mocked. She changed her rhythm just to keep him off-balance, keep him from coming, and he groaned with the effort of not releasing. He started up the rhythm under her. Sweat dripped from her nose and chin as she tried to close herself off from what he was feeling, but her own physical sensations were getting to be too much. She couldn't withhold a whimper.

Somehow he found the strength to laugh at her. He gave her fanny a light smack and his little finger strayed...

"Off limits!" Lina swatted at him. That was it! She began a faster, up and down rhythm. Her mind rode a bucking bronco inside his soul.

He gasped for air, clutching the sand, clutching at her butt, at her shoulders to slow her down. Unable to take his sensations, she blanked her mind to all but the double-loop. She lived only in the physicality of it all. Suddenly Lon arched up and held. He howled wordlessly, twitching, and then fell back to the sand. Lina shuddered and rolled off.

Lon lay there panting, his eyes closed. He let out an occasional incoherent whoosh of a word. Finally he opened one eye, then the other. "Too..." he tried to speak. "Too much."

"You can take it." Lina grinned, squinting at him triumphantly.

He shook his head. "Too deep. Much too deep." He pulled her to him. "God, that was amazing. Don't ever do that again."

She ran her fingers down his forehead, down his nose, until they landed on his mouth. "Maybe I will and maybe I won't. My sweet honeybear." She laughed softly.

"Don't you ever tell that to anybody." Londo smiled as he closed his eyes, his chest heaving.

They lay together on their blanket in the moonlit clearing. Those cells were really changing now; the process was going from minute to minute, like circuit breakers switching on, alive with potential but not hooked up to anything yet. They could both sense it although in different ways. She watched the gentle smile on his half-sleeping face.

"I want the dress," he said softly.

"The what?"

"The nightie. The chemise. I'll buy you another one just like it, if you want. I'll buy you a hundred. Just let me have the original."

She snuggled against his chest. "What, are you going to fly it from your rooftop? Oh no, make it into a cape? Frame it and hang it over your mantelpiece with the rest of your trophies?"

"I was thinking about wearing it under the costume," he said.

Lina laughed.

He leaned his head back onto the sand, watching the backlit indigo clouds amble by overhead.

"I can't decide if you're sentimental or perverted, Lon."

"Sentimental? I guess I am, about a lot of things. I want something to remind me of you, of being here."

"Londo, what–"

"I don't want to talk about it. I'm living in the here and now."

"You're in denial. You've got to talk about it sometime. Afterward. It's not long now."

"I know. I know, I know. I just don't want to talk about it now." He raised up, bringing her with him. "C'mon, kitten, let's go for a swim."

Lina sighed in frustration. Denial was not healthy, but she couldn't refuse him this, not this last time.

"Thank you, Lina," he said as they walked toward the pool.

He was sitting on the side of the pool and she was in the water between his legs, when it happened and they both knew it. Like a switch closing, like his body suddenly seeing the clear path to unlimited energy. His cells were back online at a significant fraction of his full power. She wasn't near finished, but he took a breath and then said softly. "That's it. That's enough."

She paused and went back to what she was doing. Her mind dove deeper, trying to distract him.

"Um. No, I mean it. Enough."

She lifted her head. "I can handle it." she said.

He reached down and grabbed her by the waist, easily lifting her out of the water. "Ouch!"

"See?" It took effort not to hold her like he ordinarily would because they'd become so used to their special mutual touch. Everything teetered off-balance now when he touched her. He could feel himself revving up internally. The power level must be increasing at something close to a geometric rate.

He set her down beside himself so both their legs dangled in the water. Londo stared ahead at nothing, afraid to think.

"I can handle it," Lina repeated urgently. She put her hand on his thigh.

"No you can't." He shook her off– carefully, carefully– then rose and went to gather up his clothes, dragging his feet through the sand.

She ported her chemise to her so she could put it on as she ran to him, regardless of how damp she was, how sandy it was. "So this is how it ends? Abrupt– wham, bam, not even a thank you, ma'am? It doesn't have to be like this. Come on, we said we were going to talk it out. Talk to me."

Londo's mouth set in a grim line. He'd been through something like this scene many times before. So many disappointments, so many embarrassments. This one was the worst of them all, the worst by lightyears, by kiloparsecs! He steeled himself to facing a lifeless life. How many empty years stretched in front of him?

He picked up a small rock and turned to her. Making a loose fist, he opened his hand again and a pile of dust fell from his palm. "I never made you any promises. We knew it had to end."

"You promised never to hurt me. Well, this hurts! And you're hurting yourself more, and I can't bear it. You have to stick around a while, face the situation. You can't just run. You've been running all your life, haven't you?"

He tucked his torn shirt into his pants, his back to her. It seemed strange that she wasn't wearing his shirt. He couldn't look at her. She was a symbol of the happiness he'd never ever have again. "Leave it, Lina. I'm sorry for all this. I'm... sorry."

"You shouldn't be," she said as he pulled on his boots. To do so he hovered in the air, inches above the ground. "You've changed my life around and it's been all for the good. Stay, Londo," she pleaded. "I need you to talk to me. Then we can say goodbye."

"I can't take this now. Look, I'll... I'll call you. Tomorrow or the day after."

"No you won't. You take off now and I'll never hear from you again– not even a Christmas card. Stay, Londo. Please."

His face was twisted, tortured. "I can't," he finally blurted. "Goodbye. I'll send someone to get you. It was–" He couldn't finish the sentence. Instead he shrugged on his vest and turned and leaped for takeoff.

But she jumped on his back.

In less than a half-second they must have risen five hundred feet in the moonlight, ocean and island stretching out below them. "It's not that easy, is it?" she hissed to him, ignoring the pressure in her ears. "Not that easy to get rid of me?"

Pausing in midair, he twisted around. Lina didn't even think about looking down; she was too intent on him. "You set me down and I'll just teleport right back. I mean it; I'll learn how. All the way to Montreal. And if that doesn't work, I'll, I'll *stalk* you. I can do that now, you know." Say anything to keep him shocked, keep him from going into that deep depression that was looming in front of him!

"Lina, be reasonable."

"Goddammit to hell, Lon, you have to talk this out! It'll eat you away– kill you the way nothing else can. Talk to me. I'm a good listener. I'll never say anything, never do anything to embarrass you."

He shook his head, suspended there in mid-air with her on his back. He couldn't speak.

"Trust me, Londo," she whispered. "I'm a priest."

He broke out in a laugh that was half-sob. "Lina, what am I going to do with you?" He settled her back on the ground. She released her hold on him just as he collapsed in a heap, covering his head with his hands. "God. God! Lina, what am I going to do?"

He wept. She knelt and put her arms around him, letting him cry himself out. She ported in a box of tissues from home, and he laughed miserably when he saw it, but used it.

"It's all right. I won't tell," she assured him whenever she sensed that he was getting embarrassed about crying in front of her. She made occasional passes with her hands around him that he didn't notice, funneling the grief away from him down into the earth, which accepted it peacefully. She tapped the etheric level of his heart chakra to shake out some heartache that had lodged there. She clawed a dark patch of congealed loss out of his liver, though she didn't physically touch him. All part of being a psychic healer, a counselor. She could help people even when they couldn't help themselves.

Thank you, Lord, for the ability, she said silently. Of all her clients, this man here, Londo Rand, was the most important. She just had to find a way to help him. *Angels, help her!* Where to begin?

Thank God too that Lon was the one crying. Lina felt as if life itself had been wrung out of her. She teetered on the brink of a crying jag herself. As soon as Londo truly did leave... She shook her head, trying to rid herself of that thought. As soon as she was home safe, she'd... No, she'd have to go out for groceries, cat food at the very least. Check to see if there were any bills in her mailbox and pay them. Call in to work to explain that she needed to take some sick time.

And then she'd allow herself to cry for days. Weeks. As long as it took. She'd violated her own rules this time. She'd allowed her heart to be touched, and she had a glimpse now of how badly she'd pay for making such a monumental mistake. It was going to be the worst nightmare of her life– but it wasn't here yet.

Now while he was still with her she had to stay calm for Londo's sake. There was nothing so important as helping him.

He started coming out of it after maybe ten minutes– very embarrassed. He began to say something and sniffed loudly.

"You got rid of a lot of stuff you were carrying around with you." Lina summoned authority in her voice. She had to guide him through this.

Londo wiped his eyes. "I haven't done that since... Well, since ever."

"Maybe you should have. Ah well, there's no shoulda, coulda, woulda. Just do or do not."

"Yoda." He tried a smile. It came out watery.

"And others," she admitted. "You've got a lot of abandonment issues, Londo Rand. They control your life."

"Yeah, I've had a million shrinks tell me that." He combed his hair back with his fingers, but didn't take his hands away from covering his head. Hiding from her.

"And in turn they make you abandon others."

He made a sound. It might have been "No."

"How long are you going to let yourself be controlled by something you won't even admit to? Acknowledge it and it has a tendency to go away... or at least fade to the point where you can see where it's controlling you. Then you can decide when you want to follow in the same old tracks, and when you want to move in a new direction."

He eyed her from between his wrists. "You've done this before," he accused her.

"Like I said, I'm a priest. And a psychic. And I've read a bunch of self-help books. People come to me all the time with things like this. Londo, I really can help if you'll let me."

"We screwed ourselves. We got in way, way over our heads."

"Marianis Trench deep," Lina agreed. "So now it's over. What do we do?"

He shook his head. "I don't know. I don't know."

Lina sighed. "God comes up and hits us with a cast-iron skillet." She looked at him. "All I really need to tell you is that I'm not deserting you. I'm not abandoning you. We agreed before that things would have to end now. It's not like I'm running out on you."

"It sure feels like it," Londo said. "I know it's not your fault. I know it's just damned nature. But god, it feels like it." He fell onto his side, rolling into a fetal position. "God, why are You doing this to me?"

He radiated pure misery. Lina reached to hug him.

"Don't!" he said suddenly as he froze. "I might crush you."

She pulled back immediately. "Do you crush everyone?" she asked.

"I'm used to touching you as an equal." He rolled out of his knot to support himself on his hands. "Not as I normally do people. I usually treat everyone very lightly, like you would, I don't know... eggs, maybe. Or a newborn baby." He looked at her and gave a sad smile. "That's not the way I've been touching you lately."

She agreed with a shake of her head. "So we can't touch, we can't hug... We can talk this thing through. Maybe if we worked through the abandonment issues, things would be easier."

"Lina, I've been working on those for as long as I can remember– with professionals, guys with diplomas on their walls who send out big bills every month."

"I've got a diploma on my wall. A few of 'em, in art and psychic healing. And I can send out a bill if you want one. Just give me an address for it. I'll need one for the Christmas card anyway."

That same sad smile stayed on his face as he shook his head at her. "What are your rates?"

"There's a special today on poor, pathetic paraheroes. Where do we begin? How about you skip over your problems with sex–" he flinched, but she bulled on "– and tell me when you first realized you had been abandoned by someone?"

15

L ina winced at the things he'd gone through but she asked only a few guiding questions and let him talk.

Londo could remember his mother. At least, he thought she was his mother; she was certainly the woman who'd taken care of him, who'd loved him. He'd called her Maman. She had straight dark hair worn a medium length, and brown eyes. Skin color hadn't really registered for him, but he could remember doing a crayon drawing of her: brown hair, brown eyes. Maybe all he'd had had been a brown crayon. But she'd been the most beautiful person in the world. That he remembered well.

How had her voice sounded? He could hear her telling him, *"Londo, nous irons à Toronto cet automne. J'ai des amis là-bas. Tu les aimeras bien."*

"Did you understand that?"

Lina nodded. "You were going to Toronto in the fall. She had friends there and you'd like 'em. How old were you?"

He'd been three, maybe four years old. Those were the only words of hers that he could ever remember, but they rang in his mind through the years.

He knew he had a father. He could almost see him, a memory of a memory's memory: a male face laughing with him. For this face he assigned a medium-pale complexion because he heard someone saying that this face was tanned today, and he'd noticed the coloring. Why hadn't he noticed the features instead? Brown hair? Maybe. A dazzling smile. He remembered the smile, the strong hands, the echo of a laugh he heard in his mind whenever he himself laughed. Nothing else really.

Londo distinctly recalled one day playing in the living room with the TV on while his parents were in the kitchen arguing. They'd shout at each other, then calm down, then shout some more. It wasn't the first time. While the fight went on, he hit the couch as if that could stop them, but it didn't work. A squeaky door slammed and then his mother wept. He toddled into the kitchen to find her alone and comfort her. She took him into her arms, still crying, him crying too. He fell asleep on her shoulder.

Abandoned by father, Lina guessed.

Of course he could never forget the night *they* came to take him. He'd just been tucked into his bed. He loved his bed now that the railing had been taken down. It made him feel so free. Maman was reading him a story from an illustrated book. *What book?* He didn't know.

How hot was it in the room? Not hot; there were just the sheets on the bed. The windows were open, and a warm breeze was coming through them.

Any smells? Londo tasted his memory. The soft but pungent smell of garlic hung in the air. They'd had some kind of soup and soft bread for supper.

Sounds? Maman had the radio on to a classical station. He didn't know what the selection was, but there were a lot of violins, a bit of French horn, too. It made it sound distant against the story Maman read.

Claude the Magic Horse! That was what it was! He loved that story. He had Maman read it every night. He could remember some of the illustrations now: the rangy horse strolling around its farm, talking to the other animals before it found the magic necklace that let it fly.

The book held sounds and dialogue Maman would trigger. She'd let him touch the buttons, too. Claude's voice was deep– like Mr. Ed's. He remembered now. When he'd had the bed railing, he'd stand at it and make animal noises along with the book, pretending he was fenced up like them. Then when Claude found the necklace, Maman would lift him out of his cage and hold him up in the air as she skipped around the room. He pretended he was flying, and he'd laugh and she'd laugh...

Okay, let's leave the book. The breeze through the window: can you see out the window, see what the landscape looks like?

I don't want to look. That's where they are.

Who?

They came before Maman could finish the story. She was just about to get to the part where Claude found the magic necklace. Lon loved that part best of all. He wanted to fly, too. He felt frustrated because he couldn't.

A light brighter than a noonday sun suddenly shone into the window, eclipsing the room lights. Maman had let out a little shriek and reached for something on the nightstand. He didn't know what it was, but then she dropped it and sat in the rocking chair next to his bed. She rocked gently and he shook her arm, but she stared straight ahead as if he weren't there.

Then some strange men came into the room. They were tall, very skinny, and very white with triangular heads and huge, almond-shaped eyes. They pointed a magic wand at Maman and she went to sleep there in the rocking chair. They pointed it at him and he couldn't move.

Off-balance, he sat down hard in the bed. They put a harness around his neck and shoulders, something that made him float– just like Claude the Magic Horse. He liked that. Maman must be proud of him for doing this. Then he realized that he was being taken away from her.

Maman! Maman!

A big ship overhung the yard. It was a flying saucer, just like on TV, with colored lights and a long ribbon of pulsing white light running around it. More tall white men stood around, looking anxious as if perhaps they feared police might investigate. But no one did. The night was silent, and Lon floated into the ship. That was the last time he saw Earth for years.

"Aliens!" Lina blinked in amazement. "I've never heard anything about aliens being the ones who abducted you!" She was about to add, "Are you sure?" but of course he would be.

Lon shrugged. "We didn't want to alarm people. There's enough hysteria about aliens as it is. Roswell, Area 51... Imagine what would happen if someone proved that it was all true, worse than true, worse than people imagined."

"But... But..." Lina shut up and let him talk. So he'd been kidnapped by aliens. Abandoned by his mother, in effect, Lina noted. Maybe one could even call it being abandoned by the Earth.

They'd put him in a bed and he'd protested as much as he could since he was still stunned from whatever that magic wand had done. He wasn't sleepy! He wanted Maman!

They shaved his head and roughly attached sticky patches all over it. Then they covered his body with the patches. The things looked like they were round band-aids and so he thought he'd been hurt. He began to cry.

His attendants glanced at each other at that, then at him, and from then on they put the patches on more gently, telling him through a floating button that translated their words into French that these weren't band-aids, that he was all right. They patted him and told him he was a good boy. He should go to sleep. Finally he lay back on the bed and closed his eyes.

When he woke his hair had grown out again, even longer than it had been before. This is why he noticed it in the first place– it was different than it always had been.

He seemed a lot bigger. He felt clumsy when he moved. The bed had changed. The attendants had changed, too, he thought. He looked down at his skin; it seemed pale, and he cried about that.

He thought he was sick. Was this a hospital? The attendants assured him that he had indeed been sick, but they were doctors in a very special hospital. Where was Maman? He wanted Maman! They told him that Maman was also ill, but she would visit as soon as she was well again. Maybe a few days. He must be patient.

There were a few tests they needed to do on him. Ouch! That hurt! The doctors told him that these tests would also help his maman to get well. He must be brave in order to help her. She had the same illness he had, and so they did these things to him to help her, too. That made sense.

He sobbed through more of their tests: needles and tubes that flashed red beams of light. They took blood– he didn't like that at all. They poked him and listened to the interior of his body. They put things into every orifice he had. He cowered on the bed when they weren't prodding him.

This will help your maman, they kept telling him. You're saving her life. So he took it.

One day one of them brought in a real teddy bear, *un ours en peluche*. It was black and white with big brown glass eyes and a red ribbon around its neck. Lon grabbed Ours from the doctor and never let it out of his arms. The alien doctors learned that to ensure his cooperation they merely had to invoke Maman and not bother Ours.

Ours was Lon's best friend. Lon told him everything, and the bear listened and sympathized. But as months, maybe years, went by Ours became tattered and raggedy. One morning– at least, it might have been morning; Lon never saw outside and the lights never dimmed– he awoke to find Ours gone. That was the same day they told him that Maman wasn't going to come visit. First they told him that she had died. Another doctor told him later that she didn't love him anymore and had gone home without him.

Londo was silent for a long time before he returned to the telling.

They let him out of the room every now and then, but he had to wear a special bracelet when they did. He had no idea why. There were stark white, curved corridors outside the room with many doors leading off them going to what, he didn't know.

He was usually taken to a gym– a coliseum, after his small bedroom– with a track and gymnastic bars, even a round pool. He could exercise there, but only after they'd covered him with those band-aid electrodes. They had to shave his head again, and he sat quietly while they did it, retreating inward to the stories he told himself to keep himself brave and distance the pain. This was the only place of security he had left.

Londo gave a small laugh as he recounted watching the aliens demonstrating how to run around the track, how to climb the bars, how to step into the pool to see how long he could hold his breath underwater. They looked ridiculous doing it.

Although he was initially weak and uncoordinated from his confinement, it gave him great pleasure to outrun them in their awkwardness, to learn to climb the bars like a monkey, to hold his breath longer than they thought he could.

And then one day when he went to the gym, another boy stood there. A companion, the doctors told him.

They looked at each other warily. It occurred to Londo that the doctors were a different species than he was. He'd gotten so used to them, he'd begun to think of them as being as human as himself. But this boy was about his own height, with charcoal black skin and a shaved head, covered in round band-aids.

They looked at each other and the boy said, "You aren't wearing any clothes." The floating button was translating whatever language he was speaking into French. This boy was human, but he didn't speak the same language Lon spoke, and Lon couldn't understand why.

"Neither are you," Londo said defiantly.

"They took 'em." The boy nodded at the aliens. "What's your name?"

"Londo."

"Londo what?"

"What do you mean?"

The boy looked at him as if he were an idiot. "Everyone has more than one name. I'm Trip Golombek."

"I'm just Londo." He let the aliens finish fastening the band-aids onto him. They'd done it hundreds of times before.

"What is this?" Trip asked as his eyes darted from alien to alien, then around the room.

"It's someplace to play. You run and jump, and these things–" Londo nodded at the bandages, "tell them how well we're getting."

"How well?"

"Sure. You're sick, aren't you? That's why you're here?"

"I'm not sick. They took me. I want to go home!" Tears welled up in Trip's eyes. He sat down on the indoor track and covered his face with his hands. "I want my mama!"

Londo shook off the alien doctor and ran to Trip. He held him like he wished his maman would hold him. "It's all right," he told Trip. "They won't hurt you." He realized that he'd just lied, but he wanted Trip to stop crying.

They'd hurt Trip. They'd hurt him bad.

He and Trip had spent that day in the gym trying to play in spite of Trip's enormous homesickness. Trip told him that their home planet was Earth and that this was a big spaceship.

Lon remembered how it looked from the outside. "A flying saucer," he said, and Trip agreed.

Lon told Trip that these were all doctors, but Trip said that they weren't. They were evil alien kidnappers, just like on TV. How long had Londo been here? Longer than he could remember. He told Trip about having his hair shaved, and then it growing out that long– he showed him how long it had been– and then it was shaved again. Trip didn't know how long that would take, but he knew it was a long, long time.

They'd gone to their respective rooms that night, and the next day Lon had been taken to a new room, one not as big as the gym, and so crowded with electronic equipment that they'd had to weave their way through. The doctors– no, *aliens*– strapped Londo into a big chair there. He watched as Trip came in to be strapped to a matching chair, just beyond a bank of equipment.

The aliens stood behind a smoky glass wall as a wide, blue ray bathed the two boys. It had hurt. Lon closed his eyes and grunted from the pressure, the prickling needles that it seemed to press all over his body.

He heard Trip start to scream in fright, but Lon was used to being experimented on. He was used to needles. He was used to funny lights. He gritted his teeth and took it until it got so bad that he had to scream, too. The lights stopped when he did that. Londo watched the aliens carrying the limp body of Trip out of the room.

He never saw Trip again.

There were others through the years, fifty-nine of them. He kept count on his fingers and toes, and he remembered all their names except for one. Nine of the children had spoken French. All of them were boys except for three. He'd wondered why the girls were so shy and figured it was because they were missing some important parts.

There were times when he almost didn't introduce himself when another companion came along, but they were always so distraught, some of them hysterical with fear, that he had to let them know that there was someone else who shared the human experience. He comforted them as he could, never letting them know that they didn't have much longer to live.

He tried to make them happy in the time they had. It made him feel like a traitor doing it, but it felt good to help them, too. He was their protector.

Now he called the aliens by their racial name, *Lectori*. If they were too harsh to the new companion, he'd come to their rescue. He'd demand the Lectori be more gentle, or he'd knock the Lectori's arm away from where they'd grabbed the companion too roughly. Lon berated them in the Lectori tongue, for he'd learned their language. They didn't have to keep the translator going when there wasn't another human around.

It began to dawn on Londo that he could outrace the other children, speeding powerfully around the track when they had run to exhaustion. He jumped around on the bars almost as if he could fly. He stayed underwater long after the other had surfaced, gasping. When they held the laboratory sessions he tried to fake screams so that it wouldn't last so long, so that maybe whatever the Lectori were doing to the companion wouldn't kill them. But the Lectori were rarely fooled.

How guilty he felt to be alive! Why was he here; what were the Lectori doing? Back in his room, he'd bang his head against the wall just to get the frustration out of his system. Sometimes he'd cry, wondering if anyone were missing him. Did anyone in the universe love him? No one here did.

They'd told him that Maman didn't love him, but they also told him that she was dead. He didn't want to believe either story, and he clung to the idea that somewhere out there Maman was moving heaven and earth looking for him. He made up a million stories in his head where he'd wake up one morning and there she'd be, a laser blaster in one hand and the other open, ready to hug him to her as they prepared to go home.

Londo's companions told him that this ship was in outer space. Then they had to explain what outer space was. Now Lon knew that wherever Maman was– maybe she was on that planet called Earth– it would be next to impossible for her to find him. He understood intellectually. But he kept thinking up new stories.

And his new-found friends kept dying. Depending on what kinds of experiments the Lectori were performing, they sometimes lived for as many as five days. Usually they only lasted two.

Deserted by the entire universe, by dozens of friends. Lina tried to put the pieces of his story together with some other logic, but it always came back to this. She pressed her hand against her mouth, aghast at the life Lon had had to lead.

He began to punch the walls, too. Sometimes he wouldn't cooperate in gym, but just stand there and punch the walls. He didn't want to help the Lectori in any way. He only wanted to go home, to find Maman!

There was one companion, he recalled– though he didn't want to admit it– that he'd ignored completely. He couldn't take it any more. Londo ignored the kid, who looked to be about the same age as he was, blond and brown-eyed, crying there in the middle of the track. Londo merely walked to the gym wall and punched it with all his might until his hands bled all the way down his arms. He didn't give a damn.

He never saw the kid again. Didn't even know his name.

The Lectori sat him down for a talk after that. Only he could help these other children, they said. They wouldn't kill them any more, but only if he cooperated. They knew now that the children couldn't keep up with him, couldn't take what he could take, so they were only there for quantified comparison. The Lectori would only take them as far as they could reasonably stand– if he cooperated.

How long had he been with them? How many years? One? Five? They'd had to get a new bed and later on another to keep up with how he'd grown. Time meant nothing to Lon. He had no way to measure it other than by the intervals he was allowed to sleep. The lights in the ship were always on, never even dimmed, so it was eternal day. He realized that the Lectori couldn't shave his head any more for some reason, so he tried to keep track of the passage of time by how long his hair was getting.

There came a period when there hadn't been any companions for some while. Instead, Londo bore a constant barrage of strange and painful experiments, the usual agonies with new equipment that often whined nerve-scratchingly when they used it. But now they had to tire him out before they could make him feel pain. His powers weakened when he got tired.

"I didn't know that," Lina said.

"It's not something I want to advertise. They don't weaken that much anymore, but I can still get awfully tired at times."

One day they took Londo into a room he'd never been in before. To his present-day eye it was a lounge, but to his child's mind it was a palace full of comfortable furniture with cushions. He knew about palaces. Sometimes one of the aliens would read to him from Terran children's books to keep him distracted. There were palaces in those books.

Here was carpeting on the floor, pictures on the walls. A large window looked out into blackness with multi-colored pinpoints of light shining in it.

He pressed his face against the smoothness of the glass and stared. Those must be stars. *Étoiles*. His companions had told him about them. They were a part of outer space, but they were also visible from the planet Earth. He didn't remember them.

A large picture hung in mid-air in the center of the lounge. It was just a frame that, when he came in front of it, suddenly turned into a man, a man cut off by the frame. Gradually Lon saw that the man wasn't really there. He remembered TV; the books had TVs in them. This was like that.

This was a three-dimensional moving picture of a middle-aged, haughty-looking human man wearing shiny clothes that covered him everywhere except the head. Maybe that's why the Lectori had put a robe on Londo. He tugged at it, unused to clothing.

The Lectori bowed to the screen while Londo regarded the man curiously. He seemed human enough. He had a pointy chin, but not incredibly so. The vertical, oval pupils of his eyes were the oddest part about him. Tiny ringlets of hair made his head look like it was covered with hundreds of small springs. Around his forehead he wore a wide golden circlet with a large red stone on the front.

The Lectori called him Emperor Yanist-Glory, called him Your Imperial Majesty, Your Glory. Lon watched in wonder as they groveled. This was somebody like a king, maybe. He didn't look like any king in Londo's books. Kings had thick gray beards and wore capes with fur collars. But maybe this was a kind of a king. Emperor.

The emperor looked Londo over critically. He never addressed him. He just referred to him as "the boy" to the Lectori. Londo's eyes narrowed as he studied the emperor. Somehow he knew that this man was behind it all– behind whatever had happened to him. Behind what had happened to all the other children through the years. Behind the hell that was his own life. And he knew that the emperor had realized that he knew, too. This child knew who had caused it all.

16

"Yanist-Glory. Where is he now?"

"I'm the official thorn in the imperial butt," Londo replied with a grim smile that made Lina shiver. "Gloryboy's about fifty parsecs over from Earzh. Well, the very edge of his empire is. His central world's about fifty more parsecs from there. Call it a half-day's travel to the Empire, a little over a day to Soalok and the Emperor. Close enough to spit. He knows me very well by now, though we've never met in person." He paused. "He's going to get his one of these days. And I'm the one who's going to give it to him."

He told her more.

They'd ushered Lon out of the imperial presence quickly, for now there were new experiments to be done. A few days went by, maybe a week or more, before another companion appeared.

The Lectori reminded Londo of his responsibility and he cooperated. He easily outraced the other boy, Alhad, and left him gasping on the floor. On the bars, he flipped and whirled, leaping into the air and landing lightly, as Alhad stood watching with his mouth open. Lon could almost live on the bottom of the tank now too.

The next day the Lectori carried Alhad's body out of the laboratory.

"He was supposed to live! You promised! You promised!"

The Lectori apologized profusely. They had overestimated what Alhad could take. The next one they'd give half the dosage. He wouldn't die. They reassured Londo constantly.

Two weeks later, Jorge appeared. This time Londo reminded the Lectori of what they had promised, and they agreed, how they agreed!

And they had taken Jorge's body from the lab.

For at least two weeks Lon refused to leave his room. They couldn't force him to. He realized that he had the power to deny them this, knocking them away when they tried to drag him out. He remained seated tailor-fashion on his bed and banged his head against the wall, knowing that cameras watched him.

They tried withholding his food. He paced his tiny room and hit the wall with his hands, waiting for them to bleed, but they never did. And then he noticed a very small dent in the wall. He scowled at it with interest.

Claiming hunger, the next time they approached him he allowed them to take him out. They gave him some food as a reward before he went to the gym. There he met Kurt. Kurt was doomed, either way Lon decided to play this game. Londo himself might be doomed, but there was a chance that wasn't true. At any rate, he'd be out of here. They went through all the routines: the running, the jumping– hell, Londo could fly, not just jump– The breath control.

The Lectori removed the electrodes in preparation to take Kurt back to his room. Kurt could tell that they were going to take him away from Londo and began to hyperventilate from pure terror.

"Take it easy, Kurt," Londo whispered. "Follow me."

Londo knocked down the Lectori attendants and opened the door to the gym. "Come on!" He was out of range of the translator, but Kurt got the gist of it and ran after him.

Kurt wasn't fast enough, so Lon picked him up and flew through the corridors, looking for that lounge. There it was! He remembered its window. The books had shown windows. They could be easy to break. Londo couldn't open the door to the lounge, so he pounded on it with all his might. Finally it dented, then dented some more. With a cracking sound it split open and the two boys wriggled through as Kurt jabbered excitedly in some strange language.

Alarms went off everywhere. Lon knew he had to be quick. The window showed blackness and stars.

"No!" Kurt yelled. "That's outer space! There isn't any air there! We'll die!"

But Londo didn't understand the language. He barreled at full flying speed for the window, and it exploded open in front of him.

Kurt grabbed onto a handle and braced himself– but there was only the slightest bit of wind, and that was coming into the ship, not leaving it. Kurt gaped as Lon hovered outside the window against a horizon, under the stars.

"*Viens-t'en! Enfin la liberté!*" Londo shouted at Kurt. Why wouldn't Kurt let go? He flew into the ship again and picked up Kurt, flying him out of the ship. Out into the Canadian Rockies. He headed east because that was a direction away from the ship.

Lon slowed down when he realized that Kurt couldn't take the speed. Kurt hung on tightly and didn't look down for a long time, then finally opened his eyes and looked around. They were in the middle of wilderness, but a tiny light glowed on the ground.

Kurt pointed excitedly. "People!" he said.

"*Peuple?*" Lon asked.

Kurt nodded. "Down there," he pointed again.

Lon changed course and they landed– not very gracefully– next to a house. Londo recognized it as being a house, almost like the one he remembered. Wood and windows and doors, beds and chairs that he could see faintly through the walls. "*Une maison,*" he said wonderingly.

"A house," Kurt corrected him. Eventually someone answered as he pounded on the door. Someone with a shotgun. The man was astounded to see two young, naked boys on his doorstep.

"Help us!" Kurt demanded.

"Good lord!" the man said. "Where'd you come from? Where's your clothes? Where're your parents?"

Kurt pointed back to the mountains. "A flying saucer–" he said, and then he fainted.

Lon looked at the collapsed boy on the doorstep. "Kurt?" He'd never seen anyone faint before. Kurt must be dead. "*Non!* Kurt!"

In a panic, he roared away into the night still flying east, away from his captors. He could see their saucer perched miles away on a mountainside. Londo wanted revenge, but he wanted his mother more.

"And Kurt?"

"Oh, he was okay. He's living in Australia these days, along with his family. Second wife, two kids. The guy we found took him straight to the police. They reunited him with his folks. We're good friends. When he tells his version, he doesn't faint. But he did."

But Londo didn't know that fainting wasn't fatal. He kept going, flying until he ran out of energy. He landed in a forest and slept lightly, afraid the Lectori would find him and capture him again.

When he got up, he was hungry. And scared. He knew this must be Earth, and he thought that maybe Maman was still alive. But it looked like a pretty big place, this Earth. Where was she? He flew through the skies of Canada and the U.S. looking for her, unsure whether he'd recognize her or not. She'd recognize him. Everyone he saw wore clothes, so he stole some from a clothesline somewhere– maybe Ohio or Wisconsin, he wasn't sure.

But after a few days he became frustrated searching every woman's face. Walking through the crowds of Earth, peering at women, looking lost– More than once people called over a cop because they suspected that the dirty, rumpled boy with the long hair was misplaced. But cops had a presence about them of authority, of being locked up, that Londo feared. He'd see one coming and he'd fly off, leaving astonished humans staring up into the sky after him.

Several times he just sat down and cried in frustration. He wanted his maman! Wait a minute. Toronto. She'd said Toronto. That was some kind of place. Where was this Toronto?

He landed in a city crowd somewhere where he heard French being spoken.

"Toronto?" he went around asking. "*Où es Toronto?*"

After dodging the police, he began asking kids his age. They didn't know, so he asked some who looked a little older, maybe twelve or so.

One girl looked at the sun to get her directions and pointed. "*Là,*" she said. That way. "*Deux cents kilomètres, peut-être. Peut-être plus.*" Two hundred kilometers to Toronto.

"*Qu'est-ce que c'est un kilomètre?*"

The girl looked down the street they were on. "*D'ici à là,*" she declared, pointing. That far was a kilometer.

"<What's two hundred?>" he asked in French.

She looked at him like he was an idiot, but he convinced her to show him. Toes and fingers were twenty, and do that ten times. Toes and fingers times fingers times that far was Toronto. Londo nodded thanks and took off into the sky, leaving her open-mouthed.

"*Un para!*" he heard her gasp in his wake.

Apparently the girl had no idea what the true distance was, but she had the general direction right. He found a huge city on a lake: Toronto, but Maman wasn't there that he could find.

By now Lon had seen flying people in the sky, and had a hunch they were looking for him. Flying police, maybe. Maybe people working for the Lectori.

His frustration built until he thought he would explode. At one point he stopped in the street, leaned against a building, and began to hit his head against it. Then he beat his fists against its steel coating. It started to crumble. People screamed and ran from him, but he didn't notice. He hit and hit and hit. Then he realized that people were inside the building, so he flew off before they could get hurt.

But it wasn't long before he had to hit another building. He couldn't help it. He was angry! Angry at Maman for not being there. Angry at himself for being so stupid to think that she would be. He cried and hit, cried and hit.

A red beam caught him in a cocoon.

"Easy now, fella," a calm voice said. He looked up to see a man descend from the sky dressed in red, white and black, with what skin that was showing eerily glowing red. "Easy, son," he said, and though Lon couldn't understand the language, he understood the tone. He stopped his attack on the building and warily watched the man.

"*Je veux ma maman!*" Lon declared.

"You want your..." The man said slowly. "Oh. Um. *Où... Où est... ta maman?*"

"*Aucune idée!*" Lon shouted, and beat against the red cocoon. It was made of light, but it was solid, too. He didn't want to be locked up again! Never again! "*Lâchez-moi!*" He burst from the cocoon and flew off, leaving the man staring after him.

It only lasted a second or two. The red man followed him through the sky, then backed off and disappeared until Londo thought it might be safe to land and look some more. He walked into the heart of the city with buildings towering overhead. He wandered down the streets. Searching, searching...

The sidewalk crowd slowed. People stared at someone up ahead. Curious in spite of himself, Lon wandered forward. The crowd parted to let whoever it was through.

It was a man– a man with skin as dark as Trip's had been, dressed in clothing much tighter than that of the other people on the street. It looked very dynamic with a bright, splashing symbol across his chest and a short white cape.

The man looked directly at him. "*Bonjour,*" he said kindly. "*Je crois que je peux t'aider.*"

Lon stopped. Could the man really help him? "*Où est ma maman?*" he demanded of him.

"*Je ne sais pas.* <I don't know,>" the man said, shaking his head. "<My name is Hal. What's yours?>"

"Londo," he answered defiantly. "<Where's my Maman?>"

"*Je ne sais pas,*" Hal repeated. "<But I do know that you're lost. Let me help. You're a stranger here and I can help you, Londo, if you want. Stay with me while we look for your mother. I won't hurt you. Don't be afraid of me.>"

He seemed trustworthy. He had a kind face. He was human, not Lectori. Londo was so tired, so discouraged, so lost...

Hal held up his hand, a stopping sign to someone behind Londo. When he whirled around, Lon saw the man in red descend quickly.

"Don't!" Hal called, and the man backed away, his hands in the air in clear indication that he wasn't going to do any harm. Hal walked to Londo, who didn't take his eyes off of the red man.

Hal crouched to be at eye level with Lon. "*D'accord*, <he won't hurt you now. He doesn't want to hurt you; he's a friend. His name is Rico.>"

The red man nodded at Lon. "*Bonjour...*"

"Londo," Hal supplied the name.

Rico nodded. "*Bonjour, Londo. Je ne parle pas le... la... le français, mais... je...*"

Hal chuckled. "*Il essaye. Il n'est pas vraiment bon, n'est-ce pas?*"

"*Non,*" Londo admitted. This Rico didn't speak very well at all.

Hal smiled at him, still speaking French.

"<Well then, Londo, will you come with me? I know where there's a nice bed and something to eat, and we can search for your mother from there. It's a big world; it might take a long time to find her.>" Hal paused. "<I want to be your friend.>"

Londo took a breath, considering. He looked from Hal to Rico and back. Both men seemed concerned but friendly. Not Lectori. His eyes narrowed. This could be a trick.

"Yanist-Glory?" he said, watching for reaction. Both men looked at each other with shock and then suspicion.

"Yanist-Glory!" Rico growled.

Hal turned Lon toward him, and sheer fury fired his eyes. "<What do you know about Emperor Yanist-Glory? He's a bad man, a very bad man. He lives very far from here.>"

"*Bon,*" Lon nodded at Hal, at the hatred he shared with this man. "<I'm going to kill him someday.>"

Hal turned to Rico and translated.

Londo watched as Rico raised his eyebrow and nodded at Londo. "*Bon,*" he jerked his head in agreement, and Lon smiled at him.

"*Amis?*" Hal asked, and Lon gave a definite nod.

"*Amis.*"

"*Bon. Suis-moi.*" And Hal took off into the sky. Londo laughed to see that Hal could fly, too, and followed. Rico trailed after them.

Lon was nine or ten. He'd been held captive for six or seven years; he didn't know precisely.

Hal of course was Maximus, and Rico Carapella was the then-current and legendary Galactic Guardian of the Terran Sector. Hal took Lon to his own adoptive parents' home to get him into a family atmosphere as soon as possible. While Mama

Ruth fixed one of her wonderful, fully-Terran meals for them, Rico and Hal gently questioned Londo, recording. Rico finally found a mechanical translator that could handle French so he could question Lon directly.

They were horrified at the boy's story. Rico used his ruby medallion to produce mugshots so they could confirm that it had indeed been the infamous Lectori who were in league with Emperor Yanist-Glory. He looked very grim as Lon nodded his head at the pictures between bites of pot roast and confirmed, *"C'est eux."*

Lon told them about Kurt, and Hal called the authorities. When he got off the phone, he could assure Londo that Kurt was doing fine; he'd only fainted, a concept Lon wasn't too sure about, but everyone assured him was not fatal. Kurt was already home with his family in Australia. Londo nodded, and they questioned him some more until he fell asleep on the table.

Hal put him to bed and stayed by his side all night in case he were to wake up and not know where he was.

The next day Hal, Rico and he flew to British Columbia to check out the saucer. It was no longer there, but evidence remained to prove that it had been. Rico took bags along to collect the broken plasti-glass, proof of Lectori manufacture. It could help a legal case if they could ever find Londo's captors.

Hal assured Lon that although it might be impossible to get Yanist-Glory imprisoned, they could certainly beef up their planetary security to make sure that no more hostages would be taken by the Lectori.

The courts eventually awarded Maximus custody of young Londo, since he was the only one strong enough to handle him. Custody became adoption, and Londo officially became Londo Rand. Hal had given him honest love and solid life values, and had taken him to scores of psychiatrists. For four years Lon had even moved to another planet where the advanced psychiatric professionals there took him through a major phase of his healing.

On both worlds, entire books had been written about him chronicling both his psychological problems as well as guesses about what kinds of experiments had turned this Terran boy into a younger version of Maximus.

That it was a Yanist-Glory plot against Maximus, everyone who knew the entire story agreed. How terrible that he had chosen this innocent young boy to be part of his plan. How fortunate that Lon was smart enough and strong enough to get away, and that he had found himself a good home.

Somehow he turned out remarkably well-balanced, since now he was surrounded by people who loved him. But Maximus being, well, Maximus, was gone for long stretches at a time. Lon had been farmed out to Maximus's own adoptive parents for a week or even two here and there as he was growing up. They'd been like family, but it just wasn't a steady home life.

And they'd never found Maman.

The Terran Paranorm Network had searched through every inch of Canada, looking for her as well as his unknown father.

Lina stopped with her fork halfway to her mouth. "Why in the world did they choose Canada? Just because you were found there?"

Londo swallowed a mouthful of hot biscuit as he sat in the moon-dappled shadows. "I spoke French. That and Lectori. I could remember Maman talking about going to Toronto."

"So? Londo, let's go to... Capetown next summer. Does that mean we live there?"

"Of course not."

"Now, what did your mother say?"

"She said we were going to Toronto in the fall."

"In the fall. Not that afternoon. In the fall, like it was going to be a long trip she was looking forward to. I can't believe they'd just limit the search because of that."

"Well, there was a lot more to it than–"

"Londo, you're from France."

"What? Where'd you get that?"

"I just know. In here." She tapped her head. "Give me a map and I'll point it out to you. In the Northwest... I mean Northeast, I always get my directions mixed up when I'm looking at the Eastern Hemisphere for some reason. Northeast of France. There's a town with an 'sch' in the name– it must be close to the border of Germany. Lon, I'll bet good money you came from somewhere within 50 miles of that place. Maybe you weren't born there, but there are strong ties."

"France." He gave a little laugh. "If anyone else had said that to me, I'd say they were crazy."

"Oh hell, I've had people calling me a crazy Sagittarian for years," she said. By now, they were dining off her plates from home and a dinner of a breakfast stolen from an all-night Shoney's almost on the other side of the world. Lina used half a roll to point at him. "So the ParaNet searched through the wrong country..."

Londo continued to tell her things he'd told very, very few people as he dined on stolen chain restaurant food in a tropical paradise, unable to touch his lover.

17

He truly did live in a world completely different from Lina's. He was Valiant, megaparahero supreme. He had been kidnapped by aliens, adopted by Maximus, surrounded by other megas and paraheroes all his life. Londo had been immersed in world celebrity since the day Maximus found him. He'd saved sections of the globe time and time again, and he'd saved the entire earth itself on occasion.

God had certainly gone to a lot of trouble to set up this joke, teasing the old Muttbutt with this time with wonderful Londo, just to end it so soon. But involving Londo in His joke was going too far! *That was unfair, God!*

She wanted to stay in Lon's shadow for just a few more precious hours before the universe took him away from her forever. A television image would never be real enough for her again. Seize the night, her selfish core whispered. Make up any excuse to keep him here.

It took sheer determination to shunt that urge. She knew she was selfish and egotistical– Dad had reminded her of that enough– but now she had to remember that she was a priest and had taken a vow to help. Poor Londo needed her to rise above herself. He needed– what?

There were things she did for clients, but those were so elementary... At least they were a start. Lina shook herself. The physical experience was over. No matter what she wished or how she tried to fool herself, it would never come again. What remained was the mental and spiritual side of life.

"Okay." Lina stood and brushed off her hands. "I'm going to clear out what you've covered already. It'll take a while. My question is: do we want to stay here tonight, or should we move somewhere else? That Terry Whatsherface–"

Londo felt drained and vulnerable after everything that had happened today. "Rhodes," he corrected her as he rubbed his forehead. But a part of him was amazed that he was still here. And Lina didn't hate him for being such a louse.

"– Is out there somewhere, still gunning for you. It's been two days."

"I know. But the powers are back now and we're about three days out from the hotel, no fires lit. I can see her thugs way the hell down at the far end of the island. Looks like they're leaving. They've given up. Good riddance. I'll get them later. We're safe enough."

"Are you sure?"

He looked at her and through the cool night Lina could see the warmth in his eyes. "I like it here," he said.

"Whatever you say, Londo. You're the expert." Had she ever trusted anyone as she did him? "So let's clear stuff. Don't worry; it won't be all that painful. For me. You'll be doing all the work." She gave an evil laugh for atmosphere as she sat behind Lon on the blanket, straddling him.

"Lina–"

"Oh hush, it's not that kind of technique. You just lean against me. You don't have to worry about crushing me this way. I put my fingers– hope you don't mind if they're greasy– on the pressure points on your forehead here." How odd; his skin no longer had any give to it. It was as if he were made of warm granite.

"I can't even feel them."

"You aren't supposed to. It's just to remind your brain where to store and how to process these memories. Okay, which are we supposed to start with?" she asked the air, as far as Lon was concerned. Apparently she received an answer. "Huh. Okay, I was wrong. We follow the sex trail first, then go back and do all that other stuff. Whatever."

Lon stirred in her arms. He didn't want–

"Be still." Lina made sure her fingers were in the correct position on his forehead. Moon-cast shadows of the gently-blowing palms above them played across his face. "All right, pick one of those women you had problems with."

"But–"

"Don't argue. Let's do this first one, and then you can decide if you want to continue, okay? It won't be that bad... I don't think. Now, visualize."

She didn't want to intrude, but a picture came up of a bottle blonde with squinty eyes and a phony smile. Was she jealous of her? "Think about the embarrassing moment, think about whatever it was with her that made you feel bad."

"Okay."

"Think about it, run it like a movie."

"Do we really have to do this?"

"Yes you do. Shut up. Now run the movie again, this time in slow motion."

He was still very, very tense. Then again, maybe the inhumanity of his skin made him appear that way. "Now backward." Lina paused to let him think. "Now forward, but dress her in clown clothes."

He shook his head but stayed with it. Still very tense. "Now forward, slow motion, but if it was inside..."

"It was."

"Okay, make it outside now. In a frozen Arctic wilderness. With purple snow."

"Huh."

"Run it again, regular motion. Sky is, oh, pink polka-dots. Giant parakeets make rude comments."

"Huh." This time he had a little smile on his face. He was getting into it.

"Now run it as it was."

Londo leaned against her with his eyes closed and then opened them, his mouth an astonished "O." He could remember the event as clearly as ever, but now there was no embarrassment, no anxiety. "How'd you do that?"

"It's all the remarkable science of neuro-linguistic programming. Bad experiences are filters that we can strip emotions from. Leave the memory, trash the filter. Ready to go on?"

"Eh... *oui*. Okay, I'm game."

"All right. We'll need to quantify some things next. How hot was it when...?"

They spent the night going through his traumas until they both fell asleep. Lon awoke with the morning sun in his eyes to find himself side by side with her: his arm around her, his hand on her bottom. She had huddled up to him for warmth.

He froze in terror. He'd awakened once in his life beside someone. That had resulted in a badly broken arm and ribs, a terrible accident just because he was what he was. Always since, he'd made sure of waking up alone.

Lina stirred when he scooted away. She smiled sleepily to see him. "Good morning." Her expression changed to chagrin. "Good grief, morning breath."

Lon had to chuckle at her as she covered her mouth with her hand.

She jumped up and made her way quickly to the pool. "I stink. I'm going to take a bath. I'd advise you to do the same."

"Yes ma'am. I'll do that after you get through."

"So you're going to be here when I return?" She began to pull off her gown and he turned away.

"I'll be here."

Well, that was an improvement at least. Lina had to think of something that would be an instant cure for him, but she couldn't concentrate. She was too happy that she'd helped him and that he was staying.

As she bathed she began to sing softly, then louder as she forgot that anyone might be listening. Celebratory songs of life let her express her joy. She brushed her teeth and dove down to the bottom of the pool for a final rinse. When she put her hand on the bottom to commune with the earth, the planet was warm and motherly as always.

I'm so happy, she told it.

It answered, ***Better things coming, worse things coming. Tests ahead.***

I don't care, she told Earth. ***I'll be happy right now, right this minute, with what I have. I don't dare expect any more.*** And then it was time to come up for air. She ported two towels from home for herself. Her last two she left for him at the edge of the pool.

Tucking the one around herself, she let it ride low on her breasts just to bedevil him and wrapped her hair up in the other one. "Next," she said as they passed each other. Good, he hadn't missed the cleavage.

Lina kept her back turned to him in respect for his need for privacy. She dressed while he was in the pool, porting in one of her dozen *Star Trek* tee shirts, cutoffs and finally a change of underwear– her laciest, she realized ruefully. Not that anyone would ever see them. Something had to be done about Londo. Carefully she folded her chemise and put it on the sand. If he still wanted it, he could have it.

Lon seemed as if he were going to take a while. She gritted her teeth. Drummed up her courage. Concentrated for a long, long time–

And ported herself to the beach.

Another try, another long visualization... Back to the clearing.

Now she practiced porting around the area making sure that she took her time with each attempt. She ran a psychic and physical scan of herself after each port to check that everything was where it was supposed to be, colors were true, that her butt didn't arrive on backward. It took a lot of concentration, focused attunement to her body, but she figured that as time went on she'd get better at it.

And her practice gave her an idea.

Lina looked up just in time to see Londo descend from above the treetops. She'd thought he was still in the pool, but here he was flying, flying up close, actually flying as naturally as a cloud travels the sky! And carrying bananas and a frying pan and a full basket of groceries. He hung in midair before he dropped gracefully to the sand: an angel descending to the earth on invisible wings of glory.

"Breakfast," the angel told her. "I stole a few things from the estate west of here. I don't think they'll mind. I believe I owe you a dinner."

As she watched, awestruck, he gathered firewood and lit it just by blowing on it, then produced enough from the basket to prepare fried eggs and toast with marmalade. There was orange juice and small juice glasses to go along with everything. He'd forgotten napkins, but Lina ported in some from home. She took the bananas and added brown sugar, butter and cinnamon to the pan to make fried bananas as a decadent dessert.

"Very nice," Londo said with a small smile as she finished. He washed his hands in the pool and came back in time to watch her practice more porting as he smoothed his still-damp hair with the comb that he slipped back into his vest.

"Valiant After the Bath," Lina decided the painting of the event would be. Her heart stopped for a second. He certainly looked god-like, just as he appeared on CNN every night.

"What's wrong?" Lon asked. "Did you port okay?"

Sheepishly, she admitted, "You're Valiant now, not Londo."

"Well, it's true we've never been seen together, but–"

"I've been thinking," she interrupted before he could start his arguments again. Before anything, she had to get this out. "You need a training program."

"A what?"

"Wait, wait. I'm jumping ahead of myself. Londo, are you still telepathic? Now that your other powers have returned?"

Can you hear me?

"Okay, you are. So here's what we do. Recalibrate the double feedback loop system. See how far that takes us. Wing it from there with whatever comes up, a little at a time. Set a goal, shoot for it, and if we miss, we try again."

"I am not going to risk hurting you."

"So don't. We just recalibrate and take it one– sure– step at a time. Very slowly. Keep recalibrating. I think it could work. I think we could get you to the point that you could go all the way with someone, a para, but maybe just another mega. I don't know. If we hit a snag we stop, see what happened and then figure where to go from there."

"No."

"Are you afraid of this? Or are you just trying to back away?"

When he looked at her, the expression on his face was unreadable. "*Voyons donc,* the first time we did the double-feedback we made mistakes. That was fine then. Now those mistakes could kill you in an instant."

"So we take it slower this time. We're good at the double-loop now, Lon. I'm game. How about you?"

"No. Absolutely not."

But he paused. He paused! Lina knew she saw it. Maybe she was getting through.

"Lina. What do you get out of it?"

"What do you mean?"

"I mean..." Londo swallowed and then set his jaw, staring her down. "Do you get a thrill out of making it with Valiant? Or is it something you have to prove to yourself as a psychic? Is it still something you're doing out of pity? Or maybe a story you can tell the people back at the office?"

She stood there, stunned. "How can you ask such things!"

"I have to be sure. Why do you want to be with me?"

"Why, I want to help you. I took a vow, remember?"

"And I didn't ask for help this time, priest. Why are you doing this?"

"Oh, suddenly there's something wrong with helping others?"

"What's in it for you?"

Lina turned her back on him. She didn't want to think about her own selfish reason. She didn't want to face it. She'd spent a lifetime building up barriers. This was no time to unveil a vulnerable point.

Vulnerable, he said wonderingly in her mind. **What leaves you vulnerable?**

He'd know if she tried to lie or fudge her way out of this. But how could she tell him when she couldn't even tell herself?

"What are you afraid of? Tell me. You can tell me anything." He stood behind her now, barely touching her, afraid of his own power. But he was there.

"No," she breathed. "I can't."

"You can. Tell me. Tell me."

She clenched her fists and finally released them with a shake. "Oh hell, it's just too stupid," she muttered and moved away, knowing that he wouldn't touch her. But he followed her, shadowed her so she could feel his breath on the back of her ears.

"What is? Say it out loud."

"Oh god. Okay."

She steeled herself and couldn't do it. A lump in her chest kept the words from rising.

"Say it."

She felt sick. Don't make her do this! "Okay." She tried to catch her breath, to summon up energy to make her mouth work. "Okay. I think I'm in love with you. Is that good enough?"

Her eyes welled with tears and she clapped her hands over her mouth. She made sure he couldn't see her face. *I get laid for the first time, and I fall in love with the guy! Stupid! Stupid!* She ran to the other side of the clearing, her back facing him.

"It took you the hell long enough!" he called after her. He followed her with a deliberate step, slower than hers. "You're afraid to love," he accused her. "Of course. You're not good enough; you're not worthy of love, so you turn it around and say you can't allow yourself to love someone. Like me with all my abandonment issues. I feel abandoned; therefore I abandon. You abandon people who want to love you. You deny them and you deny yourself."

Lina made a noncommittal noise.

"Just because you hate your father is no reason to hate all men!"

She shook her head. "I don't... I don't hate my..."

"And they make you tell him that you love him. *Crisse*, you don't have any idea what love is! You think it's some kind of punishment. Well, it's not, no matter how bad the circumstances are."

She wanted to leave. Now. Maybe she could teleport home. She wrapped her arms around herself, trying to hide. Pull the earth energy up around herself...

"You can't hide from me that way." He stood behind her. "Lina, say it again."

She might as well. It was out of the bag now and she couldn't outrun Valiant. "I think I'm in love with you." Barely audible, but it took all her energy. She slid to the ground in a little heap at his feet.

"Now say it with pink polka-dots."

"I'm in love with you." Her voice was muffled by her position but it was stronger, even if she didn't notice.

"Now with giant parakeets making rude comments."

"I'm in love with you." She gave a small, strangled laugh as her insides clenched.

He walked around in front of her and squatted on the sand. "Look at me," he told her in a no-nonsense voice. Slowly her head rose from the huddle. "Now quantify it," Londo said softer. "How deep is it?"

She was serious now, not afraid to meet his eyes anymore. She'd jumped in; might as well finish it off and drown. "Deeper than any ocean. Brighter than the sun. Sharp as a knife in my heart. Don't go, Lon. Don't leave me. Please."

"I'm here. I want you to listen to me, and I want you to believe me for once. Trust me. Carolina, I love you. Higher than the moon, big as the sky, tender as your breast under my hand. I love you, dammit!"

"Oh."

Did the entire universe tip onto its side? A wave of wonder and then utter rapture washed over her as she tumbled with it. Falling, falling—

He knelt next to her. "I'm crazy about you, kitten. I thought I'd been in love before, but it was never like this. Never!"

Lina rose uncertainly to her knees and laid her hand on top of his. Taking a deep breath, she said, "Then you've got to recalibrate, Lon. Please."

He smiled at her crookedly. "Yes, love. We'll recalibrate." He shook his head. "A training program. I've never heard of one like this. What's our goal?"

To fuck each other until our brains turn to jelly, Lina immediately thought.

Lon laughed.

"Oh god, you didn't hear that, did you? I don't know where that came from." Lina was embarrassed down to her toenails. Lon probably thought she was some kind of gutter trash now, she thought miserably. Dad always said she'd wind up in a gutter.

"I don't know, it sounded like an honest goal to me. I just caught it before it went through any kind of filter. If I'm going to be a telepath, I'll have to get used to that kind of thing."

"I'm used to reading other people and not being read myself. I'll watch my language next time."

"At any rate, we have Goal A." Londo grinned at Lina's blush. What a radiant face she had, even like this. "Now, where to begin?" So carefully he picked up her right hand and held it lightly between his. Human flesh was the most fragile of eggshells.

He gazed into her eyes and she into his for a long time until the unnaturalness of his touch reached Lina's mind. She looked at his hands– at Valiant's hands. The hands that could shred steel with an easy twist.

"Ah... It's not that I don't trust you, Lon," Lina said. "But I'm right-handed. Could you do this with my left hand?"

"This does not bode well..."

"Oh, hush. Just because I'm in love with you doesn't mean I can't be practical."

"*D'accord,* fair enough." He picked up her left hand, and she noticed how very rigid his touch was even though his hand trembled ever so slightly.

"Feel it from my point of view."

He tried but his attempt was clumsy. Lina decided to work on her own loop and narrowed her concentration to his fingers. She felt what he felt: a kind of static from the double barrier of his normal invulnerability and of fear because he was steeled to not hurt her.

"Relax more," she told him. She unwedged her hand from his and unsuccessfully tried to shake the immovable object until he let it swing free in her grasp. "That's better. Try again."

She returned her concentration to his hand and found herself diving deep, talking to the cells there. ***Hi, guys; it's just me. Lina. Nothing to hurt you here. You don't have to be afraid.*** She sent out loving thoughts to the cells, thanking them for doing their jobs so well. **ize my own reactions so you could... read them...*** *Good cells. Don't be afraid.***

Fear permeated them. She used her other hand to stroke the etheric level, just inches from the skin. She drew the fear out and down into the earth. Magnetic passes gathered the excess electrical buildup.

ize my own reactions so you could... *It's just me. Recognize me.* She kept her thoughts gentle and brought them up to the level of the fingers. **ize my own reactions so you could... *Recognize me. Recognize me,*** she repeated, and then expanded her awareness to the entire hand. **ize my own reactions so you could... *Calm, relax, easy.***

"What in the world are you doing?" Lon's voice brought her out of it.

"Talking to your hand, sorry. I should have been concentrating more on emphasizing my own reactions so you could... read them..." She realized that he was massaging her hand, and that it felt very nice indeed. And he knew it.

"Well, do it some more," he said. "All of a sudden I felt relaxed, and it was easy to establish the feedback. Very natural sensation, like I wasn't doing anything." He carefully placed her hand down on her leg and then ran his fingers up her arm to the shoulder. She could still feel tension permeating him.

"Hmm."

"You have an idea," he grinned, crooking an eyebrow at her. "Keep it slow, whatever it is."

"You need to relax all over," she declared. "How about a back massage? I'm not certified, but I've never had any complaints."

He shook his head. "It won't work, not with my powers. I'm invulnerable."

"So, that means you can't relax? It's the relaxation we're after. We get that, and the feedback loop might start to work everywhere."

He shook his head again.

"At least let me try."

"Eh, *rapport*, whatever."

"Awright, what a great attitude." She tried to figure out how to do this. Oh well, if she got it wrong she could always try again. And he'd let her, wouldn't he? He said he loved her. Londo said he loved her! "Vest and shirt have to go."

He obeyed, grumbling a bit about the impossibility of it all.

"Oh, lie down." She pushed him. Absolutely nothing happened. It was as if she'd tried to push a gigantic marble statue or a building or the Rock of Gibraltar.

The enormity of the task at hand hit her. Still, she couldn't afford to think about it. It might daunt him and send him back to being worse than before. "I said, lie down, please." And he did.

"Carve out a place for your face in the sand," she ordered. "I don't want you to have any excess tension right here." She drew a line across his neck and shoulders with her fingers to show him. He did as he was told.

"Okay, I'm ready," Lon said in a "let's humor her" manner. He glanced back over his shoulder at her.

"I'm not." Her voice muffled as she pulled her tee shirt over her head, then smoothed out her hair. She gave him an innocent look as he stared at the lacy, low-cut black bra.

"Anything more coming off?" he asked, raising an eyebrow.

"Maybe later," Lina said, tossing the shirt aside. "I get very warm with all the energies when I'm working. Now lie down."

Nothing like a little incentive. She got to work. Lon caught the thought and chuckled. Good. She rubbed her hands together, working up energy, as she considered his beautiful broad, ripply-brown back.

Wait. There was some oil in the product samples cabinet back at work. She could picture it on the shelf. And now it was in her hand. She poured the fragrant oil into a little puddle into her palms, then rubbed them together to warm it. Mm, roses for relaxation.

She dipped her hands down to his physical body and just let them lie there while her mind went down into the cells. **Hi, back, it's me,** Lina said to it.

She let her own strong etheric field, which ended three or four inches from her own body, brush up against Lon's, so much stronger. She'd never felt an etheric field go so far– it must extend a foot from him– but she didn't let it faze her.

Recognize me. I'm the one who loves you. Relax. Tensions out, relaxation in. All is calm. All is love.

She moved her hands around the tissue she was talking to and extended her awareness into the entire muscle. After some minutes of rubbing the area, it began to flow with the movement of her hands. The rub became a tight massage.

Good muscle, she cooed to it. She sang a wordless song softly to his body as she worked. **Relax and recognize me.**

Every few minutes she had to take her hands off and redirect the toxic energy that flowed out of the muscles away from Lon and herself, and down into the earth which could recycle it and use it well. She used her breath to bring white light into the muscles, turning the light to blue to relax them.

In a while she realized that the massage was now a normal one, with Lon's back reacting the way anyone else's muscles would. She settled into giving him a thorough treatment along his back and arms to relax him everywhere. **Recognize *me,*** she chanted to the cells as they began to ease all over. ***I will never hurt you. I love you.***

God, how she loved everything about him. She loved the tiniest cells in his body; she loved the electrical currents that crackled and flowed through the nerves, the deep colors of his blood, the strength of his bones, and his strong heartbeat that proved that he was as real as could be. She massaged the love into him and the tensions flowed away. There was nothing for them to fight; they welcomed her.

"Don't fall asleep on me, Lon," she chided gently as she eased back to take a break. He was limp under her and she regarded the job with pride and hope. She had stopped at the waistband of his pants. They'd see how this went. If she had to massage every inch of him to get this to work, she'd happily do it.

"Hmm..." He *had* been dozing, or almost. "I'm awake."

"Good. Time to roll over. Let's do the front."

"Um. Okay." He rolled on his side to lean on his elbow, blinking himself more awake.

She slid over and sat next to him. As she waited for him to assume the position, she stretched to let out the tensions in her own back. Massage was strenuous work under ordinary circumstances.

Londo paused to stretch himself, feeling in wonder the relaxing effects of the massage as he lifted each shoulder in turn and rotated it. He settled to gaze at her as she took her break, her arm resting on her knee. Some locks of hair stuck wetly to her face. A fine sheen of sweat on her body dried in the cool late-morning breeze here in the shade at the edge of the forest. It would leave her skin salty and sweet, he remembered. God, she had great breasts. Long, shapely legs. Great everything. Lush. And those green eyes...

She turned to look at something in the forest, squinting in the sunlight. The breeze lifted her hair and fanned it out around her.

Londo surged toward her. She turned to the movement, turned to look into his eyes. Gathering her into his arms, he kissed her tenderly. For a moment he concentrated on the feedback loop but then all there was was Lina and Lina's sweet mouth. He smoothed the wet hair back from her face and kissed her eyelids, then ran his mouth back down to hers. She shifted in his arms to better reach him.

Relax, he told her, told her body. ***Recognize me.***

His hands traveled over her shoulders, down her back– and into an obstacle. He unhooked the bra with little difficulty and slid it from her shoulders. "Better," he whispered to her, and then bent to his pleasurable work.

She trembled on all fours in front of him, clutching blindly at the grass as she groaned. Behind her, he knelt conscious only of giving it all he had, while monitors in his brain and hers confirmed that no physical harm was done.

Londo's breath rebounded from her warm neck as he bent over her. They rocked together like a storm building against the ocean, elemental forces of creation. He slowed and tightened and bucked with a wordless shout. So in tune with him, she let out a cry and welcomed it.

Lon released her in one way, but took her in his arms and rolled with her on the packed sand, both of them laughing and out of breath. Then he gathered her close and smoothed the thick, tangled hair away from her face so he could kiss her.

"I don't know about you, but my brain certainly turned to jelly," she said, still laughing.

"I'll tell you what happened to mine if I ever recover," he replied. "Thanks, coach." He was suddenly serious. "Thank you, Lina. Thank you so much." And he slowly kissed her all over her face, her neck, her shoulders. He loved her so much... and now they had all the time in the world.

"Anytime, Londo," he realized she was whispering in his ear. "Anytime you need me for this, all you have to do is call."

He gazed into her eyes and knew that when she looked at him she saw the scared little boy, the lonely man, the parahero, all in one. Accepting of all of them and more.

"Or if you just need me to listen, I'll be there."

"Tell me," he urged her. "Tell me. Tell me."

"I love you, Londo," she told him, speaking to his soul. "I love you forever!"

He buried his face against the softness of her as the tears ran from his eyes.

Now his dark head lay against hers as he slept. Lina regarded him wonderingly. Imagine, someone loving *her*, Lina Muttbutt, Lina the Unlovable! This wasn't some fantasy she'd dreamed up. This was the most wonderful of realities. This was the universe finally saving her, the universe finally loving her. The universe was Londo, and he was all there was.

She had Londo Rand here in her arms and eternity coursing through her soul. She had Londo to live for now, Londo to love. All her goals were shifting to make room for this new priority: protect and support Londo Rand for as long as he wanted her and beyond. There was nothing as important, as exciting, as fulfilling as that.

The prospect of living in a reality that held such a being as him was suddenly the most wonderful of fates. Here she'd thought that God spent His days playing her for a laugh, when He had been smiling on her all the time. Certainly she was the most blessed of women!

"Thank you, God," Lina whispered. She could feel the love everywhere now. It pulsed in every living thing from the tiniest speck of dust in the air to the gigantic planet below and around her. She wanted to throw her arms wide and shout her love in return. *Thank you, thank you! I love all of you!* Londo stirred in her arms, God's personal answer to her:

I love you, too.

Part Two

1

The full moon floated just above an indigo horizon. Beneath it silver rippled the South Pacific in a band that stretched toward the two of them on the shore.

Their world had narrowed to this: cool moonlight, the sound of beaching waves, and the warmth of two bodies wrapped around each other. It was all Lina had ever wanted: a snug cocoon of absolute safety. Having Lon beside her was the fulfillment of a wish she'd never dared make.

Londo lounged propped against a palm tree. He was shirtless but otherwise dressed in his famous black-on-black Valiant uniform, the vest loose over his wide, toasty-brown chest. He held Lina in his arms. She was half-clad in that terribly sexy black lingerie, wearing his gray-striped shirt with its torn right sleeve like a jacket against the comparative chill of the tropical night.

That white chemise she'd started out in was tucked securely into one of the pockets in Londo's vest as a souvenir of this precious time together.

"I love you." Londo's deep voice seemed that of the sea and sky. "*Ma chérie.*"

How miraculous that anyone would ever love her, stupid old Muttbutt! It was a day of miracles, a week, a lifetime. "I love you, too," she told him with all her heart.

She snuggled in his powerful arms. His mind and hers wrapped together as well. A hypnotic languor settled over them as they watched the moon rise over the ocean and night settle upon the land. Maybe another hour here like this, Lina thought, and then Londo would take her home. To *his* home, that was, to Montreal for a romantic day of who knew what? Their lives were just beginning again. The universe was an incredibly beautiful and peaceful place when you knew how to look at it. Love let you see it in the right light. This was what all the fuss, all the poetry and art, all the hope of humanity was about.

And yet a tiny, insidious worm of a thought squirmed through Lina's brain: Londo was Valiant. Even if she was the only woman in the universe Lon could have sex with, how long could this love affair continue before he became bored with her?

The thought gave her too much pain so she shoved it hard away, and when Londo stroked her the thought disappeared as if it had never existed. The only thing that mattered now was him.

He twisted a long lock of her curly auburn hair in his fingers. "I have a friend who's never going to believe this." Lon murmured, his dark eyes half-closed.

"Oh! He's blue!" Lina exclaimed. "Oh, sorry. I didn't mean that to sound racist. But… He's *blue*, love." The mental picture recalled a medium teal-ish-skinned, violet-haired man in a baggy yellow jumpsuit– very colorful, like TV from the Sixties. The vision Londo held of him showed him standing in what could only be a laboratory. It had that kind of feel, antiseptic and yet messy at the same time; tick-tick-tick with a machinery vibe. Futuristic.

"Yeah, that's Wiley. Wilder Mem-Bazer." Lon nodded. "It means 'Five Minds.' He's got them all tucked away in that brilliant head of his."

Funny. He didn't look like an overbearing mental giant. He seemed like he should be mowing his yard in a suburban neighborhood before the weekend family barbecue. Darrin Stephens without the attitude.

Lon smiled at her mental simile. "Eh, he's a real funny guy. You'd like him. He's crazy in his own way– not like 'The Nutty Professor' crazy. A normal guy kind of crazy."

"Schizoid? I mean, with five minds…"

"Not schizoid– although he does talk to himself. But never, ever hint to him that he might be." Londo chuckled at a memory. "He and I are members of an interstellar–"

Lina clenched his arm hard. "Something's wrong!"

A finger-thin bolt of lightning streaked by inches away from her face, blinding her for a moment.

Before she could even think, Lon shoved her behind himself and leapt to his feet. Just in time. More lightning bolts crashed through the clearing. They ricocheted off Lon without affecting him. He was Valiant now.

Lina's first instinct was to roll up like a bug and hide away from the world, but she was also very okay with cowering behind his protection. Clamping down on a whimper before it could escape her mouth, she blinked wide-eyed at the situation and hugged herself into as small a target as she could. Less for Lon to have to protect.

Londo reached out and sank his fingers *into* their palm tree. He gave a kick to its trunk. It caved in so he could snatch the entire tree as if he were grabbing a paper towel off its roll. With a whirling motion, he tossed it so it caught the brunt of four more lightning strikes. The tree blasted into shreds.

Lina wrapped her arms around her head. Tiny pinpricks of wood shrapnel stung her legs. Strange how the lightning buzzed and crackled, but never thundered. Now she clairvoyantly sensed the people who surrounded them. Weaponry, too. Through her daze it seemed time stilled.

But not for Lon. He'd jumped up and hovered in the air, tossing more trees at targets she couldn't see. Jagged lightning targeted him at an apex of hellish fury, but other than his hair standing on end– or at least through the glare Lina thought it did– he was unscathed.

But behind his cool professionalism, she could tell that he was also struggling to switch gears from the mental state he'd just been in. He searched for a more effective weapon to use.

"Hah," he said. Only Lina could hear it because he'd thought the triumph as well. He darted down and came back up with a cannon that he used as a baseball bat to attract and deflect the lightning.

Screams from the northern edge of the woods answered his attack. Wood shreds filled the air as the crossfire caught more trees.

Lina could teleport herself, but what about Lon? She'd never tried to port him before, not consciously. She dug her fingers into the calming earth energy of the sand and set herself to forget about the commotion and danger. She tuned into his body to prepare for the port.

He sensed what she was doing. "Just port yourself! Now!"

But she almost had it! Then suddenly the cold, hard barrel of a gun pressed into her cheek. Someone grabbed the back of her shirt and lifted her. He grabbed her around the waist for a firmer hold. In spite of herself she let out a squeal. Londo spun around in mid-air.

"Back off, Valiant!" the man who held her yelled. "I've got your girlfriend. Just take it nice and slow."

The man had the grip of a sasquatch and stood about as tall as one– a para? Though she was six feet tall, Lina's feet kicked in the air.

"Don't try any of your Valiant tricks. There are a dozen guns trained on her. You take one of us out and she gets it before you can blink."

Lon's eyes locked with hers. He told her, **_I mean it. I can get more done with you not here. Go home if you can. Call the ParaNet. I'll meet you later._**

Okay. She prepared for the port by taking a breath—only to have it knocked out of her as a yellow-white energy bolt blasted her shoulder. The bunched shirt had left it bare and unprotected.

"Don't move, Valiant!" someone cried out.

Lina yelped as the burning pain shattered her concentration, like grabbing a hot pan on the stove and not being able to let go. The brute who had her squeezed tighter and laughed. He hadn't even flinched at the blast. Now his touch made her skin crawl. Lights began to flash in front of her eyes and she felt faint. The white curtain of unthinking panic threatened to descend. Her phobia– Not now! Don't touch her! Don't touch!

Londo eased back down to earth, facing her and her captor. His snarl caught the moonlight. He twisted the half-slagged remains of the cannon into a pretzel and then dropped it on the sand. Its dead bulk was three times as large as he. Slowly he flexed his dangerous body in a futile challenge.

A woman's voice called, "Good boy, Londo. Stay."

2

From the tropical forest stepped the bottle blonde who had been in Lon's thoughts the night before. She was medium height, forties or early fifties, gaunt but beautiful if you could get past the cruelty of her expression.

She pointed at Lina. "That was just a sample, girl. No more spacey looks from you! If she gets that distant look in her eye again, shoot her," the woman ordered the small cadre of camoed troops whose guns were aimed at Lina.

This of course must be Terry Whatsherface– Rhodes.

Now that the need for stealth was gone, engines came to life. Trees swayed as bulky shadows lumbered beneath them. Dozens of men streamed up through the woods and from the beach– more and more and more.

Lina cursed herself. She should have sensed them and the danger! But she'd been too preoccupied just by being in Londo's arms...

Terry stepped in front of Lina. "I don't trust telepaths." She slapped her face hard. "You better not try any mind tricks on anyone here." The blow left Lina's ears ringing, but the phobic curtain of panic retreated.

"Stop it, Terry!"

Terry whirled to Lon, who stood helplessly, clenching his fists at his sides. He merited a larger focused group of soldiers. They surrounded him in a semicircle, but their readied weapons were bulky, huge-barreled and terrifying. These were attached by blinking hoses and cords to machinery others pulled behind them on tough, track-wheeled platforms.

"Why, hello again, Londo," Terry said sweetly as if she'd just noticed him. "Oh, we won't kill her. She's just to keep you in line." Terry turned her head. "Get some spots in here, damn it! What do I pay you people for?"

In response two bobbing lights came on as running soldiers carried them. They added six others to focus on Londo. The sharp accents and black shadows made the scene more unreal than it was already. In the lights Londo seemed to glow like a statue– or a sacrifice.

Port out, he commanded Lina.

Can't concentrate. Damn it, nothing like this had ever happened to her. She'd only been porting for two days. Focus!

When he spoke to Terry his voice sounded far off as Lina struggled within her own mind. "What's the plan? What mood are you in this time?"

"I didn't appreciate you blowing up my cannon the other day. I paid a lot for it. It got you good though, eh?"

As more spots lit up the clearing, Lina's guard squeezed her hard. He pinched her on the shoulder where she had been hit, chuckling when she sucked in a gasp.

"Your fault for getting involved with Valiant," he growled in her ear.

Her lips curled back, baring her teeth. She wasn't frightened any more. Dark anger rushed through her. Her concentration sharpened like the edge of a hunting blade. She'd port him into the next world for using her to threaten Londo!

"Don't, Lina!" Londo barked. He stood stock-still but his expression carried his imperious order home as no other thing could.

Lina froze. She clamped her jaw in frustration. It had been a stupid thought, but she did stupid things when she was angry.

"Don't try anything here," Lon repeated. **Let me handle it. I'll get us out of here, chérie. Terry gets too cock-sure. She always slips up.**

"And what did she think she might do?" Terry purred to Lon.

Remember, I'm Valiant. I can handle anything. You port out when you can. You stay safe! "Let her go, Terr," Londo urged the mercenary leader. "Whatever she's been here for she's served her purpose. You don't need her any more, and it's a messy business disposing of corpses."

She walked around him but eyed Lina. "We seem to have struck a little nerve, eh?" She stage-whispered to her, "He falls in love so easily."

"An interesting situation," a loud male voice from the crowd behind Londo declared. "Let's deal. I believe we have the better hand here."

Londo's face twisted. "Menlo," he growled, and a wave of sudden uncertainty rolled from him through Lina's mind before he could stanch it.

Terry chortled. "You didn't know? Oh, Lon, this is rich. You thought that I could pick up all these wonderful guns from Walmart?"

Dr. Theodore Menlo stepped into the open, and Lina blanched. "Terry, no slight to you," he said, "but there's no way in hell you could have designed these weapons."

Londo had had to tell her about Terry Whatsherface, but Dr. Menlo she'd heard of. For years the evening news had featured his terrifying international crimes. Two villains after Londo– this was very bad.

"No offense taken, Ted. You build 'em; I buy 'em."

Stuffing his hands into his rear jeans pockets, Dr. Menlo scrutinized Londo. The lean doctor's shirttails hung out above his jeans, flapping in the ocean breeze, and his long brown hair kept getting behind his glasses and into his eyes.

"So tell me, Rand, are all the powers back now? Are you at full power or a portion thereof? Absolutely invulnerable, or just a teensy bit not? Terry, can we test this now? I'd like to get a reading as close to the time of powerlessness as possible. How long has it been since your powers came back, Rand?"

Lon stood silent.

Terry watched Londo's face. "I'd be willing to bet it's been less than an hour," she offered.

"But that radar reading last night–"

Lina didn't know what Dr. Menlo was talking about until she remembered Londo leaping into the air with her clinging to his back. They must have hung above the island for a minute or two.

Terry shrugged. "I know Londo. Londo doesn't like to stick around at the scene of the crime, as it were."

"And there is an explanation for that. Our bet?"

"It's impossible. Here. Someone with an E547– you've calibrated those, haven't you?– take a shot at Valiant. Wait, not everyone. Cottle, you." She pointed at one of the soldiers and then turned to face Londo, her arms crossed over her chest as she commanded the scene. "Full power. Somewhere non-vital."

As Lina caught her breath, a man with a rifle thick as his own heavily muscled arm took aim. Lon shifted slightly, eying his attacker.

"Stay put, Lon. We still have guns on *her*."

Cottle pressed the trigger button and a long pulse of blue-white light shot out of his gun to hit Londo's left shoulder– and bounce off across the clearing. It struck one of the soldiers, roasting him before he could even scream. Lina gasped at the abruptness, the coldness as the fellow's neighbors glanced at the smoldering, blackened corpse and then shuffled back into place.

"That's good, Terry." Londo gave the woman a hard grin. "Let's do that again."

"Shut up!" Terry paced angrily. Menlo squinted and stuck out his lower lip as if he were determining voltages.

"*Eh bien*, that's one less man on the payroll. Or do you offer widow's benefits?" Londo's eyes narrowed at Cottle. "You'll be sorry. Dead sorry."

"I said, shut up!" Terry motioned to another and pointed at Lina. The man flinched, but took aim and held it.

"I'll be quiet," Londo said quickly. "Don't hurt her!"

Terry did not give the order to fire.

Lina grimaced. She was Londo's safety leash now. If it weren't for her, he could mop up these guys with impunity.

She had to port herself. Even if it were only down the beach, it would give him enough time. No– she'd port home and call the ParaNet, as he'd said. In the few times she'd had to practice her new power, distance didn't seem to affect her porting.

Home was this… She began to build the familiar picture in her mind, to feel her own body and the space it held now, then the place she wanted it to be…

She cried out as a scalding blast hit her in the stomach.

"What– Londo! Stay there!" Lina heard Terry say imperiously as she hissed in pain.

A strange man's voice from her left: "She was looking funny, Commander."

"Hold your fire! Any more and we might set off our guest here. See, Londo? She's not hurt that much, eh. My men just have nervous trigger fingers. You keep that in mind."

Londo's voice was tight as Lina opened her eyes again, gasping. "A trade-off, Terry. Her safety for my good conduct."

"We were doing that already, dear." Her laugh rang low and vicious.

Menlo brushed the hair out from his glasses and then cocked his head this way and that, taking in the situation. Then he strolled across the clearing to Lina. He kept his hands in his pockets in a play of unconcern.

"Terry," he said, "a willing bargain could work well in our favor. An hour, two hours studying him with his cooperation would be worth the lives of an entire city. Make it a day or two in exchange for the girl, Rand."

"I'll do it," Londo promised quickly. "Let her go."

A crook came to the side of Menlo's mouth. "I didn't say we'd let her go now. I will promise that we'll keep her safe. This could be a valuable study in itself." Menlo tilted Lina's chin to the left and right in a hard grip as she glared at him. "A real psychic. You know, before we started this project I was convinced that it was all hokum. Now I'm not sure at all. Are you real, girl?"

"Your wife still loves you," she said to him.

"What?"

"Your wife, the one you hide. And little… Alber… Alex. He calls you 'Poppy Ted,' doesn't he? They still love you, despite everything."

His eyes went to slits.

"She's looking for you. You didn't tell her where you were going, so she's hired someone to find you. There was a fight. She said things that she's sorry for now."

"Shut up."

"She wants to tell you that she still loves you. Dora wants you back."

"Shut up. Shut the hell up!" He jerked his chin at one of the mercenaries and Lina found herself gagged with someone's sandy handkerchief. Her green eyes flashed at Menlo.

"Didn't know you were married, Menlo," Londo said conversationally across the gap between them. "Dora, is it? I should send a card. Or are you registered somewhere?"

"Shut up, Rand," Menlo growled. He glanced back at Lina. "Here's our deal: three days with you, two days with her. The girl's released unharmed at a location of our choosing when we're done."

"Wait!" Terry cried. "What do I get out of this? I don't want him for scientific study. And I certainly don't want her. Look, I'm the one who financed this venture. I was to have full control!"

"Of course, of course." Menlo returned to Terry and Londo. "Tell you what. You keep Rand for an extra day or two for your part. Hell, Terry, you just need him for a half-hour. I'm sure he'd spare you that if he knew that every moment meant Ms. O'Kelly's safety. I'll keep track of her personally after we finish the testing."

Londo's voice rasped when he spoke. "You touch her and you're dead, Menlo. Terry, name your exchange. You have my word that I'll keep it."

"Your word. I'm supposed to trust that?"

"Absolutely."

She gave him a laugh that held more than a hint of fury. "And how many people have you fooled with that line, eh? You lie smoother than anyone I've ever known. You lie to further your own ends, to get you everything you want and then some. You lie, you liar!"

She slapped him hard, but her hand rebounded from his chin as she cringed. "Ah shit. Why can you make me so mad?" She cradled her hand against herself, biting her lip. "Shit, shit!"

"Keep on target," Menlo reprimanded her. "Remember why we're here."

"Why are you here, Menlo?" Londo asked, and Menlo turned back to him.

"Experiments. Scientific curiosity. Questions to be answered. How the hell did you evade everyone for so long? We'd actually given up on finding you until…well, until last night. And then we find you here– forty miles from the starting point."

"I have my ways."

"I'm afraid you'll have to be more exact than that."

"I explained it to some of Terry's men in the jungle. You'll find their bodies if you look hard."

Menlo raised his hand without looking back. Lina cried out behind the gag as her guard squeezed the breath out of her with his fist, setting off her burned stomach again. Her mind swam as waves of fire and phobia slapped sharply at the remains of her concentration.

"How long since your powers came back?" Menlo demanded.

"…A day. Call him off, Menlo."

"A day?" Terry asked, still livid. "I don't believe it."

"It does open up all kinds of possibilities." Menlo turned to consider Lina. "I may have won the main bet, Terry. I told you so."

"Get real, Ted."

Londo scowled at the clusterfuck. This was all his fault. He should have gotten the two of them away first thing, as soon as his powers had come back. *Idiot!*

If he could detonate two of the guns over there, he thought it would be enough of a diversion to grab Lina and run. Maybe. He hadn't missed the way none of these mercs had dropped their duty posture when one of their own had been killed before their eyes. These were cold-blooded killers.

Above all, his first duty was to protect Lina. Lina belonged to him, the most precious thing in his life. In the rough hands of her guard she looked like a pale doll. Damn that she wasn't dressed. He hated the thought of her paraded in front of these men like that, and he knew it could only hurt the concentration she needed to port out.

But she didn't seem to be readying for porting. She was a civilian. Untrained in how to react in a combat situation. Her eyes were wide on him with fright, warm pink lips parted in concern for him.

Londo didn't want her ever to be frightened again. She was his to protect. He'd get her out of here alive and well.

"Main bet?" he asked to gain him time to consider more options. "This was all to settle a bet?"

A dangerous, smug smile settled on Terry's face. "I may finally win enough to buy me that country I've wanted. Ted had a theory about you and your vaunted powers. Me– I've always thought you were a bit of a telepath. I thought if we got you together with another telepath, it might, ah, solve your little problem. But Ted– he's been researching psychics lately– he said no, let's see what a psychic healer can do. Have you had sex with her since the powers came back, sweetie?"

"Terry–"

"Did you appreciate my little gift to you? Isn't she something? She took me a long time to find."

"What?" Despite knowing Lina's mind, a sharp pang of suspicion shocked through Londo before he could shove it down. Emotions and dangerous situations didn't mix, not if you wanted to win. He was used to winning.

Terry obviously enjoyed her position here. "It took a while to find just who to get for you. Something cute. Big boobs; you always did like 'em big. Somebody smart enough for you to talk to. We did a whole computer date match-up.

"It was a challenge to test her without her knowing she was being tested. We had to make fourth-generation arrangements. You know, hire someone who hired someone else to test her. The things one has to do when dealing with telepaths–! Quite a powerful one, too, eh? We were surprised at that. Rotting away in some podunk town down in the States.

"Oh, and in the porn biz as well. A bonus there; did she tell you? She did. I can see you're not surprised. How sweet that we found someone who could use their own expertise to ease you past your virginity."

She laughed at him.

"Why, Terry?" Londo's fists opened and closed helplessly. Those snipers kept dead-eye aim on Lina. A diversion might not give him the time he needed. **Lina, you've got to take her over. Use mind control.**

3

Lina's guts clenched. This was Londo's life here. The unforgivable sin of enslaving a being's will versus saving Londo–

Even without her spirit guides shouting at her not to do it, she knew that this was a line she must never cross.

But it was *Londo*.

Then tell me how to do it, he said. **She doesn't know I'm a telepath now. And don't port anything yet besides yourself. They don't seem to know you're a teleporter. Don't give anything away.**

He wouldn't have to consider mind control if she could stop acting like a baby and port out. Lina caught Lon's eye. **Give me a minute and I'll be gone.**

Another searing blast hit her on the front shoulder. It knocked her against her guard. He shook her hard.

"I told you, no funny stuff." Terry turned to look her full in the face. "So you're the one who finally did it. Sex with Valiant– lucky girl. The power starts going up if you try anything else."

Terry turned back to Londo and Menlo and the three talked, tension thick in the air. Sometimes Terry laughed and once Londo did. They were sharp, cruel laughs.

Lina's guard surreptitiously squeezed her breast. She squirmed away as he chuckled into her ear. Then he did it again. The man next to them laughed quietly. The one on the opposite side whispered, "Real or fake, Harry?"

A thorough squeeze. "Feels real enough," Harry hissed back.

She could sense Londo start to object. **Hush, let me try something,** she told him as she squirmed, ordering the white panic back and trying not to shiver.

She disassociated herself from her body as much as she could so she wouldn't be distracted by this man's touch or her scalded flesh. Then she squirmed some more, enough to attract the attention of the other men.

And these *were* all men. Terry Rhodes didn't seem to be an equal-opportunity employer. Use all that testosterone against them.

Think of home. The soldiers nudged each other now, pointing with their chins in her direction as Harry squeezed and pulled on her. Every new, disgusting touch brought the paralyzing whiteness closer to her and she had to spend precious moments pushing it back. Numb herself some more. Think of home again.

"Dammit, Terry, call him off!" Londo exploded from where he stood. Terry turned curiously as Harry froze.

"Call who off from what? From your little tramp?" Terry asked innocently.

Many of the men smirked at Harry.

Terry set her fists on her hips and surveyed her army. "No one here would want to provoke Valiant into doing something stupid. Don't trust what the TV news shows say. Valiant has a short fuse. Everyone pay attention, stay on top alert, and *don't* make the first move. Got it?"

The smiles of the men vanished and she nodded before she turned back to Londo and Dr. Menlo.

Harry kept his hands pristinely around Lina's waist now, pinning her arms as before. Lina tried to make her communication hit a subconscious level. Plant a suggestion.

You could feel her up, she whispered into the back of his mind, hidden from his conscious. ***That way you'll keep the prisoner off balance and have a little fun, too. You'll show them all what kind of man you are.***

It wasn't control, it was just an idea. He didn't have to pay attention to it–

She was half-amazed when the guard did exactly that. But a sudden surge of intense panic surprised her as she reeled from its intensity. This was an evil man and he wished her harm!

Still he was a prime distraction. Gritting her teeth and trying not to gasp from fright, she suggested, ***Come around in front of her.***

Instead Harry grabbed her hair in his fist, yanking her head back. He pulled the gag down and forced his tobacco-breath mouth onto hers.

Keep quiet! Lina ordered Londo as she felt his rage surge.

Port the hell out!

I'm trying. My damned phobia's back; can't concentrate. You use this as a diversion if you can. I've got an idea. I'll try to give you a little more time to do whatever.

Lon wanted to shout at her not to take chances, but instead he said, **You tell me when I can move. And make sure that you're absolutely safe, baby. One hundred percent. Don't worry about the* bâtard *with you; I'll take care of him. Later.**

The guards were all intent on Harry's actions and not what her eyes might be doing. They glazed as she closed them and looked around with clairvoyance. If she ported herself out, they'd just shoot Lon with those big guns over there. Maybe the guns could hurt him. These people certainly seemed to think they could.

She made a mental sweep of just how many guns there were. No way she could port them all at once.

Harry came around to her front. He yanked her shirt fully open. Someone had taken his place at her back, pinning her arms behind her.

Don't think about them! She shook her astral head with determination and tried to step farther back from the situation. Withdraw from the real world– out of her body entirely.

She could start porting out parts. Many of the guns had an electronic feel. Non-organics were easy to port. Maybe she could grab some wires or computer chips. The others had a lot of simple springs…

Lon tried not to watch what Harry was doing to Lina. He couldn't do anything about it without them hurting her, so he forced his gaze to stay on Terry. "Why?" he demanded.

She gave him that serene smile she always used whenever she knew she held the upper hand. "Ted and I have had this bet going for years," she said. "It was time to pay off the pot, one way or another. I thought a telepath who knew you could give you a creditable illusion of the real thing."

"If you had a good imagination," Menlo said as he fastened wired sensors to Londo's bare chest.

Lon tried not to wince. Those things reminded him of other sensors from far in his past. Tortures. Friends who had died because of who he was. Damn it, he had to get Lina out of here!

If she didn't port out in another two minutes…

Menlo twirled the wires as he attached them to a small, handheld box. "I thought a psychic healer, if she were real, might be able to physically affect your body." He squinted a moment as he threaded a wire, and then relaxed when its fastener clicked into place. "I was hoping some of your powers would be affected in the process. We'll have to check that out." He shook his head. "Too many controls lost. Sloppy."

Terry shrugged her indifference. "So we got both a telepath and a psychic and said we'd figure cause after effect was observed. We lucked out with her, didn't we? Was she good, Londo? How many times did you do it?"

"So everything was to settle a bet?" Lon could read both of them as if their thoughts were shouts. Personal rivalry had indeed evolved into a sick game with them, but they both had the same outcome in sight: Londo's murder. Lina would be mere flotsam to them, someone to be killed and discarded.

"You know me, Lon sweetie. Nothing's ever simple." Avoiding the sensors, Terry zigzagged her fingers across his broad chest, bare except for the open vest. She rubbed his nipples roughly. Londo fought to remain impassive while his stomach twisted. What had he ever seen in her? Whore-bitch!

Terry didn't notice the slightest of twitches at the sides of his neck. "But now you're like you've always been: a slab of warm granite. So human-seeming, but in reality so unattainable. Too bad Ted's here; too bad all these men are here, eh? You're shaking, trembling like you did the time we–" Terry's mouth hardened into a line.

"Still so possessive, are you? Do you consider her yours?" Terry taunted him. "Maybe we *will* keep her around for insurance."

"Good idea," he said. Keep her alive. Keep her well until he could get them out of here. This wasn't a time to vanquish them. He'd just grab Lina and run. When she was safe he'd come back and take care of business. Permanently.

"Five days." Menlo snapped something on his box and the machinery began to whine in a pitch only Londo could hear. "Three days with me, two with Terry, and we let you know where to pick up the girl when it's over."

"Five days," Londo nodded. "You've got it." That would form Plan B. Sometime during those days Lina could port out to safety and then he could escape, no prob. Stick their slimy butts in jail until their very bones crumbled into dust. Maybe he'd hasten the process.

Lon's gaze darted to Lina and back to Terry. He knew Lina was hiding her eyes from the soldiers, keeping her face in the deep shadows afforded by the spotlights. None of them were looking at her eyes.

Terry was completely unaware of what was happening across the clearing. "Maybe in the last two days you've finally learned how it is to be a norm, eh? Ted didn't expect you to escape capture. I knew better. No one runs better than you."

"Are you trying to goad me, Terr?"

"Ted's cannon the other day– it managed to do a job on your powers, didn't it? Ted convinced me that it would. And I hoped you'd get injured even more after we let you run. Was that cruel of me?"

Terry's gaze swept Londo's body. She dropped her fingers to trail them along the top of his belt. Her manicured nails traced a line across his belly. "Did we manage that?" She leaned in. "Tell me," she crooned, "or I'll tell them to hit her again with the guns."

"Yes, yes you did," Lon said quickly. The guard Harry was bending down to take Lina's breast into his mouth. Her hair hid her eyes; he knew that she was up to something, but couldn't figure what. Her two minutes were up. He ground his teeth. At least she was pulling her rag doll routine. She'd hardly be aware of what the shit was doing to her.

All the mercenaries were mesmerized by the scene. That might buy the two of them time if he could figure out something. Maybe now he could move at top speed, grab her before they could refocus their weapons on him. Maybe…maybe a few minutes more before that would work. Get the soldiers feeling really loose. Watch for the signs of inattention to duty. Watch closer those who remained alert.

Blast the cannon there, there and there with his heat breath on the way out. Park Lina safely far down the beach, grab some trees and some of that rockfall he'd seen to fence this army in. Then use that radio there to call the ParaNet for cleanup. Four minutes more, mark. Four minutes to keep Terry and Menlo occupied.

"It was a dislocated shoulder, Terry," Lon said. "Lots of glass cuts. She healed me."

"I would have liked to have seen that," Menlo said. "Hm. Well, let's get the major bet cleared up. You've had sex with her since your powers came back, right? At least that's why I assume you stayed here."

"Yes, dammit."

"You lie," Terry said quickly.

"I don't lie, not where her life is concerned."

"It's an illusion. A telepathic illusion." Was there desperation in her voice?

"Not illusion," Lon told her flatly. "When do the five days start? What assurances do I have that she won't be harmed? I'll do anything to keep her safe."

Lon, I've got a lot of the small guns decommissioned, but I can't figure out the big ones, not so they won't notice before we're ready. I think I can port them out to sea pretty quickly when you give the word.

She probably could, judging from her past performances with inorganics. **You're beautiful, chérie. Forget about the big guns; just get ready to port yourself. Tell me when you're ready. I'll save those two for you to watch how I handle 'em.**

"Well, damn," Menlo muttered. "Now we'll never know exactly how it's done." He studied his famous prisoner. "I wish there'd been a way to keep some controls going during the experiment. Is the technique based more on psychic or telepathic–"

Menlo's mouth opened as he met Londo's eyes. Londo's face might be a mask of contained fury, but his eyes were out of focus and glassy.

Menlo jerked his head around to check the tableau: two soldiers working on the girl. For a moment he paused, entranced.

Menlo's explicit fantasy flashed clearly to Londo's mind.

Scum! Not with his woman!

Almost in the same instant Menlo blurted, "They're communicating with each other! They're up to something!"

"Why, Doctor," Lon calmly turned to him, the tiniest of smiles on his face. "I have no idea what you're talking about." His eyes showed cold death, and Menlo took a step back.

"Rhodes! Call them to–"

Lon tapped him on the head and Menlo dropped like a stone. "Lina, out!" he bellowed, and turned to melt the big guns behind him with a swash of his–

But he staggered before a blast.

"Londo!" Lina screamed.

"We have computer-enhanced failsafes." Terry chortled. "Did you feel that, Londo? Would you like another shot? Or do you want to stand here like a good boy? Let's watch them give your girlfriend a little burn, eh?"

Lina didn't even see the gesture that brought the thin beam of red to play a design on the back of her bared shoulder. She only felt the burn of a branding iron, searing to the bone. She shrieked. Harry held her still to the fire. Somewhere another blast went off. Londo must have moved.

She was beyond fear now. It was all or nothing. Damn that she hadn't gotten all the small guns! She'd just been using them for practice for the big ones. The branding finally stopped. She gasped as hard as she could, trying to expel the heat with her breath so she could concentrate.

Shit, now it didn't hurt that much. That meant the nerves were burnt as well.

Port the big guns, fast! One– Two– Three–

A sudden shout went up in the clearing. "The guns! The guns!"

Almost got them all, just four of the big ones left–

And a sharp, acid blast hit her from an angle in the back. It struck the unsuspecting guard behind her as well and knocked her against Harry, who let her fall in surprise. The world blacked out for a second as she writhed in pain on the ground. Heat– heat– Must stay awake, get rid of them all!

Clicks surrounded her, men trying to fire their nonworking guns. Warm liquid washed over her back and down the front of her shoulders. It was red: blood. She hoped it wasn't hers, but if her nerves were burned it could very well be. That big guy in back lay on top of her, pinning her to the ground.

"Valiant!" someone cried almost immediately, followed by a lightning flash. This time it roared with thunder. Lina squinted against it, blinked against the white dots that bloomed in her eyes to see Lon stagger to his feet after being knocked down. Bodies fell around him, caught in the blast to lie bloody on the ground.

In front of her, Harry shakily stood up to point his measly rifle at the advancing parahero. Harry's gun had been the first to be decommissioned, but he didn't know that. He swung the rifle down at Lina's head and Lon stopped.

It doesn't work, Lina tried to tell him, but her mind was spinning. Maybe he didn't hear.

Londo reached for Harry's throat–

A slice of light split the air, so bright it cut Harry in half, cut through the guy on top of her, tried to cut through Londo. He fell back from it with a howl and sat down hard.

From out of the glare Terry stood over her. Her eyes poured hate. "One more trick like that and he's dead." She twisted to watch Londo, then turned again to kick Lina hard in the face, rolling her away from the man on top. "Filthy telepath," she said. "Filthy teleporter!" She kicked Lina again in the stomach, up against the guard who fell back over her.

Through it all Lina could feel the waves of jealousy emanating from Terry. She groaned in agony as she heard Terry's mind quickly considering options and probable outcomes.

"Hit him again," Terry finally barked, "until he's unconscious. He doesn't have to be awake for this, but I think he does have to be alive. That might not be a necessary condition," she added for Lina's benefit. She ground her heel on Lina's scorched shoulder, cutting the burn in further where the nerves still held sensation. "Honey, you've just become expendable again." She turned to point at the men with the big guns. "Again! Hit him!"

Londo had pushed himself back up to stand. He began a squat that Lina recognized was a push-off to flight, but another beam shot out. Lon's knees wobbled, but he recovered, visibly gathering himself to try again.

"The rocker! Use the rocker!"

Lina's spirit guides shouted at her as loudly as if they'd been material beings. **Close your eyes!**

She clenched them shut, covered them with her hands, and prayed that Londo would be okay. *Guides and angels, come to his defense! Please, please, God!*

The world ended.

4

A roar–

A thunderclap of a roar, the sound you'd hear from within a tornado with a thousand thunderstorms without– shattered the air. The island heaved.

Behind Lina's eyelids, reality turned white, then red with neon purple ghosts. The world closed down to just the sharp stridor in her ears, a deafening blare that slashed her mind with decibels.

She clutched the now-hot sand that flowed red and opened her eyes. On top of her, the soldier's head hung limply onto her own, something that was not blood flowing from it. When she brushed it aside, the head rolled away from her. She let out a soundless shriek and tried to shake off the body.

Lina peered around. Londo! What had happened to him?!

The island was still shaking. Earth herself keened within Lina's mind. No one was standing, and there were many she knew would never stand again. Partial bodies of those who had been in the way were strewn like roadside litter. A blackened hand and forearm lay on the sand in front of her. Harry? Perhaps. There wasn't anything else of him around.

But where was– Oh! Oh god, was Londo still alive? He lay crumpled on the ground on the opposite side of the clearing. His indestructible vest hung in two pieces but was still intact otherwise. Maybe that meant that he was, too. He had blood all over him, but so did everyone: blood from the wounded, blood from the dead. Maybe that wasn't his blood. She didn't see any holes in him.

Londo! Londo!

No answer.

A black glass crater gashed open from where he'd been to where he was now. Fire blazed around a stand of leveled palm trees. Slowly some of the few remaining mercenaries rose to yell at each other. Unable to hear over the ringing in their own ears, they began using sign language, pointing at Londo, trying their guns.

She had to do something now while they were still regrouping. The headless wonder still lay on her back. Maybe they'd think she was dead, too.

Get a feel for how Londo was. Memorial Hospital back home– could she port the two of them that far? Could Memorial even begin to handle what had happened to Lon? If he were still alive? He was, he had to be!

Wait. That blue man and his futuristic lab. How had it felt? Where was it? No, that didn't matter. Just use imagination and clairvoyance to picture it. A lab, a little messy, a lot clean. Busy. Important– that suddenly occurred to her. An important place, a lab with the blue man's imprint.

He was proud of it; it was his baby. It was as big as a warehouse and it was all his, no matter whose it technically was. There were important experiments going on everywhere, personal experiments hidden among them that no one would ever know were being done. Science for the sake of learning, of helping, of satisfying his curiosity. The symbol of a caduceus superimposed itself over the mind picture. That meant it must have medical facilities. There. She had it.

She raised her head now to look at Londo. Get the feel of him, the space he took up in the universe, the signature that was his on Creation. Almost…almost…

She screamed soundlessly as something blasted the body on her back off her and pummeled her own ribs as well. Hell flamed along her side. She rolled halfway into the crater, into a roasting oven. Her back was burning, burning! Burning through Lon's indestructible shirt!

Someone grabbed her wrist and hauled her up, flinging her over his shoulder. To her shame, Lina cried from the pain. She shook her head violently to stop herself. It was all she could do to catch her breath while the heat still flashed through her flesh.

From here she could see more pieces of men. Little packets of bleeding protoplasm that used to be organs or parts of bodies lay scattered like lumps of cherry Jell-O melting in the sun, Jell-O that had been put under a broiler, black and cracking on the outside but still jiggling as the very island quivered beneath it.

Angels, help us! Help Lon, please help Lon! Ah God, help her so she could help Londo! It hurt, it hurt!

The man dumped her onto sand and stones. She just lay on her stomach, twitching from the pain. Call down the light, heal herself to the point where she could concentrate and get the two of them out of here. Someone kicked her on her unburned side and sent her sprawling onto her back. Searing pain scalded her.

She played dead. Maybe they'd think she truly was. *Heal, cells.* Release the heat, send it down into the earth. Bring cooling energy in. She had to breathe deeply for this and they'd notice– shit. But it was either heal herself a bit now or doom the both of them. Breathe for Londo, too. Breathe in healing blue, green and violet light, link him with her.

Another hard kick, this time in her throat– she gagged– and another that caught her cheek. "You're awake, you slut," she could hear a woman say through the ringing. She must be shouting. "Don't pretend that you aren't!"

A wave of saltwater crashed onto Lina. She gasped, snapping her eyes open. Someone had thrown a bucketful of water on her. She clenched her eyes for the next one, the salt sizzling into her sores as it washed part of the gore off her.

Terry studied her with a look of sheer hatred. "Let's get this started," Lina thought Terry said. Terry over-enunciated her words so her men could read her lips. "Backup operation commencing as of now. Men-lo. Menlo's backup."

One of the soldiers lifted Lina up like a wet dishrag as she shook her head to clear it.

"Put her down here."

The mercenary lowered her carefully so she was lying on top of something: Londo. He was spread-eagled under her, completely unconscious but alive. Alive! She could feel his essence as he struggled to consciousness, but he was deep, deep down. She wanted to cry in relief.

Somebody dragged her arms to match up against Londo's, her legs to do the same. A plastic netting snapped over the limbs, clamping them together.

Concentrate, Lina, she told herself fiercely. But she couldn't! Through all the burning her jaw and gut throbbed. It was so hard to breathe. But she had to. Funnel the pain into anger.

Dr. Menlo unlocked a long case by her feet. He rubbed his head gingerly now and again and once reached out a hand to steady himself. Then he drew out what looked like a slender metal rifle. Shit. What the hell were they going to do to them?

Terry sneered down at her. She had black and gray roots. "And now we get to the interesting part."

The doctor took a measurement of Lina's arm and calibrated his rifle. She hissed against the pain of the burns on her back, her shoulder and legs, and of his hand on her arm. He looked at her face, then down to her bared breasts and closed her shirt for her. Then he rolled the sleeve of the shirt up her left arm.

Standing back, he lifted the rifle and took aim. Her arm! He pressed the trigger and a red light bloomed in the barrel.

Lina shrieked as the beam cooked her flesh. Good god! The blackness… She didn't know if she wanted to surrender to it or fight it. Fight! She shook her head, gasping and sobbing.

Lon had heard her scream. He was coming out of it, fighting as hard as she was.

A hole now gaped in her forearm, maybe an inch and a half, two inches, in diameter, perfectly round and blood-free. The sudden stench of scorched meat hung heavy all around. Hopefully the hole had missed the major artery going through her arm but probably it hadn't. It had been a laser, cauterizing the wound as it cut.

Why? Why? Lina asked herself while blinking her tears away. Funnel away the haze of pain that would not stop. She had to see what was going on!

Menlo scrutinized the hole. "How about that," he said with a smile and turned away. "Score one for me, Terry. It worked."

Terry stared at the hole and then turned back to her. "Oh, it'll be just a little while longer." She gave Lina a sickly smirk of triumph but couldn't hide her revulsion.

Dr. Menlo now held curly clear tubing with a needle on one end of it, a plastic bag on the other. It looked like equipment Lina had seen at the Red Cross blood donation center. She tried to move her arm away from Lon's as a horrible thought entered her mind. The netting kept them firmly attached to each other.

The top layer of Lon's skin underneath the hole in her arm had been burned. *Burned.* But Lon was supposed to be fairly invulnerable still.

Was he able to be hurt because he was exhausted? That sickening suspicion said no. Lon's cells were now attuned to her. They were programmed not to put up resistance…as long as she was touching Londo. Oh god, what had they done?

The hole in her forearm was directly over the inside of his elbow. She panted against the agony and tried to watch the doctor through the tears of pain. He slid the needle through the opening in her arm into Lon's arm. It went in easily. Menlo chuckled. Blood rushed through the tubing into the holding bag.

"Take as much as you can," Terry instructed the doctor.

As much as you can. The blood wouldn't flow if Londo were…dead. They planned to kill him in a few minutes if he weren't dead from blood depletion.

Lina began to writhe and groan with a passion. Cover up trying to concentrate, get it together enough to port them both out. Now.

Under her, Lon stirred.

Quiet, Lon; we're going to port. She hoped he heard her. Get the feel of Dr. Five-Minds' lab again. There it was.

"Just a little painful, is it, dear?" Terry was standing over her, she knew. Lina groaned, only half acting. She caught a glimpse of Menlo attaching a new bag onto the tubing. Already!

"Doctor, when you're through there, we can begin the sperm samples. You should be able to take the first directly from Ms. O'Kelly here. She should have plenty. Cutting her open wouldn't be the easiest way, but I'd enjoy it. As a favor to me?"

Beneath her, attached to her, Lon suddenly rose up.

"Fuck. Kill him!"

Ready or not, Lina knew she had to port now. But a micro-second before she could do it, an instant of an instant before they left, the leading edge of the blast hit Lon in the back. Lina could feel shock more than pain fizzle through him like cascading firecrackers.

They teleported.

The blue man's lab– he'd had to be able to help Lon!

She knew that they'd arrived instantaneously, and that there was something terribly wrong with Lon. Something was wrong here, too. There was a different electrical charge in the air, something she felt as if the hair on her arms stood up. There was different pressure, different air content. Different everything.

They were in the lab but yet not there, someplace that was almost in real space but not quite; she didn't know. But she held them there as she tried to sort through the imbalances and finish the port. She decided to even out the electrical imbalance and pressure by feel and take her chances.

They appeared on the blessedly cold laboratory floor, a clear space in an orderly ocean of tables and plastic domes and desks. Yes, something was horribly wrong with Londo. He lay like a sack of potatoes, not moving.

And she couldn't feel his mind.

5

"Help!" Lina cried, hoping someone was around. "Help! Oh, Londo– Help!!"

Something noticed. Lights began to flash: yellow and red and strobing orange. A blue panel of solid light unrolled in the air next to them. Maybe those marks on it were words. Someone was talking loudly through a speaker, saying the same words over and over, while this blue light spoke with a different voice. It said "Valiant" at one point, so something recognized Lon, at least.

"Help us!" she cried again. She directed what concentration she had left to porting the netting that bound them together. One net gone. Two. She rolled off Londo as best she could, still attached to him on one side as that blue man ran up, shock piquing his face as he saw the two of them and recognized Valiant, who was unconscious, maybe dead.

Lina tried desperately to port the rest of the nettings off. There was blood and gore on Lon's face and chest. Running blood from the burned spot on his arm where the needle had gone in and she hadn't ported it with them. Someone rushed up behind the blue man. Lina was too dazed to concentrate on the final two nettings.

"He's been hit by some kind of weapon," she told the doctor. Wilder? Wilder Mem-something. "Can you understand English? He needs help. I think he's dying." She looked at netting number three and managed to port it off to the floor.

Her left arm could still move, but feebly. It hurt worse than hell, yet the fingers were going numb. It felt like it was going to fall off and she blinked the urge to faint out of her mind.

"I understand you," Five-Minds said in English. He crouched by Lon, holding some kind of tricorder in his hand and referring to its screen. "What type weapon did they use?"

"What? I can't hear you," she said. He tried again, this time louder, and she heard. "I don't know," she replied helplessly. A marble floated through the air to hover next to her face, echoing her words in another language. "But they got him four… no, five times with it. Four with one kind of gun, and then once with something really big. They were energy weapons, not bullets. And then something ten times worse that they called a 'rocker.' It– it left a crater. They were firing again when we left; I think some of it may have–" she choked "– caught him." *Don't die, Londo! Don't die!*

The other man, a blond with normal tan skin tones, reached down to the final netting on their legs. It dissolved into a mist at his touch. He must be a para. Lina rolled off all the way, sprawling on the floor and catching her breath as the blond man helped Wilder pull Londo up to a clear table.

The floor heaved and the room spun around her as she fought for consciousness. She couldn't control her trembling. Concentrate! Concentrate! Londo needed her!

"Oh my god," she breathed as she pulled herself up and stared at him. She had to hold her left arm with her right one. She'd automatically slipped into psychic healer mode, but she didn't need her usual visualization techniques to see what was happening. It stood out to her.

"He's imploding!"

"What?" Wilder didn't bother to look at her as he quickly arranged his equipment, peering through a square of smoky glass at Londo. He glanced to his side to examine floating displays: bar graphs, wire diagrams, virtual microscopic views, pulsating lines.

"Computer," he called loudly, "evacuate the building! Absolute priority. Get everyone out now!" In answer, orange lights started to flash and a siren began to scream in a pulsating wail that hurt even Lina's ears. "Puter, sound off in here!"

How to explain to them? "His chakras… Do you understand chakras?" Lina looked at the two men uncertainly. The blond man nodded and said a strange word to Wilder, who also nodded. The marble next to her translated it back: "Biological energy centers," it told her.

"His chakras are imploding. Every one, the minor ones, too. He can't live like that," she realized. "They know they are supposed to– God, they're blocked– They're overloading!"

Without thinking she ported up on the table to straddle Londo. Pain from her arm, pain from her shoulder and back, neck and stomach didn't register; it wasn't important. She laid her hands flat on his solar plexus and looked wildly around the laboratory. A spirit guide pointed to another section of the room.

"Watch out!" she yelled and bent to her work, left hand on him, her right pointing to that section. She funneled energy that had been surging through Londo out of him and over to the corner of the room, a safe place to dispose of it. **Whatever planet this is, please help me!**

A concerned voice answered, encouraging her to keep it up.

The living energies roared as they tore out of Londo across the room. They swirled through her like a mad whirlpool, dragging at her body unevenly until she had to scream. Hurricane wind blasted them, sending equipment flying and crashing all around the lab. And somewhere in it all the blue man was shouting at something in the air while the blond man braced himself against Lon's makeshift bed.

Lina had never seen the energies of the body appear on the physical plane before, but then she had never seen chakras implode, either. All that mattered was Londo and his life energy. Funnel out the blocked excess– get rid of it! Dump it while there was still time!

Now the blond man raised his arms in the midst of the storm. Somehow he was trying to help. Slowing down the chakras trying to burn themselves out? Whatever he was doing bought her time.

Sweat poured from her as she gritted her teeth. Breathe, breathe. Keep the energy flowing. She cried out from the pressure in her arm as the energy surged around the wound there like a living fire. Arching against the pain, she screamed again. Keep the energy flowing out! This was Londo! He must be saved at all costs! The two men shouted to each other in the background, but she couldn't spare them any attention.

"Relax, Londo!" she cried to him. "Relax, dammit! You're just making matters worse when you fight it. Damn it to hell, relax!" Suddenly the room stopped. No lightning, no wind. More equipment fell and shattered at the sudden cessation of the storm.

"No. Oh no."

"What's going on?" Wiley demanded.

The other man gestured over Londo, strain on his face. "I'm trying to speed him up now," he said frantically, "but nothing's working. Wiley, do something!"

It could only mean one thing. Lina said, "He's shut himself down. The implosions– Chakras aren't designed to work that way. It was too much. Ohmigod, ohmigod–"

She swayed there on her knees, right hand over her open mouth. She had to do something and fast. She could feel the energies slowly sliding out of the lowest chakra, leaving the second chakra… Lon was moving to the Other Side. "Jesus!" she cried as her heart turned inside-out. Not Londo!

A vision of a heart attack patient appeared before her eyes. "Clear," a doctor shouted, and an electric charge went through the patient, shocking the body back.

"Got it, thanks," she said quickly to her guides. She looked around to the blond man. "Help me," she begged, and he swung her down from the table. She ran to a spot about four feet above Londo's head and smacked the air and the energy boundary there with her good right hand. A vibration shuddered down the cord only she could see that ran into Londo's body. She smacked it again. "C'mon Londo! You're not leaving me again!" Something seemed to take. Ever so slightly, the chakra stabilized. "Good."

She moved down to his crown chakra, the spherical bioenergy center, and slapped its edges, twelve inches from the top of his head. "Always be gentle with chakras," her teachers' lessons came back to her. Not now. Not this time. Shock therapy was his only hope.

She slapped it again, and again the chakra paused in its death throes. Maybe once she got them all done, they'd help each other. She went down his body, slapping the air around him about a foot out from his body at each major chakra's boundary.

"C'mon, c'mon," she chanted. "Hang in there, Lon. Don't you dare leave me again, dammit. You promised. Come back. Come back!" She reached the root chakra, slapped it and waited. "C'mon," she whispered. Nothing. She went back up to the solar plexus chakra and held her hands above and below him on the table. Her left arm drooped and shook, but the blond man reached and held it in place for her.

"Londo!" she cried out. "Londo Falcon Rand! Come back!" And abruptly he was inside the body. More than half-dead but there. Lina breathed out with a whoosh of relief, and then realized that that had been a mistake.

She fell in a faint to the floor.

The blond man managed to catch her, but just barely. She had been so pale before, between the purple-black bruises and blistered red-black burns, but now she was absolutely white. He didn't think she was breathing. "Wiley!" he commanded as he checked for her pulse.

"I'm a little busy here, Jae!" The blue man gestured over Londo, comparing flashes of information as they displayed on the half-dozen monitor boards floating alongside the bed.

Jae lifted up Lina quickly, depositing her on another lab bed, and then swung monitors around to focus on her. "As soon as you get a moment, get the *kick* over here!" he yelled, and Wilder looked up. Jae attached a butterfly to the girl's rib cage. It should have made her suck in a breath, but Wiley only saw her twitch.

"Puter," Wiley instructed the air, "set up emergency respiration procedures at Jae's station."

Two beeps, and Jae reached around to grab two thin tubes from the table behind him. He jabbed them into either side of Lina's neck and touched the butterfly again. Another twitch, almost a breath. Green light splayed out from the ceiling above and Jae triggered the butterfly. This time she gave a great, shuddering breath and a trickle of blood came out of her mouth.

"*Grigach*," Jae muttered, trying to make sense of what the monitors were telling him. "Deep shock, Wiley. Trauma. Burns. Broken ribs, punctured lung. Her windpipe is almost swollen shut from the bruising. Tell me what to do!"

Jae held her hand and reached for communication with her weak lungs, then her blood. He coaxed compounds there to turn into oxygen, dissolved already so the hemoglobin could instantly use it. The faintest tinge of pink touched the girl's skin, but he didn't think it was anywhere near what her normal color should be.

Monitors showed that Gorgeon and the rest of the medical staff were proceeding with evacuation of patients in the med section. They wouldn't be available to help. Jae elevated Lina's feet, threw a blanket of warmed air over her and checked the monitors again. "Life signs decreasing," he reported to Wilder. "C'mon, Wiley, what do I do? Puter, give me an oxygen field here!" He touched the butterfly again.

Wiley looked at the man on the bed in front of him. Shards and shreds! This was Valiant! He couldn't do anything for him, even though he desperately wanted to, but he could do something for the woman. He hesitated a moment more, frustrated at his own inaction, and then hurried over.

Taking a quick glance at the monitors, he focused a resuscitating turze beam array on her. "It's okay, Jae," he said. "I've got her. It looks like we're not going to lose anyone in the next fifteen minutes at least." He became the epitome of efficiency as he pressed various pulse-ampoules to her neck, checking the readings from the monitors after each try.

"That hole in her arm seems blacker now," Jae noted as he caught his breath, "like maybe that lightning seared it."

Wiley glanced at the arm, then back to his monitors. "It probably did. I'm surprised we're all not burnt to a crisp."

"How is he?" Jae turned to look at Lon, so still on the table over there. The monitors over him showed an uneven heartbeat, ragged lines of registration for different body functions. At least it showed he was alive.

The girl was breathing on her own as she came out of shock. Wiley programmed nanomeds to shunt her airways open against the swelling. Now he could return to his primary patient. "I'm *skurned* if I can figure out what's going on. His whole neuro-electrical system has gone completely haywire. Readings showed him clinically dead just up to a few minutes ago. He is back, showing slight signs of stability, but I don't know for how long." He looked grimly at Jae. "What did she do? Could you see it?"

"A little. She was working with the chakras. They'd closed down and she shocked them open, allowing the life energy back. Then she actually called the spirit back down into the body. I've never seen anything remotely like it in my life."

"Calling the spirit back– Give that to me in scientific terms."

Jae shrugged. "The soul, the mind… He was leaving; he was gone, Wiley. But he came back. Lon came back when she called."

"The soul." Wiley grunted at Jae's inexactitude and looked around the remains of his beloved laboratory: tables upended, loose equipment lying everywhere, much of it broken. Experiments stopped by voice command; some would have to be restarted from scratch, sunfire take it! *Flapping dermott*, it would take days to get things back to normal in here!

The fire suppressants the puter was pumping into the huge chasm in the floor where black smoke was rising– The chemicals might interact with the chemicals in Experiment G3016. Wiley told the puter to move that table away from the hole.

Good thing that there was nothing important underneath that section of the lab to be damaged. Sensors reported the floors ripped apart at least thirty stories down. Through impervion– impervion!– supposedly an absolutely impenetrable substance. He scratched his head, which made his violet hair stand up.

"Well, I don't get any of it. Puter, cancel building evacuation. Advise everyone of quarantine conditions in here and institute same. Where the *kick* did these bio-contaminants come from? Get a force field up over the damage here to contain things." Two beeps. "I want a replay of this in broad-vision, enhanced on the extreme sides of the spectrum. Jae, get that sielwer over there and I'll bring her around again so she can keep on doing… whatever the *kick* she was doing."

Jae shook his head. "Let her sleep, Wiley," he said. "I think Lon's not going anywhere for a while yet. She'll be better off with a few minutes of rest at least. Look at her."

Wiley considered and nodded his head, then moved to view the playback, muttering to himself. A screen popped into the air above him. A man yelled from it, "Mem-Bazer, what the *skurn* are you doing in there?!"

Wiley addressed him brusquely. "Londo just teleported in– dead. But he's alive now. Just let me do my work and figure out what's going on, Stoan. Check the playbacks and leave me alone!" He gestured, and the screen folded back into the air.

Jae stood by Londo. Gently he tried to speed up Lon's metabolism. Keep the energies going in Londo's body. *I agree with the girl, Lon. Don't leave me,* he thought. The cold-rushing fear that had tightened its fist around him ever since he saw Lon lying there on the floor began to trickle out of him, but he caught it and held on. Lon was still very much in danger, but there was nothing he could really do here except to act as assistant to whoever needed him, Wiley or the girl.

The girl. Badly injured, covered with blood and gore that the table was cleaning up now. Horribly bruised, burned and swollen all over her face; her bare legs were patterned in red and blisters. That shocking hole in her arm. Some kind of deep burn on her shoulder; sensors showed a major burn on her back, too, as well as internal injuries that were minor to everything else except the punctured lung.

Londo's shirt's sleeve on her was shredded. Did that happen while he was wearing it, or while she was? Jae decided that Lon had to have been wearing it. Anything that could rip the material that way would have shredded the girl's arm as well.

The machinery of the table continued to stabilize her. Wiley would come over again after he was through with Londo and work on her. She might be pretty enough when she healed up; it was difficult now to tell. And she was wearing Londo's shirt over very little else.

Jae smiled in spite of himself and wondered if he had time to put some money on this month in the "When Does It Happen to Londo" pool. Then again, perhaps he should wait until they were sure Londo was going to pull through. It'd be a *kick* of a thing if Lon died after he'd finally discovered sex, but then Jae had never held a high opinion of the universe's sense of humor.

Besides, this girl looked entirely too vulnerable to stand up to Lon. Even the almost-invulnerable women Lon had had over the years had never been able to go all the way with him. Poor Lon would live and die a virgin, but hopefully he wouldn't die anytime soon. Jae looked again at his friend's so-pale face and wondered if anyone would notice if he held Lon's hand.

6

L ina pulled herself up through a suffocating fog of pain and exhaustion. She didn't want to, but there was something very important to do. Something…
She squinted against the bright laboratory light and licked her lips. So dry. The blue man, Five-Minds, stood next to her, holding one of Dr. Crusher's *Star Trek* hyposprays.

"Londo," she croaked.

"I've given you a stimulant," Five-Minds said.

"Okay," she replied faintly. It couldn't have been very powerful. Her throat felt clogged. It was hard to breathe and she rattled when she did. She was burned, ah god, she felt like she was still sizzling on the blackened sand like a piece of bacon in a frying pan. The agony from that blotted out everything else except her arm.

She wanted cold water to wallow in, to suck the burn out. Cold water to drink and wash her face.

But more than that she wanted to faint again to get away from the pain. Instead she wiped a thick film of sticky sweat from her forehead. Her left arm buckled as she tried to raise up. It throbbed and pulsated with raw torment in time with her heart. She couldn't feel anything below her elbow. She was afraid that if she looked, that part of her arm would be gone.

"Lo– Londo. How's Londo?"

"I'll give you some more pain killers for that."

"How's *Londo?!*"

"Here." Five-Minds pressed the shot against her neck.

She gasped at the entry point: a sharp heat sensation whose effect stopped too quickly for it to have been hot.

Something was happening. The pain wasn't going away, but a layer of insulation spread through her, separating her from the worst of it. It was a little like floating now. Ah, god, she hurt. Now she could feel the all-over pain that had been under the surface.

The blue doctor checked his instruments and turned back as if he were going to administer another shot.

"No." She tried to make that clear. He paused. Perhaps this time he'd heard her. But no, he leaned in for another one. "No!" she said loudly, and when he didn't stop she managed to lift her good hand to block his access to her neck. It felt bigger than it should have been, as if it had a huge bee sting.

"I am giving you something to lessen your pain. It comes in this tube. I put it in your body and you get better," Wiley explained slowly.

Something was funny about his eyes. They didn't move in unison. Lina tried to scowl at him, but the muscles in her face were too stiff. "And I told you no," she growled in a gravelly voice. "Try it again and you'll need a shot of your own. How the hell is Londo?!"

"Puter," Five-Minds instructed the air, for all Lina could see, "give me some restraints."

Two beeps responded.

"Puter!" Lina called, surprising the doctor. "What's the medical status of Londo Rand?"

#That information is classified level five,# a voice from the air said as Lina fumed.

"All right, I take it you know what shots are." The doctor held two glowing straps in his hands and leaned down to check attachment points on Lina's bed. He gave a start when the straps disappeared. A determined look came over his face and he picked up the hypo again with a shake. "Now, see here–"

"He's not dead, is he?" Lina raised up like a fish flopping on the beach. She couldn't twist around enough to her right side for good leverage. "Keep away from me with that thing. Tell me how he is!"

His left eye betrayed someone approaching behind her and she managed to turn her head a little. The blond man.

"No fights in hospital!" He pointed sternly at the both of them.

"He's alive?" Lina asked him anxiously. "Tell me he's alive."

The man gave her a small smile. "Yes. Hanging on, but alive."

Lina sank back down on the cushions of the table/bed. "What are you doing for him? Is he getting better?"

Five-Minds was creeping up on her and she turned quickly. "I thought you said you understood English? I said no!" She stared him down. "Well, *you* give some suggestions if you know better!"

That stopped the doctor. "…In regards to what?"

"Did I look like I was talking to you?" Lina's gaze darted around the room until she spotted Londo lying on a floating bed, a different setup than he'd been on before. "What's going on?"

"Was that addressed to us?" the blond man asked, holding his hand up for the doctor to be quiet.

"He is. He is? Then why the hell aren't you helping him?" Lina glared at the doctor. "I don't need anything. You. You get over there and help him. Please!"

"I take it that was for me. Now calm down, young lady."

"Look, if nothing else, he's Valiant. Valiant! Isn't that worth saving his life?" She struggled again to get up and this time the blond man reached out.

"Easy," he said. "I'll help you." He almost touched her wounded arm but supported her back instead. She was too exhausted, too immersed in the emergency, to draw back from his touch.

"If it's money you want, I'll pay for everything," Lina promised. "It may take me a while to pay you back, but I'll do it somehow. Every cent!" She tried to feel for the floor under her and slid off the side. "I have a house I can sell." After what seemed forever, her bare toes touched the smooth, cold floor. She stood up.

And fainted.

The blond man's face was the only thing in her line of sight. She was back in that bed. A new point on her neck hurt as if she'd been given another shot.

"Let's start again," he told her pleasantly as that marble translated his words. He had blue eyes that operated normally. "We want to help Londo. We are ready to do anything to help him. Okay? Do you understand that?"

The room was still spinning around her. "Uh huh."

"Good. Now the unpleasant truth of the matter is that Londo is Valiant, and so even in this state we can't work on him very well. We were hoping that maybe you could. Can you?"

"Um…" Her eyelids were closing on her and she forced them back open. "I don't… I can't…"

"Wiley here can get you up and around if you can help him," the man said, "but if you can't, we'd rather you stay here and get well while we figure out what we can do with him."

"Oh."

"So?"

"Just a…" Lina's eyes went unfocused, but they moved around as if she were watching something far away. "Kolaimni," she said.

The word hadn't translated. "What?"

She blinked back to focus. "A Kolaimni and a chakra balance," she told the man. "That'll start him off. He's teetering right now. It'll steady him so he can begin to heal."

"These are healing techniques?" The blue doctor, Wiley, was on the other side of her bed.

"Um hm. Yes." She was on a choppy sea, so she shut her eyes to stop the movement of the room.

"I've never heard of Kolaimni," Wiley's voice said.

"Not many have." She fought to open her eyes again and finally succeeded. "How are you going to get me up? What do I–? What's–? Oh, okay."

"Who are you talking to?" Wiley's eyes worked together to focus sharply on her. Obviously he thought she was crazy. "Do you see someone else here?"

It was so difficult to keep her eyelids open. "Don't worry about it. If you can get me up and awake somehow without too much caffeine, I can do it. I need a clear mind. Steady nerves."

"What kind of medicine is this?" the doctor asked. "Pietzallicanthic?"

Lina tried to get a grip on the bed to turn herself to her side. "Psychic," she replied. "Holistic psychic healing."

"I've got you." The blond man lifted her to a sitting position.

She steadied herself there with her right hand, wobbling in a circle. "Are you sure–" Lina swallowed painfully "– you can get me up? Londo–"

The blond man smiled encouragingly at her. "Lon can wait a few more minutes while we get you in shape. Ms.–?"

"I'm Lina. Carolina O'Kelly." She closed her eyes again while she waited. "Just don't anyone show me a mirror. That might put me into shock."

"You'll heal. I'm Jae, Jaeson Rallene. And this is–"

Lina knew. "Wiley um…Five-Minds."

"Mem-Bazer, Dr. Wilder Mem-Bazer. You can call him Wiley. He only gets really rude when he's upset."

The doctor grunted as he continued fiddling with loose instruments on a neighboring table. Lina nodded and regretted the action. "Wiley. Lon was telling me about you just before the attack. I figured you'd be the best place to bring him. Just where are we, anyway? I know we're not on Earth anymore."

"You came in from Earth?" Wilder turned to her, but one eye still focused on a floating screen. "I find that hard to believe."

"I just aimed for the lab he showed me." She looked around wonderingly. "This place." Another world!

"Wiley, it would explain those bio-contaminants," Jae said. He regarded Lina as his expression turned sour. "You're Terran."

"Terran," Wiley echoed, but his inflection was that of resignation. "That would explain the unscientific approach to medicine."

Jae took a breath and released it with a frown. "You're on Sarastor," he told Lina in an even tone. "At the headquarters of the Affiliated Systems Megaforce Legion."

"Is that something like the ParaNet? The Terran Paranorm Network?" Lina desperately tried to figure it out and fight through the dreamlike quality of her surroundings. Nothing seemed to focus except the pain.

God, how her arm hurt. Not as badly as it had a few moments ago, though; the second drug must be kicking in. Now it didn't feel like it was about to fall off. She could feel the lower length of it by thousands of pinpricks of pain.

"ParaNet? Larger scale; we're interstellar. Londo's a part-time member." Jae rolled up Lina's left sleeve and fitted a flimsy sheet of chicken wire around her punctured limb, stretching from wrist to upper arm. Wilder threaded a stretched-out piece of bubblegum through it, and when it was in place, the armature contracted to fit snugly upon her skin.

"Huh. He would be," Lina said. Don't worry about the frou-frous; concentrate on Londo.

"Tell us what happened," Wiley instructed her. He brandished another hypo and she let him administer it, flinching at the sensation. This time it was different. The hypo didn't actually touch her but it still felt like an insect sting.

"Ah. Well." Lina tried to organize the events so she wouldn't seem like a complete idiot. "There's this terrorist, Terry, Teresa...Rhodes. And Dr. Menlo. He's famous. For doing awful things. Just now– I guess it was a little over an hour before we got here– Terry attacked us," Lina felt sick inside, "and she used me to keep Lon in line. But he tried to protect me, and she let him have it with some of Dr. Menlo's guns. Big guns. End-of-the-world guns.

"I tried to get rid of them," she said helplessly, "but there were too many. I didn't understand them. And now he's... he's... What are you doing with him now? I have to work on him. Will anything I'm going to do interfere with that?" She flexed her left-hand fingers. Her arm was starting to feel as if it were a part of her again. "Oo, thanks."

"You're definitely from Earzh?" Jae asked.

"Of course I'm from Ear*th*." She accentuated the final *th* to correct him.

"Have you known him long? Are you a ParaNetter?"

"Oh no, I'm no hero. I only started to teleport yesterday. Maybe the day before that. I met Lon then when he saved me from a fire. That was tough with no powers. He saved me about a thousand times over since, but then Terry surprised us."

Jae eyed her warily. "So, number one: you're Terran. Number two: you'd only been with him a short while and already you were attacked." His chin jutted as his gaze seemed to turn inward. He muttered, "Londo, Londo."

"They weren't after me; they were after him."

"Of course. And you were caught in the crossfire." Jae's mouth tightened into a line before he asked, "He could have escaped unscathed if you hadn't been there, right?"

"Well…yes."

"He was hurt when he tried to protect you?"

"Yes." So terribly hurt. It was all her fault.

Jae turned away from her. "Next time maybe you'll think twice before you consort with one of the Rands without wearing mega-enhanced armor. They don't need to have a weak spot their enemies can use to target them."

Speaking of weak, Lon lay so still there as lights played over him. "I should start working on him soon," Lina hinted. "What are those machines doing?"

Wilder shook his head. "With Londo, there's not much stabilizing that can be done. His invulnerability defeats any external—"

Lina interrupted, "I found something out, just before he was hit that final time. We've sort of got this…bond going on. I think. He might be vulnerable wherever I touch him." She blushed at the sound of it. "If you need to give him a shot or anything I think I can arrange it."

The sheer audaciousness of the statement made Jae whirl to stare at her. Despite a whirlwind of other implications the thought that leaped foremost in his mind was, *Definitely need to get that money in on the pool.* She'd been with Lon for how many days? Undressed like that for how long?

Wilder's eyebrows had shot up at the news as well. "If that's true, I can put that to use immediately. Come."

Jae supported her as Lina followed the doctor on trembling legs. Londo lay on his floating bed, so pale. The life currents struggled to make it through his body.

"They took an awful lot of blood from him," she said as she leaned on the bed. "He bled really quickly. Faster than I've ever seen."

Jae nodded. "Lon's got to be better at everything. All right, I can help with that." He put his hands on Lon's legs and closed his eyes in concentration.

"What's he doing?" Lina asked Wiley softly. Jae was communicating somehow, connecting to the bones…

"He's speeding up the production of blood cells. Put your hand here," Wilder instructed, pointing at Lon's arm. "Let's see if this works."

She spread her fingers so he could get the hypo between them. The lines on all the monitors skewed the instant Lina touched Londo. Wiley fired. Judging from his surprised expression, it worked.

"Well," he said. "Well. Keep your hand there. I'll give him some more." He went to the other side of the station and busied himself.

Jae blinked to awareness and then looked down at her as he removed his hands from Lon. "I'm afraid to do too much with him in this condition," he said. "Probably just a little at a time would be best."

He removed the melted mass that used to be a ring from Londo's right hand. "Great shards of the orb," he breathed. "I thought these things were indestructible."

Lina noticed that Jae wore a ring on his right hand, middle finger, same as Lon. They might have been similar. She couldn't tell from the melted one, but they looked like they could have been the same size. They were certainly the same slightly iridescent metal.

"I don't want to bother you," she said, looking up at Jae. She trailed off as she took in the sight before her. He was maybe a foot taller than she, topped with a thick mass of shoulder-length, light blond hair that might have been responsible for a few inches of that "foot" estimate. His height was odd enough– Wiley's was about the same– but holy moly– there were two tiny points sticking out of the hair on either side of his head. He had pointed ears!

He was dressed in blue tights, unlike Wiley's bulky jumpsuit and equally baggy lab coat, but he wore a gray cocooned tunic like a seaman's sweater with a loose double belt and dark, over-the-knee boots. It made him look like a freakishly tall, elvish pirate.

What had she been saying? "Do y'all have any kind of aluminum pan that I can fill with salt water? No, not a pan. Not for this." She thought furiously, aware that things needed to commence very soon. "Maybe a tub. Something that I can get into and dunk my whole self, not just my arms. I've got a lot of nasty energies that I need to get rid of. Salt water will do it. I'll have to re-use it a couple of times, maybe more, while I work on Lon."

"You're serious?"

Lina was apologetic but determined. "Yes. Right now it's like working through mud. Clear the energies, and I can almost guarantee you that it'll work. Leave the energies building up– I don't think so." Her troubled eyes tore at Jae's heart. "Please find me something. For his sake."

"We may have a whirlpool here. Wiley's got a little of everything."

Wiley returned and administered the extra shots, studying his diagnostic panels after each one.

"Wiley, you still have that aquatic test chamber?"

"Yes. In the back, near storeroom number three," Wiley said without glancing their way. "Why?"

"Lina needs it. I'll fill it with warm salt water. Anything else?" Jae paused expectantly.

"Um, a robe or something, so I don't have to run around in wet clothes? Like I said, I think I'll have to use it several times. And it would be great to get out of these bloody things. But I can live without that."

"I'll see what I can find."

A nice guy, Lina thought as Jae left. Both these men were nice people. If they were part of this Mega-Legion, or whatever he'd said, they'd be heroes, too, wouldn't they? Megas meant heroes, more powerful heroes than even paraheroes. And heroes had to be nice people, just like her wonderful Lon.

With Jae gone and Wiley– she hoped he really wouldn't mind if she called him that instead of Wilder Ben Dozer, no, Wilder Mem-Bazer– just using her as a prop, she took a few minutes to study Lon's condition. It scared her. He looked too far gone, as if he were still hovering on the brink of death, but Lon was Valiant. Maybe that would tip the scales.

She must be brave for this. She conferred with her guides to perfect her healing approach. They were soon all in agreement. She was ready. That stimulant was really grabbing hold now without screwing up her mental balance. Good stuff.

Jae came trotting back. "All set," he announced. "It's back here." He showed her the way, pointed out the tank next to a bathroom and a stack of clothing he'd found, and left the area.

Dear lord, I hope it's not too alien, Lina prayed, cringing from the idea of asking a strange man how to use a bathroom. But she *really* had to go. She closed the door behind her. It clicked shut with a snap. She couldn't see any unlocking mechanism. Oh god, she was locked in an alien bathroom and Londo needed her! "Puter, how–?" she began, before she remembered she could port.

#What information do you require?# the voice of the computer asked her in English.

"Um, how do you…use this facility?" Lina asked and hoped no one was monitoring the conversation outside. The computer didn't mind her embarrassment. It showed her diagrams in mid-air that were definitely not in good taste but which imparted the necessary information. There were a variety of alternate positions displayed. Things were fairly straightforward with a couple of startling surprises. *Everything* was automatic!

The real shock came when a mirror revealed the horror that was her face: grotesquely swollen with a long line of cuts and blackened blisters on top of green and dark purple patches. She didn't recognize herself. It looked as bad as it felt.

Deal with that later, after Lon was well. Maybe he would do an Elephant Man imitation for her.

She *had* to heal him. He couldn't die!

For him she braved the hellish sting of the saltwater pool. Submerging in the center of the pool was the best way to drain the energies. **Hello...Sarastor,** she hesitantly called to the planet while she did it.

Hello. We've been waiting for you.

Now what did that mean? Planets and guides could be funny or mysterious. They had moods just like anyone else. But this one was very friendly and kind, very willing to help out. Lina thanked her, finished draining the last of the energies, and painfully pulled herself out of the tank as she tried not to use her left arm at all.

There was a real towel there with the clothing. She thought Jae might be humoring the backwater human, but right now she felt like being humored. She dried off as best she could and pulled on the thick leotard she'd found. It was black and at least two sizes too big, intended for someone much taller than her six-foot self. But it covered everything that needed to be covered. The fact that she couldn't pull the sleeve on over her left arm complicated things. It could have cleared the armature, but then it would have dug into the raw burn on her left shoulder.

Time was pressing. She still had Lon's torn and now burned shirt, so she put that on over it and fastened it shut. Something had cleaned most of the blood off it while she'd fainted. Feeling minimally presentable and a bit warmer, she returned to the main laboratory.

"I'm ready," she announced as they stood back from her. "Do you need to do anything else to him before I start?" She put the towel down and gave Londo a final psychic examination as she combed her fingers through her hair.

"Will we disturb you if we find we need to work on him while you're doing whatever it is?" Wiley asked.

"I don't know. Not during the first part at least. I'll let you know."

"Then let's see how it goes," Jae said.

Lina nodded. She explained that she'd do a rough chakra balance to get those working better, followed by a Kolaimni treatment, an etheric method that would affect the more minor chakras of the body as well. She'd probably have to repeat the procedures, and felt that they'd take much more time than they usually took. "For all I know, it may take all day."

Wilder shook his head at the gibberish. "We're not going anywhere. Will it disturb you if I record? Do you understand recording?"

"Be my guest."

Jae lowered Lon's table just by gesturing so it would be at an easier height for her. Lina pulled a stool over and sat on it even as she gathered protective white light around herself. "Um, it may not look like I'm doing anything much here during this first part, but I will be. Ah, and if I seem to be talking to myself, please don't think I've gone bonkers."

"Just a quick question, then, before you start," Wilder said. He crossed his arms in front of himself.

Typical body language: *he doesn't believe a word of this*, Lina realized.

"Have you ever done anything like this before?"

She tried to smile around her swollen cheeks. "Are you kidding? I've been taking lessons for years; even taught a few classes. I've never done anything remotely on this scale. But I can do this," she said, and even to herself she sounded confident. "I can." She could do anything if she had to, and this was top priority in the universe right now, Goal A-quintuple-plus.

She scooted the chair closer to Lon's table. "By the way, this planet says she really hates the weather control. And she says her name's Glasti, even though it's also Sarastor. Just thought you should know." She raised her hands over Londo but brought them down again. "Oh. No shortcuts. No, I can understand that."

So she stood up and passed her hands over Lon's body: front/back, side/side, from head to toe, as if she were peeling something back.

"Now I can start." Raising her hands again, she brought them out, then in toward the top of Lon's head until she touched the outer edge of his crown chakra. Carefully she tapped the back, then the front, back and forth in a slow, fluid motion, drumming out toxins and blockages.

She used her breath to help clear it, visualizing her breathing as the kind of energy breathing that the chakra did. Occasionally she'd lean in against it, wrapping her arms around the perimeter of the chakra as if she leaned on a large invisible sphere. She seemed like she was listening, and then she'd rap on one spot. Or she'd hum or sing a note.

While she was doing that, Wiley hovered around Londo applying small stickers to his chest and switching on vari-colored lines of lights. Since Lina wasn't touching Londo directly, his skin held the hardness of metal. A readout showed Wiley that

that wasn't quite as hard as usual: iron instead of impervion, soapstone instead of granite. But it was hard enough. Invulnerability did have its drawbacks in medical emergencies.

Wiley stopped and stared when Lina sang, but after a moment he went back to what he was doing– although he muttered to himself about Terrans. When he was finished, he returned to his seat at a central console next to Jae and kept track of five different screens at once.

Finally Lina leaned back in the chair and let her breath out in a heavy sigh. "Only one chakra and I need to go in for another dunk." She turned to Wiley and Jae, her audience. "First one's the hardest."

"His readings have definitely improved," Wiley confirmed for her benefit. "I'm reassigning his condition from grave to critical." Her swollen face twisted into what might have been an expression of relief.

"Wiley, I've been thinking," Jae said when she had gone. "Wasn't 'Glasti' the name of some ancient world goddess here at some point?"

"Yes, it was. The question is: if she's Terran, how does she know? My readings confirm that they may indeed have transported directly from Earth. Contamination levels are completely inconsistent with hyperspace travel. Conventional hyperspace travel, I should say."

"Any diseases we're not covered for?"

Wiley harrumphed. "I haven't had time to research that, but I don't think we'll collapse before I can spot everything. I should have preliminary vaccinations ready by this evening. Even for our Terran guest."

"It would be nice if Gorgeon were here."

"Oh yes, as if we're too busy now," Wiley said sourly. He hated being hardly more than an observer. He liked to test, to do his own lab work for major studies. "We really need another body sitting around in quarantine."

"I just mean she should look at Londo, too. As a backup," Jae added quickly so Wiley wouldn't take it as a professional insult. "I suppose Stoan's going to classify this as triple-level-5 anyway."

"Only double so far," Wiley pointed at a security warning on a nearby screen. "We'd have to mind-wipe Gorgeon if she saw any of this."

"That's not right."

"Those are the rules, Jae. I already sent Stoan a memo asking for a Need to Know exception for her." Wiley quietly busied himself with ordering new readouts as his companion sat in silence.

Jae finally said, "So the biggest question is…"

Wiley couldn't hide his grin. "Who had this month on the betting boards?" They snickered together.

7

L ina made it through two more chakras before she had to return to the tank to de-energize. Then two more and the tank. This time when she returned, they could see that she trembled and had to catch onto tables for balance as she walked back to Londo's side.

"Here." Wiley administered another shot as she braced herself against Lon's table. She straightened up, nodded, and went back to work. The final two chakras took as long as the three before them. Her hands quivered at the end of the procedure as she re-covered Lon with what Wiley could only see was air.

After submitting herself to the tank again, she found Jae working on Lon. Lina decided to let him work for a few minutes and sank onto a stool, looking expectantly at Wiley.

"His signs now are critical but stable. I'd say you could get a couple hours of sleep if you wanted."

She rubbed her eyes. "Yeah, I want. But *they* say" (Wilder wondered who *they* were) "I need to go right into the Kolaimni. A normal one takes about thirty, forty minutes." She eyed the small marble that floated above her. "Can that translate Terran time units?" She didn't think Wiley really knew all the English that he pretended to know. After all, they were– where the hell were they, anyway? How could anyone know English Out Here?

"It did. Forty minutes."

"All right. That's for a normal Kolaimni. This one's going to take a lot longer. Two, maybe three hours." She gazed at Lon but spoke to Wlley. "Can I get some more of that stimulant from you? I need an absolutely clear mind for this technique."

"Yes. But I don't recommend you stay on stims in your condition."

"And could I bother you for a little more painkiller? I really need to use both arms. But just enough to let me use the arm fairly normally, not make me spacey. Like I said, absolutely clear mind. And some water if I could, please. If it's not too much trouble."

Wiley set off to get the drugs. "Thanks," Lina called after him. She pushed herself up to stand next to Jae and blearily watched him work. Whatever he was doing, the femurs liked it. They were producing red blood cells as hard as they could, given their low energy levels. Was Jae increasing the levels by some power of his or was he merely encouraging the bones to accomplish the job themselves? She began to ask the bones by anthropomorphizing them in her imagination so she could understand them.

"Don't interrupt," Jae murmured.

"Sorry." She hadn't thought he'd even noticed her. Stifling her curiosity, she watched for a few more minutes until it seemed he was through. He turned and brushed his hands off, ridding himself of the excess toxic energy. It didn't quite clear him; Lina wondered if he knew. But he'd clear out eventually. Just look at the glow around him.

"I hope you don't take this the wrong way," she said slowly, "but I've never seen an aura like yours. Not that I've seen that many auras. I'm kind of spacey right now."

"What do you mean? No, I'm familiar with the concept of auras. Why is mine unusual?"

She peered at him. The world had begun to dissolve into the immaterial. Realizing that he had asked her a question, she explained, "It's pretty big. Very white in places, very spiritual. And all the people around you–"

"People?"

"Thousands– millions of people crowding around you. A planetful."

Jae froze but she continued, oblivious to his reaction.

"They're all, like, patting you and saying don't be sad. Don't weep for us. Don't mourn for her when she lives in you."

"Who?"

"Somebody named…Feith. She says she's alive in you. What does it mean? Who is she? I can barely hear her."

Jae pressed his lips tightly together and turned his back.

Wilder chose that moment to return. He waved his equipment near Lina's neck. There was that prickling heat for a moment. Lina blinked, took a breath and then released it, her eyes opening wide. "Hello, real world! That did the trick, thanks." The water he gave her was the best she'd drunk in her life.

Wiley adjusted the bubble gum in the armature on her bad arm as she wiped the sweat out of her eyes. She flexed the arm experimentally. Now she could move it through almost a complete range of motion. "Thanks a lot," she told him.

But she paused before she went back to Lon and glanced back at Jae. Now that she was alert, the only aura she could detect was a faint afterimage around him, and even that could have been her imagination. "I'm sorry. I shouldn't channel unless I'm absolutely clear. Never upset the client, that's the first rule."

Jae turned slightly, acknowledging her presence once again. He brushed away the hair that had fallen into his face, tried to smile and didn't make it. "I'm not upset. It's okay."

"We'll talk after I get through with this. After I get some sleep. Can you wait that long?"

Only when he nodded did she take her position next to Lon. "If he wakes up and tries to speak, get him to be quiet until I'm done," she instructed them. "Somebody remind me to do the end ritual; I always forget that part."

The latter request was not directed at either of them. They had gotten used to her talking to the air, although Wiley still made rude remarks under his breath about it.

Seated at a main monitoring station fifteen feet away, Wiley and Jae watched and sipped hot drinks. With one mind, Wiley began to compile his notes about Londo into a report as another mind compared data from an experimental trial he'd started some of his assistants on in Lab 1-C, some forty stories below this one. His other minds observed the Kolaimni process and commented to Jae.

Jae didn't reply. Instead he scratched his chest, then his shoulder, then the back of his head as he took deep but shaky breaths. Wiley's youngest mind noticed when Jae tapped a pattern on his wrist to trigger the release of internal tranquilizers.

That mind nodded to the others; Jae had been controlling his manic depression on his own for years. It was to be expected that Londo being so near death would cause him anxiety. Now Jae seemed to be relaxing. He was taking expert care of himself. Wiley should be using all his assigned faculties to study Londo's reaction to this strange technique.

Lina's fingers stroked the air as if there were a surface some six to eight inches from Lon's body. She began at one of his feet and very slowly progressed up. The other leg got the same treatment. Wiley's main desk monitor held a detailed overview of Lon's condition, and the indicators changed their readings radically as Lina's hands passed over each area.

"I have absolutely no idea what she's doing, but she's doing it well." Wiley pointed out the changing augmented colors on his charts to Jae. "Look at that." Before, it had been the entire body gradually improving in condition as she moved down. Now the effect was tightly concentrated.

"Enjoy it, Wiley. When was the last time you had a real witchdoctor doing her thing in front of your sensors? You'll write a book about this, I know."

"Probably," Wiley admitted.

Heat readings were changing along the healing front, as he'd begun to term the area where Lina worked. It seemed like a miniature weather front, with drastically different readings on either side and turbulence between. He modulated the picture to illustrate other body functions besides temperature.

Wiley noticed that Lina was arguing to the air and upped the mikes he had on her so he and Jae could hear what she was saying.

"No," she protested. "I really don't think I should mess with the major chakras at this point." She paused. "I know, but these poor chakras have been through so much. Tell you what, what if I skip them this time, do everything but them, and then when I do the second Kolaimni I pay special attention to them? Okay, will do. Thanks." And she proceeded with the technique, apparently satisfied.

"Who is she talking to?"

Jae shrugged his shoulders. "Gods. Spirit guides. Familiars. You can always ask her when she's done. She seems cooperative enough."

"That's a major plus. So who won the pool?"

Jae ran a search through the puter. "Kuttr." He chuckled a half-snort. "He places his bets in random cycles. This time he had a special rider on it, too: ten percent extra if she were a virgin."

"Hm."

"What?"

"Did I say anything?"

"Are you telling me that she was?" Jae glanced at the very female form in front of them. Imagine it pre-attack. Nah, no way.

"I fail to see how you got all that from me passing a little gas. I was just taking into consideration the fact that the young lady is a healer, and so certain physical, ah, alterations may appear to be healed longer than they actually are."

"So you're saying she was."

"So I'm saying that we should ask Londo." Wiley switched to a new set of data screens. "We may want to question him while he's still a bit dopey. He once told me that a gentleman doesn't kiss and tell."

"He's no gentleman."

"But he considers himself one."

Now Jae's snort was a full one. "But this is Londo Rand we're talking about. Londo 'Poor Me I Can't Have Sex So Everyone Stop Talking About It and Pretend It Doesn't Exist' Rand. He'll tell everyone about this one. He's going to put up a sign in the main meeting room. Maybe hang one on the outside wall of Headquarters. In flashing lights."

"And maybe not. Readings show that in addition to having died, he's just recovered from a major, and I do mean major, previous shock to his entire system. Before this latest attack."

Jae peered at the screen Wiley referred to. Dozens of lines of data streamed across it using obscure bio-physical terms. Golgi body acceleration in the presence of extensive toxiplasmic residue… "What's that mean?"

"I hate to jump to conclusions–"

"What a load of–"

"But it could have been enough to have stripped him of a considerable amount of invulnerability and strength. Remember, she said he'd rescued her without powers. She must have been talking about him, not herself. This may have been a once in a lifetime event– in which case he may not be too pleased about it."

New floating sensors leaped to flock into formation around Londo's bed. Wiley frowned as he first widened their focus, then tightened it.

"Electromagnetic radiation," he muttered to himself. "Londo but not Lina. I'd have thought that Lon would have been able to throw off almost any kind of… DemGerre." With that name he flexed his left pinky with its electronic ring, and the screen on that side began scrolling through a list of technical articles written by said researcher. He narrowed the list to one and perused it with Mind #3.

"Two years ago," Mind #2 prompted the computer without stopping. "*Lecerate Journal of Medicine*, article by Prepoe someone." The right-hand screen displayed another treatise, this one concerning focused electromagnetic effects on human tissue. Wiley's eyes tracked the screens separately and he grunted. "*Grigach* take it all," he finally concluded sourly. "They both reference Tishana research, of all things. That equals a dead end. Sunfire take that world and its censorship!"

He threw up his hands and shook them toward the ceiling, perhaps even the sky above headquarters. After a moment of strained grunting he lowered them, rolled his shoulders, and then re-aimed his sensors with merely a murmur of new curses.

Jae tried to make sense of the screens, especially the one that concerned itself with subcellular processes and reconstructive conjecture. He frowned at it as Wiley continued to mumble to himself and motion for resets and new possibilities.

"Shards, look at that," Jae said at one set. "How do you drain the power off Valiant? Could he even have gotten it up in that condition?"

Wiley glanced at what Jae was referring to. "There's stress and then there's stress. I have a model going through one of my minds that shows Lon in a room, fainting away from weakness, and then this girl walks by."

"To which he finds the strength to jump up and say, 'Pardon me, miss, but would you like to have a little sex?'" Jae grinned to himself. "While he's still dopey, huh?"

"'He's vulnerable wherever I touch him,' she said." Both of them snickered at that.

"Virgin?"

"Ah… I'd be willing to put down a reasonable amount on the theory." Wiley switched the screen on his second-left to the Legion betting boards, and let his left eye and Youngest Mind watch it as he did just that. Youngest Mind appreciated that sort of thing more than the others.

Jae glanced down at his own screen. "Kuttr will be pleased. Not just for the money."

"Yes, what is it that he's always telling Londo? 'A man's not a true man until he's bloodied himself with a battle and a virgin girl.'"

"He just said that to get Lon's goat."

"It worked. Drove Lon crazy." They laughed softly together. And watched.

Occasionally communication screens lit on their console, and they'd bring whoever was checking in up to date. To almost every inquiry from their fellow Mega-Legionnaires, Wiley would let slip the fact that he was able to administer medication to Londo because the Terran witchdoctor could manipulate Lon's invulnerability. It was very satisfying to see activity on the betting boards dramatically increase.

For the most part, Wiley ran scans in different frequencies trying to determine what Lina was doing. Sometimes Jae would suggest Wiley check some aspect and Wiley would re-tune his instruments to catch it. During the two times that Wiley left for a few minutes, taking his screens with him, Jae's gaze focused on the girl herself, and his eyes narrowed into hard slits.

Lina reached Lon's head two hours into it and paused. "Damn," she muttered as she shook her arms toward the ground. She wiped the sweat off her forehead and face, trying to use her sopping shirt to soak some of it up. Healing was very hot work sometimes, and this was complicated by the fact that she was straining so hard.

It didn't help that her good arm was stiffening up on her. She was overcompensating for the other one, which had begun to throb again. It was difficult to move her left fingers. The two Legionnaires strolled over.

"What's the matter?" Almost offhandedly Wiley administered another two shots to her.

"I hate to leave in the middle of this, but I need to de-toxify again. He should be flipped over anyway. Could you guys…?"

Wiley put on a sour expression. "Oh, you mean we get to do something?"

Jae nudged the older man. "Don't listen to him, Lina. Sure, we can handle him. Is something wrong with your hand?"

"It's just stiff again. I think I should be able to work it."

"Umph," Wiley grunted and restrung the bubblegum.

"Oh. Oh," Lina said, amazed. The feeling returned to her hand, tingling as the arm came back alive. "Hello, fingers!"

"We need to reroute the nerve signals every hour or so," Wiley said. "I'll rig a permanent patch later."

"Thanks. Be right back." She trotted off to the tank, leaving the two of them to negotiate turning Londo. As they hefted him, he groaned and stirred. They rolled him over and he sighed.

"Is that a good sign?" Jae asked hopefully.

"Seems like it to me." Wilder was cheered. "Maybe not interfering with whatever she's been doing has paid off."

"But still you don't like doing nothing."

Wiley shook his head. "Sunfire take it!"

"There's that book to be written from this."

"At least one. Maybe a whole section of the medical library if I can get it de-classified. Too bad it's just a Terran technique."

"Yes." The way Jae said it, with a slightly mocking tone, made Wiley look twice at him.

"Your people could do this," Wiley surmised, but Jae didn't reply.

Lina returned drying her head with the very damp towel. "My hair's never going to be the same after this," she complained. "Oh, and I think the tank needs more salt. It's not absorbing as much energy." She shivered.

Jae reassured her, "I'll handle it. And I'll warm up the water again."

"Thank you. Thanks a lot." She straightened her shoulders and shook her head as she turned back to Lon. "This side shouldn't take nearly as long. I went kind of deep on the front. I usually do."

"He was stirring a moment ago."

Lina's lower lip began to tremble violently. Her entire jaw worked to hold back cries she could not spare the time for. Instead she gulped four times and clamped her hands into hard fists, pounding them against her hips to snap herself back into focus on her goal. She swallowed her tears with a clatter of teeth that she knew Jae must have heard.

Her voice sounded almost steady as she said, "Let's finish this up. Remember, if he starts to talk, quiet him down. It's okay to talk a little, but not too much."

"Right." They stood back while she started the process again. It did seem to go faster. By the time she got to his mid-back he stirred again.

"Um… Hum… Lina?" Lon turned his head in her direction but didn't open his eyes.

"Hi, guy." She paused but kept her hands perfectly in position. "Don't let what I'm doing stop you from going out and moving a mountain or whatever."

He tried to smile and didn't make it. "May– Maybe not t-today."

"Okay. I'm finishing up right now. Should be about ten, fifteen minutes. Until then I want you to be quiet. You're on Sarastor in Wiley's lab, and you're much better now."

"*D'accord.*" He quieted; perhaps he slept. Lina returned to her work with a lighter heart. She reached the top of his head and paused.

"I remembered, I remembered," she muttered under her breath. She walked to midway down his body and stood over him, one foot in front of the other, arms stretched to the ceiling. In her imagination, a ball of pink light as long as Londo appeared overhead and the light flowed down to engulf him. He sighed contentedly on the table.

"Ah, *oui.*"

Lina concentrated on funneling the energy. Finally it stopped and she shook her arms out, wincing when she shook the left one.

"Uh oh," she said.

"What's wrong?" Jae had been the first to pick up on it.

"I'm finished, but I can't ground myself. Just a second." She struggled for control. The world was now a series of overlapping auras, no solids to be felt, no gravity. Wait: she could bring earth energy– make that Sarastor energy– up through her root chakra, counter the lightheadedness…

"It's not working." She tried not to let panic into her voice, much less her mind. Not grounded– she couldn't get fully back into her body. She'd wanted to finish Lon's back, but she should have stopped for a dunk somewhere during the last part. Too eager to finish. Now she had too much energy coursing through herself.

"Is there anything we can do?"

Her mind raced. She could do what she did for her clients.

"Do you have some kind of dark stones around here? Obsidian, lead, garnet, even turquoise. Something that I could hold."

Jae's voice: "Give me a minute."

Lina clutched at Lon's bed in case she lost her balance. Where was up or down? She must have swayed badly because something steadied her from behind. Even so she still shrank away from the touch.

She searched and found Jae's aura. The brightest part would be where his body was. He seemed to be talking to something, but she couldn't hear.

"Hold this." His voice came from surprisingly near, and she knew he had put something in her hands. Immediately she was falling, falling, until with a jerk that hit her all over, she fit fully in her own body.

Gravity. Objects. The lab. "Wuff." She shook her head to clear it, and it didn't take much. "I'm back, thanks. What is it?" She held up a black coffee cup. Funny, she'd thought the ones they had been using had been some kind of white material. "Obsidian." She sighed her wonder. "Usually I can't handle obsidian or turquoise. They are too much of a grounding energy for me. Thanks. I really needed that."

Jae noticed the way she clutched the cup to her, as if she desperately depended on it. "Any time."

"Okay. I've finished the Kolaimni." She turned to her patient. "You can wake up now, Londo. How do you feel?"

He stirred and stretched; tried to roll over, tried again and failed.

"Here," Jae said and helped him. "I'm here now."

"Jae. God," Lon groaned. "I f-feel like I've been run over…by a s-starcruiser." He tried to laugh. Instead he grimaced. He could barely hold his eyes open.

Lina wanted to touch him, wanted to hug him, but didn't know how to act in front of these two strange men. Instead she just put her hand on Lon's hand, feeling happiness return to her life.

She silently told him how much she loved him, delighted to feel the feedback from his mind. "I've got to go dunk myself," she said aloud. "I'll be right back."

Wiley motioned to her. "Before you go…" He waved a hypo meaningfully at her.

"Where?" she asked.

Lon opened his dark-ringed eyes curiously as Wiley pointed to a spot on his arm and Lina put her hand there. Wiley lowered the injector to the arm. "Wiley, w-what…? Hey! Ouch! How– Ow," he said, trying out the sound. He looked at Lina and tried to focus. "How the–?"

"That's right, you were unconscious when Terry demonstrated that the first time. It seems to be a side effect from, you know. It's what the whole setup was for, apparently. Maybe."

"W-what…" It was difficult for him to speak yet. Lina could see how his hands trembled with weakness. ***What'd they get out of it?***

"They took a lot of blood from you. A whole lot."

She heard him say, ***I remember they wanted to cut you open.***

I'm okay, Lon. Getting better all the time now that you're back.

His eyebrows knit together as he tried to puzzle it out. Why? Why?

Lina sighed in frustration. She was fading out again, even with this huge hunk of obsidian in her hand. "Sorry. I've really got to dunk. I'll be right back."

Jae and Wiley both noted that she hugged the mug with both hands as she ran for the tank. The two Legionnaires turned back to Lon.

Jae grinned. "Okay, Lon." He felt like dancing now, but who would understand? Lon was awake. Lon was getting well! "We want to hear all about what happened. But first you've got to tell us: where in the worlds did you find *her*?"

"Be-believe it or n-not, Jae," Lon grimaced weakly in what was supposed to be a smile, "she was a g-gift from an old…an old en-enemy." Then he proceeded so slowly to tell them of Terry Rhodes and her latest scheme.

They patiently listened as he stumbled through the short-version overview, his eyes mostly closed. He delicately skirted the issue of sex and actually dozed off at one point.

"*Too* dopey," Jae murmured to Wiley.

"Was not asleep," Londo mumbled as he woke.

"So," Jae said, "the two of you were surrounded by soldiers…" He looked up to see Lina returning, hair neat from a comb she had found in the bathroom.

She'd also discovered fresh towels and a white terrycloth-like robe or lab coat which wasn't remotely her size. It hung in bulky pleats to her ankles and needed the sleeves rolled back a foot. But it tied shut, just like robes back home. Jae was very considerate.

There in the pool at the remote end of the lab, she'd sloughed off the excess energies from the healing. She'd dried herself, tucked her underwear into a pocket in the robe, folded Lon's burned shirt neatly, placed the obsidian mug on the top of the pile, and then broken down in tears. Lon was okay. He was alive! And he was getting better. *Thank you, God!*

Thank you, thank you, thank you! I don't know how I'm going to repay you for this but I will. You can ask anything of me. Anything!

After that came mere mindless sobbing.

Londo's table had been reconfigured so he could sit up a little. Now she crossed over to him and took his hand, which returned the squeeze weakly. How exhilarating to gaze at Lon's wonderful face! He continued his story.

Backtracking to the part where they first had been attacked, he switched from that other language to English. He worked himself up, trying to get his commanding voice back, but it didn't go with the watery eyes. "And n-next time, *next* time, Lina, when I tell you to port, you port."

She wrinkled her stiff nose at him. "First of all, I sincerely hope there won't be a next time, but if there is, I'll probably be a lot faster at getting things together for a port. I mean, I've only been doing this for, what, two days now? Secondly, I was this close–" she held her blistered fingertips together– "to getting you out of there when they hit me. And thirdly, that Terry bitch had her own set of priorities. If I weren't there, she would have blasted you to kingdom come and not thought twice. Am I right?"

"Euh. M-maybe."

"So you tell me. What was she doing getting blood from you? Does she want to impress a vampire?"

"Lots of…" Londo licked his lips. He was tired of talking. "Wiley?"

The blue doctor cocked his head. "There are a number of possibilities. It could be anything, really. Cloning experiments. Power experiments. There have been theories that a blood transfusion from Londo could give the recipient parapowers."

"She wanted to have Lon's baby," Lina said quietly. "Maybe the blood had something to do with that. Her biological clock is ticking down. She was desperate; I know that much."

"Blood wouldn't–"

Lon looked at Wilder. "Sh-she also wanted a sperm s-sample. Post mortem." His gaze went to Lina, and Wilder realized what had been threatened.

"As I said, a number of possibilities, and none of them pleasant. Londo, we're going to…"

Vaguely it occurred to Lina that Wiley's voice sounded more and more distant, and the room was going dark.

Jae was the one to catch her before she fell across Londo.

"Is she okay?" Lon demanded. He blinked and tried hard to focus although his eyes refused to do so. Was Lina's face discolored? Dark rust? It seemed the wrong shape somehow, though he knew it was her by her presence.

"It's all those stimulants we had her on," Wiley explained quickly to keep his patient calm. "She's just crashed from them. Good. Now that you're stable, Londo, I can work on her."

"Why? Is sh-she hurt?" Now Lon remembered Terry slapping her and more. "Th-they hit her. Low-grade…energy weapon. Number of t-times. Burned her. And…and I thought…I h-heard her…scream…"

"She was hit hard with lasers. And yes, there are some severe burns on her shoulder and back. I should be able to handle it. There'll be a long recuperation time for her arm, but she'll be all right." Wiley began to set up another bed like Londo's.

Jae hoisted Lina into his arms. She was like a rag doll and oddly light. He looked down at Londo, meeting his eyes.

"Jae… Jae…"

"Congratulations," Jae said softly to him so Wiley couldn't hear.

"Ah, Jae… I don't… I don't…" Lon scowled as he tried to talk.

"I'm glad for you, Lon. I really am." Jae gave him a wan smile and took the girl over to Wiley.

8

L ina woke up with a start. Where was she? Oh– the lab. Sarastor, another world. The lights were very dim and tiny creaks and hisses softly leaked from the corners of the place. She was on one of those floating bed-tables. Someone had put a blanket over her.

Her arm throbbed considerably less than it had, though the chicken wire and bubble gum were both missing. She touched the spot and felt a hard, oval bandage under her sleeve. A matching one was on the other side of the arm. A dressing covered her shoulder where the branding burn was, and something thick and sticky had been applied all over her face and throat and elsewhere.

She rotated her jaw experimentally. The skin was tight but not stretched achingly taut as it had been. She could feel some big patch on her back by the way the edges scratched at her when she moved, but her back as a whole was fairly numb, as were her stomach and legs.

Her mind wasn't completely clear, but it would do.

Raising up on her good elbow, she looked around. Lon was sleeping peacefully on his bed about twenty feet from her. Further away were Wiley and Jae, passed out on couches near the double-doored entrance.

Lina secured her robe and tiptoed over to Londo on the too-cool floor. Running a thorough psychic examination of him, she checked in with her guides and the guardian angels who massed around him, healing him in his sleep.

He looked so vulnerable.

A gray blanket left his shoulders uncovered. The brawniness of those muscles was a sharp contrast to Lon's face. His skin was sunken beneath his eyes, leaving dark circles. Whitish patches blotched around his mouth.

His hair was tousled and boyish– oh, how he wouldn't like that! Automatically she reached to smooth it back, but as soon as she touched him the lines on the monitors went haywire. She snatched her hand away. Those squiggly lines went back to the way they'd been.

She couldn't touch him when she longed to reassure herself that he still lived and still loved her.

All his life he'd been unable to give a human touch to anyone else. How selfish of her to feel as if she were being punished with this short time away from him! Maybe the universe thought that she'd overstepped her place for daring to love Valiant.

So now she had her hands slapped. Now she couldn't even touch him. But tomorrow he'd be better, the next day even better. Maybe she would be able to touch him then. She could live for two days like that. But she missed his strong arms around her, the warmth of those brown eyes as he smiled at her. He had the world's most bewitching smile.

The charts bleeped and she hastily withdrew her fingers from his lips. Oh dear, oh dear!

As Lina stamped her foot, a blond head across the room raised, then lay back down to feign sleep again.

All right. If she couldn't be a lover, she could be a professional. She corrected a few minor energy points on Lon, blew out some fetid energy, and then checked in with his femurs. They were happily churning away at producing blood cells.

The monitors were a mystery and thus no help. All she could tell was that Londo's body was in a balancing mode, taking the healing she had given him and in effect digesting it. It wouldn't be wise to give him anything more for a number of hours yet.

But there was another kind of healing that people said worked anytime. She offered up a prayer to the universe. *Please watch over him.*

She begged whatever God there might be and all His angels to heal this man– if it wasn't too presumptuous of her. They'd been saved by a miracle back there on Tiawa, and again after Londo had died. One miracle more, she pleaded. He's such a good man. The universe needs him.

I need him, too, Lord. He was the only person in the entire universe who had ever loved her.

Lina knew the signs of her own body: she was up for a while. What to do until then? She tried to stretch, but her body rebelled with twinges and worse. She blew out the worst of it and wished for an aspirin. Maybe a half bottle or so.

As she turned, she noticed the room's details for the first time. It was dark from the dim light, but also darkly furnished. It was also entirely too messy to be used as a set in a science fiction movie. Hurricane Lina had visited. Overturned glass-covered table cabinets lay everywhere. Smaller chunks of debris filled the spaces between them.

Jae and Wiley had sat at a dining room-sized table with a frameless windshield. Various paths to the table had been kicked out of the piles of detritus that surrounded it.

At least one tiny section of the vast, open lab revealed some order. Over there were terrariums and engines and what seemed to be chemical setups and heat sources aimed at various materials and steaming pots of whatever, all separated onto their own display tables. They provided quiet blips and bloops of background noise.

A scurrying sound like a mouse the cats had dragged in attracted her attention. Lina wove her way through the mess toward the few neat lines of tables and gave Wiley credit for cleaning some things up as well as he had so quic– Oh! A turtle-dome scuttled into view. Well, it looked like a turtle was there somewhere under the five-foot round, undercooked, translucent crystalline pancake someone had thrown over it.

The turtle thing scooted toward an up-ended table-high cabinet. The pancake part oozed forward, formed a short bulldozer wall, and pushed. Slowly the cabinet righted itself. Next the turtle-pancake crept up the sides and overflowed it, leaving a clean surface in its wake. It slithered back down to the floor.

Pincers formed from the pancake to set various machines and containers on top of the cabinet. Some blobs left the pancake to dribble across the floor beyond downed machinery. Other blobs returned from the same direction to merge seamlessly into the pancake.

From deep within the crystalline structure, two tiny Christmas lights blinked twice, to echo twice from lights in the cabinet's baseboard. The cabinet began to move on its own. Lina was so intrigued watching the turtle-pancake spread itself over the newly-uncovered expanse of floor and the tan and blue powders spilled there that she didn't realize that the cabinet had come to her and stopped.

"Oh, sorry," she told it and moved out of its way. It now continued on its path until it came to rest in an orderly fashion, right angles to a walkway through the lab, perfectly spaced from its neighbor equipment.

Instant house-cleaning by an overgrown sorcerer's pancake. Maybe she was still dreaming? How much would something like this cost, so she could get one? The cats would certainly hate it. She wondered if it could clean litter boxes and cat barf. Worth its weight in gold, if it could!

(And where could she get some real pancakes around here? She was starving!)

Back beyond where Wiley and Jae were passed out was a little nook of a room, an intimate place with an upholstered bench that ran around three sides of an oval table. The room's walls held neat linear indentations. When she used her imagination in conference with her guides, they showed her that the lines marked some version of a microwave and fridge. This room was a break room. Too bad that she had no idea how to get to the food.

So she tiptoed back past Wiley and Jae to return to the main room. Why hadn't at least one of them gone home? Oh right, they were in quarantine. No one could leave. How long would it last?

Lina remembered reading that when people first went to the moon and returned, they'd been kept in quarantine for a month in case they'd picked up a space virus. Of course they had no idea what to quarantine for. People would know about Terran diseases here, if Lon were a member. But he was invulnerable; did he ever get sick?

Should she expect to stay here for a month? If she ported them back, would they have to stay someplace for another month on Earth? If Lon were a member here, how did he operate without going into quarantine all the time? It was rare that he didn't make the news every few days.

Lina ached for information about everything. Ignorance frustrated her.

A glow from a cluster of small, colored squares along the near wall caught her eye. **Internet,** her guides whispered.

Walking along the wall with its long desk surface, she muscle-tested herself every few feet. She clicked her right thumb against a cage made of her left-hand fingers while asking if she were near a monitor, but every time her thumb broke through to signal "no." The results couldn't be trusted. Muscle tests wouldn't work if her hand were injured. *Idiot.*

"Computer," she asked tentatively, "is there a terminal here?"

#*No.*# She jumped at the voice next to her. She couldn't tell if it was male or female.

"Can you tone down the volume? I don't want to wake the others."

#*Volume control on low,*# it whispered.

"That's better." Damn. Had she mis-heard her guides? Maybe she was just too cocky after the events of the day. Psychic anything was usually far from 100% accuracy. "Is there a station along here where I could connect into something like the internet back home?"

#*Yes.*#

Great, a computer who wanted to play twenty questions. "Do I just call you computer? Do you have a name?"

#Computer.#

"All right. Computer, please show me where this communication station is." Four feet away along the table, a rectangle of blue light appeared. It hung some three inches away from the actual wall.

She rolled a chair down to sit in front of the screen. "Can I get a medical update on Londo?"

#That information is classified security level triple-five.#

"Still? Look, I was one of the people working on him. I'm going to be working on him some more. I need to know."

#That information is classified security level triple-five.#

She stifled a curse. "Okay, it's not your fault you had a paranoid programmer. But you better watch it or I'll pull a 'Captain Kirk and the Cosmic Computer' maneuver on you. 'Norman, coordinate,' but you don't have Norman. Won't you regret that!"

The sigh of defeat Lina gave her situation sounded more like a groan. "Can I just access some information? Please?"

#Restricted files call for Legion membership and suitable security rank.#

"I don't want any restricted files. I want general, everyday information."

#Subject?#

"Um. Valiant, for one. Wilder Mem-Bazer. Jae…Rallene. Ah, Aff… Affiliated Planets Legion."

#Affiliated Systems Megaforce Legion.#

"Right, that one. And Sarastor." Since she couldn't read whatever language they had Out Here– the computer called it "Panlingua," or "Lingua" for short– she was delighted to discover that everything could be translated into English.

#First subject?#

"How about the Mega-Legion?"

#Affiliated Systems Megaforce Legion.#

"Yeah. History, mission, whatever you have. General overview, if you would."

The computer beeped twice and the screen lit up with writing that scrolled comfortably without her lifting a finger. Occasionally it would dissolve into startling 3-D video clips of paraheroes doing various heroic things: battles with criminals, rescues from natural disasters, the building of this headquarters two hundred forty-seven years ago, flashy glamour shots of the current membership.

Ooh– there was Londo. The screen changed to another member before she could fully appreciate the photo.

She did a slap-dash Reiki healing on herself as she studied, resting her hands together on her blistered, slime-covered skin and moving them as the energy lowered, to strengthen again over a new area of her body.

There were almost 500 members, or Legionnaires, so she didn't even try to learn who everyone was. Members were not only paras, but megaparas. Five hundred megaparas. Imagine! Earth had less than ten.

She recognized Jae Rallene. He went by the name "Neutrino"– a full Legionnaire, not merely Wiley's assistant. Wiley was just Dr. Mem-Bazer. Apparently "Five-Minds" was lurid enough for his parahero name, though come to think of it, Lina doubted that any parent would name their baby "Five-Minds." Wiley had probably adopted his hero name as his legal one to be efficient.

****Change your name,**** her guides told her.

"I am trying to concentrate here," she replied as she resumed her studies.

The Megaforce Legion served the Affiliated Systems, over 600 worlds (and giant artificial satellites! But darn it, no Dyson spheres or even ringworlds) in just under 400 star systems, which was the vast majority of the civilized worlds in this sector of the galaxy. Wherever the heck this sector was.

The organization consisted of both military and civilian personnel in a demi-paramilitary-ish organization. It stepped in when local government was too overwhelmed to handle an emergency. It was held in highest regard by the populace, and for good reason: they had pulled off some amazing feats over the years, had helped millions if not billions of people.

Feeling pressed for time, she switched from that subject to glance at quick entries on Wilder and then Neutrino. Oh– his entry mentioned Feith. It was Jae's home planet, it seemed. So what could it mean that Feith was inside him? Maybe it was one of those crazy guide things, where they didn't make much sense. She was going to ask for further information, but decided instead to see how far she could go on other subjects before she came back.

Valiant. Nice footage, woof! Apparently he was very active off-Earth. How in the world did he have time for it all? Lon was considered the most powerful Legionnaire.

The puter noted his high Q scores for public approval both inside and outside the Legion. He was captain of an Alpha Team, which sounded important, and Lina recalled the same listing for Jae. Lon had been nominated a couple of times for Legion Commander, but he wasn't eligible. A commander was required to be a full-time member, which he was not. It didn't help that Lon came from Earth, which apparently was not in the Mega-Legion's sector.

And yet he was as renowned here as he was at home. The listing of available information on Lon went on and on. It was as if she'd Googled "sex." There must be a billion entries.

Londo was beyond famous. He was historic. Generations from now his name would still be mentioned every day. Maybe he'd engender his own myths and folk tales. Maybe some people would think he was a god.

It would be easy to picture Maximus as Zeus and Valiant as Hercules. While Maximus stayed in the clouds with his lightning, commanding the other gods, Valiant walked among humans.

He'd walked beside her.

Those distant future people would never hear a whisper of Lina O'Kelly's name.

She shouldn't be doing this. All she was doing was driving herself crazy. Lina resolved to live in the present and enjoy everything it had to offer. She wouldn't think about tomorrow.

She got up to check on Londo again and to go to the bathroom to wash the sticky stuff off her face. There she paused and stared at her lumpy, mottled condition. It was still almost impossible to see Lina within the charred mess. A prominent patch of blisters on her left cheek resembled Australia. Angry-looking cuts added multiple Rings of Fire around the continent, especially toward New Zealand. The same condition on her legs and arms made it seem as if blister-ivy had grown all over her.

Perhaps she'd best leave the goop on.

Yesterday she'd felt like she could have healed anything. Well, anything named Londo. The emergency had plugged her firmly into a rare psychic healing "zone," though the earlier deep communion with his cells certainly helped her know the way his body worked.

Could she do the same for herself? She made a face at the mirror. Psychic healing wasn't recommended for most emergency situations. It was usually a gently holistic manner of gradual healing. Yesterday had been a fluke, a miraculous exception.

Wiley had helped bring Londo along and he'd done an amazing job on her so far. She flexed her left arm. It was stiff and she knew where the major nerves lay, for they felt like double-pointed needles inside her muscles. Still, it was lots better than waking to find it amputated. Or not waking at all.

She decided she'd handle the metaphysics and let Wiley continue with his biophysics.

Lina returned to the computer screen and brought up information about Sarastor. Sleepily she began to satisfy her curiosity about this friendly planet. The overview was written from a touristy point of view with many videos about governmental areas (Sarastor was the capital of the Affiliated Systems, or AffSys, which didn't sound so hissy before her floating marble translated it), and a lengthy section extolling the presence of the Mega-Legion's headquarters. After a while she chose a couple more subjects, one of which was very important, but she dozed off in fits and starts before she could finish them.

9

Wiley found Lina in the morning. She'd taken the blanket and pillow from her makeshift bed and had slept on the floor next to Londo, just out of reach. Wiley scanned her and frowned, then gestured at his screens to note the situation on her med record. Crossing the room, he touched some points on the wall monitor screen she'd used to see for himself what she'd been accessing during the night, though Jae had already written a quick report of his own on the matter.

Obviously she was trying to get her bearings here. She'd looked at info about Valiant. After a moment's consideration, he decided that might make sense as well. She'd wanted to know about Sarastor, and here was a request for information about Sarastor's weather control system. She'd asked if there were really a need for it and what it would take to have the authorities shut it down. Interesting.

There'd been a request for information on biocleaning. She would be concerned about getting out of quarantine as quickly as possible. He had to smile at the last subject she'd covered: birth control methods with a specific query for something called a "morning-after pill." Sensible. Nothing to worry about concerning an attempt to get sensitive files from the Legion computer. Requested subject matter also seemed to confirm a Terran point of view.

Bare-feet sounds on the laboratory floor behind him told him she was up and about. "Your bed was programmed for healing," he said without turning around. "I didn't think about programming the floor."

"Sorry. I didn't know. I was worried that Lon might wake up and need something."

"He slept the night through. I can prepare a shot for you, if you wish."

Lina blushed when she saw that he was referring to the birth control screen she'd been reading. With the blanket wrapped around herself and her pillow tucked under one arm, she tried to pat her crazy hair into place. "I suppose I do want one, if you could. Thank you. How's Lon?"

"I'm curious to see what you think about that."

"He's still badly out of balance, probably weak as a kitten– well, maybe a cat. He needs to sleep undisturbed for a few more hours. And Jae needs to tone down that blood production. He's got happy bones working like heck, but I think Londo needs all his systems easing back to normal now that the danger's over."

Two of Wiley's minds smiled to the others. Yes, this was going to be an interesting book, despite it being a Terran technique.

Lina continued: "If I were you I'd put on some soft classical music, like Pachelbel's *Canon.* Wish I'd brought my flute. Lon should drink lots of pure water. Absolutely no stimulants; he should sleep as much as he can. And a massage couldn't hurt."

"I don't know anything about the music item, but that last is definitely out of the question. He is Valiant." Wiley paused. "Unless you can supply the massage."

"I can, as long as my arm stays with me. Whatever you did has done wonders, but it still doesn't quite feel all there."

"We'll work on that today."

She tucked the blanket back on her lab bed and tried unsuccessfully to fluff the pillow. "It's not everyday that I get a hole blown through me. I'm very lucky that y'all were able to do anything for it. Thank you very much."

Wiley gave her a half-nod. For a Terran barbarian she was surprisingly polite. He'd have to keep watch for other un-Terran-like behavior. The woman could well be a sleeper agent. "It's no problem," he said, "especially since we have time to spare right now. As long as you're awake, come along with me while I prepare your shot. We won't wake the others. I have some questions for you."

She followed him. "I take it there's no tradition of psychic healing here?"

"Rumors and traditions from the distant past, but nothing that's ever been proven to work. Are you a doctor on Earth?"

She had to stifle her snort. "Heavens, no! Heck, it's only been sixty years or so since the medical profession admitted that nutrition had anything to do with health. Everyone just wants to give you a shot to cure anything instead of preventing it in the first place. Pretty stone knives and bearskins to you, I should think."

"I can understand shots," Wiley said, though he'd have to puzzle through the "stone knives and bearskins" reference later.

Wiley's central console was the windscreened desk where he and Jae had watched her work, but he chose to lead her to another station. He kicked through the debris to make a spot where they both could stand, and then moved his left hand in the air strangely, wiggling his fingers. To Lina it didn't seem to be an affectation but something deliberate. Then he took a hypo handle and pressed it against an indentation at the side of the counter.

He wore plain gold rings on all his fingers, two on each thumb. Lina noted that same iridescent ring that Jae wore was on his right hand, middle finger.

Wiley explained as he waved the hypo over her good arm, "This isn't just a morning-after solution. It's good for a year. Will that be enough?"

Lina opened her mouth and nothing came out for a beat. Wiley was assuming a long-term affair. Between the legendary Valiant and Lina Nobody?

But how long *would* it last? Could she pray for it to go on as long as a year? Lon had to get tired of her sometime. *Not going there,* she determined. *Living in the present.* "I have no idea," she admitted. "I– This just happened from out of the blue. At first I thought it would be just until his powers came back." She tried to shake away the suffocating cloud of doubt. It was like being hounded by a green-headed fly, the kind that bit and held on, chewing. If it ever shook off, it kept flitting around, trying to bite again.

I live in the present, she ordered herself.

"It's reversible, if you ever want to," Wiley told her.

The outrageousness from so many angles made her laugh. "Me– a mother? I don't think so. I'm not the mother type."

"Even for a child of Valiant?"

"What has he been telling you?" Suspicion knifed through her. Had Londo been bragging about his prowess? Had he been telling sex stories to his buddies?

Wiley shrugged his shoulders and examined two screens before he pressed the hypo to her arm.

"I'll kill him. What did he say about me? Or has that been classified, too?"

"I doubt if you'd be able to access it. And you should know that it's illegal to threaten the life of a Legionnaire." Wiley looked like he enjoyed the strangled sound she made.

Change subject before she said something that would get her deeper into trouble! "Okay. Okay. So,... If you don't mind me asking, which eye do I look at?"

"Say again?" One of Wiley's eyes maddeningly turned to the left to examine her while the other remained focused on the first screen.

"They aren't coordinated well," Lina said. "I mean, first one looks at me and then it's off on its own and the other looks at me, and then neither does. Londo says I have to start looking people in the eye, but your eyes keep switching back and forth. I hope I'm not rude, that it's not a medical condition or–"

"I have five minds," Wiley said, returning his complete attention– or was that attentions?– to his screens.

"And two eyes."

"I can utilize visuals from two separate bio sources," he told her.

"Only two? That must be boring for the other three minds."

"With only two eyes," Wiley clicked a ring against the tabletop, "I've added three computer links and two direct digital broadcast receivers to my senses with optional analog transition. I can pick and choose from seven source modes, and am considering adding enhanced visuals to my ocular nerves this coming year, which will give me nine total."

"But do you get HBO?" Lina asked.

"Hm?" Wiley began to turn to her.

"Bad joke. Sorry. I take it you don't drive? I mean, depth of field must not kick in when you do the roving eye routine."

"Since I don't go out on many missions I don't require three-dimensional sight," he said. "When I need it, I coordinate eye movements. That also allows me to concentrate on the mission at hand with an extra mind."

"Oh." Lina scratched her bad arm and encountered only hard bandage. "It's so deathly quiet. Can we turn on some music, please?"

"Again a music reference. Why?"

The sourness of his expression surprised her. "To keep from going crazy, I guess. It helps me to concentrate. And like I said, Lon could use some for relaxation, even while he's asleep."

Wiley looked like he'd just eaten a lemon soaked in vinegar. "I'm aware of the music of Earth," he said. "Londo has the same problem with quiet that you do." He shook his head as he returned to whatever it was he was doing to the desktop. "Sarastor and most of the planets of the AffSys have very little non-percussive music. The Terran form is a primitive expression of raw emotions: love, lust and violence set to tones and drums."

"What idi– Ah, who decided that?"

His ringed fingers drummed their own pattern on a row of colored lights, though Lina didn't think he noticed. "Combining music and words is shamanistic ritual. Does it have to do with the magical traditions of Earth's Timeless Realms?"

What peculiar ideas they had Out Here! "Of course not. We make music because we like it. It's an art."

He made a noise that didn't sound as if he were convinced at all.

So she changed subjects and discovered that there was no chance of getting a change of clothing. The Mega-Legion had matter transmitters to zap stuff around electronically, but no larger receivers in this lab, at least not to be used under quarantine conditions.

"And I keep my replipons in my other labs," Wiley added as explanation.

"Oh." Whatever that or those was or were. It boiled down to: no clothes beyond what they'd come in with.

Lina snugged the oversized robe around herself as she told Wiley what she'd theorized from the night's research about quarantine and quick cures.

He said, "You were reading about biocleaning in hyperspace, which is the way we get from star system to star system. Hyperspace is different from normal space. Biocleaning can complete in just minutes there. But apparently you didn't come through hyperspace."

"And…?"

"It will take longer. About three days."

"Three–? And how long to get back to Earth– via hyperspace, so I don't have to go through quarantine again?"

"Approximately one day."

"Four days, plus today for finishing up on Londo…" She counted on her fingers and bit her swollen lip.

That brought both his eyes to bear on her. "You're concerned about something."

"First of all, who's going to feed my cats? My cat sitter is scheduled to stop looking after them, oh, tomorrow or the next day. And secondly, I guess I'm out of a job."

"Your job?"

"I only had one week off, not two. My employers will not be pleased when I finally appear god knows when."

At that he faced her, leaning back on his desk. "But when you tell them that you saved Valiant's life–"

"Yeah, like they'll ever reverse a decision just because it was a mistake. Oh well, I hated that job. I was going to leave it anyway." She looked at him sharply. "But I can't let my cats starve."

"Cats." Both Wilder's eyes swiveled. One rolled up and to the left, classic memory-retrieval position while the other went its own merry way. "Small domesticated mammals kept as pets," Wiley decided.

"Yes. Hungry small mammals. Can I get to some more information about biocleaning? When we arrived, I knew I wasn't equalizing everything I should, but we were in a hurry. Maybe I can learn how to bioclean."

"I can arrange that. In the meantime we'll arrange for your cats' care. We are the Legion."

He said that last part the same way a pharaoh would say, "So let it be written; so let it be done." The certainty of it cheered Lina.

"Tell me," Wiley continued, "how long did the actual port take? Was it all done in one hop or more? Exactly how is the process accomplished?" He gestured at the air and recording screens swung around to either side of Lina.

She scrunched her shoulders so they wouldn't bump into her, but they seemed rather immaterial for computer screens. Lina explained as much as she recalled.

"And how did you compensate for the difference in conditions between departure and arrival points?"

"I uh… There was *this* and *that…*" Running out of descriptive words, she tried to mime the feel of things. She found her hands making balancing motions as she wobbled back and forth like a surfer, and thought that explained the technique very well.

Wiley frowned very hard at it all. "We'll come back to that," he told her.

He showed her the tapes of Lon and her on the table, her funneling energy out of him like lightning bolts from her hand, and Lina explained what she had been doing. She wondered at the bolts of energy crashing through the floor, at the power involved. She knew she was a decent healer, but this?

This had been a case of Divine Inspiration and probably a couple kazillion guardian angels working through her. *Thank you, Lord*, she silently repeated and knew they all heard her.

As Wiley went through highlights of the rest of the process she decided to try various healing passes on him so he could have his own experience.

His face took on a boyish look as he strove to feel something, but then he shook his head. "Nothing. But apparently something about it works." Wiley touched a spot on the black desk. "Gorgeon," he said.

After a moment came an answering female voice. "Here, master."

"Don't call me that."

A round, friendly middle-aged woman's face with a distinctly orangish hue set against a white cap appeared on the table's surface. She looked expectantly at Wiley.

"I want you to hear some new medical theory." Wiley turned to Lina. "The doctor's in the Legion's Med Wing. The… occurrence yesterday is now classified information, so do not mention anything concerning it to her, but this general research isn't."

"Classified?" Lina was puzzled. "But if Dr. Gorgeon's—"

"Just call her Gorgeon."

"If Gorgeon's in the Legion–"

"I'm a Legion employee, not a Legionnaire," Gorgeon said pleasantly. That white cap with ear flaps she wore now looked like medical wear instead of something out of Olde Holland. "My security level is four point two."

Wiley nodded. "And Lina's is Special Need to Know for this episode. Medical emergencies almost always end up under Gorgeon and her staff's care, except in the…oddball," Wiley tasted the Terran word, "case like this."

Gorgeon had been eying Lina's disfigured face with concern. Her image rose from the table to hover 3-D in midair so she could get a better view of the entire patient. "I think your guest needs to see us immediately," she said, "or was the rumor I heard about a quarantine in Lab 1-A true? The commander's had everyone scanning the entire complex for bio-contaminants. I even saw young Nud Littel carrying a bio-unit along the visitors' floors way after his bedtime last night."

"Commander Magnos is merely being overcautious as always. Better that than the opposite. Let's just say that Lina will see you in two days," Wiley replied. "This is Lina O'Kelly of Earth."

Gorgeon's bodiless head tilted to the side as she calculated. "Valiant's home world. Rumors are certainly flying lately."

"Then you'd better report them to Security, shouldn't you? Gorgeon…"

"Ready and waiting, sire."

"Don't call me that either."

Was there a touch of passive-aggression in Gorgeon's manner? Though she said it pleasantly enough, Lina thought she sensed frustration underneath.

She recalled her lessons of the previous night. This Mega-Legion likely meant big celebrity status. Did some of the members exploit that? Did the people they employed run up against a wall of social elevation when trying to deal with them?

She might be reading too much into this. The frustration level wasn't that great, and Wiley and Jae were very friendly and approachable, definitely not the über-celebrity type. As for Gorgeon– Lina's guides liked her very much. Thumbs up and pats on the head for her.

Wiley still spoke to Gorgeon. "I want you to see this. Now Lina, put your arm here." He adjusted a floating sensor ball.

Wiley had Lina demonstrate astral body stretching. Halfway through, Gorgeon heaved a quick, exasperated sigh as if she'd been through something like this before.

"May I assume we're talking metaphysical anatomy? It would help if someone gave me background on what the *kick* we're looking at." Her head jounced from side to side as if she might be flapping her arms about to make a point, but the screen didn't show that much of her.

Somehow Wiley managed to disguise Londo's image as he ran a playback of yesterday for Gorgeon, so an observer would have thought the person brought back to life in his lab could have been anyone. That is, if rumors hadn't been rampant.

What kind of weapon could kill Valiant? came clearly from Gorgeon's concerned mind, though she never spoke Lon's name aloud.

Computer-enhanced color fields filled the air around the body, flickering like sputtering candles as Lina worked. Lina watched the playback with as much wonder as the others.

Every now and then Gorgeon asked a question and Wiley would ask Lina to elucidate on this technique or that one. That she'd taken courses with textbooks excited him until he learned that the textbooks had originally been channeled from disembodied entities. Oh, he didn't like that concept! "Scientific method," he grumbled under his breath.

Gorgeon didn't mumble. She merely pursed her lips and pressed her eyelids almost shut. There was something akin to *the blind leading the blind* in her thoughts about Lon's healing, but also great relief that the hero was back among the living, along with tremendous curiosity to examine these new techniques in controlled conditions. The frontiers of medicine should be advanced whenever possible so people could be helped.

Lina tried to be patient within the flood of doubt coming at her from both directions. It took effort not to hear strong thoughts especially when they were so concentrated, as they were with these two focused doctors.

When she made Wiley perform a basic astral visualization exercise, his screen recorded a faint afterimage of his hand expanding and then retracting.

Gorgeon exclaimed, "Look at that!"

"But I was merely imagining I was doing it," Wiley protested.

Lina recalled a teacher's lesson. "Thoughts are powerful. They come before actions, which allow creation. Or even more basic than that: I think; therefore I am."

"I'll have to think about that," Wiley said with a quirk to his lips.

Gorgeon gave a pleasant snort. Minutes later she was exclaiming again as Wiley refined his scans so they could almost see the structure of Lina's etheric body, but only when she concentrated on it.

"This is a network that ties body systems together?" Gorgeon asked. She demanded Wiley take physical readings, too, so she could compare changes on that plane.

When Wiley took Lina's hand or arm to position it under his recorders, Lina gritted her teeth but tried not to pull away from the touch. Gorgeon must have noticed, for she asked her if she needed new painkillers, as if touching had physically hurt. Politely declining, Lina tried to cover up her phobia better.

Jae found them while they were experimenting and smiled to see Wilder so fascinated with something totally new. "Good morning." He kept his voice low so as not to disturb Londo. He'd already checked to see that Lon was very much improved.

Lina looked up and froze. Had she been so out of things yesterday not to notice?

Jae was breathtakingly beautiful. Maybe the most beautiful being she'd ever seen!

10

Jae was shaking his shoulder-length, night-tangled hair into place and didn't notice her amazement, thank goodness. More slender and maybe a half-foot taller than Lon, he walked with a sure dancer's ease. His lean face held the roundness of youth, balancing a slight beard stubble, narrow nose, and a mouth wide enough to turn an ordinary smile into a mischievous grin. His eyes were such a bright blue they seemed to shine on their own. Glints of matching blue peeked through his hair: tiny earrings.

It wasn't that his looks were so perfect. He was good looking, yes, but there was something else that sent him over the top. A cosmic sense of grace, she decided. It was like he and the universe walked in tune with each other.

Then again, maybe those were her pain meds talking.

That glamour sloughed off when he made a face and squeegeed his tongue between his teeth. He smacked his lips, then wrinkled his nose as he woke up more. Adjusting his belts over his tunic sweater, he stretched his back and rolled his shoulders. "You're looking a *kick* of a lot better today, Lina. I'm beginning to think that purple is not your normal skin color." At last he considered himself awake. No, a final scratch behind his neck finished the job.

"Morning, Jae," Wilder nodded absently as he paid attention to Gorgeon's detailed analysis of mitochondrial metabolic rates.

Lina was not going to stand here like a gawking para-groupie! "Good morning," she drawled. Mustn't embarrass either of them. "I was hoping you'd be up soon, before I needed to start on Lon. We have to talk."

That caught Wiley's attention and he turned one eye to Jae.

"She saw something in my aura yesterday," Jae explained. He ran his fingers through his hair to push it out of his eyes, and again Lina saw that the tops of his ears had an elongated elfish tip. His deep almond skin would have marked him a member of the Californian surfer elf clan, if there was one.

"I apologize for the way I presented it. I didn't want to upset you," she said, reminding herself fiercely that she was not on Earth anymore. After all, here was Wilder Mem-Bazer, with his skin a beautifully subdued shade of teal as he stood in this set that would out-*Star Trek Star Trek*. It all combined to give a breathtaking sense of unreality and cosmic cosmopolitanism.

"Sometimes I'm too eager to get things done. I went too long without a break during the Kolaimni." She paused. "I read that you change sub-molecular structure and reactions. I was wondering how you came up with that obsidian mug. That's pretty amazing."

Jae shrugged. "That's what I do."

"I heard you talk to the spirit of the mug, or maybe the deva of its structure. Something about crystalline patterns. It listened to you," she said wonderingly, "and it changed."

Wilder's ring-covered fingers paused over his monitors. "That's an odd idea," he said. "Is she right? People have always wondered how Feithi–" He stopped suddenly and both eyes blinked in unison for once. Then he said, "Lab transmission out, Gorgeon."

"Aye aye, master." Gorgeon's disappointed image vanished.

"Is it?" Wiley asked Jae.

Jae's features evened out, the smile fading. "People have had lots of theories," he hedged, "but I want to hear some more from you, Lina."

"I read a little about you last night. The computer said that you came from Feith. That Feith was a planet, not a person. I think I need to do a reading for you."

"Wait a minute," Wilder insisted. "First of all, please review for me what you discussed yesterday."

Lina regarded him. "I don't want to seem rude, but I don't like third parties around when I channel. They interrupt with inappropriate questions. They often make the client uncomfortable."

Jae smiled warningly before his features slipped back into neutral. "That's okay. I trust Wiley to hear whatever. And he won't ask too many questions, will he?"

Wiley made a noncommittal noise.

Lina tried to persuade Jae. "This might get pretty personal. You can never tell."

"Wiley has a blackmail file on everyone and mine's bigger than most. Will it bother you if we record for him?"

"I always record so my clients can review later. Can we sit somewhere?" Standing up for so long, her knees were beginning to wobble.

They moved to that little break room. Lina settled herself at the table, linking with the universal white light for spiritual protection. This was a service she'd performed many times before. She planted her bare feet flat on the floor to connect with the grounding energy of the planet.

After she straightened her chakras she announced, "This will be a general reading with time for a few questions. Don't let me go over oh, thirty minutes or I'll get too tired to work on Lon, okay?"

"All right." Jae looked at Wiley, who touched one of his rings and then nodded.

Lina took a deep breath, released, and began the familiar visualization routine. "Okay. Whew, it's hard working my way through the crowd around you. So many people. Who here is best qualified to speak for the group? All right, thank you. Go ahead."

She listened, stretching her senses to feel who might be there. Quick impressions of faces passed through her imagination as the whispers focused down to one voice.

"He's an elderly gentleman, but he looks very young, as if he were in his forties, maybe even thirties. His name is, ah… Smolenk. Smlenk. No, it's Sim Lenk. Two words, said very fast."

"My grandfather." Jae breathed shallowly. "He always talked fast."

"Slow down, please. He says, 'Hello little Jaeson, you've grown well and strong. Rest assured that you are well-loved, too. Everyone sends you their love. But you've let fear into your heart, hate and fear and it has cost you dearly. Cost you the heritage that you would have received naturally if you had just let it. But that is water under the bridge, so to speak. You could not have been taught that because…because there was no one left to teach you any better.' What does that mean?"

Before Jae could ask if she were asking him or his grandfather, she answered her own question. "'Feith is no more. Feith is dead.'" Her forehead creased in puzzlement. "But Feith is a planet. He keeps saying that Feith is dead and gone. How do you kill–" She gasped so hard it hurt. "Oh my god. Oh my god!"

Lina scrambled off the bench and shook her arms to clear the horrific energy. "Oh my god." She clapped her hands to her mouth. She looked at Jae, then at Wiley, then back at Jae. "All those people– I didn't know," she whispered.

The past's death cries howled in the ether. Trillions of beings, not only people but animals, plants, even the rocks themselves– stripped of their physical anchors to the universe in a few shared moments. For a second Lina couldn't breathe. She arched her back as sensation flashed through her. It had been heat. Some kind of Armageddon, supernova heat–

Jae nodded hollowly. "An accident destroyed the world and everyone on it but me, back when I was a child."

"An accident? An entire planet?!"

"Some military exercises nearby…got out of hand." His voice grated. "A weapon pointed the wrong way."

She squinted at him. "You don't think it was an accident. You saw something."

No accusation or emotion showed on Jae's face. "It wiped out the perpetrators as well, so we'll never be sure. I was the only survivor."

Wiley said, "Every final report cited technological failure." But his lips tightened, and his nose wrinkled as if he smelled something terrible.

"I'm…so sorry," Lina said, unable to decide what words were appropriate for genocide.

"It was a long time ago. I've gotten used to the situation," Jae said.

"No you haven't." With alacrity she took her seat again, gathering the white light around her. She asked it to project onto Jae, too. He must be protected! "You've never accepted it. It wears at you, it eats at your soul. It's torn your life apart and it's all you can do still to hold it together. It's getting worse. Isn't it? Isn't it?"

"Ah… Yes," he admitted, and concerned surprise bloomed on Wilder's face.

"And they're telling you, it's like the whole planet's population is gathered around, reaching out to reassure you. They're saying it's all right, that they're all right. You volunteered while they left. What do you mean?"

She paused again, listening. "'You were the one who willingly stayed behind to teach, to carry on, to make sure that Feith, all she was in spirit and culture, lived on.' That's wonderful. The others…um. Could you repeat that? Oh. The others, everyone on Feith, from animals to people to the very planet itself– They were all ready to advance to the next level of development. They all needed to shed their physicality. To die."

She took a breath, trying to gauge Jae's reaction to all this, but the information swept her along. "They chose a quick death."

She had to give an ironic laugh at this point. "They weren't stupid. They didn't want to suffer. This one took place in seconds. More efficient than *manna-line*," [Jae inhaled sharply, that a non-Feithi should know that word] "to take care of everything at the same time. Moments for an entire planet to return to spirit." Lina was absolutely serious at this point. "They made a choice that would serve two purposes simultaneously."

A sharp metaphorical image came through: the Washington Mall swarming with people carrying signs, their free hands raised in "V" salutes into the air as they sang, *All we are saying…* "A, a cause? A peace protest?"

"That weapon," Jae murmured, "is now forbidden for any world to use."

But she was almost oblivious to his comment, her pupils pinpoints. "Oh my god." She bit her knuckles at what she saw, but bulled on.

"There was one chosen, one who volunteered. You, Jae, before you were born the plan was in place, and you volunteered to remain behind. For that you are honored in a special place by the others. And loved.

"But Sim Lenk observes without judgment that you have adopted hate and fear into your life, embraced them in a way that Feithi should not. 'Hate and fear are not part of Feith, but you are eaten up with them. Go back and remember yourself, remember Feith. See past the fear, see past the pain and remember.

"'It is time to teach Feith. She lives inside of you, waiting for you to show her to the galaxy. It is the teacher who learns the most. Teach and learn, Jaeson.'"

She blinked, coming back down a couple of notches. "Did you understand? You volunteered to be the survivor. You are supposed to teach your culture. The people, the planet you left behind– they're all okay. They're where they're supposed to be. They did not suffer overmuch when they died. They love you dearly and wish you well. There is nothing for them to forgive, for everyone, including you, did as they were supposed to."

Lina studied Jae. He leaned forward, his elbows on the table, arms crossed at the wrists, head cradled there, looking into space. He was silent for a long time and Lina waited patiently for him.

"So I was supposed to survive."

"Yes. You– your Higher Self, I suppose– volunteered to be the one. There had to be one."

"And everyone else? Where are they now? My grandfather... my parents, my sister? My friends?"

Lina searched for an answer. "It's beyond my comprehension. Another...dimension? A much higher vibration than ours. Totally non-physical, but it's not angelic in nature. I think. Akin to angelic, maybe that's the concept, a first or second cousin. But life goes on evolving there even as it does here, and there they've just begun in a new series of cycles. Oh, they think it's exciting."

"In heaven?" Jae had heard from Londo about Terran concepts of heaven.

"No, it's not a *bardo*, or between-lives cosmic kind of state. They are living their learning lives now in a world just as real as this one but so different– I wish I could get a handle on it. Going ahead of you."

Jae considered. "And me? I'm going to join them when I die?"

Lina asked. "It's your choice. If you wish to be with them, you can. If you want to remain in this dimension, to help or whatever, it's still your choice."

"So I'm supposed to give up the Legion and teach now, is that it? How? And what exactly?"

Lina appeared to ask and look puzzled. She asked again and still looked puzzled, but smiled through it. "The line they're giving me is this: 'Don't quit your day job.' Do you understand the concept? That you can teach, but shouldn't give up what I assume is the Legion? Hang on… Uh huh. Okay. Say that part again?" She paused.

"They say that you'll know what to teach when it comes that you have to, that you'll recognize the opportunity. It will be as obvious as if a ton of bricks had fallen on you. Do you understand bricks?"

"Bricks. Yes."

"There are three planets… I don't get it. Three worlds that you'll specialize in, or maybe live on. It's unclear. You're definitely going to move, but this is something else. Oh. They're being deliberately vague. They're shutting a door to that information and locking it away. Showing me that they have the key and I don't, nyah, nyah. In a nice way."

Sheepishly she shrugged. "Sorry. Can't help you in that department. I've heard of that happening to other people, and they've always said thank goodness they didn't know at the time, that things turned out for the best because they didn't."

Jae scowled before his mask of indifference fell back into place. "All right. I'll know what I'm supposed to do when I'm supposed to do it, and I shouldn't leave the Legion, right?"

"Probably not. Free will is always up to you, of course," Lina added quickly. Many people didn't realize that part. "This is just advice."

"Is there anything else they can tell me about the future?"

She asked and then laughed when she heard the response. "I'm sorry. It's just so clichéd, and they're laughing, too. A new love, new job, new home, a new life. Happiness, if you will embrace it. It depends on your attitude.

"Hang on to the hate and fear that you have brought into your life, and it will continue miserably, maybe even…" she paused and tried to push away the gruesome image of Jae lying in some empty room, his wrists slit and the blood pooling everywhere, "worse than that.

"Set about to rid yourself of the darker emotions, to grasp what life has to offer and what you have to offer life, and…" Oh, that was so much better! No image, but a wonderful feeling blossomed within her like a rainbow, like spring after a hard winter. "Well, fulfillment awaits. Your happily ever after. The stuff that dreams are made of."

Even Jae had to smile at that. "I suppose I want to make the better of the two choices. Do they have any ideas how I can get rid of my, ah, darker emotions?"

"Five minutes," Wilder warned.

"Right," Lina said. "Let's get the Higher Self involved here, okay, guys? And how about a guardian angel or two? Ah, there they are, in the crowd." She paused for a half-minute, communicating. "You're kidding," she said. "Say that again. I must not have gotten that right." Pause. "Tell me three times; I can be stupid." Pause. "Okay, got it. Yes, I'll tell him. Thank you. Thank you all for the information. Good bye."

She blinked, clearly coming back to the here and now as Jae waited expectantly. "Well?"

She gave an embarrassed little laugh. "I don't know what it means, but they kept saying it over and over. 'Tell him to stick around Londo and you,' they said."

"Londo…and you?" Jae asked, his head tilting to the side.

"That's what they said. I repeat, I don't know why. Sorry. Sometimes they can be very strange that way. Sometimes they seem to get a kick out of being mysterious."

Jae pushed back in his chair, his gaze far away. "Well. Good enough. Thanks. You've given me a lot to think about."

Lina couldn't tell him about the blood. Don't alarm the client! Still, she had to make sure that he kept on the right path. When she left here to go back to Earth, she'd have to arrange for someone to watch Jae. Londo might have some ideas.

Had she come all the way to Sarastor to rescue Lon and then see his friend die?

11

Wilder switched off his recording instruments with a wiggle of two ringed fingers. "It's not every day I get a live event to add to my anthropological section on extant superstitions. Although after yesterday I rather expected a few more fireworks. It was a very vague reading," he decided.

"I wouldn't say that," Jae said. Thoughtfully, he scratched his neck. "I wouldn't say that at all."

"Lina, you'd read about Feith being destroyed."

She was used to skeptics. "I never got that far in the personal histories. I was going to go back, but I fell asleep."

"Then Londo must have told you."

"The only name from here that Londo mentioned was yours." She gave Jae as much of an apologetic grimace as her swollen face would allow. "We were attacked right after that," she explained.

Too quickly, Jae grinned at the consternation on Wiley's face. "She's got you. Face the facts. Besides, I remember this kind of work back when Feith was alive. People did it all the time for advice and communications. It was as normal as breakfast. Anyone else hungry?"

"That's the only hard fact I can affirm right now," Wiley declared. "Let's get the food units up and running. Any preferences?" He rose from his chair and looked at Lina expectantly.

Her stomach overruled the shock of the death vision. *Jae will be all right. We'll see to it.* A quick breakfast wouldn't hinder Lon's healing, and she needed the fuel. And something to drink. You'd think a lab of this size would have a water fountain somewhere!

"If it's not any trouble, I became a vegetarian about two days ago," she said.

"We can cater to that easily. Two days–"

"When I became a teleporter. A lot of things happened then." Her eyes automatically went to Londo, who was still sleeping soundly in the large room. How she needed to talk with him!

"He'll be out for another few hours," Wiley said, following her gaze. "Oh, yes. Jae, Lina says to turn down the happy bones."

"The what?"

Lina huffed at Wiley. "I think I said that the bones were very happy doing what Jae told them to do, but that he should return them to normal working condition now."

"Happy bones." Wiley shook his head and made a note on his notepadd.

Jae peered over his shoulder at what he was writing. "I wouldn't say that either," he commented about the note.

"But you would agree to the phrase 'happy bones'?"

Jae shrugged. "Well, they are." He went to Londo's bed and held his arms over him for a minute, two minutes, as the other two watched from the break room.

"Can you tell what he's doing?" Wiley quietly asked Lina.

"I can almost hear it," she told him. "I don't want to ask Lon's body. When I tried that before, Jae said I was interfering."

"You say he's talking to…what?"

Lina turned to him. "Is there some reason he hasn't told you himself?" she asked.

"The Feithi were always secretive about how their abilities worked."

"Well then, if Jae decides that you should know, I suppose he should be the one to tell you."

Wiley grunted.

A food dispenser in the cozy nook– too bad there wasn't one for clothing– produced a breakfast of super-chewy granola. Jae explained to Lina that it was a favorite of his. Wiley stuck to a cream of wheat lookalike that went down fast, so he could get back to his endless studies and experiments.

Jae showed her how to use the laundry in the bathroom. Her clothes could cycle through and be ready by the time she finished a water shower. She was rather leery of the thing he referred to as a sonic shower. Supposedly it was a lot quicker than water and involved that pancake thing somehow, but to Lina's mind quicker was not necessarily better, and she'd had enough of loud noises yesterday. Besides, the hot water soothed many of her overall aches, though it didn't wash away the soap-resistant goo. The process merely made the goo cleaner.

All ablutions finished and her hair in its usual, neat single braid, she sat in a tailor position on her bed table while Jae took his turn in the bathroom. Lina used the energy of Sarastor to clear out the vibrational debris left in the lab from yesterday. Her teachers had always taught her to keep her space clean, but she had been sorely remiss last night. Of course, there had been good reason for it.

Wiley walked past, absorbed in his screens.

She asked, "Do you have any white candles?" Then she had to explain *candles*.

"This is a state-of-the-art laboratory!" He acted as if she'd insulted him. Wiley gestured at the general ambiance of light and the places at desk stations where focused light came from nowhere, like she'd never seen anything electrical before.

"Thanks anyway." Lina tucked her robe tighter around her cold feet. She placed angels in the corners of the lab for protection, imagining them holding their own candles. The angels who had positioned themselves around Londo the day before, nodded approval. She could sense their link with Raphael, who usually appeared in healing ceremonies, even though they must be light-years from Earth. Well, what did distance matter, anyway? Time and space were an illusion.

She meditated for ten minutes to ground and calm herself, and then checked on Londo. He was so much better, she could hardly believe the difference in the signs. Communing with the angels in attendance, she was told there should be a special ceremony after the Kolaimni.

She began to panic. Her Kolaimni textbook with all the non-standard ceremonies was back on Earth. Only when the angels assured her that she could channel it satisfactorily did she calm down.

As Wiley's baseball-sized recorders hovered silently around her, Lina got through half Lon's chakras this time before she had to clear her energies. The other half went as well. She tried to explain things to Wiley as she went, but found that her words dragged farther and farther apart as her attention was rightfully diverted to what she was doing. At last she shut up and just did her work.

Wiley and Jae sat at their station watching monitors recalibrated since the morning's experiments. An occasional exclamation told Lina that they must see what she was doing. She was curious to see it herself.

But she had to focus to strengthen Lon's etheric field. She pictured the etheric as a complicated blue web comprising the energies and memories holding the physical body together in perfect health. Remind the cells of their optimum function, of their connections with each other. The cells dazedly began to link in. She didn't have Jae or Wiley turn Londo for fear of interfering in the process. Instead, she worked on his back by intent.

But it was taking so long! She was trying to be so careful with precious Londo. The shots were wearing off and she was so, so tired and achy.

Jae came up behind her. "Lean on me if you have to," he said quietly and reached out to steady her.

The shock of the stranger's touch triggered her phobia.

"Easy," Jae told her as she jumped.

"I'm sorry." She gritted her teeth as she held back the white wall of fear that had so unexpectedly appeared. "Please don't touch me. Please!"

He backed away hurriedly. "I'm sorry," she said again. He'd just been trying to help. Damned fear! She shook the unwelcome energy out of her arms and returned to work.

It was just before the final ceremony, which would have roused him anyway, that Londo woke. He watched her as she stood with her hands raised toward the heavens, her feet in almost fourth ballet position. She chanted as she channeled, speaking a language she didn't understand. The translator hovering next to her didn't know it, either. Then the chant became a song as pink energy streamed down to fill Londo, who lay back trying to feel the extent of it all.

"Did I miss the dead chicken?" Lon asked her lazily when she appeared to have finished.

"We're sending out for it later," Lina replied. "You want extra crispy or original recipe?" Lon was back, this time for good! The tension that had held her together suddenly released.

She caught herself from sinking to her knees. Instead she stepped back from the table to finish properly: she shook out her arms, her left one very gingerly. The pain-killers had stopped working. Right now perhaps amputation *was* the best solution. She had to grit her teeth with each movement. Hot electric knives vibrated up and down every nerve she had left. To make matters worse, her back had begun to sear down to her bones.

It took intense concentration to imagine hoses from Sarastor rising to cover her arms and suck the excess energy of the healing from her like a vacuum cleaner. Then she had to attend to clearing the room's vibrations.

But she couldn't suppress as big a smile as her face could handle for Londo. *Thank You. Thank You!* "There. Good morning or afternoon, or whatever it is."

He brought the back of his table up to sitting position. The blanket drooped to expose more of the broad chest and powerful arms that set Lina's pulse pounding. He reached out to pull her to him to kiss her, and his arm barely shook. Then he kissed her again.

"Good morning, *chérie*." He smiled that Londo smile. "How are you feeling? They said you'd been hurt pretty bad." His bleary gaze swept her face and clearly realized the extent of her condition for the first time. "Ah, shit. Poor baby. Does it hurt? It does."

His concern showed so baldly that she wanted to cry from happiness. He still cared! She smoothed his hair back from where it stood on end. "I'm fine, just a little sore. Don't worry about me; how are you?"

The right corner of his mouth crooked as the others approached, and he spoke low. "I could use a back rub just like the one you gave me before." He gave her a sly look.

"Then I'd say you were feeling much, much better," she whispered. She eased her hand back from Londo's, but he took it back.

"What's the matter?" he asked her. "Ashamed of me?"

Wiley and Jae's approach didn't give her a chance to reply. She let Lon hold her hand while he spoke with them. She wanted to fade into the woodwork– or rather, plasticwork. Lon was back. They wouldn't be interested in anything she had to say now. She'd run through the entire gamut of her abilities and then some– by a mile. There was nothing left she could do; time for the hook to appear from side stage and pull her off.

"You've got better color to you today. Blue didn't suit you," Jae observed as Lon held out his other hand for him to grip. "Welcome back from the land of the dead."

"A trip I'm not anxious to repeat." Lon used English for Lina's sake. It didn't bother the others, since their own translator units hovered next to them.

"I don't think you'll have to, Londo," Wiley said, tossing something in the air as he came. It was small and caught the light, but it twirled too fast for Lina to make it out. "I've recorded the entire process to my satisfaction."

"Then it's settled, eh. I don't need to die again." At Lon's laugh, Lina's insides relaxed completely. All was well. "*Assez.* Do you guys have any breakfast left? I can smell it."

"Time for lunch, maybe," Jae said.

"Good. Lina said you were sending out for fried chicken. Jae? A little help here?" He and Lina had to drop their hands as Jae stepped between them to ease Lon up to a full sitting position. One at a time, Londo swung his legs over the side of the table.

Lina's good fingers clamped over her mouth. "Should you be trying that?" she squeaked.

Wiley shrugged. "Londo's not the average patient. If you feel like standing, Lon, I'd say go ahead. You may need this, though."

He handed Londo what he'd been tossing: a ring like what he and Jae wore. Londo chuckled when he saw it and put it on his middle right-hand finger. He clenched and unclenched his fist. "Feels good, Wiley. Thanks. I don't feel so naked without it."

"Rand calibration test," Wiley said into his own matching ring, and Lon's brows went into a minor scowl as he concentrated on his ring.

"Up two points," he told it.

"Rand calibration test," Wiley repeated, and again Londo considered his ring.

"It's good for now," he finally declared and glanced at Lina. "It has a… Have you ever used a vibrating beeper?"

"Not lately."

"I think it's like that, a little pulse vibration," Londo explained.

"In Lon's case, an earthquake," Jae said.

Londo pondered his ring. "Very funny, Jae. It also communicates silent messages."

"A secret decoder ring." Lina nodded to Jae. "Everyone should have one."

"But then everyone would be in on the secret messages. What fun would that be?" Jae countered pleasantly.

Lon wobbled slightly. "And how have you been treating Lina?" he asked them as he steadied himself with a hand on the table.

Wiley crossed his arms in front of his chest and assumed Lecture Mode. "I've incorporated a neuro-patch on her arm in order to reroute the–"

Jae knocked on the older man's head. "Hello? Anyone home?"

Wiley stopped speaking and gave Jae a level stare with both eyes.

"I'm going to get you a dictionary," Jae told him. "One for each mind."

Wiley frostily ignored Jae and turned to Londo.

"I *meant*," Lon said, "have you been treating her well? I think she looks a lot better than she did yesterday," he squeezed her hand, "but you haven't been ignoring her, have you?"

"I assure you," Wiley said gravely, "we have not."

"*Bon.* Now, she feels to me like she needs styrifin," Lon said. "A lot of it. Can we get her down to Gorgeon to–"

"Quarantine," Jae told him. "Plus Triple Level Five security."

"Oh." Londo scowled as the situation sank in. "Oh."

Wiley's brow creased as he aimed a scanner at Lina. "Styrifin indeed. Interesting. How did you know? Lina, if you're in pain you need to say something."

As Wiley busied himself getting another set of shots ready for Lina, Londo nodded his head. Even though he was still sick and in quarantine, he was in control again. Things were as they should be. "Good. Consider Lina my guest here. That means that you, Wiley, will not perform endless tests on her or have her running mazes. And you, Jae, will neither mentally nor physically torment her in any way. I have my eye on you."

"Not even a footsie flop? It's not often that we have bare feet running through the lab." Jae looked disappointed.

What's a footsie flop? Lina silently asked Lon.

Is that what it translated as?

What is it?

"And you, Lina, will communicate out loud when in the presence of others. A guest does not talk behind her hosts' backs."

"Yes, Londo. Sorry."

"A footsie flop is… Have you ever left a bag of doggie doo on someone's doorstep?"

"Of course not. Ouch." Even if those shots didn't break the skin, they *hurt*. Lina gave Wiley a fierce frown but he didn't seem to care. She forgave him after a second or two when her pains dissolved into a faint, irksome fog.

"No, of course you wouldn't. But you know what one is. A footsie flop gives pretty much the same effect, minus the flames."

"Flames?" Jae perked up.

"No fires in my lab without my permission!" Wiley declared. "I'll start handing out demerits at the first sign of smoke."

"No flames." Londo cuddled Lina. "We'll warm things up in here enough. Things got pretty hot back on that island, didn't they, *chérie*?"

She squirmed and tried not to blush. "Hush, Lon."

He wrapped his arm around her neck, and she ducked her head to hide in his bulk. "Mine," he declared. "Jae, make a note of that. No putting the moves on Lina. Lina, you watch out for Jae here. He thinks he's a sex machine. But I don't think he can match anything we pulled in the last few days!"

"Londo!"

Lon laughed as she gently batted at him.

Jae planted his fists on his hips. "I bet Wiley you were going to hang a sign at the main entrance," he said. "How big will it be? Are you going to be issuing a statement to the media?"

"Londo! Make him stop!"

"Jae, you're upsetting my little kitten here. There will be no media involved." Lon freed a hand to rub his nose. "At least for now. But I am going to throw a party. I think the occasion calls for one. How'd you like that, Lie? You like parties, don't you? We'll have one as big as you could wish for."

She gave him a final bat and disengaged herself. "You throw one as big as *you* want, Lon. I will be home. Where it's quiet. Where there are no crazy sex maniacs running around."

"Not even me?"

"More liquor for the rest of us." Jae eyed Lina up and down before he turned back to Londo with a sly elf's grin. Londo returned it triumphantly.

"Hold this," Wiley instructed Londo and passed him a hand-sized dumbbell. "Right hand."

"Lon's right-handed," Jae informed Lina.

"Aren't most people?"

"Not any that I'd noticed."

Lon held the variable-weight dumbbell for a minute, then shifted position to hold it more steadily.

"No, that's enough," Wiley told him. "Left hand."

"People around here are ambidextrous," Londo said. "I don't know why."

Lina was about to offer a quick theory she'd read but decided that might be presumptuous, what with folks Out Here having all this medical tech. They probably gave prenatal inoculations to tweak all kinds of things. Too bad they couldn't control the temperature better. She shivered.

"You need some more clothes," Lon said as he handed the weights back to Wiley. "Got anything else in here for her to wear?"

Wiley clicked at something invisible in front of him. "We weren't prepared for contaminated people beaming directly into the lab from across the galaxy. At least, ones who didn't bring their luggage with them."

"Sor-ree," Lina muttered darkly. She hadn't planned on being a burden.

Londo bent down to his boots– Lina wondered that no one had removed them through all this– and grabbed at the table before he fell over. Lina and Jae both pushed him back up. "Socks," Lon said abashedly. "She can have my socks." His mouth twisted. "Maybe after I wash them," he added.

"You're sweet," Lina said. "But you need warm feet, too."

"Lon's sweet feet will stay warm with just his boots," Jae assured her. "We'll see just how sweet those toesies smell now, why don't we?" With a great deal of fuss he began to pull at Londo's boots until Lon waved him off with dire threats, and promises to Lina that he'd launder the socks in a few minutes.

Through it all Wiley kept staring at the air about a foot or so in front of his face. Lina realized that he'd been doing that every so often.

Lon caught her thought and explained, "He's got polarized viewscreens he uses for high security matters."

Without warning, Jae jabbed at one of Wiley's many plain rings, and in fact a floating screen did appear just in front of Wiley's right shoulder at easy reading distance.

Lon nodded at it as Wiley touched his ring and swatted at Jae. The screen disappeared again. "When it's polarized, it follows the movements of his eyes. It only focuses for his retinas. And he has a third eardrum rigged up to handle audio from it."

"How cool." Lina blinked. "Except for the third eardrum part, I mean." Different world. Different tech age. She shivered again.

Lon reached out to twine his fingers through Lina's, grinning at Wiley's vague displeasure. "When we get out of here, I'll take you shopping. As I recall, you weren't wearing too much on the island." His eyebrows came together as he recalled. "That man– that *bâtard* who had you. He didn't–"

"He was caught in one of the blasts," Lina told him. "There wasn't much left of him."

"*Bon. Skurny bon.* Let's hope his end was painful. When I get back, I'll make sure every last one of them get what they deserve."

Lina let out a squeak.

He considered for her sake. "With due process of law, kitten. Don't worry; I'll take backup. We'll make it quick."

That seemed to mollify her. "How much of it do you remember?"

Lon scowled. "I remember that it hurt like hell. I remember that you got one hell of a lot of the guns. For a moment I thought we were home free, Lie."

"I missed a few," Lina admitted. "I was working as fast as I could, but I didn't understand them. I didn't want to give it all away before everything was disconnected. I didn't want them to notice."

"What's done is done, *chérie*. I'd say you did extremely well for your first– and last– combat situation." Londo smiled at her and turned to the others. "We need to borrow this one trick of hers for covert ops. Go ahead and show 'em, go on."

That caught Wiley's attention. "Covert ops?"

"Show what?" asked Lina.

"That cover up thing you do. The hiding."

"I'm sure they'd want to see me hide."

"What I want to know is how you managed to do it, Londo." Jae considered the two of them and for a moment Lina wondered what he meant by that. His jaw jutted, his eyes squinted as if he were angry at something. Was he still upset by the morning's channeling?

Jae continued, "How did you manage to stay alive for two full days without powers?"

"Very nicely, thank you," Lon replied. He arched a reproving eyebrow at Jae.

"I've seen you in combat practice," Jae said. "You cheat. You and all those powers of yours. Invulnerability– you blunder into things and expect your thick hide to protect you."

"I was the picture of finesse," Londo crowed. "Perfect timing. They didn't stand a chance against me."

"Except for that guy who was about to tie you up and blow your head off," Lina teased. "And the one who burned your back. And then you talking so loudly when they had listening equipment–"

"They don't want to hear about any of that," Londo said quickly.

"Oh yes we do," Jae told her. "So Lon couldn't keep his mouth shut? What, was he bragging about himself?"

"I think I need to hear this, too," Wiley told them all, "just for the official record. Debriefing."

Lina caught her breath. "I was just joking. He– he brought us through alive and well. Right up until that part at the end, and that wasn't his fault."

She shouldn't have made fun of Londo, not here. Stupid! Sometimes her mouth got ahead of her brain. Trying to tease Londo in public, as if he were a normal person– She had to remember that this was Valiant. "That island was swarming with soldiers. And jungle. And a couple of volcanoes. No one else could have gotten us out alive. No one!"

Londo's eyes crinkled. "That's my girl," he said softly, squeezing her hand.

Wiley gave the two of them a sour look. "All right," he said, "how many casualties do you think these mercenaries suffered?" He directed his notepadd at Londo.

Lon sighed, trying to remember. "*Voyons*. Three committed suicide while in custody at the house. During the trek across the jungle I went up against maybe… How many would you say, Lina?"

"Twenty more?" she ventured.

Lon kept hold on her hand as he watched her expression. "More like twenty-six. How many dead of those?" he asked. "I counted eleven."

"Fifteen," she said tightly. "It happened later, after we'd gone. The angels told me."

"I'm sorry. You know the situation we were in."

"I understand it. It's a shame that they chose to end their lives that way."

The way she looked at things. "I think it's very nice that we didn't choose to end our lives at their hands." Londo sighed and shook his head. "And when they confronted us… *Eh bien*, we were stuck. That was my fault entirely."

"I don't know how many died there." Lina blew out a breath as she thought. "Maybe thirty, thirty-five. Maybe a lot more. It was hard to tell."

"Thirty-five? From what?"

"From the guns they threw at you, Lon."

"What was this?" Wiley leaned forward and Jae crossed his arms, cocking his head.

As with many accident victims, Lon hadn't retained some of his short-term memories. He could remember the initial energy attack, but Lina had to tell them of the grisly scene afterward. "The more they fired at Lon, the more of their own men they took out."

"That would explain part of the blood we found on you two," Wiley nodded. "Were these clean cuts or–"

"Wiley," Londo said sharply. He held up his hand to fend off Wiley's questions.

"No, that's okay." Lina swallowed as the picture came back to her and did her best to describe the bodily injuries. Wiley wanted to know if there were clean holes or tears, discoloration around the contusions or not, if the blasts came with a shimmering of air beforehand, if beams seemed tight or affected the area overall. Did any of the guns ricochet off objects? Did they just affect bodies, or…?

Lina apologized again and again for not noticing something that might enable Wiley to begin to reconstruct what kind of weapon could affect Lon that way. She tried her best to explain what she'd seen through a fog of pain.

"…Like broiled, runny Jell-O," she finished.

Londo made a wry face. "I don't think I'm ever going to eat Jell-O again."

"I'm sorry."

"*Mais non*, I'm sorry for getting you into that mess. I should have evacuated us both as soon as I was able. It was completely stupid and unprofessional of me."

"And I should have sensed all those guys. I don't understand why I didn't."

"For the same reason I didn't." Lon tipped her chin up so their gazes met. Both their faces softened into silly smiles. They didn't even notice the buzzer at first.

"Go ahead," Wiley answered, and a long screen appeared in mid-air in front of their group. It morphed into a life-sized man standing in their midst. Lina jumped. Lon hugged her to him with a reassuring squeeze.

"It just the phone," he murmured to her. "Hologram."

The athletic-looking man wore what must be a costume because the tight, cobalt blue outfit had a repeating-line insignia on the chest, too bold to be a normal fabric design. He was dark-haired with a grayish blue cast to his hair, sharp blue-black eyes under bushy eyebrows, and chiseled cheeks that were also distinctly blue, though in contrast to Wiley, in ultramarine.

Is the color balance off? Lina asked Lon. He shook his head but paid attention to the screen.

The man turned to them as if he were actually there in the room. "Good afternoon, Londo. Glad to see you're back with us."

"Hi, Stoan. I decided to drop by at the last minute." Londo gave an easy grin.

There must have been a translator inside the phone because Lon's use of English didn't seem an impediment. "How is he?" Stoan looked at Wiley expectantly.

"He's just finished his second round of treatment," Wiley said as he produced that tricorder thing again. He ran it around Londo and checked its screen, then glanced at the various screens around Lon's table. "I'd say he's well along to full recovery. Knowing Londo, maybe two days back to full strength. Maybe more. Are there going to be any more treatments?" Wiley looked at Lina.

She shook her head. "Rest is the only thing he needs now." For once in her life she'd done a fantastic job, she thought proudly. She'd come through when she'd needed to.

Stoan gave the stranger a measuring look that couldn't conceal a flash of revulsion at her appalling condition and turned back to Wilder.

"Oh yes," Wiley said. "This is Lina O'Kelly of Earth. She's the teleporter and, ah, psychic healer I told you about last night."

It occurred to Lina that this was the commander of the Legion she had read about early that morning. The written word suddenly matched up with this conversation. He was Stoan something; she forgot his hero name. His mega power had to do with magnetism and polarities. She had put the name Stoan together with magnetism, and had pictured a magnetic stone, even though the name was drawled out: sto-wan. She figured it was Southern for "stone."

He had been commander for three terms now, indicating how well he was thought of in the organization, for the rank was an elected one from the membership. She nodded her head politely at him and saw him dismiss her as he concentrated on his friends, the famous heroes.

Jae must have seen it, too, because he added, "If it weren't for Lina, Londo wouldn't be alive."

Stoan again considered Lina, and turned to Wiley. "Surely that's not–"

"Oh, it is. I think that given enough time I could have stabilized him, but we didn't have that. He was dead within moments of arrival. If he hadn't blown up Headquarters by imploding and causing a daet-hold reaction, he would have died permanently before I could even have started treatment."

Lon tugged at Lina's arm and she turned to him to see puzzlement in his eyes. She smiled and patted his hand. **They have tapes; you'll have to watch 'em,** she told him. **Look over there.**

Londo looked across the room and saw the blasted floor, the visible net of energy holding in quarantine conditions from the fracture.

That's impervion. "Impervion!"

You made quite a mess, Lina chided silently.

"Londo?" Stoan was asking.

"Oh, sorry." Lon brought his attention back to the commander. "Lina was just telling me that I needed to look at the tapes to see what happened."

"Telling you–"

"Lina's telepathic. Oh, and for the official Legion record, so am I as of about two days ago. It seems to be a permanent condition," Lon told the commander.

Stoan scratched his head in consternation. "Telepathy? I want to hear more about this. Wiley, when does your quarantine end? I'd rather communicate in person." He pointedly looked at Lina. Obviously he didn't want to talk in front of unimportant strangers, non-Legionnaires. Lina could understand that.

Wiley said, "It will be another two days as well."

"Two days?!"

"They teleported directly from Earth. They didn't come through hyperspace, didn't have access to any kind of biocleaner–"

"All right. Two days." Stoan whipped around to face Lina, staring her down. "Have you ever practiced mind control?" he demanded.

12

The question took Lina aback. She shook her head vigorously. "No, I can't do that. It wouldn't–"

Stoan cut her off before she could say "be ethical" and went back to Wiley. "I want regular reports about Londo's condition. And any more powers that may appear."

"Right."

"Do you need anything in there?"

"Being in quarantine," Jae put in, "it's difficult to grant any requests." He crossed his arms and puffed out his cheeks at Stoan with a raised eyebrow for emphasis.

"Ah, yes. Right. Well. Good luck; I'll see if maybe we can't reroute protocols later today just this once. Don't kill each other before quarantine ends. At least you get out of helping with repairs. Thirty stories of damage…" Stoan shook his head as Londo straightened, clutching Lina's shoulder.

"Thirty stories? Of impervion?"

****You were trying to die on us,**** Lina said gently. ****You did die. Just for a few minutes.****

****I thought Wiley was kidding.**** Lon's brows furrowed; his eyes moved as he struggled to remember.

"Luckily it's along a route that's away from structural elements or important conduits," Stoan said.

Lina didn't like to be accused of mind control. "Luck like heck. I aimed it that way," she said defiantly. She was tired of people trying to criticize her when she'd done a good job! She got that at work. Darned if she was going to take it here. "*They* told me where it would do the least harm."

"They?"

Jae took a guess. "Your guides? The same entities you channel with?"

"That's right," Lina said.

"Where are they?" Lon whispered to her.

"All around you."

In absolute seriousness he bowed to the empty air. "Thank you. Thank you all."

Lina could have melted with pride. He'd remembered to be polite.

"Entities," Stoan drawled. "Wiley?"

"*Skurned* if anything registers. But then it took a few tries to get even moments of the Kolaimni treatment to show up on sensors."

Londo squeezed Lina. "You're kidding; it actually records?"

"I told you, you need to look at the tapes." She smoothed his hair with an intimate gesture that Stoan caught.

The Legion commander now noticed how Londo had the woman encircled in his arms, how she leaned against him, her hand on his arm. He glanced down and searched on his personal drive for one particular section of information. There it was. The betting boards had paid off– with bonus points. He frowned at Londo and Lina.

"I'll review your records, Wiley," Stoan said quickly. "Kinrol out." His image rolled up vertically and then disappeared.

Lina's jaw dropped as she caught what Stoan had been thinking. **Londo, is there an office pool on you?**

"Oh *marde*," he muttered. "I'd forgotten about that."

Lina hissed. "Isn't anything private around here?"

"Not much. There are long stretches of monitor duty when nothing happens. People get bored. Don't take it personally, kitten."

She sighed. "It's difficult not to. Oh well. I need to dunk myself and detox. I'll be back in a few minutes."

"I'll come with you." Londo slid off the bed to stand, catching himself on the edge. "Whoa."

"Londo!" Lina grabbed him before he could fall.

"I'm okay," he said.

"You are not! You get back into bed right now."

"I'm fine." Gingerly Lon shook off Lina's hand and then released his own hold from the bed. He straightened slowly. "See? Fine. Let's go. I need to shower."

Jae caught him when he tried to take his first step. "You've always been the subtle one," Jae jibed.

Lon steadied as Lina supported him on the other side. He took a hesitant step, and the one after that was steadier, the next steadier still.

"No sex back there," Wilder ordered nonchalantly as he returned to the main computer station.

Lina thought she'd never stop blushing. "Is there somewhere I could go to die of embarrassment?" she asked. "Not that I want to inconvenience anyone, mind you."

Jae laughed at the both of them, his eyes almost dancing as he saw Londo up and about. "This is just one of the benefits of quarantine," he said. "By the time all this is over, we'll know each other much too well." He scratched his chin at Londo. "Lina gave me a pretty personal reading this morning, so I think it's time we came up with something for Wiley."

Londo gave an evil snort. "I'll see what I can do."

"Good. If you need any more bodies back there, just tell me and I'll come running."

Londo laughed again and hit the air a millimeter above Jae's arm, an air-blow. "You'll be the first I call," he said, and turned around when he felt Lina release him.

She hurried to the back of the lab, her hands over her ears. "I'm not going to stand around and be embarrassed any more than I have to," she declared. "I am going to learn how to bioclean so I can get out of this camp of crazies as soon as is humanly possible!"

Lon patted Jae's shoulder and Jae stepped back. Lon took a few steps on his own, testing his balance. He tried a trot and stumbled, then managed a brisk walk. "Lina!"

She turned in shock. "Lon, you shouldn't–" He was still sick! Her fault to push him like this!

He caught up with her and took her in his arms. "I'm okay, all right?" He looked around to see that Jae was watching them. He cocked his head at him, and Jae turned away with a bow. Or was he offering his rear end as a comment? Lon took Lina's hand and walked with her to the back of the lab.

It was private next to the ocean tank, close to the bathroom.

Lon's arms around Lina were strong enough to make her feel safe. His lips on hers held the same heat as before. The body that pressed against hers was the only one she'd ever allow in this position, the only one she wanted. She stopped worrying and gloried in the physical presence of living Lon.

His fingers pressed into her until she gave an involuntary cry. Blister, cut, burn or bruise; she didn't know which one he'd found.

He jerked away and then fastened upon a new spot, holding her as if she were made of butterfly wings. She wrapped her arms around his neck and clung to him. The tears began to return.

"I was afraid I'd lost you," she whispered.

"I'm better now," he assured her. His mind sank into her skin, activating the double feedback loop. He kissed her a little harder now that he knew where not to touch. "As a matter of fact, I'm feeling fine." He let his mouth wander down her neck to the shoulder that didn't have a bandage on it.

"Mm, sticky sweet." He smacked his lips on the medical goop that covered her.

She giggled. The universe was once more the happiest of places. The weakness of her knees was a good thing, not a sickness. The sparks that his soft lips left on her skin were sweet ones and not painful in the least.

She gave a lighthearted sigh and pushed away. "You are a walking hormone, honey, do you know that? Come to think of it, so am I lately. But you have doctor's orders. I don't think we should push it. *I* can tell that you aren't feeling well, even if you put on a good show. Now come on; I have to detox and get rid of energies."

He eased back reluctantly. "All right. But I'm going to find a way out of here for us before I go crazy and bust down a wall. And you– you don't port home without me. Promise. Promise me."

"I promise I'll tell you before I try it." Lina tiptoed to kiss him on the nose. "I really have to detox now."

She dropped her robe, leaving just the lopsided leotard as she prepared to get into the tank.

His fingers brushed the bandages over her arm. "Damn, Lie, what did they do to you? There's a hole."

"That was some kind of laser rifle. They burned through me to get a spot to stick a needle into you. I guess they didn't figure that they could have just done like we did last night with the shots. Or maybe they just wanted to be gruesome."

"*Crisse*. It was all my fault. I'm supposed to know better than to get people into these situations. Does it hurt much?"

"I think I could stand another shot. Now that you're up and around, maybe I'll have Wiley anesthetize the hell out of it. He's been wanting to all along."

"Good." Londo grasped her firmly around the waist and looked intently into her eyes. "I never wanted you to get hurt. That will never happen again. I swear I won't let it."

"I am not going to get hurt." She smiled and tried to brush his hands away, but he was holding her too tight. He was much too serious.

"Look," she told him, "here we are on *Star Trek* and there's Doctor McCoy up front. He can cure a rainy day, you know." When Londo frowned at her, she said softly, "He'll give me another shot. It won't hurt, darling. And it's so much better than it was. Wiley's a miracle-worker. Don't worry about me. You just worry about getting well yourself."

"I'll talk to Wiley about it."

"I can talk to him." She poked her finger at his chest. "You'll be in the shower, right? They've got nice showers here."

Gradually his frown worked itself into one of those wonderful crooked smiles. "You can detox and then join me," he suggested.

"Might not be a good idea."

"Might be a very good idea, *chérie*. I bet you you'll like the shower I have in mind."

"I bet you Wiley won't like it one bit."

"So we won't invite Wiley."

"I think we need to keep on his good side." Lina chuckled him under his chin. "At least for a couple more days."

He sighed acquiescence. "Maybe just one. Maybe less."

"But we aren't going to do anything to get him mad at us now."

The grunt he gave was unenthusiastic. "*Non*, not right now."

"Good, the brain is beginning to kick in. We have to set our goals." She ticked them off on her fingers: "Detox. Shower."

"Shot for you."

She nodded. "Yes. Lunch. Way out of here."

"Right. I'm starving." He grinned and then kissed her thoroughly.

She rearranged the pillow on her bed, tucking the sheets in hospital fashion, just to have something to do while she waited for Lon to return. Some vague aftereffect of their telepathic bond let her know his muscles were stiff and sore. He was enjoying the warmth the shower offered while he could still feel it as a norm. Lina hoped the lab had access to unlimited hot water.

"We need to talk."

Lina caught her breath and whirled. It was that Stoan man, the commander, standing right next to her! Apparently he found her shock amusing, damn it. She tried to compose her features.

A black bar hung over his head. It had writing on it. Some of it scrolled while other words remained stationary. It was all foreign, of course, so it didn't make a lick of sense. The only thing it told her for sure was that the commander hadn't violated quarantine.

"You're a hologram," Lina said.

"And you are Terran," he said.

He'd said it like that was a bad thing. Lina didn't bother to concede the insult and instead remained silent.

"You know what a hologram is," Stoan went on. He paced two steps in front of her, keeping his eyes on her. The bar stayed above his head.

"Sure."

"Earth has such technology."

"Of course." She wasn't going to tell him such things were rare. "Londo has one on his uniform. It's a movie."

Lon had that pin that– whoops, didn't work any more. On the other hand, its new symbol was also a holo-movie, even more spectacular than the original. She smirked at Stoan. So there for Terran equality.

"That pin is from us. It's official Legionnaire ID."

"Oh." Damn. "Well, it looked like one of ours." Fake it, baby. And whatever you do, don't tell him you broke it!

His left eyebrow twitched at that anyway. Lina kept her face as calm as she could, even while recalling all those TV programs that showed how easily careful facial study could reveal lies.

As a telepath she was rotten at reading faces. She relied too much on non-physical signals for communication. Still, part of her training had been in body-mind observation. That was good for general personality traits, not so great for specifics.

She noted what she could. His posture was rigid and he kept pacing, two steps, turn and stop, two steps, turn and stop. Right shoulder ever so slightly low: daddy issues. Hips also slightly forward under that puffed-out chest. He thought himself a very powerful man, dominating his competition by his very presence. Footsteps were solid.

Maybe he'd been trained in body-mind too, only his class had been called "How to Make Your Enemies Cower Before You." He stared at her like he was trying to peel her brain back with his eyes.

"I am not a mind controller," she blurted. Damn.

He came to a full stop at that, his hands behind his back. He looked down at her. "Can you prove that?" he asked.

"No. Can you prove I am?"

His nose crinkled ever so slightly as he gave her a hard smile. "No."

"So we're at an impasse."

"The Legion is never at an impasse."

Again with the pacing. "Valiant is one of my top men."

"Not *the* top one? Valiant?"

"If he weren't part-time, he might be. Tell me, where are you from?"

"Earth, of course."

His tone was snide. "Of course. Not Soalok?"

"Soalok?" She'd heard that word before. "Oh. That's the Empire, right?"

"Right." He drew the word out. "How about Tishan? You've heard of that?"

"Uh…no, I think."

That garnered a laugh. "Just a Terran who doesn't know her galactography, eh?"

"They don't teach that in our schools."

"It's all easy enough to check. I've begun looking into it already."

"Oh." She didn't know what to say to that. She was innocent, so this should clear her, right? "Good. Thanks."

That seemed to throw him. He recovered quickly. "Until you're cleared, you are not to try to break into secured information."

She chewed on that. "What kind of information would be secured? I mean, I don't want to accidentally–"

"There will be no accidents. We are the Legion. You try anything suspicious, and we'll slap you in a cell. A quarantined cell if we have to."

"Uh. Okay."

"We will investigate you so thoroughly your skin will peel. Worse than it already is."

What a jerk. "That's okay. I have real good skin lotion back home."

"If you can get to it."

"I have my own private mode of transport."

"That's yet to be determined."

"Sure." She checked out the inside of her middle finger fingernail, giving him a surreptitious bird that this alien commander would never recognize.

Lina felt very naughty. She'd never flipped anyone off before. It felt good. She'd have to do it again sometime.

"What's your interest in Valiant?" Stoan asked abruptly. "Did you have something to do with the attack? Who was behind it? How well do you know Teresa Rhodes and Dr. Menlo?"

"Other than them trying to kill me, I don't."

"We'll see about that."

With no further word, he shrank vertically to a central bar and then disappeared.

Lina blinked at the effect before she realized that Jae had been sitting across from her on a lab table, hidden from her view by Stoan.

He eased off his table and paused before resuming his business. "Have a nice talk?" he asked. "Getting to know everyone?"

13

L ondo rounded the corner just in time to miss Jae's comment. Lina needed another shower, too, to wash away the sweat and salt water and Stoan's presence. So not only were Londo's enemies against her, but his employer and friend were as well. Shit.

Right now Lon's condition was more important than that. She hurried to him. He leaned on her as they made their way to the break room.

As they entered Jae was ahead of them, already reaching into that cabinet from which meals appeared. He brought forth a loaded plate and steaming mug. "Londo's favorites," he said and set them down on the table as Londo eased himself onto the banquette.

This was worse than Jae watching her squirm before the Legion commander. Londo was hers to help. Lina glowered at Jae.

Jae gave an ingratiating shrug. "You'll have to learn these things."

Dammit, he was right, but he didn't have to be so smug about it. He knew what Londo ate while on Sarastor, and could operate the food cabinet. Lon's plate did smell very good.

But Lina could feel Lon's twinge at it. "Lon, can you stomach this now?"

"Of course I can." But he didn't hurry toward the dish as a whole, just the soft gray stuff that was heaped on one side.

"How about some soup instead? Can we put this in a fridge for later? Do they have chicken soup here?" Her question switched from Londo to Jae, who frowned at her.

"Chicken soup," he parroted the English. With a glance at Londo, he turned to configuring the meal cabinet. What he brought out was a double-handled soup bowl.

"Thanks, Jae," Lon said as he wrapped his unsteady hands around it.

It smelled good enough, though clearly it wasn't chicken. Lina could see some kind of somethings in there which she hoped were healthy veggies. Londo sipped a few times before he gave a good chug. After that it was back to sips until he settled down to using a spoon.

Lina relaxed. Londo had what he needed. He was getting better.

Jae leaned against the counter with his own mug. He seemed expectant. Or maybe he was just watching Londo closely.

"Stop staring," Londo said into the bowl. "It's good."

Jae grunted and then attended to his food.

"Well," Lina said into the silence. "Guess I'll take a shower now. If you're in good hands."

Jae's sour expression now refocused on her.

"And you are." Lina squeezed Lon's arm before sliding out of the banquette. He nodded to her before returning his attention to the meal at hand.

Lon and Lina sat in front of a small window in the outer wall of the lab while Wiley stood behind them. Londo had handled three more shots and had a network of sensors taped to his bare chest.

"You sure you're not cold?" Lina asked him.

"Not a bit. And if I feel a chill–" He pushed his chair closer to her and wrapped his arm around her shoulders. "Warmer," he pronounced to Lina's smile.

Wiley said, "Here's a concentrated burst of biocleaning rays, *aksel*, set for ten seconds. Starting now."

Lina stared at the microwave-sized compartment within the window. It looked exactly the same now as it had before.

"Can you see them?" Lon pointed at it. "Narrow yellow rays. They leave a green glow on surfaces for maybe a half-second."

Lina shook her head. "Nothing."

"I always thought it was kind of pretty. Too bad no one else could see it. Well, except Hal."

"Maybe if the rays had something to work on I could figure it out," she said hopefully.

Wiley thought a moment. "The compartment is sealed. Port something in if you can. Make it disposable. Such a concentration of *aksel* will probably destroy it."

So she chose an object and focused on porting. "Jeez, the electrical difference is so great…" After two minutes a folded black tee appeared in the compartment. "I've always hated that shirt," she told Londo as Wiley noted the incredibly short time it took to transport something in from Earth.

Londo merely swore fluently.

Wiley triggered the *aksel* again and Lina watched. "I don't– Oh. Is that what it is." The shirt began to burn and turned into ashes in seconds.

She turned to Wiley. "Okay, I got it."

"Do you think you can mimic the effects?"

"No. *They* say that those are an outside force. I'd have to be able to produce those rays myself. Guess I'm stuck with constant quarantines."

Londo set down the nutri-drink he'd been sucking through a straw and told her, "What you need to do is forget being a biocleaner. Try to filter what you port. Just don't let anything harmful through. You can do that, right?"

"Biofilter?" Lina chewed over the concept. "I might. Why didn't I think of it?"

"You would have eventually," Lon assured her with a pat. Ordinarily Wiley would have separated them so Londo could heal fast, but he'd laced Lon's drink with special medi-nanites that would direct Lon's healing process as well as see to potential internal problems. With Londo's defenses down whenever he touched Lina, the nanites could do their job fairly well.

"All right. We'll call this phase two." Wiley signaled the computer to clear the compartment.

Now Lina chose to bring in a plastic chess pawn. "It's here," she immediately announced for Wiley's benefit. "Just not quite here. It's *outside*." She held it in that phantom space to compensate for atmosphere and potential, then tried to tune into all its germs and shove them away before letting the pawn materialize.

Londo scanned it with a handheld padd. Just three minutes from Earth to Sarastor! In all his travels he'd never heard of anything remotely like this.

"It's a start," he told her. "Contamination is significantly less compared to the shirt, but still *très dangereux*. Let's try it again. You can do better."

He held the padd for her to see, but it was in a strange language, or in Terran notations so obtuse that Lina had no idea if they were supposed to make sense. But they did to Londo. Everything Out Here did. He was as much at ease here as he would have been on Earth. The exotic and alien were his home.

Not hers.

Wiley cleared the compartment and Lina brought in another piece, a rook this time. She held it outside as she tried to go through every microscopic particle of it, but suddenly–

"Whoops."

They looked at her.

"It's gone. Not back to Earth. It's just– gone."

Wiley made more notes. "So there's a time limit on how long you can hold something in stasis." He checked his screen. "Five and a half minutes, approximately. We'll need to get an exact reading later."

"Terrific, now I've got a time limit," Lina grumbled. "Maybe it's just a case of practice shaving some time off the process."

"You're on the right track," Lon encouraged.

An hour later she apologized for not improving quickly enough. She was getting better at screening some of the contagion out of the objects, but also crept closer to her time limit. Wiley was fascinated when she brought in a knight just as it dissolved in front of their eyes.

"Subatomic cohesion breaking down?" he theorized, and replayed the moment through his sensors. "Reversion to dark matter?"

"Shit," Lina muttered.

"I think that was very cool," Lon soothed. He eased back into the chair beside Lina and handed her a cup of hot tea made of nutri-mins. "Drink," he told her. He waited for her to comply, and then stood up to massage the back of her neck. She leaned against his hands. "Don't sweat it, kitten. Take a break. You'll get this."

"But probably not before quarantine ends naturally," she complained and sighed. "I wish someone would turn on a radio, Muzak at the very least. I'm going crazy with the silence."

Lon chuckled. "I know what you mean. But they don't have music here."

"So Wiley said." Lina stretched and Lon rubbed her shoulders around the bandages. He had magic hands. His wide fingers knew her so well. "Too bad we can't pick up any TV. We could use that as background noise."

"*Voyons*, the classics," Lon mused, and then broke into song: "*Come and listen to a story 'bout a man named Jed...*" He drawled it out, yodeling on some of the notes as he did a cowboy grapevine-and-hitch across the floor. Lina couldn't help but laugh.

"Londo!" Wiley looked very cross indeed. Music in his lab!

Londo grinned and kept going. Lina wanted to join in, but between him and Wiley's expression she laughed so hard she couldn't even speak. It didn't help when Londo took off on his own vocal version of the banjo ending, air-picking his way to a grand finale. Lina applauded and Londo bowed graciously to both her and Wiley, who stood with his arms folded across his chest practically under his chin.

"Are you quite finished?" the doctor huffed.

"I've got lots more," Londo threatened.

"I will not stand for any more of this Terran barbarism in here," Wiley declared. "What you do in your own quarters, behind your own doors, is your business. But you are a guest in my laboratory, and you'll keep some decorum or I'll file a complaint. You can't stand to have too many more demerits."

Londo made a show of prissily settling back in his chair. (It involved a great deal of shaking his butt and shoulders.) It was a difficult feat to achieve when one had his broad musculature.

"I hardly have any demerits on file," he claimed. "And I bet I can come up with something that will earn you some demerits if I really try." He nudged Lina. "Terran barbarians. Huh."

Lina stage-whispered back, "At least we barbarians keep the temperature in *our* laboratories to a decent level."

She'd been sitting tailor-fashion, cocooned in her giant robe, her stockinged feet tucked up under her for warmth. Wiley had made some comments about Terrans who didn't know how to sit in a civilized manner, but she'd ignored him.

"It's fine in here," Wiley said. "So you can control indoor conditions on Earth?" he asked Lina.

She grunted at him stupidly. "Ugh. Fire good."

One of the colored squares in the wall lit up as Wiley touched it. Londo jumped out of his chair and cowered, covering his eyes. "Fire bright!" he squalled. "Fire burn!"

He let out a series of shrieking monkey cries and bounded about this cleared area of lab, his knuckles dragging the ground. He noogied Jae as he bounced past, and then hopped back to Wiley. There he bowed down monkeylike and made motions of kissing Wiley's feet. "Ci-vi-lized!" he ooked. "Not Terran!"

"Point made." Wiley sighed.

Lina had never seen such a showman as Londo. "How do Leos do that?" she wanted to know.

"Is that what it is," Wiley said sourly. "And here I thought he was merely insane." He let a beat pass. "Or Terran."

"Ouch." Lon straightened until he was on eye level with Wiley. He had to rise in the air to do so, his feet entirely leaving the ground; Wiley was over a handspan taller than he. "Step outside and say that, pardnah." Out of the corner of his eye he glanced at Lina. **Amused*, chérie?***

I'd pay double admission to watch your act, Lon. What say when quarantine is over, we shanghai everyone here to Earth? I think they need a few lessons in real civilization.

Lon gave her a grin of agreement at that.

Jae sat well away from them at the wall's communications station. He'd been talking to several people: mundane Legion business, apparently, but making a little show of not participating in the great porting experiments. "Hey Lon," he called now, "if you don't have anything else to do– and it seems you don't– L-PIC wants you."

Londo muttered something dark under his breath. "Tell 'em I'm sick," he said out loud.

"It doesn't look like it to me. C'mon, I'll share some with you."

"Share some what?" Lina asked Lon.

"Interviews. All the time interviews," Londo grumbled. "None of my mission reports have been released to the media lately, so these will be the little gossipy kind." Giving a tight, saccharine smile, he undulated his shoulders and raised his hands like he was handling the Queen's tea service, pinkies extended. Then he bared his teeth. "I hate the little gossipy kind."

"Just tell them you're not dressed for it."

Lon's vest had been torn in half, and he hadn't put on the shirt Lina'd ported in with, so he'd been walking around spectacularly bare-chested. Wilder had made a few remarks about proper Legionnaire deportment and Jae had accused Londo of showing off for Lina. Lon had ignored both of them. He'd chivalrously sacrificed both his shirt and socks for Lina to use in addition to her robe.

He gave her a squeeze now and added his mischievous smile. "That's no problem around here. You take a break and watch, why don't you? Get your mind away from this."

He talked to Jae and Jae's screen for a few minutes before the two arranged some chairs in a cubicle just outside the break room. As Wiley helped them, the equipment behind them shimmered and disappeared behind an illusion of a smooth, neutral-colored wall. It displayed an oval emblem with a child's version of a bird, a "V" with wingtips, flying through it. It was the same emblem as on everyone's rings, so it must be the logo for the organization.

Lon disappeared into the bathroom and came back with his hair perfectly styled. Jae just shook his head violently and patted his mop of hair into position, grinning superiorly at Lon. Then they took their places in the chairs. Three baseball-sized metal globes hovered at eye-level in front of them. A monitor scrolled down from the ceiling.

"Lower," Lon directed in Lingua, and the screen descended to slightly below their eye level so they could see it comfortably. "That good for you?" Lon asked Jae.

"Fine."

Lina walked up behind Wiley. "How come you aren't in this, too?" she asked as the others talked back and forth about technical setup.

Wiley shrugged. "The press doesn't like to interview me."

"Why not?"

"They say I talk down to them. They can't understand what I'm saying."

"I bet you it's the eye thing. You seem quite comprehensible to me, and apparently I'm just an idiot barbarian. Then again, maybe it's the translator."

"That reminds me." He turned and adjusted the translator marble so that it set almost in her ear canal. "Don't want any–"

"Feedback," Lina finished for him.

That surprised Wiley. "So Earth does have some technology," he said.

"Of course it does. If this interview was supposed to be just Lon, why is Jae sitting in?"

"Lon will do it if Jae's there. That's the only way any more that Lon does this kind of interview. If they have Londo alone, interviewers have a tendency to ask him embarrassing personal questions. This way they skip that. Besides, everyone knows that Jae and Lon are best friends."

"*Best* friends?"

"Mm. They grew up here together. They're practically the same age."

That explained a lot of Jae's possessive attitude. Oh great; Lon's best friend disliked her. Still Lina's mouth quirked. "And they're both a little looney tunes." That made Lon glance at her from across the room with a sparkle in his eyes.

"They've both had a lot of advanced psychiatric treatment, if that's what you mean, yes. For a newsgroup to request Valiant and wind up with Neutrino and Valiant is a definite coup for them. Now quiet, they're ready to begin." He pointed at a screen he had scrolled down for himself to watch. It bloomed to life.

There sat Lon and Jae, the same as they were sitting now, but Lon was in full uniform and Jae wore gloves and a cape, with a bodysuit and tight vest. His outfit was vivid blue and white, unlike the neutral sweater he was really wearing, and there were blue metallic triangles prominent on each shoulder.

Lina hadn't realized how gray Lon's skin really was until she saw the color-corrected version onscreen. There it was a healthy, light brown. Still, in person he was looking far better than he had yesterday.

He was indeed the all-Canadian guy next door: easy in his handsomeness and athletic bulk, his face not too chiseled, but not round at all. His noble nose was ever so slightly larger than normal and a bit Roman in attitude. Lina chuckled to herself. Large noses were sometimes a sign of a large ego. Londo had no doubts about how wonderful he was. Such a Leo!

The two Legionnaires greeted the interviewer, seen screen-within-screen, and Lina wondered if the reporter were manufactured CGI, too.

Does this mean that they could be sitting there stark raving naked if they wanted?

Wiley gave a start at the sudden telepathic contact but recovered speedily. **I doubt if they'd do that with me handling the feed,** he returned in the exaggerated, word-by-word way non-telepaths had to speak to telepaths. **The controls might slip accidentally.**

Lon was talking to the reporter. "*Eh bien*, I just got in from Earzh," he said as if it happened every day. For some reason Lon's problem with "th" bothered Lina when it came to the name of their home planet. Otherwise, his accent was ridiculously romantic.

"Someone there tried to kill me and didn't quite succeed. And when I arrived here," he shrugged, "I got stuck in quarantine for a couple days."

"Quarantine?" the reporter blurted with alarm. "Bio-weapons? Bio-chemicals?"

"No, no, nothing like that. Our biocleaning unit didn't work."

Jae pretended to elbow Lon in the side. "So who does he drag into quarantine with him? Valiant, next time, *ask*."

"Sorree."

"It's boring in quarantine. Particularly a quarantine that you're unprepared for. If we'd known, we could have invited the usual party crowd over for a few days of fun."

The reporter asked, "But you're still relatively safe?"

Lon made a sick face. "You haven't been locked up with Neutrino for two or three days. I never know what he's going to do."

They spoke of some mild practical jokes they'd pulled on each other and said some strange things that Lina could only figure were jokes or puns that the translator unit didn't catch right. Wiley certainly chuckled at some. The reporter slapped his chair arms as he laughed, the ultimate appreciative audience.

Lina was fascinated. It was just like any celebrity interview, except that it was live, she was here, and there was Lon…and Jae. Jae was a big celebrity, as was Wiley. She had to remember that. They were all special.

Hell, that wasn't her Londo up there, that was Valiant. She swallowed as she watched him. He knew nothing of her world of office cubicles, staring at computer screens day after day, and scraping to live from paycheck to paycheck. One day he'd…

She swatted at the green-headed fly that buzzed her mind. *I'm not going there*, she told it.

The interviewer ran tapes of first one and then the other hero in flying action, then a tape of both of them working together. Considering how fast this interview had been arranged, he'd gotten his material organized quickly.

Lon would talk about such-and-such that they did, and Jae would pepper Lon's monologue with rude comments. When Jae had to talk about his own feats, he would explain them by making the rude comments about his opponents, while Lon added his own description to Jae's actions: "Wait, wait, I like this clip. Look, there you go: 'I must defend this commission with my honor as a Legionnaire,'" Lon mimicked Jae's voice cunningly, 'but mainly because that's where all my secret Union Fund-bale traffic is kept!'" The reporter laughed and laughed at that, but Lina had no idea why.

"I don't have Fundbale," Jae sulked.

"Do too."

"Do not." Jae wobbled his head with superiority. "I purged them just in time. I wasn't sucked in like *some* people I know."

"*I* never had Fundbale."

And so it went, with obscure references to things and other people, other Legion-naires maybe. Looking over the heroes' schedules, the reporter asked about upcoming events: political functions, major interviews…

"So, Valiant," the reporter asked. He never called Lon "Lon," nor Jae "Jae," nor did either of them refer to the other by their civilian names. "There are two dozen Legionnaires represented in the AffSys United Charities Date Sweeps for the Izers next month. I see your name is on the list."

"Eh." Lon rubbed his nose as he wrinkled it. "I may have to pull out of that. I don't think my girlfriend would approve."

Lina stopped breathing. Lon's *girlfriend*. He meant her! Her!

Lina wasn't the only one surprised. The reporter sat slack-jawed, so Jae took over the interview.

"Girlfriend?" he asked Lon, assuming the posture of the reporter. "Valiant, are you saying that you're involved with someone now? After all these years? After all these long, long, looong years of singledom?"

"Why yes, Mr. Neutrino," Londo answered gravely. "I think I'll be taking her to the Izers. She's never been."

"Valiant!" the reporter recovered. "You aren't joking here, are you?"

"I doubt it she'd like it if I joked about it."

"You're involved with someone."

"Very involved, yes."

"A Legionnaire? Orenya?"

"No, not Orenya, not a Legionnaire, and…hm. I don't think it's a good time to give out her name. I haven't discussed this with her."

"Haven't discussed the Izers?"

Lon shifted in his chair. "Going public. This is the first time I've even called her my girlfriend." He glanced at Lina and flashed her a quick grin. "I think I shocked her."

"So it isn't as involved as you suggest? Is she there with you? Can we meet her?"

Lina met Lon's eyes and crossed both arms in front of her chest. Her in this robe and sock feet and Australia on her face and bruises and cuts and a hole in her arm and god knew what her hair must look like… Good lord, how could Londo stand to look at her, much less drag her in front of a camera?

Lon chuckled at the steely glare. "I think she's feeling a little shy today," he told the reporter.

"Valiant, I don't think that that's shy," Jae said just loud enough for the camera to catch. "I think that's more an 'if you try to make me come over there, I'll personally throttle you for everyone to see' look."

Lon cocked his head as he regarded Lina. "*Peut-être*, could be." He made a palms-up gesture to the reporter. "She's not really dressed for it."

"She's not dressed at all." Jae leered in Lina's direction. "Can't someone get her a robe at least? Let's have a little decorum here at Mega-Legion HQ!"

"Okay, okay," Lon said as fire blazed in Lina's eyes. He held up his hands in surrender. "She's dressed. She's proper, but she's also shy. Let's not bring her out here. Neutrino, I remember a time when you appeared on camera in somewhat less than regulation Legion gear…"

Londo launched into a story that had the reporter hiccupping as he tried not to lose complete control, while Jae exclaimed, "It's a lie! It's all lies!" every few seconds. They laughed their way out of the interview with Jae covering Lon's mouth with his hand and Lon blathering on even as the reporter thanked them. Wiley's screen went blank.

Lon grinned at Jae, who huffed at him in exasperation. Lon got up and stretched his spine slowly, then arched his back and stretched his arms out in front with hands clasped.

"If I'm well enough to do that," he decided, "I'm well enough to get a little real work done." He turned to Lina and held up an index finger. "Give me five minutes. Business."

But five minutes turned into ten and then fifteen. He used the corner to unscroll one of those vid screens and a few others besides.

Lina couldn't even sit near Londo. "Official business," he told her. "I'm afraid it's classified. I'll make it quick."

She caught a glimpse of an overgrown praying mantis, and Lina recognized it from the night before as being a Legionnaire. Or perhaps related to that mantis-y Legionnaire. How would one tell mantises apart?

Finally he turned away from his screens and started to stand, smiling at her that his call was over. But one screen beeped and he turned.

"Sorry," he told her. "It's the High Senator of Dramenglad. I've been trying to get hold of him for weeks." When he'd finished there, the Queen of Fell had to speak with him. Then some other official, then another.

So Lina returned to her porting practice. It was difficult to keep her mind on it when she was trying hard to learn everything else. This was Londo's world, so completely different from Earth. If she wanted to understand Lon better, she'd have to understand what he did here.

He seemed entirely comfortable talking to that queen, and then to some ambassador or interstellar minister. He must do that kind of thing every day.

And now she was Londo's girlfriend. Why, she wouldn't have the first idea how to begin to talk to such important people. What would they think of her? Just a Terran barbarian. They'd wonder why Londo deigned to say hello to her, much less...

Valiant's girlfriend.

The phrase carried an intense combination of thrill and fear. Was that really who she was? Did that make the two of them like the other couples she'd known through the years? None of them had murderers stalking them in order to score some insane kind of brownie points.

Still… Londo's girlfriend.

She sank into a happy daze considering the ramifications of that, once both of them were healthy again. And alone.

At last Lon seemed to glance over to her, but she realized he was looking past her shoulder. His eyes widened. His mouth opened in surprise and–

fzzWHUMP!

14

Lina jumped in her chair and whirled.

Wearing a bulky helmet and face shield, Jae pointed a wide rifle at a target along the far wall while Wiley studied a phalanx of monitors nearby.

Though that area of the lab had previously been straightened to a gridwork pattern by the crystal pancake, many tables had now been moved back to make a long, clear alley to the target.

"Setting four." Again Jae fired, and again the muffled sound of destruction made her jump.

She was sure it was muffled, for the target disintegrated into fizzy, glowing bits even though it seemed made of metal. Another popped up to take its place.

That was six inches of dimensional ceramic, Lon told her silently so he wouldn't interrupt what the minister on his screen was saying. **That's what they make warships out of. Space-faring warships.**

"Eight inches thick this time," Wiley announced.

"Setting five," Jae replied.

And yet with a *fizz-WHUMP,* the target again disintegrated. With this destruction Lina realized that she was looking through a distorted wall of air that looked as though it had been super-heated. Each time Jae fired, the distortion went wild as if a shock wave had slammed into it, and Jae stumbled back a pace or two before he regained his balance.

Jae walked to the new target, as thick as the last. On the edges of her sensitized awareness Lina could hear him silently speak to it. He waited for it to obey his commands, and then returned to his position. "Setting five." Again he fired.

This time the target took a few seconds to disintegrate.

"Huh," Londo said, which must have confused the minister before Londo returned to his screen conversation. It didn't help that Lon frowned in disapproval.

Weapons practice continued for some time. Lina returned to her window. As she lost herself sorting through contagion at a microscopic level in some place that wasn't quite *here*, she stopped hearing the shots altogether. It was just her alone in that silent *elsewhere*.

The disappointment of losing another knickknack to the void brought her out of it just as Jae breezed past her.

He placed his palm on Londo's shoulder. "That's enough," he said.

Lon looked pale, glassy-eyed. He said a few words to his screen and signed off, passing a hand through hair damp with sweat.

Lina jumped up. Why hadn't she sensed the problem? But Jae was already there, already taking care of Londo. She could only wring her hands as Jae asked, "Are you all right?"

"Yeah, I'm fine." Lon trembled as he got up from his chair. "Just a little tired."

Jae steadied him as Lina rushed to Lon's other side, but he waved her off, trying to maintain his manly image in her eyes.

"Get some rest, Legionnaire," Jae ordered. "You're still recovering from being dead. I'd call Gorgeon and have her order it, but she's out of the loop on this."

"Maybe I will take a little nap," Lon admitted. He reached to take Lina's hand. "You won't mind if I do?"

"You heard Doctor Jae. Sleep if you feel tired."

"And you do the same. You're still pretty banged up. Mama Ruth always says that sleep is the best healer."

Wiley called Jae from the firing range.

"I've got him." Lina gave Jae a reassuring smile as she eased Londo over to lean on her. Jae gave a reluctant nod and went to join his colleague.

Lon nudged her as they hobbled to his bed. "We could sleep at the same time."

"I think I should work on biofiltering for a little while more. Let's see what else I can destroy." Lon was leaning heavily on her. "Do you need some pain shots?"

"Just tired."

"All right. Lon, how loud was that gun, really?"

He gave a little *hmph*. "Loud enough to blow your eardrums right out of your head if they hadn't had the dampers on. Be thankful that we have such good shields here." But his forehead creased. "Jae should be wearing body armor."

"Could he be hurt?" The vision of Jae lying in his own blood came back to Lina. She had to talk with Lon about that, but not now.

"It's an experimental weapon, Lie. Jae likes to cut corners when he thinks he can get away with it. He claims he thrives on danger. I've tried to talk him out of these stunts, but…" He spared a dark look toward his friend across the room, who didn't notice. "He'll be lucky if he doesn't get demerits. Wiley lets him get away with it, but someone else had to notice."

"Someone?"

"We're being watched, *cherie*. There are monitors all over the lab."

Lina clutched her free hand to her chest. "Not near the pool in back!"

"Probably not. I'm sure Wiley turned off the monitors back there to give you privacy." He crooked an eyebrow at her. "You went skinny-dipping?"

"Near enough. Once." Or was it twice? She'd been kind of blurry when she de-toxed.

"Not to worry, kitten. Wiley doesn't believe in naked. In fact," Lon leaned to whisper, "he was scandalized by your bare feet."

Lina glanced down at the offending appendages, now baggily covered with Lon's borrowed but warm socks.

"Is that why he doesn't turn up the heat in here? So I'd cover up? Is that a culture thing or a Wiley thing?"

"The heat's a Wiley thing. It's his lab. His heat. His floor. And you have violated that space just being here, not to mention those bare feet of yours."

"Oh dear."

Lon chuckled. "He has to get used to life throwing a spanner into his control issues now and then. Besides, I think he's on the verge of forgiving you, what with all the new ideas about porting and healing. If you're still cold and bug him about it again, I bet he'll turn up the heat. By at least a half-degree."

Lon paused. "I'd do it myself, but I wouldn't want to get on his bad side. For not being a team leader, Wiley carries a lot of weight here. Technically he ranks above me."

"And what's your rank? 'Team leader' is not a rank. You're a 'captain'?"

He rubbed his nose as he tried to explain. "It doesn't translate well. There's a lot of if's and but's and circumstances involved." He motioned to Jae. "Jae outranks me, but I outrank him, too. It all depends. The Legion's built for fluid action; that's one reason why it's as good as it is."

"And the ParaNet knows about you being in the Mega-Legion?"

"They have to. They grant me leave to come here, and vice-versa."

"I'm glad you aren't full-time, or I'd never get to see you on CNN."

He gave a small smile at that. "I used to be."

"Used to–? Oh." The years before Valiant had moved to Canada and gone to university, there'd rarely been a Valiant sighting. Maximus had said that he was away. All Lina knew was that the evening news wasn't exciting for a long, long time.

"You weren't at some kind of boarding school."

That generated a soft laugh. "No. Here. With the Legion and as many psychiatrists as Hal could find."

Poor Londo, recovering from his long childhood ordeal. Lina was grateful that he'd found Maximus and that Maximus had cared enough to help him so. If Londo had managed to find his birth parents, they wouldn't have been able to help him nearly as much.

"You made good friends here," she surmised. "I'm glad." But she cringed at a new popping from Wiley and Jae's direction. "Even if they do have strange hobbies. They do that kind of stuff for fun?"

"Couldn't get out to go to the firing range and it's got to be done." Londo eased down to sit on the edge of his bed. "You haven't mentioned it."

"Mentioned–?"

"You don't mind if I say you're my girlfriend?"

As she drew back the blanket so he could lie down, she blushed with the warmth that he exuded. "If, if it won't embarrass you, Lon."

"Of course it doesn't. You still love me, right?"

She looked earnestly into his wide brown eyes. Did he truly not know the answer to that? There was a hint of anxiety there. "I'll always love you, Londo. Always. It's just that... that..."

"That you'd rather keep this hushed up so you can hide away."

She nodded shyly.

"Tell you what, kitten. I'll get you a little badge that says, 'Taken,' and that way I won't have to worry about anyone trying to steal you from me, eh?"

At that she had to shake her head. "There won't ever be anyone else, love. You don't have to worry about that." Never ever anyone else for her. But Londo was Valiant; he'd have lots of loves in his life. He deserved them.

"You see that I don't. I'll see that I don't."

He placed his hands on both sides of her neck, his thumbs against her chin, as he looked first at the right side of her face, then at the left.

"Ah, *chérie*," he sighed, "I am so sorry. Wiley says you'll heal up in time. I'll take you to see Gorgeon the second we're out of here. She's much better than Wiley," he added in a whisper.

"Is it awful?" Lina asked of what he saw in her.

"It's only awful because I was the cause," he assured her.

"Even Australia?"

"Aus–?" He suddenly laughed. "I see. It does look like it. Oh, jeez." He pulled her to him. "Never again. I'll keep you safe. My fault entirely. Stupid, stupid. And I'll take you to the real Australia when we get back. I'll take you everywhere. You've always wanted to travel. I'll show you the world."

"The whole world?" Lina asked against his cheek.

"Not only Earzh but other worlds too. This planet is just the beginning. Sound good?"

"Sounds wonderful. But you don't have to–"

"Want to. Not have to." He gave her a final squeeze and released her. "I'm going to conk out for a while. Miss me?"

Lina glanced around to see if anyone was looking and kissed him. "Sweet dreams," she whispered.

Now she couldn't concentrate when she tried her porting. Londo's girlfriend! Wonderful Londo loved her. Most perfect Londo! Her brawny honeybear with the strong arms and the voice that made her bones melt.

He could make her body come alive. It pleased him. She wanted to please him, for he had given her so much. To be able to touch, much less touch *him* was a miracle and would always be.

She would never take her two steps back from the real world again, so long as he was around.

(But how long would that be?)

What would it be like when they got back home? Lon would take her out on dates, wouldn't he? She blushed at her own faint reflection in the biocleaning compartment glass when she thought of how those dates would end up: Londo curled up sleeping in her little bed beside her.

She jumped when Jae touched her shoulder. "Congratulations," he said.

"On what?"

Jae nodded his chin toward the corner where they'd had their interview. "Now the entire sector knows that Valiant has a girlfriend."

"I wish he hadn't said anything."

"But he did." Jae slid into the seat beside her. He fiddled with the lights on display. "Do it again," he told her.

She ported– yet another chess piece destroyed, this time quicker than most. Jae's face was expressionless as she frowned at the compartment.

He said, "The media is already inundating Legion PIC with demands for information about you."

"Whatever for?"

He looked at her levelly. "He's *Valiant*," he said, drawing out the word for emphasis.

"Oh."

"He's the most famous Legionnaire there is. A legend in his own time. I'm sure that's the same way on Earth?"

She nodded miserably. Jae knew. Who wouldn't? He knew that she was a Muttbutt who didn't deserve Londo Rand. She'd been fooling herself.

Jae bulled on: "People have made a big deal about Londo and all his publicity romances. Most people never knew the truth."

All?

"Bernita," Jae began ticking them off without her asking out loud. "Felzann. Ramone fa Telischar– she was cute, but she didn't last long. The Nawps." He gave a little laugh at that. One by one the names came out until he ended with, "Aiko– that's Orenya. You've heard of her, of course."

"No. She's famous?"

"They don't come more famous than Aiko." His gaze raked her, measuring her behind his words. "He's never mentioned her on Earth?"

"No." She licked her lips. "There were just celebrity dates. Set-ups. And Forte, just a couple times. I suppose with the press knowing about a couple of times, that must have meant that they were together for a while, right? Londo values his privacy."

"Londo values people not knowing that he's– he *was* a virgin," Jae said. "That's changed. Thanks to you. I imagine you're about to become quite the celebrity."

"No." It came out less than a whisper.

"Don't you want to be famous? Lon's a Mega-Legionnaire. That's as much celebrity as you can be. People are impressed by celebrities on Earth, I know. Lon's brought printed magazines back with him."

"No."

Jae continued as if he hadn't heard. "People here are obsessed with fame. They'd do anything for it. You'd do anything for Londo, right?"

"Not for that reason! What we have is private." She spat the word. "Private! Not for other people to know about!"

"Lon's going to make sure people know," Jae told her. He played with some of the bright lights on the table in front of them, but he watched her from the corners of his eyes. "It's been a long time coming. It's taken a toll on him through the years. Doubting his own manhood, hearing the jokes behind his back and if anyone can hear something behind his back, it's Lon. You'll be wide open to public scrutiny within another day. Bet."

"No one would be interested in me."

"And on Earth?" Jae settled back in his chair as if mentally scheduling the timeline for that news release.

"They don't know about us there," she finally said. "I'll ask him not to say anything."

"So you'll stay locked up behind his doors?"

"Behind my own. I'm nobody." Jae was Londo's best friend; of course he'd be concerned. "I, I told him…" She took a breath. "I told him that I won't tell anyone. Whenever he gets tired of me, I'll go quietly. I won't raise a fuss. I won't embarrass him. You don't have to worry about it."

Jae studied her as she bit her lip. "Do it again," he instructed.

Lina didn't want to seem the suffocating girlfriend, so she tried to make her stroll to Londo casual once he was sitting up after his nap. He blinked a few times at the world until the blank look slid off his face. It was still marred with dark circles under his eyes. His cheeks were sunken more than they should be, but they were better.

"Can I get you a–" she began when one of those communication screens rolled down from the ceiling. Two chimes sounded.

Londo glanced at the writing that floated in mid-air and paled.

"What is it?" Lina didn't like how it had affected him.

"It's, erm." He looked like he was trying to catch his breath.

Lina looked around for Wiley. Did Lon need medical help?

"It's something I need to take," Londo told her quickly.

When she turned back to him his color was still pale, but his shoulders were straight and he seemed alert. "Sure," she said. When he looked at her expectantly, she added, "Oh," and moved away. It must be one of those security calls.

But the female exclamation of "Londo!" behind her made her turn. The screen had expanded to full-figure…and what a figure! Slender, definitely female even from the back, and clad in shining, skin-tight gold.

Whoever it was, was almost exactly Londo's height– though that could be something to do with the screen, Lina thought. The woman had black, close-cropped hair. Each lock had been capped on the end in a flat, triangular gold bead, so the effect was more golden jewel than hair.

With a wave of Lon's hand, both sides of the sound cut off from where Lina could hear it, though the conversation went on. Did Londo hesitate in talking? Was it the illness or something else? He was trying to look cheerful.

The woman put her hands on her contrapposto hips and shook her head at Londo. The gold-tipped hair danced.

Lina caught her breath when Jae sidled up from nowhere next to her. "Well well," he said *sotto voce*.

She couldn't help herself. "Who is she?"

"You really don't know Orenya?" He began to walk toward the studio wall to Lon's far left. Lina kept up with him.

"Just what you told me. That's Orenya?" She glanced back at the private conversation, now able to get a better view of Orenya's front. Was that why Jae was practically steering her this way? Or did he really need to fiddle with one of the panels on the wall?

"Everyone's heard of Orenya."

"She must be a Legionnaire."

Damn, but she was gorgeous! Skin darker than Lon's, heavy-lidded eyes and a wide, smiling mouth. Her gold suit seemed as if it had been dipped in oil, so the lights flickered on every bit of female anatomy. Lina could see now that it was tight, but not quite skin-tight. Tight enough.

"A very famous Legionnaire. As famous as Lon."

"So that's…a business call."

Jae chuckled.

"Is it?" Lina demanded. Over there, that golden Orenya person laughed with Londo, though she couldn't hear it out loud.

"Valiant and Orenya," Jae told her. "The tabloid shows run rumors that they're a twosome."

For a moment the room seemed to swim in front of Lina. Londo and another woman. Not someone from his past, but from the now. Why couldn't she breathe?

"Everyone here knows," Jae said. He wasn't checking that panel but his fingernails. "Her civilian name's Aiko Fallow. Londo never mentioned her once?"

No he hadn't. The dog. Why he and this Orenya woman– Obviously lovers. Obviously they had–

Wait. Londo'd been a virgin. So Orenya couldn't be his lover.

Or she could, to an extent. Lon had said that before he met Lina he could handle a few bases.

"Third base," Lina surmised and tried to recall what all the stops were.

"Say again?"

Whose ballpark was Londo playing in?

15

L on's heart thudded in his chest. "Aiko," he said and was glad it didn't come out as a squeak. He didn't have to fake the smile and once-over he gave her. She was a glorious woman.

"I just got in. They told me when I arrived. I called as fast as I could."

Now he had to control the smile, make it seem relaxed and easy. "I'm fine. Now."

"I was afraid from all the reports that you'd be, well, just a tad on the dead side. They said you didn't look too good when you arrived, dearest. Sunfire, you could have died!"

"Actually–" Lon began but decided against telling her that he had.

"You're sure you–"

"They've been taking good care of me," Londo assured her. "I'll be back in full form in a few days."

Aiko's brows contracted. "Few days? Valiant takes that long to recover?"

"Maybe Wiley's just being cautious."

"Him?" Aiko frowned her disapproval.

"I don't know why you and Wiley can't get along."

"They said you were in some kind of quarantine. It is viral?"

"Interstellar travel."

"What?"

Lon scratched the back of his head, which allowed him not to look her in the eyes. "I came in by teleport, not hyperspace."

Aiko opened and closed her mouth, then looked thoughtful. "How–"

"It's something new. Came in handy, didn't it?"

She crossed her arms over her gilded chest. "What aren't you telling me? Is Stoan having you guinea pig R&D's gadgets again? Is Wiley behind this? I swear I'll–"

"Don't blame Wiley," Londo said quickly. "He's just as surprised as I was. He's been in here doing his best to get me back on my feet."

"So this–" she waved her hands to indicate his condition– "wasn't due to the R&D?"

"No. Good thing we had it, though, as things turned out."

She shook her head. "I need to know–"

"Not now. I'll be out of quarantine in two days." He linked her to the countdown clock and she glanced at it from her end.

"What's going on, Lon?" she asked. "What is it you're not telling me?"

"Less than two days, *chérie*. I'll take you out to lunch. There's someone I want– Ah, maybe not."

"Not?"

"Not lunch. We'll have a long talk in two days. The moment I get out of here."

The left side of her mouth curled into an impish smile and she lowered her eyelids seductively. "My place or yours? I bought some lingerie with you in mind."

He couldn't help himself. He gave her an evil grin before he stanched it. "Maybe not that long a talk. Don't plan on it being that long, Aiko."

Puzzlement creased her forehead.

"Give me two days. Don't listen to anyone about me, any reports until then. Promise me. I'm really kind of dizzy here. Need to rest and all that," Londo said quickly, giving her a pained look.

She pursed her lips and then said, "I'm late for debriefing."

"Then you should go. Don't want to get you any demerits."

"I think I can handle a couple."

"Two days, Aiko. Two days." Londo hoped she couldn't see the guilty sweat on his skin. Maybe she'd think it was illness.

"I'll check back," she promised, and the screen rolled back up into the ceiling.

Crisse, how am I going to tell her? He moaned at the thought, but behind the screen were two people standing, watching him. Jae and Lina.

Make that *blabbermouth* Jae and Lina.

Londo groaned.

That brought a shocked look to Lina's face. She ran to him. "Londo, are you all right?"

She thought he was sick. He put a hand to his stomach the way that norms did when they didn't feel well and said, "Maybe I got up too fast."

Jae's sharp eyes mocked him.

Lina pulled at the blanket as if she were going to cover him. "Can you make it to the break room? Maybe you need some coffee. Or some juice. Or cold water."

"Maybe." He drew it out so he sounded pitiful. Jae cocked his head at him.

Lina helped him off the bed and then tucked the blanket around his bare shoulders. "We'll get you hydrated and see how you feel, okay? And then you can tell me all about Orenya."

Londo choked and stumbled for real. Jae, damn him, let out a short round of his patented machine-gun laugh: "Hah-hah-hah!"

"You told her," Londo growled.

"And why didn't you?"

"Told me what?" Lina asked innocently as she lent her shoulder for him to lean on. "Jae just said that the tabloid shows–"

"I never had time to tell you about her," Londo said. "I wasn't keeping anything from you. There was nothing to keep from you."

"Does Aiko know that?" Jae asked from their side.

"You stay out of this!"

"Just speaking up for her since she can't be here."

"I– We– You–" Lon sputtered.

"Let's get you hydrated," Lina suggested. Lon could hear the steel in her voice hiding the hurt.

During an uncomfortable break room session Lon assured Lina that rumors about him and Aiko were exaggerated. He didn't think he convinced her and he couldn't try to read her as that might reveal that perhaps he wasn't telling the entire truth of the matter. Surely he was entitled to keep some secrets, especially when they might hurt someone else?

At long last he thought he succeeded in diverting her attention to other subjects. Then he got up and moved the sectional privacy screens that had been around his bed to hers. He firmly suggested she take a nap– the girl didn't know how to take care of herself– and came back later with half-completed debriefing reports to watch her sleeping peacefully. Healing units irradiated her in blue and violet glows. The worst of those horrible blisters had disappeared, leaving patches of scabby red and brown in their wake. The hole in her arm was still as raw as ever. Gorgeon would be in charge of healing that.

Her attending translator unit suddenly bounced up in the air and flew toward him.

Deftly Jae caught it, closing his fist around it as he came up behind Londo. "Badly hurt," he told Lon quietly in Lingua. "She could easily have been killed. She was dying until Wiley caught her."

Lon didn't answer.

"A hostage for Valiant, caught in battle by mistake. When will it happen next? She's no Legionnaire. Where's her training? When have you ever hung around with anyone– anyone!– who didn't have a solid background in self-defense?"

"Be quiet, Jae."

"Come back to the real world, Londo Rand. Girlfriend to Valiant: why don't you just pass out invitations to all your enemies with maps detailing the best spots for ambush?"

"Shut up."

"I just don't want you to get hurt."

"Like hell. I know what you want."

"I don't want her to get hurt either. She seems nice enough, but nice never saved anyone from an assassin. Of course, she might be pretty when she heals up, and I've seen pretty save a couple people once or twice. But sooner or later, Lon-Lon…"

"Don't be an ass about this, Jae. I'm warning you once only."

"Who's being an ass? We've made plans. Maybe I should remind you of them."

"Plans go wrong. Circumstances arise that make shreds of the best plans, you know that."

"And you can stand here and tell me this as cold and callous as if you were giving a mission report. Thanks a lot, Valiant, you bastard. You're making the worst mistake of your life. That's my one warning to you. In all the time we've known each other, have I ever deliberately misled you? Shards, man, if you can't think of Lina's safety, think of Aiko. This'll kill her."

"It won't." Lon's jaw set tight, his teeth clenched. "Aiko's tough. She's not that involved. Others have blown that all out of proportion."

"You haven't even told her yet, you coward. Think, Londo. For once in your life, when it comes to dealing with people as people, think! Sometimes you can't apologize your way out of a mess. Sometimes people don't forgive."

"And sometimes people go too far. Drop it."

Londo walked deliberately away from him. The blond Legionnaire watched him go and then released the translator. It sped back to float beside Lina's head as she slept.

"Fine, if that's the way you want it," Jae muttered. He watched as Wiley called Londo over to his examining table. Wiley loved his experiments, and to have Londo be the focus of them was making his day, maybe his week. He was talking excitedly. Londo was trying to be patient with his friend, but kept grumbling about how he'd had his fill of being experimented on long, long ago.

Jae sat down to a screen and called up the commander behind a fluctuating privacy field that the otherwise-occupied Londo and Wiley would never notice. He was fortunate. Not only was Stoan Kinrol available, but Andrisenon Nemlor, the sub-commander, sat with him in his office. She was in civvies and not on official duty. A Legionnaire's work was never done.

"Jae!" Stoan exclaimed, surprised and then troubled. "Has something happened? Is Londo all right?"

"Londo is fine," Jae began.

"Then that woman…" Stoan's eyebrows came together as he frowned.

"Is she really a mind controller?" Andri quickly asked.

"I don't know," Jae told them irritably. He was getting in one of his moods again and he fought against the feeling, trying to remain rational. He should have triggered his tranks to dose him before he made this call. "The woman is a problem. She's going to be a bigger problem."

"I knew it," Stoan muttered.

"What do you have, Jae?" Andri asked.

"We know she hasn't tried anything on Wiley," Jae said. "He always has a relay set up so that if one of his minds gets controlled, the others will have time enough to warn someone before the controller can take them over as well."

"No alarm yet," Andri said as she double-checked screens from the information padd that hovered over her left hand. "Are we sure that this woman is trouble? I want to trust Londo's judgment when it comes to people."

"Londo is in no state to judge character," Jae told her. "He's in flat-out, don't-tell-me-anything-I-don't-want-to-know love. And lust. He's not listening to sense right now."

"If that's not mind control–" Stoan began.

Andri regarded him sourly. "I've always suspected you didn't have a romantic bone in your body," she said. "Why can't Londo fall in love? If what the boards are saying is true–"

"It's true," Jae told her. "And apparently the two of them can still have sex even now."

"Convenient," Stoan said. "And I find it highly unlikely. Have you considered that it's all a telepathic illusion?"

"I don't think it is. She can manipulate his invulnerability, but it's not done on a conscious level. He touches her as if he were a norm."

"Lucky girl." The corner of Andri's mouth quirked. She caught a lock of her short, pinkish hair and twirled it around one finger thoughtfully. "If you ever find out how they do it, I know a lot of women who'd be very interested in learning the technique."

Jae looked her up and down measuringly. "You come over to my room after I'm out of quarantine and we can experiment, maybe figure out ourselves how they do it," he teased.

"You wish," Andri fired back, obviously not really interested.

"People," Stoan interrupted. "Haven't you had every woman in the Legion yet, Jae?"

Andri challenged Jae with a smile, "He hasn't had me."

"That's another thing I respect you for," Stoan told her. "Now back on track. We've been researching mind controllers, Jae. Up till now they've had to have a brain implant."

Jae shook his head. "She doesn't have the standard obvious implants. But how do we know that that's the only way to do it? Lately the Empire has been focusing on mind control. Maybe they've come up with a new technique."

"I wouldn't put it past them," Stoan growled.

They sat for a few moments in silent thought. Andri was the first to speak. "So what if all we're doing is conjuring up bogeymen? Afraid of shadows in a dark room? What if the woman's exactly what she purports to be?"

"A Terran witchdoctor?" Stoan drawled. "Oh come on, Andri."

"Do you have any other ideas? Besides her being a controller? Who's she working for? What's her motive?"

"Controlling Valiant is enough of a motive for anyone," Stoan replied. "Control Valiant and you have how much power behind you? Control Valiant and you could take over a sector. Not the AffSys, but probably the Terran Sector. It's primitive enough. And it's right next to the Empire.

"My bet's on Yanist-Glory being behind this. The timing's right. We've been waiting for final reports from operatives behind the border to hold a summit about this. It's an all-out security threat to the AffSys. Mind control is a threat to every rational being."

He pointed at Jae. "You watch yourself as well. If she should control Valiant, Neutrino…and even one of Mem-Bazer's minds, she could pose a direct threat to the AffSys. I wonder if that wasn't her plan in the first place."

Andri nodded, her hands clasped in front of herself. "And yet," she said, "what if she's just another of those Terran megas? That world has far too many megas. Where do they come from? Londo and Hal have convinced us that there's no mega-based genetic experiments going on there. What if she's just another freak para? What if she became involved with Londo by a coincidence? It would be understandable that if he ever got…" She paused.

"Laid," Jae said and she rolled her eyes but continued.

"If Lon ever got laid, and *especially* if he had the prospect of continuing to get laid, he'd let himself fall in love with the woman. Everyone knows he's got that sentimental streak. Surely it would follow, wouldn't it? I've noticed that Hal has some peculiar ideas about love and sex as well. Lon could have picked it up from him. Shards, *he* probably picked it up from Mike and Ruth. They've been married forever, I think."

"And yet look at what Hal married," Stoan said. "So you think that this is Lon's sentimental side taking over, Andri? And you, Jae, is this sentiment, does this affection seem logical to you?"

Jae shrugged. "Lon told us that Terry Rhodes had conducted a worldwide search to find a physical and mental type that would appeal to him. Lina fit the bill."

"Really?" Andri asked. "A Terran?"

"Not jealous are you?" Jae flashed a grin that disappeared just as quickly. "She's everything he's been interested in, judging from what he's told me. And she seems nice enough. But she's just too shy at times. She's very timid and then the next moment she's taking command. She's teaching Wiley, for orb's sake. She's from Earth– Earth!– and yet she's made the adjustment to Sarastor with considerable ease. I think she must have been in these types of surroundings before. She's too polite for a Terran. Too clean. I think she's been exposed to Imperial society."

"But she saved Lon's life," Andri contributed. "She was dying herself and she worked until she dropped to save him."

"How lucky she did that in Legion Headquarters, where we have the equipment to save her life," Stoan said darkly. He drummed his fingers on his desktop.

"I want you to keep her under close observation," he finally told Jae. "You keep a list of everything she does, anything that is even remotely suspicious. If we're going to build a case against her, we have to have a mountain of circumstantial proof. Mind controllers are *kicking* hard to pin down even if you have trained telepaths on the trail."

Jae nodded. "We'll need someone to contact the Terran ParaNet to see if they have any information on her. It's impossible that she just sprang from nothing one day. She's left a record somewhere."

Stoan checked his calendar on the edge of his screen. "I've got meetings taking up the rest of my day," he said, "but I'll get to that first thing in the morning. As long as you people are quarantined, we have some time to play with on this. We'll put the full weight of the Legion behind the request. The ParaNet will jump when we call. Keep your guard up, Jae. Kinrol out."

Jae deleted the privacy screen to find that Wiley and Londo were still engrossed in their experiments. He went about his ordinary official business and even played a few remote games with some other Legionnaires when he got bored, dribbling the tiniest atoms of gossip about Londo and his girlfriend, the Terran witchdoctor, to their hungry ears. Not to Aiko's.

At one point he felt eyes on him and turned, half-wondering if this were what mind control felt like when it started. But Lina was still asleep on her table. Instead, it was Londo catching Jae's attention. He jerked his chin toward the break room. Jae excused himself from the game and met him there behind a privacy screen. Wiley didn't even notice.

16

Lina worked in front of her little window for another hour. Try as she might, she couldn't tune out the constant barrage of incoming calls along the wall. Jae took most of them. He didn't bother to keep his voice down, and the accusing reiteration of *"Terran witchdoctor!"* and *"Valiant!"* from both sides of the conversations made her cringe.

She wasn't just a Muttbutt; she was a troglodyte, straight out of the deepest cave of, god help her, Earth, with a bone stuck in her frazzled hair. They expected her to jump around and shout, "Ooga booga!" Even Londo had made jokes about her whirling a dead chicken above her head.

Another "witchdoctor" mention caught her ear. Maybe it came from just a Legionnaire and not the outside world. But Legionnaires were not "just's"; they were big celebrities, she reminded herself, and Londo was the biggest of all.

She watched him as he bustled shirtless about the lab, helping the turtle pancake straighten up. His condition had improved so much! He lifted two experiment stations off a pile of fallen equipment as if they were two paperback books. He set them down carefully and continued his task, choosing two or three others at a time, then switching to hold up a cubicle-sized metal table as the pancake swept underneath.

How many times had she watched him on TV lifting trucks, boats, even airplanes? How many times had she watched him change the course of world events?

Once he caught her looking at him and broke into a grin. To her utmost astonishment, he juggled three stations high in the air, *da-dee-da-daah*ing a circus ditty to go with it, until Wiley ran up to yell at him for mistreating his equipment.

Londo was Valiant.

He was world-famous, had been in every magazine ever published, every newspaper. CNN had a weekly show just about him and Maximus. E! network had squadrons of reporters solely assigned to cover him and all the Valiant groupies and wannabes. The Parahero International Information Network devoted half their broadcast day to chronicling just the activities of the Rands.

Lina was the only person in the universe Lon could have sex with. Did he love her because of that, or did he love *her?* She shook herself but that green-headed fly buzzed around her, no matter how hard she tried to swat it away.

I live in the present, she told it. *I'm not going to think about the future.*

Don't be an idiot, it retorted.

Sex was overwhelmingly important to Lon and now she could do something about it for him. But if he could have had sex with someone else, and she was just someone he'd met, would he even give her a second glance?

Should she insist on a better explanation about Orenya? Was it true what Jae said? If it was, didn't that make Lon a liar? That Terry bitch had called him that, a liar. But Lina knew Lon's heart. It was steadfast. It held by hard ethics. Could a heart like that lie? To a person he loved?

Lina knew there'd come a day. He would leave to be with– who? Whoever they would be, they'd be beautiful and elegant and famous. Maybe their pictures were already in a magazine she had at home. Maybe they'd be from Out Here. Orenya.

Lina saw herself in that near future, waving goodbye so bravely, assuring Londo that she would be all right. But day after day, night after night…decade after decade she'd sit before her TV and watch him and love him, cherishing every move he made before the international cameras.

A gentle kiss on the back of her neck brought her out of her reverie with sweet surprise. "This bandage looks scratchy," Londo said as he touched her shoulder. "Does it hurt?"

"It's probably time that that was changed," Wiley observed. He'd been talking on screen with a smart-looking woman, maybe the president of a university. Or a country. Or a star federation. Now Dr. Mem-Bazer was forced to talk to Lina Muttbutt. "Unless you've healed yourself today?" he added.

Lina rubbed some moisture from the corner of her eye before anyone could notice it. She said, "I Reiki'd last night. It's not my best technique. If my friends Sue or Dinah were here, they could work on me. I mean, if I ported in Sue's homeopathics with her."

Wiley's fingers poised in a frozen gesture. "Full names?" he demanded more than asked.

"And so the security check begins," Londo whispered to her as he slid into the next chair with only the faintest of winces.

She dutifully shared the information as she wondered how Sue and Dinah would be contacted by the Mega-Legion. It would probably be done subtly. Would they see through the ruse to realize they were involved in interstellar games?

Then Wiley asked her about Reiki, why she didn't know how to teach it and then why she couldn't afford to learn that level. He didn't understand classes that didn't offer scholarships to gifted students.

"Even teachers have to eat," Lina told him. "And some do barter. Like I barter with my clients."

Londo turned to the doctor. "All this psychic hoodoo is news to me, too. I always thought these people were charlatans. They're the subjects of jokes. I'm learning better. You should have seen him, Wiley– that storm deva the other day. It was amazing."

"I've seen plenty since your arrival," Wiley assured him.

Lon propped his head on his hand to gaze at Lina as he leaned against the counter. "So where do you find cheap teachers?"

Wiley took notes furiously as she detailed everything from ads in the back of New Age magazines to Facebook to neon hand signs along the highway. "You have to watch out for the scam artists. A lot of them are easy to spot, but some are real pros. That's why psychic work is illegal in so many places."

That caught Wiley's attention. "Illegal?"

Londo earnestly placed his hand over his heart. "I almost had to arrest her." He leaned back in his chair with a smirk.

"Oh hush, Londo. It's legal in most places if you do it to practice your religion. That's why I became ordained. The law can't touch religion. Wiley, that's in the First Amendment to the American Constitution." She counted them down on her fingers. "Freedom of speech, freedom of religion, freedom of… ah, something else, I think."

"Right to bear arms," Lon said, his eyes half-closed. Maybe he was bored with her. Maybe he was just resting them. They were still pretty bloodshot.

"That's the Second Amendment," Lina corrected.

Jae looked up from where he was working on some computer project of his own next to them. He seemed to have decided not to distance himself so much. Was he always this up-and-down, this manic? Lina recalled that she hadn't discussed Jae with Londo yet.

"Then it's all a religion?" Jae asked.

"Oh no. It's a non-religion, but according to the law if you're ordained, you're practicing a religion. Counseling clients by any appropriate means is part of a priest's legal duties."

"Religion." Londo made a rude noise. "Buncha cults with good publicity."

"Maybe," Lina hedged, "but religion can introduce people to spiritual concepts. And it's important for heritage purposes, you know, to carry on traditions and culture."

Lon opened one eye and regarded her doubtfully.

"People need solid foundations in their lives."

"Religion's the excuse behind too many wars," Lon grumbled. "They're all cults that make people who don't know how to think, think whatever the religious leaders want them to. They make everything 'us' against 'them.'"

"A lot of religions sponsor some good charities. I seem to recall a few on the Valiant Endorsements list."

Lon grunted into his chest at that. Then he rolled his head to focus on Lina. "Jae's ordained." Lina turned at the news.

Jae frowned at Londo for a moment before he said, "It was common to be ordained on Feith. We show our service to the universe by taking vows to help whenever asked."

"That's what Lina's vow was." Lon gave him a meaningful look.

Jae's return glance was emotionless. "There wasn't religion on Feith. Everyone was encouraged to discover how the universe spoke uniquely to them."

Lina tried to imagine it as Jae spoke to Londo.

"If what she said was true, it worked," Jae said. "My people all evolved and moved beyond the physical."

"What are you talking about?" Lon came to attention and swung around in his chair. Jae told him about the reading that morning.

"And you were the *volunteer*," Londo mused. "That puts a different spin on things."

"It does. Lina's given me something to think about. Along with whatever that was about sticking with you two."

"What was that?"

Lina shook her head. "I don't get it. But it's what *they* said."

Jae explained. "*They* told her that for me to change my attitude, I should stay around you two. If you don't mind, I think I'd like to see what they mean about that."

"As long as you know when to back off," Londo said pleasantly as he put his arm around Lina.

"I'm not stupid."

There was something about the way he said it. Since Lina had taken her nap, Jae's face had been emotionless, as if he wore a mask. It was a beautiful mask, but she didn't like it. She much preferred to see him smile or pout for real.

Lina was about to ask what the problem was when a tickle tapped at her brain. She tensed up immediately. Londo felt it through their link.

"What's the matter?"

"Something's wrong," Lina said, fishing for it. "My house– Someone's there."

"An intruder?"

Her mouth twisted as she tried to get a picture of the scene. "No, they're not going in. They're putting mail… No, a package in front of the door. They've got a, a UPS truck or something parked out on the street."

"A delivery."

Something was very off. "I think it's nighttime. UPS doesn't deliver at night. And I haven't ordered anything." She fished some more. "The deva of the house, he sits on the roof and oversees things. He's very excited in a bad way about the package. Explosion? I think it has explosives in it. My cats– If they get near it–! Oh, Londo!" She clutched him in terror.

"Wiley, where can she port it to here?"

Wiley's eyes rolled counter to each other as he thought. "Porting a small bomb. How powerful?"

Lon held Lina protectively. "About a 3.2, maybe 3.5?" he guessed. "Knowing Terry Rhodes–"

Lina blinked. "Terry Rhodes?" But of course; who else?

Wiley clicked his tongue against his teeth. Was he smiling? "Put it over here."

Lon peeled Lina out of her chair to follow Wilder to another section of the laboratory where a man-size transparent booth was embedded in the wall. Wiley nodded at it. "This will contain an explosion that size. I can seal it against contamination." He used one of his rings to do it. "All right, port away. Let's see what you've got."

Lina couldn't help trembling. "Should I try a biofilter?"

"No, just port it in." Three floating balls flew in to take formation around the booth. With his hands folded, Wiley clacked his rings together as he waited expectantly.

"Okay. I can't visualize… There it is. Carefully." She bit her lip as she concentrated for more than a minute. "Shit," she said as it materialized and simultaneously exploded. The booth shook. Debris struck the glass only to ricochet back and forth in the confining space before sliding to the floor.

Both of Wiley's eyes focused on the cataclysm. "Yes!" he said. "Excellent!"

"I didn't get the electrical potential balanced. S-sorry." A bomb! A bomb at her house! Her cats in danger!

And all because she knew Londo.

"An interstellar teleport combined with a Terran-manufactured bomb," Wiley said even as he began to run play-backs. "Very interesting."

Lon massaged her shoulders. "Terry must think there's a chance you could still be alive. I guess she wanted to cover every contingency."

Lina clutched at Lon's arm. "If she thinks I could still be around, how about you? You'd be the one she'd be concerned with. Are there any bombs at your place?"

He rubbed his nose. "And how would I know? I'm not… clairvoyant, that's the word. Don't know my household devas. Do apartments have devas? But I have neighbors who might be hurt. Can we get a patch through to the ParaNet? Who's on comm duty here?"

"A chance for another bomb? Let me configure the connection," Wilder said. It took a few minutes, but a 3-D screen soon appeared in the air next to the lab's central desk. It cleared into a view of a small room covered with monitors: regular TV screens, Lina noted. Background music played at medium levels, the latest from the Devil's Owed.

At the main console sat the Bolt, his visor pulled back so you could see his face and brown hair clearly. He was drinking a Snapple through a curlicue fun-straw. When he realized Londo was on the screen, he jerked straight up in his chair, eyes wide.

"Eff it all!" he exclaimed. "You cockeffing shit!" He hit his desk with his fist as he directed a few more f-combinations Londo's way. "We've been wondering if you were alive or what! Where the eff have you–"

"*Salut* to you too, Gary."

Now the Bolt used both fists to pound his console. The effort seemed to calm him. "We've been searching for you everywhere. The last we heard was the Armageddon call." He eased back and gave a snort of a resigned sigh. "Effing suckass effer. So you're off-planet. No wonder no one could find you."

"*Oui*, I'm on Sarastor for a few more days yet. I was wondering if you could do me a favor."

"You could have put in an effing Cancel Emergency call!"

Lon frowned. "Sorry. Too many things have been happening. I forgot. *Mea culpa*. Cancel emergency."

Bolt grumbled as he typed a quick message, then hit a "send" button. "Okay. Okay, a favor after he gives us all effing heart attacks. What is it?"

"There could be a bomb planted at my apartment. Maybe at Starhaven, but I don't think Terry knows about that place."

"Terry Rhodes again, huh?" The tone was easy, but the eyes glinted, the face tightened.

"In spades," Londo said as his own gaze darkened. "That bitch was the problem the other day. Could you transport down and check things? Keep your distance, of course. If you could take a visual display with you and patch into this channel, it would help."

"Sure thing. Give me a moment." Clicking his visor into place, the Bolt dissolved into a crackling blur. He reappeared with what looked like a rubik's cube. "Let me put things on automatic." His hands moved in blurs of speed, giving off tiny sparks. "Okay, beaming down." He nodded at Lon and streaked out of the picture.

The screen showed the empty room for a moment before it faded into a picture of a condominium hallway with homey striped wallpaper and potted ferns in brass buckets. Front and center was a door with an apartment number on it: 2817C. Bolt pointed at a large UPS-marked box in front of it. "Bumeff bomb. Or is it your latest beer club selection?"

17

L ondo's hands balled into fists. *"Crisse!* So much for building security. Stand clear; it could be on a proximity fuse."

"Sure thing."

Wiley craned his neck at the scene. "It can't be sensitive to motion if they delivered it– by hand, I presume?"

Londo grunted affirmative.

"Unless they remote-triggered a motion sensor later, of course." Wiley's squadron of sensor balls dipped and realigned themselves in mid-air to get a better view.

Lina shifted so she could see the screen clearly, too. Bolt could see her now, standing next to Londo as she said, "It's the same thing, but more so. Let me see if I can put a scale on it."

Bolt cocked his head. "English? Or are those Legion translators getting better?"

"English," Londo confirmed as Lina concentrated.

"Okay, I've linked the deva of your apartment with the deva of my house, and they're comparing. Yours says that this is… One, two, three, oh, 40 times as powerful."

Wiley gave what Lina could have sworn was a soft squeak of pleasure. She turned to him. "Do you have some place that would contain that? I'll be extra-careful this time with the potentials. I think I can do it. I know what I did wrong."

"Absolutely, but not in this lab. We have holding cells that would handle it, all impervion walls." He tapped a finger against his upper lip, so deep in thought that his eyes moved in unison. "Ah, I know exactly the one. Well-monitored, very well indeed. Good acoustics."

"Can you show me a picture of it?"

Wiley touched a ring and the picture with the Bolt went to split-screen to show a lackluster cube of a room in dim light. Apparently Bolt could see it, too, because he studied something just to the left of his camera.

"That's the place," Wiley told her. "If you can't do it, then just hold it to your time limit. It would be interesting to examine the device, but it's not essential." He actually bit his lip before he added, "But if you can bring it in, I'd appreciate it."

Jae harrumphed; he'd come over to stand behind them. "Lina, one of Wiley's hobbies is loud explosions."

"To each their own. *Chacun à son goût* and all that," she said to break the grim set of Londo's mouth.

"*Marde*, your accent is terrible." But he smiled.

"English or French?" she asked. "Okay, here goes. Let's see if I can get it here in under four minutes, unexploded."

Bolt folded his arms across his chest. "Four minutes? Earth to Sarastor? That I'd like to see."

"She's been practicing most of the afternoon," Lon said as he watched her stare at the screens, then close her eyes. Bolt jumped as the package disappeared from the hallway.

He said, "I'll check the rest of the place and then buzz over to Starhaven."

Lon nodded, squinting at the screen as a flash of light zipped through the door and back. The lightning-Bolt coalesced back to human form in front of the camera, which was still floating in the hallway. "All clear here. The place is a wreck, though. As usual. When are you going to hire an effing maid?"

"Nobody likes a nag, Gary."

The Terran part of the split-picture blurred as the ParaNet's mechanical transporter took effect. Then Bolt stood on a rocky mountainside with long rows of windows in its undulating face. Lon glanced over to see if Lina could see the picture, but she still had her eyes closed. It was sunset there, but enough light lingered for Bolt to search inside and out. It helped that using his power furnished his own illumination.

"All clear here, too," he reported with a sneeze. He slapped at some newly-settled dust on his shoulder and then looked at Lina's image curiously.

"Okay, it's coming through. I'm pretty sure I've got it," she announced. On the other side of the screen in the empty room, the package appeared. It held steady, just sitting there. Nothing exploded. "Time?"

Wiley's mouth opened and turned into a grin: the proud father seeing his child arrive in the world. His eyes flashed triumph, though not in concert. "Three and a half minutes. Very good indeed."

"It's still a biohazard, but at least the electric potentials are perfectly matched." Lina breathed a sigh.

Bolt scratched his cowled head, his mouth screwing in different directions as he tried to make sense of the screen. "That's Sarastor. Eff."

Londo wiggled his eyebrows at him. "Right. You're going to have to get back in training, Gary, because you've got competition now. Tell the Network I'll return in a few days. We're waiting out a quarantine here."

"Sure thing. Anything else I can do?"

"Um…" Lina chewed on her lip, wondering if she should say anything.

Lon gave her a nudge of encouragement. Bolt looked from one to the other with an inquiring glance before he shrugged his shoulders and gave his head an infinitesimal shake as if to say, *no way.*

"Ask," Londo told Lina.

She summoned her courage. "W-would it be too much trouble for you to call my work and tell them I'm in quarantine? Tomorrow or the day after I'll be overdue and it would be nice to still have my job when I get back. A call from a ParaNetter might keep the position open for me a while more."

Inside she squirmed. Here she was worried about her little desk job when she was surrounded by people who saved entire worlds on a daily basis. Even worse was what the Bolt would think of her if he ever figured out what she did at work. Lots of people had the wrong idea about healthy porn.

"Sure. Tell them you're on Sarastor?"

"Oh no! They think I'm on Tiawa in French Polynesia. I'd port you in a pad and pencil, but I'm having a little problem with biohazards. Oh, of course. Wait."

Bolt jumped as a pen and piece of paper from Lina's office appeared in his hand. It held the corporate name. Unlike some of the companies within the corporation, that wouldn't be familiar to anyone.

"The main number's on the pad," she told him and gave him a name and extension. Bolt wrote it down. The receptionist would answer with the corporate name. He'd never know.

"Please tell her Carolina O'Kelly's in quarantine, home in a few days. If you could throw in something like a world emergency or the end of the universe so they wouldn't fire me, I'd appreciate it."

"Sure thing. Anything else?"

Lon nudged her. "The cats? Your family?"

She gave him a smile now that she didn't have to worry about her job. "Porting without seeing both ends is out, but maybe I can zigzag cat food into one of the containment compartments here and then back home. There wouldn't be any contamination that way, would there? I mean, if it works."

She'd have to repay the grocery store when she returned, and the cats did need real human attention… Oh well, they had each other to play with. She'd have to get the knack of this real soon, but she'd always worked best under a deadline. "My parents won't even notice that I'm gone," she told Londo.

"That's it? *D'accord*, see you in a few days, Gary. Rand out."

"Good to see you're still with us. Effass."

The screen cleared and disappeared.

Lina gulped. "Did I actually talk to the Bolt? I mean, *the Bolt*?"

Lon chuckled and hugged her to him. "Gary's just a regular guy. Just like me."

"I would never make the mistake of calling you a regular guy." She ran her fingertips across his shoulders. Even when she set aside the fact that he was Valiant, Londo was the most special man in the world. Her protector. She gave him a thankful kiss and he shifted his hold on her so he could draw it out. The tip of his tongue grazed her bottom lip. Just that much ignited a fire within her and she opened to him, eager for more.

The air clicked as another screen flared to life in front of them. Londo muttered a curse onto Lina's lips. Stoan's face appeared.

"Feeling better, are we, Londo?"

"Ahem. Yes, Stoan, Feeling much better now."

"What the *kick* are you people doing up there? We just registered an explosion a few minutes ago, and now there's a sizable explosive sitting in one of the IM-area holding cells."

"Lina's porting in some bombs from Earth. Boobytraps for us. We thought some innocent bystanders might get caught by them, so we elected to bring them here. Wiley wanted to play."

"I didn't get the first one exactly right," Lina said. "It went off. Sorry."

Stoan gave her a measuring stare that she didn't like in the least. Londo tightened his grip on her under it.

"So tell me. Is it Lina or Carolina?" Stoan asked.

"Carolina for long, Lina for short," she replied, trying not to sound nervous. Should she call him "sir?" He didn't seem much older than Lon, maybe in his mid-thirties– young but mature. The bluish cast to his skin should have given him a death pallor, but the color was a living one. It merely made him seem…distant. Cold. He needed some yellow in it to warm it up, like Wiley had.

"So tell me, Carolina," Stoan said. "Can you teleport anything anywhere?"

"I don't know. I just started doing this, what, three days ago? So far so good on anything I've tried."

"Could you handle, say, this entire building?"

Lina shook her head. "Oh, no. Much too big. I think I'd better stay in the human size range. Maybe something a little bigger, but not much."

"Can you sense the entire building?"

Lina concentrated. Get the feel of this room, its connections to the larger building, the space it took up in the world… It wasn't a good time for her meds to start wearing off. She tried to ignore that and extend her senses. "I…think so. It would take me some time to go through the entire place and map it out, but given a few days– No, jesus, how big is this place? Big. Given a few weeks, maybe, I could."

"With all security systems mapped out, too?"

"What are you getting at, Stoan?" Londo snapped.

"I know what he's getting at," Lina said. "It would be a rough map, but I think I could get a reasonable percentage of the things that would make sense to me. I don't know about the odder stuff. Maybe; maybe not."

Stoan gave Londo a hard look. "What kind of security clearance would you give Carolina if you were in my shoes?"

"I'm not in your shoes. I know Lina well enough by now. I'd trust her with my life. I already have."

"She's been in our system."

Lina didn't like the way this conversation was going. She didn't like that this man was using her to embarrass Londo's position here. "Wiley checked after me. He knows exactly what I've accessed, and he seemed to be perfectly all right with it."

"How much more time do you have on the quarantine?" Stoan asked.

Lon looked at his padd. "A day and a half."

"I'm thinking about coming in there. Just as a backup."

"To what?" To make things worse, a quick sensation of burning flesh flashed across Lina's back. She was too angry to breathe into it, so it lingered and sizzled before finally fading away.

"That's not needed," Londo told Stoan as he squeezed reassurance to her. ****Let me handle this.****

The squeeze pulled the tight, healing skin of her side. He released instantly. ****Sorry.****

"Can you transport me in there directly?" Stoan peered at Lina's expression.

She tried hard not to scowl, but had to pause before answering. "That's odd."

"What?" Londo wanted to know as Stoan's eyes shuttered on Lina.

"He's got, I guess that's a magnetic field built up around him," she said to Lon and then addressed herself to Stoan. "Is that your normal field, or are you increasing it for some reason?"

"I'm in my normal mode," he said.

Lina thought he might be lying. She shook her head. "It feels weird. I wouldn't advise porting you. I'm not sure I can port a field like that and keep it intact."

Stoan looked strangely satisfied, and Lina concluded that he thought that here was something she couldn't control. He didn't realize that she could port him, but that his field would be wrecked to hell if she did.

"I could set up an emergency airlock for the lab and enter that way. Or use our own transporters," Stoan said smugly to Londo.

"And that way we'd all have to stay here another three days while we waited for you to go through decontamination." Londo's voice was liquid as he tried to ease the situation. "Stay put for another day, Stoan. We're fine in here. Everything's under control."

"That's what I'm afraid of," Stoan said tightly. He stared down Lina.

Damn it, he was trying to turn Lon against her! "I do *not* control minds! I am not controlling anyone." She tried to think through all the information she'd gathered. "Don't y'all have any telepaths around? I thought there was one on the membership list. Londo, you said you knew a telepath. Is she a Legionnaire?"

Stoan glowered at her. "Psyche's not here now. She's on a mission. She doesn't seem to be in the same class as you; she doesn't talk to *spirits* and *angels*." He named the two snidely, as if he were talking about children's fantasies. "She doesn't bring people back from the dead."

"None of that is telepathy. At least, I don't think it is."

"I've already left messages for Chim," Lon interrupted. He used the name as if this Chim might be the same person as Psyche.

"Then we are at an impasse since I believe that this is all telepathic in nature. Chim tells me that mind control is theoretically something a strong telepath can do, if one has the right intent and skills. Even without implants."

Londo pulled Lina back from where she'd advanced to the screen to face down the Legion commander. He stepped in front of her as a shield. "So when she returns she can scan Lina and everyone else in here and confirm that no one's being controlled."

Stoan shook his head. "Have a lesser telepath scan a more powerful one? Or one just as powerful, with more tricks up her sleeve? I'm not willing to do that."

Lina raised up on her toes to emerge from the shelter of Lon's shoulder. She couldn't come across as a coward. Londo would reject her sometime in the future, but by god he wasn't going to do so now over something like this! "Well, dammit, what would prove it to you?"

Easy, Lina. Lon raised his hands to increase the barrier between the two. "Let's slow down here, everyone," he said. "Stoan, I've been thinking. If you can't find any grade-8 or above teeps nearby, then why not just call up the Tishana and ask them to interview Lina? They can use their own controller protocols, use whatever security they want. Surely we can set up an independent link so there'd be no possibility of them getting into Legion communications."

"No. I'm not willing to go that far yet."

"Then let Wiley put together some likely tests and tape Lina doing whatever. You can submit the tape to the Tishana without endangering Legion security."

Stoan rubbed his mouth.

Lina caught her breath. "All I'm asking," she said carefully, "is what can I do to prove that I'm not controlling anyone?"

The Legion commander studied her for a long time, and Londo, too. "I'm not sure. I'll think about it and get back to you. You're still in quarantine. I'll have an answer ready tomorrow morning."

"Wonderful," Lina said without enthusiasm.

"Stoan, we can go ahead and–" Londo started, but the screen went blank and disappeared.

18

"Nice guy." Lina made a sour face at Lon.

"Actually, he is. He's just concerned at the circumstances." Londo took her in his arms again and hoped they wouldn't be interrupted this time. **I'm ready to tear down a few walls around here,** he told her. **Does Wiley have any more bomb rooms? Hell, I'd be willing to share the place with that bomb, if it meant we could get a few minutes of real privacy.**

He laughed suddenly. "*Bin-bin,* that's it. That's it exactly." He grinned at her.

"What? I was kidding about the bomb."

"Instead of Earth-to-Earth porting, we do Sarastor-to-Sarastor."

"If you recall, love, we are biohazards. Can't go anywhere."

"Yes, and we are in Mega-Legion Headquarters."

"Huh?"

"Jae." The other two Legionnaires had discreetly absented themselves from the general vicinity, but now Jae turned in his chair in front of a workstation to face Lon.

Londo said, "Emergency systems in Headquarters carry throughout the building. Any chance of there being biocleaning agents in the mix?"

"Biocleaning. I suppose so." Jae turned to his terminal to check. "Yeah, emergency biocleaning available in case of biohazard leak or attack. Not just here and in the medical sector, where you'd expect it, but everywhere."

"*Oui,* I thought I remembered it. I know the seals on individual quarters are pretty tight. Are they biohazard tight?"

Jae gave a grudging conspiratorial grin at Londo's eagerness. "As I recall, they're made to be airlocks. The original HQ designers were a paranoid bunch. You'll have to tell the computer to activate the special lockdown."

"Good enough. Wiley?"

The azure genius was standing at a bank of monitors overlooking the room the bomb was in. He turned at his name.

"What are the chances of the prisoners making a break for it? Port into quarters, activate emergency airlock procedures, emergency biocleaning system?"

Both Wilder's eyes narrowed at them. "The environmental factors would work, yes. But I said no sex, Londo, and I meant it."

Lina covered her mouth with her hand, trying not to laugh.

"All we want is a little privacy," Londo urged.

"If privacy is all you want, use the break room."

"I don't want the break room," Londo's voice came out ever so slightly as a growl.

Wilder said, "You may think you're healthy, Lon, but you're still healing. I've been thinking about separating you two for the rest of quarantine. No more nanites. Without the link weakening you, you could recover completely by the time we're released."

"No," Lina and Lon said simultaneously.

Wiley's mouth twisted either in a smile or grimace. "I suppose we could postpone that. For a while."

Londo scowled his famous scowl at him, but Wiley wasn't impressed.

"Because any introduction of foreign substances will create a new quarantine condition," Wiley began.

"When they return," Jae put in, "we'll turn the biocleaning system in Lon's quarters up to full. That'll get rid of any life forms, foreign or domestic, within a half hour," he added for Lina's benefit.

She nodded warily. The bland mask Jae had made of his face seemed a trifle friendlier for some reason, but still reserved.

"So let's go," Londo said. Gingerly he put his arm around Lina's waist. "Puter, put bio-tight force fields around all plants in my room."

Wiley held up his hand. "Just a moment. I need to change Lina's dressings. And give you both some injections."

"Oh, good," Lina said.

"Are you sure you need to give me a shot?" Lon asked. "Or are you just getting a kick out of finally being able to?"

Wiley gave him a rueful smirk. "Maybe a little of both."

"Stop egging him on, Lon." Lina pushed Londo and he wobbled away from her.

"Whoa!" Jae cried.

"Do that again," Wilder ordered.

What were they so upset about, Lina wondered? "Do what?"

"Push him."

Lina looked at Londo and he shrugged. She pushed him, and he wavered from the force of it. "So?"

"You forget, Lina," Lon said with a smile and an innocent hand to his heart. "Valiant *ici*."

"Hm?" Then she remembered trying to push him when he'd first gotten his powers back. It had been like pushing against the Rock of Gibraltar.

Wilder got his handheld sensor out and ran it up and down, inches away from Lina.

"What does it say?" she asked curiously.

"It said that you seem to be a normal, if injured, human being. The last time I looked, normal human beings couldn't budge Valiant. Invulnerability is one thing, but getting past his strength is quite another."

Now Wiley ran his tricorder around Londo. "Hm. Valiant is still Valiant-like. Do you feel back up to full power, Lon?"

"I'm getting there. I'm not mega yet, but I'm enough."

"So how does this happen?"

"Well," Lina began. What to say?

"It happened when you gave me that back massage," Londo nudged her. "That was some massage."

"When you had no powers," Jae said.

"No, when I had full powers. Lina said I needed to relax, so she decided on a massage."

They were all looking at her. She stamped her foot. "Well, he wouldn't relax, so I told his cells to recognize me."

"Recognize you?" Wiley was taking his notes again.

"You know, not be afraid, not put up any defenses. Cells have a rudimentary intelligence. Oh, is that how the shot thing works? All I was trying to do was to get him to relax enough to let me give him a massage."

"Apparently you got him to do a little more than that," Wiley said and cocked an eyebrow at Lon.

"Oh *that*," he said, laughing. "That's a double-feedback telepathic loop."

"We'll talk while I change Lina's dressing," Wiley said, moving to chairs near what had become his medical section.

"You aren't going to write a paper about this, are you?" Londo asked cautiously.

"The question is how much I'll publish." Wilder gave a faraway smile while his left eye focused on his invisible screen. "I might be persuaded to keep some aspects private. I always appreciate blackmail material. As if I don't have enough on you already. Lina, sit here."

Lina dutifully sat, and was about to take off Lon's shirt when she realized Jae still stood next to Londo.

"Privacy?" she asked.

"Here," Lon said, and swooped his fingers in the air between them. A shimmer cocooned her from the others. "Good?" Lon's voice came to her as if from a distance.

Not that good, but what else was she going to do? Apparently Jae couldn't take a hint, and Londo truly thought this was enough.

Men.

With a sigh she divested herself of her robe and shirt, leaving just the leotard with its off-kilter bodice. She still wore it without the one arm on, to avoid most of the bandages.

Wiley'd want to get to all her major injuries, so she dropped the leotard to her waist and then tied the arms of Lon's shirt around her neck, letting the body of the garment cover up her front. The weight of the robe wrapped around her waist secured it– for the most part– and hung down to warm her legs. Back and arms were now bare.

With these few moments to herself, just her and her bandages, Lina could focus on the aches and stings that congealed in patches and then ran in definite paths within her body. If not for Wiley she'd have died along with Londo.

And now Terry the Bitch had tried to bomb her house.

Would she try again? Were Lina's cats in danger? What would Dr. Menlo do? He'd been implicated for that poison gas massacre in Guatemala, hadn't he? Would he gas her house?

She couldn't port gas, could she? Hell, think back to how she'd reacted back there on the island. She couldn't do anything, just flailed about in victim mode while people used her to hurt Londo.

Involuntary images from the news came to her: countless criminals attacking Valiant. More often they threatened innocents since their weapons could do so little harm to him.

If she were going to follow him, they'd be aiming at her.

"Yo, Lina?"

She called all done and the privacy screen disappeared. It was nice to see that Londo had placed himself between her and Jae, blocking most of his view.

Wiley lifted the dressing on her shoulder. She flinched at his touch though the material slid off easily.

"This is healing nicely." The skin was brownish red where there had once been a brand going all the way to the bone. Now it was just a severe case of sunburn.

A screen showed her the burned patch on her back. It was flaking white with a thin layer of regenerated skin underneath. Wiley told her that tonight he'd program her bed for deep regeneration in that area, with special attention to the nerves.

"But she'll be all right?" Londo asked.

"In a few days. Perhaps a week for this area."

Wiley reached in a drawer and sorted through a jumble of containers, finally producing a small bottle of what he termed *bartol flea*. "For the next two days you need to spray this every four hours or so on your back," he told Lina. "Use it sparingly. Gorgeon can handle it from there. Now let's see how this is doing." He snapped off the dressing patches on her left arm, revealing the black-crusted, two-inch hole underneath.

Lina glanced away; it looked worse now than it had before. Londo made a sound of dismay.

"It's doing well," Wilder announced, "but I'm surprised that it isn't doing better. I would expect another miracle healing."

"I couldn't figure out what kind of technique it needed. Maybe a Kolaimni or magnetic, but I haven't had the time."

"Take some time. Ask your guides; that's what they're there for, right? I'll strap a regenerator on it tomorrow and you'll wear it for two weeks, maybe three. I'll let Gorgeon make the final decision. You'll have a scar, but eventually you'll have full use of the arm."

As Wiley rigged that hard patch again on either side of the forearm, Lina could see that the inside of it was lined with a spiderweb of multi-colored tubing.

"I'll take you to Gorgeon first thing when we're out of here," Londo assured her. Then he turned to Wiley. "No offense."

Wiley grunted. It did not sound like a happy grunt.

"Thank you," Lina told her doctor. She pulled the robe up around herself and secured it. She could adjust everything else later when she was alone.

Wiley scanned her head. "Londo said you'd had a head injury," he prompted.

"A brick or something caught me," Lina told him.

"That's got to be what's causing the porting," Londo said. "The power will go away when the bump heals, right?"

Jae peered at her past the top of Lon's ear. Lina pulled up the collar of the robe so that the lower half of her head was covered as well.

"You're practicing medical theory without a degree again." Wiley double-checked his findings. "Hm." He ran the sensor around her again and checked. "I think it may be just the opposite," he pronounced. "I see some old trauma here that seems to have been corrected by this more recent event. When did you receive the original brain injury?"

"Brain injury?" Lina jumped off her stool.

"I take it that means you didn't know you had one," Wiley said dryly.

Jae scratched at his scraggly whiskers as Lon wrapped Lina in his arms. "There now," Lon cooed. "There's no brain injury now?"

"Scar tissue. What's not healed will in the next few days."

Lon rocked her back and forth. "All better now, eh. She was attacked once when she was a kid," he volunteered. "And there were other times when she was hurt pretty bad."

"What did the doctors tell you?" Wiley asked Lina. "How did they treat the brain damage?"

"They never said anything about brain damage," Lina replied slowly from where she curled under Lon's chin. She didn't know what to think. "I just got stitches and stuff."

At Wiley's blank look she added, "For bad cuts. Other times than that, I was almost never taken to the hospital unless I broke a bone. I fell a lot back then. What, you think I had this power all along? That all I needed was for someone to clunk me on the head with a baseball bat?"

"That's the cure for amnesia," Londo solemnly told her. "For this you needed to be clunked with a brick." He kissed the top of her head, and she emerged to give him a wan smile.

Wiley mused over his findings. "I can't see where this would prompt such a development," he muttered. "This part of the brain controls non-linear subconscious processing."

Lina piped up hopefully, "So the porting's permanent? Ha," she added for Lon.

"Ask me in ten years," Wiley said, bemused. He wondered if the accident could be duplicated. "You say you fell a lot back then?"

"Was pushed, I bet," Londo said darkly.

"Lon!" Lina's eyes flashed at him. Don't give away family secrets!

"Some balance centers could have been affected as well. Here's an anesthetic for your arm." Wiley gave her a couple of those fast-burning shots through the robe and the pain completely vanished, leaving her a little spacey.

Maybe *more* than a little. "Ooo. Too much," she giggled with a snort. Then she giggled at that.

"What'd you do to her?" Londo demanded. He held her at arm's length to study her. "You okay, kitten?"

"Juuust fine. Um hmm."

"Undo it, Wiley. Now."

Wiley clicked his hypo twice as he turned to him. "Londo, she's going to be out of it for some time. You don't want to take advantage of someone who's not in full possession of their faculties, do you?"

Londo scowled at him as Jae let out a quick bark of a laugh. "That's a dirty trick."

Wilder chuckled evilly. "I said no sex for a while more, and I mean it. You're not the only one injured. Now you're next. Lina, I need your hand, please."

Lina hardly let him place her hand where he wanted. "I can do it; just point where you want it," she said. But she kept dropping her hand as she giggled at her inability to keep it steady. Jae started to hold her hand in place at Wiley's direction as he grinned at Londo, but Lina growled, "Don't touch me!"

"Don't take it personally," Londo told Jae as Lina shook his hand off.

She tried to hold still while Wiley administered the shots. Lon set his jaw and glowered manfully as if the doctor were performing anesthesia-free surgery. Wiley compared his new readings with those previous, then gave Londo another shot.

"Ouch." Lon rubbed the site. "You did that on purpose."

"Maybe."

"Oh hell, we'll stick around here for a little while longer," Londo said. "What do you want to know…about us?"

"How you do it, of course."

"The Big Question," Jae added. He made no move to leave when Londo included him in his dark glare.

Londo's scowl deepened. "*D'accord*, you bastards. It's a… telepathic psychic thing."

"That tells me a lot," Wiley muttered. "More information."

"Double feedback loop," Lina said. She discovered that her stool could turn, and she did so now. Londo steadied her.

He did *not* feel comfortable discussing this! "One person tries to feel what the other person feels. Tactile, not emotional. And the other person does it too, for resistance and calibration."

"Double feedback loop de loop," Lina repeated.

Wiley squinted measuringly at the two of them. "And how does the other technique work? The cell recognition?"

Londo shrugged his shoulders. "I have no idea. All I felt was a massage. A great massage." His smile returned as he watched Lina's careless abandon of anything except the ride she was getting.

"All you have to do is talk with the cells," she said cheerily. "You have very nice cells, Londo. They're just scared, defensive." She made itsy-bitsy spider finger crawls in Londo's direction. "Putting up their little force fields all over, teeny tiny force fields. Whoo, Tilt-a-Whirl!"

Londo caught her before she could fall and she cackled with glee. "I never throw up on the Tilt-a-Whirl. My roommate did, all over the midway. Just *bwaff*, and there went two chili dogs and a whooole lotta nachos and some funnel cake besides. It was really gross. I had to drive us home with her ralfing out the window all the way back, I-40 after dark, and me without a driver's license." She snickered behind her hand.

"Force fields," Wiley urged the drunk girl. "What's this about force fields and cells?"

"Oh, *that*," Lina waved her hand disparagingly at him, but just managed to throw herself off-balance. Londo straightened her. "I talked to them, told them not to be afraid any more. It was just me. Lon's always telling me to relax. Well, that time I told *them* to relax." For some reason she felt like laughing, so she did, just a little.

Now ignoring her, the men talked with Jae letting out an occasional exclamation of surprise, like when he said, "How many times?!"

Londo just gave an embarrassed grin while Lina could feel the not-so-hidden boast inside him. "Maybe a little more often than that. I didn't keep track. Much. We didn't know how long we had before my powers came back. We thought each time would be the last."

Jae slapped the side of his thigh. "I'm adding that to your official listing of powers," he laughed.

"You do and you're dead!" Londo glared at him.

Lina was just extremely glad she was too drunk to be embarrassed. She didn't even blush when Wiley looked her up and down and then grinned. "A healer. Of course." She just made a face at him and spun on her stool, curling her toes to reduce wind resistance. She was nothing if not efficient.

They only asked her a couple of questions, for she had a tendency to giggle or stick her tongue out and lose track of what she'd been saying. At one point Wilder took her hand and she drew back. He nudged Jae, and Jae took her hand; she snatched it away. Londo took her hand, and she snuggled to him.

Wiley shook his head and made a time notation on his screen. "A phobia for touching. I can remember her doing that now. I'd put it down to cultural differences or injury."

"*Eh bien*, none of this gets out, right?" Londo said occasionally, just to make sure.

Lina could understand Wiley being there for intellectual curiosity, but she couldn't Jae's presence.

*******Jae's practically a brother,******* Lon explained. ******T'inquiète pas. *Anything you say to him he'll keep under wraps.*******

"Oh," Lina said. "Say, is that an affectation or what?"

"What?"

"*Eh bien. D'accord. Voyons.* I had a French teacher who used to spout off small talk for five minutes at a stretch when he was pissed at us. Which we got him a lot. So is it real?" She turned to Jae. "Does he do that in Lingua, too?"

"*Eh bien*," Jae replied with a straight face and Lina could hear the French through the translator version, "he certainly does."

Lina nodded. "AffecTAtion then. A very cute affwect… affwect… thing." She pecked Lon on the cheek.

Wilder was searching through a drawer in another cabinet. Now he turned around with what looked like an ice pick in his hand.

"What's that?" Lon asked.

"Nothing for you to be worried about," Wiley assured him. He held the pick in front of him like his tricorder, point out. "Take her hand, will you?"

Londo squinted at him, trying to figure out what he was up to. He kept his arm around Lina's waist and took her hand with his free hand.

"No, just hold her hand," Wilder instructed. "One hand."

Lon let go of her except for one hand while Jae hovered behind the wobbly woman to make sure she didn't fall off the stool. She cocked her head at Wilder, then at Londo. When Jae reached out to steady her, she said, "Watch it," but didn't make any other comments when he quickly retreated.

"It's okay, *chérie*," Lon assured Lina. "We're just keeping you– hey!!"

Wilder looked pleased as he measured the distance between where he'd poked Londo with the pick and where Lina's skin first touched Lon. "Did it really hurt, or are you just complaining?" Wiley asked.

"It really hurt," Lon sneered, reaching for the pick. "Here, I'll show you how much."

Wiley easily dodged out of Lon's way.

"Sorry about this," Jae said from behind him and stomped on Londo's booted foot.

"OW! HEY! Jaeson Rheoboth Rallene–!" Londo lunged up suddenly, facing down Jae. Lina wobbled back in her chair. Jae caught her and used her as a shield.

"I see some problems with this," he told Londo.

"Leggo!" Lina protested, slapping at Jae. "Leggo leggo!!"

"Very interesting," Wiley noted on his padd as Londo hurriedly collected Lina from Jae. "Problems. Yes."

"Hell," Lon muttered. After the moment that his invulnerability had snapped back on, his foot felt fine. He looked at Lina. "Remind me not to carry you through a crowd of people shooting at me," he said.

"I'm a stupid drunk, Lonnie-Wonnie," she replied blithely. "I didn't know that before."

"I'll remind you. And don't call me 'Lonnie.'"

"Here," Wiley told Lon and handed him the dumbbell from before. "Hang on to that. One hand on Lina."

"One hand, check." Lon held the dumbbell in his right hand as Wiley increased its weight. Fifty kilos, one hundred… Lon groaned at two hundred kilos and flexed his arm and fingers after setting the instrument back down, Wiley having brought the weight back to one kilogram.

"Hurt?" Jae asked.

"I'd like to see you do that. Jeez," Lon muttered as he read readings over Wiley's shoulder. "Only two hundred? Felt like…" He rubbed his right arm. "A lot more."

"Once more. Ring off. Arm around her." They repeated the experiment but this time Lon floated up into the air a foot, supporting Lina and holding the weight as Wiley took it up to three hundred kilos before Londo's feet involuntarily touched the ground.

"Control check," Wiley announced, and this time Lina was left on the ground as Londo floated in the lab with the barbell. One ton, two tons…

"Without her you're within expected parameters of your recuperation. I just don't understand," Wiley said as Lon handed the instrument back to him. "Jae, what do you make of it?"

Instead, Lina broke out into song. She performed a Broadway tune about wanting adventure and love as if she were performing to the back of the theater.

When she was done Londo cheered and threw her an imaginary rose, which she caught and "smelled" before clasping it to her chest. Even so, he said, "Maybe you ought to lie down."

"It's his fault, not mine," Lina accused Wilder, using what must have been a rather floppy rose to point with. "He knew he was giving me too much. Don't they have the Hippy-cratic Oath out here? 'First, do no harm.' Or are we all too cibilized for ethics?"

"She brings up an interesting point, Wiley," Lon said. Wilder just gave a little *harumph*. "I sense major demerits in your future."

The room spun a couple degrees around Lina before it stopped. "Dooo– Do we want to trade ethics? I'm a priest and a telepath and a psychic. Triple whammy." She hummed some ominous theme. "I know things about people. Know things about you."

Again she pointed at Wilder, this time without the rose. "Wiley Coyote, every now and then I hear what you're thinking while you're pretending to check test results. Now, if I didn't have any ethics…"

"Yeah?" Lon asked. "What did you hear?"

Wiley grimaced. "Perhaps she does need some of that painkiller neutralized." He reached around to get another ampoule ready.

"Damn straight. I'm not anyone's guinea pig. Oh god, I'm a vegetarian now."

Jae seemed to be enjoying the show. "You don't want to be?" he asked as Wiley administered the shot.

"Wuff. That's getting better. No, I wanted to be a vegetabubble… begetarian. I only had one meat left to give up. Poor ol' mad cows. And I sneak bacon, too." She splayed her fingers across her face and then dared a peek to see Lon's judgment.

"Bacon?" he asked.

She nodded sadly. "Babe Bacon. Poor piggy Babe!"

"I see your point. I liked Babe."

"Babe?" Jae asked.

"But I eat bacon, too," Londo assured her.

"Arnold the Pig. He was smart as a dog," Lina added before she grabbed Londo by his arm and joggled it. "You'd never eat a dog, would you?"

"Absolutely not! Never."

"Good. I will bacon no more forever."

Lon stroked her braided hair while she quieted down as if the drugs were wearing off. Instead she began to mumble to herself. "One minute I ate meat, the next– bam. Begetarian. I didn't even get a chance to have my last hamburger. Everything's happened so quickly in these past few days. It's like…" She knocked her head against Londo's chest. "I'm just paranoid. Stupid ol' Muttbutt."

Londo took her by her shoulders and turned her to face him. Her eyes were still half-closed; her lower lip sagged. He gave her a soft shake so she'd pay attention. "Don't call yourself that," he ordered. "I don't want to hear you say that name again, *comprends-tu*?"

He brushed a lock of hair out of her face. How did she really feel about him, about all that had happened? Did she really think this rushed? He couldn't blame her. "So things have happened a little quick. It's like what?"

"Like pulling the Chariot card from the Tarot. The universe is rolling, the road is rough, and you can only hang on for dear life."

"Sometimes that's just the way it is," Jae said. Was there an echo of regret in his voice?

"And sometimes you end up being run over," Lina said darkly.

"Have you been run over?"

"You may have noticed us yesterday, hm?"

"But you got back up."

Lina blinked and frowned at herself as something kicked in inside her. The world looked a little clearer, but it was still difficult to concentrate. "And we're okay now. I'll keep that in mind. But the ride's not over yet." She looked at the floor. "Hey, Sarastor, Earth told me better and worse things ahead. Are they over, or still on the event horizon?"

She heard the world laughing at her. **You still have too much in your system. Yes, Speaker to Worlds, they are still on the move. Better things, worse things. Follow your heart and you'll choose the correct path.**

"Follow my heart, huh?" Lina closed her tired eyes. This alien world still spun around her. "Planets have no real perception of human life, you know that?"

"You talked to this world?" Wiley asked.

"What did she say?" Lon wanted to know.

Lina wanted to crawl into her own little corner to catch her breath. Maybe it would be nice to be in that corner with Londo, just so she could feel safe and sleep. Well, maybe not sleep if Londo was there. Touching him made everything inside her rev up in a very satisfying way. Woof.

"Lina? What did Sarastor say?" Londo repeated.

She gazed at him with a hungry, crooked smile. "Mainly that I'm still drugged too much. That things aren't over yet. 'Speaker to Worlds,' she called me; that's new. Earth usually says something like 'Little One' or 'Child.' Guess that's the difference between Earth and Sarastor, huh?"

"What was that about following your heart?"

"'Follow your heart and you'll choose the correct path.' Unquoth the raven."

Lon turned to the doctor. "Dammit, Wilder, sober her up! I need to speak to her in private. With her mind absolutely clear."

Jae turned away– probably laughing at them, Lina thought.

Wiley checked the remaining level in his hypo. "Oh, all right," he grumbled, and gave Lina another shot.

She blinked and took a breath. And another. The world focused. The roller coaster was sliding in to dock. "Thank you. In the future, Doctor Mem-Bazer," she said evenly as she drew herself up straight, "I would appreciate it if you did not treat me like a child who cannot control herself. I am not an animal or a mentally incompetent human being, and I don't appreciate being treated like one."

"I didn't–"

"Yes you did. You didn't believe that I was mature enough to assess the situation and act accordingly. And you used me as a tool against Londo."

Wilder pressed his lips together. Both his eyes focused on her. "I did. I apologize. I won't do it again."

She smiled at him. "Thank you. Apology accepted."

Lon put his arms around her. "So are you sober now?"

"Quite, and quite thoroughly pain-free, too."

"Good. We need to talk." He turned to Wiley. "Can we go to my room now, doctor?"

"I repeat, no sex." Wiley heaved a sigh of surrender. "For a while yet."

"*D'accord*. Lina?"

"We aren't being gracious. Does anyone else want to get out of here? I can provide the transportation."

Jae considered. He seemed calm enough, but Lina knew he was upset about something. He'd been through so much in his life, it was no wonder that he had these moods. At least he'd found a socially acceptable mask to wear when he was upset, this emotionless face with the sharp eyes peering out from behind.

"When you two arrived yesterday," he said, "I was helping Wiley with some compound experiments. I'll finish up so I can resume my duties when quarantine is over."

"Good enough," Wiley said. "And after we're done, if we can get done tonight, I need to finish analyzing all the data I've gathered in the last day."

Lon nodded. "*Bon*. Lina, I can get some clothes shipped into my quarters."

"Then what are we waiting for? I'm tired of running around half-naked. Can you picture your room in your mind?" She gave a little laugh. "What, you only have one piece of furniture?"

"No sex," Wiley warned again.

"That's better," Lina said as Lon took her hand and pictured another room. For two minutes she concentrated on the both of them, on their destination, and then they were gone.

"Anyone taking any bets?" Jae asked.

19

L on's room was suddenly *there* around them. Lina sucked in her breath.

"Computer," Londo barked at Systems. "This is not an emergency, but utilize emergency air lock procedure for these quarters. Also begin bio-cleaning at the same levels as in Laboratory 1-A."

Two beeps of acknowledgement sounded.

"Lon, this isn't a dorm room, it's an apartment!"

Londo hadn't realized just how eager he'd been to get her into a place that was his, all his. Having Lina in his life had knocked him completely off-balance. She commanded such great power over his thoughts and body. Now the tables were turned, perhaps. Here he was in command– even if she held all the cards.

But he had other games he could play. As she turned to take in his place, he twisted her farther around to enfold her in his arms. Her eyes widened when she looked up to him, but she parted her lips as he bent to her.

Automatically their thoughts twined as they had days before. Her unfinished questions he met with bold suggestions. She might call them demands. Damn but it was good to have her back like this. They had to get naked. Now. He'd been too long without her.

When he pulled at her robe's belt, she pushed away. "No sex, remember? We can keep this just to this level, can't we?"

Lina always tried to deny what she felt. She needed a little encouragement now and then. The belt fell to the floor and he explored under her robe with his hands and mouth.

Her throat vibrated beneath his lips as she whispered, "Londo, no. Love, we can't...do this."

But her eyes were black with the same desire that fired him. He pulled her to the floor– gently, gently!– and clicked his belt buckle open.

Lina used the slight freedom to frame his head in her hands. She kissed him soundly on the mouth.

"Dearest Londo, no. I mean it. I can't think when you do this. Someone's got to keep their sense now. Getting you healthy is more important than sex."

She wasn't serious.

"I am," she said, and he saw her jaw set, her shoulders straighten. Maybe she was.

"You are a killjoy."

"No, Wiley is. Let's blame him for this."

"He said for a while. Define 'a while.' I say that 'a while' has passed. C'mon, *chérie*."

"You're still hurt."

"Am not. C'mon, baby."

"Are so. Look me in the face and tell me you don't feel bad."

Lon gave her his silly, crooked smile. "I'm a Legionnaire. I can rise above the pain. I feel myself rising right now."

"You are such a walking hormone."

"Yes, darling Lina."

Her responding smile made her blistered face crack. She winced.

Lon grimaced in sympathy– and guilt. He ran his fingers down her cheeks as if he could heal her. "I am so sorry, kitten," he said. At her questioning expression he added, "The healing time is for you, too. I should have never gotten us into that mess."

"You've already apolo–"

"I can't beg your forgiveness enough. I was stupid. Beyond *idiot*. Your safety is everything to me. Your health is as well."

With that he put his arms more sedately around her and rose into the air, shifting her so she was cradled against him.

Talk was actually a better tactic, he reasoned. Talk and talk some more. She liked talk. Then some sex. She liked that, too. Then he could accomplish tonight's mission, no sweat.

They glided an arm-length or two above the floor across the room. Lina held on tightly. She feared Lon would overtax himself. Still, it was thrilling. Flying! In Londo's arms!

Here out of the entryway, the living room stretched even farther than it had seemed before. "Ohmigosh, look at this place," she said. "It belongs in *Architectural Digest.*"

"I may have gotten some ideas from there," Lon said. He swung them vertically and set her feet down on the floor. "We will take a tour," he announced.

Lina gave him a suspicious look.

He countered it with a Sunday school face. "It'll put a better spin on the 'a while' definition," he said.

That made sense, so Lina tucked her robe back into place. She pulled her thick braid out from the collar and flipped it behind her but Londo caught it. He used it as a rein to guide her around. "Living room," he began.

This room alone was bigger than Lina's entire house. Furniture was very masculine with crisp corners and tight upholstery, no patterns except a stripe or two. Occasional live plants thrived blurrily behind blue glows she supposed were force fields.

It was all homey if military, but… "It needs some outside light," Lina suggested as she walked in small arcs so she could see everything. Even with the occasional abstract black and brown stripe, the white walls were oppressive.

Lon grunted and then said to the air, "Computer, full window view of…Saturn, from Mimas."

Instantly great windows stretched from ceiling to floor along every wall. It seemed they were high over the canyons of a frozen moon. A spectacular Saturn hung on the horizon, her rings almost vertical.

Lina jumped and clapped her hands to her mouth. She spun to face Lon. "Holy shit!" She laughed. "That's amazing!"

Lon sauntered cockily toward her, very sure of himself now. "This is Mega-Legion HQ," he explained. "The outer perimeter has to be constructed of solid impervion for defense purposes. Windows would be a weakness. We have viewscreens instead." He slid his arm around her waist and felt her arch her back against him. "Want to see the bedroom now? If you remember, we've never had sex on a real mattress. That might be amusing."

"I would like to see the bedroom. And kitchen, and whatever else you have here. That's what a tour usually entails, isn't it? And I assume you have the facilities here to take a shower. All this medicine gunk makes me feel filthy. I can't seem to get clean."

"I know what you mean. I could handle another shower." He pulled her closer, capturing her gaze with his.

But her will was just as strong. "Alone. I want a warm shower. You need a long, hot soak to get rid of some of those aches and pains."

"I won't feel the heat."

"Maybe you're just a little more vulnerable now than you think you are. I never heard of any invulnerable guys feeling like they needed to take an aspirin."

"You're one hell of a nosy psychic."

"If you won't pay attention to what your own body's telling you–"

"Oh, I know what my body's telling me." His eyes danced with hers. "C'mon, Lina." He made it into a soft song. "C'mon, Lina. C'mon, Lina."

He was being silly, and she couldn't help herself from grinning at him. Just the same, she pushed away. "Let's finish the tour. And then I'll get that shower."

"You'll just need another one afterward. I was planning on a long, sticky session. We'll have to change the sheets at least twice." He ran his finger along the line of her shoulder blade, considering. "No, we'll finish off with a bath for two, with bubbles and champagne." With an approving nod to himself for his plan, they moved on.

Lon's kitchen was of surprisingly humble proportions. It was too small even to be called a kitchenette.

"Why prepare meals in your room when you can use the Legion cafeteria?" Londo said. "It's open 20 hours a day. We get room service too."

"Twenty–"

"Sarastor's day has 20 hours. It's the equivalent of about 27 Terran hours."

Next stop was his private trophy room. There was an official one somewhere else in the building, but this was for "just a few personal things," though the room was the size of a modest shoe store and crammed with spotlit displays.

He pointed out some oddities: a puck from last year's Stanley Cup semi-final with signatures of the entire winning Canadiens team. A mannequin wearing his original costume, the spandex-and-cape classic parahero design that had lasted with a few variations until he'd entered college. A fishing pole that Maximus had given him on their first vacation together, that he'd broken because he couldn't control his strength yet.

"The dress is going in here," he told her and then snapped his fingers. "*Zut!* I forgot–" He touched his ring. "Wiley!"

Wiley's voice came from the ring as if he were standing here with them. "No, you do not have my permission to have sex."

"Yes, yes, you *frickurn*, no sex yet. My vest. You haven't trashed it, have you?"

"It's still here somewhere. I assumed you had a storage room worth of items in it that you'd want to transfer to the new one, so I haven't given it to the kol-vanasche."

"*Bon.* It's got something very valuable in it. Do *not* dispose of it. Rand out." Londo grimaced over the now-silent ring. "Aw *marde*, now he's going to look. Wiley's got five times the curiosity of a normal person. He's only cataloged my vest three hundred times already. And Jae'll probably put something vile in it just so I can find it."

"Don't worry," Lina reassured him. "I'll beat them up for you if they even smudge the leather."

She put her arms around him and they continued the tour. A dining room of impressive size. A small conference room, of all things, big enough to hold six people comfortably around a table. A receiving room.

"What do you receive?"

He shrugged vaguely. "It's for official parties. You know." But she didn't, not at all.

There were even more rooms, including two guest rooms, but nothing like the master bedroom. That was big, even palatial; spacious and hollow. Crammed bookcases lined two walls. His bed was larger than a kingsize, and a guitar sat on a plain chair next to it. Yet with all that, three-quarters of the room sat empty.

"You need something else," she said, trying not to sound critical. "A table with pictures on it. Maybe a little seating arrangement for fourteen. And a grand piano."

"Maybe a woman in here," he said softly. "You figure out what I need and I'll get it. Imagine whatever you want, and I'll make sure it's here for you." He took her hand and gazed into her eyes. "You'll like Sarastor. It's… It's better than *Star Trek*."

He'd caught her by surprise. "As if you'd know," she said automatically, but pondered the invitation to return. Oh, wouldn't that be wonderful!

"So when we get home I'll watch and we can compare. And then we can come back and you can tell me how great this place is."

"Lon, I…" Her gaze seemed so helpless. "When I've had a chance to think about it, I thought that you would just, well, visit me whenever you wanted."

"You'll be back here." Lon's smile was the warmest there was. "Don't worry about that. I want you to–" He suddenly perked up, his eyes unfocusing instead of sharpening. "Do you feel that?"

Lina could sense something too. She went over to the far wall of the room and touched it. "What is it? Is someone listening?"

Lon had to concentrate as he looked through the wall. Impervion was difficult to see through, but he could see a shadow there, enough to guess. "Puter," he said. "I want to send a verbal message to Neuron in her bedroom. English to Lingua."

Two beeps of acknowledgment.

"Deegel, can you quote me regs on privacy in quarters?"

"Lon!" A sweet, feminine voice sounded flustered. "What do you mean?"

"You know exactly what I mean. Do I have to build a Neuron-proof wall? I'm sure I can figure one out."

"And I'm sure I don't have the faintest idea what you're talking about. Are you out of quarantine now?"

"No, I am not. We'll have to flush out my quarters when we leave."

"Don't expect me to come over there."

"We hope you don't. You'll just get infected, probably come down with some kind of horrible, disfiguring disease. You know how Earzh is."

The woman's voice contained a shudder of revulsion. "I'll be sure to stay away. And I'll remind Aiko, too."

Londo's right hand made a fist. "You should tell everyone that, not just Aiko. I'm sure they'll all understand."

"You may want to check the betting boards, Lon. There's a lot of action on them these days."

"Rand out," Londo snapped.

Lina watched him. "Ah, the problems of apartment living," she said lightly to diffuse the mood. "Neighbors."

Londo nodded at the wall. "Deegel's a Legionnaire. Her para name's Neuron. She's got a little trick she can do where she touches something and transfers physical sensations."

"How handy that she's right next door," Lina said archly. "Next bedroom down."

"You'll notice that my bed doesn't touch the wall. And the legs are on insulators."

Lina had to laugh as he bent down to show her the clear disks under each leg. "Oh dear," she chuckled. "She's really causing you some problems, isn't she?"

"She's a royal pain."

"And Aiko? She's Orenya, right?" Lina tried to make it sound casual, but Lon's glance at her was sharp.

"I told you that I had experimented with women…"

"Deegel?"

He frowned. "I had a weak moment once. Once. Makes me ashamed to think about it. She said that she thought she could–"

"But she couldn't."

"She keeps telling me that she's figured it out now. Like I said, it was a long time ago."

And what if she had? This Deegel was another Legionnaire, a celebrity like Londo. Like the very famous, very beautiful Aiko. "That's okay, Lon. And you don't have to tell me any more about Aiko." To fight the urge to freeze in her uncertainty, she began to walk around the room. Make it look like she was considering decor.

Lon said, "Aiko was before I met you, remember that."

"Heck, we just met." What was it Jae had said? *They don't come more famous than Aiko.*

"And I'm just reminding you of that. Aiko and I have been friends for a very long time. Not as long as Jae and me, but long enough."

She couldn't stand not knowing. She blurted, "Are you still just friends? Or are you closer than that? For real, Londo. Should I back off and give you two space?"

In a flash Lon crossed the room and took her hands. "Don't you think that for a second! You're the most important woman in my life! Aiko knows that we can never be lovers. She has real lovers of her own. It's just that we get together every now and then for– She takes pity on me. She humors me."

"She probably doesn't do either," Lina said softly. It sounded like a practical match. Moreover, Aiko was a woman Lon had been attracted to even though they couldn't have sex.

But Lina's heart clenched at the thought. Lord, let her have a little more time with Londo before she had to give him up! "You'll need to talk with her, Londo. Is she telepathic?"

"No. She's very strong and damned near invulnerable, but she couldn't do what we do."

"But she's more than a friend." Lina turned from him and saw another door. She opened it just to think of anything else. "If we're going to–" Suddenly she began to laugh. "Ohmigosh!" She tried to control herself, but the laughter burbled underneath her words. "Do you have enough?"

In the closet hung at least thirty of his uniforms: thirty black vests, thirty pairs of black faux leather pants, thirty pairs of black boots, and drawers in which she could easily imagine thirty finely-brocaded gray-striped shirts neatly stacked. Some others came in non-standard colors: stark black and white, all-blue, magenta…

Londo scowled. "I have to keep a few variations of my costume for special occasions. And even my clothes can get torn– you should know that. It takes a hell of a long time to replicate the fibers. I get dirty when I work hard. I don't like wearing filthy clothing all day."

"I'm– hee hee– sorry." Lina put her hand over her mouth. "For a minute it just looked like a shrine to Valiant." She giggled to herself and shut the door, looking for something else to change the subject. "I didn't think paraheroes played musical instruments," she finally decided to say, pointing at the guitar.

"I do."

Even without the additional mutters she could tell she'd pushed the wrong button with him. Her comments about the closet echoed within his mind, answered with something about Normals not understanding his life, laundry taking too damned long, and by god he wasn't all that different from others, was he? He did *not* have a huge ego. Why did everyone keep telling him that he did?

"I happen to be damned good," he finished, his mouth still discussing the guitar.

"You're damned good at everything, honey. Okay. More books," she said as she paused to read the spines and let him cool down. To judge from the selection, Lon's interests ran to adventure, architecture, sailing, and the children's books she already knew about.

On top of the bookcase were some photographs. One, she realized with a start, was of Maximus in civilian clothing, tank top and shorts, waving from the deck of a sailboat. Another showed a middle-aged Black couple, smiling into the camera. Those were Lon's "Mama Ruth" and "Papa Mike," his adoptive grandparents; she recognized them now.

There was also a 3-D shot of Maximus, Lon and Jae, all in uniform and looking very buddy-buddy. Heroes. Celebrities. Part of a reality that didn't include Muttbutts.

"You have good maid service here," she told him and hoped that he couldn't detect the quaver in her voice. "No dust anywhere."

Lon led her to a utility closet next to the guest bathroom. Like the inside of a spaceship, blinking lights and banks of info screens lit when he opened the door. He explained some of the processes: laundry facilities, automatic housekeeping equipment that he called a *kol-vanasche* (that pancake thing), and so forth.

Lina nodded in awe at it all. This tiny room freed his time so he could concentrate on the important things in life. "I'll take two of each," she declared.

"You'd have to keep them here," he explained. "This kind of technology is forbidden on Earzh."

"Ah. Prime Directive stuff."

"*Quoi?*"

"*Star Trek*. The Prime Directive orders non-interference with existing cultures."

He thought and nodded his head slowly. "*D'accord. Star Trek.* Do you realize that you're living in a fantasy world?"

She gazed happily at the equipment blinking in front of her. "I certainly do," she said with a sigh.

He laughed and, choosing the safe spots to hold, picked her up under one arm like a bag of laundry so she'd screech. "Earzh to Lina. *Pardon:* Sarastor to Lina. Coming back to reality now. Please make sure your seat belts are fastened. We're running into some turbulence on reentry."

He bounced her up and down as he walked back into the living room, enjoying the litany of mild curses she spouted, and then flung her on the couch. He showed her how the solid black coffee table could turn into a state-of-Sarastoran-art communications panel, how a tri-D mini-stage would appear if you commanded it with the correct gesture.

Just for now, Lina decided to ignore all the new technology so she could enjoy Lon's magical presence. She scrolled through his music library. Finally– time for some music around here!

"Look at all this jazz!"

"I like jazz. That's one of the reasons I moved to Montreal."

Londo seemed to have the entire iTunes catalog on his system. Lina tried to figure how he had the music organized and finally found a few familiar sections.

"I've never even heard of some of these Beatles albums."

"I've got them all," he said. He'd brought in some glasses from the kitchen filled with dark golden liquid. Now he collected pillows from other chairs and arranged them on the couch to form a nest for two.

"So many playlists. Are they all yours?"

He shrugged. "I rack up a lot of boring travel time, so I make lists. I'll copy whatever ones you want."

"Here's the Billy Joel that I knew you must have." She turned to him with a warm look, remembering their first night together when he'd sung to her. "Oh, a couple of nice soundtracks. Do you mind?"

"Whatever you want."

Out of Africa began its sweeping, lonely melodies of two lovers who could never align. "Music. Hallelujah." She leaned against him but he drew her closer. That made it easier to run her palm across his bare chest. He really was spectacular. She chuckled softly. "Was Jac right? Are you showing off for me?"

"*Euh*... Maybe." His eyes, his slow smile held glints of deviltry as he regarded her, letting his gaze slide along her body. "Why don't you make yourself comfortable, too?"

"I don't think Wiley would want me to."

"Wiley's not here. I don't want him to see you comfortable."

It was heaven to be able to touch him again. Her hand slipped down to that minefield of a waist, all taut and bumpy with muscles. His skin shone slightly as if he'd oiled himself. Maybe he was covered with slimy salve, too, but on him it was sexy. It made her fingers slide so easily. She played with the hills and valleys of his chest, shoulders, and oh my, those marvelous arms, watching the warm shimmer of his tanned skin against her fingernails.

His hand slid under the neckline of her robe.

"Doctor's orders," Lina unwillingly murmured.

20

"**S**auce for goose." Lon's hand swept down from her shoulders as he kissed under her ear. He released the shirt she still wore around her neck. Then he caressed her, cupped her, and his lips lowered to the base of her neck as she arched to him.

Londo shouldn't do this; he wasn't well. With a blink back to consciousness, she gave his thigh a sharp rap and sat up, brushing his hands out of her robe. "'For a while,'" she declared.

"Liiina…"

"'For a while.'" She placed his hands demurely on his lap and batted them away when he objected

"So what do we do now?" he pouted.

"We talk. Like civilized humans."

"Not like Terrans?"

"What is it with all the Terran barbarian stuff around here?" Lina asked. "Where did they get these ideas?"

"Have you looked around, eh?"

Lina frowned at the room, at the electronic display in front of them. "So they've got a little technology," she told him. "Big deal."

"Actually…"

She harrumphed and bounced self-righteously on the couch. Then she asked, "How good are you with the guitar, really?"

"Oh, we're changing subjects, are we? The guitar." He made a face at the universe in general and then rolled his eyes in surrender. "*Ben*… I learned as an exercise to control my touch, but even with all that I still need special strings. Here I've got just the acoustic. I'm good. Real good."

The leer he gave her told her that he knew he was good at something else. They talked of Lon's life and hobbies– he had his license in architecture as well as construction– and Lina thought he was so sweet to pretend that what she did day-to-day could be interesting as well. They went off on impersonal editorial tangents, yet underneath it all was the knowledge that they were playing out the time until they would adjourn to the bedroom.

Time slipped by but the night hours lasted forever. "Yet?" Londo would ask, and Lina would check and shake her head. They'd both heave sighs and then fish around for a new subject.

It turned out that, though he liked the perks, Londo wasn't really that fond of being a parahero and fighting crime. "I'm too busy to get anything important done," he told her. "It's always the same, somebody wanting to push their way through life over the backs of others."

"You have to admit you're pretty good at your job."

"*Ouais.* But it's like putting a bandage on a gaping wound. I'm tired of stopgap. I want to go after the source. No, I want to do something–" he sought the concept, "– bigger. Huge."

They gazed at each other and again that spark of heat flushed through them both. As they discussed the world he looked into her eyes like he could see through to her soul.

They switched from social studies to TV. Then he told her of good times playing sports with the Legionnaires who could keep up with him, and smiled anew. Lina's heart raced to see his dear features light up. His was not a magazine-mannequin face, but rather that of the All-Canadian male next door, honest and strong, handsome and true.

"What else?" Lina finally whispered. "Tell me everything, anything."

"I most like being with you, my beautiful Lina. Talking with you. Hearing the crazy spin you put on life. And I like making love. I like that a lot."

She raised up a bit as if to say something and then nestled to him, burying her head under his chin. If only it could be forever like this.

He rubbed her arm against the bandages. "Does that hurt?"

"No." Her voice was small and shy.

"As God as my witness, *chérie,* I never want you hurt. I would have done anything not to have it happen. I won't ever do that again. I learned my lesson. I swear–"

"Hush, darling." She raised her face to meet his. "It's over and there's nothing we can do to change it. This last batch of painkillers took away just about all the pain.

It makes me just spacey enough to start to consider going against doctor's orders. But not spacey enough to actually do it."

She kissed him lightly on the mouth. "Londo Rand, I almost lost you yesterday. I did lose you, but you came back. And I'm not going to run the chance of losing you again."

"You're not. Not ever."

"What was it like to die?"

"You're the one who talks to ghosts. You tell me."

She massaged his hand. "You're so accepting of things. Me, I don't believe even when it's right before my eyes. I know what it is I think I see, and I know what I've been taught. And I know people with near-death experiences who've told me what they remember. But we're all operating from our own paradigms, unable to see the complete truth. What was it like for you, Lon? Were there angels? Was there a light that was pure love?"

He sighed. "I don't remember. There was just… I thought I heard you scream, and I heard them threaten you, plan to kill you, and then… I don't even recall getting hit with the big one."

"Ah."

"Ah." They sat there in each other's arms, content for a while. "So what do you think it's like, Lina? Who runs all this? Do you think there's anything to all this religion crapola?"

"I've seen listings of angelic hierarchies," Lina said slowly, "but people I talk to say that everyone and everything is equal in God's sight. Once I heard somebody say that we were all little sparks of God's mind that want to know our own individuality, our own gifts. Maybe it's that God can only see the overall view of things, and so we split off from Him to see the bits and pieces. Somewhere along the line there's got to be some kind of communication that lets the universe put the whole picture together. Maybe that's what the Higher Self is for. I don't know."

"So you do believe in God."

"I believe in something. Used to be I couldn't even say the word 'God.' There's something that makes that word scary, and the Big Guy, or the guiding consciousness or quantum field, whatever it is that so many people say is pure love, well, you shouldn't be scared of love. So I started to say 'the universe' instead. Lately I've found myself saying 'God.' I'm not married to the word, though. It comes with a lot of crap baggage."

She shifted in his wonderful, safe arms. "There's something there; can't you feel it? There are devas for countries and worlds, why not a deva for the universe? Of course, that's only a very tiny part of it. There's everything that's created, and then there's this huge, even more infinite *something*, a potential that's the uncreated. Other dimensions. Other things we can't begin to name. There's a force there that's behind absolutely everything.

"That song, 'God is Watching Us from a Distance,' has it exactly a hundred eighty degrees wrong. God's inside us. We're little pieces of God, or we're growing around an inner core that's God or connected to God. He or She or It is watching and experiencing everything from within us. Within me, within you, within this table, within all the germs and the thoughts going around."

Lon's mouth moved as he thoughtfully digested it. "So that's what you believe."

"Until I come up with something better. Yes."

"The old man with a beard," Lon said. "I remember pictures when I was very young. He rode on clouds. Someone told me that this was God, and that He was watching over me and keeping me safe.

"He didn't keep me safe. He threw me into Hell and then turned His back on me. I tried saying my prayers every time I went to bed, but there came a day when I realized that no one was listening. No one cared. So I stopped. And every time that one of my friends was carried out of the lab, dead, I hit the wall with my fist and pretended that it was the face of that Old Man with the beard."

Lina stroked his arm. "After you came back to Earth, how was it then?" she asked quietly.

"I'd gotten out without His help. I was on my own. I found my own friends, my own guardian. Hal became my god for a few years. A not quite all-powerful god, it's true, and more human than most gods, but he was a serviceable substitute."

"He accepted your offerings?"

Lon frowned, which involved sticking out the left corner of his lower lip and then rolling it so that the right corner protruded.

"He saw that I was hero-worshipping him, and he nipped it in the bud as best as he could. Mama Ruth and Papa Mike took me to a few churches to get me to settle on something, but I wasn't too interested in Christianity. It's too confusing, too many people thinking they're in the same faith and saying things completely opposite of each other.

"So they took me to some Jewish synagogues, and although it was interesting as history, I wasn't impressed with the basics. They took me to Muslim mosques, to a Buddhist shrine– that was all right but too quiet. And there was a Hindu place… Then I went around to see if there was anything I could stomach left. I like bits and pieces of Native American stuff. Taoism. Aboriginal Dream Time? I don't get it, but that may be that I'm looking at it from the wrong angle." He shrugged his shoulders.

"But it seemed to me that almost every religion had some version of that Old Man with His beard who was telling me what and how to think, and that it was bad just to be who I was already. I don't like people telling me what to do."

"So are you an atheist or an agnostic?"

"I try not to classify myself. I don't like restrictions."

"*Don't fence me in*," Lina sang softly. He'd been restrained through too much of his childhood.

"Exactly." He shifted his position on the couch slightly so he could look more directly at her. "You understand me," he said.

"So when you say you don't remember anything when you died," she asked, "does that mean that you don't want to remember or that there was nothing there for you to remember or that you just don't remember? You could solve a lot of questions for yourself, or at least figure out where you're starting from, if you could recall something."

"I just… There was a feeling," he said. "No images, nothing else. Just this feeling of peace, an absolute lack of worries. I felt like I could have taken off without caring about what I was leaving behind, or what catastrophes would take place if I weren't around to stop them."

She turned to him and gave him a gentle smile, rubbing his bare chest. His brave heart was beating so strongly. "I'm so grateful that you decided not to go. Honey, you're tense. What's wrong?"

"There was just that one thing that I kept thinking about," Lon said. He looked past her and then back into her eyes. He seemed like he wanted to say something. Lina waited, curious.

"I came back because I heard you calling me." Londo paused for a moment. "Lina, marry me."

21

"What?" Just like that. Cold shock thrilled through her.

Taking her hand in his, Lon said, "We'd be so good together. I love you; you love me."

"You're serious." She whispered because she couldn't breathe. "You can't be."

"But I am. Marry me." He pulled her closer to him with one hand, keeping her hand in his other. "No more loneliness ever. No more empty nights for either of us."

He moved in to kiss her, but she sat straight up and pushed him back. "We've known each other for how many days? Four? Maybe five? Heck, we could still count it in hours. Londo, you don't ask someone to get married after four days."

"I just did. What, do you want us to date for three years before I pop the question? We know *now*. Marry me, Lina. C'mon."

"Oh no, again with the 'c'mon.' No, Londo. It's just the sex. We're both new at this and we're a little– no, a lot– crazy. We can't think straight."

He pulled gently at her good arm.

"Look, Lon, I told you." She tried to slow the pounding of her own heart and speak softer. Maybe she could get through to him. "Anytime you need me, I'll be there for you. Always and forever."

"So let's make it official. Let me make an honest woman of you."

She jumped from the couch and then scrambled behind it, out of his reach. "Oo, Lon. Think! Marriage is more than sex. Personally I can't quite believe it right now, but they say the sex becomes a minor part of the relationship after a while. Where would that leave us?"

"A happy couple drooling in the old folks home, waiting for our great-grandchildren to come and visit. And the sex will *never* be minor."

With his chin propped on the arm that lay across the back of the couch, Lon watched her pace. He knew her mind so well now. She was going to say yes. It might be in a minute or in a year, but she'd accept. There was no way she could refuse him. He smiled into his elbow so she wouldn't see his look of triumph. He'd always gotten what he wanted, and now he wanted her. It was that simple.

Lina laughed because there was nothing else she could think to do. "Grandchildren! You know, Lon, most people usually discuss the matter of children before they decide to get married."

"I was thinking about five or six, *peut-être* a dozen."

"Oh yeah, keep me barefoot and pregnant. I've never even given it a thought! I'm not good around kids."

"You'll get used to 'em."

"Cats. I have lots of them instead. Seven. All spoiled rotten."

His jaw dropped. "Seven cats? Seven cats!"

Lina poked her index finger in his face. Get him to focus on real life! "Yes, Lon. I'm the crazy cat-lady who lives at the end of the road in the run-down house."

He grinned and then lay down on the couch, singing, *"Our house is a very, very, very fine house. With seven cats in the yard..."*

"Again with the singing! Lon, I love you, but no. Has anyone ever said that to you? No. In French that's *non*. I'm sorry. I'm so–" She blinked hard. "I'm going to take that shower."

She ran to the master bathroom, the one farthest from the living room, and closed the door. Londo laughed out loud now that she couldn't hear and sank back on the couch, giving himself a victory arm-chug.

So she'd said no. She didn't mean it. Humming merrily to himself, he formulated a rough wedding schedule checklist but then an idea hit him. It blocked the rest of his mind from functioning. He scowled at himself for his stupidity. That had to be the problem. So what could he do about it? He lay back in silence and thought while the shower started.

He knew this would be a very long shower. Was she sniffling in there? She did it quietly as if she knew he could hear her. He could have peeked at her through the walls but he'd been taught privacy.

Londo kept a black silk robe in his closet for Aiko. It might be a welcome change of pace from the white terrycham coat Lina wore. He opened the bathroom door, called, "New robe!" and threw it in, then closed the door. After a pause he heard her say "Thank you" in a very small voice.

She was frightened, he realized. Running scared. Women weren't supposed to act this way after a proposal from the man they loved, were they? But Lina wasn't like any other women that he knew.

Maybe… Maybe it was time to back off a little. He'd pressed his advantage as far as it could go for now. More pressure and she really might say no when the decision-making was over. She was right. No one had ever said no to him, not for anything important. He didn't want this to be his first experience.

Wandering in frustration, he paused at his communications desk. With a groan of dread he sat down. In moments the image of a dark-skinned woman with short, gold-tipped hair appeared on the screen. She smiled radiantly at him.

"Londo!" Aiko exclaimed as her gaze traveled over his face and then his bare shoulders. "You're looking well. Very well. Maybe a little tired."

"I'm fine, *cherie*," he said gently. Her smile faded to seriousness at his tone.

"You brought someone with you." Her eyes lost their shine. "The witchdoctor."

"Yes."

"Roads and shadows. This is going to be one of those conversations. Sunfire take it all."

"One of what conversations?" But he knew what she meant.

Her voice was flat. "You want us to remain friends."

He had to look down at the desktop before he could face her again. "Is that all right with you? Is there anything I can do to make the transition smoother? I didn't tell you… before… because I was trying to figure a way you wouldn't get hurt, and we could still be friends. It was all happening so fast. I couldn't think of anything. You know me; I screw these things up so badly. But I do want us to remain friends, Aiko– always. You are very dear to me. In many ways."

"Do you love her, Londo? I've heard that, apparently, things have gone well physically for you."

"They're still going fine. And yes, I love her. I just proposed to her."

That caught her by surprise. "Proposed? A marriage contract?"

"She said no."

That took her by surprise, too, but the moment had passed and now waves of hurt and anger washed across her features.

"So after you've proposed to this…woman, after you've announced to half the sector that you have a new girlfriend and she's not me, you finally decided to give me a call."

"I'm sorry, Ko-ko. *Si desole*. I should have called you first thing, as soon as I'd sorted things out. It was inexcusable of me not to discuss this with you before I said anything public. Anything. Trying to show off. I was a coward."

"Yes," she said harshly. She bit her lip and put her hand over it to hide it, then turned away from the screen.

"I'm sorry," Londo repeated. "The last person I'd ever want to hurt is you."

The woman nodded, her face still averted. "I should expect Londo to be L-Londo." She took a breath before she turned back. "So," she said, and Londo could see her shaking herself to composure. "You…proposed, and she said no."

"Um, yes."

"Let me get this straight. She's had wild sex with the galaxy's most eligible hero for days now–"

"Who the hell have you been talking to?"

"Jae, of course. At least he tried to break it to me gently. He was a little late. And now apparently– even though your powers are back and you can still do it– How the bloody blaze does that happen, Londo?"

"Privacy, Aiko. Let's just say that a non-telepath couldn't do it."

"That's another thing. Jae says you're suddenly a telepath, which would make any bond closer automatically. And she says no?"

"She'll say yes. Eventually."

"Stoan says she's a rogue telepath and a controller."

"You know how Stoan can overreact with mind control. And he doesn't like anything that isn't status quo. Once we're engaged, he'll come around."

Aiko frowned at him. "You're pushing her too hard, Lon. By the longest road, I know you. If she's the kind of woman you'd like, she won't appreciate that. I wouldn't."

"I'm backing off."

"Where is she?"

"In the shower."

Aiko's eyebrows raised. "Without you. How atypical."

Londo shrugged at her bitter tone. "She needs quiet time."

She gave him an ironic glare. "How about that? Londo Rand is actually taking someone else's emotional needs into consideration. Has the galaxy stopped spinning?"

"I know you're feeling–"

"I'm going through a little shock now, Lon. Maybe anger. Maybe sheer murderous fury. But you'll have to admit that you run pell-mell over people. They don't like that. I never have."

"I'm sorry. I don't want to hurt anyone, especially you. Am I as bad as I was?"

Her face softened into a sad, fond smile. "No. Not at all. You're quite semi-pleasant to be around anymore." She paused. "Are you absolutely sure? Just because you're in the throes of the Wonder of It All doesn't mean that you two would make a good choice for marriage partners."

Lon nodded. "I know. I'm sure I'll get the same lecture from Hal if I can ever get hold of him."

"I don't consider him an expert on the subject." Again those exquisite eyebrows arched.

"And you are."

"I've been married before. I know what doesn't work."

"This will. I know down to deeper depths than I even knew I had. Aiko, we've shared minds. I know her; she knows me."

"Bright sun. You're a telepath now. How does all this happen at once?"

"It just did. Things started happening, and then more things rolled into place, and it avalanched from there."

"So you're under an avalanche of new emotions, new sensations."

"One of which is love. It's real and it's going to last."

Long moments passed before she spoke again. "I saw it," Aiko said slowly. "I was watching the lab monitors and I saw the way you looked at her. Shards. Andri saw it too, I know."

"You were watching us?"

"Andri was curious about what the mind-controlling witchdoctor was doing up there and Wiley was feeding us impossible figures about travel times from Earth to Sarastor."

The left side of Aiko's mouth twitched into the smallest of smiles. "I was watching because you were running around half-naked. You know, Londo, most of our female members were tuning in just to see you in that condition. You really must become more aware of the monitors. Civilized people simply don't dress like that, even if they have just been blasted halfway to the next galaxy and survived."

"I'll keep that in mind next time, *chérie*. Sorry."

Aiko nodded, pondering. "It has to be a fairly equal partnership. Marriage between a para and a norm… Oh. She's not a norm, is she? Oh Londo, a witchdoctor? Even so, who is she to stand up to Valiant?"

"I'm not going to walk all over her!"

"See that you don't. Remember what happened to me when I was married. I got too full of myself and things fell apart." The longing stood starkly in her eyes. "And now look at me: alone again."

"I know you'll find someone. It's been all I could do to keep men from launching themselves at you while I was around."

She gave him a little smile at that, a tight nod as she forced herself to maintain. "You've told her about certain…problems?"

"That, and she's got some of her own. We're going to work through them together."

"And she's Terran."

"Very."

She looked away and then back. "I won't be there for you. Not in that way, not if you get married. But I'll be there to listen if you need me. You'll have to give me time to adjust." She sighed and closed her eyes. "A lot of time."

"Thank you, Aiko. You're the best. You tell me what you need– for anything– and I'll make sure you have it."

"You've told Jae about the proposal, of course."

"He knows." Lon heaved a sigh. "That's likely why he contacted you. I'm sorry. I should have."

"I won't say that this hasn't come as a tremendous shock, Londo Rand. But I'll get over it and who knows, maybe I'll even come to like her."

"Give her a chance. She's very nice, very loving. Very smart, too."

"Not so smart if she turned you down."

"She's going to say yes, I tell you." His eyes grew moist as he gazed at her. "Papa Mike will kill me when he finds out. He adores you. Mama Ruth and Hal both love you, too. And I love you. I'll always have a place in my heart for you, *cherie*."

She tried to smile at that. "Give me some time, Londo. I'll be okay. I'm…I'm glad you finally found someone."

After the screen went blank Lon could hear Aiko's sobs through two stories of impervion.

Time not to screw things up with another woman. Londo waited outside the bathroom door, a towel draped around his neck to make things seem more like home, and deliberately thought bland thoughts. Eventually the door opened and Lina emerged in the black robe, her wet hair unbraided and her face pale as death under the bruising and burns.

"*Enfin.* At last," he said, trying to make it light. "My turn now." He breezed past her to close the door behind him. Give her some more time to herself. Besides, he might really need another shower. He'd almost died– no, he *had* died– yesterday, and dying and healing were hard work. He wanted to look his absolute best for his lady.

He watched her through the walls while he was in the shower. She walked like she was asleep, wandering through his bedroom. She tried the bed. That could be a good sign. Then she drifted through his trophy room, looking a long time at all the awards. She kept running her hands through her hair, pulling on it as she thought. Finally she walked into the living room and stood there gazing at the view of Saturn that was so real.

She sat on the couch, where she combed her hair absently. Lon smiled as he watched her soft auburn hair coil around the comb. Real curls, real boobs, real love… Everything about Lina was the truth except for the lies she told herself. He'd show her, but gently.

Mustn't scare her. Charm and subtlety…and maybe a little truth. He wasn't used to telling the truth, but for her he would. She'd think less of him if he didn't. Of all the people he knew, he didn't want Lina to think badly of him.

Should he bring up–? No, let that wait. One step at a time. Being honest didn't mean telling everything at once.

The soundtrack had cut off long ago, so she reprogrammed the music. Some color had returned to her cheeks. It was time for Londo to come out of the shower.

He entered the living room with dry hair and wearing a cham wrap that left his chest, arms, and lower legs bare. She liked his body. He set refilled glasses of *rava* on the coffee table and sat down on the couch, but gave her some space.

"We need to talk," she said as John Legend played in the background. She leaned forward over her knees, her hands clasped together: a semi-fetal position closed off from him.

"About what, we will talk?" he asked.

With a very small laugh she rolled her eyes at him.

"*D'accord.*" He leaned back to drape his arm casually upon the back of the couch. "But let's let the proposal itself go for a while. What else do you want to talk about?"

"I don't know you. I know a lot about you but I don't know so much more."

"So what do you want to know? I'll tell you."

"I don't know. Plans, dreams for the future. Were you serious about the six kids? How you manage to juggle the Network and this Mega-Legion and everything else. Whatever. You talk, I'll listen."

He took one of those fascinating curls and fondled it for a moment before he spoke. "Well, eh, I wouldn't mind six kids. I want to have a real family. I missed out on that."

"Don't you think it's irresponsible to have more than two in an overpopulated world? Especially if you're a famous hero, setting an example for everyone."

"I can't be responsible for people copying me. I just do the best I can and what anybody thinks is their business. But as for six…I guess I could be happy with two. And there's always adoption for the rest."

"Do they let megaheroes adopt kids?"

He tilted his head and raised a meaningful eyebrow at her. "They let Maximus."

"Oh of course. Duh."

Lon propped his elbow on the back of the couch as he lounged. "Lately I've been thinking about moving away from Montreal, too."

"Whatever for?"

"I thought the southeastern United States might be interesting."

Lina shook her head ruefully. "If you're talking somewhere around me, I'd have to advise against it."

"So I should cancel the tent I ordered, eh? I was going to set up camp in your back yard and howl at the moon every night."

That brought a wan smile to her lips. "You'd scare the cats. I hate to quote Terry the Bitch, but 'podunk' is a good description of Eno Valley. It would be much too boring for you. I've been thinking about moving to the Appalachians anyway. I like mountains."

He raised up hopefully. "Do they have to be the Appalachians? How about the Rockies?"

She barely had time to register a question on her face before he commanded, "Computer, show summer view from Starhaven."

The view of Saturn abruptly changed, and a glorious panorama wrapped through the windows of the room of towering Terran mountains stretching into blue infinity behind a long and wide mountain valley. Nearby deer grazed in a meadow of waving wildflowers and grasses. Hardwood forests blanketed the slopes. A long lake that even distance couldn't make small lay sparkling below in the sun.

"Ta dah." Lon spread his arms to encompass the vista.

"Ohmigosh. It's so beautiful." Lina stood up so she could have a good view of all the "windows," and looked back toward Lon. "Is it yours?"

He sat back on the couch so as not to interrupt her view. "I bought the property a few years ago. I've got a little place up there that I'm building. It's really nowhere near finished. That's my vacation home. I call it Starhaven." He raised a glass of *rava* and toasted the mountain vista.

"And this here was just a 'room.'" Lina laughed. "How big's the little place?"

Londo smiled in spite of himself. "Big enough. There's plenty of room for expansion."

"Where is it? Alberta?"

"No, it's in the States. Wyoming."

"Londo, how old are you?"

"Twenty-nine, thirty, somewhere in there. It's hard to tell precisely. How old are you?"

She sat down next to him as he took a drink. "Twenty-six," she said. "Londo, what do we do if I'm pregnant?"

22

Londo sprayed yellow *rava* across the back of the couch.

"P-pregnant?" he sputtered. "You're not… You're not…"

Coolly Lina dabbed at the mess with the sleeve of her robe. "Why haven't you mentioned anything about birth control now that we're back in civilization?"

He scrutinized her innocent look. "You're playing with me. You're not pregnant."

"You never asked. All that time in quarantine, all those medical monitors."

Lon got up to retrieve better toweling from the kitchenette. "I never had to worry about it before," he said as he returned and sopped the mess from both the couch and Lina's sleeve. "It never occurred to me. Now tell me. You're not–"

"No. And I had Wiley give me one of the very wonderful shots that they have here. It's good for about a year. One hundred percent safe, one hundred percent sure, and only one side effect."

"Which is?"

"Zero periods. I know two or three billion women back on Earth who would kill for birth control like that." She searched for another question. "What do you call Maximus to his face? 'Dad?'"

"No, I call him Hal. You can, too."

"Oh god."

"No, he doesn't like to be called 'God.' Marry me, Lina."

She bit her lip. "You haven't thought this through."

"How so?"

"We've both been turned upside down in the last five days. Hell, Londo, you died. What happens when the real world snaps back?"

He settled back on the couch, drawing her to him. "We'll still be together. Always and forever. Do you really see that changing?"

"Forever's a long time." She tried to laugh and didn't make it. "Up to now we've been on our best behavior with each other. You've never seen me when I get on a stubborn streak or when I'm really hateful. You've never heard me let loose and cuss. You don't know—"

"I know the real you," he whispered. He could be so tender when he wanted. "We've shared minds. You know me. It's the details that we don't have any idea about. We've got a lifetime to learn about those. It'll be fun." His eyes narrowed slyly. "And there's no one who can out-curse me. Not in this sector of the galaxy."

She covered her trembling lips with her hand, determined not to cry. "Back home… Back home, I hear them talking all the time. That before they get married couples should sit down and discuss all the domestic things that can ruin them. How much money they make; who's going to handle it. Who makes supper; who washes the dishes. Who cleans the bathroom, for god's sake." She regarded him helplessly. "What do you want in a wife? What do you expect?"

"You're putting labels on things that shouldn't have labels. All I want is Lina O'Kelly. We'll figure everything else as we go."

"Are you sure you're not Sagittarian?" She planted her hand on his bare left pectoral and frowned at it. Touch. A few days ago she hadn't been able to touch anyone and now she was drunk with human contact and he, with sex. Or was that vice versa? "Oh Lon, what have we gotten ourselves into?"

She started to turn away from him, but Lon caught her shoulder. "We're not *them*. We're not like *them*. Why should we do things *their* way?"

He cocked his head at her, giving her the Command Frown he'd practiced so hard to achieve when he first became a team lieutenant. "Around here I'm considered an outstanding combat leader. I'm the best at sizing up situations and making decisions. I see us now. Marriage is the correct move for us."

"But that's just it." She rubbed her hands on her knees as if she could rub out the problem. "You're the biggest hero around, even out here halfway across the galaxy or wherever the hell we are." She looked lost. "I'm nobody, just Lina O'Kelly from some podunk town in North Carolina. What would people think if they ever found out? How long would it be before you were bored to tears with me?"

She didn't let him respond while she eased away from him. "You're *Valiant*— the big kahuna himself. You should have, I don't know, a royal consort. Someone who can keep up with you on the social and parahero circuit. Not some hick— Good god, Lon, I'm a pornographer. What would people say?"

He started to speak, but she interrupted him. "I've had so many friends get married, and I've seen so many of those marriages end in divorce. Most of them messy, people's lives torn up. They start hating each other. I don't want you to hate me. Why can't we just leave things the way they are? When you get tired of me, there won't be any muss or fuss. I won't cause you any embarrassment."

Londo wanted to take her in his arms but he stayed where he was, resting his head on his hand. "I don't know the statistics on marriage," he said. "It's what, 50 percent divorce? Higher, lower?"

"I don't know."

"Let's call it fifty percent. What about the other fifty? And how many of them are telepaths? How many people have shared minds like we have? You're a part of me now. Don't you feel the same?"

A tear rolled down her cheek as Lina sat silently. She finally nodded, pressing her quivering lips together.

"God, I want a family so bad. I want a beautiful, loving woman to come home to. I want kids and I want you to be their mother. I want to know you even deeper than I do now. I want you on my arm at every event I attend. I want to make love to you every day of my life. I want to wake up with your arms around me.

"I want so many things, and now at the middle of them all is you. I can't imagine living without you."

He scooted closer to take her by the hand. He didn't mean to scare her, but it came out fierce. "I don't want you to find anyone else. Oh, I know you say that you're never going to, but you're a passionate woman, Lina O'Kelly. If I let you go you'll find someone else. I couldn't bear the thought of you lying with another man."

He pulled her to him tightly, locking her in his commanding gaze. "You're mine. You believe in fate. It's like the universe brought us together. Say it, Lina. Say it. Tell me. 'I'll marry you, Lon.'"

She shook her head with a small smile. "Londo Rand, you can be a wonderful, sweet bully bear. I do love you so much. But this–" She looked down at his hand clutching hers. "Possession," she breathed. "You want to make things in your life permanent by owning them. It's not control, it's fear of abandonment. I will not marry for fear. Either yours or mine."

Immediately he dropped his hand and turned away so she couldn't see his shame.

"It won't work," she whispered. "At the very least, let's let a little time go by. Let's not rush into a huge mistake."

Lon sighed. "You will live with me, won't you? So we can see how it goes?"

"Live with–" She caught her breath.

With renewed hope he swung back to her. "Choose your place, Starhaven or Montreal. Move in, cats and all."

"You can't be serious."

"I'm not. What I want is for you to marry me. Live with me at the very least, *chérie*. That way you can get used to the idea. If you want we can be engaged with no set date. Will that make it easier for you? I'll buy you a ring as soon as we get out of quarantine, as big a diamond as you could wish for."

"Honey, I don't care about diamonds. I just don't want you to make any commitment that you'll be sorry for later."

"There you go again, trying to tell me what to think. Let me make my own commitments. Make one of your own."

Londo edged closer, then over the front of the couch until he was down on one knee in front of her. "I'll give you anything. I don't think I can live without you." Even as he said it, he could hear the horrible echo within her. "Don't!" he warned, but it was too late.

She'd overheard her father telling her mother the same thing too many times. Her parents were stuck in a sick marriage. Londo shook Lina gently but insistently. "I'm not him, *chérie*. We're us and this is our life. This isn't some sickness on our part. It's a healing, us together."

Desperately he squeezed her hand between the two of his as she sat, her head down and hair hiding her face from him. He let her have her time.

She shook her head. "I'm an idiot."

"Never."

But still she shook her head. "I can't. Dearest Lon," she finally whispered, "Please. It's too soon. Let some time go by. I want you to realize… I want you to be really sure."

He knelt silently. She was miserable, desolated because of his question, when he'd thought that it would make her so happy. This had not been his plan.

"I'm losing you, aren't I?" he murmured. "You think I'll leave you someday, so you've imagined it happening already. You're slipping away from me without me ever going. Is that right?"

She shook her head but he could feel it inside her.

"I'm here," he said. "The thought of leaving has never entered my mind. It never will."

Time for making her see her own truth. "Just tell me one thing, Lina, and I won't ask again until you want me to."

She brushed her hair back as she raised her head, her liquid green eyes gazing down into his. "What?"

"Will you let me love you forever? With or without marriage?"

Her breath caught at that. He could see the puzzlement in her own eyes as she searched her soul.

"That's it, isn't it?"

"It's… It's…"

"That's the real reason why you don't want to marry me. You have a hard time accepting love." He jumped up and slammed his right fist into the opposite palm. "Damn, I want to take those parents of yours and throttle them! How could they have done this to you?"

She cocked her head at him. "What do you mean?"

He searched for the proper words. "You're the most loving person I've ever known. You give and give, and you keep saying 'Let me help.' But there's something missing."

"What?"

He sighed and studied her face to see how she'd take this. Then he sat back next to her so he wouldn't be towering over her. That might frighten her. Over the years he'd learned from the best psychiatrists.

"I've been thinking, *chérie*. You're afraid to be touched. I know, I don't count. But I've seen you now with others, and I see how you're still avoiding it. You aren't afraid to touch someone when you're healing them. You're giving love then. But when the chance that it will be reciprocated comes along, when someone wants to touch you, you can't do it.

"And then that other time. When you said love was like a knife in your heart– I think you meant that almost literally, whether you were conscious of it or not."

"Lon–"

"You've got a knife in your heart, kitten, and it stops the flow of love from others. What is it, you don't think you're worthy of being loved? Is that what it all boils down to?"

She was silent for a few moments. "I've always known something was wrong. I was too embarrassed to let some other healer try this problem. Look. I'm closing up just talking about it." She tried to unroll from her hunched position.

"*Chérie*, you can tell me anything."

"Don't you see? I can feel all this love coming from you and it's like I'm standing in the middle of a flowing river… *I am a rock, I am an island…*"

Her words came in fits and starts as she tried to explain. "That night when we first made love– It was an absolute miracle that I got to that point. I can't believe it happened still. To get beyond this it would take another miracle, and miracles just don't happen that often, not in this world. I'm stuck. Oh, Lon, you deserve someone who can take that love so you won't be wasting it. Someone who's worthy of you. I'm a hopeless case."

Lon smiled and pulled her to him. She leaned her head on his shoulder, her hand on his chest. "*Mon petit chou*," he said, "I am reminded of a great coach who once told me that to accomplish my goal I had to do a little at a time, see how it went, and go from there. Sometimes miracles happen in small steps. Sometimes miracles happen because people work hard for them." Miracles had come true for them. They would again.

"So, coach, what do I do?" Her voice was muffled against him.

"As I recall, first we set a goal."

They both recalled their previous goal, which had to do with a literal use of the f-word. "And how would we phrase it? Politely, that is."

"Hmm. *D'accord,* I've got it. We're going to fix you up so that you can accept love with the same passion that you give it so well. To the point where, if I should ask, 'Carolina O'Kelly, will you marry me?' you would answer," and he pitched his voice to a falsetto, "'Yes, Londo Rand, even unto eternity.'" He hoped she'd chuckle and release her tension.

But she was quiet for a moment before she whispered, "That sounds perfect."

His heart stopped for an enchanted moment. "*Bon. D'accord,* just tell me where to begin."

"I was hoping you'd have some ideas about that, coach." She leaned back to look up anxiously at him.

"Oh. Ah. I could wake a few psychiatrists I know, but you're good with all this metaphysical stuff. Let's start there, eh. How about these chakras that you're always talking about? Are any of them involved?"

"Chakras." Lina let out a breath and frowned in thought. "The obvious one is the heart chakra, but the one underneath it, the solar plexus chakra, deals with interactions with people. I've been trying to work on them for years but maybe I'm too close to the problem." She paused. "Or…"

"Or what?"

She looked puzzled as she chewed on a knuckle. "You remember when we first did the double-loop? You went too deep. What happened? What did you experience?"

Lon thought. "*Voyons.* I can't remember. Do you mind? Reenact the crime?" He slipped one shoulder of Lina's robe down and paused, waiting for her reaction.

"You beast. I'll just bet you can't remember. Doctor's orders."

"Doctor's orders. I really can't; this is strictly scientific method. Right?"

"Oh, all right." She started to shrug out of her robe, but he reached over and slid it off her shoulders, down to her waist, leaving those magnificent breasts bare. She pulled her arms slowly out of the sleeves and he watched the jiggly results with delight. Lifting her chin, he gave her a quick kiss. Then he ran his hand carefully across one bandaged shoulder, down to cup a warm breast, his thumb barely grazing the nipple.

"I believe it had been about here." A lot of things had started from this position. His imagination– and his body– lurched into high gear and it took real effort to stanch it.

"Mm, scientific method." She cooed in appreciation of his approach, then caught herself. "Wait. Science. Whiteboards and calculus. Read chapter seven. Cold desks. Final exams." She licked her lips and set her jaw determinedly. "Okay, do it."

He let his mind sink into her skin, something so natural now he wondered why he'd ever had trouble with the technique. He felt what she was feeling from his fingers as he massaged and squeezed gently. Then he sank deeper to sense the emotions within.

She breathed shallowly. On the surface she was holding back so neither would get too excited– doctor's orders.

Easy, Lon.

He tried to merge with her to feel her emotions instead of diving deeper. Just expand himself inside her like a breeze filling a sail. Almost like sharing minds, but not quite. Feeling what she felt…

Try a higher vibration.

Vibration?

Hum a note, then hum a third or a fifth higher. Pay attention to it.

It sounded silly, but she was the expert in these things. He tried a note, then raised it a third, then a fifth. Was anything happening? It seemed now like he could almost feel something, almost experience…something. Just out of reach.

Higher, if you can.

He thought of the two chakra centers, so close to where his hand massaged, and hummed the octave, then went another third higher as he tried to delve deeper inside her.

This was eerie. Maybe he'd gone too far. A sudden, cold fear clenched him that he would experiment on Lina this way. In his ignorance he might hurt her–

Wait, that fear wasn't his, though it almost felt like it was. She must be the one who was afraid. What else did he feel that wasn't himself? Cautiously, Londo tasted his own emotions to get a bearing.

Without warning, savage self-hatred crashed upon him. It ripped through and tore at his very being. It smothered him in its wash as he fought against drowning. Shame, disgust directed inward. *Not good enough!* Separated from the rest of the world because he was a lowly creature, filled with faults he could never make up for. *Ugly! Absolutely unlovable!*

Moments illuminated for him, lightning flashes of the past. His parents pushing him away, never holding, never telling him they loved him, never the small touches that bring a family together. Mom told him that he had to love Dad, but Dad punished him every time he tried to show him that love.

Home was filled with sarcasm and the pointing out of shortcomings. Never rewarding the good things; always dwelling on the bad. An overabundance of painful "accidents." Locked up to consider the sin of being himself.

He scared them, he could tell. They couldn't force him into their mold. Mom was terrified for him, telling him to *hide, hide. This is wrong, don't let your father find out. Don't do it; it's bad. Be normal! Be miserable like us.*

And the more they feared him, the more judgmental they became, the more Dad punished, the more Mom pulled away with her own fears. But he couldn't bring himself to be what they wanted him to be. He told himself over and over that he was normal, but he wasn't.

Hide away from them. Learn that others would always betray him in the end. Love equaled betrayal. Love hurt. *Don't reach for love. Don't touch love and you won't get hurt.*

It made him independent, even strong– but hollow inside.

There came a time of darkness, of total singularity, shut away from the world. Hell on a cold concrete basement floor lying forever in the dark. A leg badly broken and no one else caring about it.

There in that basement the entire universe separated into a level higher than where he lay. Everything in it was equal but he crawled below, always apart. That separation was made as clear to him as death.

What had he/she been, ten? Younger? A choice: reconnect or die. Reconnect! Just don't allow yourself to be touched. Keep yourself separate from the rest, hiding on that lower level. But don't let it lower to death where Hell might be permanent.

Something changed slightly for the better in the family then that Londo couldn't catch, but he'd already jumped to a new path. He'd distanced himself from the world, taken his two steps back from it. He couldn't touch anything physically, but he needed to keep some kind of connection.

So he touched people with love, not flesh.

Now as he lay drifting on the waves of Lina's mind, Lon sensed things that amazed him: Past life echoes– he was certain that that was what they were– repeated the idea that it wasn't safe to receive love.

The little girl in Ireland, the youngest of a large family, desperately loving her mother but abandoned to die during the Potato Famine.

The Egyptian general holding the cold, dead body of his eight-year-old son in his arms. Three sons born and loved, now three sons dead. Grieving with his last ounce of strength.

The African tribesman whose wife criticized his every waking moment, humiliating him in front of the entire village until he volunteered to lead a hunt for a savage leopard. It was a virtual suicide that would make her sorry for the things she had said about him, wouldn't it?

Lon realized that there were thousands of years of the same tape running in Lina: fear the world, don't trust it. Don't let it love you; you're unlovable anyway. Love hurts. Love betrays.

He'd gotten in too deep. Now he struggled to come up for air. He needed to separate from her. Rising terror made the breath catch in his chest. He wasn't good enough at these mind games to handle all this. Where was he? How could he get out?

But wait. Was that him thinking that, or just him soaking up all these negative energies?

Lina, he announced to all that he felt coming from her, including those past lives, **you are a wonderful woman. Just think: you've been through all this and yet you've given so much to the world! How many people have you helped? How have you turned my life upside down?**

You don't have to be alone anymore. I love you, Carolina, and it's time you learned how to love yourself. If you don't love yourself, who will? I will. I love you.

A pink rose blossomed in the darkness in front of him. It enveloped him with love as its sweet perfume drifted to him. **I love you, Londo,** he heard. But the petals formed a barrier around him. She still wouldn't accept his love.

Wait– one petal unfolded, creating a break in the wall. What did it mean?

Anthropomorphize, a faint, unfamiliar voice whispered to him. He imagined Lina there, the petal draped around her like a sari.

If you love me, I will pay the debt with love, she told him. **But please, it must stop. If I lose myself in you without limit, you'll betray me. You'll hurt me.**

I will never betray you. Can't you receive something without feeling obligated?

You pay for what you get, she replied. **Cash up front and no warranty. If you ask for too much, the universe will punish you. That's how the world works.**

No it's not. Loving should be voluntary, not an obligation. It should be done with joy, not guilt and embarrassment.

I can't do that. Haven't I gone far enough already? It will destroy me if I try more. I don't want to die! No! The sari'd girl covered her face with her hands. That blasted petal began to grow again, reforming the wall between the two of them.

Yes you can! Lon batted at the petals but they stood fast. **You won't get hurt– I'll never ever hurt you, love. I promise you. Lina!**

Lon. He heard his Lina call him. **Lon, you may have gone too deep. I can't sense you well. Come back.**

23

Lina told him, **Lower your vibration. Think of your body, think of your feet.**

So close, but this time he knew she was right. He hummed to himself, lower and lower, and tried to feel his body around himself again. He was coalescing, focusing to solidity. Almost back… His body gave a jerk and he opened his eyes to see Lina crouched and holding his feet. She'd put the robe back on.

"Good, you got back all right. I'm just grounding you. A little more…"

The room swayed around him, but he was here. She got up to sit next to him on the couch, rubbed his hands, and that helped too.

"Lina, it was *incroyable*. There were even past lives there. And your childhood."

She was terribly embarrassed and tried to cover it up by talking briskly. "I can imagine. Aren't I a mess? Did you run into the Egyptian general? I thought I sensed him. I've been working on him a lot lately."

"Yes, he was there. And you aren't a mess, *pas du tout, chérie*. You've been hurt. Let me help. You've had some bad experiences that programmed you to not being able to accept love without feeling guilt or embarrassment."

She stopped rubbing his hands for a moment. "Guilt or embarrassment. That's new."

"*Bon*. But in turn it's forced you to be more loving toward the world, and that's your greatest gift. That's why I love you, Lina. It's all that love inside you."

Lina's eyes filled with tears. She put his arms around him and held him close.

"Thank you, Lon. That's the nicest thing anyone's ever said to me."

"Someone should have said it a long time ago. It's their fault they didn't, not yours."

"So did you find anything that we can follow up on?"

He thought and then that crooked smile came to his face. His eyes narrowed with deviltry. He jumped up, scooping her into his arms as if she were a feather.

She let out a laughing screech. "Londo, what in the world–?"

He laughed right back at her and carried her to the bedroom. "I have an idea."

"Londo– Lon, doctor's orders!"

He dropped her on the bed and she bounced, still laughing. He bounced in right next to her.

"'For a while,' quote unquote, and we have faithfully fulfilled the prescription," he declared. "Hang on, *un moment*." He touched his ring. "Wiley?"

"Uff." Had he awakened him? Good. "Here, Londo. Are you all right? What's up?"

"Reporting in: no sex yet. Rand out." Lon chuckled with the moment as communications cut off. "That was just for the record," he explained to Lina.

Now he sat on his knees getting serious again while she lay there, propped on an elbow. "The problem that I saw just then was that you're operating on a give-and-receive process in addition to low self-esteem. If someone gives you something, you feel the obligation or guilt to give them something in return.

"You can't accept a gift at face value without feeling the need to do an equal whatever in return. So you begin to devalue what you've been given. You think that since it was given to lowly little you, it must be throw-offs."

He pointed sternly at her. "Believe me, what I'm offering you is not second-hand. It's real, it's primo, and it's going to last forever."

She flushed pure rose and scrunched her head between her shoulders.

"That's another thing," Lon told her. "Love makes you feel guilty and embarrassed. Those aren't feelings you want to experience. Therefore love that's offered to you can't be worth much."

"Huh. That's pretty deep. Absolutely true, but deep too. I'm impressed."

"Be quiet." He slapped the mattress and she jumped. "Ah, now you know what it's like to be on the other side of the psychiatrist's couch.

"*Donc*," he continued, "the lesson is to be able to accept something without feeling the need to do something else in return, and also to accept that thing with positive feelings. *Comprendu?*"

"Ooookay…"

"I want you to be happy when you accept my love. I don't want you to think that yes, you're happy now but I'm going to dump you any day, so you get to wallow now in the sadness that you're going to go through then. I'm not leaving you, Lie."

She looked at him, her disbelief stamped on her face.

"No. Never. I will camp in your backyard. I'll follow you to work. I'll loiter outside the ladies room when you go in."

"There are laws against that."

"Like any cop's going to try to go up against me." That crooked grin dawned on Londo's face and Lina's pulse raced to see it. "But I won't have to do that. I'm starting your training right here, right now. What I'm going to do for you is to give you a night of pleasure."

Lina chortled.

Lon bounced sharply on the bed to stop her. "*Vraiment*. I'm going to do everything to you that you like, and you'll enjoy it. And you're not going to do a single thing to me in return."

"Oh come on, Lon."

"No. Not a thing. You'll be severely punished if you do one pleasurable thing to me. You are going to take this and enjoy it, do you hear? The guilt will come if you don't."

"But there's so much pleasure in giving, too."

"That's the one pleasure you won't get tonight. Just think of me as your love slave, *d'accord?*"

"If I can be yours some other night," she giggled.

"Wrong answer. You are never going to reciprocate! You are not going to do anything to me in return for this."

"Honeybear, this is too silly."

"It is not. You've spent the last four days doing everything I wanted and needed, and now I want to do this for you. You *will* lie there and enjoy this!"

She giggled again, entirely embarrassed and knowing that Londo must hear her heart pounding so hard and fast. He was such a Leo! "Okay, where do we begin? Or rather, where do *you* begin, slave?" She waved an imperial hand at him to commence.

"*Eh bien*, let's see." He quickly began to unfasten his wrap and noticed that she was watching him very attentively, so he slowed it down, added a little action to it and a few measures of growled "bow chicka wow wow" striptease music. She grinned at him, blushing. She had such a pink blush.

"Very nice," she said. "Let me get a few dollar bills." She gave him an appraising glance. "Maybe some tens."

"No compliments, mistress! No tips, either."

"The love slave will desist from his comments," she ordered grandly. She was a deep rose down to the neckline of her robe. "And he will refer to me as, as…empress.

I've always wanted to be an empress. Catherine the Great, Czarina of all the Russias!"

"Back to earzh, empress. You'll be yourself during this. You. Lina." He moved in to undrape her, making sure that his hands caressed her soft skin as they moved the robe. Her breathing changed; her skin warmed. He eased up behind her, bringing his hands around to cup her shoulders as he nuzzled her neck, so careful of the bandages.

"You stand above all empresses in my heart. Forever, kitten. Now tell me what pleases you," he whispered next to her trembling cheek.

"Ooo, that does. I love the sound of your voice. It sends shivers up my spine."

He whispered his love to her and then moved his mouth to kiss down her neck. She quivered under his attention. He deepened the feedback loop to search out more pleasures for her.

Women and their heightened sense of touch. She was sensuousness itself as he moved over her.

He would ask and after a while she began to admit to him what pleased her the most. He fell to his task gently but thoroughly.

She shied away from a selfish core of lust that she kept so tightly bound inside, but he played with it, urging it to unfurl and demand for herself. He wanted it to be selfish. He nibbled at its edges, coaxing, coaxing…

"C'mon, baby," he whispered to her. "You can do it."

She thought about squirming away but the things he was doing–! She was breathless; she couldn't talk, but he found just where she wanted him to touch her, he knew just how she wanted to be touched.

She cried out her resistance to him. He responded by repeating his vows of love and faithfulness. "You are my empress, my goddess of love," he told her. "I bow down before your power." He worshipped her in body and mind. "Command me. Command me!"

Lina knew she couldn't stay trapped in this dead end she had created for herself. At some point she either had to give up– and that would mean giving up Londo, too– or she had to fight for him.

Even if that meant fighting herself.

Despite all his promises, Londo might someday leave, and she knew that would destroy her. But where could anyone get a guarantee in life? Why did she expect God to reach down and deliver a written lifetime warranty into her hand?

Sometimes you had to take a chance, close your eyes and jump. Sometimes you had to break the repeating pattern of your life and change, for good or bad, just to get to a different place. Surely in these past few days circumstances and Londo had forced her to jump farther than she ever had. Could she do it again?

A year ago, a week ago– Where had she been? Cowering from life. Now she had touched another human being. She'd made love to Londo. He loved her. She'd helped him and then saved his very life when no one anywhere else could have.

Did that mean that she was truly Lina Muttbutt, lowest of the low?

Londo called her beautiful. He told her she was brave. He said she was sexy and smart.

Was there a chance that he was right, even a little?

"*Je t'aime plus que tout.* I adore you," he whispered in her ear. Londo said that, Londo who was the most wonderful man in the universe, who was Valiant, who had proposed a lifetime of marriage to her.

She had faith in Londo.

She had faith in herself.

Lina took him then. She wrapped her body around him and reached inside his mind to cherish him, to lust for him. To have him every way she could, his mind naked and open to her touch so she could know him like no one else had ever known him before. To have him in body and soul.

He was hers! She could ask anything of him, she could want anything of him. She could receive anything from him that he offered.

She was good enough. She deserved this.

She kissed him again and again afterward, memorizing his face by touch and then tangling her fingers in his soft hair as she kissed his chest and arms. She brushed her hands over his body to pleasure the both of them. Lon sighed with delight and wonder at her reactions.

She purred, "There has never been another man in the entire universe as wonderful as you. I love you, I love you so much."

"And can you feel how much I love you?"

Lina opened her eyes to meet his. "Darling, I'd have to be dead not to feel this. You made me live again. You're incredible."

"My love for you is infinite. There's no way for you to match it, so don't try. Accept it. Take it; it's yours."

"I love you, Londo. Forever and ever."

He could feel it in her. The dam had broken; the flow could reach her. She truly knew his love now.

And with the flow was a return current, a warmth that he'd never known before. She gave her entire heart with no hesitation. She was his and she knew that.

Her eyes were bright with adoration and softly she began a song that seemed written just for her to sing to him. She had a most beautiful voice, clear and bright and filled with love.

There was love all around, but I never heard it singing.

No, I never heard it at all,

'Til there was you.

She sniffed and hugged him tightly. Londo held her in awe, held the universe in humble amazement. All at once life seemed to steady and the future stretched clear and wonderful and perfect. God was in His heaven; all was right with the world.

"Us together," Londo murmured as he stroked her hair. "Forever. You beside me."

She nodded against his chest. "For the rest of our lives," she said as she ran her hand down his arm, "and even beyond."

She was made of love, tender and deep, reflecting and strengthening his own.

The love itself seemed to echo through the room like a physical thing, making it misty. No, making it clearer, Londo realized, yet with a mysterious, golden glow. Something was happening to the room but it didn't upset him.

Rainbows encircled them. A golden-white light shone down. They were showered clean from their lovemaking with love itself. Presences lived in the light, great and powerful and benign with loving thoughts.

A voice: "Two of the three have accepted each other. Receive the blessings of the Three Worlds. Take these as gifts for your union."

The two of them were now dressed– in what, Londo couldn't tell. The light was too bright for even him to see through, but it wasn't uncomfortable in any way. He looked at Lina in his arms, and she, at him. "It's not me," she said, and then caught her breath–

They hung beyond time itself. The two of them, their higher selves: their true and perfect selves, forever a part of each other, forever joined, yin and yang. Lon caught the words, "twin souls" but it hadn't come from Lina. She moved toward him to kiss him against the curtain of eternity. He wrapped her in his arms to seal her promise. They were one.

And then they were floating above a floor, surrounded by that mighty light as it faded. Lon supported Lina in mid-air, trying to hold on to the moment.

"Wiley, all your recording equipment had better have caught that!" Jae's voice exclaimed as he and the doctor scrambled out of their makeshift beds and ran toward the two.

Unwillingly Londo touched down. "Twin souls," he said in wonder, stroking her cheek as Lina gazed into his eyes. "What does it mean?"

"Twin souls are…soulmates. Real ones, not the cliché. Some people say that when human souls were created they were androgynous, and at some point they split in two, male and female, yang and yin. I'm not sure about the yin and yang part, but twin souls are definitely… companions from the beginning of Creation. Yes."

"So that's…us?

"It feels like it," Lina said, ignoring Wiley and Jae. There was only Londo.

A slow smile came to Lon's face. "Carolina O'Kelly, would you do me the great honor of marrying me?"

She gave him a dazzling smile of her own. "Oh yes, Londo Rand. Even unto eternity." And they kissed while Wiley and Jae looked at each other.

24

"Hold it! Break it up!" Wilder yelled, but they were oblivious to the others for some time. Finally Londo turned to blink at their surroundings: Wiley's lab.

"How did we get back here?"

Lina dreamily said, "Wasn't me." Londo! Londo!

"*Aussi bien.*" It was unimportant next to other things. "Gentlemen, I'd like you to meet my fiancée, Ms. Carolina Angelina O'Kelly, of the North Carolina O'Kellys."

Lina giggled and he waggled his eyebrows at her.

"I thought I told you no sex," Wilder grumped. "Did you even wait five minutes?"

"The prescription was 'for a while,' unquote, and I feel much more than fine."

Lon grinned at them all as Wiley demanded to know what had just happened here. Some of his sensors had caught vague lights and murmurs but others hadn't registered anything they could quantify beyond going off-scale across the spectrum.

Lon merely said, "It was a miracle," and let it go as if miracles happened every day.

Lina beamed at Londo, beamed at Wiley and Jae and the universe and said, "Wasn't that nice? Wasn't that wonderful?" She didn't let Londo go. She'd never let him go.

Jae finally elbowed Wiley. "Give them a little while on this," he said as he came out of his own amazement. "They're obviously in shock."

To which Wiley muttered darkly and snapped, "Report, Legionnaire!" to Londo, who tried to make it clear to the scientist that they really had no idea.

As Wiley tried to coax some sense out of his foolishly-smiling teammate, Lina noticed the cream-colored, floor-length dress she wore and smoothed out the material. It was lace over a satin underdress, the lace a surprisingly bold yet delicately wrought pattern of three symbols– no, a fourth one peeked out from behind– over and over. The same held true for Lon's satin coat: four symbols, but his were embroidered into a subtle brocade.

"What is this?" Lina asked, interrupting Londo. She craned her neck to check her back. The strapless underdress belled out because it was hooped, and the off-the-shoulders lace overdress trailed behind her in a long train. There were tiny gold dome buttons for accents and a simple gold chain at her throat. She could feel a wreath of blossoms in her hair, smell the soft fragrance of the flowers there. Her hair was up and securely pinned under the flowers. Her ears held what felt to be button earrings.

"It's a wedding dress," Lon answered. "A beautiful faerie gown for my beautiful princess bride."

Lina caught her breath. "Does this have something to do with that special effects hoodingus from your TV interview?" **Are we still naked underneath the illusion?**

"It's no illusion, chérie. Wiley?"

Wiley already had two tricorders going, giving the puter orders for more focused scans even as he kept replaying the previous event. "No illusion as far as I can detect," he said.

He ran his instruments over Lon's outfit: also with the same cream as Lina's accents, but overall much darker, a cafe latte tan and rich mocha. Instead of Old South, Lon styled a Napoleonic gentleman. His vest reversed the colors, and tight pants were tucked into knee boots. A row of gold buttons ran down either side of the high-collared tailcoat. Pink-blooming ivy peeked out of a buttonhole.

"Bon. Jacson, m'man." Lon clapped the blond Legionnaire on the shoulder with such ease that no one noticed the care he took to do it. Even so, Jae stumbled from the friendly blow. "You're still ordained? You haven't resigned from the priesthood since this afternoon?"

Jae's face had gone tight and masklike. "Of course I am."

"Marry us. Right now."

Lina clutched at Londo. "What? Oh Londo, you can't– We don't even know what's–"

"Hush, wife-to-be. We have made a decision, and I think we should follow through before you change your mind."

"Londo! You're the craziest, most wonderful man I've ever met. But this is impossible!"

"You saw it; it's all impossible. C'mon, twin soul, let's get married. The universe or at least three worlds, whatever they are, agree to this match. We seem to be dressed and ready. Jae, can you do it? I mean, would you do us the indescribable honor of officiating as we take our vows?"

Jae stood there with his mouth open, his mask cracked in shock. "She's right, Londo, you're crazy. You can't have discussed things. She doesn't know what she's getting into."

"We can talk later. Time to do this now," Lon insisted. "C'mon, Jae."

"I am not going to play a part in this!" Jae exploded. "It's craziness! It's... It's dangerous for her. Lina, he didn't tell you, but he's got people after him all the time. Now they're going to have a new target. You."

"I'll keep her safe," Lon said quickly. "There's a–"

Jae interrupted him, gesturing in the air in a quick motion. "Priority call. Commander Magnos!" he called.

From the air, a familiar voice grumbled, "Umm…" There came a snort, then, "Jae? What time is it? Has something happened?"

"Yes, something has happened. Londo is getting married," Jae announced, folding his arms in front of his chest and giving Lon a hard look. "And he's doing it now."

"Come, Jae," Londo said amiably, "we don't have to get Stoan–"

"What?" A screen scrolled down from the ceiling. There was the commander rising up from under his bedsheets, unmindful of the disarray of his cropped hair. He wore something close-fitting, so black the style wasn't apparent even when the screen disappeared to display him as if he were standing there with them. "Londo, explain!"

Lon held out splayed arms. "What's to explain? Stoan, go back to bed. Or watch if you want. I'd like that. I just want to marry Lina, and I want to do it before she has a chance to change her mind. Happens every da–"

"The *kick* it does." Stoan glared at Lina. "No. I forbid this."

"What?" Lina blurted.

"Stoan, you can't–"

"I certainly can, Legionnaire. You know the rules as well as I. 'No social interaction of a nature contrary to proper appearances shall– '"

"Hell, Stoan, I've been sleeping with her outside of wedlock with no birth control. On a lot of worlds that's a felony. So we're making this official, legal."

"A Terran!" Stoan snarled.

Lina opened her mouth to retort, but Lon put a restraining hand on her arm.

"So am I. Hush, love, let me handle this. Commander, if you try to block this I'll file an official protest."

"Do it. Have the forms in my office first thing in the morning. We'll have them processed by the end of the week."

"*Saint-ciboire de tabarnac!*" Londo slammed his fist against a table and then winced as it shattered to dust beneath the blow. "Aw, *marde*. Sorry, Wiley; I'll replace it. But Stoan, we're getting married *now*. The Legion might not officially recognize it, but that's tough."

What was all this? Lina clapped her hands over her mouth. How could this man try to stand in their way? **Lon, will it be legal?**

"Hell yes, it'll be legal, *chérie*. The Legion's a powerful organization, but it's not that powerful."

"Just test us," Stoan warned. "You want me to wake some lawyers now or in the morning?" His eyes sharpened on Lon. "Are you afraid you'll have second thoughts if you wait?"

"I have given full consideration to this."

"Have you? Really?" Stoan walked to a desk that only partially appeared in the room and then pulled some screens of his own around himself, ticking off items they couldn't see. "If it's real, it can wait a few days. We need to check O'Kelly's background. We don't want to damage the reputations of either the Mega-Legion or you."

"They're not going to be damaged, *skurnit!*"

Stoan kept checking different areas on his screens. He certainly seemed the calm businessman now. "You've worked hard all your life to get where you are today," he soothed. "What you don't need is a catastrophic mistake to blot your record. What you don't need is to be…swayed in the wrong direction by someone you truly don't know."

"Do you only have one telepath on this world?" Lina exclaimed. "Can't you get someone in here to clear me? I am not a mind controller!"

Stoan regarded her with clear distaste. "Perhaps you even think so," he finally said. The screens in his room rolled back up into nothingness. "Perhaps Terrans don't realize the danger, or don't place a value on people having independence of thought."

"Stoan!" Londo barked. "Enough of this crap. I mean it. Lina is not a controller in any way. She's—"

Jae interrupted evenly: "What have you told Hal about this, Lon?"

That stopped Londo. "…I haven't been able to get in touch with him. He's gone off somewhere."

Stoan shook his head, obviously thankful of Jae's new tack. "You want to get married, even if Hal isn't there."

"I'm sure that Lina could port him in if we could just find him. He could wear a quarantine suit–"

"You're getting married without Hal," Jae said. "What's he going to think about being left out?"

Londo's teeth ground against each other. "I… He…"

Stoan rested his chin on the palm of his hand, the picture of a reasonable man trying to talk sense to the insane. "You're getting married, but Hal won't be there. Or your grandparents. Think, Londo. If you were in a clear state of mind, would you even consider such a thing? The most important people in your life, not witnessing your wedding contract? I don't think so." He paused. "All of this– What will Hal think?"

The air whooshed out of Londo's chest. His shoulders slumped and he stared at the floor. Lina started to reach out to him, but Jae caught her hand and pulled her away from Londo. "Let him work this out," he whispered fiercely to her. "Don't make a mistake here."

"A mistake?" she asked helplessly. There was Londo, who had been so adamant about professing his love to her, about them getting married, living and loving together forever. Lon didn't seem so sure now. She sank against Jae.

God, he was backing out! Her heart began to shrivel at the thought. Could she talk him back into it? If he needed to be talked into marriage, was it right for them to consider it in the first place?

Londo was impulsive. He believed in fairy tales. Now maybe he was coming back to the real world. No one could really love her, could they? Especially Londo Rand, the most wonderful man alive. How could she have been so stupid to ever think–

"No," Londo said softly, and Lina caught her breath in horror. This was when he'd turn to her and tell her that they had to wait. Or that it might be best for them to go their separate ways for a while, maybe a few months, to make sure they were being sensible about all this.

Possibilities flashed through her mind, scenes of less and less Londo in her life. Finally a picture of him resuming his Valiant role in Montreal, forgetting about the silly girl from North Carolina. Reading his Christmas card from her with an expression of embarrassment at the entire affair.

No.

That was wrong. Londo didn't have the right to do that to her. He'd sworn his love and by god she was going to hold him to it. He would not disrespect her. Lina gathered herself to remind him very clearly of that, but before she could he said–

"No!" Londo straightened to stand at full height. "If I know Hal, he'll welcome Lina with open arms, even if he does miss this. If he gets my messages, he'll call and we'll port him in, but if he doesn't– Well, these things happen. He'll understand. We'll have this marriage now, with or without the Legion's official sanction, Stoan. You know I'd much prefer with." Londo gestured to the air much as Jae had before. "Priority call. Subcommander Nurunori!"

A second screen scrolled down to add another person to the room. Here was a pink-haired woman sitting on the edge of her partially-seen bed but looking more composed than Stoan. "I've been monitoring, Lon," she said tiredly.

"Andri, what's my legal standing here?"

"Legal? Talk to the lawyers. Give them a few hours to sleep, but–"

"Internally," Londo insisted. "How much of this is Stoan's bluff? How much can he impede this?"

She pulled one hand down her face and looked to her left, as if Stoan were there with her, even though with their screen set-up he was on her right. She must have a second screen there. "Unless the woman is a proven mind controller, I don't see how you can block this, Stoan. It's a little quick– it's a *kick* quick, Londo– but it's not entirely unheard of. But Lon, a Legion wedding should be careful, correct, planned and–"

"And a media circus," Londo growled. "No. Now. Here. We can have the circus later."

Wiley cleared his throat at that. "We've had some unusual phenomena associated with all this," he announced and held up his padd to the two outsiders. Stoan and Andri both looked to the side of their screens as if seeing the readouts there.

Andri wrinkled her nose. "What is this?" she puzzled.

"Lights?" Stoan scowled. "Voices? How did you manage this, Londo?"

"I didn't."

"Then *you*," Stoan accused Lina and turned back to his poor deluded comrade. "Londo, think. Think!" he pleaded. "I want to come in there and pound some sense into that invulnerable head of yours!"

"It's dangerous, Lina," Jae said from between gritted teeth. He still held her by her upper arms. "Has he told you, really? Have you had a chance to think about it? We're talking *Valiant*. How many enemies does he have who'd love to get back at him? *Grigach*, how many enemies does Maximus have, too? You'd be the weak link in the family. Anyone can see that."

Jae scowled horribly at Londo. "Anyone with half a mind. And here Stoan is practically giving orders for you to be arrested for mind control as soon as quarantine is over. You can't get married under the shadow of that suspicion. Lon's crazy, Lina– has he told you that? Have you suspected? He is not entirely sane."

Lina's lower lip trembled. "I know a lot more about Londo than you think I do. I'm a reasonably intelligent person. I can guess that things might be a little danger- ous, but I'm a nobody. No one would want to hurt me."

"Tell that to Terry Rhodes, to Doctor Menlo. How many dozens, hundreds of others are out there, Lina? Do you know? Did he tell you? You'll have to spend the rest of your life locked up behind impervion to stay safe."

"She's a teleporter." Londo's voice was dead calm as he stared evenly at Jae. "She can port out of trouble."

"She didn't do it before."

"I'm sorry." Lina pulled at her hands. "I'm new at all this. I'll get better at my porting. I'll practice, I promise. And my guides will help protect me, right?"

"Guides!" Stoan exploded. "Guides and Terrans and witchdoctors! Wiley, how much time is left on this *skurny* quarantine?"

Wiley checked his padd and did a double-take. "That can't be right," he muttered as he reset. He huffed at the padd again and said, "Puter, scan the laboratory for extra-Sarastoran contamination."

"No contamination present," the impersonal voice replied.

Wiley's mouth opened and closed before he burst out, "What the *skurny kick* of sunfire is going on here?!"

Lina tried to do a psychic scan of the room but didn't get anything. She was too upset. "Are we out of quarantine?" she asked and it came out ever so slightly as a whine. Londo pointedly removed Jae's hands from her, then took her into his arms even as Wiley held his scanning padd toward them.

Jae looked at them oddly. He openly stared at Lina as if he'd never seen her be- fore, first at her face, then her shoulder. Tentatively she touched her cheek. No bumps, no crust. No map of Australia?

"Report, Mem-Bazer," Stoan snapped. He'd jumped up out of bed and was walk- ing rapidly as his screens kept pace with him.

"Look at you," Londo said to her in wonder. "I didn't even notice."

But Wiley could only make an unintelligible sound before he managed, "Lina is healed, even her arm. Completely, and it never registered with me either. No scars, no bruises, no burns… Hard to tell with Londo, but prelim scans indicate him at 100%. There is no more reason for quarantine. This entire area is clean. And then you two appear here in a blinding light– I practically expected a…a band of Terran angels to shout 'hallelujah!' What-is-going-on?"

Jae shook off his shock. "You have to listen to them, Lon," he hissed. "Listen!"

"Could we get some privacy, please?" Lina asked. She didn't like the waves of anger and fear coming off Jae, the utter block that Londo had thrown up unconsciously to stop those waves from hitting him. Jae was Lon's best friend!

"Are you trying to cover up something?" Stoan asked harshly.

Andri cut in. "Stoan, maybe a few minutes of privacy–"

"Giving a mind controller a few minutes alone with her victim is like–"

Lina didn't hear the rest. She pulled Jae away from the screens while Londo followed her. Somewhere in the back of her mind the ability to touch someone besides Lon startled her, but this was no time to worry about that.

It was just the two of them and Jae as the others argued. "Jae, all I know is that I love Londo so much that I don't want to live without him. If something happens to me– or to him– at least we'll have this much to take with us."

Londo squeezed her shoulders.

"I've been through this before," Lina added. "My best friend got married and she did it pretty quick, too, though not this quick. She called me up in the middle of the night after just two dates. 'I'm getting married,' she said. She waited a couple months for the actual ceremony so she could have a fancy wedding. Which she borrowed money from me for. That she never paid back."

Lon made an offended noise but Lina merely shrugged. "We'd been friends for years and she was always asking me for money. A little here, a little there. A big chunk there at the end, even though Chad was fairly well-off. But I had no idea everything else was going to change as much as it did.

"After she got married I managed to talk to her twice. Then she called me and told me that my concern for the loan indicated that I was not her true friend so she wasn't going to pay it back. And that her marriage was more important than any friendship. She said not to bother her again."

Jae looked away for a moment. "Did you? You let it drop for her?" There was silence in the room.

"Yes," Lina said. "I didn't hear from her again until she wanted me to testify against her husband at the divorce. And to help pay for it. She said he'd abused her emotionally and that she'd always been loyal to me. She wanted me to tell the judge that her husband beat her. She wanted me to fake some photos for evidence."

"Did you?"

"Of course not. Look, I learned about friendship from her, about false friendships and true ones and how you don't mess with a true one. Jae, I'm not asking you and Londo to break off your friendship. When we're married he'll owe me time, but he also owes you time as his friend. I won't begrudge you that. We all need all the friends we can get, but he especially needs you. Wiley says you've known each other since you were kids. You must have helped each other through some terrible times."

"But Lon never told you about me…before," Jae said slowly.

"Heck, I've only known Lon for a few days. He told me about this friend he wanted me to meet. I think that must have been you."

"It was," Londo said quickly.

"I love him, Jae, and I know I'm going to love him forever. I promise you I'll do everything in my power to make him happy. I will try never to do anything to embarrass or diminish him. If you see me doing something you don't think I should, just tell me and I'll stop. Please give us your blessing."

Jae turned away and leaned against the wall on an elbow. His fingers tangled and pulled in his hair.

"I know it's sudden," Lon said. "It would mean a lot. Tell you what; we're out of quarantine. This afternoon– no, make that tomorrow– we'll all go out and have lunch together somewhere private and we'll talk about everything you think we need to talk about. Everything."

"Someplace where they serve stiff drinks," Jae muttered.

"It'll be a long lunch and we will both listen to whatever you have to say. Maybe we'll even take some advice. Will that be acceptable?"

"I guess I never really believed this day would happen." Jae swallowed as he turned around slowly. "I know we talked about it. A lot. But–"

Stoan's voice came from behind them. Lina turned to see the real man entering the lab. He was as tall as Wiley, and had a wine-colored robe wrapped around himself though he wore a black, booted jumpsuit underneath. Even in person his skin held that icy bluish cast.

"Jae's made some valid points, Londo," he briskly said as he joined them. "Danger. You're used to having people around you who can take care of themselves."

He seemed the picture of arbitration now, although Lina could feel panic radiating from him. He really believed that Londo was the one in danger, Valiant, the man who could be a supremely powerful weapon if he fell into the wrong hands.

"Publicity, plus your reputation, plus Hal's… Could even Mega-Legion Headquarters be safe enough for someone who– I'm making this assumption– has had no defensive training?"

"I'll teach her," Londo offered.

"And Legion protocol. You must know that you can't do anything spontaneously around here. Not a member of your standing. This needs to be orchestrated, publicized…*delayed*. I'll get Legion PIC started on this first thing in the morning. I'll call

all my contacts and have them flag down Hal, wherever he is. We can get Ruth and Mike here–”

“And hold up everything,” Londo growled, “while you pile the red tape all around us. We can go almost anywhere to get married and you wouldn't be able to say anything about it. Michi would be a great world to have a wedding, wouldn't it? I know a resort there.” He turned to Lina. “We can be there in three hours, no quarantine.” He gave Stoan a dark look. “No red tape.”

“I can have you drummed out of the–”

“Stoan!” Now it was that pink-haired woman, Andri, who hurried in. She stood Jae's height, tall and slender, wearing ballooning trousers and slippers under her robe. “Don't say something that could get you impeached. There's nothing we can legally do to stop this wedding; certainly nothing morally. But we can have her investigated after the fact, quietly and off the record.”

“Quietly?” Stoan's face seemed to close in as he considered. Finally he announced, “For that, there must be no mention of this marriage outside this room.”

“Are you standing as witnesses?” Wiley asked curiously. He kept peering at everyone as if he'd been presented with the most curious data ever. “Just the six of us to keep this secret?”

“A secret marriage?” Lina couldn't believe what they were asking. “That's crazy! For how long? You expect us to–”

“Easy, *chérie*,” Lon told her.

Acrid fury filled Lina's veins. How dare they? “I mean it, Londo. I want to know how long, and I want it in writing. I don't believe in secrets. And a secret marriage– what, do you want everyone snickering at us until we announce?” She gave Jae a hard glance. She'd heard him on the phones talking about Lon and the Terran witchdoctor. At least he had the grace to look contrite.

“It's very important for you to announce, isn't it?” Stoan eyed her shrewdly.

Lina frowned. If their marriage was going to embarrass Londo– she didn't want that!

“It won't embarrass me,” he told her.

“I don't want you getting in trouble over this,” she insisted.

Londo squeezed her shoulder. “Secret marriages are out of the question, Stoan. We go public right away. Call in L-PIC afterwards.”

“No.”

Andri spoke softly into Stoan's ear, as if she'd forgotten that Londo could hear her whispering from a mile away. Stoan answered her and she replied, then Stoan nodded. “Secrecy outside of Legion Headquarters,” he declared, “until we get an investigation and a qualified telepath clears her.”

"Hal?"

"Hal's cleared. But not Ruth or Mike."

"How long does that mean?" Lina asked Londo suspiciously.

"Say…a week. Two at the most," Andri offered.

"Okay. Can he put it in writing?"

Stoan's eyes were slits. "We are officially recording now. Four or five days should be enough, Londo. Five days of secrecy. And if the investigation turns up something, you both disavow all knowledge of this," he ordered. "The marriage will be annulled and wiped from the record."

The wedding was on!

25

"You sure your record's clean, *chérie*?" Londo asked her, giving her that crazy lopsided grin of his.

"There was just that one time I tried to take over the world. That doesn't count, does it?"

"*Mais non.* It's only Earzh; no one here will mind." He glanced back to Stoan. "She was arrested once– once!– for participating in a legal protest. Charges were dropped. And there might be a little mixup in her record as to age."

"Age?" Stoan asked. Andri had produced a padd for her own notes.

"I sort of lied about my age when I was younger," Lina said uncertainly. "There are things you can do on Earth only if you're old enough. I, ah…fudged a bit."

"So she could survive," Londo told them. "It was nothing even approaching criminal intent. She just needed to be able to get jobs, education and living space until she was of legal age."

"We'll see," Stoan said, turning on his heel. "I'll find out what kind of telepaths with security clearance are on this planet. I'll have somebody here today." He strode out of the lab. The double doors swung shut without rebound behind him.

The tension in the room eased immediately as they all stared after him. Finally Andri spoke. "It has to be today?" she asked Londo.

"As soon as possible," he replied. "We're already dressed for it."

She shook her head. "You and your 'gotta do it now' mentality. But not in here. Sorry, Wiley, but this place is still a wreck. You know video CGI isn't permitted for official records; this will look horrible. Plus there are too many classified experiments going on."

Wiley sank down in a chair, overcome by the press of events. "They'd just destroy the areas I've managed to clean anyway," he said abstractedly.

She nodded. "Puter, warm up VR Room 2." Two beeps sounded. "VR is legal enough."

Lon gave her a grateful smile. "Thanks, An; I owe you."

"Consider it a wedding present, one that I'd better not have to take back. We've all been worried about you lately, Londo."

"In that case, how about Room 17?"

She gave him a little frown. "Isn't that too big for this? How many witnesses do you want?"

"Everyone. Drag in people off the street," he grinned. "Send up fireworks."

"Security, Londo. Headquarters personnel only."

"I was just joking. Look, Andri, weddings are a big deal on Earzh, the biggest parties in a person's life. Room 17?"

Making a show of shaking her head and sighing, she nodded. "Okay, okay. Puter, change that to VR Room 17. You really want lots of people there? *Grigach*. Wiley, is this kosher?" (Lina started at the translation.) "Do they really do this on Earth? I remember Hal's wedding."

Wiley inclined his head slightly. "Hal's was an exception. I believe both he and Londo mentioned the oddness of such a small ceremony."

"All right, a big party– at this time of morning. Let's wreck everyone's sleep schedules and not just mine. Puter, activate non-emergency wake-up chimes for Legion members, families and assisting personnel in Headquarters, security level 2 or higher. Secure guests also, but level 3 and higher; no other civilians. No reporters no matter what their security level. Jae, do you want to explain to everyone what's going on? They'd probably forgive you easiest for waking them up. Who else? We need a secure judge with the contract–"

"Jae's officiating," Lon said quickly. "Jae? You've got to." He turned to his friend.

Jae chewed his lip as he considered. "Lunch tomorrow?" he asked.

Lon nodded. "A very long lunch. We don't leave until you say we can. Officiate for us. Please."

Jae sighed and straightened his shoulders. "Oh, anything you say, Lon. Might as well join the rest of the lunatics here. So. We're having a wedding in Headquarters today." He rubbed his hands together, his expression shifting into an expression of curious expectation. "A wedding! How many people are here?"

"A wedding!" Londo swung Lina around, her skirt billowing around her. She grabbed at her train to keep it from sweeping lab tables clear. "Everyone put on their party hats– I'm going to marry the woman I love!"

Lina laughed gaily as Lon's sparkling eyes erased any gloom from the day.

"Jae?"

"Sure, Londo. Let me get some proper–" As they looked at him, Jae's clothing changed. He gave a start when he realized what had happened and then peered down at himself.

In contrast to Lon and Lina's outfits, his looked informal: a short-sleeved, cream tunic over a long-sleeved tan undershirt with a line of gold trim, and loose, mocha trousers that were gathered at the ankles. The symbols were subtly knitted into the soft material of the outfit, but the design also stood out stark and large on the priestly dark-brown stole that draped over his shoulders. The small blue-stoned earring he'd worn was now a simple, small gold hoop.

"Eep!" The suddenness startled Lina.

"What the–" Andri sputtered.

Londo laughed. "Welcome to the club, Jae. What, nothing for the chief witness?" Everyone looked expectantly at Wiley, but nothing happened.

"Thank you for that," he said to Lina.

Andri cocked her head at Lina. "I really could have used a new outfit. You sure you couldn't come up with something?"

"I tell you, it's not me. I know when I'm porting. I think."

Wiley was skeptical. "Subconsciously–"

"What, I could do something like this? With lights and voices and dressmakers? All hands, reality check!"

Lon shook his finger at them. "*Non non non*, there's a faerie godmother lurking around here somewhere. Come on, come on, before the clock strikes midnight! Let's drag everyone out of bed. I've been up all night convincing Ms. O'Kelly to go for it. I don't want her to back down now."

"All Sagittarian tendencies on alert and committed, Cap'n Rand." Lina saluted him smartly. She was deliriously drowning in his smile, the one that meant that he loved her. Forever. "I'm jumping."

"Good. Jae?"

"Wiley, I'm putting you in charge of invitations and explanations. See who's up. Hell, see who's not up. It's not every day that Valiant gets married." Jae laughed helplessly; this situation was impossible! "Give me a few minutes, Londo. I'm going to set up the VR room personally."

The Legion's subcommander said, "And I suppose I'll get dressed."

"We'd appreciate that, Andri," Lon called after her as she left. He picked Lina up in his arms and kissed her. She didn't resist in the least.

Between kisses, she did manage to say, "Lon, you better straighten up. I don't want people to say you were drunk when we got married. It might not look good."

He laughed. "You can't get me drunk. It's impossible. But I'll behave, Carolina, ma'am."

"Good. Now let's get this over with before I faint or throw up or something. I don't want the tape of this to make it on *Funniest Home Videos*."

"Nervous?"

"As hell. How about you?"

"*Pas du tout*. This feels right all the way." He was suddenly very serious. He let her down and held her close. "Now, really, are you okay with this? Jae… Jae did bring up some valid points."

She looked into his warm eyes and took a breath. "I'm game if you are. Now and forever. Let's do it."

That slow and dazzling smile of his! "It's going to be rough at first, kitten. There's going to be a lot of media attention on this."

"Oh, Lon, does there have to be? Do we even have to announce? I mean, to the media? To our friends, fine."

"Ashamed of me?"

"Londo–!"

"Yes, dearest love, we have to announce. You don't have any idea how people are always trying to set me up or put me on those damned most eligible bachelors lists. I want to rub it into some people's faces that I'm marrying the most beautiful, most amazing girl on Earzh. And I want all of your suitors to know that you're taken."

"I don't have any suitors. Just one absolutely crazy fiancé."

"And I think you haven't been looking at your life clearly. You probably have hundreds of men following you with their tongues hanging out. You never even noticed."

"And you have the world's biggest imagination." She smiled at him. Such a wonderful face. Such a wonderful soul. "Ohmigosh," she realized. "We're getting married!"

That stopped him. "Ohmigosh," he said, too, his eyes open wide. Then they narrowed with mischief.

"What?" she asked him. "Oh no, Londo, you're not doing this just for the shock value."

"You should know better than that, soulmate. It just occurred to me that this situation raises the potential for a lot of, shall we say, rightful repayment for some things. Merely in a humorous way." He rubbed her back as he smiled to himself. "Ah, the fine art of the practical joke. Let me strategize for a while."

"A quiet marriage, Londo. Let's not get anyone mad at us."

"A quietly wild marriage, Lina. We'll have such fun. And we'll go everywhere together."

"I'm not comfortable in public."

"That's because you were afraid before." He hugged her tightly. "You aren't afraid if I'm here, are you?"

"No," she whispered. "I'm not afraid. But Lon, do you really think–"

He put his index finger on her nose. "No arguing with team leader," he ordered.

She grimaced at him. "Team leader is fine when you're doing your Valiant thing," she told him, "but this is something else entirely. Eventually, Londo Rand, you are going to have to compromise."

"Com-pro-mise." He tasted the word as if he'd never heard it before.

"I'm serious. I'm not going out there and pledging myself to obey you. This isn't the nineteenth century."

"Actually, it's the thirty-fifth," Londo said, looking around. "Here, at least."

"Londo."

"Compromise." He appeared to consider. At length.

"Londo."

"*D'accord*, we'll try it. But if I don't like it, I reserve the right to change my mind."

"Seven cats."

"Seven cats, check."

"Pornographer."

He groaned. "How about we just pass you off as an artist? Until everyone gets used to you?"

"Is it really going to cause that much of a problem?"

"Maybe if you keep at it. But you hate the job, right?"

"Darling, I was going to quit anyway. Really I was. That's what the whole vacation was about, the first step in getting away."

"Then how the hell is it going to be a problem?" He stopped as a sudden thought hit him. "Your employee discount is still in effect until you quit, right?"

She chuckled. "They've probably fired me by now."

"Let's hope not. *Voyons.* The headlines will read: 'Valiant Weds Porno Queen.'"

"Oh shoo. Headlines?" Once again, the fact that he was Valiant struck her and she wrung her hands.

"*Chérie*, that's who I am. Marry me for that as well." He paused. "Two kids, plus."

She started to say something, then nodded. "Two kids," she agreed.

"Plus."

"To be negotiated. Not guaranteed."

He considered and grunted his approval.

"Oh, Londo, you don't smoke, do you?"

"Horrible habit– never. You don't smoke, don't drink, no drugs…" His forehead creased as he tried to remember what he'd felt of her mind. "Right?"

"Right."

"PC or Mac?"

"Mayonnaise or Miracle Whip?"

"Paper or plastic?"

They went through a list of life's important choices, each satisfied with the other's answer until they got to: "Artificial or real Christmas tree?"

"Artific–"

"Aw, Lie–"

"Now, Londo, why should anyone kill a beautiful tree just for a couple weeks of–"

"Okay, okay, we'll talk about it some more. When the time comes." He chuckled her under the chin.

She beamed up at him. "Our first Christmas," she said, visualizing them still together months from now.

"Lots and lots of Christmases," Lon assured her as he shared the vision of them together always. Then he grew serious. "Lina…I have to tell you something."

"What?" He was so solemn-looking!

"Jae was… Jae…" As he was trying to get it out, Lon saw movement across the room. "Later," he told her quickly. "When we have more privacy. We'll cover it at our lunch, *d'accord*?"

"Whatever you say, honeybear."

Wilder was getting up from the personal consoles, turning to look at them. "Have you changed your minds? Or did you have some more special effects stored up that you want to show me?"

"We have not changed our minds," Londo replied with a sniff. "Puter, Lina O'Kelly is my guest. I vouch for security for her." Two beeps. "Come, wife-to-be; you've been stuck in this messy old lab for too long."

He took Lina's hand and gave her a mental picture of a corridor many floors below them. One minute later they ported out into Mega-Legion Headquarters.

*Your Presence is
Cordially Requested
at the Wedding of*

*Alpha Team Leader
Londo Falcon (Valiant) Rand
and
Ms. Carolina Angelina O'Kelly*

*Affiliated Systems
Megaforce Legion Headquarters*

Sarastor

The port meant that they arrived before anyone else except Jae. From a darkened hall double doors opened at their approach, and they stepped into Technicolor as a brilliant, rolling expanse of deep summer bloomed before them.

Someone had found a meadow, surrounded it with a distant forest, placed it under an afternoon sun… and set it in the middle of Mega-Legion HQ. Lina knew it couldn't be real. But it was.

The breeze was fresh and infused with the essence of warm grasses. The colors were just off Earth-normal, all under a green firmament. Jae stood nearby, his back to them as he studiously watched a circular white rostrum appear in the middle of the meadow. It then began to grow a perimeter of four slender columns.

He turned at their approach and dusted off his hands as if he'd just finished all the landscaping with a trowel. "Is this appropriate?" he asked.

"It's beautiful," Lina breathed. "Was this…Feith?"

Jae gave the sad ghost of a smile. "A little fancied up, but yes, this was Feith."

Lon looked at Lina in amazement. "You understand VR rooms?"

"I thought I might not, but I know a holosuite when I see one."

"Holosuite. I like that." Lon addressed the marble that hovered overhead. "Translator, from now on erase 'VR room' and substitute 'holosuite.'" It double-beeped acceptance. "Jae, this is perfect, thanks. Does this mean a Feithi ceremony?"

"I thought I might give it a try– if that's what you want."

"What other kind would we have in here, with you as the minister? This will make it even more special."

That obviously pleased Jae. "Open-air is all right? I remember Hal's wedding."

"This is much better. His was, ah, irregular."

Jae looked around, checking the perfection of his creation. "It will be informal but completely legal by Feithi custom. I don't know Terran law."

"It'll hold up there," Lon said for Lina's benefit. "There's precedent."

Lina breathed a sigh of relief at that. "Thank heaven. I don't think I could go through this again."

"Are there any Terran traditions that you want mixed in?" Jae asked.

Lina glanced toward the door, camouflaged as a tree leaning on another one. Through the gap in the middle came Wiley in a clean and surprisingly tailored yellow lab coat along with three other people in parahero costumes.

"It's traditional on Earth for wedding guests to be naked," Londo said loud enough so they could hear him. One of the costumed people opened his mouth as if to say something, though nothing came out. The other two looked at each other, then at Londo.

"Right." Wiley drew out the word until it whined.

Lina half-turned to Jae as if she were speaking with him. Amid all this unreality and freedom from the lab she felt completely silly. "It's to honor the fertility of the couple," she said, matching Londo in volume. "It makes the transition to the post-ceremonial orgy easier, too."

Jae began to lift his stole over his head. "Does the minister also get naked?" he asked.

"He leads the orgy," Londo announced.

"They're kidding," Wiley explained to his companions as the three on the podium frowned at him. "Strange Terran humor."

"*Eh bien*, if you're going to be so prudish, we don't want to see what you have under there! Go clothed for all we care!" Londo gave them a dismissing wave of both hands and then imperiously crossed his arms in front of himself. "Wimps!" He turned his back on them. "Are they getting undressed yet?" He grinned at Jae.

Jae still held his stole in mid-air. "No," he reported. "So much for the wedding of the year. No, of the decade. That would have gotten you some real publicity, Lon."

"*Pas mal*. Too bad."

"Real Terran traditions. What do you want?" Jae settled the stole back into place.

Lina watched a swarm of topaz insects making their way across the wondrous landscape like traveling baubles of stained glass. All this for them. They shouldn't ask for any more.

But Londo beat her to it. "No, Jae, no Terran accouterments. I'm not sure how far we can stray from the Feithi ceremony and have it hold up on Earzh. An off-world marriage has to be the traditional form of the alien civilization involved."

Two distinct spots of light in the sky caught Lina's eye: tiny moons. She gave a sigh. She'd almost been convinced it was Earth on a greener day than usual. So pretty, but odd. If only…

"What, *chérie*?"

"Nothing."

Londo squeezed her hand. "C'mon, Lina."

"Oh, Londo, this is fine. More than fine; it's gorgeous."

Londo glanced at Jae. "You are not going to hurt Jae's feelings. Jae?"

"Depends on what kind of changes she wants."

"Lina?"

"It's just that, um, back home it's spring."

Lon nodded. "Slush in the streets, icicles melting off the roofs."

"No, really spring. We're jumping so fast into this. It's a shame that we've jumped all the way into summer as well. When I left the trees were just starting to bud. My daffodils and crocus were blooming."

"Spring okay with you, Jae?"

Jae turned around in a circle and scratched his neck thoughtfully as he perused his work. "Puter, change scene to springtime," he said.

As he talked specifics to the program and waved his hands in that conductor-like way people communicated with electronics, Lon told Lina, "See? It's okay to ask for what you want."

"But he was so kind to do it in the first place. I didn't want him to think I didn't– Oh."

The landscape changed like a cloud lifting. Thousands of shades of early greens washed the surrounding forested hills. Nearby small groups of trees covered themselves in glorious, full blossom. Wildflowers ran riot in the meadow in all the colors of the rainbow.

"Oh my," was all Lina could say.

Garlands of flowers cascaded over the tops of the columns trailing white and pink ribbons that danced in the slight breeze. An occasional petal floated through the air. Lina pulled on Lon's sleeve and pointed out the changes so he too could admire each nuance.

"Yes, I think he's been hiding a talent for landscaping from us," Lon said. "Very nice. Thanks, Jae."

Then Lina heard another sound of approval and realized it came from the growing audience. There must be three dozen people here. A handful of sleepy children gazed at the landscape as if still dreaming. These strangely-dressed adults weren't just paraheroes, they were part of families that happened to contain heroes like Londo.

Slipping his arm around Lina's waist, Lon held out his left hand to the air. "Puter, give me a large bouquet of flowers. Match in general the kind the bride's already wearing, but larger blossoms, long stems. A ribbon wrapped around them to match the ones on the columns." A bundle appeared in his hand and he presented it to her.

Lina held the flower illusion to her nose. It smelled of fresh rain with a dash of honeysuckle. "It's almost too beautiful now."

"I can tone it down," Jae offered.

"No!" Lina blurted. "Sometimes you want a little excess. Isn't that right, Lon?"

"Excess is good," he said gravely. "But I don't think this is too excessive."

"It's excessively romantic," Lina sighed. She held her bouquet tightly to herself, not believing yet. This was a dream, or maybe a TV program, and she was an actress playing a part next to the world's most wonderful, most exciting man.

But no, this was real, this was now, this was Lon and her forever. A miracle. "Can we get started? My nerves are going to kick in soon."

Jae studied the growing crowd who milled about on the grassy slope rising beyond them. "Let's wait a few more minutes. You don't want to deprive everybody of Valiant's wedding, do you?"

She'd done it again. Lina hung her head. "I'm sorry. I keep forgetting who he is, Valiant-wise."

This was historical. And more important even than that–

The bouquet bobbing dangerously, Lina grabbed Lon's lapels. "Photographer!" She was going to say more but Lon gently detached her.

"Done," he said as he clasped her free hand between his. "We're recording already."

Behind his back, Jae motioned the computer to begin doing so.

"Good." Lina breathed a sigh of relief. "I'll need to watch this once it's all over. To see how it went." Her face softened as she gazed at Lon. "To watch you."

Lon nodded. "To show our grandchildren." He gave a modest shrug. "And the world." Then he grimaced. "And Hal."

Automatically Lon reached for a pocket he didn't have. "Jae?" he asked instead.

Jae patted himself down, but either found no pockets or whatever was supposed to be in pockets. He gestured to the front row of the crowd. "Wiley. A moment."

Wilder stepped up and the three men conferred over a pocket device Wiley produced. Then he resumed his position and Londo turned to Lina. "No word from Hal yet. He's going to miss this after all."

He rubbed his nose harder than Lina had ever seen him do, his mouth grim. "Can't be helped," he finally decided. "Papa Mike and Mama Ruth. Chim. And–"

Lina squeezed his hand and he nodded. He told her, "We'll throw a huge party later with everyone. My friends, yours, and any family you want to include. We might even invite some of this bunch back." A sideways nod indicated the meadow's occupants.

There must be well over two hundred here. Lina tried not to think of them, turned away…and something glittered on Jae's stole.

"What is that?" she asked.

Jae looked down and touched the decoration. A downward-pointing triangle balanced on a horizontal line set upon a circle. It was embroidered in metallic gold on the stole's left shoulder.

"How about that?" he said. "That's the symbol of the spiritual order I belong to. Interesting that– Whoever– included it." He raised the stole's edge and revealed the same symbol underneath, embroidered on his tunic.

A sense of expectation filled her as Lina looked down at her own dress. There it was, the same symbol. "Because," she said as she lifted her necklace to show him. The symbol was a subtle part of the linkwork on the left. "That's the symbol of the order I belong to. An order that supposedly only exists on Earth. The Order of–"

"Uriel," they both said together. Jae's mouth opened and closed.

"Londo," Lina announced, "I am going to faint. Catch me." She raised her arms to either side to make it easier for him.

Lon smoothed a tendril of her hair though he remained alert for wobbling. "No you won't. You'll be great. This is a day for miracles."

Jae scratched himself thoughtfully behind his right shoulder. Finally he said, "Yeah. Let's get started."

He adjusted his stole but Lon gave it a perfecting tweak. As Jae walked toward the dais Londo took formal parade hold of Lina's arm.

"Wait," he decided, and switched sides so he was on her right. From there he took her other arm and patted it. "A bit of Terran tradition no one will object to."

"You're sure about this?"

"Absolutely legal, *chérie*. Ah, here we go."

The crowd quieted. "Good morning," Jae told them. "Very, very early morning." His voice carried throughout the area. His attitude was easy as if he'd rehearsed this.

"I'm so glad you could join us on this special occasion. Legionnaires, families and friends– Most of us have seen some odd things in our time, strange and wonderful things. We've had some pretty odd things happening here for the past couple days and some very strange things took place just a little while ago. And now we have a wonderful thing. Our good friend, Valiant– Londo Rand– is getting married."

People applauded as Londo led Lina to center stage. Despite knowing that Lina was so nervous, Lon would never have guessed it. She walked gracefully, with a peaceful presence that calmed even him. She had made a jump of faith for him, and now she strode steadfastly on her new path.

Jae's next statement was lost on him because he was admiring the way she looked: like a bride. His bride. And the trusting way she gazed at him made him want to take her into his arms. She felt so good in his arms.

Pay *attention, Londo, you handsome devil.*

With a smile he did so.

Jae spoke of the universal consciousness creating new groups of souls that would be linked through eternity, and of the just-discovered fact that here indeed were two of those, together at last in incarnated form. He called upon the entire cosmos, created and uncreated, to witness the marriage and strengthen it through time.

As if an invisible curtain were drawing back, a long, draped table appeared in front of them with three plates of foods and a rough pottery jug. Pouring from the jug into a low, almost flat bowl with handles, Jae offered it first to Lon and then to Lina. He told them that this was the sweet wine of desire and good fortune.

Lina sniffed and made a face over it. "Ew, it's real."

"She doesn't like alcohol," Lon whispered to Jae.

"This much won't kill her."

Then they went on to the other things: pressing a fingertip dusted with salt on each other's tongues, chewing on bitter herbs, eating a sour wafer. Then once more the wine, which Lina stoically drank without comment.

"The cycles of life include all of life's experiences," Jae told them and the crowd. Every now and then his eyes would flicker to the left. Lina was sure that one of those invisible computer screens hung in the air so only he could see. It probably held the traditional script for the wedding.

"All things come around again. Now you are required to face everything, that which you deem good and that which you deem bad, together."

He picked up a pink spool of ribbon and gave one end of it to Lon. Lina received the end of what was on a white spool. Then Jae walked around the couple, intertwining the spools and passing the thick ribbons through each other in lavish falls of color that sparked in multicolored speckles whenever they touched and as they gathered on the ground.

"Is this strict tradition?" Londo asked out of the side of his mouth as Jae circled behind.

"Absolutely." Unbeknownst to them at first, Jae spread his arms to the crowd for attention and began to juggle the ribbons high into the air, which evoked a fireworks of sparks and audience applause. Jae stuck a silly one-legged pose to his left and juggled. Then a pose to his right and juggled some more. To the crowd's delight, he kicked a ribbon into the air with his left heel.

Lon looked at Lina, who held one hand over her mouth so she wouldn't laugh, and then decided to give Jae a doubtful look. "Traditional?" he asked.

"Traditionally informal. Life is not a serious affair."

With that the two balls of ribbon popped back into Jae's waiting hands and he returned to the business of knotting. He finally came to a stop in front of the two and handed the ends to them, keeping a length in his own hands.

"Marriage," he announced, "unites you both. It is a mystery of life, the two who become one." He yanked at both ribbons and with a magical sparkle spray all knots fell away, leaving one long straight ribbon in Lon and Lina's hands– a ribbon that was just one now, pink with white stripes.

For a moment Lina wondered if she should applaud like the rest of the spectators. Londo certainly had a twinkle in his eye at which Jae wrinkled his nose in triumph.

"But never forget," Jae continued in solemn tones as the audience quieted, "that you are individuals, and acting as individuals, you need to work at mastering this unity every day."

His gaze targeted Lina's face. "Now you sing to Londo."

"Uh. Say what?"

Jae nodded encouragement. "A song that reveals your heart."

"Jae," Lon warned. "This has to be traditional."

"Absolutely. One hundred percent."

"*A cappella*?" Lina whispered.

Jae listened to the translation for the phrase, which seemed to go on for some time.

"If this is so informal," Londo told her in low tones, "you don't have to do it."

"*A cappella*," Jae finally decided, pronouncing the words in English, or rather Italian. He stood expectantly.

Lina blinked at him.

"A little warning would have been nice," Londo growled his friend.

Jae shrugged. "If you want to skip this most important–"

"*When you're weary*," Lina murmured.

"– step, you…" Jae's words trailed off.

Lina turned to look Londo fully in the face. "*Feeling small*," she sang in a tiny voice.

As her gaze moved over his features, finally settling on his eyes, her voice became stronger, more sure. With her song she pledged that she would stand behind and beside him always, a bridge over the troubled waters of life.

When her last note subsided, Lon stood staring at her. With a slight jerk he woke from his trance. "I do," he said. "I do, I do!"

Lina squeezed his hand. "I do too, honey, but I think that's a Terran tradition."

Lon grinned at her. "Didn't I say she was something, Jae? That was beautiful, *chérie*. I can't–"

"Your turn, Londo."

"I uh I…" It was Lon's turn to blink at Jae. "Oh. Right. *Crisse de calisse de tabarnak*, Jae–"

"Londo!" Lina squeaked. "I don't know exactly what you just said, but I don't think it was something you should say at a wedding. Particularly your own."

Lon winced. "Sorry. But d–" He cut the curse short and grimaced mightily. "You could have told us, Jae."

"Didn't think you'd play along."

"We should have had a rehearsal," Lina admonished the both of them.

Lon nodded. "With a rehearsal dinner afterward. Anyone else hungry?"

"Song, Londo. Now."

A rare look of panic washed across Lon's face and Jae let him stand there silently for a long minute. Finally Lon nodded, turned to Lina and took her left hand between his.

There must have been excellent amplification in this meadow, for the wedding party could clearly hear even the back rows of the audience as they laughed in expectation at Mega-Legionnaire Valiant singing like a barbarian. But his voice came strong and baritone.

"*I'll be the hero you've been dreaming of,*" he pledged to her and sang that he'd always love her, never leave her.

A tiny part of the very back of Lina's brain hoped that her smile wasn't too big, too dopey, before it gave in to the rest of her and melted at Valiant publicly singing a love song for her. He would always be her hero! "I do," she told him after he'd finished.

"See that you do." He breathed a sigh of relief and stopped himself from looking around to measure how the audience had taken it.

"Repeat after me," Jae instructed. He was plainly reading from some invisible cheat-sheet. In turn they took their vows:

"I promise to love and cherish you in heart, mind and body through the cycles of time and fortune's wheel. I promise to help you face the challenges of life, to aid you in leaving the universe a better place for having been here, and to better enable you to see the spark of God that lies within you."

As the last syllable faded across the meadow, Jae whirled around, one arm outstretched with pointing finger. A golden glow followed it, hanging in the air and enlarging until it encapsulated the three of them like a cocoon.

Jae lifted a fist. "Let the universe hear," he commanded. Somewhere a gong sounded. "Let the universe recognize this couple, forever united. What do you give each other to signify this–"

"Forever?!" a voice bellowed from the audience.

Lina's shoulders constricted in dismay.

Stoan strode on stage. "What's this about forever?" he demanded of the two of them, then of Jae.

Jae stood calmly as the golden glow dissipated. "Feithi marriages are eternal," he said.

"Not 'until death do us part'?" Londo asked.

Jae gave him a stern look. "Beyond death."

"Eternity?" Lon considered and then broke into a smile for Lina. "I believe that's what we agreed to an hour or so ago."

He was wonderful. Lina almost glowed as she gazed at him. "Yes, we did. Eternity will do just fine. Or at least until the stars pass away."

"Longer than that," Lon assured her. He gathered Lina close to him and turned to Jae expectantly.

Stoan put a hand on Lon's shoulder and the other hand on Jae's, trying to separate them. Only Jae could be moved. Lon of course was Valiant.

"Stop the wedding," Stoan commanded.

"Vows have been made," Jae said.

Stoan growled, "Vows can be un-made."

"If you lack civilized ethics." And then he quite pointedly called Stoan, "Barbarian."

The audience collectively inhaled.

Suddenly Jae struck Lina as being so very alien, so...*different*. On a much higher vibration than anyone else here. Despite his youth he was ancient in some way, and wise beyond reckoning. In some invisible fashion he towered above them all.

She blinked. Jae? But the image held.

Feithi, Lon told her but there was awe in his thoughts as well.

The Last Feithi faced down the Affiliated Systems neanderthal.

The Legion commander had to speak from between gritted teeth. "We do not do permanent marriages. Give us a contract marriage, Jae."

Jae opened his mouth to reply, but Londo turned to his leader. "On Earth marriages are lifetime contracts. Jae's is merely a bit longer than that."

"It's–" Stoan sputtered.

"Even the Legion doesn't have jurisdiction over us after we die," Lon said lightly. "Lifetime or beyond, we are willing."

"No. We must have time to investigate."

Jae sighed. "There is–"

Everyone turned to look at him. He gave Lon and Lina an apologetic look. "You two are young for a Feithi marriage. There was an out if people were under age..." His eyes looked up and to the right in memory. "Fifty or so. Early marriages were not encouraged."

Lina started to say something but Jae waved her down.

"They were allowed. But there was a provision, an annulment period. I think there was something like six months' time that the couple had to back out of the marriage honorably. Youthful indiscretion could be a valid excuse."

"Mem-Bazer!" Stoan barked.

"Checking now," Wiley said from the audience. Lina turned around at his snort to see what he was up to. Studying those invisible monitors of his, it seemed.

"Jae?" Wiley looked up. "Release."

With a sigh, Jae made a few motions to the air to signal the computer system. "Only duo marriage legalities," he told it, and Wiley turned with renewed interest to his screens.

"Jae has censored specific information about Feith on the Nets," Londo quietly explained to Lina. Before she could ask, Lon added, "Since he's the last survivor, technically he owns all things Feithi, including information."

Lina's mouth formed an "O" just as Wiley said, "Got it. Yes, yes… Yes, Commander. Marriage partners under age 60…which would be about 57 in Sarastoran years, and ah, 62 or 63 in Terran years… Half a year trial period to test the marriage. Annulment accomplished by simple verbal and written decree of a priest. Oh, interesting." Wiley looked up at them. "By 'written,' it says that the decree can be handwritten and affixed to a wall in a public forum if need be. Web posting is optional."

"Half a year," Stoan mused as he rubbed his chin between thumb and forefinger. With a grimace he nodded at Londo. "We'll give it five days for our secrecy period. You have five months more to get out of it altogether."

And then he had the nerve to sneer sourly at Lina. She felt herself flush in rage that he would interrupt such a holy service, that he'd dare to come between Londo and her!

Jae waved Stoan away with the tips of his fingers. Stoan stayed for a beat, just to show them who was boss, and then retreated into the audience where he stood glowering.

Jae closed his eyes and took a deep breath. He let it out in a whoosh and then regained his normal posture. "Where was I?" he asked the two of them.

Lina blinked. Wedding again. Wedding again! She broke out in a smile. "There was a gold swash," she said, imitating Jae setting it, "and sound effects."

Jae bobbed his head from side to side as he looked to his left and silently mouthed bits and pieces of what he read in the air. "Ah," he finally announced. "Here we are."

Again he set the golden glow. Again the gong sounded. It was funny, Lina thought, how that gong seemed to cement the occasion by vibrating through them all.

"Yeah," Lon whispered to her.

"Let the universe recognize this couple, forever united," Jae announced. "What do you give each other to signify your commitment within this lifetime? A symbol. It must be physical and unchanging," Jae prompted.

"A ring?"

Jae beamed at his friend. "Yes. Perfect. That's right; Hal had rings at his wedding. Where're your rings?"

"Uh oh," Lina said. She looked at Lon and he looked back blankly– maybe a trifle hysterical. No, he was just flustered. Lon didn't get hysterical. Yet there was a wild look in his eyes.

"Rings?" The edge of the word squeaked. Just a bit. He cleared his throat. "Computer, let's have–"

"Real rings, Londo," Jae said. "They can't disappear when we leave the room. These must be permanent–"

"Oops," Lina said. She held out her hand. On it lay a beautiful, large gold ring.

Lon opened up his clenched palm. There sat a smaller version.

"It wasn't me," Lina said defiantly before Stoan could accuse her. She turned the ring this way and that. The band was sculpted as entwined vines. A large diamond sat snugly in the center of a crest or seal made up of a starburst that held a circle that held a triangle.

When she looked at Londo's ring, it was the same except that the stone was green. It was breathtaking. "Emerald?" she asked him.

He peered at it. "Diamond," he said. "This metal doesn't look normal."

"Why should it?" Jae asked.

"Starburst, circle, triangle," Lina breathed. She caught Lon's eye and he cocked his head at her. These were the symbols that Lina had seen back on the island, a message from her guides.

"Are *they* behind this?" Lon asked.

Slowly Lina shook her head. "I think it was a relayed message. From Whoever it was with all the stars."

Lon nodded. "Makes sense to me." Stiffly he turned his back on his commander's glare, faced Jae, and said, "Jae, pray continue with the ceremony."

Jae patted the air down in a circle in front of him. "Calm down, calm down, everyone," he told the muttering audience. "Just a little miracle in the midst of things. Nothing to get excited about. Let's go on.

"These rings act as a physical anchor and reminder of your vows. Put the ring on her finger, Londo, and repeat after me: This ring is a material symbol of my vows to you and commitment to any children resulting from our union in this lifetime. Wear it and remember."

Did the universe always do things like this for soulmates? Londo would ask Lina later. He slid the ring on her trembling finger and repeated the words.

She licked her lips at the totality of the import. She was getting married. This faerie ring sealed her to Londo forever. His fingers held her hand in his and a slow smile came to his face. **With this ring, I thee wed,** he whispered to her.

He held his left hand out for her and she slid his ring over his knuckles. "This ring is a material symbol of my vows to you and commitment to any children resulting from our union in this lifetime. Wear it and remember." **With this ring I promise I'll always love you.**

"By your vows and by the symbols you wear," Jae intoned, "you show the universe that you are united for all eternity. Now turn and face these people."

Lina and Lon turned, his hand around her waist, and Lina gazed out at the veritable sea of guests of all ages, strangers to her, then back at Lon.

This was his world, and now she was a part of it. Forever. There would be no more hiding two steps back from reality. From now on she would have to summon the courage to deal with life as the cosmos dished it out. As wife to Valiant she would have to do so with her head held high.

Jae held his arms out wide. "Who here bears witness to this marriage?"

"I DO!" The audience cried as one. Some of the younger children laughed and clapped their hands at the sudden roar that they were able to participate in. Why did Lina's gaze go to where Stoan stood silent with arms crossed?

Jae nodded. "Let the record so show. Now, witnesses: behold husband and wife!" He was about to say something else when Lon raised his hand in a stopping gesture.

"Terran tradition," Londo announced. "Just one won't harm anything at this point. There is a sealing of the marriage contract."

"Uh oh, here comes the orgy," someone in the audience stage-whispered a little too loudly.

Londo pointed a warning at them and then turned to take Lina in his arms for a quick kiss. He went back for another much longer one, silently promising many more later. "*Now* it's official," he declared for the cheering crowd.

Epilogue

The Four spoke to each other quietly, despite the fact that they were many, many parsecs apart. One was farther even than that. Her voice was a whisper, but if the others were still enough they could hear it. Another, though, was not in the mood to be calm.

****The pot has finally begun to boil. At last! I cannot wait much longer!**** Aldierra was always anxious these days.

I thought for a while that things would fall apart. I thought we'd have to settle for lesser choices.

Hal would not be such a lesser choice if something were to happen to Londo.

I prefer Londo. I was relieved when he chose to return to physical life. He fits in much better than Hal could. He is the magnet around which things are attracted.

But Lina is the heart of the matter. She will gather more than the other two can ever hope.

***At least we have the three coming together now. Finally! I want to push them, to shove them, to make sure they– ***

Patience, Aldierra, the whisper said. ***I realize you are frustrated now, but you must have patience. Keep in mind that this is bigger than you, although we all hope it will help your situation, or at least resolve it once and for all. Remember: together the three will gather the billions– the trillions or more if things go well. They will change the course of the galaxy if they pass all their tests. And if they trust their hearts. They will work for you, but the larger picture is that they will work for all, for us and all our sisters.***

They considered that. Sarastor asked, ***Is there a way to avoid this coming death? She still has a few lessons that could be learned in this lifetime.***

It is a part of the plan. This will be the death that signals the birth of the Three Worlds. It is necessary. She is needed more on the Other Side now to guide and foster than she is in the incarnated world. There will be other lifetimes to learn her lessons.

She has agreed?

She does not know, but she has agreed since before she was born. If the elements were in place, this would be the time for her to shift. All has been set in proper motion. Now we sit back and let things ripen. Not long. This is the cusp when decisions and chance tighten into a knot to anchor a new path.

I confess that even after all these billions of years, these next few days will seem a long time.

You have always been impatient. When you are old like me, you will understand.

Feith, I don't think I will ever fully understand you.

Sweet Earth, we are all destined to perfection. You will understand everything someday.

Illustration by Colleen Doran. Copyright the artist.

Don't miss the next chapter in the Three Worlds saga...

Lost in the Stars

Three Worlds vol. 2

by Carol A. Strickland

"Carolina O'Kelly Rand, you are under arrest for suspicion of mind control. You'll have to come with me," Jae Rallene told her in a strange, tight voice.

"A-arrest?" Lina asked. She stared up at the so-tall Legionnaire with the startlingly beautiful face. Her head was still whirling from the events of this night. Now this?

She clutched the abundant white lace of her wedding dress because she didn't know how else to hide her shaking hands. Londo wasn't here now to protect her. Londo and all the other Mega-Legionnaires had been called away from his own wedding reception for an emergency, to rescue a wrecked hyperspace ship.

Jae grimaced as he ran his hand through the mop of sun-gold hair that framed his head and shoulders. For a moment the points of his elf-like ears showed and then were covered again.

"Look, Lina, the commander didn't specify that you were to be put in a holding cell. I'm going to declare you under house arrest, and I'll define what that house is. I'm your confinement officer; that means that whatever I say you take as an order."

She gave a dazed nod at the best friend of her new husband. She should have been expecting something like this the moment the four of them got out of quarantine. Stupid of her not to.

But everything was topsy-turvy now. House arrest? She had a faint idea of what that entailed on Earth, but here– a far-flung world totally unknown to her, with a technology beyond her imagination– what did that mean?

Mind control had to be a major crime, possibly on terrorist level. Did they have lawyers Out Here? And if so, how would she contact one?

Londo would know, but Lon wasn't here.

Leave it to sour Stoan Kinrol, the Mega-Legion's commander, to railroad a charge like this against her. No one Out Here would believe she, the Terran witch-doctor, was innocent, would they? To them Terrans were barbarians– except for Londo, the most powerful being this side of forever.

Jae lifted the minister's stole that he had worn to officiate at the wedding. He regarded it a moment, then folded it into a black square and tucked it under his arm.

"I suppose this last miracle was asking for too much." Lina tried to smile bravely about her minutes-old marriage, but had to hide her trembling mouth with her hand.

The holosuite's walls echoed Jae's words now that it stood empty and colorless: "Central command is being transferred to Lab 1-A. That's standard procedure with a skeleton staff. Wiley hardly ever goes on missions with the rest of us. He's in charge now."

"Wiley?" Dr. Wilder Mem-Bazer was both a theoretical and practical physicist– with five minds in one body.

"He's not just Wiley; he's a high-ranking Legionnaire. Think of him as a major when it comes to these situations." The marble that floated next to Lina translated the position as well as the rest of Jae's sentences into English.

At Lina's jerky nod Jae added, "All you have to do is stay in the lab under watch until everyone gets back. We'll need to run a few tests, ask you a few questions. If we get a quorum in the meantime, don't worry. You won't be going into any cell. If I'm called away, you will stay with Wiley, is that clear?"

"Yes. Thank–" Her voice broke and she whirled from him, tears erupting. She was alone. She wanted Londo! He'd make everything all right again.

Londo was a brand-new telepath. The power had likely catalyzed by her mind-talking with him so much in the past few days. It hadn't occurred to him to warn her about the silence of hyperspace, but when he'd entered it, flying under his own power, it had been as if her insides had been sucked out, trying to follow him to wherever he was bound. She couldn't find him anywhere.

Where had all this helplessness come from? When had she stopped being her own person and started relying on Londo instead? In her entire life she'd made her own way in the world. Now why was she clinging to a husband for what she should be providing herself?

She wasn't going to put that burden on Lon. He was the famous Valiant, after all; he had enough problems to deal with.

Embarrassed to weep in front of Londo's friend, she fought for control. A loudly voiced sob. She couldn't choke it down and it echoed in this auditorium. "I'm sorry," she managed to say. She sniffled her way to a semblance of order and held her hands over her face, breathing purposefully to get rid of the redness and puffiness that must be there. "I seem to... I don't seem to be–" she sniffed– "in control of my emotions these days. Give me a minute, please."

"Sure," she thought Jae said.

God, what he must think of her. He'd warned Londo before they got married, hadn't he? He'd told Londo that she was a weakness he didn't need, a target for his enemies. He'd told her that Londo needed to explain the situation to her before they got married. But Lon had convinced Jae to officiate at the wedding. Didn't that mean that Jae approved of her, even a little?

With a shake, she straightened herself. Being wife to the great mega-parahero Valiant meant that she couldn't allow her actions to detract from his reputation. "I'm sorry," she repeated, but now she turned around to face Jae. "It won't happen again. It's just... everything at once."

Now she blinked not to get rid of tears, but because they were back in Wiley's warehouse-sized laboratory– or rather, in the little break room just off the entrance to it. She hadn't ported. They'd accused her of teleporting to arrange the strange things that had been happening lately, but it hadn't been her and her new power of interstellar teleportation. "How–?"

"You knew we had our own intra-planetary transporters," Jae gave her a small smile that might have tried to be encouraging. Obviously he was uneasy around females on a crying jag. "I just saved us a trip. You okay now? You look all right. A little red around the nose."

"No, I'm fine." A snuffle betrayed her. "How does this house arrest work? Do you need to get my fingerprints or a-anything? Do I get to call a lawyer?"

"No. Come on," Jae told her brusquely. "There might be time to see the last off. Watch the dress."

He strode away from her. Lina grabbed on to the lace train of her wedding gown to make sure that it didn't sweep across machinery or into any of the boxy experiment stations here in the main lab. It was the size of a warehouse and dim, most of the front third gridded with enclosed tables that contained a variety of monitored experiments. In the past few days she and Lon had benefited from medical stations Wiley had rigged. Jae had set up a shooting gallery along the far wall to while away quarantine.

It looked like *Hoarders* could shoot a full season of episodes with the piles that took up the place. In the far reaches of the lab equipment the size of cement trucks sat buried amongst the flotsam.

Unfortunately, Lon's minutes-long death throes two days ago had created an indoor hurricane, from which the warehouse's automatic cleaners were still trying to recover.

She followed Jae to the central data desk where Dr. Wilder Mem-Bazer had already settled.

The aqua-skinned genius with the subdued brush of violet hair was talking to a 3-D screen hanging in the air. "Systems are checking in full blue. I've got you cleared for hyperspace insertion coordinates EF-679-45. Three minutes."

"Right." It was golden Aiko herself, known as the hero Orenya, who filled most of the screen, with the hint of a person or two behind her. She was in love with Lon, who'd neglected to ease her into a breakup. He'd proposed to Lina before he'd told Aiko what was going on– only hours ago.

Aiko still held her courageous, cover-up smile from the wedding. And there was something odd…

"Coordinates noted," she said as she checked her subscreens. "Time marked. All other Legion passenger ships are clicking out of comm range. There goes the hospital ship, mark. Robot drones are checking in; I'm giving them the go-ahead now. Time for us, I suppose. We'll see you in about four or five days, Wiley. Oh– there's the bride herself."

Aiko nodded to Lina. "Congratulations again. Sorry we have to take him away from you for a while. On my world we have a saying: 'Dark start, bright finish.' We'll continue that party when we all get back. He'll be fine; don't worry."

"Thank you." Lina tried to bring up a genuine smile, but her very bones quaked in horror. "Good luck to you all."

"We don't need luck; we are the Legion. Take care of business, Wiley. Jae. Hyperspace insertion mode commencing. Fallow out." The screen blanked.

Fighting back a scream, Lina turned quickly from the screen. She clapped both hands to her mouth and then realized that Jae was still staring at the space in the air where the screen had been. His almond-brown skin had gone pale.

"You saw it too," she accused him. Her speech diffused the scream that wanted to explode from her. Wilder caught the words and turned toward the two of them.

"What's the matter with you? I can understand Lina being upset, but you, Jae..." He paused. One of his eyes targeted Jae and the other, Lina. "What the *skurn* is it?"

Jae tried to speak, then tried again. "Aiko... She's not coming back."

"What? What do you mean?"

Lina put her hands on Jae's shoulders, surprised that she could do that much as he stood there paralyzed. She said, "He means that she's g-going to be killed. Real soon." She squeezed her eyes shut, exhaled as much of her fear as she could. Nothing to be done…

Wilder turned to his control board and then back to them. "They're gone; no further direct communications possible until they return to normal space. What's this about?"

Jae choked, "I saw the Mark of Ramseur on her– the Feithi death sign."

You can pick the format and store you want to buy from here:
http://www.CarolAStrickland.com/fiction/lost.html

ABOUT THE AUTHOR

When you think of strong women and strange worlds, think Carol A. Strickland.

Although born in a small town in Illinois noted for its Nineteenth Century demonic possession cases, Carol claims that all those voices inside her head are a result of having stories to tell and books to write. Even so, her strange devotion to and study of Wonder Woman would seem to indicate an abby-normal brain.

A one-time comics letterhack and outspoken member of various comics message boards, Carol has found herself the basis for two comic book villains (at times her opinions have not been taken well by the books' creators) (both villains were soundly thrashed) (and both, for some perverse reason, were male) and had one superhero wear her costume design. (Light Lass!)

Carol has also become an award-winning painter. Along with her writing, she exercises this skill in her secondary hours (both of them) as she waits for the lottery to free her 9-to-5 time to more fulfilling pursuits.

Trademarks Acknowledgement

The author acknowledges the trademarked status and trademark owners of the following workmarks mentioned in this word of fiction:

Adventureland: Walt Disney Productions

Band-Aid: Johnson & Johnson Corporation

Big Mac and McDonald's: the McDonald's Corporation

Biography: A&E Television Networks

Bullwinkle: Ward Productions, Inc.

CNN and CNNi: Cable News Network LP

Coke and Sprite: The Coca-Cola Company

Cosmopolitan: Hearst Communications, Inc.

Frisbee: Wham-O, Inc.

Jell-O and Miracle Whip: Kraft Food Holdings, Inc.

Hershey: Hershey Foods Corporation

James Bond 007: MGM Inc.

Jeopardy!: Jeopardy Productions, Inc.

Kleenex: Kimberly-Clark Corporation

Luke Skywalker and *Star Wars*: Lucasfilm Ltd.

Pepé Le Pew: Time Warner Entertainment Company, LP

Playboy: Playboy Enterprises International, Inc.

Shoney's: Shoney's, Inc.

Snapple: Snapple Beverage Corp.

Star Trek: Paramount Pictures Corporation

Velcro: Velcro Industries B.V. LLC

Walmart: Wal-Mart Stores, Inc.

"An Innocent Man," written and copyrighted by Billy Joel, is used with permission.